PANEL ON THE DEMOGRAP
ECONOMIC IMPACTS OF IMM

JAMES P. SMITH (*Chair*), RAND, Santa Monica, California
ALAN J. AUERBACH, Department of Economics, University of California, Berkeley
GEORGE J. BORJAS, John F. Kennedy School of Government, Harvard University
J. THOMAS ESPENSHADE, Office of Population Research, Princeton University
RICHARD B. FREEMAN, Department of Economics, Harvard University, and Labor Studies, National Bureau of Economic Research
JOHN F. GEWEKE, Department of Economics, University of Minnesota
CHARLES HIRSCHMAN, Department of Sociology, University of Washington
ROBERT P. INMAN, Department of Finance, Wharton School of Business, University of Pennsylvania
GUILLERMINA JASSO, Department of Sociology, New York University
RONALD D. LEE, Departments of Demography and Economics, University of California, Berkeley
MARY C. WATERS, Department of Sociology, Harvard University
FINIS R. WELCH, Department of Economics, Texas A&M University

BARRY EDMONSTON, *Study Director*
KRISTIN McCUE, *Research Associate*
JOEL A. ROSENQUIST, *Senior Project Assistant*

COMMITTEE ON POPULATION

COMMITTEE ON NATIONAL STATISTICS

The National Academy of Sciences is a private, nonprofit, self-perpetuating society of distinguished scholars engaged in scientific and engineering research, dedicated to the furtherance of science and technology and to their use for the general welfare. Upon the authority of the charter granted to it by the Congress in 1863, the Academy has a mandate that requires it to advise the federal government on scientific and technical matters. Dr. Bruce M. Alberts is president of the National Academy of Sciences.

The National Academy of Engineering was established in 1964, under the charter of the National Academy of Sciences, as a parallel organization of outstanding engineers. It is autonomous in its administration and in the selection of its members, sharing with the National Academy of Sciences the responsibility for advising the federal government. The National Academy of Engineering also sponsors engineering programs aimed at meeting national needs, encourages education and research, and recognizes the superior achievements of engineers. Dr. William A. Wulf is president of the National Academy of Engineering.

The Institute of Medicine was established in 1970 by the National Academy of Sciences to secure the services of eminent members of appropriate professions in the examination of policy matters pertaining to the health of the public. The Institute acts under the responsibility given to the National Academy of Sciences by its congressional charter to be an adviser to the federal government and, upon its own initiative, to identify issues of medical care, research, and education. Dr. Kenneth I. Shine is president of the Institute of Medicine.

The National Research Council was organized by the National Academy of Sciences in 1916 to associate the broad community of science and technology with the Academy's purposes of furthering knowledge and advising the federal government. Functioning in accordance with general policies determined by the Academy, the Council has become the principal operating agency of both the National Academy of Sciences and the National Academy of Engineering in providing services to the government, the public, and the scientific and engineering communities. The Council is administered jointly by both Academies and the Institute of Medicine. Dr. Bruce M. Alberts and Dr. William A. Wulf are chairman and vice chairman, respectively, of the National Research Council.

Acknowledgments

This report reflects the efforts of many people. The panel was established under the auspices of the Committee on Population, directed by John Haaga, and the Committee on National Statistics, directed by Miron Straf—both of whom were instrumental in developing the study and provided guidance and support to the staff. At a number of critical times, John Haaga offered useful advice and always found a way to help us meet our obligations in a timely fashion.

The panel gratefully acknowledges the funding received from the U.S. Commission on Immigration Reform. Commission staff, including Susan Forbes Martin, Lindsay Lowell, and David Howell, were helpful to the panel throughout the study.

The panel benefited greatly from a set of papers we commissioned: by Susan Carter and Richard Sutch on long-term population and economic effects of immigration on the United States; by Kevin Murphy and Gary Becker on the role of immigration in economic growth; by John Hagan and Alberto Palloni on immigration and crime; by Edward Funkhouser and Stephen Trejo on the economic effects of immigration on women; by Thomas MaCurdy, Thomas Nechyba, and Jay Bhattacharya on a conceptual framework considering fiscal effects of immigration; and by Daniel Trefler on economic models of immigration and trade. In addition, William Frey and Kao-Lee Liaw prepared a paper that analyzed the effect of immigration on internal migration and state distribution of the U.S. resident population. The National Academy Press expects to publish a volume containing revised versions of some of these papers.

The panel did considerable new research, with the aid of some expert consultants. Peter Brandon prepared fiscal estimates from the Survey on Income and Program Participation. Michael Clune conducted the panel's case study of the fiscal effect of immigration in California. Deborah Garvey worked with panel member Thomas Espenshade on the panel's use of their ongoing study of the fiscal effect of immigration in New Jersey. Tim Miller collaborated with panel member Ron Lee on lifetime estimates of the fiscal effect of immigration. And Michel Vanderhart assisted panel member Finis Welch in estimating price effects of immigration.

I also acknowledge the contribution of Mendelle T. Woodley's superb editing skills in the preparation of the report. Mendy was there from the beginning and helped us translate our thoughts into clear English sentences. Our report also benefited from a final copy editing by Christine McShane, of the National Research Council staff.

No panel with a task as complex and challenging as ours could perform its duties without an excellent, well-managed staff. In particular, the overall report would not have been possible without the dedicated efforts of four staff members. The panel is indebted to Karen Foote, program officer, who handled administrative matters for the first year of the panel's work. We appreciate very much the work of Joel Rosenquist, senior project assistant, who skillfully guided the report through numerous rounds of editing in preparation for publication and ably and cheerfully handled the large number of administrative tasks presented by the panel. Kristin McCue, senior staff officer, made major contributions to the panel's work. Working with the panel's chair, she coordinated much of the work for the study of labor markets and directed the preparation of considerable data analysis for Chapter 5. More than this, she also worked with the study director on revising and reviewing drafts of the report, offering constructive advice on the panel's work and helping to bring the report to publication. Finally, we are indebted to Barry Edmonston, study director, who managed the overall work of the panel, organized and managed a complex set of activities, and helped us to meet our deadlines. Barry worked on all aspects of the project and was always dedicated, responsible, and in good humor.

I close by expressing my appreciation to fellow panel members for their willingness to devote long hours to this project. They worked together well and patiently, a critical element in such a far-reaching project. A number of panel members prepared drafts for the panel's use. Some of their contributions have greatly assisted the preparation of chapters; others appear in the appendices. Although the work was difficult and the requests I made of their time bordered on the unconscionable, all panel members responded in an extremely helpful way. This project has been one of the most intellectually stimulating experiences of my life. The reasons are simple—an important public issue and a group of intelligent, and highly motivated panel members. I am in their debt.

James P. Smith, *Chair*
Panel on the Demographic and
Economic Impacts of Immigration

Contents

SUMMARY 1
Impact of Immigration on the U.S. Population, 3
Economic Impacts of Immigration, 4
Fiscal Impacts of Immigration, 8
Social Dimensions of Immigration, 12

1 THE IMMIGRATION DEBATE 14
Immigration Policy, 15
Who Wins? Who Loses?, 16
Is Immigration "Too" Costly?, 16
What Did the Panel Do?, 17
A Road Map, 19

2 BACKGROUND TO CONTEMPORARY U.S. IMMIGRATION 20
A Word About Terminology, 21
U.S. Immigration Laws and Trends, 22
Background to Immigration Numbers, 30
Current U.S. Immigration Policy, 37
Immigrant Characteristics, 52
Comparison with Other Countries, 62
The Canadian Case, 65
Conclusions, 67
References, 68
Appendix 2.A: Admission of Immigrants into Canada, 71

3 THE FACE OF THE U.S. POPULATION IN 2050 76
Background to Population Change, 78
A Projection Model, 81
National Population Growth, 93
Implications of the Size of the Population, 98
Age and Sex Composition, 99
Immigrants and Their Children, 110
Racial and Ethnic Composition, 113
Conclusions, 122
References, 123
Appendix 3.A: Population Projection Model, 124
Appendix 3.B: Population Projection Assumptions, 131
Appendix 3.C: Sensitivity of Population Projection Results, 133

4 IMMIGRATION'S EFFECTS ON JOBS AND WAGES: FIRST PRINCIPLES 135
First Principles: Labor Market Effects of Immigration, 136
Growth and Immigration, 153
Conclusions, 164
References, 165
Appendix 4.A: Immigration in the Two-Good, Two-Factor Model, 166
Appendix 4.B: Assessing the Labor Market Benefits and Costs of Immigration, 170

5 IMMIGRATION'S EFFECTS ON JOBS AND WAGES: EMPIRICAL EVIDENCE 173
The Economic Gain to Immigrants, 174
Trends in Immigrant Skills, 181
Differentials Across National Origins and the Decline in Immigrant Skills, 185
Who Are the Immigrants?, 190
Economic Assimilation, 196
Emigration, 204
Trends in Employment, 205
Occupations and Jobs, 209
Impact of Immigrants on Native Earnings and Employment, 219
Immigration and Native Migration, 228
Price Effects of Immigration, 230
Conclusions, 235
References, 237
Appendix 5.A: Observed Wage Growth of Men and Women, 240
Appendix 5.B: Calculation of Shares of Expenditures Attributable to Immigrant Labor, 251

6 DO IMMIGRANTS IMPOSE A NET FISCAL BURDEN? ANNUAL ESTIMATES 254
Introduction, 254
Estimating the Annual Fiscal Impact of New Immigrants, 257
Estimates of the Annual Fiscal Impact of Immigrant-Headed Households, 270
Conclusions, 292
References, 294

7 THE FUTURE FISCAL IMPACTS OF CURRENT IMMIGRANTS 297
Introduction, 297
Dynamic Incidence, 298
Kinds of Impacts, 302
The Heterogeneity of Immigrants and Intra- and Intergenerational Mobility, 306
The Age Profiles of Taxes and Benefits, 308
Aggregate Cross-Sectional Fiscal Impacts of Immigrants and Their Children, 316
Constructing Longitudinal Age Profiles, 323
Baseline Results, 325
The Average Impact of an Incremental Immigrant, 331
Alternative Scenarios, 336
The Timing of Fiscal Impacts, 341
Interpreting the Results, 344
Summary, 349
Key Conclusions, 352
References, 354
Appendix 7.A: Intergenerational Educational Mobility, 355
Appendix 7.B: Net Present Values for Immigrants and Natives, by Scenario, 358
Appendix 7.C: Discussion of Data Sets for the Study of Fiscal Impacts, 362

8 THE SOCIAL DIMENSIONS OF IMMIGRATION 363
Integration of Immigrants into American Society, 365
Effect of Immigrants on American Institutions, 382
Attitudes Toward Immigration and Interethnic Relations, 389
Immigration and Interethnic Tensions, 393
Conclusions, 395
References, 397
Appendix 8.A: Analysis of Polling Data, 402

BIOGRAPHICAL SKETCHES 407

INDEX 413

THE NEW AMERICANS

Summary

Throughout its history, the United States has been a nation of immigrants. The door may not always have been wide open, but it has never been completely shut. The current debate over the wisdom of high rates of immigration is not new; it stretches back even to colonial times. There are concerns about the effect of immigration on the economic prospects of native-born residents, on population growth, and on the ability of immigrants to interweave themselves into the social fabric of the nation.

Responding to these concerns, Congress in 1990 appointed a bipartisan Commission on Immigration Reform to review the nation's policies and laws and to recommend changes. In turn, the commission in 1995 asked the National Research Council to convene a panel of experts to assess the demographic, economic, and fiscal consequences of immigration. The panel was not asked to answer all the current questions about immigration, let alone to set out alternative policies or to make recommendations among them. Rather, it was asked to lay a scientific foundation for policymaking on some specific issues, to provide as rich a background as possible against which the commission could do its work.

The panel's charge was to address three key questions:

- What is the effect of immigration on the future size and composition of the U.S. population?
- What is the influence of immigration on the overall economy?
- What is the fiscal impact of immigration on federal, state, and local governments?

This report summarizes the panel's work.

As long as there is a virtually unlimited supply of potential immigrants, the nation must make choices on how many to admit and who they should be. Throughout U.S. history, legislation and regulation have dealt with five generic issues: how many immigrants to admit; within that number, who should be let in and who should be excluded; how to deal with refugees; how to handle illegal immigrants; and whether immigrants and citizens should be treated the same.

The modern era of immigration policy dates from the 1965 Immigration and Naturalization Act. This act removed the quotas for immigrants based on national origins and replaced them with a preference system based primarily on family unification and, to a lesser extent, on occupational skills. One consequence of the 1965 legislation has been a decline in the labor market skills of new immigrants relative to those of native-born workers. This decline has accompanied a decrease in immigration from more prosperous Western Europe and a rise in immigration from Asian and Latin and South American countries. Recent legislation, notably the Personal Responsibility and Work Opportunity Reconciliation Act of 1996, restricted access to public assistance programs for noncitizen legal immigrants, and set a lifetime limit on public assistance for all residents.

In 1994, there were nearly 800,000 legal immigrants. This number is considerably smaller than the number in the peak year of the early twentieth century wave of immigration—1.3 million immigrants in 1913. Moreover, since the resident population has more than tripled during the course of the twentieth century, the number of immigrants in the earlier decades represented a much higher proportion: 13 immigrants per 1,000 resident population in 1913, compared with 3 immigrants per 1,000 residents in 1994. However, immigration now plays a greater role in population growth than it did eight decades ago: it accounts for 37 percent of total growth, partly because of the decline in the fertility rates of residents.

Besides legal immigrants admitted for permanent residence, there were in 1994 some 22 million visits by aliens admitted for short stays—students, tourists, short-term employees of international companies. Most stay no more than a few weeks, but others live in the United States for several years; some overstay their allotted time and swell the number of illegal immigrants.

Between 200,000 and 300,000 illegal immigrants enter the United States each year, 40 percent of whom first enter legally as nonimmigrants. Mounting concerns about illegal immigration led to the passage of the Immigration Reform and Control Act of 1986. First, by requiring employers to check prospective employee's legal U.S. immigrant status and by setting financial and legal penalties for employers who knowingly hire an illegal immigrant, it sought to reduce the attraction of jobs in this country for illegal immigrants. Second, it provided for legalizing the status of those illegal immigrants who could prove their long-term residence—estimated to be nearly 3 million.

In census and survey data, it is not always clear whether foreign-born persons are legal or illegal immigrants or whether they are nonimmigrants who are temporarily in the United States. In this report, we refer to either foreign-born persons or immigrants, unless we wish to distinguish a particular type of immigrant.

IMPACT OF IMMIGRATION ON THE U.S. POPULATION

What influence will immigration have on the size and composition of the U.S. population over the next half century?

To answer that question, the panel developed a demographic model that projected the population to the year 2050. This model projects an initial population under various assumptions about fertility, mortality, and international migration. It places special emphasis on understanding the effects of immigration on the total population, its age structure, the size of the foreign-born population, and the ethnicity of its descendants. The model adds a generational perspective to demographic projection by distinguishing immigrants and their descendants, along with the current native-born population, using data on fertility, mortality, exogamy (rates of intermarriage), and ethnic affiliation that vary by generation and ethnicity.

In our projections, we used five alternative assumptions about the numbers of immigrants in the coming decades: a continuation of the current number of net immigration, high and low immigration (a 50 percent increase and decrease from current levels), and two extremes—zero net immigration and twice the current rate.

If net immigration continues indefinitely at its current levels, there will be 387 million people in the United States in 2050, 124 million more than at present. Immigration will play the dominant role in that growth, accounting for 80 million, or two-thirds, of the increase. Even if net immigration were halved, to 410,000 a year, the population would still rise to 349 million. And if it were increased by half, to 1,230,000 a year, the population would be 426 million by the middle of the 21st century.

Immigration will also affect the age distribution of the resident population, with crucial implications for public policy. Under current immigration policy, enrollment in kindergarten through grade eight will increase to 53.7 million by 2050, 17 million more than the 36.8 million in 1995. If immigration were cut in half, that number would be 47.3 million; and if it were 50 percent higher, it would be 57.6 million. High school enrollments will rise from 14.0 million in 1995 to 20.3 million under the medium assumption about immigration—and to 2.5 million more or less than that under the high or low assumptions.

The U.S. population is aging: the number of persons aged 65 years and older is expected approximately to double between 1995 and 2050, no matter what immigration policies are adopted. With a low immigration assumption, the absolute size of the population aged 65 and over will be 73.0 million in 2050; with the high immigration assumption, it will be 80.6 million. The proportion of older people in the total population will be smaller with higher immigration, however: there will be 27 older people for every 100 people aged 20 to 64 years in 2050 assuming high rates of immigration, compared with 30 assuming low rates of immigration.

Our demographic model also projects the racial and ethnic composition of the future population, divided into four mutually exclusive groups: non-Hispanic whites, blacks, Hispanics, and Asians (American Indians, Eskimos, and Aleuts are excluded from presentation in the report, but are included in the analysis for the total population). In addition to the rates of immigration and levels of childbearing, these projections depend critically on two parameters—rates of intermarriage and racial/ethnic affiliation, which is the extent to which individuals of multiple ancestry choose to identify with a given racial/ethnic group.

Under any immigration scenario, both the absolute and the relative sizes of the Asian-ancestry and Hispanic-ancestry populations will grow rapidly. Assuming continued net immigration at current levels, the size of the Asian population will increase from 9 to 34 million in 2050 (growing from 3 to 8 percent of the population). This growth stems mainly from the large fraction of Asians in the immigrant population. Similarly, fueled by higher fertility, high rates of immigration, and high affiliation rates, the Hispanic population will grow substantially over this period. Assuming continued net immigration at current levels, and current rates of intermarriage and ethnic affiliation, the Hispanic population will rise from 27 million in 1995 (about 1 in 11 of the population) to 95 million in 2050 (about 1 in 4 of the population).

These projections incorporate the assumption that current levels of intermarriage will continue, and thus that the proportion of people with multiple ancestry will increase. Multiple ancestry adds complexity and ambiguity to ethnic definitions, and it is possible that, by the middle of the next century, ethnic and racial lines will be even more blurred.

ECONOMIC IMPACTS OF IMMIGRATION

The second charge to the panel concerned the impact of immigration on the U.S. economy. Economic theory points to possible effects on the employment and wages of domestic workers, U.S. trade with other countries, the growth rate of the economy, and the prices people pay for goods and services. To address these issues, the panel relied both on theoretical insights on what the likely effects would be, and on empirical estimates of the magnitude of the actual effects.

Using a basic economic model, with plausible assumptions, we show that immigration produces net economic gains for domestic residents, for several reasons. At the most basic level, immigrants increase the supply of labor and help produce new goods and services. But since they are paid less than the total value of these new goods and services, domestic workers as a group must gain.

The gains to the domestic economy come from a number of sources. On the production side, immigration allows domestic workers to be used more productively, specializing in producing goods at which they are relatively more efficient. Specialization in consumption also yields a gain.

Immigration thus breaks the rigid link between domestic consumption and domestic production. From this perspective, the effects of immigration are comparable to those of international trade. That the two processes are so similar suggests that, when trade is relatively free, any change in the number of immigrants will affect the incomes of domestic workers less than it would have without trade.

In our baseline analysis, we assume that the U.S. economy is characterized by constant returns to scale—that is, growth in the size and scale of the economy neither reduces nor increases the productivity of labor and capital. Existing research has not convincingly demonstrated that, in the aggregate, either decreasing returns due to fixed factors or congestion effects, or increasing returns, are more compelling alternatives. We caution, however, that we would not extrapolate far beyond current levels and say that immigration flows much larger that those considered in our demographic projections would always produce economic gains. With far larger flows, and over long periods of time, the uncertainty about increasing or decreasing returns to scale would have to be resolved with sound empirical evidence.

Even when the economy as a whole gains, however, there may be losers as well as gainers among different groups of U.S. residents. Along with immigrants themselves, the gainers are the owners of productive factors that are complementary with the labor of immigrants—that is, domestic, higher-skilled workers, and perhaps owners of capital—whose incomes will rise. Those who buy goods and services produced by immigrant labor also benefit. The losers may be the less-skilled domestic workers who compete with immigrants and whose wages will fall. To the extent that immigrants specialize in activities that otherwise would not have existed domestically, immigration can be beneficial for all domestic residents. In this case, there is little substitution of new immigrant workers for domestic workers, and domestic consumers gain from the lower prices of these services.

In the long run, assuming constant returns to scale, immigrants can affect rates of economic growth only to the extent that they differ from the native-born—if, for example, they arrive with a different mix of skills from those of native-born workers. To have an effect on growth rates, this difference between immigrants and natives must persist over each new generation. If the children of immigrants—or, if not the children, the grandchildren and great-grandchildren—come to be just like the native-born, then all that immigration does is augment the population and the scale of the economy; it does not change the rate of growth of income per capita.

Overall, in the massive and complex U.S. economy, immigration is unlikely to have a very large effect on relative earnings or on gross domestic product per capita. Among the legions of factors that affect the economy, many are far more critical than immigration, including savings and investment and the human capital of U.S. workers. Immigration over the 1980s increased the labor supply of all workers by about 4 percent. On the basis of evidence from the literature on labor demand, this increase could have reduced the wages of all competing native-born workers by about 1 or 2 percent. Meanwhile, noncompeting native-born workers would have seen their wages increase, and both competing and noncompeting workers may have benefited as consumers.

Overall, barring sizable immigration-induced economies or diseconomies of scale, the most plausible magnitudes of the impacts of immigration on the economy are modest for those who benefit from immigration, for those who lose from immigration, and for total gross domestic product. The domestic gain may run on the order of $1 billion to $10 billion a year. Although this gain may be modest relative to the size of the U.S. economy, it remains a significant positive gain in absolute terms.

Potentially, immigration may have much larger effects on certain parts of the labor market—workers in geographic areas that receive large numbers of immigrants or those with low levels of education. However, comparisons of geographic areas with different levels of immigration show only a weak relationship between native wages and the number of immigrants in a city or state. Furthermore, in these studies the numerically weak relationship between native wages and immigration is observed across all types of native workers, skilled and unskilled, male and female, minority and nonminority. The one group that appears to suffer substantially from new waves of immigrants are immigrants from earlier waves, for whom the recent immigrants are close substitutes in the labor market.

While some have suspected that blacks suffer disproportionately from the inflow of low-skilled immigrants, none of the available evidence suggests that they have been particularly hard-hit on a national level. Some have lost their jobs, especially in places where immigrants are concentrated. But the majority of blacks live elsewhere, and their economic fortunes are tied largely to other factors.

There are a number of problems with studies based on local labor market analyses. If native workers and firms adapt to the entry of immigrants by moving to areas offering them better opportunities, then there is no reason to expect local-level correlation between the wages of natives and the presence of immigrants. The wages of all competing native workers would fall, not just the wages of natives working in the cities where immigrants cluster.

Some studies have investigated the impact of immigration on aggregate labor markets, rather than on local labor markets. Such studies estimate the effects of changing the relative proportions of skilled to unskilled workers to simulate the effects of the supply increases brought about by immigration. This approach also has its limitations, as it relies on an assumed underlying model of the economy. But plausible estimates based on this second approach show that, since 1980, immigration has been partly responsible for increasing the supply of high school dropouts by 15 percent, relative to the supply of workers with at least a high school education. Based on previous estimates of responses of wages to changes in supply, the supply increase due to immigration lowered the wages of high school dropouts by about 5 percent, that is, about 44 percent of the total decline in wages of high school dropouts observed between 1980 and 1994. This wage reduction is concentrated in a declining proportion of American workers. By 1995, high school dropouts represented less than 10 percent of the American workforce.

The evidence points to the conclusion that immigration has had a relatively small adverse impact on the wage and employment opportunities of competing native groups. This effect does not appear to be concentrated in the local areas where immigrants live, but instead is dispersed across the United States. This dispersal comes about in part because competing native workers migrate out of the areas to which immigrants move. Over the last two decades, immigration thus played some role in explaining the declining wages of high school dropouts, but little part in the expanding wage inequality for any other group of native workers.

Immigration most directly affects the welfare of the immigrants themselves. Immigrants expect to gain from immigration, or they would not come. Wages are higher in the United States than in less economically developed countries, such as Mexico and the Philippines. In addition, the spread of wages is broader in the United States than in most of the developed sending countries, such as Western Europe and Canada. Because of these differences, emigration to the United States should be attractive to most workers from less developed countries and to more highly skilled workers from many developed countries.

Once in the United States, the foreign-born on average earn less than native workers. This gap between foreign-born and native workers has widened recently. Among both men and women, those who have arrived most recently and those who come from Latin America earn the lowest wages. Even though recent new arrivals are better educated than their earlier counterparts, the education of the native-born has improved even more, so that the gap in skills, and thus in wages, has widened. This relative decline in immigrant skills and wages can be attributed essentially to a single factor—the fact that those who have come most recently have come from poorer countries, where the average education and wage and skill levels are far below those in the United States.

Part of this growing wage gap may stem from the influx of illegal immigrants, who are generally more poorly educated, but it is not due exclusively to them. There is also evidence of widening in the gap among legal immigrants, brought about not only through shifts in their countries of origin, but also through changes in the composition of refugees and more severe limits on the entry of certain highly skilled immigrants (specifically, physicians). Over time, the wage gap closes for some—significantly for immigrants from Europe and Asia, and at least modestly for some others—but not at all for those from Mexico.

Employment rates of recent immigrants have also fallen relative to those of natives. However, immigrants catch up to natives relatively quickly, so that after some years in the United States their employment rates are quite similar to those of natives.

What jobs do immigrants do? A higher proportion of immigrants than of the native-born work in many jobs that call for high levels of education: they are college teachers of foreign languages, medical scientists, economists. But they are even more disproportionately represented in many of the lowest-paying jobs: as waiters and waitresses, agricultural graders and sorters, private household workers. Immigrants also account for a disproportionate number of workers in many occupations that require little education but much skill, such as tailors, dressmakers, and jewelers.

FISCAL IMPACTS OF IMMIGRATION

How do immigrants affect the revenues and expenditures of the various levels of government in the United States? Does additional immigration raise the amount that current residents must pay in taxes to receive a constant level of government services? Fiscal impacts are a much more important policy issue today than for earlier immigrant waves, because the relative size of all levels of government is so much larger.

Fiscal impacts are typically measured through estimates of the annual difference between taxes from immigrant households and the cost of government services and benefits to those households. The panel outlined how the fiscal impacts of immigrants on the native-born should be measured within a single year, and then directed a study based on that methodology for California. In addition, the panel made use of an existing study of annual fiscal impacts on New Jersey that also follows the same general methodology.

These annual calculations provide one picture of the United States today as a consequence of past immigration policies, but they cannot be used to predict the long-run cost to taxpayers of admitting additional immigrants. For this reason, the panel also directed a study of the long-term fiscal consequences of new immigrants. The long-term analysis takes the annual calculations as a starting point, and then projects revenues and expenditures into the future, under various assumptions about the course of immigration policy, fiscal policy, and the economic assimilation of immigrants and their descendants.

Measures of Annual Impact

The panel's calculations of annual fiscal impact required data on government spending, taxes, household income, and program participation by household members. They also required assumptions and estimates about the incidence of business and real estate taxes, the degree to which the costs and benefits of various public services are affected by additional beneficiaries, and other characteristics of the economy. The panel's calculations for the annual fiscal impacts were made for households as the unit of analysis, rather than individuals, because households are the primary units through which public services are consumed and taxes paid. Ideally, the revenues from and expenditures on U.S.-born children of immigrants should be included in estimating the fiscal impact of immigrants, and this procedure was followed in the panel's estimates of long-run fiscal impacts. However, for the annual estimates, only those U.S.-born children who remain in the parent's household were included. As a result, the analysis tends to overstate the net fiscal burden of past immigration, because it generally includes U.S.-born children of immigrants in immigrant households when they are of school age (and hence costly), while excluding them once they have reached working ages and moved out on their own to become contributors (or at least a lighter burden).

At the state and local government levels in New Jersey, the net fiscal burden from immigrant-headed households in the 1989-90 fiscal year is estimated to be $232 per native-headed New Jersey household, measured in 1996 dollars. A similarly constructed estimate for California from the 1994-95 fiscal year gives a net fiscal burden of $1,178 per native-headed California household, again measured in 1996 dollars. On average, immigrant-headed households from these two states make small positive net contributions to the federal government, equivalent to a reduction of $2 to $4 per year in federal taxes for resident households nationwide. (There are indications, however, that immigrants outside California have a more substantial positive impact at the federal level.)

New Jersey and California both have large numbers of immigrants and, as a consequence, the net fiscal burden on native residents in those states imposed by immigrant-headed households is relatively high. If the net fiscal impact of all U.S. immigrant-headed households were averaged across all native households in the United States, the burden would be considerably lower—on the order of $166 to $226 per native household.

There are three main reasons why immigrants receive more in services than they pay in taxes in these annual calculations: (1) immigrant-headed households include more school-age children than native households on average, and therefore currently consume more educational services; (2) immigrant-headed households are poorer than native households on average, and therefore receive more state and locally funded income transfers; and (3) immigrant-headed households have lower incomes and own less property than native households on average, and thus pay lower state and local taxes.

Across the immigrant population, the size of the net fiscal burden imposed on native residents varies significantly. It is by far the heaviest for households of immigrants originating in Latin America. Immigrants from Europe and Canada actually make an average net fiscal contribution. These differences arise because households of Latin American immigrants tend to have lower incomes and to include more school-age children than do other immigrant households.

Looking forward, any fiscal burden from new immigration will be shared by the households of current immigrant residents as well as native households. For example, if the United States added 916,000 new immigrants per year—an increase of about 10 percent in current immigration—and with those households located the way current immigrants are, they would increase the annual net fiscal burden on New Jersey households by about $20 per household, and they would increase the burden for California households by about $90 per household. For all U.S. native households, the net fiscal burden would be about $15 to $20 per household.

These estimates of the current-year fiscal impact of immigrant households do not provide an estimate of the long-term effect of immigration on public finances, for three reasons. First, new immigrants who are a net cost to the public sector in the current year's accounting (for example, those with children in school) may ultimately offer a net contribution, as their children finish school and become workers and taxpayers. And new immigrants who are helping to solve the nation's funding problem in the near term for Social Security and Medicare through increased payroll taxes are likely to become recipients of Social Security and Medicare benefits later in life, and so could turn out to represent a fiscal burden over their lifetimes.

Second, the fiscal benefit or burden from additions to the U.S. population depend crucially on the future paths of government spending and tax rates. Burdens today can be shifted onto future residents, both native and immigrant, through government borrowing. Only a long-term fiscal accounting can reveal these redistributions across generations, and hence offer an accurate picture of the long-run consequences of new immigration.

Third, the economic characteristics of the different generations of current foreign-born residents differ substantially. The annual measures for the current year combine the taxes and government expenditures associated with older immigrants who have been in the United States for many years with the taxes and spending associated with younger, recent arrivals.

Long-Term Measures of Fiscal Impact

Only a forward-looking projection of taxes and government spending can offer an accurate picture of the long-run fiscal consequences of admitting new immigrants. The methodology used by the panel for these long-run measures is an extension of the methodology of the annual calculations. Initially, tax payments and benefit receipts are estimated for individuals by immigrant status, age, education, and time in the United States; those estimates are then used to determine how adding an individual with particular characteristics would change government spending or revenues. Moving to an estimate of the long-term fiscal impacts requires making assumptions about future taxes and expenditures; the characteristics of new immigrants; how the differences between immigrants and natives in factors such as fertility rates and earnings change over time; and the discount rate used to combine costs and benefits in different years into a present value. The panel considered a variety of assumptions, which in turn generated a range of estimates. These illustrate how estimates of the fiscal impacts of immigration depend on future decisions about how many and which immigrants are admitted and about how the United States deals with the serious budget imbalances expected when the baby-boom generations retire.

The difference between immigrants and the native-born in program participation and program expenditures per capita varies greatly across types of government programs. For some programs, such as Social Security and Medicare, immigrants receive proportionately lower benefits than the native-born. For other programs, such as Supplemental Security Income (SSI), Aid to Families with Dependent Children (AFDC), and food stamps, they receive proportionately more. Combining the costs of benefits from all programs, there is little difference between immigrants and the native-born. Immigrants are more costly than natives during childhood because of the costs of bilingual education, and they are less expensive than natives in old age. Over a lifetime, these differences tend to balance out. Program participation is affected by policy changes such as those made by the 1996 Personal Responsibility and Work Opportunity Reconciliation Act, which denied means-tested benefits to noncitizen immigrants. If we assume that immigrants are naturalized after the required five-year waiting period, these restrictions turn out not to increase significantly the present dollar value of the long-run fiscal benefits of admitting a new immigrant.

On balance, the panel's estimates of the fiscal impact of immigration are affected more by differences in future earnings between immigrant families and the native-born than by differences in program participation. The lower earnings of immigrants mean that they pay lower taxes, and these tax differences are much more substantial than the differences in benefits.

Taking the difference between taxes paid and benefits received at each age, immigrants (like others) are costly in childhood and in old age, but are net payers of taxes during their working ages. For this reason, the long-term net fiscal impact of an immigrant (measured as a present dollar value) varies greatly with age at arrival. Immigrants arriving at ages 10 to 25 produce fiscal benefits for natives under most scenarios, whereas immigrants arriving in their late sixties generally impose a long-term fiscal burden. In fact, most immigrants tend to arrive at young working ages, which partly explains why the net fiscal impact of immigration is positive under most scenarios.

The long-term fiscal impact of an immigrant also depends on his or her education: immigrants with more education have more positive long-term fiscal impacts. For example, under one set of plausible assumptions, the net present value of the fiscal impact of an immigrant with less than a high school education is –$13,000; in contrast, the net present value for an immigrant with more than a high school education is +$198,000.

If the only policy goal were to maximize the positive contribution of immigration to public-sector budgets, that could be achieved by policies favoring highly educated immigrants and not admitting immigrants over age 50.

Although the average fiscal impacts of new immigration measured in present values are found to be positive under most scenarios, the impact of an increase in the annual flow of immigrants would initially be negative overall for a couple of decades before turning positive. The timing and extent of such a period depends crucially on federal fiscal policy. Given that near-term fiscal burdens will be offset by later fiscal gains, the present-value estimates of the long-term fiscal impact will be sensitive to the choice of a discount rate for comparing future expenditures and revenues with current ones.

Finally, under most scenarios, the long-run fiscal impact is strongly positive at the federal level, but substantially negative at the state and local levels. The federal impact is shared evenly across the nation, but the negative state and local impacts are concentrated in the few states and localities that receive most of the new immigrants. Consequently, native residents of some states, such as California, may incur net fiscal burdens from immigrants while residents of most states reap net fiscal benefits.

SOCIAL DIMENSIONS OF IMMIGRATION

How well are immigrants and their descendants integrated into American society, and how does immigration affect important American institutions? These are complex research issues, in which speculation and public discourse often run ahead of conclusive research findings. Despite fears in the past about the effects of immigration on the social fabric of the nation, few socioeconomic differences now separate the descendants of immigrants from Europe. Whether the same generational progress will characterize present-day immigrants and their children remains to be seen. Early readings suggest that some recent immigrants and their children—especially Asian Americans—match native-born whites in education and occupation, although not in incomes, fairly quickly.

Residential segregation is another visible measure of social distance. Recent immigrants tend to cluster in neighborhoods with others from their country of origin. But with convergence in socioeconomic status across generations, most immigrants disperse from the ethnic neighborhoods where they first tend to settle, and integrate with the overall population.

This residential movement has parallels in intermarriage among immigrant groups. Today, the children, grandchildren, and great-grandchildren of immigrants from various European countries and of various religions—once so distinct as to be referred to as "races"—have intermarried to such an extent as to virtually erase differences in education, income, occupation, and residence.

The picture is similar on the sensitive issue of the English language. Many immigrants arrive with at least a working knowledge of English. The 1990 decennial census found that three-fifths of the immigrants who came in the 1980s spoke English well or even very well; and of those who had been here 30 years or more, only 3 percent reported that they could not speak English well.

Attempts to draw empirical conclusions about the relation between immigration and crime rates founder on problems of measurement. Crime rates rose from the 1960s until about 1990, and since then have declined; there is no obvious link with trends in immigration in this period. Studies at the local level have found no association of immigrant concentrations with crime rates, with the exception of high rates of nonviolent crime near the borders.

Americans have always been ambivalent toward immigration, welcoming flows of foreigners in one era, blocking them in the next. In the past 50 years, polling data have charted a deepening opposition to immigration, linked in part, it appears, to economic concerns. Interethnic tensions have surfaced, especially in areas of high unemployment and poverty. Attitudes are by no means monolithic, however: Americans of African, Hispanic, and Asian descent are more accepting of immigration than non-Hispanic whites are. At present, about 68 percent of non-Hispanic whites favor decreasing immigration, compared with 57 percent of blacks. Asians and Hispanics are even more favorable toward immigration than blacks. Persons with more education tend to accept immigration more than those with less education. Finally, attitudes toward immigrants are no more negative in states with large immigrant populations than in the rest of the country.

1

The Immigration Debate

Throughout its history, the United States has been a nation of immigrants. Some came in search of economic opportunity, some for political, religious, or artistic freedom, some to reunite with their families. Their welcome depended on the idea that the newcomers conferred benefits on the nation: in scientific knowledge, artistic accomplishment, entrepreneurial talent, a richer cultural diversity, or simple additions to the labor force needed for the country's geographically and industrially expanding economy. Yet one has only to remember the Alien and Sedition Act of 1798, the Chinese Exclusion Act of 1882, or the ebbs and flows of immigration legislation in this century to know that the current debate about immigration is nothing new. Although the door has never been completely shut, it has been—in varying degrees—only partly open, as Americans continue to debate the costs and benefits of receiving and integrating immigrants, in both economic and social terms.

In the last years, concerns have been raised about how well recent immigrants are doing in the labor market, whether their job skills match the changing employment needs of the country, and whether they adversely affect wages and jobs for current U.S. residents. These concerns have been sparked in part by the influx of illegal immigrants and by the belief that they—and even legal immigrants—impose heavy costs on government at all levels and may reduce the well-being of the native-born. Beyond concerns about economic costs and benefits are equally pointed social and cultural questions: How will immigration, whether legal or illegal, affect the racial and ethnic composition of the population? The primacy of the English language? The level of crime? The American culture?

Responding to the intensification of concerns about immigration and undertaking to review immigration policy and to consider changes in immigration law,

Congress, in the Immigration Act of 1990, created the bipartisan U.S. Commission on Immigration Reform to assess current trends in immigration and to recommend changes in immigration policy. Among its other responsibilities, the commission was to assess the impact of immigration on labor needs, on employment and other economic conditions, and on the demographics of the United States.

The commission, in turn, requested the National Academy of Sciences to convene a panel of experts to explore the demographic, economic, and fiscal consequences of immigration—to address some of the questions raised above. The panel was not asked to answer all the current questions about immigration, nor did its mandate extend to setting out alternative policies or making policy recommendations among them. Rather, the panel was asked to provide a scientific basis for policymaking, providing as rich a background as possible against which the commission could do its work.

IMMIGRATION POLICY

U.S. immigration policy has always balanced a number of competing goals—economic, social, humanitarian. As long as there is a virtually unlimited supply of potential immigrants, the nation has to make choices about how many immigrants to admit and, within that number, who should be selected. At times in the complicated, never-static history of immigration policy, exclusion has been a matter of simple numbers, based on some notion of what the economy and the society could absorb. At other times, people have been excluded on specific grounds: national origin, race, health status, education, language ability, and job skills, among others. The criteria are obviously linked to the objectives, and the priorities may shift: for example, when other countries practice repression, the nation's historic role as a refuge takes precedence over concern about applicants' facility with English. Freely admitting highly skilled technical workers may mean turning away the more poorly endowed who are fleeing oppression; freely reuniting families, without regard to the degree of relationship or the capacity for self-sufficiency, may tax the society's ability to integrate the newcomers. Choosing policies, then, requires careful consideration of goals and, in turn, careful consideration of the trade-offs to be made in terms of both numbers of immigrants and their characteristics.

A second avenue open to policymakers for affecting immigration involves the ways that immigrants are treated and integrated into the United States after their arrival. The successful adaptation of immigrants, including refugees and legalized immigrants, depends on the ways in which they are treated differently from the native-born—through local programs that find places to live for refugees, job search programs, and English-language programs. Overall, these avenues of policy determine how many immigrants we have, who they are, and how they influence U.S. society—and thus, in the long run, the characteristics of the foreign-born population.

WHO WINS? WHO LOSES?

The choice of goals for immigration policy depends in part on the priorities assigned to the welfare of three groups with different stakes in the debate: people who were born in the United States, people who were born elsewhere but have come to live in the United States, and people who live in other countries. Even if the native-born receive primary consideration, inevitably some will be winners and some losers. Some may largely gain from immigration because the goods produced by immigrants, with their lower wages, will now be cheaper. On the other side of that coin, some native-born Americans may see their wages or even their jobs jeopardized as they compete directly with immigrant workers. But even among native-born Americans who may lose economically, attitudes toward immigrants vary by ethnicity and by the strength of ties to prospective immigrants in other countries. And simple adherence to the economic interests of the native-born may be complicated when foreign policy or social and humanitarian concerns dictate attention to the concerns of the other two groups.

Another complication in setting immigration policy lies in the way it impinges on government at all levels. Policies that set the number and the kinds of immigrants to admit into the country are made at the federal level. These policies need not, however, result in the same pattern of costs and benefits for states and cities. Each level has its own sources of revenue and its own responsibilities for expenditures. What may, on balance, largely benefit one governmental level may impose heavy costs on another. Since immigrants are not spread evenly across the states, they may confer more benefits or impose more costs on the states or localities in which they are concentrated. Consequently, the net impact of immigration on the fiscal positions of individual states may vary widely.

IS IMMIGRATION "TOO" COSTLY?

In the past three decades, immigration policy has been debated especially in the context of concerns about illegal immigration. Mexico, with which the United States shares a long, porous border, is only the most obvious source of clandestine migrants. Dramatic tales of Haitian boat people and dangerously overcrowded Chinese vessels highlight the issue. Whatever the interdictions of illegal immigration, in the coming decades the magnet of higher-paying jobs in the United States is unlikely to weaken for people from poor countries with dim prospects for finding well-paying jobs with potential for advancement in their home countries.

In this context, there are four primary questions raised in the debate.

First, does immigration, on balance, yield economic benefits or economic costs to U.S. residents? Even if the benefits outweigh the costs, does immigration potentially lower the employment and wages of some native-born workers? For example, the decline in real wage rates over the past 25 years for men with less than a college education has drawn special attention to the status of this group since they are the most likely to compete directly with immigrant labor. Although always part of the debate on immigration, these fears have been heightened in recent decades by sluggish economic growth. The recession in the early 1990s deepened this concern.

Second, how are the immigrants themselves doing? Have their educational attainments and occupational skills declined over time? Are they able to assimilate during their lifetimes into the mainstream of American economic life? However well the immigrants themselves do, what are the prospects for their children and grandchildren? On the answer to these questions turn policies for admitting immigrants—in terms of both numbers and characteristics.

Third, how can federal policies ease the mounting tensions between the federal government and states and localities over immigration issues? Poor economic conditions and budget pressure in areas of high immigration have spurred demands that the federal government curb both legal and illegal immigration and reimburse states for the costs of immigration.

Finally, what will the population of the United States look like in 50 years? If the "new" immigrants from Asia and Latin America continue to account for the larger share of immigration, will the size, ethnicity, and racial composition of our society be much different by the middle of the next century?

WHAT DID THE PANEL DO?

In the light of the intensity of the recent debate, Congress gave the U.S. Commission on Immigration Reform a mandate to review and evaluate the implementation and impact of U.S. immigration policy, and to report to Congress its findings and recommendations. To address some of the questions in the ongoing debate, in 1995 the commission requested the National Academy of Sciences to convene a panel of experts to explore the demographic, economic, and fiscal consequences of immigration. Through its Committee on Population and its Committee on National Statistics, the National Research Council convened a panel of 12 experts in economics, demography, and sociology to address three key questions in the debate:

What is the effect of immigration on the future size and composition of the resident U.S. population?

What is the influence of immigration on the overall economy, especially on national and regional labor markets?

What is the overall fiscal impact of immigration on federal, state, and local governments?

In answering these broad questions, the panel faced a complex set of theoretical and empirical issues. Immigration affects the economy not only through labor markets, but also through the relative prices of goods, capital flows across national borders, international trade in goods and services, and the supply of entrepreneurs or risk-takers. Moreover, in the labor market, immigration acts through changes in sheer numbers, as well as in the age, sex, educational attainments, occupational skills, and fluency in English of the immigrants. These changes are manifest not only in changes in wages but also in changes in the rates of employment and unemployment of the native-born.

The panel also focused on the assimilation of immigrants into the labor market, an issue that is important for several reasons: the degree of assimilation helps to determine the long-run labor market effects of current immigration; it affects the fiscal impact of immigration through governmental revenues and expenditures; and it influences how well the immigrants adapt culturally. Studying this issue called for looking at the types of jobs and occupations that immigrants start with in the United States, at their occupational mobility, at their wages relative to those of native-born workers, and at their success in integrating into American society over time.

In considering fiscal impacts, the panel assessed the contributions that immigrants make to revenues as well as to costs. Furthermore, we did not confine our study to the net impact in a single year; rather, we focused on the fiscal impact over the immigrants' life cycle and over those of their descendants.

What about the effects of immigration on the size, distribution, and composition of the nation's population? Immigration affects the population, again not only through its numbers, but also through emigration, intermarriage, childbearing, and mortality. Thus the panel studied the distribution of the population in terms of geography, age, ethnicity, family composition, and immigrant generations. Shifts in the age or geographic distribution of the population impinge on the fiscal balance; changes in ethnicity or family composition alter the social and cultural scene. And the changes immigration brings about are different depending on whether it is legal or illegal.

To address these questions, the panel met regularly beginning in 1995. These meetings were characterized by lively, vigorous discussion of existing research on immigration and the interpretation of these empirical studies. Where the current literature was deficient, the panel had background papers prepared to synthesize available studies or to present new frameworks and evidence. This volume draws on these papers, which were discussed at a conference in September 1996 and which will be published by the National Academy Press. The topics addressed include the labor market role of female immigrants, the historical role of immigration, a theoretical framework for addressing the fiscal impacts of immigration, the association of immigration with criminal activity, and the theoretical labor market impact of immigration.

Regarding the fiscal impact of immigration, the panel relied on an ongoing study of New Jersey, a case study of California conducted by the panel, and a study of the national longitudinal effects of immigration. The panel also developed quantitative evidence on the effects of immigration on the prices of goods and services. Finally, the panel prepared new population projections for the United States to provide a better understanding of the demographic consequences of immigration.

In addressing all these issues, the panel sought to identify the positive as well as the negative effects of immigration. Because it confined its study to the scope of its own expertise, this list of issues does not exhaust all possible consequences of immigration. We did not, for example, investigate the important implications that immigration may have for the nation's educational system or the environment. Our emphasis instead was on our collective areas of expertise: the structure and change in the population and in the economy.

A ROAD MAP

This volume reports the results of the panel's work. It first establishes a context for studying the impact of immigration with a short history of immigration laws and trends and a review of current immigration policy. Chapter 2 also provides an examination of recent immigrants into the United States—who they are, where they came from, what they are like, where they go once they arrive. Chapter 3 reviews the demographic effects of immigration—on population growth, the geographic distribution of population, its age structure, and its ethnic-linguistic composition. Chapters 4 and 5 look at the impact of immigration, legal and illegal, on jobs and wages, of both immigrants and the native-born; it identifies winners and losers, pays special attention to the effects on women in the labor force, and lays out scenarios for the short- and long-term future. Chapters 6 and 7 address the fiscal impacts of immigration—its effects on governmental revenues and expenditures. The social consequences of immigration are the subject of Chapter 8: the effects of immigration on crime, social elites, and social cohesion.

2

Background to Contemporary U.S. Immigration

At many times in the last two decades, photographs of our planet from outer space would have revealed movements of people on a massive scale. People have moved in response to the growing interdependence of the major economic powers and to the wide disparities between countries in income and employment opportunities. Migrants have also been driven by political factors—witness the large-scale shifts of populations from Eastern Europe and the former Soviet Union after the break-up of the Soviet hegemony and the famine- and war-induced migrations in Africa. By the early 1980s, 77 million people were living outside their country of birth, 14 million of them (about one in five) in the United States.

Because of its commanding economic position and its long-held reputation as a haven, the United States continues to attract immigrants—although movements of refugees and asylum seekers affect many European countries, Australia, and Canada as well. Temporary movements, stimulated in part by the demands of multinational companies for the rapid transfer of their employees, have become a major concern for developed nations. And fears about illegal immigration are not confined to the United States; other developed countries have experienced large, and often organized, flows of illegal immigrants. These developments highlight the need for a better understanding of the historical context for the global changes that form the backdrop to U.S. immigration.

In this chapter, we briefly outline the landmarks of this country's immigration legislation to highlight their role in shaping the historical ebbs and flows in the number of immigrants and in their characteristics. Second, we describe the main features of the long-term swings in these features of immigration. We detail the main characteristics of contemporary immigration laws, as shaped by our current "preference system." We then highlight the numbers and attributes of the other foreigners who come to our shores—the nonimmigrants and undocumented immigrants. Finally, we compare U.S. approaches to immigration with those of other countries.

A WORD ABOUT TERMINOLOGY

For clarity's sake we first define a few terms that will be used in this volume. *Immigration* and *emigration* generally refer to movements of people into and out of the United States. Foreign-born persons who enter the United States for residence are *immigrants*;[1] residents of the United States, whether native- or foreign-born, who leave the country to settle elsewhere are *emigrants*. *Net migration* is the difference between the two. If the number of people entering the United States exceeds the number who leave, net migration will be positive and immigration will contribute to America's population growth.

A distinction is made between *legal* and *illegal* (or *undocumented*) *immigrants*. Among those who intend to reside permanently in this country, *legal immigrants* apply for and receive permanent resident visas, "green cards" allowing them to live here indefinitely. Although illegal immigrants are often lumped together as if they formed one homogeneous group, people become *illegal immigrants* in three ways. The first way is by entering the country illegally; they enter without inspection and at some place other than a lawful point of entry, usually across a land border. The second way is by staying beyond the authorized period after their legal entry, as some foreign students do. And the third way is by violating the terms of their legal entry; tourists become illegal immigrants by taking jobs here.

Most people who enter the United States legally do not intend to become permanent residents. These people, referred to as *nonimmigrants* by the Immigration and Naturalization Service (INS), are authorized to stay in the United States for a specified length of time. The types of visas granted reflect the purpose of the visit to the United States, of which tourism is by far the most dominant. In addition, foreign students may study in the United States for several years; foreign diplomats and foreign members of the staffs of international organizations also have nonimmigrant status. This report largely ignores nonimmigrants, except when pertinent to its focus on the economic and demographic consequences of immigration.[2]

---

[1]The Immigration and Naturalization Service (INS) has a more restricted use of the term "immigrant." In INS usage, an immigrant is an alien admitted to the United States as a lawful permanent resident. Under the INS definition, such undocumented aliens or foreign students on a temporary entrance visa are not immigrants, even though they may be enumerated in the decennial census and included in federal government surveys. We note in this report when there a different usage for the term "immigrant."

[2]Although we do not explicitly address this group, nonimmigrants are indirectly included to some extent in our report because they are included in census data, pay taxes, influence public opinion polls, and constitute a stock of persons who may become illegal immigrants.

Finally, *refugees* and *asylees* are a special group of foreign residents who have fled their own countries because of a fear of persecution. The distinction between these two groups is that *refugees* apply for admission to an Immigration and Naturalization Service official outside the United States (think of Cubans seeking to flee Castro's Cuba), whereas *asylees* seek protection within the United States or at a port of entry (think of a defector from a foreign ballet company on tour in this country). Refugees and asylees are generally admitted to the United States as nonimmigrants, although their status may be adjusted later.

Although these are useful formal definitions, much of the evidence presented in this volume is based on data compiled by the Bureau of the Census, which frequently do not permit distinctions based on these terms of law. For example, the Census Bureau typically presents information on foreign-born persons without regard to their immigrant status. Many foreign-born persons enumerated in the decennial census are immigrants, but some are nonimmigrants and some are illegal immigrants. Census data also do not designate the visa status at the time of arrival in the United States, so we do not know whether a person may have entered the United States as a legal immigrant, as a refugee, or as a nonimmigrant who subsequently adjusted his or her status to permanent resident.

Moreover, census data on immigrants by period of arrival do not correspond to INS data on annual immigrant admissions. In INS data, immigrant arrivals are dated by the year in which an alien is admitted to the United States as a permanent resident; respondents to the census, however, are directed to provide the date at which they came to stay in the United States, which may be different.

U.S. IMMIGRATION LAWS AND TRENDS

During the last century, many restrictions on immigration have been placed into law by the federal government. These restrictions have dealt with five generic issues that have always been at the core of the country's political dialogue on immigration policy. First and most basic, how many people should be allowed into the United States? Second, within that number, who shall be let in and who shall be excluded? In those decisions, what weights should be assigned to nationality or race, family ties, economic contribution, and economic self-sufficiency?

Third, how should the United States deal with the unique problems that refugees pose? Fourth, what resources should be devoted to interdiction and deportation of illegal or undocumented immigrants, and what sanctions should be imposed on American institutions that deal with illegal immigrants, whether in the workplace, the schools, or hospitals? Finally, to what extent should the United States treat immigrants, whether legal or illegal, differently from citizens—in the right to vote, treatment by the criminal justice system, and eligibility for publicly provided services.[3]

---

[3]An important aspect of immigration is the meaning and criteria for U.S. citizenship. Chapter 8 presents a comparison of citizenship requirements in the United States and in other countries, as well

Immigration legislation over the past century has embodied the ever-evolving answers to these questions. Ebbs and flows in the volume and composition of immigration have not always been dictated by conscious policy decisions and legislation, but they certainly have been shaped by them. This section describes that evolution and also reviews recent legislation of special significance.

Until 1875, no direct federal legislation restricted admission of aliens into the country or the automatic qualification of immigrants and their children as citizens. States and the federal government did, however, impose some restrictions on immigration before 1875. In the colonial period, several colonies enacted laws to prohibit the entrance of criminals. After independence, many states restricted the entrance of paupers from outside the United States. And, before 1875, certain federal provisions affected immigration, such as laws to prohibit Chinese "coolies" on American vessels. But even when there was little federal immigration legislation, immigration has been a subject of ongoing discussion throughout U.S. history. Changes in public policy have quickened in this century, which has witnessed periodic and significant revisions in federal immigration policy.

Table 2.1 provides a brief summary of major federal immigration legislation. The initial federal attempts at controlling immigration dealt not with overall numbers, but instead with the types of people who were admitted. The first restrictive immigration law, passed in 1875, prohibited persons who were destitute, engaged in immoral activities, or physically handicapped. Direct and blatant exclusion of people based on their race was a major focus of early immigration legislation. The Chinese Exclusion Act of 1882, for example, was largely a response to racism and to anxiety about threats from cheap immigrant labor. Until 1860, virtually all immigrants to the United States were from Germany, Ireland, and the United Kingdom. After 1860, growing numbers came from Scandinavia, China, and South America, drawn by the job opportunities in the expanding American West. In the 1860s, for instance, about one-third of the western miners were Chinese.[4] As the numbers of immigrant laborers increased, so did opposition from native-born labor groups. This was the impetus behind the Chinese Exclusion Act. It limited the number of Chinese allowed to enter the United States; later amendments ultimately prohibited immigration of Chinese altogether.

The Immigration Act of 1891 broadened the role of the federal government in monitoring and regulating immigration. Creating the Office of Immigration, the precursor to today's Immigration and Naturalization Service, this act directed the superintendent of immigration to enforce immigration laws under the supervision of the secretary of the treasury.

Concern about Asian immigration, originally specific only to the Chinese,

---

as a discussion of recent naturalization trends. For a background on the evolution of the concept of citizenship, see Klusmeyer (1996).

[4] Many others, experienced in mining operations, came from Chile, Peru, and Mexico.

TABLE 2.1 Major U.S. Legislation on Immigration

Legislation	Provisions
Chinese Exclusion Act, 1882	Restricted immigration of Chinese laborers for 10 years. Prohibited Chinese naturalization. Provided deportation procedures for illegal Chinese in the United States.
Immigration Act of 1891	Provided the first comprehensive immigration laws for the United States. Established the Bureau of Immigration within the Department of the Treasury. Directed the Immigration Bureau to deport unlawful aliens.
Immigration Act of 1924	Imposed the first numerical limit on immigration. Began a national-origin quota system, which greatly restricted immigration from countries outside Northern and Western Europe.
Immigration and Nationality Act of 1952	Continued national-origin quotas. Set a quota for aliens with skills needed in the United States.
Immigration and Nationality Act Amendments of 1965	Repealed the national-origin quotas. Initiated a 7-category visa system for family unification and skills. Set a quota for Western Hemisphere immigration for the first time and set a country limit of 20,000 immigrants for the Eastern Hemisphere.

expanded to the Japanese in the early twentieth century. The 1907 Gentleman's Agreement with Japan—so called because it was arranged with the cooperation of the Japanese government—restricted immigration from that country. Japanese immigration was formally and unilaterally prohibited in the Japanese Exclusion Act of 1924.

Even though the distinctions made in successive pieces of legislation may seem peculiar in today's light, each "new" wave of immigrants always has seemed different from its predecessors. For example, the sharp increases in the 1880s in "new" European immigrants—from Austria-Hungary, Italy, Greece, Poland, and Russia—provoked a strong reaction in the United States. This reaction intensified with the wave of immigrants in the first two decades of the new century—more than 1 million immigrants each year for several years, over half of whom were from Italy, Russia, and Austria-Hungary. And concerns became more urgent because the rise of immigration coincided, for some years, with periods of economic weakness and high unemployment in the United States. The Dillingham Commission, one of several appointed around this time to examine

TABLE 2.1 Continued

Legislation	Provisions
Immigration and Nationality Act Amendments of 1976	Extended the 20,000 country limit for the Western Hemisphere.
Refugee Act of 1980	Established the first systematic procedures for refugee admission. Removed refugees from the preference system for visa categories. Began a program for refugee resettlement.
Immigration Reform and Control Act of 1986	Started employer sanctions for knowingly hiring illegal aliens. Created a program for legalizing illegal aliens already residing in the United States. Increased border enforcement.
Immigration Act of 1990	Increased legal immigration ceilings. Tripled the numerical limits for employment-based immigration. Created a diversity admissions category.
Illegal Immigration Act of 1996	Introduced a pilot telephone verification program for employer to authenticate the legal immigration status of potential workers. Expanded restrictions on access of legal immigrants to welfare benefits. Increased border enforcement.

immigration, recommended that immigrants be required to be literate and that the ban on Asian immigrants be continued. Congress followed these recommendations in 1917 when it required immigrants over age 16 to be literate in English or their own language, and it banned those from certain "barred zones" in Asia.

Immigration slackened during World War I but resumed at a high level after the war, despite shortages of jobs and housing in this country. Then, public opinion shifted again. In response to the economic situation and with widespread public support, Congress enacted the 1921 Quota Act. This important piece of legislation and its follow-up in 1924 set the broad outlines of immigration policy for the next half century. Most important, it dictated that the favored few would come from countries that had already sent large numbers of immigrants. Using data from the 1910 census, the act limited immigration to 3 percent of the foreign-born population, by national origin, already in the United States.

In 1924, Congress reduced immigration to 2 percent of the foreign-born groups in the United States according to the 1890 census population. This cut immigration from Southern and Eastern Europe further. This change, like that using the 1910 census, was temporary, and new national-origin limits went into effect (after several postponements) in 1929. The national origins system put into place then limited immigration from the Eastern Hemisphere to approximately 150,000.[5] Each nation received a quota based on its proportion of the population according to the 1920 census. This system increased immigration from Southern and Eastern European nations compared with using the 1890 census of the foreign-born, but it still gave the largest quotas to the countries in Northern and Eastern Europe. The 1924 act also barred aliens who were ineligible for citizenship, thus excluding Asian immigrants (except for Filipinos) who, as a group, had been declared ineligible for U.S. citizenship in previous naturalization legislation.[6]

During the Great Depression and World War II, few immigrants came to America. The quota of 150,000 from the Eastern Hemisphere—in practice from Europe, because immigration from Asia was barred—was not fully filled because the United States at times made it difficult for immigrants to enter. Various groups feared that immigrants might take jobs from native-born Americans and they wanted tight enforcement of laws to prevent immigrants from becoming public charges. For the Western Hemisphere there were no quotas, either for the entire hemisphere or for individual nations. Immigrants had difficulty, however, finding employment, and local, state and federal governments sent many Mexicans home instead of placing them on welfare.

By the 1940s, there were substantial numbers of Hispanic residents in the southwestern region of the United States. Some Hispanic residents were descendants of original settlers in the area, having resided there prior to its incorporation by the United States. Others had entered in previous decades from Mexico, although many Mexicans were deported from the United States in the 1930s during the Great Depression.

An unintended consequence of the 1920s legislation was an increase in illegal immigration. Many Europeans who did not fall under the quotas migrated to Canada or Mexico, which were not subject to national-origin quotas; subsequently they slipped into the United States illegally. In response, during the 1920s, additional funds were regularly granted to establish the Border Patrol and to expand its operations. By the early 1930s, the Bureau of Immigration aimed the bulk of its attention at exclusion and deportation.

---

[5]The Western Hemisphere comprises North, Central, and South America as well as the Caribbean. The rest of the world makes up the Eastern Hemisphere.

[6]Congress acted to cut Filipino immigration during the Great Depression of the 1930s when it gave the Philippines an annual quota of only 50 visas. When independence came, immigration from the Philippines was scheduled to be barred like all East and South Asian countries. However, this changed after World War II. In 1943 Congress gave China a small quota and allowed Chinese immigrants to become U.S. citizens. It did the same for the Philippines and India in 1946. Other foreign-born Asians were not to regain the right of citizenship through naturalization and immigration until 1952.

From 1943 to 1964, the United States authorized a special program for the admission of temporary agricultural workers from Mexico and other Latin American countries. Initiated as a way of aiding agricultural production during World War II, in 1947 the program became the legal basis for the Bracero Program, which lasted until 1964. This program allowed seasonal agricultural workers to be admitted on a temporary basis from Mexico to meet U.S. agricultural labor shortages. In practice, the federal government operated reception centers near the Mexican border that screened applicants who arrived from Mexican recruitment centers. The program oversaw the transportation of the farmworkers to the work sites and ensured that employers provided transportation and wages. Employers were required to pay the prevailing wages in the area, to employ the workers for at least three-quarters of the contract period, and to provide free housing and meals at reasonable cost. By the early 1960s, critics of the program were claiming that Braceros adversely affected the wages, working conditions, and job opportunities of resident farmworkers (Martin, 1996). At the same time, increased mechanization was reducing the heavy reliance on agricultural workers for several crops and political support for the program from farmers had weakened. In the final stages, the Mexican ambassador asked the U.S. government to continue the program, but President John F. Kennedy supported only a final two-year extension, and the program ended in 1964.

Although immigrants were relatively few throughout the 1930s and 1940s, there were large numbers of applications for refugee admission from Europeans fleeing Nazi persecution. Applications for legal admission into the United States increased following World War II—and so did illegal immigration. It was also clear by the late 1940s that many of the old immigration laws were outdated. Faced with large numbers of refugees seeking entrance into the United States, special legislation was required for each group. The national-origin quotas severely limited the numbers who could be admitted from Asia and Eastern Europe, yet many from these areas who wished to immigrate had desirable occupational skills. Congress responded by passing several laws permitting displaced persons and refugees to enter the United States outside the quotas.

President Harry S Truman believed that special legislation for refugees was not enough. He appointed a special commission in 1952 to examine immigration and naturalization law. Although the commission recommended substantial changes, Congress took no action. President Dwight D. Eisenhower also wanted the system liberalized, but reforms were delayed until 1965, when major amendments to the Immigration and Nationality Act were enacted. These amendments removed quotas and placed all countries on an equal footing with similar numerical quotas. Although only 20,000 immigrant visas could be issued to any single country in the Eastern Hemisphere, by the new rules, immigrants who had immediate relatives (spouses, children, and parents) in the United States would not be automatically excluded because of their national origin. The 1965 act also placed the first numerical limitation on immigration from the Western Hemisphere.

Thus, amid the complex workings of the 1965 preference system, the main outcome was that about 80 percent of the numerical limits were allocated to family members, mostly U.S. citizens; the rest went primarily to those with desirable job skills and their dependents.[7] A major feature of the 1965 reforms was that the number of immediate relatives of U.S. citizens was "uncapped" and not subject to numerical limits. In 1965, few policymakers foresaw that this provision would increase immigration, particularly from developing countries.

One of the unintended consequences of the 1965 legislation was that, in its wake, the labor market skills of successive groups of new immigrants (as measured by wages and education) gradually declined relative to those of native-born workers. The countries favored by the old 1924 national-quota system had become increasingly prosperous over time, and, with that prosperity, their citizens had become better educated and more skilled. In the 1950s, three of the top five sending countries of immigrants to the United States were in Europe—Germany, the United Kingdom, and Italy (the second was Canada and the fifth was Mexico). By contrast, the two European countries in the top 10 in the 1990s have been Poland and Ireland—and Ireland only in the single year 1994, because of a special provision favoring Ireland in the Immigration Act of 1990.[8] Instead, Mexico has risen to the head of the list of sending countries, followed by the Philippines, Vietnam, the Dominican Republic, and China; the introduction of the 1965 rules has seen a dramatic increase in other Asian immigration. These countries are much less prosperous than those favored by the old national-origin system. Not surprisingly, their immigrants tend also to be less educated and less skilled, although a large number of professionals have come from Asia. This shift in major sending countries brought about by the 1965 legislation toward those of lesser economic development continues to have a major effect on the composition of U.S. immigration.

The 1980s and 1990s witnessed four major pieces of new legislation. Before 1980, the admission and resettlement of refugees had been governed by several pieces of legislation, including laws dealing with such special groups as Indochinese refugees. Refugees had been admitted to the United States with the humanitarian goal of offering protection to those fleeing persecution. The Refugee Act of 1980 modernized refugee policy and provided a systematic way of deciding who is a refugee. It also established a program for settling and assisting

---

[7]Refugees are admitted under separate rules, and they may convert their status to permanent residence after arrival in the United States. If refugees are counted along with legal immigrants, then about 74 percent of all immigrants are family preference immigrants.

[8]If refugees and legal immigrants entering the United States from the nations of the former Soviet Union are counted together, then this group would also rank as one of the top 10 sending countries in the 1990s.

refugees and established better coordination between the president and the Congress on this issue.

A major focus of recent legislation has been how to deal with problems associated with illegal immigrants, including the large numbers already living in the United States. The primary purpose of the Immigration Reform and Control Act of 1986 (IRCA) was to decrease the number of illegal immigrants by limiting their flow and by legalizing the status of illegal aliens already residing here. To accomplish the first goal, IRCA strengthened the Border Patrol and established penalties for employers who knowingly hire illegal immigrants—the so-called employer sanctions. It also set up a program that would admit agricultural workers when not enough native farmworkers were available; however, this program has not been used to date. The result of IRCA was the legalization of about 2.7 million persons who were residing in the United States before 1986 as illegal immigrants. The role of employer sanctions has been widely debated (Fix, 1991), but those established by IRCA, even in combination with a strengthened Border Patrol, may not have significantly diminished the flow of illegal immigrants (Bean et al., 1990).

The Immigration Act of 1990 substantially revised the laws relating to legal immigrants for the first time in 25 years. It continued the policy of family reunification by allowing an unlimited number of visas for immediate relatives of U.S. citizens; it addressed labor issues by reducing the number of visas for unskilled workers, simultaneously increasing the number of visas for priority workers and professionals with U.S. job offers; it made available 10,000 visas for investors with $1 million or more that they intended to use to create employment for at least 10 U.S. residents; and it promoted a more heterogeneous immigrant stream by opening "diversity" immigrant visas for "underrepresented" countries (countries that were adversely affected by the 1965 immigration amendments), with 40 percent of the visas for the years 1992 to 1994 reserved for Irish applicants.[9]

The vigorously debated Illegal Immigration Act of 1996 also sought to reduce illegal immigration in two ways. First, it set up a pilot project through which employers can verify by telephone the immigration status of potential workers. This effort is aimed at stemming the use of fraudulent identification records and thus hindering illegal immigrants in their search for work. Second, the act bolstered the Border Patrol by adding guards and by strengthening the physical barriers where crossing traffic is heaviest.

Although immigration policy is not their principal focus, several pieces of recent legislation have a bearing on immigration and offer examples of the ways in which the federal government has been developing immigrant policies. The

[9]The 1990 act also specifically legalized some Central American and Asian refugees who were residing in the United States in 1990 and offered naturalization to certain Filipino veterans of World War II.

Anti-Terrorism Act of 1996 was concerned primarily with strengthening the prevention of terrorism in the United States and imposing the death penalty for acts of terrorism. The act sets out criteria for the exclusion of foreign-born persons who are members of terrorist organizations and precludes asylum for them. The act broadens the range of offenses for federal prosecution, permits faster deportation procedures (for nonviolent crimes), and authorizes state and local police to arrest illegal immigrants.

The Personal Responsibility and Work Opportunity Reconciliation Act of 1996 has several features of great importance for U.S. immigrants. First and foremost, during the first five years of their residence in the United States, it restricts access to and use of public assistance programs for legal immigrants who are not citizens. It also bars noncitizen immigrants who have been here for more than five years from some federal welfare programs. It thus increases the incentive for permanent-resident aliens, especially poorer ones, to apply for naturalization after the requisite five years because citizenship is a prerequisite for welfare eligibility. The act also sets a lifetime limit of five years on the use of public assistance by any individual—a restriction that applies not just to legal immigrants but to all residents.

The exclusion of immigrants from public programs is not without precedent. For example, before current welfare reforms, some permanent residents whose entry was family-based had part of their sponsor's income taken into account in determining eligibility for three federal assistance programs—Supplemental Security Income (SSI), Aid to Families with Dependent Children, and food stamps) in their first three years in the United States (the first five years for SSI). (The sponsor is the person who promised to provide support for the immigrant as part of the immigration process.) Until the early 1950s, most Asian Americans who were foreign-born could not become naturalized citizens and so they could not vote or, in some states, own land. In another situation, Mexicans who came to the United States under the Bracero Program were not eligible for citizenship, nor could they apply for state or federal public assistance programs. Until an immigrant becomes a U.S. citizen, he or she does not have the right to vote. Finally, the Constitution provides that no immigrant can become president of the United States. Although always part of the national dialogue on immigration, the extent to which distinctions should be made between the native-born and the foreign-born has become an increasingly intense part of the debate.

BACKGROUND TO IMMIGRATION NUMBERS

Immigration affects the size, composition, and distribution of populations, at any particular time and also, with continued immigration, over time. From a policy perspective, it is important to distinguish between flows and stocks of immigrants. *Flows* refer to people moving into the United States over a given **period of time**—say, the number of people admitted in calendar year 1990, as tallied by the Immigration and Naturalization Service.[10] *Stocks* consist of immigrants resident in the United States at a given **point in time**—say, as enumerated in the 1990 census. In general, policy most directly affects the flows of immigrants into the United States rather than the accumulated stock of all immigrants. Such an emphasis is understandable since, when compared with longer-term residents, recent immigrants are more likely to experience problems of economic and social adjustment, and they are likely to affect the community more immediately and more visibly.

Although it is important to monitor and analyze contemporary patterns of immigration, they must also be placed in a longer-term perspective. Doing so not only aids in the detection of emerging trends, but also promotes understanding of the unique characteristics and problems of the stock of immigrants at any particular point in time. In the remainder of this section, we briefly sketch the history of American immigration.

Volume of Immigration

U.S. immigration has been characterized by several wide swings. The data that have been compiled since the inception of official record keeping in 1821 reveal the boom in immigration from the late decades of the nineteenth century through the period immediately preceding World War I (see Figure 2.1).[11] This period, one of rapid urbanization and industrialization in the United States, saw especially large immigration from Southern and Eastern Europe. The peak year for admission of new legal immigrants to the United States was 1907, when almost 1.3 million immigrants entered and added more than 3 percent to the U.S. labor force.

After a trough during World War I, the Great Depression, and World War II, immigration increased steadily in subsequent decades. Compared with Europe

[10]The monitoring and description of the scale of U.S. immigration are relatively straightforward functions performed mainly by the Immigration and Naturalization Service and the Bureau of the Census. These sources confine their presentations to the factors of immigration: the number involved, the countries of origin, the key demographic characteristics of immigrants at the time of entry, and the visa categories under which they enter the United States.

[11]U.S. immigration statistics have undergone many changes since the first registrations in 1820. In the early decades, only arrivals at seaports were counted. It was not until 1904 that data on immigrant arrivals became reasonably complete. Such statistics do not include a large number of immigrants from Canada in the 1800s, as well as European immigrants who arrived by ship in Canada and subsequently entered the United States by land routes. During the 1871-80 decade, an estimated 311,000 Canadians emigrated to the United States (McInnis, 1994). This number increased to 517,000 in the 1880s and remained large but decreased to 328,000 in the 1890s. Large numbers of European immigrants also entered the United States by land, using the cheaper fares that were available for ocean travel to Canada. Most of these Canadian and European immigrants were not counted in U.S. immigration statistics until late in the nineteenth century. Immigrants from Mexico who entered the United States by land routes in the 1800s also would not have been counted in official statistics.

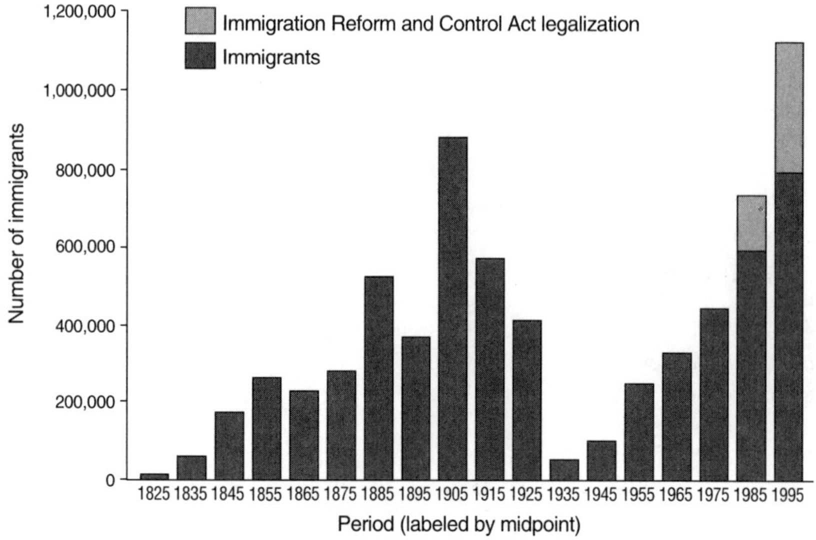

FIGURE 2.1 Average annual number of legal immigrants into the United States, 1820-1995.

and many other areas of the world, the United States enjoyed a high degree of political freedom and economic prosperity. Its expanding manufacturing and construction sectors offered ample job opportunities for a new wave of immigrants. The 1965 liberalizing changes in immigration legislation prompted even further increases, as the United States began to receive new immigrants from Asia and Latin America. At the same time, illegal immigrants began appearing in significant numbers. Since 1965, both the de jure changes in immigration law and the de facto situation regarding enforcement that has affected illegal immigration have dramatically altered the pattern of countries of origin.[12]

As the result of the liberalizing changes, coupled with the steady allure of the U.S. economy, immigration has had considerable influence on population growth in the United States during the twentieth century. Any meaningful discussion of that impact must deal not only with sheer numbers, but also with the ratio of immigrants to the resident population. Figure 2.2 presents the same immigration

[12]One complexity in Figure 2.1 deserves special mention. About 2.7 million formerly illegal immigrants received amnesty in 1986 and were allowed to seek permanent-resident status beginning in 1989. As these legalized aliens adjusted their legal status, the Immigration and Naturalization Service recorded them as new immigrants. A large proportion of the "immigrants" in official government data from 1989 to 1992 were persons who in fact had resided in the United States since before 1986. In 1991, for example, the INS recorded a total of 1,827,000 new immigrants; 1,123,000, or 61 percent, of those immigrants were IRCA legalization residents. The balance included 443,000 new arrivals and 261,000 persons adjusting from refugee and other forms of nonimmigrant status.

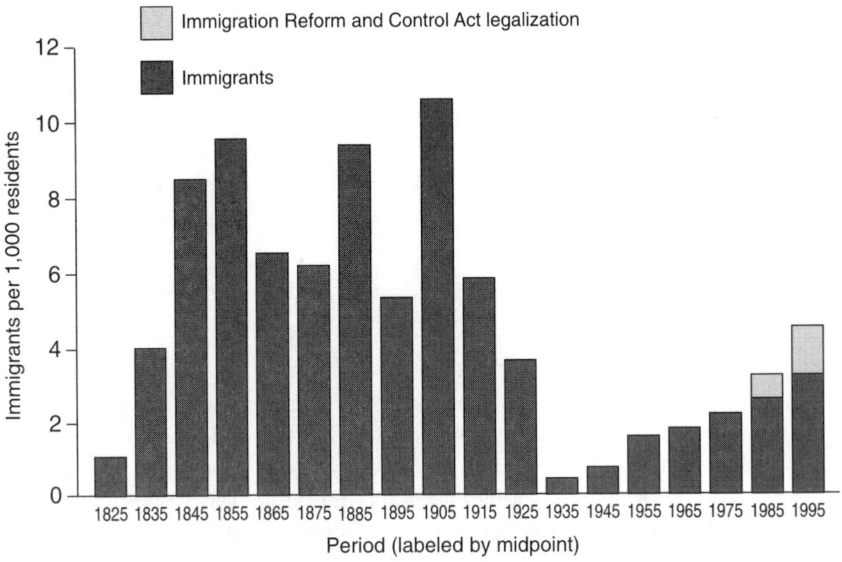

FIGURE 2.2 Average annual number of legal immigrants into the United States per 1,000 residents, 1820-1995.

data that is arrayed in Figure 2.1, but expressing the annual number of immigrants relative to 1,000 U.S. residents. This relative measure is a much better index of the nation's ability to absorb, both economically and culturally, a given number of immigrants.[13] Figure 2.2 puts the volume of current immigration in a very different light. For example, the U.S. population was 263 million in 1995, more than three times the 76 million of 1900, and it will probably reach about 277 million in 2000. The number of immigrants has grown, too, but the ratio to total population is now about one-half that of the early twentieth century—5 per 1,000 for 1990-2000 compared with 11 per 1,000 in 1900-1910.[14]

Another way to look at immigration and population change is to ask how much of population growth is attributable to immigration. Assuming a continuation of current trends through the end of the decade, the U.S. population will

[13]National figures do not reflect regional concentration of immigrants, which may be particularly important for cultural effects. A later section of this chapter highlights the geography of U.S. immigration.

[14] This trend was not smooth. As war and depression hampered immigration in the 1920s and 1930s the ratio fell off to 1 per 1,000, then turned upward with the resumption of immigration in the 1950s.

Relative net immigration is also lower than it was a century ago; it was 4.0 percent at the beginning of this decade, compared with 6.5 percent in the first decade of the century. The differences are less for net immigration than for gross immigration alone because of the much higher levels of emigration (both in relative and absolute terms) early in the twentieth century.

grow by 22.1 million. Net immigration will be 8.2 million, or 37 percent of the population change for the 1990s. Even though immigration is now at a much lower rate than it was at the turn of the century, it plays a greater role in population growth than it did then—37 percent compared with 28 percent for the 1900 to 1910 decade. The reason lies with the other contributor of population growth—the number of births to the resident population, which has dropped with the decline in overall fertility rates.

The Impact of Immigration on Population

Changes in the foreign-born population lag shifts in immigration. As immigrants enter the country, they affect the composition of the population in several ways. First, they can alter the racial and ethnic composition of the population if their proportions on those dimensions differ from those of the resident population. Second, new immigrants add to the foreign-born population, thus increasing the fraction of the population that is foreign-born. The size of the foreign-born population derives principally from past levels of immigration, but it is also affected by emigration and mortality. High levels of recent immigration combined with little emigration would increase the size of the foreign-born population. As time passes, mortality begins to diminish entry cohorts so that the numbers of foreign-born decrease if they are not replenished by additional immigrants.

The foreign-born population then represents the cumulative number of past immigrants, diminished by mortality and emigration. Figure 2.3 charts the number of foreign-born residents over time; Figure 2.4 expresses that number as a fraction of the U.S. population.

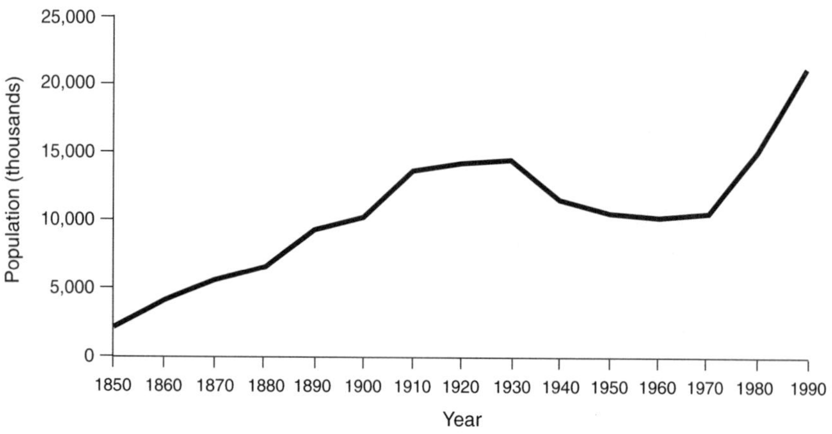

FIGURE 2.3 Number of foreign-born residents in the United States, 1850-1990.

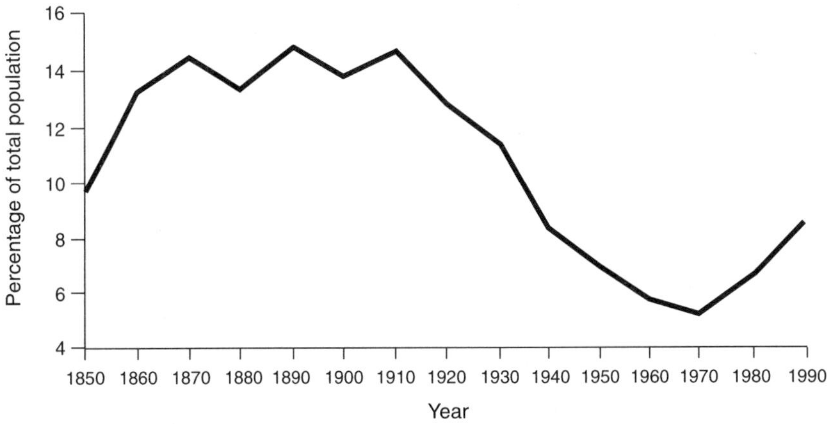

FIGURE 2.4 Percentage foreign-born residents in the United States, 1850-1990.

The size of the foreign-born population in the United States has reflected, with a lag, the changing course of immigration. Approximately 2.2 million foreign-born persons resided in the United States in 1850, accounting for 9.7 percent of the total population. With the continuing heavy immigration of the late nineteenth and early twentieth centuries, the foreign-born population grew steadily, reaching a peak of about 14.4 million in 1930. At the same time, it increased as a proportion of the U.S. population. The proportion peaked at about 15 percent in 1890, but it changed little between 1860 to 1920, hovering around 13 to 15 percent, because the native-born population grew at the same rate as the foreign-born population during that period.

With the decline in immigration and with considerable emigration during World War I, the Great Depression, and World War II, the foreign-born population decreased in both number and proportion as mortality reduced the aging wave of immigrants from the turn of the century. From 1930 to 1970, the number of foreign-born residents in the United States declined to 10.5 million, roughly the same as in 1900. The proportion of foreign-born in the total population began decreasing earlier, after 1910, as the native-born population grew relatively more rapidly. It reached a low in 1970, when it accounted for only 1 out of 20 Americans.

The large increase in immigration that began in the 1960s ended the 40-year decline in the foreign-born population. By 1995, the number of foreign-born persons residing in the United States reached 25 million, the highest level in the nation's history. Their current proportion to the population, however, is less than two-thirds of that which prevailed from 1860 to 1920: just over 8 percent of the population was foreign-born in 1990 versus 13 to 15 percent at the turn of the century. Assuming that immigration and emigration continue at current levels to

2000, the foreign-born population will increase to about 28 million and the percentage will increase to about 10 percent, a ratio still considerably below those of a century ago.

Country and Region of Origin of Immigrants

Our review of the history of immigration legislation indicated that the national origin of immigrants into the United States has experienced large shifts twice: in the period from about 1880 to 1920, immigration from the United Kingdom (including Ireland at that time), France, Germany, the Benelux countries, and the Scandinavian countries decreased and immigration from Southern and Eastern Europe increased. More recently, a greater proportion of immigrants has been originating in Asia and Latin America.

With these recent shifts, the composition of the foreign-born by national origin has changed; Figure 2.5 displays these historical trends. As a companion to this series, Table 2.2 lists the region of origin of the foreign-born population in selected census years from 1850 to 1990. Before the Immigration and Nationality Act Amendments of 1965 changed the national-origin quotas, Europe and Canada were the dominant sources of U.S. immigrants. Almost two-thirds of immigrants during the 1950s came from these areas. The rest were from Asia (6 percent), Mexico (12 percent), and other countries of Latin America (14 percent).

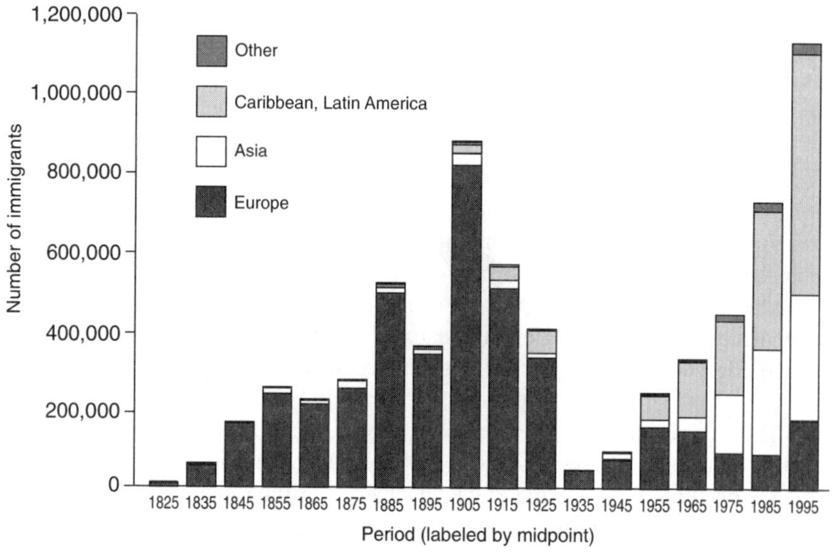

FIGURE 2.5 Average annual number of legal immigrants into the United States by region of last residence, 1820-1995.

TABLE 2.2 Region of Origin of Foreign-Born Population in the United States, 1850-1990

Region of Origin	1850	1900	1950	1970	1990
Canada and Europe	97%	98%	89%	67%	26%
Caribbean and Latin America	1	1	6	19	43
Asia	0	1	3	9	25
All others[a]	2	0	2	5	6
Total Foreign-born population (in millions)	2.2	10.3	10.4	9.6	19.8

[a]The all other category includes Africa, Oceania, Pacific and Atlantic Islands, persons born at sea, and persons with no reported region of origin.

Source: U.S. Bureau of the Census (1975: Part 1; 1993).

As the number of legal immigrants rose during each of the past four decades, from 2.5 million in the 1950s to 6 million in the 1980s, their racial and ethnic composition has also changed.

Immigration from Europe and Canada has decreased steadily both in absolute and relative terms during the past four decades. By the 1990s, only about 14 percent of legal immigrants came from these traditional sources.[15] In relative terms, the biggest gain has been by Asia, which had 6 percent of legal immigrants in the 1950s and 44 percent in the 1980s. About 2.6 million Asians entered legally in the 1980s, more than all immigrants in the 1950s.

Latin American immigration expanded from 26 percent of legal immigration in the 1950s to 40 percent in the 1960s, where it has remained since. In the 1980s, Latin America accounted for 2.4 million of legal immigrants. Mexico is the largest single source of legal immigrants, accounting for 12 to 14 percent of the flow during each of the past four decades. When illegal immigration is included, Latin America far surpasses Asia as the source for immigration, and Mexico becomes the predominant single source of immigrants into the United States.

CURRENT U.S. IMMIGRATION POLICY

U.S. immigration policy has revolved around five fundamental factors: social, economic, diversity, humanitarian, and national security. Although current

[15]The availability of diversity visas has lifted the European share to about 20 percent in recent years.

debate tends to emphasize the economic aspects of immigration, immigration policy has historically been based on a broader set of policy goals, especially on the principles of family reunification. The social goal of family reunification is principally to unite nuclear families. It has strong and sustained political support from its main beneficiaries—U.S. citizens who wish to sponsor their family relatives for immigration to the United States.

Some aspects of the economic goals for immigration may conflict—for example, allowing workers to enter who have skills and can secure U.S. employment, yet guarding the wages and employment opportunities for resident workers.

One aim of the 1990 Immigration Act was to diversify immigration into the United States. In a major reversal from the early decades of the twentieth century, the stream of immigrants in recent decades has been dominated by Hispanics and Asians. The effort became to promote pluralism by expanding the proportion of European immigrants.

Fulfilling the goal of humanitarian assistance, about one-fourth of the immigrants admitted into the United States since 1945 have been refugees and asylees. Refugee admissions as a proportion of total immigration, including illegal immigration, has decreased in recent years, now accounting for about 15 percent. These admissions have been guided by the goal of offering protection to those fleeing persecution. The current legislative framework for humanitarian admissions is the 1980 Refugee Act, which has three goals: to base admissions on recognized international criteria; to create a more manageable flow of refugees; and to establish a program for resettling refugees with financial, medical, and social support. Since 1980, U.S. policy has recognized that many refugees arrive in the United States without money, family, or ways of making a living.

Emigration

A substantial proportion of immigrants leave the United States. Some fail to find jobs or to adjust to life here. Others discover better opportunities back home. A few decide to move to a third country.

There have been emigrants as long as there have been immigrants. Some of the first colonists eventually returned to England. After the War of Independence, many U.S. residents moved to Canada, primarily to New Brunswick and Nova Scotia. Many turn-of-the-century immigrants from Italy, Greece, and Poland went home. It appears that a substantial proportion of immigrants at the turn of the century, particularly males, moved to the United States on a temporary basis. They earned income, accumulated some money, and returned after several years to their home country. These temporary immigrants were, in some ways, similar to the temporary farmworkers who were admitted to the United States under the Bracero Program from 1943 to 1964 and possibly also to recent illegal sojourners to the United States.

Information on emigration is important for several reasons. In terms of simple numbers, emigration is part of the equation that yields net immigration—which, after all, is what implants lasting effects in the U.S. economy and population. Even in the short term, the admission of 1 million immigrants a year would have vastly different consequences, depending on whether, say, all of them stayed or 500,000 among them returned. Beyond mere numbers, emigration alters the characteristics of immigrant cohorts; we discuss in Chapter 8 the issues in connection with language. Similarly, virtually all labor market tests of the ability of immigrants to assimilate into the labor market follow cohorts of entering immigrants. If large fractions of a cohort emigrate and we do not have good estimates of the selectivity of this emigration, then it is impossible to know whether the cohort successfully assimilated or not.

Emigrants select themselves, but why? They may be the most skilled, drawn by better job prospects in other countries, in which case the average labor market success among those who remain is lowered. The less skilled, too, may be drawn by better prospects elsewhere, thus improving the average quality of the remaining cohort of immigrants.

Demographic information on emigration is particularly scarce and elusive. Estimates of the level of emigration are periodically updated, but these contain a substantial range of estimates. There is some information on the relationship between emigration and variables such as country of origin and sex. However, definitive knowledge is lacking on the relationship between emigration and many important behavioral variables, including fertility, the use of public assistance programs, and labor force characteristics.[16]

Some demographic studies have sought to identify the influence of sex and schooling on emigration (see Jasso and Rosenzweig, 1990:138-148). They suggest that men tend to emigrate more than women do, and, at least in earlier periods, that those with more schooling tend to return more than those with less. Interpreting these observations calls for caution, because the information is limited and because it is not current.

Still, available studies suggest that a high proportion of illegal immigrants are sojourners: they come to the United States for several years but eventually return to their home countries. According to studies by Douglas Massey and his colleagues (Massey et al., 1990), a high proportion of Mexican illegal immigrants return to their original villages after one or more prolonged periods of working in the United States.

These caveats aside, available estimates suggest that between roughly 35 and

---

[16]Little is known on these topics because the data on emigration are weak: the United States does not record and link departures of individual immigrants with original arrival data; it does not have, at present, any ongoing longitudinal surveys of immigrants that would provide information about emigration; and, finally, information on illegal immigration is scanty.

45 percent of immigrants emigrate—either to return to their home country or to move to a third country (Jasso and Rosenzweig, 1990:124). Gross legal immigration numbers of about 800,000 per year, therefore, overstate the net effect of immigration.

Immigrants have a lesser or greater tendency to return to their home country, depending on where that is. Europeans have the highest rate of emigration, followed by those from the Western Hemisphere and from Asia. These numbers are of obvious importance for assessing the net immigration rates of people from these regions. The differences between gross and net immigration figures are generally greater for European countries than for Asian countries, for example, because of their higher emigration rates.

Using data from the 1990 decennial census and from the Current Population Survey in conjunction with demographic estimates of immigration and mortality, Census Bureau demographers Bashir Ahmed and Gregg Robinson (1996) suggest that emigration currently totals about 300,000 per year. Given about 800,000 legal immigrants a year, emigration claims about one-third of immigrants.[17]

Legal Immigrants

The tension among policy goals becomes clear in examining the complex set of rules governing entry of legal immigrants. Current U.S. policy sets limits on both the overall number of immigrants and the number of immigrants in various categories. In pursuit of varying policy goals, however, these limits are tempered by exceptions. Categories are temporarily changed to accommodate new needs for humanitarian assistance, and new categories are introduced to allow for special cases. Given this complexity, it would be impossible to completely describe current policy in a few pages, so the following gives only its outlines—intended both to give a general idea of current policy and to illustrate its complexity.

Current U.S. immigration policy sets a flexible annual limit on the number of new legal immigrants, and then uses a complex preference system to decide which applicants will be given visas. The baseline annual limit now stands at 675,000 immigrants, down from 700,000 during the 1992-94 fiscal years. The annual

[17]One specific use of emigration estimates is by the Social Security Administration, which must make assumptions about the proportion of immigrants who may depart from the United States. How many will not need retirement benefits? How many will be eligible for benefits? How many who are eligible will not apply? Answers to these questions cannot be lightly given because of their important fiscal repercussions. At the moment, the Social Security Administration assumes that about one-third of immigrants will emigrate and will not need retirement benefits (see Duleep, 1994, for a detailed discussion). Although this assumption appears to be consistent with the demographic estimates cited above, it may not accurately measure the demand emigrants will make on the system: many will have worked the required number of quarters to qualify for overseas payment of the retirement benefits.

limit is flexible in the sense that it may be higher in a given fiscal year if some of the preference visas went unused in the previous year. It is also not an absolute limit, in that the number of immigrants in a given year can exceed the cap because some categories of immigrants have no numerical limits—spouses, minor children, and parents of adult U.S. citizens; children born abroad to legal permanent residents; refugees and asylees who are adjusting their status to permanent resident; and a few other groups such as Amerasians and persons eligible for legalization under IRCA.

Numerically limited immigration consists of two broad categories with separate limits—family-sponsored preferences and employment-based preferences. These are subdivided into groups, each of which is allotted a certain number of visas based on immigration levels in the previous years. Table 2.3 gives the categories of admission with their limits and numbers of admissions for 1995. Admissions for a particular category include dependents of immigrants admitted under that classification, where applicable. Unused visas in higher preference subgroups may be reallocated to lower preference subgroups within that same category. Small differences between the numerical limit and the number of actual immigrant admissions may also occur because immigrants who are granted visas have four months to use them and may not decide to enter the United States until the following year.

In addition to the limits on overall numbers, there is a provision requiring that no more than 7 percent of family or employment preferences go to immigrants from any one country. Because of uneven demand within the categories, visas in one country may go unused while applicants from other countries are denied visas because their country's limit has been reached.[18]

Most recent immigrants were admitted on the basis of family ties to persons living in the United States. In 1995, relatives accounted for almost two-thirds of total admissions. Spouses and minor children of U.S. citizens made up 31 percent of total admissions. Those admitted under employment-based preferences and refugees accounted for most of the remainder of total admissions: 12 percent and 16 percent, respectively. Even among employment-based admissions, family ties are important: as can be seen in Table 2.4, over half of immigrants admitted in 1995 on employment-preference visas were spouses or children of those entering for employment purposes.

Because relatives of U.S. citizens account for such a large fraction of current immigration, that group would be affected by any sharp decrease in the number of immigrants admitted into the United States. Although admission of close rela-

---

[18]This rule, however, has exceptions—special provisions exempt a large portion of the second-family-preference visas allocated to spouses and children of permanent residents from the per-country limit to help to reduce a large backlog in applications for these visas from some countries, for example Mexico.

TABLE 2.3 Allocation of Permanent Residence Visas, Fiscal Year 1995

Type of Visa		1995 Limit	1995 Admissions
Family-sponsored preferences, total		253,721	238,122
1st	Unmarried adult children of U.S. citizens	23,400	15,182
2nd	Spouses, minor children, and unmarried adult children of permanent residents	114,200	144,535
3rd	Married adult children of U.S. citizens	23,400	20,876
4th	Brothers and sisters of U.S. citizens (at least 21 years of age)	65,000	57,529
Employment-based preferences, total		146,503	85,336
1st	Priority workers	41,858	17,339
2nd	Professionals with advanced degrees or aliens of exceptional ability	41,858	10,475
3rd	Skilled workers and professionals, Chinese Student Protection Act, and needed unskilled workers	41,858	50,245
4th	Special immigrants	10,465	6,737
5th	Employment creation ("investors")	10,465	540
IRCA dependents		0	277
Diversity immigrants		55,000	47,245
Immediate relatives of U.S. citizens		none	220,360
Children born abroad to permanent residents		none	1,894
Refugee and asylee adjustments to permanent resident		none	114,664
Miscellaneous categories (IRCA legalization, Amerasians, parolees)		none	12,563
Total			720,461

IRCA = Immigration Reform and Control Act of 1986

Sources: Data from U.S. Immigration and Naturalization Service (1997:Tables A and 4).

TABLE 2.4 Admissions by Detailed Category, Fiscal Years 1993 and 1995

Type of Admission		1995	1993
Family-preference admissions, total		238,122	226,776
1st	Unmarried adult children of U.S. citizens	11,219	9,636
	Children of those unmarried adult children	3,963	3,183
2nd	Spouses of permanent residents	38,828	43,033
	Children of permanent residents	59,574	41,450
	Children of those spouses or children	12,558	14,121
	Unmarried adult children of permanent residents	24,174	23,221
	Children of those unmarried adult children	9,401	6,483
3rd	Married adult children of U.S. citizens	5,719	6,475
	Spouses of those married adult children	5,052	5,667
	Children of those married adult children	10,105	11,243
4th	Brothers and sisters of U.S. citizens	19,332	20,983
	Spouses of those brothers and sisters	13,293	14,014
	Children of those brothers and sisters	24,904	27,267
Employment-preference admissions		85,336	147,012
1st	Aliens with extraordinary ability	1,194	1,259
	Outstanding professors or researchers	1,617	1,676
	Multinational executives or managers	3,922	5,088
	Spouses and children of 1st preference immigrants	10,606	13,091
2nd	Professionals holding advanced degrees	4,952	13,801
	Spouses and children of those professionals	5,523	15,667
3rd	Skilled workers	9,094	12,813
	Professionals with a baccalaureate degree	5,792	9,560
	Spouses and children of skilled workers and professionals	23,262	28,434
	Chinese Student Protection Act	4,213	26,915
	Needed unskilled workers	3,636	4,405
	Spouses and children of unskilled workers	4,248	5,562
4th	Ministers and their spouses and children	1,993	2,291
	Other religious workers and their spouses and children	2,506	2,909
	Miscellaneous[a]	2,238	2,958
5th	Employment creation	540	583
Immediate relatives of U.S. citizens, total		220,360	255,059
Spouses		123,238	145,843
Children		48,740	46,788
Parents of adult U.S. citizens		48,382	62,428
Children born abroad to permanent residents		1,894	2,030

continued on next page

TABLE 2.4 Continued

Type of Admission	1995	1993
Dependents of IRCA-legalized permanent residents, total	277	55,344
Spouses	105	17,145
Children	172	38,199
Diversity immigrants	47,245	33,468
Refugee and asylee adjustments, total	114,664	127,343
Cuban refugees	9,579	6,976
Other refugees	97,248	108,563
Asylees	7,837	11,804
Amerasians	939	11,116
Miscellaneous other adjustments and arrivals[b]	7,357	21,866
Total	720,461	904,292

IRCA = Immigration Reform and Control Act of 1986

[a]Employees of U.S. government abroad, Panama Canal Act, foreign medical graduates, retired employees of international organizations, juvenile court dependents, aliens serving in the U.S. Armed Forces, and the spouses and children of such immigrants.

[b]Includes displaced Tibetans, employees of U.S. businesses in Hong Kong, Cuban/Haitian entrants, former H-1 nurses, parolees from the Soviet Union or Indochina, miscellaneous other adjustments, American Indians born in Canada, and children born subsequent to issuance of visa.

Source: U.S. Immigration and Naturalization Service (1994:Table 5; 1997:Table 5).

tives of U.S. citizens seems to have broad support, even some of these immigrants have aroused misgivings. For instance, concern that sham marriages were being used to gain admission led to passage of the Immigration Marriage Fraud Amendments of 1986. Under these amendments, an immigrant who is admitted based on his or her recent marriage to a U.S. citizen or permanent-resident alien receives a conditional visa and must show the Immigration and Naturalization Service that the marriage was and is still intact at the end of two years, a condition that 94 percent of the cases reviewed in 1994 satisfied. A second concern has been use of Supplementary Security Income (SSI) benefits by immigrant parents of U.S. citizens. Without a history of work in the United States, most such immigrants are not eligible to receive earned Social Security retirement benefits, and SSI becomes an alternative source of income for some elderly people with few other resources. Partially in response to this concern, the recent welfare reform legislation has cut off immigrants' eligibility for SSI until they achieve citizenship.

Immigrants with family ties to U.S. citizens account not only for the majority of current immigrants, but also for the vast majority of those who are on waiting lists for visas. As Table 2.5 illustrates, as of January 1994, about 3.6 million people were on the U.S. State Department lists of persons registered for visas, most of whom had registered as family-preference immigrants. Two preferences had over 1 million registrants: spouses and minor children of permanent residents and brothers and sisters of U.S. citizens. Waits for visas are particularly long for applicants from the Philippines, Mexico, and India. For example, in December 1996 immigrant visas for brothers and sisters of U.S. citizens from the Philippines were issued to those whose U.S. relative had petitioned for their immigration in November 1977 (Bureau of Consular Affairs). Given the growth in the number of registrants in this category since 1977, recent applicants can expect an even longer wait if current immigration provisions are maintained.

In the employment-preference categories, the majority of admissions are of skilled workers or those admitted on the basis of high levels of education, along with their dependents. Executives and managers of multinational corporations are also an important component of these admissions, accounting for 58 percent

TABLE 2.5 Immigrant Waiting List, January 1994

Type of Preference		Number
Family Preferences, total		3,462,147
1st	Unmarried adult children of citizens	63,499
2nd	Total	1,498,075
	Spouses, minor children of permanent residents	1,047,496
	Unmarried adult children of permanent residents	450,579
3rd	Married adult children of citizens	257,110
4th	Brothers and sisters of citizens	1,643,463
Employment preferences, total		149,974
1st	Priority workers	8,315
2nd	Professionals with advanced degrees, aliens of exceptional ability	11,159
3rd	Total	125,083
	Skilled workers and bachelor's degree holders	30,735
	Unskilled workers	94,348
4th	Special immigrants	5,241
5th	Employment creation ("investors")	176
Total		3,612,121

Source: U.S. Commission on Immigration Reform (1994:Table 6:198).

of all priority workers in 1995. The majority (56 percent) of employment-preference immigrants in 1995 were born in Asia, with China, the Philippines, and India sending the largest numbers. A relatively small number of unskilled workers are admitted each year as employment-preference immigrants. This unskilled category accounts for the largest backlog of applications for employment-preference visas, with about 94,000 registrants in January 1994, of a total of about 150,000 in the employment category.

Diversity immigrants fall outside the preference system but also face numerical limits. In 1994, Poland, Ireland, the United Kingdom, and Canada together accounted for 92 percent of the immigrants admitted under the temporary version of this program. The permanent version of this program, which started in 1995, provides 55,000 visas to nationals of countries that have sent fewer than 50,000 legal immigrants to the United States over the previous five years. Applicants from eligible countries must have at least a high school education and two years of work experience. The 55,000 visas are allocated to six broad regions in proportion to their populations (excluding ineligible countries) and then are distributed to applicants from eligible countries within those regions through an annual lottery. For the 1998 lottery, the majority of visas will be allocated to Africa and Europe, from which Great Britain and Poland are excluded.

Total immigrant admissions vary substantially from year to year, due both to legislated changes and to changes in the number of visa applicants in the categories that are not oversubscribed. To illustrate these shifts, Table 2.4 includes detailed admissions for 1993 as well as 1995. The higher level of immigration in 1993 was due in part to special provisions for particular immigrant groups: the allocation of 55,000 additional visas specifically for the spouses and children of IRCA-legalized permanent residents in fiscal years 1992-94; the allowance for certain Chinese nationals to adjust their status to permanent resident as employment-preference immigrants, put in place by the Chinese Student Protection Act in October 1992; and provision of visas for Amerasians, for whom admissions peaked in 1992. The difference between admissions in the two years also reflects changes in the number of admissions in certain categories; the number of immigrant spouses and parents of U.S. citizens admitted into the United States was substantially lower in 1995 than in 1993, as were employment-preference immigrants.

The Changing Size of Government

The America to which the immigrants are arriving today differs in salient ways from the America of earlier immigrant waves. One of the most critical lies in the changing role of government at all levels. Immigrants have always affected governmental outlays and receipts, and cries that they bankrupt school budgets or the dole were often heard in the nineteenth and early twentieth centuries.

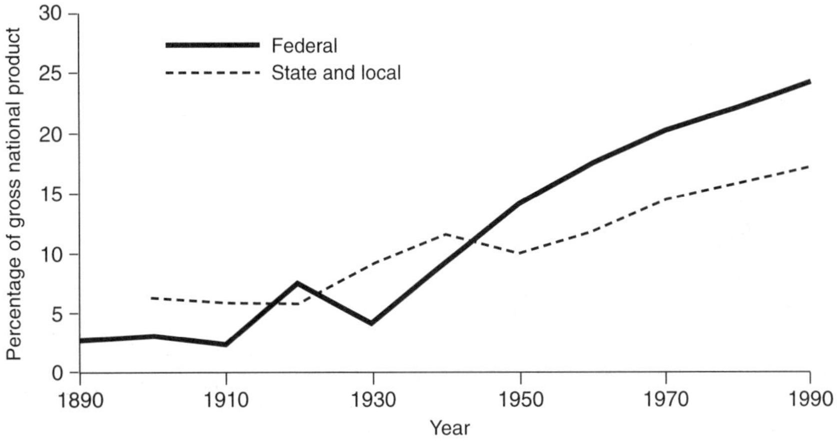

FIGURE 2.6 Government expenditures as a proportion of gross national product, federal and state and local governments, 1890-1990 (percentage). Source: U.S. Bureau of the Census (1975, 1996).

On this dimension, America is very different today. To demonstrate this difference, Figure 2.6 presents government expenditures as a fraction of gross national product (GNP) for federal, state, and local units.[19] During the last decades of the nineteenth century and the first few decades of the twentieth, the relative size of governments was low and stable. Expenditures at the federal level were only 3 percent of GNP and those at all levels accounted for less than 10 percent. Any assessment of the fiscal effects of these earlier waves of immigration, whether positive or negative, must be considerably less important in an overall evaluation of immigration. Figure 2.6 shows how different our world has become. Starting with the initiatives of the New Deal, government spending at all levels expanded rapidly, with little sign of abatement. By 1993, the federal government allocated about one-quarter of the gross domestic product (GDP), and state and local governments nearly one-fifth. Combined, the share of government spending in the country's economy has expanded four-fold from the time of the immigrant waves at the beginning of this century.

Nor it is only the level of government that has changed. Figure 2.7 divides the federal government spending into four categories: national defense, interest on the public debt, veterans benefits (largely veterans of the Civil War in the early periods), and other government expenditures. The principal historical trend

[19]A portion of the federal budget consists of outlays to state and local governments. There is some double counting in Figure 2.6, but it is a relatively small amount and does not significantly alter these trends.

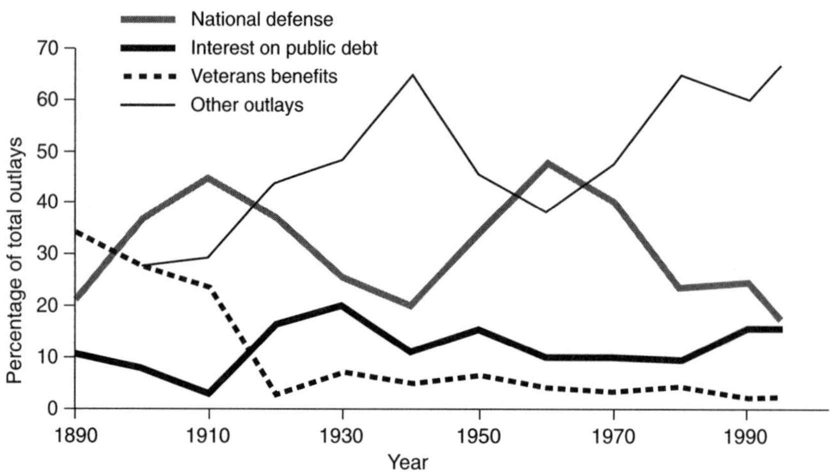

FIGURE 2.7 Outlays of the federal government by major categories, 1890-1996. Source: U.S. Bureau of the Census (1975, 1996).

is the decline in the first three categories in favor of the fourth. For example, in 1900 other government expenditures accounted for 28 percent of the total: today it represents 66 percent.

This shift in type of spending is important because immigration largely represents a net fiscal benefit to natives in the first three categories, but a net fiscal cost in the fourth. As we argue in Chapter 6, national defense and interest on the national debt are public goods. Having immigrants pay for some of these public goods reduces the amount that natives have to pay. Similarly, immigrants who arrived after the end of the Civil War contributed to the pension payments of those who participated in that war. The final category, however, includes all government transfer payments, for which immigrants are included as beneficiaries.

These simple figures alone argue that the fiscal effects of immigration should assume a much large role in our immigration debate than they did in earlier times. This conviction is reinforced by an examination of the changing composition of government spending. Because these effects are potentially so much larger, we will devote two chapters in this volume to them.

Nonimmigrants

Although this report concentrates on the economic and demographic effects of legal immigrants, two other groups of foreign-born people enter this country and ultimately affect attitudes toward immigration: nonimmigrants and illegal immigrants. The size and demographic composition of these two groups are briefly discussed.

TABLE 2.6 Nonimmigrants Admitted, by Class of Admission, Fiscal Year 1994

Class of Admission	Number
All classes	22,118,706
Tourists (temporary visitors for business or pleasure)	20,318,933
Students	394,001
Temporary workers and trainees (and their families)	229,195
Transit aliens	330,936
Treaty traders and investors (and their families)	141,030
Exchange visitors and families	259,171
Intracompany transferees and families	154,427
Foreign government officials	105,229
Representatives of international organizations	74,722
Others	111,182

Source: U.S. Immigration and Naturalization Service (1996:Table 39).

As explained above, a nonimmigrant is an alien admitted into the country for a specific purpose and period of time. Most nonimmigrant categories are subject to no restrictions on the total number of admissions, but length of stay or of employment is often limited. Consequently, the number of nonimmigrants admitted in recent years far exceeds the number of legal immigrants. As Table 2.6 documents, more than 22 million nonimmigrants arrived during 1994, more than 25 times the number of legal immigrants admitted in that year. These numbers grossly understate the relative importance of legal immigrants, since many nonimmigrants stay for only a short time. On one hand, these statistics also may count some individuals more than once, since many nonimmigrants make more than one trip in a fiscal year. On the other hand, they leave out many nonimmigrant arrivals; for example, tourists from Canada or Mexico are not counted when they cross the border.

Nonimmigrants come for a variety of purposes. More than 9 in every 10 (approximately 20 million) were temporary visitors or tourists, most of whom visit for only a few days or a few weeks. The next two most important categories are students and those who were admitted for some type of temporary employment or training.

Nonimmigrants have nontrivial economic effects on this country. Foreign tourists pour money into many large U.S. cities—especially New York, San Francisco, Los Angeles, Miami, and Washington, D.C.—as well as into major tourist sites, including national parks and theme parks. More than 500,000 foreign students, most of whom have financial support from abroad, are in the United States as nonimmigrants; they form an important part of undergraduate, graduate, and professional programs and constituted about 4 percent of U.S. college enrollments in 1990 (Institute for International Education, 1996).[20] Nonimmigrants who enter the United States for temporary employment range from international opera stars to employees of international companies who come to the United States for short-term training or work.

Nonimmigrants are a component of larger immigration processes. Although the overwhelming majority of nonimmigrants leave the United States after satisfying the terms of their U.S. admission, it is thought that about 40 percent of resident illegal immigrants originally enter the United States as nonimmigrants, usually as tourists or students, and then overstay their visas or work illegally. Nonimmigrants are also an important source of subsequent immigration. A substantial number of foreign-born college students complete their education in the United States and, responding to suitable employment opportunities here, eventually seek permanent-resident status so that they can live and work in the United States.

Illegal Immigrants

The increasing ease and relative cheapness of travel and improvements in information have greatly spurred illegal international immigration around the world in recent decades. Although most developed countries experience them, illegal flows into the United States have been comparatively high, especially from Mexico. In other countries experiencing large-scale immigration, such as Australia and Canada, illegal immigration has stirred less concern, mostly because it is assumed that it has been negligible.[21] (It is more difficult to slip into these two countries because the one does not share a land border with any other country and the other shares one only with the United States.)[22]

Illegal immigration has accounted for a substantial proportion of overall population change due to international migration to the United States. Figure 2.8 shows the average annual number of legal and illegal immigrants by decade. During the 1980s, illegal immigration accounted for about 225,000, or about one-fifth, of the 1.4 million average annual immigrants. Illegal immigration into the United States is not new, but no demographic estimates are available for these earlier periods.[23]

---

[20]The total number of foreign-born students enrolled in college in 1990 was 1.9 million, or 14 of total college enrollments of 13.8 million (U.S. Bureau of the Census, 1993: Table 3; 1996: Table 231). About one-fourth of foreign-students in college are nonimmigrants; the remainder are immigrants, or entered as immigrants with their parents.

[21]Illegal immigration exists in other countries (Martin and Widgren, 1996), although the volume and importance of illegal immigration is particularly noteworthy in the United States.

[22]Other countries, such as Germany, have long land borders across which illegals may cross but have only small resident illegal populations. In the case of Germany, the government maintains strong internal controls that seem to reduce illegal immigration.

[23]Immigration laws in the late 1800s prohibited the entrance of paupers and the feeble-minded, although some of these persons entered the United States as illegal immigrants. After the enactment of the Chinese Exclusion Act, illegal Chinese immigrants continued to enter the United States, attracted by job opportunities in mining, railroads, and other fields.

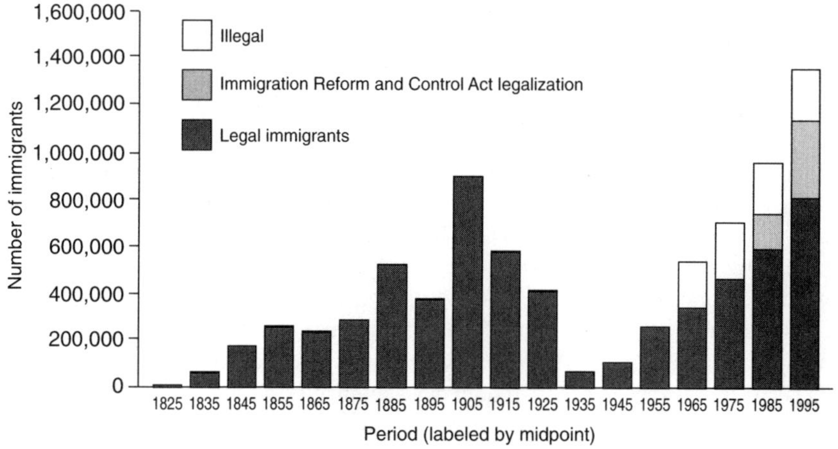

FIGURE 2.8 Average annual number of immigrants, legal and illegal, into the United States, 1820-1995. Source: Passel and Edmonston (1994:Figure 2.1). Data for the 1990s from the Immigration and Naturalization Service for legal immigrants and from the Bureau of the Census for illegal immigrants.

The characteristics of illegal immigrants emerge in studies about those who sought amnesty in 1986 under the general provisions of IRCA (as distinct from those who applied as agricultural workers). The heavy majority of the formerly illegal aliens were from Mexico (70 percent), and most were working-age men (Neuman and Tienda, 1994). Most illegal immigrants reside in only a few states, with about 40 percent living in California.

One effect of IRCA was to greatly reduce the number of illegal immigrants residing in the United States—in a sense by redefinition, because it gave amnesty to those who could prove long-time residence. Yet, even with this fiat, tougher border enforcement, and the requirement that employers check new employees for legal residence, the number of illegal immigrants is estimated to have reached about 3 to 5 million in 1996, about the same level as before IRCA (Warren, 1996).

Current estimates of net illegal immigration are in the range of 200,000 to 300,000 per year, with some consensus that the number has been closer to the high end of the range in recent years (Warren, 1996; U.S. Bureau of the Census, 1996). A lot more people go back and forth across the border illegally. Moreover, it is believed, about 40 percent of the net addition of illegal immigrants were those who entered the United States legally, as nonimmigrant students or as tourists.

Although the United States has long directed the Border Patrol to restrict the entry of illegal immigrants, public concern about large numbers of illegal immigrants has come only in recent decades. The 1986 enactment of IRCA provided a more extensive program of control of illegal immigration. IRCA was designed to reduce illegal immigration through several means: by using employer sanctions to weaken the magnet of work for illegal immigrants, by legalizing formerly illegal immigrant farmworkers and thereby providing a legal labor force for agriculture, and by increasing the resources available for detection and apprehension of those trying to cross illegally into the United States from Mexico. Implementing the amnesty conditions of IRCA has been widely regarded as successful (Gonzalez Baker, 1990); following the 1986 legislative program, the flow of illegal entries appeared to decrease for several years (Passel et al., 1990). The latest estimates are that it has increased since then to about 275,000 per year, on average (Warren, 1996). Employer sanctions have proved difficult to enforce because of the increased use of fraudulent documents and the limited resources of the federal government. At the same time, there has been little success in developing a fraud-proof system that employers could easily use to verify the legal status of job applicants.

Population increases from illegal immigration have continued in recent years. Although many persons actually enter the United States illegally and about 1.5 million persons are apprehended each year as illegal immigrants, these numbers are misleading for policy discussion. First, many of those apprehended are arrested more than once, and INS data thus involve double- or triple-counting of people. Second, and just as important, many persons who enter as illegal immigrants subsequently return to their home country. Greater resources have been allocated to the Border Patrol to prevent the entrance of illegal immigrants.

Before the enactment of IRCA in 1986, it was estimated, 3 to 5 million illegal immigrants lived in the United States. As a result of IRCA's legalization program, more than 3 million persons sought legalization and, at last count, about 2.7 million have become legal residents. The 1986 legalization reduced substantially the size of the illegal immigrant population. But by 1996, the flow of new illegal entrants had brought the number to an estimated 5 million (Warren, 1996).

Illegal immigrants enter the United States by many routes. Although most of the public attention has been on clandestine crossings of the land border with Mexico, they account for about 60 percent of illegal immigrants. The rest enter legally and then overstay their visas. Restricting the growth of the illegal immigrant population, therefore, calls also for programs that address this group of would-be residents.

IMMIGRANT CHARACTERISTICS

Gender

In earlier periods of immigration to the United States, immigrants were predominantly male. Figure 2.9 shows that this sharp gender imbalance did not give

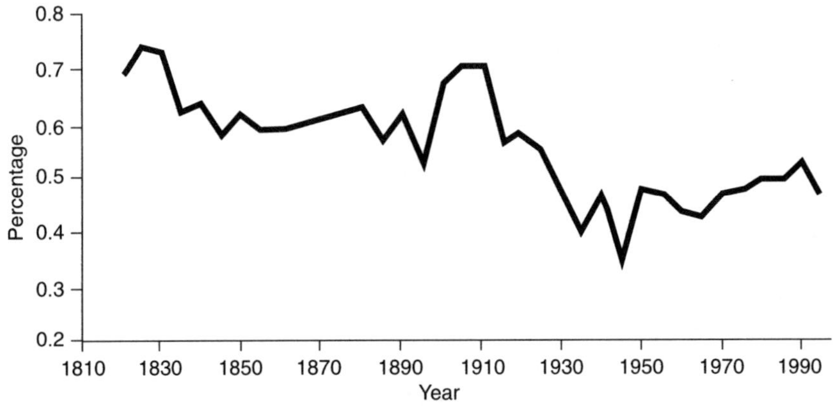

FIGURE 2.9 Proportion of immigrants who are male, 1820-1990. Source: U.S. Bureau of the Census (1975, 1996); U.S. Immigration and Naturalization Service (1994, 1996, 1997).

way to relatively equal numbers of women and men until the 1930s. This historic imbalance was even more pronounced among prime-aged adults. Among immigrants in their late twenties, the ratio of men to women was greater than 3 to 1 (Carter and Sutch, 1996). This tilt toward men should not be surprising; in virtually all contexts, men have been historically more migratory than women, especially when economic betterment was the primary motive for moving. As U.S. immigration policy changed and family reunification became a more dominant reason to come to the United States, the gender balance shifted. Since the 1930s, cohorts of immigrants—the successive groups of immigrants who arrive in a given period of time—have been more equally split between men and women (Carter and Sutch, 1996). In 1995, for example, women accounted for slightly over half of all legal immigrants—54 percent.

Why should the proportion of males and females matter for the way immigrants affect American society? A male-dominated immigrant pool has the following implications: without mates from their home country, many will eventually return home. Others will marry outside their group; their children will be of mixed parentage, with looser ties to the original home country. Men are also far more likely to engage in criminal activity, so that the crime rate associated with immigration may be higher.

The differences may also appear in the labor market. Women still work less than men do. With more women in the immigrant pool, the aggregate effect on the job market of a given number of new immigrants will generally be smaller. Since women hold different types of jobs than men do, different segments of the labor market will hear the competitive footsteps of these immigrants.

Because the sex ratio among immigrants is close to that among the native-born and is unlikely to change in the foreseeable future, the gender composition of immigrants is unlikely to have any significant effect on how immigrant outcomes differ from those of natives.

Age

New immigrants have always been disproportionately young adults, a pattern that continues to hold. Figure 2.10 compares the age distribution among 1992-94 immigrants to that of the U.S. population. The differences are especially marked at the extreme ends of the scale. Taking the native-born population as the standard, people aged 15 to 34 are substantially overrepresented among new immigrants, whereas those in the older age groups are significantly underrepresented. Children and those aged 35 to 44 account for about the same proportion among immigrants as among those already in the United States.

Young adults comprised an even larger fraction of immigrants in the earlier waves of U.S. immigration (see Figure 2.11). Since then, the age distribution has shifted gradually toward both children and older immigrants. This shift has mirrored changes in immigration policy, especially as family unification moves to center stage. In addition, longer lifespans and easier travel made migration more attractive to older people.

The concentration of immigrants among young working adults has fundamental implications for U.S. society. Immigrants are more likely to be workers, and they will make fewer demands on social programs geared to the elderly. As an illustration, current immigrants are more likely than the native-born to be paying into the Social Security system and less likely to be receiving benefits. Their presence in the United States may be beneficial to the current balance of that program, an issue we address in depth in Chapters 6 and 7.

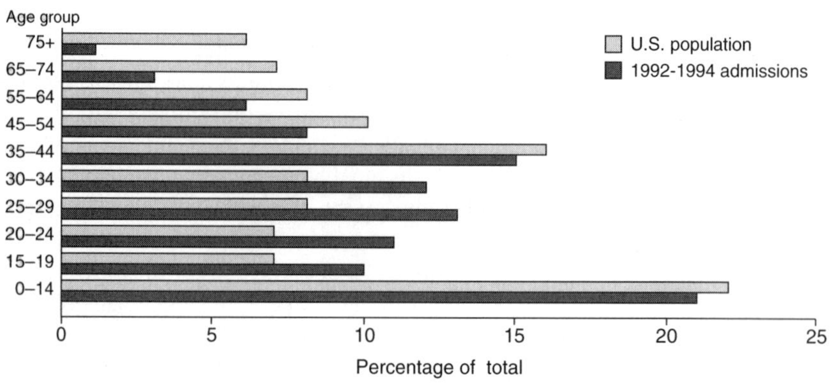

FIGURE 2.10 Age distribution of 1992-1994 immigrant admissions and 1990 U.S. population.

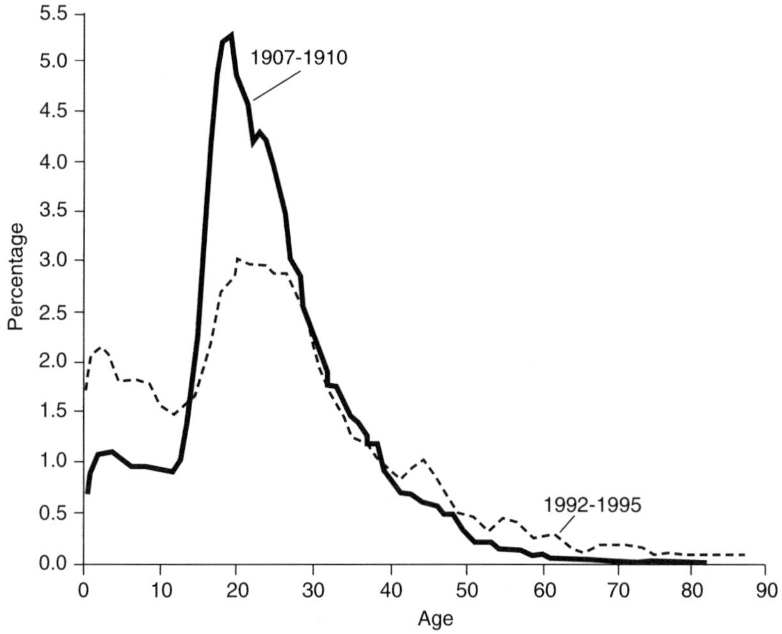

FIGURE 2.11 Age distribution of immigrants, 1907-1910 and 1992-1995.

The recent shift toward both more younger and more older immigrants means that immigrants may make greater demands on social programs that redistribute resources to those age groups than immigrants have in the past. Spending on education may be affected by these changes, both through increases in the number of children overall and through the need to help those with special needs (for example, non-English-speaking children). Public support programs, such as SSI and Medicaid, also reflect the influx of more elderly immigrants (when they were eligible under these programs). These fiscal impacts of immigration, and how they are affected by the age structure of immigrants, are explored in depth in Chapters 6 and 7.

Family Structure

Because family composition interacts with so many economic and social outcomes, it is central to the way immigrants influence U.S. society. For example, it affects whether immigrants will be eligible for many public assistance programs, how much they will work, and the costs of educating their children. It may also be relevant to such cultural concerns as trends in marriage and in extramarital childbearing.

There are many ways to characterize families but, no matter which one is used, immigrants and the native-born are not the same. As Table 2.7 shows, compared with the native-born of the same age, new (1995) immigrants are more likely to be married and are less likely to be divorced, widowed, or separated. The differences between the native-born and all foreign-born residents are smaller, but the same general pattern holds. The image of immigration in this country is not one of lone, young men with little attachment to place, family, or country. Instead, it is couples who have married and are starting families. These higher marriage rates are not surprising, since family reunification receives such high priority in our system. In choosing between a woman married to a green-card holder and an unattached single woman, the current policy selects the married women.

This image of a family-oriented immigrant is reinforced by examining the kind of families in which immigrants live. As Table 2.8 reveals, consistent with their higher rates of marriage, recent immigrants have a greater likelihood of living in family households (people living together related by blood or marriage)[24] than the average native, especially if there are minor children present. These households are slightly more likely to include the spouse of the householder and so to constitute a married-couple family.[25]

Many immigrant families have a male head but with no wife present: such a household is more than two and a half times as common among recent immigrants as it is among the population in general. The greater frequency of male-headed family households with no spouse is at least partially accounted for by householders living with their extended families—comprising, say, siblings, parents, cousins, grandchildren, other relatives, or a combination of any or all of those.[26] By virtue of the larger number of other relatives, immigrant families are larger on average, including 3.85 persons, compared with 3.16 for the United States as a whole.[27]

---

[24]A word about definitions. Statistics on groups of people living together use the terms families and households. They are not interchangeable: the first comprises people living together who are related by blood, marriage, or adoption. The second includes these family households, but also includes unrelated people living together—unmarried apartment mates, for one example—and people living by themselves. These latter, then, are nonfamily households. In all cases, the householder is the person (or one of the persons) whose name is on the lease or deed for the housing unit.

[25]The difference between immigrants and others in the fraction of households having female householders is fairly small—10.8 versus 11.6 percent. As a percentage of family households, however, the difference is a bit larger: 13.7 percent of immigrant families have a female head, compared with 16.5 percent of all families.

[26]Immigrant family households, indeed, are in general much more likely to include relatives other than a householder's spouse and children, with an average of 0.75 other relatives per immigrant family household, compared with an overall average of only 0.18 other relatives.

[27]The difference between average household size is even greater: immigrant households include 3.65 persons on average, compared with the overall U.S. average of 2.63. This difference reflects in part a much lower proportion of immigrants living by themselves. Overall, 9.1 percent of the U.S. population live in a single-person household, compared with 3.6 percent of 1980-90 immigrants.

TABLE 2.7 Marital Status of Immigrant Admissions, 1995 and U.S. Population, 1990 by Age Group (percentage)

	Men		Women	
Age Group and Marital Status	Immigrants	U.S. Population	Immigrants	U.S. Population
25-34				
Never married	34.8	36.1	18.8	25.0
Married	63.9	54.0	79.7	60.8
Widowed	0.1	0.2	0.2	0.6
Divorced	1.0	7.3	1.1	9.8
Separated	0.2	2.5	0.2	3.8
35-44				
Never married	14.5	13.4	10.2	10.0
Married	82.4	71.1	85.4	69.1
Widowed	0.2	0.4	0.8	1.6
Divorced	2.5	12.1	3.2	15.4
Separated	0.4	2.9	0.4	3.9
45-54				
Never married	5.7	6.8	7.7	5.6
Married	90.3	77.4	82.5	70.3
Widowed	0.6	1.1	4.0	5.2
Divorced	3.1	12.1	5.3	15.7
Separated	0.4	2.7	0.5	3.3
55-64				
Never married	3.7	4.8	7.5	4.5
Married	90.9	69.0	72.0	66.3
Widowed	2.3	12.5	15.1	15.9
Divorced	2.8	7.5	4.9	11.0
Separated	0.4	6.2	0.5	2.2
65 and older				
Never married	3.7	4.8	9.5	5.5
Married	84.3	73.1	46.1	38.6
Widowed	9.7	13.9	40.5	49.4
Divorced	1.8	4.7	3.6	5.5
Separated	0.4	3.5	0.2	1.0

Sources: U.S. Immigration and Naturalization Service (1997:Table 14); and U.S. Bureau of the Census (1993:Population Characteristics, Table 34).

Finally, immigrant women have more children than the average resident of the United States, another contributor to differences in family and household size (see Table 2.9). As we discuss in the next chapter, the greater rates of childbearing among immigrant women are an important factor in the effect of immigration on American society.

TABLE 2.8 Household and Family Type of Immigrants Who Arrived 1980-1990 and of U.S. Population, 1990 (percentage of all households)

Type of Household	1980-1990 Immigrants	United States Total
Nonfamily households	21.0	29.8
Family households, total	79.0	70.2
With own children under 18	52.1	33.6
With own children under 6	19.6	15.5
Type of family		
Married-couple families	59.2	55.1
With own children under 18	41.7	25.6
With own children under 6	16.1	12.4
Family with female householder, no husband present, total	10.8	11.6
With own children under 18	7.2	6.6
With own children under 6	2.0	2.6
Family with male householder, no wife present	9.0	3.4

Source: U.S. Bureau of the Census (1993:Foreign Born Population of United States, Table 2; General Population Characteristics, Table 36).

TABLE 2.9 Children Ever Born to Female Immigrants Who Arrived in 1980-1990 and U.S. Women, by Age of Mother (children born per 1,000 women)

Age of Mother	1980-1990 Immigrants	All U.S. Women
15-24	404	305
25-34	1,361	1,330
35-44	2,200	1,960

Source: U.S. Bureau of the Census (1993:Foreign Born Population of the United States, Table 1; Social and Economic Characteristics of the Population, Table 16).

Geography

Immigrants have always moved to relatively few places, settling where they have family or friends, or where there are people from their ancestral country or community—in short, with people with similar backgrounds and nationalities. This phenomenon, observed in earlier waves of immigrants, characterizes the first decades after arrival in the United States; thereafter, their children may dis-

TABLE 2.10 Intended Destination of Legal Immigrants Entering the United States, 1974, 1984, and 1994 (percentage)

State	Destination 1974	Destination 1984	Destination 1994	Actual Census Population 1990
California	21	26	26	12
New York	20	20	18	7
Texas	5	8	7	7
Florida	7	6	7	5
New Jersey	7	5	5	3
Illinois	6	5	5	5
Other states	34	30	32	61

Note: Total number of immigrants by year: 1974 = 394,861; 1984 = 543,903; 1994 = 804,416.

Source: U.S. Immigration and Naturalization Service (1975; 1985; 1996); U.S. Bureau of the Census (1993).

perse more widely.[28] Most immigrants live in a handful of states and in less than a dozen major metropolitan areas. This extreme geographic concentration implies that any state or local fiscal effects of immigration will likewise be concentrated in a relatively few communities. Similarly, labor market effects of immigration may also be more pronounced in the places where most immigrants live.

In 1990, 76 percent of immigrants arriving in the United States in the 1980s resided in only six states: California, New York, Texas, Florida, New Jersey, and Illinois (in descending rank order of the numbers of recent immigrants in the state in 1990—see Table 2.10). California and New York alone account for over 40 percent of new immigrants. Figures 2.12 and 2.13 show the state of residence for newly arriving legal and illegal immigrants in 1994. By and large, recent immigrants are going to the same places that immigrants went to 10 and 20 years ago—the majority to those same six states.

---

[28]The regional concentration of current immigrants seems to be similar to that at the turn of the century, with slightly more than three-fourths of immigrants going to the top 10 destination states. The current state destinations for immigrants differ from 1900, however: California was not a top 10 state for immigrants in 1900, but it now receives the largest number of new entrants.

We lack up-to-date information on the dispersion of immigrants and their offspring because the 1980 and 1990 censuses did not collect information on the nativity of parents. Previous census analysis (Lieberson and Waters, 1988) on ancestry reveals that European ethnic groups continued to be regionally concentrated. The residential concentration is often modest, however, within metropolitan areas. There are few American cities with large, concentrated European immigrant settlements so characteristic of the turn of the century.

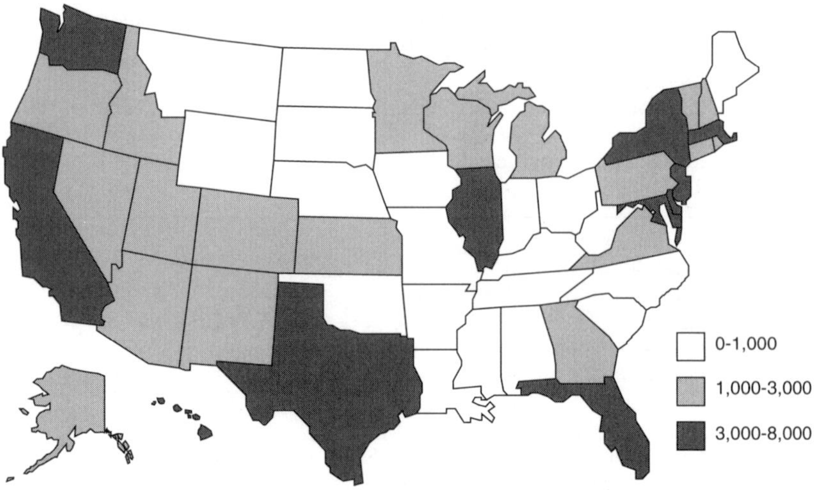

FIGURE 2.12 Legal immigrants entering the United States in 1995 per 1 million residents by state. Note: total number of immigrants for the United States in 1995 was 720,461.

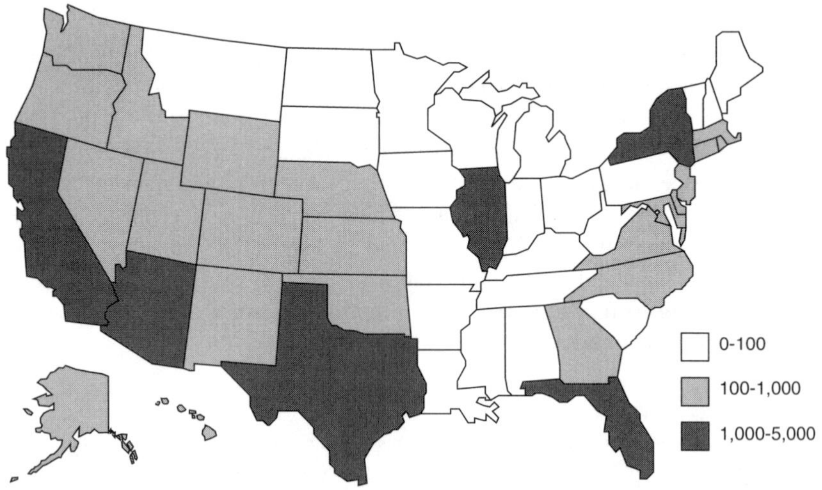

FIGURE 2.13 Illegal immigrants entering the United States in 1996 per 1 million residents by state. Note: net illegal immigrants entering the United States in 1996 estimated to be 275,000.

The differences in state destinations for legal and illegal immigrants are modest: some states have relatively large numbers of legal immigrants compared with their numbers of illegal immigrants (the New England and northern Great Lakes areas, Maryland, Pennsylvania, and Washington); others have higher numbers of illegal immigrants compared with legal immigrants (Nebraska, North Carolina, Oklahoma, and Wyoming). The mix of illegal and legal immigrants appears to reflect the balance of demand for farmworkers (attracting illegal immigrants) and employment opportunities in expanding larger industries (attracting primarily legal immigrants).

This concentration need not be static. On one hand, the foreign-born population in a state may decrease if many immigrants move to other states or if they are very old and will soon die. On the other hand, the foreign-born population could increase if other immigrants resettle in the state. However, the state distribution of the foreign-born population closely resembles that of new immigrants. In 1990, one-third of the foreign-born population resided in California and another 14 percent lived in New York. Texas and Florida each had 8 percent, and New Jersey and Illinois 4 percent each. Combined, these six states accounted for over three-fourths of the nation's foreign-born population. The remaining quarter of the foreign-born population were widely distributed across the other 44 states and the District of Columbia.

The geographic concentration is even more pronounced than state-level data indicate because most immigrants live in remarkably few metropolitan areas. According to the 1990 census, over 93 percent of the foreign-born population reside in metropolitan areas, compared with 73 percent of native-born residents. About one-half of the immigrants who entered the United States during the 1980s lived in eight metropolitan areas in 1990: Los Angeles, New York, Miami, Anaheim, Chicago, Washington, D.C., Houston, and San Francisco—again in rank order. The two metropolitan areas with the highest proportion of foreign-born in 1990 were Miami (46 percent foreign-born) and Los Angeles (33 percent foreign-born).

The patterns of immigration (foreign-born arrivals) and internal migration (by both immigrants and native-born within the United States) are often interrelated. In many instances, the same forces that attract immigrants into a state entice internal migrants from other states. In other cases, the arrival of new immigrants into a state may induce out-migration by some native-born workers with whom they may compete. These patterns varied widely among the major immigration-receiving states in the 1980s. For example, California and Florida attracted a sizeable number of internal migrants as well as a large number of immigrants during that period. By contrast, New York, Texas, Illinois, and New Jersey received many immigrants, but experienced a large number of departures to other states. For these four states, population gains from immigration were largely offset by losses from internal migration. The degree to which native workers move out of an area under pressure from new immigrants will be a critical element of any analysis of the labor market effects of immigration. This issue is addressed further in Chapter 5.

COMPARISON WITH OTHER COUNTRIES

The United States has not been alone in receiving large numbers of immigrants in recent decades. The same forces that draw people to the United States—global interdependence, wide disparities in economic circumstances, and political upheaval—are incentives to immigrants into other countries as well. Although often in other languages, the same rhetoric that characterizes domestic debates about immigration are carried on almost verbatim in many other countries. Concerns about economic competition from immigrant workers, crime, the cost to domestic taxpayers, and the loss of cultural uniqueness are mainstays of the political debate on immigration policy across Europe, Asia, and Africa. On the major issues of immigration policy—the numbers of immigrants to admit, who they shall be, how to treat them during their stay—the solutions adopted vary widely. This variety can be used to test the wisdom or limitations inherent in U.S. policy choices.

Table 2.11 documents international differences in three salient dimensions of the scale of immigration: the number of immigrants, the rate of immigration per 1,000 residents, and the percentage foreign-born. Among European countries, immigration has increased greatly in recent years. In 1990, European countries combined received more than 2 million immigrants, almost twice as many as the United States. However, this number hides wide differences among countries. Several European countries, along with such countries as Kuwait, Canada, and Australia, currently receive proportionately more immigration than the United States does. In contrast, other European countries, such as the United Kingdom, Denmark, and Finland, as well as Japan, admit few immigrants relative to their domestic population.

The uniqueness of the United States is not in how many immigrants it has relative to its population, but in its position as the only large country that is attracting significant numbers of immigrants. The other countries with large populations—China, Russia, and India—have not been magnets for immigrants from other countries. Consequently, America dominates other countries in terms of the fraction of all international migrants who live within its borders—23 percent of all immigrants arriving in 1990 in the countries listed in Table 2.11.

The percentage of foreign-born is an index of the persistence of immigration over longer periods of time. For example, Kuwait, Israel, and Australia rank at the top in the fraction foreign-born, but Australia and Israel are in the middle in terms of the number of new immigrants in the population. This discrepancy indicates that Israel and Australia's current restrictions on immigration are quite tight in comparison with its past. The United States, with 9 percent foreign-born, is in the middle of the range; Switzerland, Canada, and Australia, for example,

TABLE 2.11 The Role of Immigration in Selected Countries, Calendar Year 1990

Country	Immigrants per 1,000 Population	Number of Immigrants (thousands)	Percentage Foreign-Born in Country
Kuwait	150	325	60
Austria	16	123	6
Switzerland	15	101	16
Germany	11	842[a]	4
Canada	8	213	17
Australia	7	121	23
Sweden	6	53	6
Netherlands	5	81	5
Norway	4	16	3
Denmark	4	26	3
Israel	3	15	42
United States	3	656[b]	9
France	2	102	8
United Kingdom	1	52	3
Finland	1	7	1
Italy	1	43	1
Japan	1	82	1

[a]The high number of immigrants into Germany reflects, in large part, the arrival of "Aussiedler," that is, persons of German origin from Central and Eastern European countries with a constitutional right to come to Germany. About 400,000 Aussiedler arrived in Germany in 1990. The flow of Aussiedler increased from 1986 to 1992, before Germany established a ceiling of 225,000 per year in 1993, with a waiting list for the remaining Aussiedler who wish to come to Germany.

[b]In addition to the 656,000 nonlegalized immigrants in 1990, there were 880,000 persons who adjusted their status to permanent resident under the terms of the 1986 Immigration Reform and Control Act. Most of the legalized residents who adjusted their status had lived in the United States since 1982. If the total of both the legalized and nonlegalized immigrants are combined, there was a total of 1,090,000 new permanent resident aliens in 1990, comprising 10 new aliens per 1,000 population.

Source: International Centre for Migration Policy Development (1994:53); United Nations (1991:Tables 28, 30, and 31; 1996:Table 3); Organization for Economic Co-operation and Development (1995).

have over 15 percent. Several countries, including Finland, Italy, and Japan, have relatively few foreign-born persons.

Within their own numerical limits, countries also differ in their policies concerning whom to admit. This variety is revealed in Table 2.12, which divides immigrants in 1991 into four categories; employment related, family reunification, asylees and refugees, and those admitted based explicitly on ethnicity.

TABLE 2.12 Composition of Immigration, by Type of Admission, Calendar Year 1991 (percentage)

Country	Employment Related	Family Reunificaton	Asylee/ Refugee	Ethnic Background
France	47	19	19	15
Austria	43	12	45	0
Australia	37	50	14	0
Netherlands	33	17	42	8
Canada	29	42	29	0
Norway	29	36	35	0
United States	29	49	21	0
United Kingdom	28	40	28	4
Switzerland	27	31	43	0
Germany	20	14	46	20
Finland	19	21	25	35
Denmark	12	32	55	0
Sweden	7	49	44	0

Source: International Centre for Migration Policy Development (1994:55).

Employment-related immigration is defined on the basis of a labor permit issued before entry. For European countries, labor immigration also includes foreign labor within the framework of the free European Union and Nordic labor circulation zones. Family-reunification immigration is based on a residence permit issued to kin of a resident in the country. The category labeled "ethnic background" refers to "Aussiedler" visas in Germany[29] and groups allowed to immigrate into France, the Netherlands, and the United Kingdom because of colonial obligations. A U.S. program of this kind extends the right to immigrate to past employees of the Panama Canal Company, an obligation undertaken as part of the Panama Canal Treaty to turn the canal and the Canal Zone over to the government of Panama. In the case of Finland, the category comprises ethnic Finns arriving from the former Soviet Union. Finally, refugees are those from other countries who are fleeing persecution.

Several European countries use a "guest-worker" system in addition to permanent residence immigration. Germany, for example, has received a large number of temporary guest-workers from Turkey, who entered Germany on specific work contracts for a limited time. Some guest-workers have remained in Germany for many years and have recently availed themselves of the German asylum

[29]Aussiedler admissions are ethnic Germans from other parts of Europe. Under laws passed in Germany in the early 1950s, ethnic Germans have a right to settle in Germany upon establishment of their German ancestry.

system to seek permanent residence. Germany has enacted a series of visa obligations and special control measures for guest-workers, but it has had continued problems with regulating the increasing number of asylum applications.

A significant proportion of immigrants into European countries—two in five—are refugees, almost twice the proportion for the United States. Labor migration plays roughly the same role in many European countries and in traditional immigrant-receiving countries, including the United States—about one-third of total immigration. Where the United States stands apart is in the relative numbers of family-oriented immigrants.

As shown in Table 2.13, the source countries for immigration are diverse. Among countries receiving immigrants, the top three source countries vary greatly. Although Mexico is the major source country for immigration into the United States, Mexico is not a major source country for other immigrant-receiving countries. Other countries also tend to receive specialized immigration flows: only the United Kingdom tends to receive a significant proportion of immigrants from Australia and New Zealand.

Canada and the United States receive immigrants from a large number of countries. Less than one-fourth of immigrants into these two countries are from the top three sources. This contrasts with the situation in several other countries, such as France, where most immigrants are from only two or three countries.

Although the concern of this report is with immigration into the United States, the United States also supplies immigrants to other countries. Australia is the only major immigrant-receiving country that receives a substantial proportion from the United States. In addition, although the United Kingdom, Japan, and Israel do not receive a large volume of immigrants, persons from the United States constitute an important source of their immigrants.

THE CANADIAN CASE

Any time immigration is restricted, there must be a mechanism for choosing immigrants. Countries have adopted a wide variety of procedures that emphasize different factors. Which set of rules is chosen has large consequences for the composition of immigration. Canada offers an interesting contrast to the United States, because it places less emphasis on family unification and more on employment skills, admitting more than one-half of its annual immigrants on economic grounds.

A comparison of the United States and Canada illustrates how immigration selection works in another country. It is not meant as an endorsement or criticism of the Canadian immigration system, nor that the United States should place more weight on a point-based preference system that stresses employment skills.

The Canadian immigration system, which has been operating for two decades, begins by setting a total for immigration for planning purposes, along with projected immigration in several components (Citizenship and Immigration

TABLE 2.13 Top Three Sending Countries for Selected Immigrant-Receiving Countries, 1989

	Top Three Sending Countries			Percentage of All Immigrants From Top Three Countries
Country	First	Second	Third	
Kuwait	Jordan (16%)	India (10%)	Pakistan (6%)	32
Switzerland	Yugoslavia (13%)	Portugal (10%)	Italy (8%)	31
Austria	Yugoslavia (23%)	Poland (17%)	Czechoslovakia (13%)	53
Germany	Poland (35%)	Turkey (9%)	Yugoslavia (6%)	50
Canada	Hong Kong (11%)	Philippines (6%)	India (4%)	21
Australia	United Kingdom (19%)	New Zealand (14%)	United States (6%)	39
Norway	Denmark (12%)	Sweden (12%)	United Kingdom (7%)	31
Sweden	Iran (16%)	Finland (12%)	Norway (8%)	36
Netherlands	Turkey (12%)	Morocco (10%)	Germany (9%)	31
France	Algeria (73%)	Morocco (8%)	Tunisia (2%)	83
Israel	U.S.S.R. (15%)	United States (10%)	Argentina (10%)	35
United States	Mexico (9%)	Philippines (8%)	Vietnam (7%)	24
Denmark	Sri Lanka (9%)	Turkey (6%)	Iran (4%)	19
United Kingdom	United States (11%)	Australia (9%)	New Zealand (5%)	25
Finland	Sweden (57%)	U.S.S.R. (6%)	Norway (5%)	68
Italy	Germany (24%)	Switzerland (16%)	France (8%)	48
Japan	United States (24%)	China (13%)	Korea (12%)	49

Note: A number of countries follow the U.N. definition of a long-term immigrant as someone who arrives in the country with the intention of staying one or more years. Such a definition would include intra-company transfers, for example, of Americans to Japan for extended work. In the United States, such intra-company transfers would be classified as nonimmigrants; the Unites States does not report nonimmigrants to the U.N. as immigrants.

Source: United Nations (1991:Table 28).

Canada, 1996a). Canada's legislation requires that the government make an annual announcement of the number of immigrants and refugees that Canada plans to admit over the next five years. This number is determined after consultation with the provinces, government organizations, and other appropriate institutions.

Canadian immigrants fall into three broad classes. First, Family Class immigrants are sponsored on the basis of family reunification by Canadian citizens and permanent residents who are living in Canada. Second, Independent Immigrants, including those under the Business Class, are selected for their special occupational skills and experience, assessed in a point-based preference system. Third, Convention Refugees are admitted in accordance with Canadian laws governing refugee admissions and are evaluated not on a formal point system, but on their education, job skills, knowledge of English and French, and ability to adapt successfully to Canadian life.

The Canadian immigration system is distinctive in its selection of immigrants under the Independent Class. Immigrants are evaluated on 10 factors and admitted to Canada only if they score a minimum of 70 points. Most of the factors are related to labor market skills, including occupation, practical training, experience, ability to communicate in English or French, and general education. Canadian immigration officials maintain a fairly detailed list of occupations, which are updated periodically, that indicates the "value" of occupations and their labor market demands. If an applicant, such as a janitor, has an occupation with a very low score, he or she will be denied admission. An applicant with a university degree, in contrast, receives the full 16 points available for education. The appendix to this chapter describes the point-based system in more detail and presents examples of the factors and their scoring.

The September 1996 projection for 1996 immigration into Canada was for 199,000 to 205,000 total immigrants and refugees. Of these, 52 percent will be admitted on economic grounds (42 percent under skilled workers and 10 percent under one of the three business classes), 31 percent will be admitted under the Family Class, 13 percent will be admitted as refugees, and the remaining 4 percent will be in an "other" category.[30]

CONCLUSIONS

Throughout this country's history, immigrants have arrived, ever changing in their numbers and composition and presenting daunting economic and social challenges to successive American generations. The nation's history offers abundant legislative experiments alongside the 200-year history of successes and fail-

[30]The "other" class of immigrants includes persons admitted under the live-in caregiver program, special immigrant categories, humanitarian and compassionate admissions, and provincial and territorial nominees.

ures of the immigrants themselves. And the experiences of other nations assure us that we do not stand alone in deciding how many and which citizens of the world should be permitted to join our national experiment.

As long as there is a virtually unlimited supply of potential immigrants, the nation has to make choices on how many immigrants to admit, and within that number, who should be selected. Since colonial times, successive waves of immigrants have forced us to make these choices. The answers, in regulations and legislation, have reflected the nation's notion of itself and, often, reactions to the characteristics of the immigrants.

An important piece of national legislation was the Immigration Act of 1924, which established a system of national origins quotas for immigrants. The 1924 act restricted total immigration, with limits set for annual immigration by country or nationality based on its relative proportion of the population according to the 1920 census. Because there were relatively fewer persons from some countries with high immigration demands, this system resulted in large reductions in immigrants from Eastern and Southern Europe and essentially ended immigration from Asia.

Impeded by the Great Depression and the Second World War, immigration slackened during the 1930s, and the pressure of legislation eased. But after the war, as applications for both legal and refugee admissions rose, it became clear that many of the old immigration laws were outdated. This eventually led to the second major piece of legislation, the Immigration and Nationality Act Amendments of 1965, which abolished the national-origins quota system that had been governing U.S. immigration for more than 40 years. The 1965 act replaced national-origin, race, and ancestry quotas with a preference system based on family reunification and special occupational skills or training. The 1965 act also was the first legislation that placed numerical limits on immigration from the Western Hemisphere.

With the 1965 legislation, the emphasis of immigration policy shifted to a new approach, introducing employment-based preferences to a system with family-sponsored preferences. Family ties clearly dominate, accounting in 1995 for two-thirds of admissions; moreover, nearly half those admitted in this category were spouses or children of men and women with preferred occupations.

REFERENCES

Ahmed, B., and J.G. Robinson
1996 *Estimates of Emigration from the United States*. Washington, D.C.: U.S. Bureau of the Census.

Bean, F.D., B. Edmonston, and J.S. Passel, eds.
1990 *Undocumented Migration to the United States: IRCA and the Experience of the 1980's*. Washington, D.C.: The Urban Institute Press.

Bureau of Consular Affairs
1977 *Visa Bulletin*. U.S. Department of State 7(69):2.

Carter, S.B., and R. Sutch
1996 The Economic and Demographic Consequences of Immigration to the United States: Quantitative Historical Perspectives. Paper prepared for panel. Department of Economics, University of California, Riverside & Berkeley, September.

Citizenship and Immigration Canada
1996a *Canada's Immigration Law.* Ottawa, ON: Minister of Supply and Services Canada.
1996b *Applying for Permanent Residence in Canada: A Self-Assessment Guide for Independent Applicants.* March 1996 version downloaded from the Web Site of the Canadian Consulate in Buffalo, New York.
1996c *Occupational Demand List, as of February 29, 1996: List of Occupations Open to Prospective Independent Skilled Worker Immigrants.* December 1996 version downloaded from the Web Site of the Commission for Canada, Hong Kong.

Duleep, H.O.
1994 Social Security and the emigration of immigrants. Pp. 97-128 in *International Social Security Association, Migration: A Worldwide Challenge for Social Security.* Geneva, Switzerland: International Social Security Association.

Fix, M., ed.
1991 *The Paper Curtain: Employer Sanctions' Implementation, Impact, and Reform.* Washington, D.C.: The Urban Institute Press.

Gonzalez Baker, S.
1990 *The Cautious Welcome: The Legalization Programs of the Immigration Reform and Control Act.* Washington, D.C.: The Urban Institute Press.

Institute for International Education
1996 *Open Doors 1995/6.* New York: Institute for International Education.

International Centre for Migration Policy Development
1994 *The Key to Europe: A Comparative Analysis of Entry and Asylum Policies in Western Countries.* Vienna, Austria: International Centre for Migration Policy Development.

Jasso, G., and M.R. Rosenzweig
1990 *The New Chosen People: Immigrants in the United States.* New York: Russell Sage Foundation.

Klusmeyer, D.
1996 *Between Consent and Descent: Concepts of Democratic Citizenship.* Washington, D.C.: Carnegie Endowment for International Peace.

Lieberson, S., and M. Waters
1988 *From Many Strands: Ethnic and Racial Groups in Contemporary America.* New York: Russell Sage.

Martin, P.
1996 *Promises to Keep: Collective Bargaining in California Agriculture.* Ames: Iowa State University Press.

Martin, P., and J. Widgren
1996 *International Migration: A Global Challenge.* Washington, D.C.: Population Reference Bureau (May).

Massey, D.S., K.M. Donato, and Zai Liang
1990 Effects of Immigration Reform and Control Act of 1986: Preliminary data from Mexico. Chapter 6 in F.D. Bean, B. Edmonston, and J.S. Passel (editors), *Undocumented Migration to the United States: IRCA and the Experience of the 1980's.* Washington, D.C.: The Urban Institute Press.

McInnis, Marvin
1994 Immigration and emigration: Canada in the late nineteenth century. Pp. 139-155 in T.J. Hatton and J.G. Williamson (editors), *Migration and the International Labor Market, 1850-1939.* New York: Routledge.

Neuman, K.E., and M. Tienda

1994 The settlement and secondary migration patterns of legalized immigrants: Insights from administrative records. Chapter 7 in B. Edmonston and J.S. Passel (editors), *Immigration and Ethnicity: Immigration and the Adjustment of America's Newest Immigrants.* Washington, D.C.: The Urban Institute.

Organization for Economic Co-operation and Development

1995 *Trends in International Migration, Annual Report, 1994.* Paris: Organization for Economic Co-operation and Development.

Passel, J.S., F.D. Bean, and B. Edmonston

1990 Undocumented migration since IRCA: An overall assessment. Chapter 9 in F.D. Bean, B. Edmonston, and J.S. Passel (editors), *Undocumented Migration to the United States: IRCA and the Experience of the 1980's.* Washington, D.C.: The Urban Institute Press.

Passel, J.S., and B. Edmonston

1994 Immigration and race: Recent trends in immigration to the United States. In B. Edmonston and J.S. Passel (editors), *Immigration and Ethnicity: Immigration and the Adjustment of America's Newest Immigrants.* Washington, D.C.: The Urban Institute.

United Nations

1991 *U.N. Demographic Yearbook, 1989.* New York: United Nations.

1996 *U.N. Demographic Yearbook, 1994.* New York: United Nations.

U.S. Bureau of the Census

1975 *Historical Statistics of the United States, Colonial Times to 1970, Bicentennial Edition.* Part 1. Washington, D.C.: U.S. Department of Commerce.

1993 *1990 Census of Population.* The Foreign-Born Population of the United States. 1990 CP-3-1. Washington, D.C.: U.S. Department of Commerce.

1996 *Statistical Abstracts of the United States, 1996.* Washington, D.C.: U.S. Department of Commerce.

U.S. Commission on Immigration Reform

1994 *U.S. Immigration Policy: Restoring Credibility.* Washington, D.C.: U.S. Commission on Immigration Reform

U.S. Immigration and Naturalization Service

1975 *Statistical Yearbook of the Immigration and Naturalization Service, 1974.* Washington, D.C.: U.S. Department of Justice.

1985 *Statistical Yearbook of the Immigration and Naturalization Service, 1984.* Washington, D.C.: U.S. Department of Justice.

1994 *Statistical Yearbook of the Immigration and Naturalization Service, 1993.* Washington, D.C.: U.S. Department of Justice.

1996 *Statistical Yearbook of the Immigration and Naturalization Service, 1994.* Washington, D.C.: Department of Justice.

1997 *Statistical Yearbook of the Immigration and Naturalization Service, 1995.* Department of Justice.

Warren, R.

1996 State Population Estimates: Legal Permanent Residents and Aliens Eligible for Naturalization. Office of Policy and Planning, Immigration and Naturalization Service, Washington, D.C.

APPENDIX 2.A
ADMISSION OF IMMIGRANTS INTO CANADA

Because Chapter 2 is concerned with U.S. immigration and the U.S. immigration system, this appendix describes how immigration selection works in another country. We illustrate the selection system in Canada, not because we wish to endorse it, but because Canada admits a large number of immigrants and has emphasized the admission of immigrants based on employment skills.

Classes of Immigrants

Immigrants and refugees are admitted to Canada without discrimination on the basis of race, national or ethnic origin, color, religion, or sex (Citizenship and Immigration Canada, 1996a). They are selected according to universal standards that assess their ability to adapt to Canadian society and to settle successfully. Canadian immigration includes three broad classes of immigrants. The major components of Canadian immigration are Family Class, Independent Immigrants, and Convention Refugees as well as members of Designated Classes.

- Family Class immigrants are sponsored on the basis of family relationships. Canadian citizens and permanent residents, age 19 years and over and living in Canada, have the right to sponsor certain close relatives who wish to immigrate to Canada. Relatives eligible for Family Class sponsorship include wife or husband; fiancé(e); dependent son or daughter (under 19 and unmarried, full-time student, or with disability); parents or grandparents; brothers, sisters, nephews, nieces, or grandchildren who are orphans, unmarried, and under 19 years of age; children under 19 whom the sponsor will adopt; and any other relative if the sponsor does not have any of the above or any family in Canada.
- Independent Immigrants comprise persons selected on the basis of special occupational skills and experience, business immigrants, assisted relatives, retirees, and other independent immigrants. Immigrants in the Independent class are assessed against formal selection criteria. The point-based preference is described in the section below. This class includes skilled workers, assisted relatives, and three types of immigrants within Canada's Business Immigration Program. Assisted relatives include applicants who have a Canadian relative who is willing to help them or relatives who do not qualify under the Family Class of admission. There are three categories within the Business Immigration Program: entrepreneurs,[31] self-employed persons,[32] and investors.[33]

---

[31]To qualify as an entrepreneur, a person must be able to demonstrate to a Canadian immigration official that he or she intends and has the ability to establish, purchase, or make a substantial investment in a Canadian business that will make a significant contribution to the economy. The business must create or continue at least one job in Canada for a Canadian citizen or permanent resident other

• Convention Refugees are refugees admitted to Canada in accordance with Canadian laws governing refugee admissions. Canada defines a refugee in accordance with the United Nations Convention on refugee status. Groups of at least five Canadian citizens or permanent residents, 19 years of age or greater, or local organizations that are legally incorporated may sponsor Convention Refugees. Refugees are not subject to a formal point system for evaluation. Nevertheless, Canadian visa officers take into account the refugee's level of education, job skills, and knowledge of English or French as a guide to determining whether the applicant will adapt successfully to Canadian life.

POINT-BASED PREFERENCE SYSTEM

Canada uses formal selection criteria for admission of the Independent Class of immigrants. The criteria are used to determine whether independent immigrants are likely to become successfully established in Canada. The criteria's factors and weights are designed to meet Canada's demographic and labor market needs. Emphasis is placed on the applicant's intended occupation, practical training, work experience, education, ability to communicate in French or English, and personal suitability. Employment-related factors account for about half of the total possible units of assessment that can be awarded.

In order to be admitted to Canada as an independent immigrant, the applicant must receive a minimum number of points. Immigrants must also have an occupation that is in demand or can be easily absorbed in the labor markets. In most cases, applicants are also required to have at least one year of work experience in their intended occupation.

---

than the entrepreneur and his or her dependents. The applicant must also have the ability to provide active participation in the management of the business.

[32]A self-employed immigrant is an applicant who intends and has the ability to establish or purchase a business in Canada that will create employment for that person and will make a significant contribution to the economy or the artistic or cultural life of Canada.

[33]To immigrate as an investor, the applicant must have proven track record in business and have accumulated a personal worth of $500,000 or more (about $375,000 U.S.). Investors are admitted in one of three tiers: (1) provinces with less than 10 percent of landed business immigrants require a minimum investment of $250,000 (about $187,000 U.S.) for a minimum holding period of 5 years; (2) provinces with 10 percent or greater of landed business immigrants require a minimum investment of $350,000 (about $263,000 U.S.) for a minimum holding period of 5 years; and (3) investors with a minimum net worth of $700,000 (about $525,000 U.S.) and an investment of $500,000 (about $375,000) for a minimum holding period of 5 years are eligible for immigration to all provinces in the third tier. The investment must be in an accepted project that is of significant economic benefit to the province. The project may not involve residential real estate and must contribute to the creation or continuation of employment opportunities for Canadian citizens or permanent residents. Some provinces, such as British Columbia, have established special investment funds, authorized by the province, so that investors can deposit their investment easily. Such provincial investment funds hold the funds for the minimum period and pay a guaranteed rate of return. At the end, the investor receives the investment with the interest payment.

Occupations that are in short supply in specific provinces are referred to as "designated occupations." Additional points, as well as priority processing, are awarded to an applicant in a designated occupation.

Not every independent immigrant is assessed on all of the selection criteria. Applicants are assessed on only those factors that actually reflect their ability to become successfully adapted. Since occupation is not a relevant factor in selecting self-employed applicants, for example, it is not assessed for this category. Rather, more emphasis is placed on ability and experience by it making it possible to gain bonus points for being self-employed. Skilled workers are evaluated on all the factors. Assisted relatives are assessed on the same factors as other independent immigrants, but they receive bonus units of assessment if they have a relative in Canada.

This section describes the operation of the Canadian point-based selection system for immigrant admissions in 1996 (Citizenship and Immigration Canada, 1996b). Prospective independent immigrants to Canada are assessed on a point-based system; they must obtain a qualifying score to receive an immigrant visa. In addition, prospective candidates must have valid passports, be able to support themselves and their dependents in Canada, be of good health and character, and pay administrative fees.

The Canadian point-based system scores an immigrant on 10 categories. In 1996, the candidate needed to score 70 points in order to qualify for an immigrant visa. Applicants with scores less than 70 are refused a visa. Several of the factors relate to employment. Arranged employment is a guaranteed offer of employment from a Canadian employer. The employment must be approved by the Canada Employment Centre, and the applicant must be qualified for the arranged employment. Designated occupations are occupations identified by the province or territory as being especially in demand in that region (Citizenship and Immigration Canada, 1996c). The list of these occupations changes periodically and varies among provinces and territories. Points are calculated (in 1996) on the following:

Factor	Maximum Points	Points Calculation
(1) Age	10	0 points for 17 increasing points for 18 to 20 10 points for 21 to 44 decreasing points for 45 to 48 0 points for 49 and over
(2) Education	16	0 points for less than high school diploma 5 to 15 points for various types of high school and post-secondary training 16 points for four-year university degree

(3) Specific Vocational Preparation	18	The score for this factor is based on whether the applicant has a designated occupation, and length of training, education, and/or apprenticeship for Canadian work (for example, an aerospace engineer receives 18 points, a locksmith receives 11 points, and a janitor receives 0 points)
(4) Occupation	10	0 points if there are no listed occupations for which the candidate is qualified; if the applicant scores zero on this factor, then then are automatically refused a visa Intermediate points awarded on the basis of the candidate's qualified occupation (for example, an aerospace engineer and a locksmith both receive 5 points) 10 points if the candidate has arranged employment in Canada or has a designated occupation with high specific occupation preparation value
(5) Arranged Employment/ Designated Occupation	10	0 points if no arranged employment or a designated occupation 10 points if the person has arranged employment or a designated occupation with high specific vocational preparation 10 points for a member of the clergy with a congregational position offering employment 10 points for full-time employment in a family business approved by the Canada Immigration Centre
(6) Work Experience	8	The points are calculated based on the specific vocational experience (factor 3) and the years of experience; a maximum of 8 points is awarded to an applicant with the maximum specific vocational experience and 4 years or more experience in the occupation
(7) Language Ability	15	0 points if the person speaks English and French with difficulty Intermediate points are awarded based on the reading, writing, and speaking of English and French 15 points if the person is fluent in both French and English

(8) Demographic Factor	8	These points are set by the federal government to adjust the volume of annual immigration; 8 points are awarded in 1996
(9) Personal Suitability	10	These points are awarded based on a personal assessment of a Canadian visa officer; the points are based on adaptability, motivation, initiative, and resourcefulness; the purpose is to predict whether the applicant and family will be able to settle successfully in Canada
(10) Relative in Canada	5	5 points are awarded if the applicant has a brother, sister, mother, father, grandparent, aunt, uncle, niece, or nephew as a permanent resident or Canadian citizen living in Canada

3

The Face of the U.S. Population in 2050

How will the population of the United States change on the way to the middle of the 21st century? How will immigration—current and future—contribute to that change? This chapter seeks to answer the second question, which in turn will help answer the first. It focuses on the characteristics of immigrants and their descendants and explores how they will change the demography of the United States over the next six decades.

Immigration is not the only force at work shaping the size and the structure of the United States in the coming years. It will interact with other demographic forces, already in place, that also play a large role in what the country will look like by the middle of the next century.

First, in the two decades following World War II, the baby boom greatly increased the annual rate of U.S. population growth and provided birth cohorts from 1946 to about 1963 that were much larger than those of either the decade before or after. The baby boom and the subsequent baby bust will have major ramifications over the next half century: the population will age as the baby-boom generations become older; when they eventually retire, the number of retirees will be much larger than this country has ever seen.

Second, the future level of mortality among the elderly will have fundamental implications for their numbers. These changes, in turn, will affect their demand for private and public pensions and for health services. Because the small baby-bust generations will be the workers at that time, a relatively few income-producing residents will be providing for the older generations.

Finally, volatility in the volume and composition of immigration affects the U.S. population across many dimensions: its size and rate of growth, its age and sex composition, and its racial and ethnic makeup. In the future, a major source of variation in population change may lie in the volume and characteristics of immigration.

Population change inevitably has broad social and economic implications. Changes in the age composition of the population affect school enrollments and policies. The number and educational levels of the population in the early and middle adult years are critical for the future labor force and its productivity. And the numbers of elderly and how healthy they are become major determinants of pension needs and the health care system. Population change may also produce ripples across many other critical aspects of American life, in the needs for housing, the crime rate, savings, and voting.

Immigration has consequences for all these aspects of population change. In its relatively large flows and wide variety, immigration as the United States experiences it adds both to the numbers of people in the nation and to their diversity. Immigration works its longer-term effects through other dimensions as well.

First, not every group of immigrants into the United States bears children at the same rate. Immigrant groups with persistently high fertility rates will grow over time, absolutely and in relation to other immigrant groups. Second, not every group of immigrants has the same life span—that is, their mortality rates differ; these, too, may change over time and thus shift in their relation to one another.

If immigrants have a higher fertility rate than does the resident population, the nation will grow younger on average. And if immigrants have a higher mortality rate—that is, if they die at an earlier age—that trend will be reinforced. Again, the differences among groups of immigrants also matter, and so do the shifts within groups and between groups as the generations unfold.[1]

Previewing the U.S. population in 2050, then, calls for making assumptions about the numbers of people entering and leaving the country, about the numbers from various racial and ethnic groups within the totals, and about the fertility and mortality rates of individual groups. Moreover, it calls for assumptions about *exogamy* and *ethnic affiliation*—the degree to which groups intermarry and the way the descendants of intergroup marriages identify themselves.

This chapter offers a view of how future immigration will alter the U.S. population.[2] To paint that portrait, a framework is used to ensure consistency for

---

[1]Even the apparently simple flow of immigrants into the country is not completely straightforward. The relevant concept is net immigration, the difference between the number of those entering the country and the number of those leaving it, whether foreign-born or native-born. These flows respond to various economic, political, social, and family concerns, in the United States as well as in the sending countries, that themselves may be volatile.

[2]The panel is aware that our population projections may be of great interest to those with environmental concerns. Different immigration assumptions, as will be seen, have substantial influence on the future path of population size and growth for the United States. The panel was not charged with examining the environmental repercussions of population change and does not discuss these issues in this report. The panel does not have particular expertise in environmental studies and did not give special study to the effect of immigration on the environment.

alternative assumptions about the future course of immigration and emigration and their associated demographic implications. This work has several purposes:

- To evaluate the assumptions concerning demographic developments in the years 1995 to 2050;
- To present alternative results so the sensitivity of assumptions can be assessed;
- To explore the national implications for population change from specific variations in immigration; and
- To use the population results to describe the implications for economic and social policies.

On the basis of our population projection model, this chapter examines the effects of immigration on the future course of the U.S. population. We first examine why immigration is important for population change. Next, a model for population projection is briefly described, and the alternative assumptions used here to illustrate future population change are set out. Against this background, the heart of the chapter is a discussion of the main effects of immigration on the U.S. population over the next six decades.

BACKGROUND TO POPULATION CHANGE

The number and age structure of the population are determined by fertility, mortality, and migration. The last factor has attracted considerably less attention in formal models than the first two, which have been extensively examined by means of stable population models and their various extensions.

At the simplest level, that of total population numbers, only net migration appears in the demographic balancing equation: population change = births − deaths + net migration. Thus, net migration series are typically used to examine the effects of immigration on population structure. For most of its history, the United States has attracted large numbers of immigrants. In recent years, the estimated net inflow has been around 800,000 people, including illegal and legal immigrants and refugees. This figure reflects immigrant flows into the country and emigrant departures of both immigrants and native-born residents. Although the net figure is important from the demographic accounting perspective, gross inflows and outflows are necessary for many purposes of policy and analysis. To cite one example: immigrants who are not U.S. citizens are ineligible to vote, but emigrants who are U.S. citizens are eligible to vote by absentee ballot.

Role of the United States in the World Population

The world population has been growing at a historically unprecedented rate

TABLE 3.1 World Population by Region: Actual Population, 1950-1990; Projected Population, 2010-2050

	1950	1970	1990	2010	2030	2050
World total (in millions)	2,520	3,697	5,285	7,032	8,671	9,833
Percentage of world population						
World	100	100	100	100	100	100
Africa	9	10	12	15	19	22
Asia	55	58	60	60	60	58
Europe	21	17	14	10	8	7
Latin America and the Caribbean	7	8	8	9	9	9
North America	7	6	5	5	4	4
United States	6	5	4	4	4	4
Other Countries[a]	1	1	1	1	0	0
Oceania	1	1	1	1	0	0

[a]Other North American countries, by United Nations definitions, include Bermuda, Canada, Greenland, and St. Pierre and Miquelon.

Source: United Nations (1995:Tables A.1 and A.2); population projections by the panel for the United States, 2010-2050.

for the past century and numbered an estimated 5.8 billion in 1996. In 1990, the U.S. population accounted for 4 percent of the world's population (see Table 3.1). Since 1950, the U.S. population has been declining as a proportion of the world's population, decreasing from 6 percent in 1950. If we rely on the world population projections prepared by the United Nations (1995), anticipating results for the United States that are discussed later, the population of the world and the United States will grow through the year 2050.

Because we project that the United States will experience moderate population growth for the next six decades, its proportion of the world's population will remain constant at 4 percent. Some other regions, such as Europe, will account for a diminishing proportion of the world's population over the next six decades, and regions such as Africa are likely to increase their relative proportion.

Although not everyone outside the United States wishes to or realistically will seek to emigrate to the United States, these results also provide evidence that the number of potential U.S. immigrants will increase in the future.

Population Projections

The population projections reported in this chapter take the 1995 U.S. population and calculate future growth by making assumptions about the level of births, deaths, and net immigration. The initial 1995 population is characterized by age, sex, race/ethnicity, and immigrant generation—whether the person is of the first generation (foreign-born) or is its descendant.

We examine four racial or ethnic groups of primary affiliation: Asian and Pacific Islander (taken together and referred to as Asian in this chapter), black, Hispanic, and white.[3] In federal government statistics, Hispanic status is defined for purposes of establishing a Hispanic population, which may be reported in any of the four races. In practice, the Hispanic population mainly reports itself as either white or "other" race (the latter includes individuals who do not check a specific, listed race but write in such responses as "Mexican"). The official current classification is based on an arbitrary separation of race and ethnicity, defining Asians, blacks, and whites as "races" and not ethnic groups. We refer to the four groups broadly as ethnic groups in this chapter.

The main implication of the official classification system is that population projections for the Hispanic population overlap with the overall projections for the main race groups in official government projections. For the projections presented here, we calculate a base population in which the white, black, and Asian groups do not include any Hispanic component.[4] This avoids a double-counting of Hispanic persons.

We rely on a population projection model that makes assumptions about several parameters: immigration and emigration; mortality, fertility, and exogamy; and ethnic attribution. In the next sections, we set out the model we used to make our projections and the demographic assumptions that underlie them. For a technical, detailed description of the model and additional information about the assumptions used in the projection model, see Appendixes 3.A and 3.B, respectively.

---

[3]Government statistics include Native Americans as a fifth racial group. The size of this group is relatively small and, because immigrants include few Native Americans, we have excluded them from presentation in this report. Data for the total population, however, includes separate estimates for the three Native American groups—American Indians, Eskimos, and Aleuts.

[4]One needs to remember that the Asian and Hispanic populations are very diverse. In addition, white and black populations are diverse and represent different ethnic origins. Immigrants may report themselves with a primary racial or Hispanic affiliation, but they include persons from many quite distinct countries. Some Asian and Hispanic ethnic groups, of different origins and cultures, have variations in fertility and mortality levels, as well as in propensities for emigration. For example, the Asian population includes immigrants from China, Korea, India, Vietnam, and Japan, among others, and the Hispanic population includes immigrants from Mexico, Guatemala, the Dominican Republic, Argentina, Chile, and many other countries. These within-group differences may be as important as the across-group differences we model in this volume. We do not, however, attempt to model these within-group demographic differences in this report.

A PROJECTION MODEL

This report uses a new demographic model for population projections. Similar to standard cohort-component models, this model forecasts an initial population under certain assumptions about fertility, mortality, and international migration.[5] Our interest in projecting the future population, however, places special emphasis on the size of the foreign-born population and the ethnicity of its descendants. In an important innovation, therefore, the model arrays the population by generation: a foreign-born first generation (the immigrants), a second generation (sons and daughters of immigrants), a third generation (grandsons and granddaughters of immigrants), and fourth and later generations. Because the model requires fertility, mortality, and migration by generation, it takes a somewhat different form from that of conventional demographic models.

Standard cohort-component projection models do not distinguish immigrant generations. Such a model has several limitations for our projections. First, it does not incorporate the changes in fertility and mortality that occur within a generational framework (Werner, 1986). Second, its specification of emigration is inadequate, usually assuming a fixed number of emigrants or a number based on a certain percentage of the total number of residents (Miltenyi, 1981). Finally, it provides no information on such important aspects of ethnic groups as the number who are foreign-born and native-born (Tabah, 1984). In particular, it has questionable assumptions about rates of intermarriage and ethnic attribution.

The new model presented in this chapter overcomes some of these limitations. By distinguishing the population by immigrant generation, it improves the description of population dynamics influenced by immigration.

With the model used here, we make no attempt at a pinpoint prediction of future population. Rather, the implications of a credible set of assumptions about basic demographic processes are examined on the basis of state-of-the-art research. Projections for the immediate future—say, 15 to 25 years, for which current research provides credible parameters—have much higher analytical credibility. Beyond that, population projections must be seen as much more uncertain.

The simulations of the model reported here are designed to generate the racial/ethnic distribution of the U.S. population implied in assumed interactions of the basic demographic process. Except for arithmetic errors, the projections presented here must, in a special sense, be accurate because they derive logically

[5]Among various methods for making population projections, cohort-component approaches are commonly used for making projections by age and sex. Cohort-component methods involve making separate assumptions for the components of fertility, mortality, immigration, and emigration. The method is usually applied to separate birth cohorts, by sex. The total population is obtained by combining the projections for age-sex groups.

from the assumptions of the demographic model. Hence, it becomes all the more necessary to explicate the new generational model and to buttress the assumptions we have made.

We stress that the projections for ethnic groups are not necessarily accurate predictions for the future course of the population.[6] Supported as they are by the latest evidence, our assumptions about fertility and mortality are reasonable, yet leading researchers vigorously debate the dynamics of these demographic processes. Furthermore, immigration and emigration may follow a variety of plausible courses in the coming decades. Recent history suggests, for example, that one or more new countries may be the source of a major surge of immigration, whose size, composition, and origin are uncertain.

An Immigrant-Generation Approach

Standard cohort-component population projections move a population through time by estimating its survival under the conditions of mortality (its survival from one period to the next), fertility (the births to the population and their survival during the projection period), and migration (the survival of immigrants during the projection period and the survival of the population until emigration). Such projections take into account the age and sex distribution of the population, but they do not treat immigrants and their descendants explicitly.

The population projections presented here are distinguished by their explicit treatment of the generations of the immigrant population. They address the four generations of each racial or ethnic group defined above. Characterized from this perspective, the population includes a foreign-born component (the first generation) and a native-born population (the second and later generations).

A generational perspective has several advantages for examining the future population of immigrant groups and their influence on the nation. First, the generations themselves may be useful numbers. Those in the first generation speak the language and hold many of the cultural values of their countries of origin. Their children typically grow up speaking their parents' native language at home and adhering to many of their parents' cultural values, even while speaking English and absorbing U.S. culture. To know the generational distribution of a racial or ethnic group, therefore, is to know a lot about its acquisition of the English language and of U.S. values.

Second, generational characteristics refine the modeling of immigrants, who usually enter the United States as first-generation, foreign-born individuals, and

---

[6]Population projections have had a long history of debate about viewing their results. In general, most demographers emphasize the analytical credibility of the projection model, the plausibility of the assumptions, and the usefulness of a range of assumptions for understanding future population change (Romaniuc, 1990).

of emigrants, whose rate of leaving the United States varies greatly with the number of foreign-born members of a racial or ethnic group. The model also permits varying the assumptions about fertility and mortality rates by generation. Conventional population projection models generally make the unreasonable assumption, for example, that childbearing patterns are the same for all generations—that, in other words, immigrants acquire the fertility levels of the resident population upon arrival in the United States. Demographic research, however, suggests that fertility differences exist for immigrants but that they diminish with later generations.

A Generational Perspective

To sum up, our modified cohort-component approach adds a generational perspective to the characterization of the initial population by age, sex, and ethnicity used by standard population projections. The base population is moved forward in five-year intervals, with successive application of the demographic dynamics: births are added to the population. Deaths are subtracted. And net migration is added, depending on the combination of immigration and emigration. Thus, the model requires assumptions about the fertility, mortality, and migration flows for the age-sex groups in each generation.

For our approach, assumptions made about the generational dynamics are also important, inasmuch as they affect the results and interpretation of the projection.

Most users of population projections need to be able to regard them as plausible. "Plausible," in this context, means that the conditions for demographic dynamics could be regarded as likely for the future course of fertility, mortality, and international migration. Thus, a critical aspect of population projections is scrutiny of the assumptions made about the demographic dynamics.

Our approach assumes a relatively general model for each of the demographic processes on a generational basis (the formal model is presented in Appendix 3.A). For mortality, each age and sex group in each generation experiences its own schedule of death rates. Deaths in a generation reduce its numbers. For fertility, births to a generation add to the next generation.[7] Births to foreign-born immigrants (the first generation) are members of the second generation and will thus, given the time intervals used in the model, add to the 0-4 age group in the second generation in the next interval of the projection. In our approach, the latest generation is the fourth and their descendants. Births to the third generation and to the fourth or later generations will, by definition, become members of the last generation group.

[7]The discussion here assumes that the generation membership of the parents is unique—that is, either both parents always have the same generation or only the mother's generation is considered. We discuss mixed generational models in a later section.

International migration also calls for assumptions about the generational composition of migrants. Immigrants to a population are almost exclusively foreign-born.[8] Emigrants from the United States are predominantly members of the first generation: people who have emigrated to the United States and then decided to return to their country of birth. A relatively small number of native-born residents, second or later generation, also emigrate from the United States.

Base Population

The base populations were defined for July 1, 1995, and rely on information from April 1, 1990, the date for the 1990 U.S. Census of Population, and post-census estimates made by the U.S. Bureau of the Census (1996a). The age-sex distributions for the four immigrant generations in each ethnic group were taken from fitted projections of the U.S. population for the years 1880 to 1990. To obtain their numbers by generation, the projections were scaled, by ethnic group, to the 1970 census (for the first, second, and third and later generations) and the 1980 and 1990 censuses (for the native- and foreign-born). Finally, the population figures were scaled to the post-census age-sex distributions for the total population, by ethnic group, estimated by the U.S. Bureau of the Census (1996a).

For this chapter, we include estimates for the 1995 population by single and multiple ancestry. We consider two types of births in these projections: single-ancestry births are those to parents who have the same racial or ethnic identification; multiple-ancestry births are births to parents whose racial or ethnic identifications differ. Single ancestry, in the context of this chapter, means that a person reports a racial or ethnic ancestry that is the same as his or her primary racial or ethnic identification.

To obtain estimates of single and multiple ancestry, we used the 1990 census to divide persons in each of the four main racial/ethnic groups into two groups: (1) single-ancestry persons, who reported that both ancestries were the same as their racial/Hispanic-origin identification and (2) multiple-ancestry persons, who reported one or more ancestries that differed from their racial/Hispanic-origin group identification.

Overall, the proportion of multiple ancestry for the four main racial/ethnic groups varies a lot. About 7 percent of the U.S. population reported multiple ancestry in the 1990 census. Of those who reported their primary ethnic affiliation as white, about 6 percent reported one or more ancestries that were not white. Of those reporting themselves as black, about 7 percent reported one or more

---

[8]There are small numbers of immigrants to the United States who are native-born persons with foreign citizenship who immigrate. For example, a foreign-born couple residing in the United States may have children born in the United States and, subsequently, return to the country of their own birth. If their children later return to the United States, they would be immigrants from the second generation.

ancestries that were not black. The comparable figures were 8 percent for Asians and 9 percent for Hispanics.

Fertility Assumptions

Fertility is the starting point of any demographic projection model. Higher fertility rates will make the future population larger, and subgroups with higher than average fertility will grow relative to others.

Since 1971, the Census Bureau has published fertility estimates in a special supplement to the Current Population Survey (CPS) in June of each year. The survey asks women several fertility questions, including how many children they have ever borne and whether they have had a child within the past year. Starting in 1994, the CPS has also asked about the nativity of the respondent and the parents of the respondent. Using the CPS nativity data, we tabulated the population for the foreign-born (first generation), sons and daughters of the foreign-born (second generation), and native-born of native-born parents (third and later generations).[9]

There is apparently some underreporting of births in the CPS, when compared with vital statistics for registered number of births. Births are registered for a calendar year, whereas CPS data on reported births are from July of the preceding year to June of the survey year. We tabulated the number of births from vital statistics and the CPS by race/ethnicity, along with the adjustment factors to scale CPS data to the known level of births by race of mother.[10]

Age-specific fertility rates for the four major racial/ethnic groups were estimated using recent fertility data from the June 1994 CPS and the tabulations for 1994 of the National Center for Health Statistics (NCHS). Separate estimates were made for the first, second, and third and later immigrant generations (fertility levels for the third and fourth and later generations were assumed to be the same). Overall, the following total fertility rates were assumed for the starting period of 1995 to 2000: 1.81 for the white population, 2.33 for Asians, 2.34 for blacks, and 2.63 for Hispanics. As the generational composition shifts, the pro-

---

[9]The CPS has two important limitations for fertility estimates: undercoverage of the population and underreporting of births. The first results from omitted households and from missing persons within sample households. Although the CPS has lower rates of undercoverage than do other large federal household surveys, its undercoverage is about 8 percent lower than that of the 1990 census (Shapiro et al., 1993). Undercoverage rates vary with age, sex, and race. For some groups, such as black males aged 20 to 29, the rate is estimated to be as high as 34 percent compared with that of the 1990 census. Although the CPS is adjusted for undercoverage, the extent to which the weighting procedure corrects for fertility reporting bias due to undercoverage is unknown.

[10]Fertility estimates derived from the CPS are subject to sampling variability. To provide a range of the variability, we calculated standard errors for some of the fertility estimates. For the native-born white population, we calculated that the total fertility estimate of 1.81 has a standard error of ± 0.04.

TABLE 3.2 Fertility Estimates for U.S. National Population Projections by Race/Ethnicity and Immigrant Generation, 1995-2050

	Immigrant Generation			
Race/Ethnicity	Overall	First	Second	Third+
Total	1.98			
White	1.81	1.82	1.82	1.81
Asian	2.33	2.54	2.17	1.80
Black	2.34	2.76	2.53	2.31
Hispanic	2.63	3.23	2.63	2.04

Source: Panel estimates based on June 1994 Current Population Survey data and 1994 National Center for Health Statistics birth registration data.

jection shows declining overall total fertility levels for the heavily immigrant-oriented groups, such as Asians and Hispanics.

We used the June 1994 CPS to make fertility estimates for the major racial/ethnic groups for the first, second, and third-plus generations, using the adjustment factor described above (see Table 3.2).

In a number of important ways, our fertility assumptions are not very different from those used by the Census Bureau in their demographic modeling. The overall estimate of the fertility rate of the population, 1.98, is only slightly lower than the 2.02 assumption made for the 1995 Census Bureau's baseline population projection. The new estimate for the white population of 1.81 is also similar to the previous assumption of 1.83. There is little difference in the fertility levels by immigrant generation for the non-Hispanic white population.

The fertility estimate for the black population from the June 1994 CPS is slightly lower than the Census Bureau's projections. Reductions appear as the generations progress, with a decline to 2.3 children per woman by the third and later generations.

The 2.33 fertility estimate for the Asian population is considerably higher than the assumption of 1.92 used in the 1995 Census Bureau projections. We assume different fertility levels for each immigrant generation, with higher fertility for first-generation immigrants and a decline to 1.80 for the third and fourth generations. Fertility rates for Asians three or more generations out are similar to those for the white population.

Fertility estimates in the June 1994 CPS for the Hispanic population appear to be lower than those assumed in the Census Bureau's projections.[11] Moreover,

[11]From the June 1994 CPS special supplement on fertility and from births to Hispanic women reported in 1994 to the National Center for Vital Statistics, we estimate total fertility rates of 3.23 for foreign-born women and 2.31 for native-born women, yielding an overall total fertility rate of 2.63.

there is a large decrease in fertility with the progression of the generations. The estimate for the third and later Hispanic generations is 2.04, higher than that for the white and Asian groups but substantially lower than the current observation for the overall Hispanic population (2.63).

To evaluate the relationship of variations in fertility to the course of future population change, we make alternative assumptions about the levels of lower and higher fertility levels. In general, we assume lower and higher levels of fertility that are similar to the low and high fertility assumptions used in the Census Bureau's projections. The low and high fertility assumptions used in this report differ from the Census Bureau's, however, in two ways. First, as noted above, we assume different total fertility levels for some racial and ethnic groups. Second, because we make assumptions about fertility for immigrant generations, overall fertility levels will change as the generational composition shifts in the future. For lower fertility in 1995, we assume overall total fertility rates of 1.55 for the white population, 1.98 for the black population, 2.04 for the Asian population, and 2.18 for the Hispanic population. For higher fertility in 1995, we assume overall total fertility rates of 2.08 for the white population, 2.70 for the black population, 2.62 for the Asian population, and 3.08 for the Hispanic population. Although we hold total fertility rates constant within immigrant generations, we emphasize that overall total fertility rates may change over the projection period, as each race and Hispanic group shifts its immigrant generation composition.

Mortality Assumptions

We assume that mortality follows the trends specified in the medium series of the national population projections for 1995 to 2050 made by the Census Bureau. On that basis, overall life expectancy at birth increases from 75.9 years in 1995 to 82.0 years in 2050 (see Figure 3.1). We make separate assumptions about mortality for males and females and for each of the four main ethnic groups; and we assume that mortality is the same for immigrant generations within each of the ethnic groups.[12]

Using estimates for 1995 of the generational composition of the 1995 native-born Hispanic population, we estimate total fertility rates of 2.63 for the second generation and 2.04 for the third and later generations. Such fertility variation suggests that there is a substantial decline in fertility levels with increasing generational residence in the United States. Over time, as a greater proportion of Hispanics are native-born and as a greater proportion are third and later generations, overall Hispanic fertility levels are assumed to diminish in our projections.

[12]The Census Bureau estimates 2050 mortality by projecting the 1980 to 1990 trend. Because the 1980 to 1990 trends varied for racial/ethnic groups, this method results in lower mortality in 2050 for some groups that had higher relative mortality in 1990. Asians had longer life expectancy than Hispanics in 1990, for example, but are projected to have lower life expectancy than Hispanics in 2050. Although mortality assumptions could be investigated further, the panel did not conduct investigation in this area.

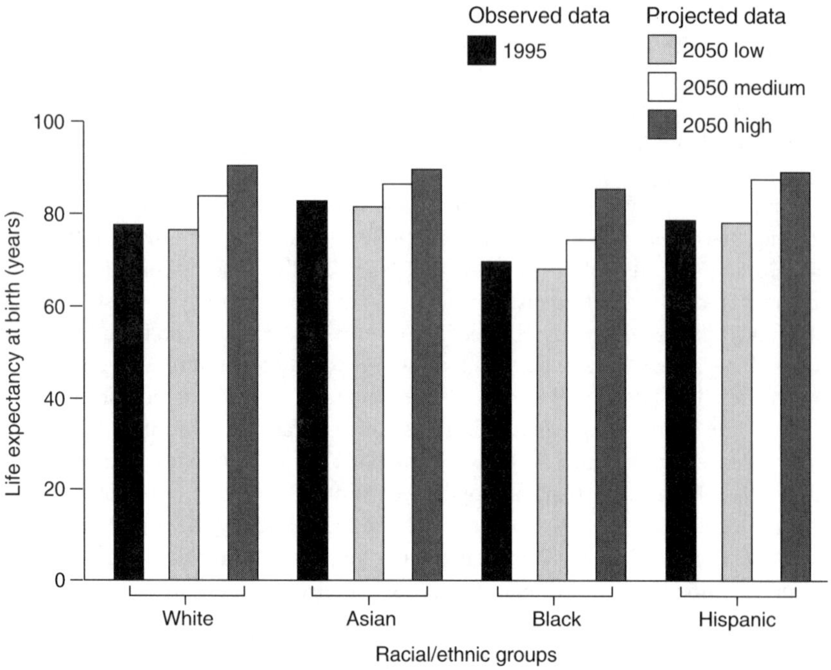

FIGURE 3.1 Mortality assumptions for national population projections.

Assumptions about lower and higher levels for future mortality help us assess the sensitivity of future population change to mortality variations. We use the same lower and higher mortality assumptions as are used for the Census Bureau's 1995 national population projections. For the low, medium, and high mortality assumptions, we assume the same levels of mortality, by sex and for each race and Hispanic group, for 1995. For 2050, we assume the mortality levels shown in Appendix 3.B: Table 3.B1.

Assumptions About Immigration

We make five different immigration assumptions about net immigration—termed zero, low, medium, high, and very high—in order: 0, 410,000, 820,000, 1,230,000, and 1,640,000. The medium assumption of 820,000 is close to the average for the period 1990-95 and includes the assumption of about 225,000 net annual illegal immigrants. The zero assumption implies both zero immigrants and zero emigrants, providing a context for discussing the overall net impact of immigration on population change. The low assumption of 410,000 assumes a decline to immigration levels that are close to net immigration during the 1980s. The high assumption represents possible expanded legal immigration through modifications of immigration law. The very high assumption suggests greatly expanded immigration.[13]

For the actual population projections, we make separate assumptions about immigration and emigration. For the five net immigration assumptions, we assume immigration levels of 0, 700,000, 1,040,000, 1,360,000, and 1,720,000 in conjunction with emigration levels of 0, 290,000, 220,000, 130,000, and 80,000. We assume a racial/ethnic distribution, with an age-sex composition, that is the same as that made in the Census Bureau's 1996 projections. Because of the need to make assumptions by immigrant generation, however, we assume that all immigrants enter into the first generation (in other words, no immigrants into the United States are native-born persons) and emigrants are selected as follows: 95 percent are from the first generation, 5 percent are from the second generation, and none are from the third or later generations.[14]

The age, sex, and ethnic compositions for the medium assumption were derived from recent data of the Immigration and Naturalization Service and from estimates of the characteristics of illegal immigrants. For the medium assumption, we assume net illegal immigration of 225,000; for the low assumption, 115,000; for the high assumption, 320,000; and for the very high assumption, 404,000. We vary the age, sex, and ethnic composition of immigrants for the different immigration assumptions, based on the legal and illegal components of net immigration.

Exogamy Assumptions

Exogamy is defined as marital and nonmarital unions between people of different racial/ethnic backgrounds. Why is exogamy important when projecting future populations? Suppose that the population consists only of Italians and Norwegians. Suppose further that each couple has two children. If Italians marry only Italians, then the future size of the Italian population will be a function only of the demography of Italians. All progeny of Italian parents would presumably report themselves as of Italian ancestry. But the two children of an Italian and Norwegian couple may report themselves as Norwegian, so that the Italian ancestry is not represented in the second generation; or they may report themselves as

---

[13]The immigration assumptions do not correspond to specific alternative immigration policies. For example, there could be changes in the visa preference categories for types of family members; we do not model such policy changes in our projections. Rather, the varying immigration assumptions are projection parameters that we vary in order to understand how variations in demographic changes depend on the overall volume of immigration.

[14]These proportions for the generational composition of emigrants were derived from a historical reconstruction of the U.S. population (see Passel and Edmonston, 1994). Such a generational composition is consistent with the notion that most emigrants are foreign-born persons who return to their country of origin, taking their native-born children with them.

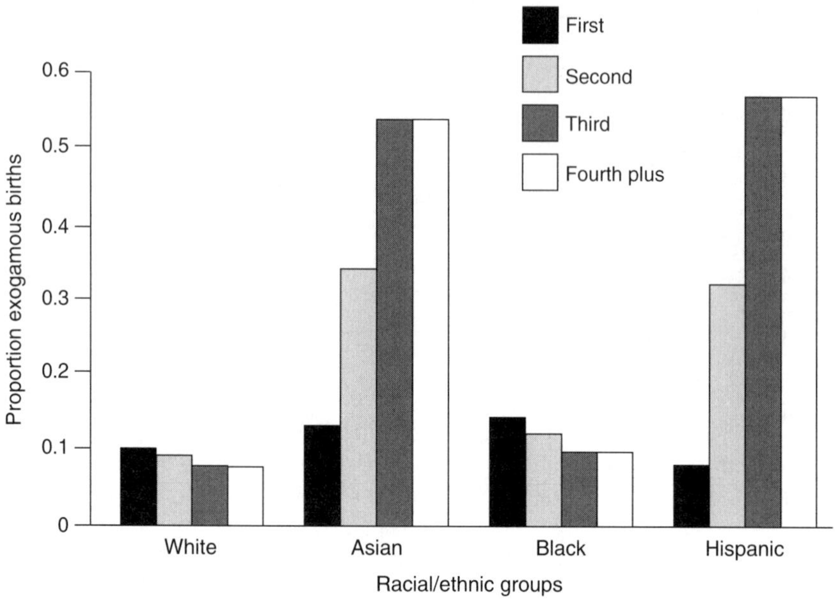

FIGURE 3.2 Exogamy assumptions for national population projections.

Italian, so that Norwegian ancestry is not represented; or each may claim one of the ancestries. Each may also report herself as of multiple ancestry. These real-life possibilities suggest the importance of assumptions about exogamy.

Conventional population projections assume that persons of different major racial/ethnic groups do not have children together and that all children will be of the same racial/ethnic identity as their parents. We address changes in the racial/ethnic identification in two ways in this chapter. First, we take into account the possibility that children may be born to exogamous unions—to parents of different racial/ethnic identification. Second, we take into account that children of multiple ancestries may report ancestries different from the ones their mothers report. *How* they report matters for population analysis and also complicates it.

Using 1990 census data, we estimate intermarriage rates by nativity (that is, for the foreign-born and the native-born) and by racial/ethnic ancestry (see Appendix 3.B: Table 3.B2). If those who themselves are the offspring of an intermarriage are more likely to enter into an interracial or Hispanic/non-Hispanic marriage, intermarriage estimates using data for all persons would be an overestimate for single race/ethnicity persons.

Figure 3.2 presents exogamy rates for racial/ethnic groups based on the data described above.[15] Nativity influences intermarriage in racial/ethnic groups. In

[15]To calculate exogamy rates for single-ancestry persons, we assume that the ratio of single-ancestry to overall intermarriage rates provides an estimate for adjusting the overall exogamy rates, sepa-

1990, foreign-born and native-born whites had similar intermarriage rates. The rates for Asians and Hispanics, however, were higher for the native-born than for the foreign-born. For blacks, intermarriage rates are lower for the native-born.

Whether one is of single or multiple ancestry also matters. Intermarriage rates are higher for persons of all racial/ethnic groups who themselves report multiple ancestries, including a racial/ethnic identification that is different from the primary one. There is considerable variation, however, in intermarriage rates for persons of multiple ancestry compared with those of single ancestry.[16]

To calculate estimates of exogamy by generation, we note that earlier work with 1970 census and survey data, mostly analyzing Hispanics, revealed a roughly linear increase in intermarriage rates for the first, second, and third generations (Gurak and Fitzpatrick, 1982). If we take the native-born population as an estimate for the second-plus generations and locate the estimate appropriate for the generational composition of racial/ethnic groups in 1990, then the native-born estimates for the white and black populations reflect primarily the third and later generations. We use the native-born information as an estimate for the third and fourth generations and estimate the second generation by averaging estimates for the first and third generations.

The native-born estimate for the Asian population is for a population centered on about the 2.6th generation. We assume that the fourth-plus generation is the same as the third. For the Hispanic population, we center the native-born population at 2.5.

Data on exogamy are available from several sources for the U.S. population. Although some data on intermarriage are available, data on intergroup nonmarital unions are not. We can approach exogamy using what is known about intermarriage, recognizing that information on currently married couples differs from data on births to parents of different racial/ethnic origins. For these population projections, we rely on data from the 1990 census on intermarriage rates for the foreign- and the native-born. For the native-born, we assume that the generational pattern for the second and third-plus generations, for each racial/ethnic group, was simi-

---

rately for the foreign-born and the native-born. For example, the intermarriage rate for foreign-born whites is 2.4 for single ancestry and 2.7 for all ancestries. We assume that the ratio of the two, 0.89, offers an estimate for adjusting the exogamy rate of 11.7. Thus, we derive the estimate of 0.89×11.7, or 10.4 percent exogamy for the foreign-born white population.

[16]Data on intermarriages by race/ethnicity in decennial censuses measure existing marriages. Although the flow of new marriages affects the stock of existing marriages, such effects lag shifts in new intermarriage patterns by several decades. This lag has implications for population projections, which rely on assumptions about the intermarriage levels for modeling fertility. Ideally, we would prefer estimates on the race/ethnicity of new marriages. Intermarriage data from the census have a handicap for population projections: a significant proportion of births occurs to persons or couples who are not married. We use special tabulations from the National Center for Health Statistics based on complete birth registration data for 1994.

lar to that reported in the 1970 census. Finally, we use NCHS data for births in 1994 on the race/ethnicity of mothers and fathers, for the native- and the foreign-born. Our overall results are that 92 percent of births to a white mother have a white father; 90 percent of births to a black mother have a black father; the ratio is 66 percent for Asian mothers, and for Hispanic mothers it is 68 percent. We use separate estimates for immigrant generations, so the initial overall exogamy rates change over time, increasing particularly for the Asian and Hispanic groups, since they have a greater proportion of persons in the later immigrant generations (Appendix 3.B: Table 3.B3 presents the final exogamy estimates for the population projections).

Assumptions About Racial and Ethnic Attribution

Assumptions about racial and ethnic attribution are crucial for population projections. Think of a child born to two parents, one of whom is Asian and the other is not. Now consider two possibilities: one, the child never identifies as Asian; the other, the child always identifies as Asian. In the first case, no children born to an Asian/non-Asian couple will identify as Asian; the only persons in the next generation who will do so will be single-ancestry Asians (those with an Asian mother and father). In the second case, all multiple-Asian-ancestry persons will report themselves as Asians. The Asian population will grow more slowly in the first case, because exogamous births will not be counted in it. In the second case, the Asian population will grow more quickly, because births to either Asian men or Asian women, regardless of the ethnicity of their partners, will add to the size of the next generation's Asian population.[17]

Conventional population projections make a simple assumption that children will eventually report their ethnicity to be the same as their mothers. In our projections, we make a number of alternative assumptions. Here we refer to conventional population projections as the baseline assumption for the attribution of racial/ethnic identification for multiple-ancestry persons. If no multiple-ancestry children identify with a specific racial/ethnic group, we call this the extremely low attribution assumption. If all multiple-ancestry children identify with

[17] In the 1990 census, Hispanics would be reported as a member of any racial group, including the reporting of "other" race. Both foreign-born and native-born Hispanics reported themselves in large numbers in the white and other racial categories. About 40 percent of Hispanic respondents reported themselves as "other" in the 1990 census; most of the rest reported themselves as white. Overall, more than 97 percent of people reporting themselves in the "other" category were of Hispanic origin. Such census reporting complicates the analysis of racial and ethnic attribution because respondents could report both a racial as well as a Hispanic identity. This may overstate the preference for Hispanic identity and, conversely, understate their preference for other identities. If persons of multiple ancestry, including Hispanics, were asked to report only one primary ethnic identification, like other respondents, this might decrease the number in the Hispanic category and increase the number in the white category.

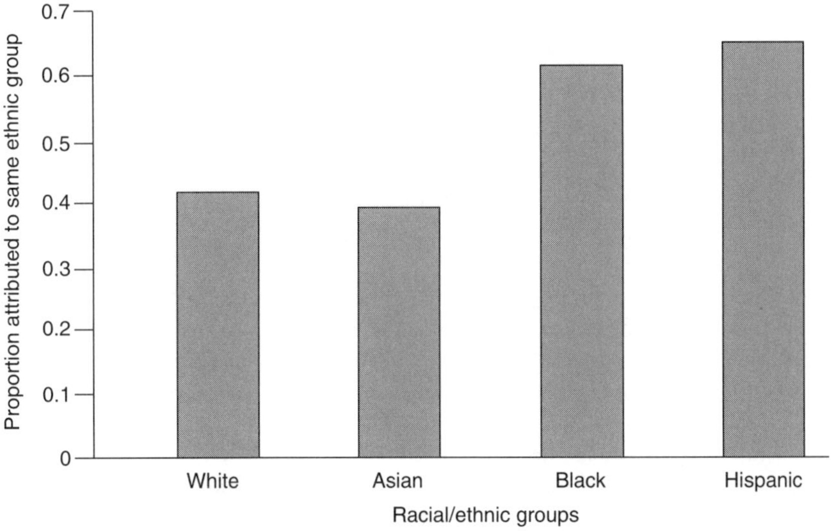

FIGURE 3.3 Racial/ethnic attribution assumptions for population projections.

a particular racial/ethnic group, we call this the extremely high attribution assumption.

Neither of these assumptions is plausible. To provide more realistic bounds, we examined data on actual racial and ethnic attribution. This information underlies a medium assumption about racial/ethnic attribution rates for multiple-ancestry persons. We assume identification rates that are 20 percentage points lower and 20 percentage points higher, respectively (see Figure 3.3).

In summary, we rely on six different assumptions about the combined effects of exogamy and racial/ethnic identification to illustrate future change in the racial and ethnic composition of the U.S. population. Two extreme and unrealistic assumptions capture the possibility that either none of the multiple-ancestry persons or all of them will choose to identify a particular ethnic background as their primary affiliation. Current attribution rates form a medium assumption, in contrast with a continuation of the conventional baseline assumptions for population projections. And we vary the current attribution rates to illustrate realistic changes in low and high attribution rates (see Appendix 3.B: Table 3.B).

NATIONAL POPULATION GROWTH

The United States is currently the third most populous nation in the world, after China and India. How large will the United States become in future decades? Will its rate of growth, which has slackened in recent decades, revive? And how much difference will immigration make?

Immigration can play a critical role in determining the future size of the U.S. population. Within the population balancing equation, population growth could rise substantially if fertility or net immigration rises or if mortality declines. The rate of fertility, which has been below the replacement level for almost 20 years, shows little evidence of reviving sufficiently to alter the course of population growth. Our mortality assumptions incorporate mortality declines over the projection period, which will lead to higher levels of natural increase and population growth. Population growth will be even higher if there is an even greater improvement in life expectancy.[18]

That leaves immigration as the most likely factor acting to spur population growth in the coming decades. Apart from the additions its net numbers make to the population, immigration, because it alters the age and racial/ethnic composition of the population, influences the rates of fertility and mortality that are the basic components of population change.

Demographic change has three main effects: on population size, on population composition, and on population growth. We draw attention to changes in the national population size and growth in later sections of this chapter.[19] Age composition is one of the most important compositional effects, because immigration alters relative numbers of the school-age population, young adults, and the elderly.

Table 3.3 lists our projections of the future size of the American population under five alternative immigration assumptions. It is important to remember that this country's population will continue to grow well into the next century, even if net immigration was immediately eliminated forever. Under the assumption of zero immigration, the population of the United States will grow slowly, reaching a peak of 311 million in about 2035.[20] Thereafter, it will very slowly decline, because, as the baby-boom cohorts age, deaths will outweigh births.

Table 3.3 also demonstrates that population growth will be significantly higher under any of our scenarios of positive levels of immigration. According to

[18]The sensitivity of the overall population results to alternative fertility or mortality assumptions are described in Appendix 3.B.

[19]We do not present projections for states or other subnational population groups. The Census Bureau makes population projections for states; however, their projections do not separately display different immigration assumptions. Most states also prepare population projections, although they do not appear to examine separately the effect of different U.S. immigration assumptions.

[20]The projections reported here differ from but are close to those prepared by the U.S. Bureau of the Census (1996a). The Census Bureau's median series projection begins with the same 1995 base population of 263 million. The Census Bureau's projected population for 2050 is 394 million, 7 million or 2 percent greater than this projection. Because we make similar immigration, emigration, and mortality assumptions, the reason for the difference is that our projections assume overall lower fertility levels. We make separate fertility assumptions by immigrant generation, including the notion that fertility decreases with greater generational residence in the United States. The Census Bureau's projections do not distinguish fertility levels by the native- and the foreign-born.

TABLE 3.3 Population of the United States, 1995-2050

	Immigration Assumption				
	Zero	Low	Medium	High	Very High
Assumed net immigrants per year (thousands)	0	410	820	1,230	1,640
Population (millions)					
1995	263	263	263	263	263
2000	272	275	277	279	281
2010	287	295	302	310	318
2020	298	313	327	341	354
2030	308	330	351	373	393
2040	310	341	370	400	429
2050	307	349	387	426	463

our medium immigration assumption (under which current levels persist indefinitely into the future), the size of the population will be 327 million in the year 2020 (an increment of 29 million compared with the zero immigration scenario). Although the rate at which population is growing will decline, **the absolute size of the American nation will continue to expand until, by the year 2050, the population will be 387 million.**[21] **Allowing immigration to continue at its current levels for the next 55 years will produce a population that is 80 million people larger than it would have been if all net immigration ceased instantly. These additional people are the direct effect of the 45 million more immigrants over this period. Then come the dual indirect effects of the descendants of these immigrants (compounded by higher fertility rates among immigrants) and of their lower overall mortality rate due to the relative youth of immigrants.**

Immigration, then, will obviously play the dominant role in our future population growth. Of the 124 million additional people living in 2050 under the medium immigration assumption, 80 million will be the direct or indirect consequence of immigration.

Table 3.3 also displays what population growth would be under realistic ranges of alterations in immigration policy. **For example, if, on one hand, net**

[21]The average annual rate of population growth will decrease from 0.9 percent between 1995 and 2000, to 0.8 percent between 2015 and 2020, and to 0.5 percent between 2045 and 2050. Since the average number of net immigrants remains constant in this projection, the decreasing annual rate of population growth is attributable mainly to a slowing rate of natural increase. This, in turn, is due primarily to a substantial increase in the number of deaths associated with the greater number of persons in the ages of high mortality.

immigration were halved, to 410,000 per year, growth would be slower, but the population would still rise to 349 million by the middle of the next century. If, on the other hand, net immigration were to increase by half, to 1,230,000 a year, the population would rise to 426 million by 2050. In either policy scenario, the population will be different from that under the medium immigration assumption—and by more than the simple addition or subtraction of immigrants, since the descendants of these immigrants will also be part of the future nation.

Although, in light of the current debate, very high immigration is not a realistic policy option, Table 3.3 also illustrates population growth under that scenario. The outcome is a steady increase to 463 million in 2050.[22]

Components of Change

What underlies the effects the various immigration scenarios have on population? Although the five immigration scenarios in the population projections assume a constant annual number of net immigrants, the annual net immigration rate[23] will change as the population grows. That rate is one of the two elements in the rate of population growth; the other is the rate of natural increase—that is, the crude birth rate minus the crude death rate. Table 3.4 lists crude birth and death rates as well as the rate of natural increase under our five alternative immigration scenarios. We first examine the contribution of net immigration to annual population growth.

Besides simply adding people to the population, immigration has other repercussions for population change. By shifting the age-sex composition of the population, immigrants alter the likelihood of all residents of dying or having children. Immigrants may have a different age distribution from other residents, or they may have different childbearing rates, and thus they may affect the number of deaths and births.

In the absence of net immigration, the crude birth rate would decrease between 1995 and 2050, the crude death rate would increase, and the rate of natural increase would decline to zero (see Table 3.4). These results would occur because the population would slowly become older, with a smaller proportion in the childbearing ages (15 to 44) and a greater proportion in the higher mortality ages (65 and over).

---

[22]After rising a bit through the end of this century, the rate of increase will ease back to levels not much above the current rate.

[23]The net immigration rate is sensitive to assumptions about the annual number of net immigrants. That rate varies in the years 1995-2000 between 0 and 6 per 1,000. Over time, however, as the population increases, the rate falls for all the assumptions about immigration. Under the medium assumption, for example, it decreases from 3 per 1,000 in 1995-2000 to 2 per 1,000 in 2045-50. Even very high immigration yields a net immigration rate of less than 4 per 1,000 by 2045-50.

TABLE 3.4 Components of Population Growth, Selected Years, 1995-2000 to 2045-2050

	Immigration Assumption				
	Zero	Low	Medium	High	Very High
Crude birth rate (per 1,000)					
1995-2000	14.4	14.5	14.6	14.7	14.8
2005-2010	13.3	13.7	14.0	14.3	14.5
2015-2020	13.1	13.6	14.0	14.3	14.6
2025-2030	12.6	13.2	13.8	14.1	14.5
2035-2040	12.5	13.3	13.9	14.3	14.6
2045-2050	12.6	13.5	14.0	14.4	14.8
Crude death rate (per 1,000)					
1995-2000	8.9	8.9	8.8	8.8	8.7
2005-2010	8.9	8.6	8.5	8.4	8.2
2015-2020	9.3	9.0	8.7	8.5	8.3
2025-2030	11.2	10.7	10.2	9.8	9.4
2035-2040	12.8	12.0	11.3	10.7	10.3
2045-2050	12.6	11.7	10.9	10.4	10.0
Rate of natural increase (per 1,000)					
1995-2000	5.5	5.7	5.8	5.9	6.0
2005-2010	4.5	5.1	5.5	6.0	6.4
2015-2020	3.8	4.6	5.2	5.8	6.3
2025-2030	1.4	2.6	3.5	4.3	5.0
2035-2040	–0.4	1.4	2.6	3.5	4.3
2045-2050	0.0	1.9	3.1	4.1	4.9
Net immigration rate (per 1,000)					
1995-2000	0.0	1.6	3.1	4.8	6.3
2005-2010	0.0	1.4	2.9	4.2	5.6
2015-2020	0.0	1.3	2.7	3.8	4.9
2025-2030	0.0	1.3	2.5	3.5	4.5
2035-2040	0.0	1.3	2.3	3.3	4.0
2045-2050	0.0	1.2	2.2	3.1	3.8

Under the medium immigration assumption, the crude birth rate would decline slightly between 1995 and 2050. The proportion of the population in the childbearing years would rise modestly, and there would be a continued influx of immigrants, some of whom have higher fertility than do the native-born. The population would have a greater proportion of older persons, however, and the crude death rate would increase from 8.8 per 1,000 in 1995-2000 to 10.9 per

1,000 in 2045-50. Overall, the rate of natural increase would decrease almost in half, from 5.8 to 3.1 per 1,000.[24]

IMPLICATIONS OF THE SIZE OF THE POPULATION

Under any of our positive net immigration scenarios, the size of the U.S. population will be higher in the future than it would be if net immigration were zero at this moment. The increase in the total size of the population in most of these positive immigration worlds would not be trivial. As we have just seen, simply holding immigration to current levels would mean a net addition of 80 million Americans by the year 2050. Should we care about whether the 2050 population is the 387 million implied by current immigration levels as opposed to the 307 million implied by the absence of net immigration?

Although we do not answer that question categorically in this volume, we spell out some important elements of the answer. Our reticence rests in part on our conviction that knowledge about many of the crucial parameters on which an informed answer should rest is still lacking.

The future size of the population is important for labor market, fiscal, social, and environmental reasons. Chapter 5 spells out our analysis of the labor market effects. As we explain there, the critical issue is the extent to which a larger population size for the United States may be associated with some economies or diseconomies of scale. For example, if the U.S. economy is characterized by economies of scale, then a 10 percent increase in population will mean more than a 10 percent increase in national output. For some specialized products, businesses with access to the large U.S. market may have a substantial advantage, compared with doing business in a country with a smaller market. Similarly, in large part, the net fiscal impact we estimate in Chapters 6 and 7 will simply be scaled up or down by the size of the immigration flow, as long as the composition of immigration remains constant.

It is less clear what the comparative advantages and limitations are for social and environmental matters. Some have argued that there may be some important congestion effects from a larger population. These congestion effects may reveal themselves in more crowded highways, schools, and parks. From an environmental perspective, a large and growing population places greater demands on the environment, other conditions being equal. Probably more important, however, from a demographic perspective, is the extent to which the population resides in environmentally sensitive areas and the per capita environmental effects of the population.

---

[24]Given the very high immigration assumption, the crude birth rate would remain virtually unchanged, the crude death rate would increase moderately, and the rate of natural increase would decline from 6.0 per 1,000 to 4.9 over the next half-century.

However, it should be noted that immigration involves primarily a redistribution of the world's population, not an absolute increase. Indeed, since the fertility of immigrants tends to decline after they come to the United States, total world population will be slightly lower. The potential for negative environmental effects (congestion and the like) must then be primarily local. From a world perspective, (negative) environmental effects in the United States may be counterbalanced by possible (positive) effects in the sending countries that are losing population. Total consumption by immigrants will typically be higher in the United States than in the places they left (which, after all, is one reason they immigrated). But efforts to abate environmental effects at any given level of consumption may also be higher in the United States. A weighting of the factors should enter into an evaluation of the environmental effects of immigration.

AGE AND SEX COMPOSITION

Even with zero net migration, a population's age and sex composition will shift if the characteristics of the immigrants and emigrants differ. The general effect of migration on the population structure over the past decades can be illustrated by comparing the actual age and sex compositions in 1995 with what they would have been in the absence of migration since 1950 (see Table 3.5).[25] It can be seen that the effect of net migration has been noteworthy over this period in terms of both the population and sex composition.

In the absence of migration since 1950, the U.S. population would have numbered about 225 million in 1995, about 14 percent fewer than the actual 263 million. However, the impact of migration on sex composition would have been trivial: the actual population distribution has slightly more males and slightly fewer females than the hypothetical population with no migration.

Immigration would, however, have influenced the age composition for both males and females. In general, migration would have made the population younger, adding to the proportion of the population aged 10 to 39 years and reducing the proportion who are aged 50 to 79.

Sex Composition

As our illustration just suggested, **the impact of alternative immigration**

[25]The data (more readily available for immigrants than for emigrants) suggest that immigrants are more concentrated than emigrants in the young adult ages, 15 to 29 years. Emigrants tend to include more children and older adults, reflecting a tendency for emigrants to be families with children. Nevertheless, the general age and sex distributions are similar for immigrants and emigrants. The zero-migration compositions were obtained by applying appropriate cohort survival values to the 1950 U.S. population (who would have been 45 years and older in 1995) and to the age-zero population (the annual number of observed births) in each subsequent year to obtain a complete set of estimates for 1995.

TABLE 3.5 Age-Sex Structure of the U.S. Population in 1995 in the Absence of Migration Since 1950

	Hypothetical Population Under Assumption of No Migration				Observed Population					
	Number (thousands)		Percentage of Total		Number (thousands)		Percentage of Total		Ratio of Observed to Hypothetical Population	
Age Group	Males	Females	Males	Females	Males	Females	Males	Females	Males	Females
0-9	17,065	16,583	7.6	7.4	19,862	18,941	7.6	7.2	99.6	97.7
10-19	15,436	15,092	6.9	6.7	18,952	18,038	7.2	6.9	104.9	102.4
20-29	15,506	15,276	6.9	6.8	18,593	18,263	7.1	6.9	102.5	102.2
30-39	18,487	18,442	8.2	8.2	21,995	22,166	8.4	8.4	101.8	102.8
40-49	16,010	16,423	7.1	7.3	18,560	19,129	7.1	7.3	99.2	99.6
50-59	10,482	11,147	4.7	5.0	11,994	12,782	4.5	4.9	97.4	98.0
60-69	8,532	10,146	3.8	4.5	9,227	10,745	3.5	4.1	92.4	91.5
70-79	5,860	8,015	2.6	3.6	6,555	8,965	2.5	3.4	95.4	95.2
80+	2,061	4,306	.9	1.9	2,622	5,478	1.0	2.1	109.7	108.3
Total	109,439	115,330	48.7	51.3	128,311	134,509	48.8	51.2	100.3	99.7
Both Sexes	224,769		100.0		262,820		100.0		100.0	

Sources: The hypothetical 1995 population, under the assumption of no migration since 1950, is derived by surviving the 1950 population, by age and sex, using period life tables and adding annual births using period fertility rates, and surviving births, by age and sex until 1995. The observed 1995 population is taken from estimates of the U.S. Bureau of the Census (1996a:Table 2).

TABLE 3.6 Ratio of Males to Females, 1995-2050

	Net Immigration Assumption				
Year	Zero	Low	Medium	High	Very High
1995	.954	.954	.954	.954	.954
2000	.959	.958	.958	.958	.957
2010	.965	.963	.962	.961	.961
2020	.964	.962	.962	.961	.960
2030	.963	.960	.959	.959	.958
2040	.963	.961	.960	.960	.960
2050	.966	.964	.964	.963	.963

scenarios on the future balance between men and women is negligible (see Table 3.6). The sex ratio was favorable to females in 1995 and is expected to remain so throughout the projection period. In 1995, there was 0.954 male per female; put another way, the population was 51.1 percent female. By 2050, the ratio is expected to change slightly, to 50.9 percent female. The range of variation in the sex ratios across our alternative immigration assumptions varies only between 0.963 and 0.966.[26]

Throughout the next century, males will outnumber females before middle age because more boys than girls are born. After age 50, the relatively higher mortality of men decreases their ratio to women and eventually results in a markedly higher number of women at the older ages. None of these age patterns in the sex ratio will be altered, no matter which immigration assumption prevails.

Age Structure

In contrast to the situation for sex composition, **immigration will significantly affect the age structure of the future population.** As Chapter 2 demonstrates, immigrants are concentrated in the age groups from 20 to 40 and are relatively scarce in the over-60 group. In the zero-migration assumption, the population will be much older than it would be if current immigration persists. Thus, the aging of the population, which is already obvious, would become even more pronounced if immigration stopped altogether.

Perhaps the single most common index of population aging is the median age of the population—the age that divides the younger half of the population from

[26]We assume that there are more females in all of our immigration assumptions, ranging from 56 percent female for the low immigration assumption to 52 percent female for the high and very high immigration assumptions. The impact of a slightly predominant female immigration flow is modest and changes the sex ratio for the total population only slightly.

the older half. Although the median age, viewed over time, is a useful summary indicator of population aging, it does not capture many important compositional changes so crucial for public policy decisions. Population aging usually involves a decreasing proportion of young people and, correspondingly, an increasing proportion of the older ones. For many issues, it is helpful to separate younger and older groups and present estimates of their population size and change. But, first, we discuss the relationship of immigration and median age.

Median Age

Population aging is not a new phenomenon in the United States. In the 1800s, the median age of the U.S. population was under 20, a reflection of high fertility levels that produced a population with a large number of children. The median age has been steadily rising for more than a century, reaching the historically unprecedented level of over 34 in 1995.

As the results below indicate, the median age of the population will continue to rise, changing as much in the next 55 years as in the previous 55 years. This rise is a consequence of continued low levels of fertility and the aging of the numerically large baby-boom cohorts. Over the next half-century, the impact of the baby-boom cohorts of the 1950s will be clear. Under all the net immigration assumptions, the future population will continue to age (Figure 3.4). Under the medium assumption, the median age will rise to 38.5 years in 2030 and then level off at about 38 years. Under the low net immigration assumption, the population

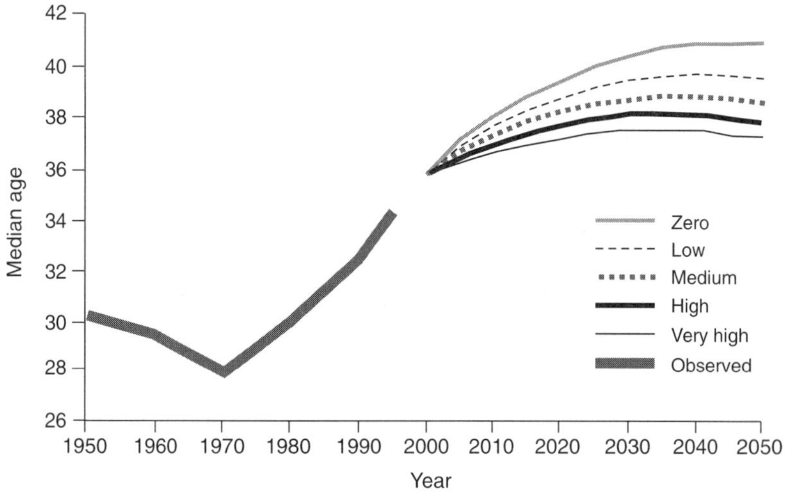

FIGURE 3.4 Median age of the U.S. population: Observed population, 1950-1995; projected population under five immigration assumptions, 1995-2050.

will reach a median age of 39.3 years in 2035 and then stabilize at about 39 years. The more numerous the immigrants, the more youthful the population over the projection period. With high net immigration, the median age of the population will reach 37.9 years in 2035 and then decrease to 37.4 years in 2050.[27]

School-Age Population

Public policies for education are perhaps the ones most obviously influenced by demography. Immigration makes a difference for the size of the school-age population, virtually all of whom do attend school—directly as young children enter as immigrants and indirectly because many immigrants are in their child-bearing years. What will the next decades hold for the school-age population?

The projections for the school-age population are subject to considerable uncertainty because they depend on projections of future fertility as well as on those for the immigration of younger persons. Since the 1980s, the school-age population (aged 5 to 19 years) has been increasing steadily, to number 56.2 million in 1995. Under the medium immigration assumption, it will expand throughout the projection period, reaching 77.3 million in 2050. With low net immigration, the school-age population would expand more slowly—to 67.9 million in 2050—whereas under the high net immigration assumption, there will be 86.6 million in 2050.[28]

If school enrollment rates, by age group and nativity, are unchanged from 1995, we can make estimates for future school enrollments.[29] **The number of school-age children will expand rapidly. Under current immigration policy, the K-8 enrollment will increase to 53.7 million in 2050, compared with 36.8 million in 1995 (an increase of about 17 million). The school-age population in 2050 will be 6.4 million lower if immigration flows are cut in half and 3.9 million greater if they are increased by 50 percent.**[30]

---

[27]Under the zero net immigration assumption, the population will reach a median age of 40.6 years in 2040 and then stabilize at slightly above 40 years. With very high net immigration, the median age of the population will reach 37.3 years in 2030 and plateau at about 37 years.

[28]If net immigration is zero, the school-age population will expand slightly—from 56.2 million in 1995 to a peak of 57.6 million in 2000—then decrease slowly, to 57.0 million in 2050. Under the very high immigration assumption, there will be 95.8 million in 2050.

[29]The kindergarten to grade 8 (K-8) enrollment, combining public and private schools, was 36.8 million in 1995 (U.S. Bureau of the Census, 1996b: Table 231).

[30]In 1995, foreign-born students comprised 6 percent of the K-8 age group. In 2050, the proportion foreign-born of the K-8 age group would be 2, 4, and 5 percent for the low, medium, and high net immigration assumptions, respectively. Under each of these three assumptions, the K-8 enrollments would increase, although the proportion foreign-born of the students would decline. Comparable figures for the K-8 enrollments in 2050 are 39.8 million under the zero net immigration assumption and 66.5 million under the very high net immigration assumption.

Similarly, high school enrollments for grades 9 to 12 were 14.0 million in 1995. These enrollments would increase to 20.3 million under medium net immigration—with a range of about 2.5 million more or less under low and high immigration assumptions.[31]

In light of the geographic concentration of immigrants, it is important to remember that not all school districts will be affected equally by immigration. In fact, most school districts in this country will feel no consequences, no matter what happens with immigration.[32] Other districts, especially those in the urban areas of the large immigration states, will be keenly sensitive to any changes in immigration policy.

Young Adults

Young adults, aged 15 to 24 years, are a crucial component of the population, given their unique economic role and place in the economy. These young adults are part of a special transition group who move on to postsecondary education, enter the labor force, and experience the highest rate of unemployment. They also are the ones who consider forming a household, getting married, and starting a family. They acquire the right to vote and are a critical recruitment pool for the Armed Forces. After peaking in the early 1980s, the numbers in this group have begun to increase again in the 1990s. Young adults numbered 35.9 million in 1995. Under the medium immigration assumption, that number will expand to over 42 million by 2020, and to almost 51 million by 2050.

With low net immigration, the young adult population will increase more slowly, from 35.9 million in 1995 to 44.7 million in 2050. Therefore, cutting immigration flows in half, a sharp departure from historical immigration policy, results in a young adult population that is 25 percent smaller 53 years from now then it would have been with continued current immigration levels. Under the high net immigration assumption, growth will be at a faster pace, with the young adult population reaching 56.6 million in 2050.[33] The next chapter discusses the implications of such a change on the labor market outcomes of native-born workers.

The implications of these changes for college enrollments can be derived

---

[31]Under the zero net immigration assumption, school enrollment in grades 9 to 12 in 2050 will still be greater than in 1995, increasing to 15.1 million. Under the very high net immigration assumption, the 9 to 12 grade enrollment will increase to 25.3 million.

[32]Most school districts have relatively few foreign-born students because recent immigration is concentrated in a few states, usually in metropolitan areas. Although the regional and state concentration of immigration may shift in future years, it is still likely that most school districts will receive few immigrant students.

[33]Under the zero immigration assumption, the young adult population will increase to 38.0 million in 2050. Under the very high immigration assumption, growth will be steady, to 62.3 million in 2050.

from our model.[34] College enrollments of 14.2 million in 1995 will increase to 19.4 million in 2050 under the medium net immigration scenario, assuming that college enrollment rates are unchanged from 1995 for the foreign-born and native-born in this age group. College enrollments will increase to 17.1 million under low net immigration and 21.8 million under high net immigration.[35] **Therefore, enrollments for U.S. colleges will grow about one-third by the middle of the next century. These enrollments will be incremented or decremented by more than 2 million students by the plausible range of immigration assumptions.**

Working Age

The impacts of demographic trends on growth in the labor force, which comprises those aged 20 to 64, have received less public attention. The compositional changes associated with the sharp decline in fertility rates since the early 1960s appear to have been masked by the higher rates of immigration since the end of that decade, and by the noticeable increase in the participation of women in the labor force. However, policymakers continue to be puzzled by the high rates of unemployment among youths and by the continued higher unemployment of some minority groups. How many people will be in the labor force years in coming decades? And what role will immigration, with its impact on the age and sex composition of the population, play in that number?

Under all assumptions, the working-age population, at 171.5 million in 1995, will continue to grow throughout the projection period. By 2000, under the medium immigration assumption, this group will climb to 183.6 million, and by 2050, to 240.2 million, a 40 percent expansion from 1995.

Under the assumption of low net immigration, the working age population will increase gradually, to 215.7 million in 2050, or 26 percent greater than 1995. Under the high net immigration assumption, the increase will be to 265.2 million in 2050, or 55 percent above the 1995 level.[36]

---

[34]These estimates assume no trade-off between changes in immigration policy and the number of young adults who seek nonimmigrant student status. If immigration were severely restricted, for example, persons who strongly wished to enter the United States might seek to enroll in college so that they could apply for a nonimmigrant visa.

[35]Under the zero net immigration assumption, college enrollments in 2050 will be slightly higher than in 1995—14.5 million. Under the very high net immigration assumption, college enrollments will increase to 23.9 million in 2050.

[36]Under the zero immigration assumption, the working age-population will increase modestly, to 189.1 million in 2050, or a 10 percent increase from 1995. Under the very high immigration assumption, the increase will be to 289.1 million in 2050, or 69 percent above the 1995 level.

Elderly

The number of elderly in the population has importance for private and public pension programs, for health care, and for a host of services related to aging and retirement. As the population ages, the maintenance of the real level of public services to the elderly can impose an ever-increasing tax burden on future generations. The nation will face two unattractive alternatives: either the elderly will receive less public services and suffer a decline in their standard of living, or future generations must draw down their resources to maintain that standard of living.

Unlike that in the population at younger ages, future change in the population aged 65 years and older is known with a fair degree of certainty because persons reaching this age in the projection period have either already been born in the United States or will be survivors among future immigrants. This population will grow rapidly in the coming years, both in numbers and as a proportion of the total population. It stood at 33.6 million in 1995, and could double—from 73.0 to 80.6 million, depending on the net immigration assumptions. Under the medium assumption, the elderly population will rise to 39.1 million in 2010, then will increase steadily as the baby-boom cohort begins to reach age 65 in large numbers. It will grow to 53.0 million in 2020 and, by 2050, to 76.8 million.[37] **Although the impact of immigration on the size of the elderly population is not trivial, it certainly plays only a supporting role. No immigration policy, no matter how restrictive, can reverse the underlying trend. The big news, therefore, over the next half-century is the guaranteed substantial growth in the number of people past age 65—the size of that population is likely to double.**

The "oldest-old" (those over 85) represent an important age group because they have the highest rates of hospitalization and nursing home use, factors that are forces driving health care costs. Variations in immigration, however, do not account for substantial differences in the size of the population aged 85 years and older. Under the medium net immigration assumption, the oldest-old age group will increase from 3.6 million in 1995 to 17.7 million in 2050 (a fourfold increase). Assuming the low and high net immigration levels provides a range for this age group of 17.4 to 18.1 million.[38] **Although the oldest-old population will expand greatly during the next half-century, immigration will have little effect on its size**. People who will be over age 85 in 2050 are at least 32 years old

[37]Under the zero net immigration assumption, the population aged 65 years and older will reach 69.1 million in 2050. Under the very high net immigration assumption, the elderly population will increase to 84.4 million in 2050.

[38]Under zero net immigration, the population aged 85 years and older will increase to 17.1 million in 2050. Under the very high net immigration assumption, the oldest-old will reach a level of 18.4 million in 2050.

today. Because most new immigrants who arrive in the next decades will be younger than that age, immigration flows will not fundamentally alter the size of this age group. Rather, the size of the oldest-old population will depend mainly on future trends in mortality.

Dependency Ratio

One useful concept in population analysis, the ratio of the number of people in their "dependent" years to those who are in their working years, is especially relevant to the study of immigration. Variations in age dependency reflect in an overall way the contribution of variations in age composition to economic dependency. Dependency ratios based on age, it should be emphasized, do not equate with economic dependency. We report three dependency ratios here: (1) a youth dependency ratio, for the number of persons 19 years of age or under per 100 persons in the working years, aged 20 to 64 years; (2) an elderly dependency ratio, relating persons aged 65 years and over to those in the working years; and (3) an overall dependency ratio relating these two groups together to those in the working years.

Youth Dependency

As can be seen in Figure 3.5, the youth dependency ratio reached a peak in the 1960s as the large number of those born in the baby boom were of school age.

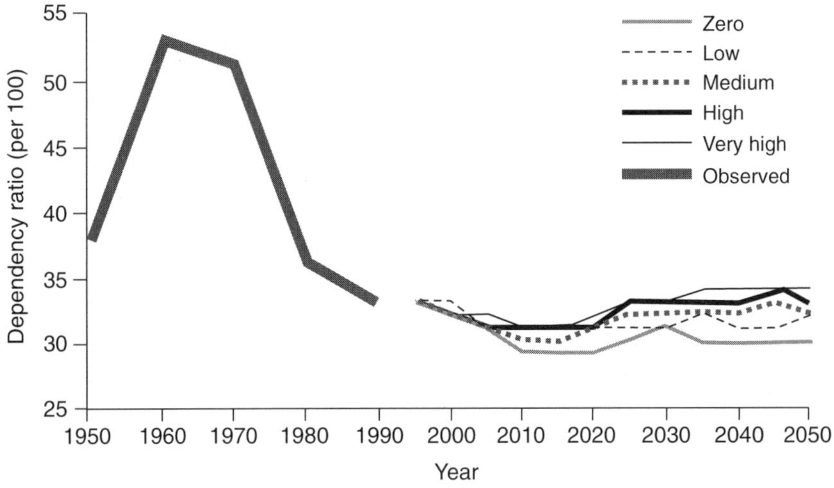

FIGURE 3.5 Youth dependency ratio: Observed population, 1950-1995; projected population under five immigration assumptions, 1995-2050. Note: dependency ratio defined as number of dependents 0-19 years of age per 100 persons aged 20-64 years.

The ratio has declined in recent decades to 33 youths per 100 persons in the working ages. As the figure shows, variations in immigration have relatively little effect on the youth dependency ratio because they tend to change the numbers of persons in both the youth and the working-age years.[39] Under the medium net immigration assumption, the youth dependency ratio will decline slightly to 32 per 100 in 2050. Under the low or high net immigration assumptions, the youth dependency ratio will range from 32 to 33.[40]

Elderly Dependency

As the population has aged, the elderly dependency ratio has been rising for the past three decades. Regardless of the level of immigration assumed, this ratio will increase substantially (Figure 3.6). From 20 elderly persons per 100 in the working years, the ratio will rise to over 29 per 100 by about 2050. Although immigration will not offset these notable increases in the elderly dependency ratio, it will influence the eventual level. Under the low net immigration assumption, the elderly dependency ratio will increase to 30 in 2050. Under the high immigration assumption, the elderly dependency ratio will increase to 27 in 2030.[41]

Overall Dependency

These two dependency ratios—for youth and the elderly—can be combined into a single dependency ratio. However, it is important to remember that such a combination can be misleading. For example, current estimates indicate that the governmental budgetary costs of adding another older person is about four times higher than that of adding another child.

In 1995, there were 53 people in age groups that typically do not work for every 100 persons of working age in the United States (see Figure 3.7). Changes in the dependency ratios will be similar for all immigration scenarios until about 2025. Under the medium assumption, this ratio is projected to decline for the next 15 years, to a low of 48 in 2010, then increase, reaching 61 in 2050. The

---

[39]Although immigration is not a critical determinant of the youth dependency ratio, higher levels of immigration tend to produce a population with more children per 100 persons in the working years. On the other hand, a future population with zero immigration would have slightly fewer youths per 100 persons in the working years.

[40]Altering the net immigration assumption has little effect on the youth dependency ratio. Under the zero or very high net immigration assumptions, the youth dependency ratio will range from 30 to 34 per 100.

[41]If zero immigration is assumed, the ratio will peak at 34 per 100 in 2035, before diminishing somewhat to 32 per 100 in 2050. At the other extreme, should very high immigration prevail, the ratio will peak at 27 per 100 in 2030, almost 20 percent less than that associated with zero immigration, and diminish to 27 per 100 in 2050.

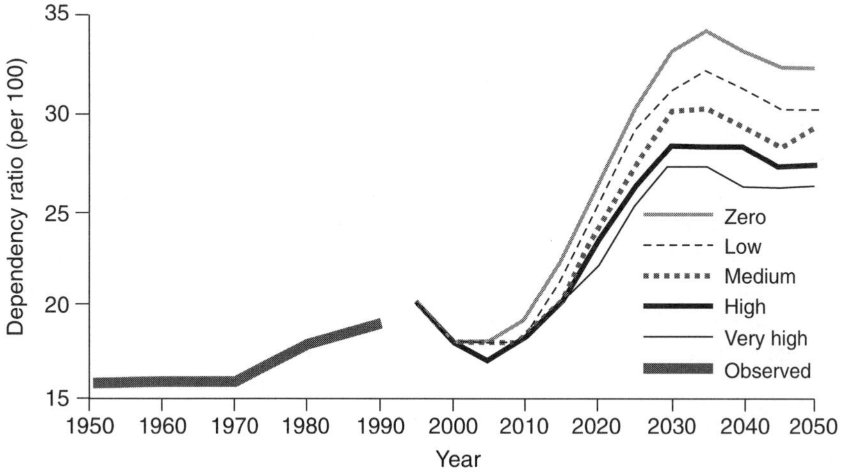

FIGURE 3.6 Elderly dependency ratio: Observed population, 1950-1995; projected population under five immigration assumptions, 1995-2050. Note: dependency ratio defined as number of dependents 64 years of age and older per 100 persons aged 20-64 years.

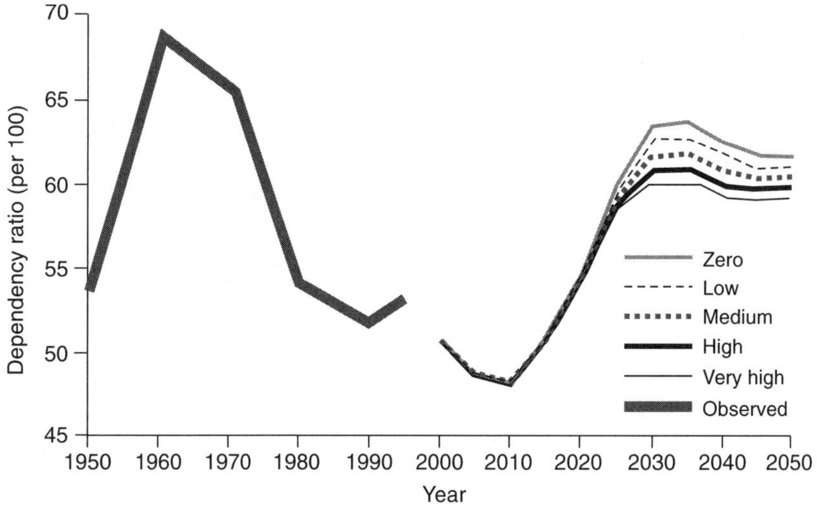

FIGURE 3.7 Overall dependency ratio for observed population, 1950-1995; projected population under five immigration assumptions, 1995-2050. Note: dependency ratio defined as number of dependents per 100 persons aged 20-64 years.

increases after 2010 are due primarily to the increase in the number of the elderly, as the baby-boom cohorts begin to reach age 65. At the same time, growth in the working-age population will slow, as smaller cohorts born after the fertility decline of the 1960s come to dominate the labor force.

Under the low net immigration assumption, the dependency ratio will decline to 48 in 2010, increase to a peak of 63 in 2035, and then again decrease, to 62 in 2050. Under the high net immigration assumption, the overall dependency ratio will decline to 48 in 2010 and then increase to a plateau of 61 in 2030.[42]

We anticipate the evidence presented in Chapter 7 by observing that relative fiscal costs vary by age group. The relative fiscal costs for youths, including education and other programs directed at the population less than 20 years of age, are approximately $1 for every $4 of programs directed at the elderly, including Social Security, health care, and other programs for the population aged 65 years and older. Chapter 7 discusses these fiscal implications of population trends in more detail.

Summary of Effect of Immigration on Age Structure

The age structure of the U.S. population will change over the next 50 years, regardless of immigration. Figure 3.8 displays the absolute change in population at five-year age intervals for our medium, low, and high rates of immigration. Under our medium immigration assumption, between 1995 and 2050, there will be an increase in each five-year age group. Two age groups are particularly noteworthy. First, the group aged 25 to 55 years (the working-age population) will not expand as much as other age groups. Second, there will a rapidly expanding number of elderly persons.

Immigration policy will have a declining influence on the population as the age group considered increases. In the extreme, different immigration assumptions have little influence on the rapid growth of the population aged 80 years and over. The elderly population of 2050 has, to a great extent, already been born and are currently younger working residents. Although a smaller number of immigrants would reduce the elderly population in 2050, lower immigration would not substantially alter the unprecedented increase in the size of the elderly and the oldest-old age groups.

IMMIGRANTS AND THEIR CHILDREN

The levels of future immigration are obvious key determinants of changes in

[42]Under the zero immigration assumption, the dependency ratio will decline to a minimum of 48 in 2010, peak at 64 in 2035, and again decline, to 62 in 2050. Under the very high immigration assumption, the dependency ratio will decrease to about 48 in 2010 and then steadily increase to a plateau of about 60 in 2030.

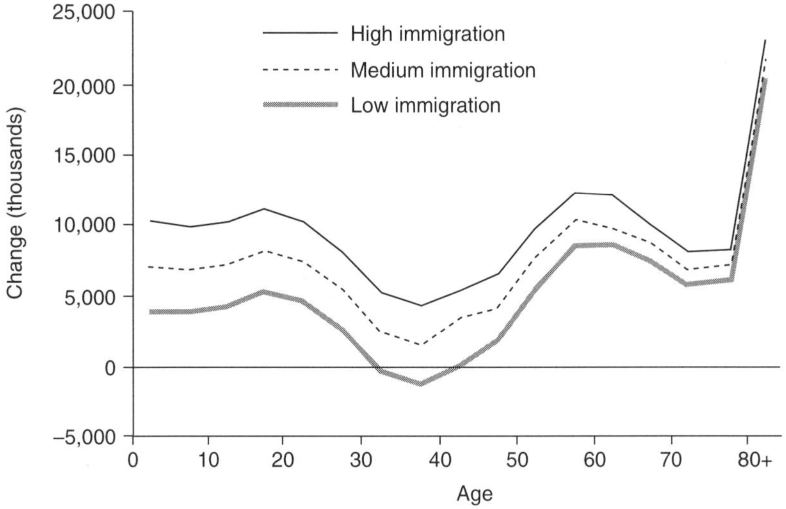

FIGURE 3.8 Population changes in the U.S. population, 1995 to 2050, by five-year age group, by alternative levels of net immigration.

the size and composition of the foreign-born population. Those changes will, in turn, affect the growth of the second immigrant generation. There is, however, a time lag in the effect of immigration on changes in the second generation, because it takes some 30 or 40 years for changes in immigration to result in substantial shifts in the number of their children.

The foreign-born population has been increasing since 1970 and numbered 25.2 million in 1995. Under the medium net immigration assumptions, the foreign-born population will grow throughout the projection period, nearly doubling and reaching 46.7 million in 2050 (see Figure 3.9). Under the low assumption, the foreign-born population will peak at slightly less than 30 million and then begin to decline, although in 2050 it will be above current levels. Only under the zero assumption will the foreign-born population decline over the next 55 years, as its members gradually age and, given the mortality rates of advancing age, die. Under the very high immigration assumption, the foreign-born population will expand rapidly, growing at an annual rate of 2.2 percent and reaching 85 million in 2050.

With below-replacement fertility and medium net immigration, the U.S. population will experience only slight changes in its immigrant generational distribution (see Figure 3.10). All immigrant generations will increase, and so will the proportion of the population in the first, second, and third generations. The number of people in the fourth-plus generations will rise from 176.6 million in

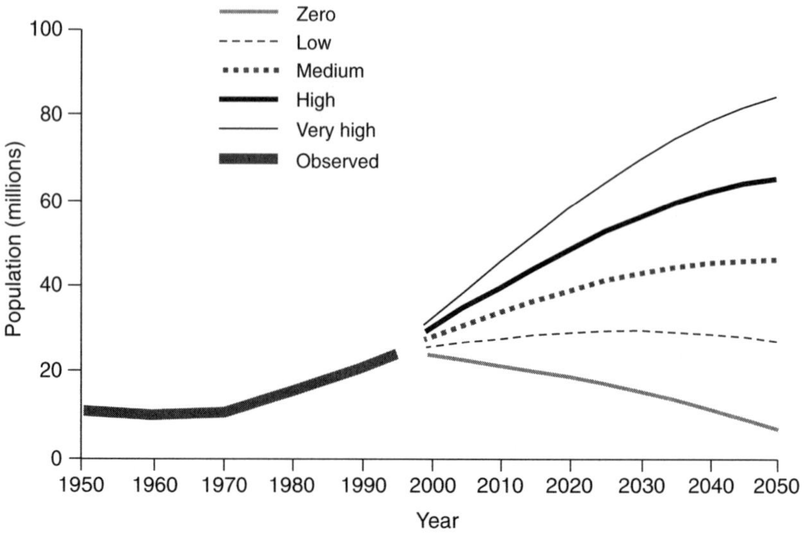

FIGURE 3.9 U.S. foreign-born population: Observed population, 1950-1995; projected population under five immigration assumptions, 1995-2050.

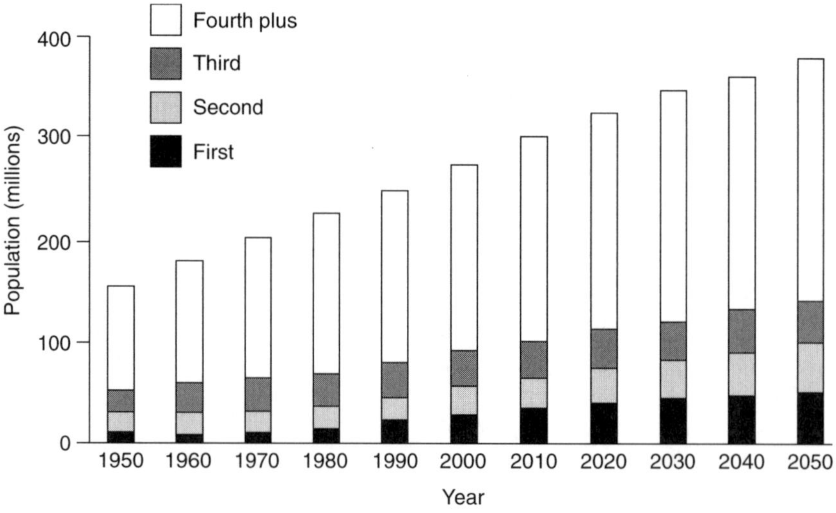

FIGURE 3.10 U.S. population by immigrant generations: Observed population, 1950-1995; projected population under medium immigration assumption, 1995-2050.

1995 to 240.0 million in 2050, although they will account for a slightly smaller proportion of the total population.[43]

RACIAL AND ETHNIC COMPOSITION

As described earlier in this chapter, projecting the future population by racial and ethnic groups in the conventional way involves making assumptions about fertility, mortality, and immigration for each group—independent of the other groups—and projecting the group as if it were a closed population. As Hirschman (1996:22) argues, this approach, however logical the exercise may seem, suffers from two limitations, one methodological and the other interpretive. First, the critical assumption of ethnic groups as ascriptively defined populations with fixed boundaries may be a very tenuous one, historically and for the future. Second, racial and ethnic population projections are being used, often without careful thought or reflection, as firm demographic evidence to show that American society and culture is being threatened by continued immigration.

The growing rate of intermarriage among whites, blacks, Hispanics, and Asians (although most intermarriages are of whites with other groups) ensures that the future of the United States will not be a set of distinct cultures and languages, let alone a unique ethnic identification. If there are many intermarriages, then more people will have multiethnic parental ties and more children will have multiple ancestry, possibly weakening traditional ethnic boundaries in the United States.[44]

With these important caveats in mind, even if net immigration is zero, the future racial/ethnic composition of the population will not remain static. Differences in fertility and mortality among groups in the present population will see to that. Because there are a large number of younger people in the U.S. population, the population will continue to grow in the future, even without further immigration. This population "momentum" is inherent to the age structure of each of the racial and Hispanic groups, although there will be future growth in the absence of

---

[43]Not shown here are separate results for the generational composition for each of the four major racial/ethnic groups. These results show that the first generation of Asian and Hispanic populations will continue to increase, along with a consequent rapid growth of the second and third generations. Asians and Hispanics will be predominantly immigrant-oriented for the period of this projection.

[44]Deepening problems beset the definition and measurement of racial and ethnic identification in government statistics, and there are strong efforts to both modify and maintain current ethnic categories. Much of the demand for change stems from concerns about the ethnic identification of children from racial and Hispanic intermarriages. After earlier waves of immigration from Southern and Eastern Europe about a century ago, the second and third generations saw rapid increases in ethnic intermarriages, resulting in shifts in ethnic identification. Population projections that rely on a conventional definition of race and ethnicity may become increasingly anachronistic.

immigration. The age structure of the white population, for example, has less momentum for future growth, whereas the Asian and Hispanic populations will continue to grow, even if they receive no further immigrants.

But net immigration is unlikely to be zero, and it will significantly affect population growth in two ways. First, the level of immigration matters. Each immigrant directly adds one new person to a racial/ethnic group. Second, beyond simply their numbers, the procreativity of immigrants—that is, their ages and fertility rates—matters, for succeeding generations. A young immigrant in a group with generally high fertility rates will add the most descendants, whereas an elderly immigrant will add few. Beyond this, exogamy and the self-identification of multiple-ancestry persons influence the racial/ethnic composition of the population. Hence, the future growth of racial/ethnic groups will be a complex product of several interacting factors.

Given our assumptions—that the current level and composition of immigration, of exogamy, and of kinds of racial/ethnic identification will continue, the racial/ethnic composition of the population will experience a pronounced shift in the next decades. In 1990, according to the 1990 census, 75 percent of the population was white. The remaining one-quarter was divided thus: 12 percent black, 9 percent Hispanic, 3 percent Asian, and about 1 percent American Indian. If we assume medium net immigration levels, constant exogamy conditions, and the medium level of racial/ethnic attribution for multiple-ancestry persons, the white population will increase from 194 million in 1995 to a peak of 211 million in 2025 and then start to fall (see Figure 3.11 and Table 3.7). **By 2050, the white population will have become relatively less numerous and drop from 75 percent of the total population to only 50 percent.**[45]

The black population, meanwhile, will increase substantially, from 32 to 54 million. Its share, however, will change only a little, from 12 to 14 percent of the population. The black population will grow primarily because of higher fertility rates and very high attribution rates (children with one black parent are more likely to report themselves as black). Immigration will play a secondary role for population change for the black population. The range of the projected black populations for 2050 varies only from 52 to 56 million for the low to high net immigration assumptions.

In contrast, both the Asian and Hispanic population will grow rapidly under current immigration policy. The Asian population will expand at annual rates

[45]The white population is likely to change little in the future, compared with the growth of other ethnic groups. The white population is characterized by slightly lower fertility, low immigration relative to its population size, and attribution rates that are below 50 percent. Nevertheless, over one-fifth of immigrants add to the white population, and variations in net immigration levels matter. The range of population size for the white population varies from 191 to 211 million in 2050, based on low to high net immigration, compared with a population of 194 million in 1995.

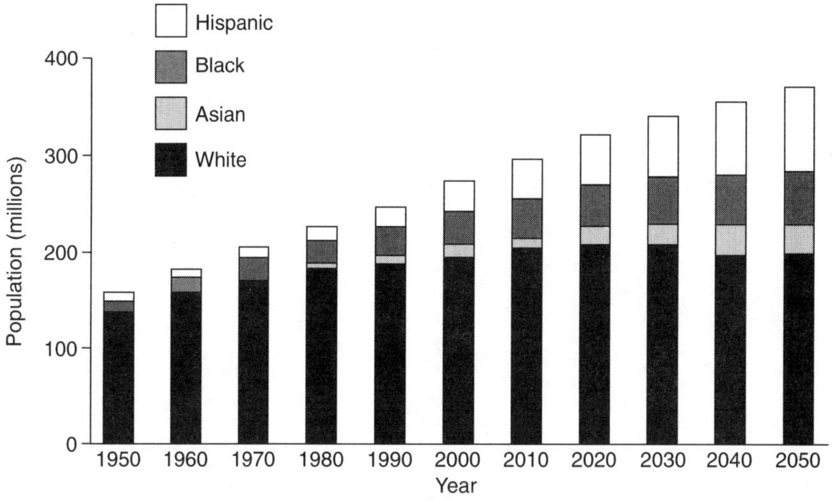

FIGURE 3.11 U.S. population by racial/ethnic group: Observed population, 1950-1995; projected population under medium immigration assumption, 1995-2050.

exceeding 1 percent for the next half-century. **The size of the Asian population will increase from 9 million in 1995 to 34 million in 2050 (growing from 3 to 8 percent of the total population). The growth of the Asian population is principally fueled by immigration. Although fertility levels for the foreign-born Asian population is slightly above average, the sizable future growth stems from the large number of immigrants added to the Asian population.** Based on the low to high immigration assumptions, the Asian population in 2050 may range from 26 to 42 million.

Fueled by heavy immigration and by high attribution rates—more than 50 percent of multiple-ancestry persons report themselves as Hispanic—the Hispanic population will grow substantially over the projection period. It will rise from 27 million in 1995, or about 1 in 11 of the total population, to 95 million in 2050, or about 1 in 4. The growth of the Hispanic population is driven by multiple factors: immigration, higher fertility rates, and high attribution rates. Although immigration is the principal factor, the Hispanic population will grow significantly in the future even if immigration were to cease. Because of their higher fertility, especially of the foreign-born, the Hispanic population will almost double by 2050, even in the absence of immigration. Under the low to high net immigration assumptions, the size of the Hispanic population will increase to 77 to 113 million in 2050.

One caution in interpreting these results arises from our assumptions about current conditions of exogamy and ethnicity persisting into the future. In fact, intermarriage has been changing during recent decades, especially for Asians and

TABLE 3.7 U.S. Population, by Ethnic Groups and Level of Net Immigration: Observed Population, 1950-1995; Projected Population, 2000-2050 (millions)

	Level of Net Immigration				
Population	Zero	Low	Medium	High	Very High
White					
1950			134.4		
1960			155.0		
1970			170.4		
1980			180.4		
1990			187.1		
1995			193.6		
2000	197.4	197.6	198.4	199.1	199.9
2010	201.7	202.4	204.8	207.1	209.8
2020	203.6	204.8	209.1	213.1	217.9
2030	202.8	204.6	211.0	216.9	223.9
2040	196.6	199.1	207.6	215.4	224.7
2050	187.6	190.7	201.4	211.2	222.9
Black					
1950			15.7		
1960			19.1		
1970			23.0		
1980			23.0		
1990			30.0		
1995			31.6		
2000	33.5	33.7	33.8	33.9	34.1
2010	37.0	37.6	38.0	38.5	38.9
2020	39.9	41.1	41.9	42.9	43.4
2030	43.6	45.3	46.5	47.8	48.9
2040	46.1	48.5	50.1	51.8	53.4
2050	48.4	51.6	53.7	55.9	57.9

Hispanics. In addition, current rates of racial/ethnic attribution may change as the population becomes increasingly diverse. This sensitivity can be illustrated by varying assumptions about racial/ethnic reporting, holding constant the immigration assumption at current levels.

Table 3.8 presents results with alternative ethnic attribution assumptions. We start with some unrealistic extremes. Very low attribution assumes that no multiple-ancestry persons identify with the ethnic group and very high attribution assumes that all multiple-ancestry persons identify with the ethnic group. A more realistic range can be obtained by using what we label as low and high attribution rates. Low and high attribution levels reflect ranges around the medium attribution rates that are based on 1990 census data: low is 20 percentage points less than the reported 1990 levels, and high is 20 percentage points greater. In between, half attribution assumes that 50 percent of multiple-ancestry persons iden-

TABLE 3.7 Continued

	Level of Net Immigration				
Population	Zero	Low	Medium	High	Very High
Asian					
1950			.7		
1960			1.1		
1970			1.8		
1980			3.7		
1990			7.3		
1995			8.8		
2000	9.6	10.3	10.8	11.4	11.9
2010	11.0	13.4	15.1	16.9	18.6
2020	11.3	16.5	19.6	22.9	25.9
2030	13.5	19.9	24.4	29.3	33.7
2040	14.3	22.9	29.1	35.6	41.7
2050	14.9	25.9	33.7	42.1	49.7
Hispanic					
1950			4.0		
1960			6.3		
1970			9.6		
1980			14.6		
1990			22.4		
1995			26.9		
2000	29.8	30.9	31.7	32.5	33.3
2010	35.2	39.3	42.2	45.2	47.9
2020	40.3	48.1	53.7	59.5	64.6
2030	45.2	57.6	66.5	75.6	83.8
2040	49.4	67.4	80.2	93.4	105.3
2050	52.8	77.2	94.7	112.7	128.8

tify with the ethnic group. This midpoint comes close to a biological view in which 50 percent of children identify with the parent's ethnicity.

The Asian population has moderate rates of exogamy and of self-identification—less than 50 percent (see Appendix 3B: Tables 3.B3 and 3.B4). As a greater proportion of the Asian population is accounted for by the second, third, and fourth-plus generations, the projection reflects the increasing level of exogamy. Overall, the size of the Asian population in 2050 for the spectrum of assumptions, from low to high attribution, is within a range of 31 to 37 million.

Although the Hispanic population is expected to expand rapidly, its growth will be magnified by moderate levels of exogamy and attribution rates above 50 percent (see Appendix 3.B: Tables 3.B3 and 3.B4), resulting in growth rates greater than baseline assumptions. Unless the extremely low attribution conditions prevail, under the more reasonable low to high attribution assumptions, the

TABLE 3.8 U.S. Population, by Ethnic Groups and Level of Ethnic Attribution: Observed Population, 1950-1995; Projected Population, 2000-2050 (millions)

Population	Very Low	Low	Half	Medium	High	Very High
White						
1950			134.4			
1970			170.4			
1990			187.1			
1995			193.6			
2020	191.0	207.0	210.0	209.1	211.3	215.3
2050	175.5	195.2	203.9	201.4	207.8	220.3
Black						
1950			15.7			
1970			23.0			
1990			30.0			
1995			31.6			
2020	37.5	41.6	41.9	41.9	43.0	43.7
2050	43.2	51.1	52.3	53.7	56.4	59.2
Asian						
1950			.7			
1970			1.8			
1990			7.3			
1995			8.8			
2020	17.3	19.1	19.8	19.6	20.2	21.4
2050	27.9	31.3	35.2	33.7	36.5	42.9
Hispanic						
1950			4.0			
1970			9.6			
1990			22.4			
1995			26.9			
2020	43.7	51.5	52.2	53.7	56.0	57.9
2050	64.5	85.0	87.8	94.7	105.5	115.2

Note: Assumed level of ethnic attribution for multiple-ancestry persons is: Very low = 0 percent; Low = .2 less than medium assumption; Half = 50 percent; Medium = attribution rates estimated from 1990 census data, see Table 3.B4; High = .2 greater than medium assumption; Very high = 100 percent.

Hispanic population is likely to increase in number from 85 to 106 million in 2050.[46]

These projections imply substantial growth in multiple-ancestry persons, re-

[46]The white population has low exogamy rates and attribution rates below 50 percent, resulting in population growth that is less than expected from conventional baseline assumptions. It will reach a maximum about 2020 to 2030 and then decline for all attribution assumptions except the extremely high one. For the plausible range of low to high attribution rates, the white population will range in size from about 195 million to about 208 million in 2050. The black population has relatively low

gardless of the reported primary ethnic identification. Table 3.9 shows changes in the single and multiple ancestry categories for ethnic groups. Overall, in 1995, about 7 percent of the population reports one or more different races or Hispanic origins than their primary race or Hispanic identification. The percentage of the population reporting multiple-ancestries will increase from 7 percent in 1995 to 21 percent in 2050, assuming that intermarriage continues at current levels. There is substantial variation in the proportion of multiple-ancestry persons for ethnic groups. Trends for the white population are similar to the overall population, but the increase in the proportion of multiple-ancestry persons is somewhat lower for the black population. But the relative gain in multiple-ancestry persons is especially high for the Asian and Hispanic populations, reaching 36 and 45 percent, respectively, in 2050. The major implication of these trends is to raise questions about the primary racial and Hispanic identification of the large number of persons of multiple ancestries.

Projections of the type presented here must be placed in a historical context. Early in the twentieth century, public interest focused on fertility differences between the "new" immigrants from Southern and Eastern Europe and the older "American" stock. Indeed, Theodore Roosevelt warned in his inaugural address about immigration bringing on the "suicide of the race."

Had there been population projections by European ethnic groups during the period of peak European immigration (1880-1920) that tried to forecast what the U.S. population would look like by 1950 or 2000, those predictions would certainly have been wrong if they assumed that groups would not intermarry at all and that all future descendants would report the same ethnic identity as their mother (or father). Such projections would have seriously overestimated the proportions of some European groups and underestimated others. Hout and Goldstein (1991) remind us that the number of self-reported Irish Americans in the 1980 census could not possibly have come about purely as a result of immigration and the fertility of Irish immigrants: the number is simply too large. Rather, most of the growth in Irish Americans must have resulted from intermarriage and the choice of many children of intermarriage to claim Irish ancestry.

Projections made at the turn of the century would have been in error for two reasons. First, they would have had to deal with all the vagaries of population projections about fertility, mortality, and immigration. Common to all projections is that the world changes, that basic demographic parameters will vary in the future in ways that cannot be fully anticipated, and thus that assumptions

---

exogamy rates and high attribution rates for multiple-ancestry persons. The medium attribution assumption suggests that the growth of the black population will be slightly greater than conventional baseline projection results. The results in 2050 under the low to high assumptions are clustered within a narrow range, from 51 to 56 million.

made about them may err. Second and more important, such projections would have missed the subsequent changes in the social meaning and functioning of the ethnic groups themselves. These changes are discussed in detail in Chapter 8.

As these findings make clear, the ethnic affiliation of Americans in the future is subject to some uncertainty. Today, many people have parents and grandparents who are of the same ethnic origin, using the broad racial and Hispanic groups current today. But a substantial and growing number have links to two or more ethnic ancestries, allowing wide latitude in how they may choose to identify themselves.

To display this blurring of single and multiple ethnic linkages, Table 3.9 displays estimates for single and multiple ancestry of the current and future U.S. population. Of the 8.8 million persons in 1995 whose primary ethnic identification was Asian, the vast majority (8.1 million) had only Asian ancestry. In addition, there were another 1.5 million persons who reported some Asian ancestry—of whom only 0.7 million self-reported that they were Asian. The net result is that in 1995 there were an additional 800,000 persons who had some Asian an-

TABLE 3.9 Population by Ethnic Groups by Single and Multiple Ancestry, 1995, 2020, and 2050 (millions)

	Population by Ancestry			
	Single Ancestry	Multiple Ancestry	Total: All Ancestries	Percentage Multiple of Total
White				
1995	181.7	15.5	197.2	7.9
2020	192.0	24.3	216.3	11.2
2050	167.9	44.8	212.7	21.2
Black				
1995	29.4	2.7	32.1	8.4
2020	39.6	4.3	43.9	9.8
2050	49.0	8.0	57.0	14.0
Asian				
1995	8.1	1.5	9.6	15.6
2020	17.4	4.1	21.5	19.1
2050	26.7	15.0	41.7	36.0
Hispanic				
1995	24.4	4.9	29.3	16.7
2020	43.9	14.2	58.1	24.4
2050	61.7	50.7	112.4	45.1
Total[a]				
1995	245.0	17.8	262.8	6.8
2020	294.5	32.7	327.2	10.0
2050	306.7	80.6	387.3	20.8

[a]The total population includes American Indians, Eskimos, and Aleuts.

TABLE 3.10 U.S. Population by Race and Hispanic Origin: Observed Population, 1950-1995; Projected Population, 2000-2050 (percentage of total population)

	1950	1970	1990	1995	2010	2030	2050
Total[a]	100	100	100	100	100	100	100
White	87	83	76	74	67	59	51
Black	10	11	12	12	13	13	14
Asian	1	1	3	3	5	7	8
Hispanic	3	5	9	10	14	20	26

[a]The total U.S. population includes American Indians, Eskimos, and Aleuts.

cestry but who identified themselves as non-Asian. Overall, 16 percent of all persons with Asian ancestry had multiple ancestry.

Now, let us go to the future and see what our model presents about the multiple ancestry of Asians. If all persons of some Asian ancestry identified themselves as Asian, the reported population could be as high as 42 million in 2050. Instead, if only single-ancestry persons reported themselves as Asian in 2050, the population could be as low as 27 million. The projected Asian population of 34 million in 2050 is between these extremes because only a fraction of the multiple-ancestry Asian population will identify themselves as Asians. The salient secular trend is the increased blurring of the lines of ethnic boundaries. By the middle of the next century, more than one-third of all of those with some Asian ancestry will have multiple ancestries, compared with only 8 percent today.

There is even greater latitude for variation in the future Hispanic population. In 1995, there were an estimated 4.9 million persons with multiple Hispanic ancestry (17 percent of all persons with some Hispanic ancestry). By 2050, through high fertility and continued intermarriage, the multiple-ancestry Hispanic population will expand to 51 million persons, or 45 percent of all persons with some Hispanic ancestry. If only single-ancestry persons reported themselves as Hispanic in 2050, the Hispanic population will be 62 million (17 percent of total U.S. population). If, instead, on the high side, all persons with any Hispanic ancestry reported themselves as Hispanic, the population could be as high as 112 million (29 percent of the total U.S. population).[47]

This blurring of ethnic boundaries illustrates some of the ambiguity inherent in any ethnic projection. With this caveat in mind, Table 3.10 shows the projected fraction of the future U.S. population by ethnic group. Today, three-quar-

[47]Taking all ethnic groups into account, including the white, black, and American Indian populations, the multiple-ancestry population is estimated to increase from 18 million in 1995 to 81 million in 2050. By 2050, we estimate that 16 percent of the population will have overlapping ancestries among the current classifications.

ters of the population identify themselves as non-Hispanic whites. By the middle of the next century, the fraction will decline to about one-half (51 percent). The two groups that will expand in relative terms are Hispanics and Asians. We project that the Asian population, which today comprises 3 percent of the population, will rise to 8 percent in 2050. Similarly, the relative size of the Hispanic population will more than double over this period from 1 in 10 to about 1 in 4.

CONCLUSIONS

This chapter paints a demographic portrait of Americans over the next half-century, taking the contribution of immigration into account. Our projections are based on a set of ethnic and generational specific rates of fertility, mortality, exogamy, and ethnic affiliation. This future population is simulated under five immigration scenarios, wherein the baseline scenario represents continuation of current policies of about 800,000 net immigrants per year. In addition, our simulations use four other immigration assumptions: net immigration of zero, 410,000 per year, 1.23 million, and 1.64 million per year. We consider net immigration levels of 410,000 (about one-half current levels) and 1.23 million (about 50 percent greater than current levels) to be realistic bounds for likely variation around current policies.

We project a 2050 population of 387 million, 124 million more than the 1995 total of 263 million. If current immigration flows continue, there will be about 45 million immigrants arriving in the United States between 1995 and 2050. These immigrants, plus their descendants, will add 80 million people to the population. **Continued current levels of immigration will add substantial numbers to the future U.S. population, through the combined effects of adding new people and maintaining higher average fertility levels. If immigration is one-half current levels, the U.S. population will increase to 349 million; if immigration is one-half greater than current levels, the population will expand to 426 million in 2050.**

Immigration will have a negligible effect on the balance of men and women in the future population, but it will significantly alter the age structure of the population. No matter what happens to immigration flows, the U.S. population will become older, as the large number of people in the baby-boom years reach retirement. Immigration has its largest impact on the youngest age groups in the population, with diminishing impacts on older age groups. **Immigration will increase primary school, secondary school, and college enrollments, compared both with current numbers and with a future scenario of lower immigration. Immigration will increase the size of the labor force. The elderly population will increase substantially in the future, although immigration will play a supporting role in its expansion.**

Even if immigration ceases immediately, the racial and ethnic composition of the U.S. population will change. Differences in fertility and mortality levels and variations in the age structure of current ethnic groups imply that some would grow more quickly and some more slowly. The growth momentum for the white population, for instance, is less than that of the Asian and Hispanic populations—even in the absence of immigration.

Immigration is unlikely to be zero, however. If current immigration policy continues, the Asian and Hispanic populations will experience much more rapid growth, increasing relative to the total population. In 1995, 74 percent of the population was white, 12 percent black, 10 percent Hispanic, and 3 percent Asian. By 2050, the relative size of the white population will decline to 51 percent, the black population will increase only slightly to 14 percent, and the Asian and Hispanic populations will reach much higher levels, 8 and 26 percent, respectively. **The Asian and Hispanic populations will increase under any immigration scenario. By 2050, the absolute and relative sizes of their populations will more than double.**

The current extent of intermarriage and the ethnic self-identification of children of multiple ancestry are critical parameters of our projections. Assuming that current levels of intermarriage continue, there will be a large increase in the number of persons of multiple ancestry, especially for Asians and Hispanics. The multiple-ancestry population will increase from 18 million in 1995 to 81 million in 2050 (a growth from 7 to 16 percent of the total population). Such a population will add complexity and ambiguity to the ethnic definitions used. **The proportion of the U.S. population with multiple ancestry will continue to increase under any immigrant scenario. By the middle of the next century, the social meaning of ethnic and racial lines will become increasingly blurred.**

REFERENCES

Gurak, D.J., and J.P. Fitzpatrick
1982 Intermarriage among Hispanic ethnic groups in New York City. *American Journal of Sociology* 87:921-934.

Hirschman, C.
1996 Race and Ethnic Population Projections: A Critical Evaluation of Their Content and Meaning. Revision of a paper presented at the 13th SUNY, Albany Conference "American Diversity: A Demographic Challenge for the Twenty-First Century," April 15-16, 1994.

Hout, M., and J. Goldstein
1991 How 4.5 million Irish immigrants became 40 million Irish Americans: Demographic and subjective aspects of the ethnic composition of white Americans. *American Sociological Review* J9:64-82.

Long, J.
1991 The relative effects of fertility, mortality, and immigration on projected age structure. Pp. 503-522 in Wolfgang Lutz (editor), *Future Demographic Trends in Europe and North America*. New York: Academic Press.

Miltenyi, K.
1981 Population Projections: Problems and Solutions. Report of the Workshop on Population Projections, Budapest, Hungary, March 1980. Department of Technical Co-operation for Development, United Nations, New York.

Passel, J.S., and B. Edmonston
1994 Immigration and race: Recent trends in immigration to the United States. In B. Edmonston and J.S. Passel (editors), *Immigration and Ethnicity: Immigration and the Adjustment of America's Newest Immigrants*. Washington, D.C.: The Urban Institute.

Romaniuc, A.
1990 Population projection as prediction, simulation, and prospective analysis. *Population Bulletin of the United Nations* 29:16-31.

Shapiro, G.M., G. Diffendal, and D. Cantor
1993 Survey undercoverage: Major causes and new estimates of magnitude. Pp. 638-663 in *Proceedings of the 1993 Bureau of the Census Annual Research Conference*. Washington, D.C.: U.S. Department of Commerce.

Tabah, L.
1984 Population Projections: Methodology of the United Nations. Papers of the United Nations Ad Hoc Expert Group on Demographic Projections, United Nations Headquarters, 16-19 November 1981. Population Studies Number 83. Department of International Economic and Social Affairs, United Nations, New York.

United Nations
1995 *World Population Projections*. New York: United Nations.

U.S. Bureau of the Census
1989 Projections of the population of the United States, by age, sex, and race: 1988 to 2080. Prepared by Gregory Spencer. *Current Population Reports*, Series P-25, No. 1018. Washington, D.C.: U.S. Department of Commerce.
1996a Population projections of the United States by age, sex, race, and Hispanic origin: 1995 to 2050. *Current Population Reports*, P25-1130. Washington, D.C.: U.S. Department of Commerce.
1996b *Statistical Abstracts of the United States, 1996*. Washington, D.C.: U.S. Department of Commerce.

Werner, B.
1986 Family building intentions of different generations of women: Results from the General Household Survey, 1979-83. *Population Trends* 44 (Summer):17-23.

APPENDIX 3.A
POPULATION PROJECTION MODEL

The panel's population projection model forecasts a population by age, sex, and four generation groups for a period of five years, using survival rates by five-year age groups for each sex and generation, five-year age-specific fertility rates for each generation, and the number of migrants by age, sex, and generation during the five-year period. The projection handles four generations: the foreign-born (the first generation), the sons and daughters of the foreign-born (the second generation), the grandsons and granddaughters of the foreign-born (the third generation), and all higher-numbered generations lumped together. A FORTRAN program, designed for use on microcomputers, implements the basic immigration generation model. The program displays results for each generation as well as the total native-born (the second and higher generations) and the total population. Although a special procedure handles each five-year projection, the main population projection program can make projections for a period of 5 to 100 years.

The model requires the following data: (1) initial female population in five-year age groups, by generation, (2) initial male population in five-year age groups, by generation, (3) five-year survival rates for females during each five-year period, by generation, (4) five-year survival rates for males during each five-year period, by generation, (5) annual age-specific fertility rates (for five-year age groups) for the beginning and end of each five-year period, by generation, (6) female immigrants and emigrants by five-year age groups during each five-year period, by generation, (7) male immigrants and emigrants by five-year age groups during each five-year period, by generation, and (8) sex ratio at birth. In addition, several parameters control various options of the computer program and permit alternative input data (such as using Coale-Demeny model life tables instead of age-specific survival rates).

Consider a population defined with the following characteristics:

$$P_x^t$$

population size for age x at time t,

$$S_x^{t,t+5}$$

rates for population age x surviving to age x+5 during the period from t to t+5, and

$$F_x^t$$

age-specific fertility rates for women age x at time t. Survival rates are derived from the life table person-years lived values in the standard fashion, with

$$S_x^{t,t+5} = L_{x+5}^{t,t+5} / L_x^{t,t+5}$$

We assume five-year age groups here, so the population age x represents the age group x to x+4.

Model With No International Migration. For a population projection with no international migration, the closed population is affected only by fertility and mortality processes. The survival of the population at the beginning of a five-year projection period is:

$$P_{x+5}^{t+5} = P_x^t S_x^{t,t+5} \tag{1}$$

and

$$P_{x+}^{t+5} = P_{x-5+}^t S_{x-5+}^{t,t+5} \tag{2}$$

for the last, open-ended age interval, where $x+$ is the population age x to the end of life, and each equation is separate for males and females.

We calculate the total births during the five-year interval as:

$$B^{t,t+5} = \frac{5}{2}\sum_{x=15}^{45} P_x^t\left(F_x^t + S_x^{t,t+5}F_x^{t+5}\right) \tag{3}$$

where P is for the female population only. Then the population aged 0 to 4 years at $t+5$ is:

$$P_0^{t+5} = B^{t,t+5}S_0^{t,t+5} \tag{4}$$

and would use the sex ratio at birth to calculate the number of male and female births. P and S are also separate by sex, and

$$S_0^{t,t+5}$$

indicates the survival from birth to age 0-4 for the appropriate sex during the period t to $t+5$.

Model With International Migration. The basic population projection model can be modified to include the effects of international migration. Define

$$I_x^{t,t+5}$$

as in-migrants age x during the period t to $t+5$ and

$$O_x^{t,t+5}$$

as out-migrants age x during the period t to $t+5$, each separate by sex. Then the net migrants age x during the period t to $t+5$ is

$$N_x^{t,t+5} = I_x^{t,t+5} - O_x^{t,t+5}$$

The impact of international migration on the population alive at the beginning of a five-year projection period is:

$$P_{x+5}^{t+5} = P_x^t S_x^{t,t+5} + \frac{N_x^{t,t+5}\left(1+S_x^{t,t+5}\right) + N_{x+5}^{t,t+5}\left(1+S_{x+5}^{t,t+5}\right)}{4} \tag{5}$$

and

$$P_{x+}^{t+5} = P_x^t S_x^{t,t+5} + \frac{N_{x-5}^{t,t+5}\left(1+S_{x-5}^{t,t+5}\right) + N_{x+}^{t,t+5}\left(1+S_{x+}^{t,t+5}\right)}{4} \qquad (6)$$

for the open-ended age category.

Equation 3 for total births is affected by migration and reflects births to the resident population plus births to the net immigrants during the period:

$$B^{t,t+5} = \frac{5}{2}\sum_{x=15}^{45} P_x^t\left(F_x^t + S_x^{t,t+5} F_x^{t+5}\right) + B_I^{t,t+5} \qquad (7)$$

where births to net immigrants is:

$$B_I^{t,t+5} = \frac{5}{2}\sum_{x=15}^{45} \frac{N_x^{t,t+5}\left(F_x^t S_x^{t,t+5} F_x^{t+5}\right)}{2} \qquad (8)$$

The population aged 0 to 4 years is also altered by international migration:

$$P_o^{t+5} = B^{t,t+5} S_0^{t,t+5} + \frac{N_0^{t,t+5}\left(1+S_0^{t,t+5}\right)}{4} \qquad (9)$$

where P, S, and N are separate by sex and the sex ratio at birth is needed to calculate the number of male and female births.

Model With Population by Generations. The population described above is distinguished by an age and time index (and is assumed to be separate by sex). Consider now a population indexed by k generations, where k=1, 2, 3, and 4: k=1 indicates the first generation, k=2 indicates the second, k=3 represents the third, and k=4 indicates the fourth and later generations. For the survival of the population alive at the beginning of the projection period equation 5 becomes:

$$P_{x+5,k}^{t+5} = P_{x,k}^t S_{x,k}^{t,t+5} + \frac{N_{x,k}^{t,t+5}\left(1+S_{x,k}^{t,t+5}\right) + N_{x+5,k}^{t,t+5}\left(1+S_{x+5,k}^{t,t+5}\right)}{4} \qquad (10)$$

and equation 6 becomes:

$$P_{x+,k}^{t+5} = P_{x,k}^t S_{x,k}^{t,t+5} + \frac{N_{x-5,k}^{t,t+5}\left(1+S_{x-5,k}^{t,t+5}\right) + N_{x+,k}^{t,t+5}\left(1+S_{x+,k}^{t,t+5}\right)}{4} \qquad (11)$$

for the open-ended age category, where

$$S_{x,k}^{t,t+5}$$

represents the survival values for the kth generation and

$$N_{x,k}^{t,t+5}$$

indicates the number of net migrants for the kth generation. In general, the number of immigrants by generation

$$I_{x,k}^{t,t+5}$$

is non-zero for the first generation (k=1) and zero for the second and later generations (k=2,3,4). Immigrants are generally not native-born persons. On the other hand, this model makes apparent that emigrants by generation

$$O_{x,k}^{t,t+5}$$

may have non-zero values for all generations. Hence, observed values of net migrants by generation

$$N_{x,k}^{t,t+5}$$

are usually positive for the first generation (representing net immigration of the foreign-born) and typically negative for the second and later generations (indicating some emigration and negligible immigration of the native-born).

In a female-dominant model,[48] a mother in the kth generation would produce an offspring in the k+1 generation. The population aged 0 to 4 for the first generation would derive solely from immigration (it is logically impossible for a mother to give birth to a foreign-born child in the United States):

$$P_{0,1}^{t+5} = \frac{N_{0,1}^{t,t+5}\left(1 + S_{0,1}^{t,t+5}\right)}{4} \tag{12}$$

separate for each sex. The population aged 0 to 4 years for the second and third generations results from births to mothers in the first and second generations, respectively, plus the effect of net migration:

$$P_{0,k}^{t+5} = B_k^{t,t+5}\frac{S_{0,k-1}^{t,t+5} + S_{0,k}^{t,t+5}}{2} + \frac{N_{0,k}^{t,t+5}\left(1 + S_{0,k}^{t,t+5}\right)}{4} \tag{13}$$

[48]We use *female dominance* here to mean the model derives the generational characteristics of children from the mother. This is to say that the generational characteristics of the father have no relevance for the offspring in the female dominant perspective.

for k=2,3 and for each sex separately, where the sex ratio at birth is needed to calculate the number of male and female births and where:

$$B_k^{t,t+5} = 2.5 \sum_{x=15}^{45} P_{x,k-1}^{t}\left(F_{x,k-1}^{t} + S_{x,k-1}^{t,t+5} F_{x,k-1}^{t+5}\right) + B_{I,k}^{t,t+5} \tag{14}$$

We would ordinarily assume that births to net immigrants during the period

$$B_{I,k}^{t,t+5}$$

would be non-zero only for the second generation. The population aged 0 to 4 years in the fourth and later generations results from births to third-generation mothers plus fourth- and later-generation mothers along with the effects of net migration:

$$P_{0,4}^{t+5} = B_3^{t,t+5} \frac{S_{0,3}^{t,t+5} + S_{0,4}^{t,t+5}}{2} + B_4^{t,t+5} S_{0,4}^{t,t+5} + \frac{N_{0,4}^{t,t+5}(1 + S_{0,4}^{t,t+5})}{4} \tag{15}$$

for each sex separately, where total births during the period are obtained using equation 14.

However, the female-dominant model does not correspond to the classifications used in U.S. censuses or surveys for most recent immigrant ancestor. A kth-generation female might marry a male of a different immigrant generation, and their offspring would not necessarily be the k+1 generation. If a third-generation woman produces an offspring in union with a first-generation man, the child would report ancestry relative to the father (the most recent immigrant generation of the parents) and indicate second-generation ancestry. Because some females marry males with a lower-order immigrant generation than themselves, the observed generational composition of births (and the resulting population aged 0 to 4 years) is always a lower order than implied by a female-dominant model.

To make the model correspond to data collection methods, consider a matrix

$$G_{k,m}$$

which indicates the proportion of births in the mth (m=1,2,3,4) generation born to women in the kth generation, subject to the condition

$$\sum_{k=1}^{4} G_{k,m} = 1.0$$

for k=1,2,3, and 4. In the female-dominant model

$$G_{1,2} = G_{2,3} = G_{3,4} = G_{4,4} = 1.0$$

and all other cells in the G matrix are zero. A model incorporating the G matrix, where mothers of the kth generation produce births in the mth generation is:

$$P_{0,m}^{t+4} = \sum_{k=1}^{4}\left[G_{k,m}\left(B_k^{t,t+5}\,\frac{S_{0,k}^{t,t+5} + S_{0,k+1}^{t,t+5}}{2} \right)\right] + \frac{N_{0,m}^{t,t+5}\left(1 + S_{x,m}^{t,t+5}\right)}{4} \qquad (16)$$

for m=1,2,3,4 and separate by sex. The empirical challenge, in this case, is to estimate the intergenerational birth matrix

$$G_{k,m}$$

The population projection model requires information about the probability that a kth generation mother gives birth to a mth generation child. The fertility assumptions for the model determine the overall chances of having a child; the intergenerational birth matrix therefore affects the generational distribution of births, and not the fertility process itself.

Data are lacking on childbearing by parental generation, for both parents, for racial/ethnic groups in the United States. We used data from the 1989 Current Population Survey (CPS) to make estimates of this matrix, examining births to parents for the first, second, and third-plus generation for the Asian, black, Hispanic, and white non-Hispanic populations. We then adopted an iterative procedure to develop estimates that fit both the CPS data and the known overall number of births (U.S. Bureau of the Census, 1989). This procedure produces approximate estimates for the intergenerational birth matrix. We estimate, for example, that births to third-generation Hispanic mothers are distributed roughly as 30 percent in the second generation, 20 percent in the third generation, and 50 percent in the fourth-plus generation.

Our current analysis of intergenerational births is preliminary. However, analysis of the 1989 CPS data suggests that the intergenerational birth matrix is affected by the generational distribution of males and females. In a population with a high proportion of immigrants, the chances are greater that a native-born person will marry a foreign-born person and produce a child with a more recent immigrant generation. Populations with few immigrants, in contrast, would have an intergenerational birth matrix that more closely resembles the female dominant perspective.

For the population projections presented here, we assume that each racial/ethnic group has an intergenerational birth matrix in 1990 that is estimated from 1989 CPS data, for the particular racial/ethnic group. Over time, we assume that the matrix changes, depending on the generational distribution of males and females in the population at the beginning of the projection period.

APPENDIX 3.B
POPULATION PROJECTION ASSUMPTIONS

This appendix presents detailed tables for the population projection assumptions. The tables that follow provide the assumptions used in the projections for fertility, mortality, immigration and emigration, exogamy, and ethnic attribution for multiple-ancestry persons. These appendix tables do not show assumptions made for American Indians, Eskimos, and Aleuts; the text and the tables do not present results for these population groups because they are relatively small and not affected by variations in immigration. Tables, graphs, and information for the U.S. total population, however, includes estimates for American Indians, Eskimos, and Aleuts.

TABLE 3.B1 Mortality Assumptions for Life Expectancy at Birth for U.S. National Population Projections by Race and Hispanic Origin, 1995 and 2050

	1995			2050		
Race/Ethnicity	Low	Medium	High	Low	Medium	High
White						
Male	73.6	73.6	73.6	72.6	81.9	87.5
Female	80.0	80.0	80.0	79.8	85.3	92.9
Asian						
Male	79.6	79.6	79.6	78.6	83.9	87.5
Female	80.2	80.2	80.2	79.8	85.0	89.3
Black						
Male	64.5	64.5	64.5	62.2	69.5	80.8
Female	74.3	74.3	74.3	73.4	78.8	89.8
Hispanic						
Male	74.9	74.9	74.9	73.1	84.4	85.5
Female	82.2	82.2	82.2	81.7	89.6	91.4

Source: Mortality assumptions made in national population projections of the U.S. Bureau of the Census (1996a).

TABLE 3.B2 Intermarriage Rates by Race/Ethnicity and Nativity, 1980, and by Race/Ethnicity, Nativity, and Racial/Ethnic Ancestry, 1990, Aged 20 to 29 Years

		1990		
Race/Ethnicity	1980	Overall	Single	Multiple
White				
Foreign-Born	1.9	2.1	1.8	5.5
Native-Born	1.7	2.0	1.8	4.3
Total	1.7	2.0	1.8	4.4
Asian				
Foreign-Born	—	48.0	38.3	91.7
Native-Born	—	79.7	71.6	90.9
Total	48.6	63.7	54.0	91.5
Black				
Foreign-Born	—	9.1	7.3	17.1
Native-Born	—	5.4	5.6	6.3
Total	3.1	5.4	5.4	6.8
Hispanic				
Foreign-Born	—	18.9	18.3	33.5
Native-Born	—	50.8	45.7	56.0
Total	29.2	37.0	36.2	48.1

Note: rates are shown as the percentage of persons in marital unions who are married to a person of a different race or Hispanic status. — = estimate not made.
Source: U.S. Bureau of the Census microdata files, 1980 and 1990.

TABLE 3.B3 Exogamy Estimates for Ethnic Groups by Immigrant Generation

	Immigrant Generation			
Race/Ethnicity	First	Second	Third	Fourth+
White	.10	.09	.08	.08
Asian	.13	.34	.54	.54
Black	.14	.12	.10	.10
Hispanic	.08	.32	.57	.57

Source: Panel estimates using 1990 census microdata and 1994 birth data from the National Center for Health Statistics.

TABLE 3.B4 Racial and Ethnic Attribution Rates for Multiple-Ancestry Persons for Racial and Ethnic Groups

	Level of Ethnic Attribution					
Race/Ethnicity	Very Low	Low	Half	Medium	High	Very High
White	.00	.22	.50	.42	.62	1.00
Asian	.00	.19	.50	.39	.59	1.00
Black	.00	.41	.50	.61	.81	1.00
Hispanic	.00	.44	.50	.64	.84	1.00

Source: Panel estimates from 1990 census microdata.

APPENDIX 3.C
SENSITIVITY OF POPULATION PROJECTION RESULTS

Different assumptions for each component of population change lead to shifts in population size. Using alternative assumptions for immigration, fertility, and mortality—each projected under low and high assumptions—we obtain changes in the projected population size. These variations can be compared with the medium-level projections, assuming medium levels for immigration, fertility, and mortality. Table 3.C1 shows results for these projections.

In the intermediate 10 to 15 year period, different assumptions about immigration and fertility could increase or decrease the population size by 2 to 3 percent (see Table 3.C2). In the long run, by 2050, different mortality assumptions will result in population size differences of 6 to 7 percent. In contrast, the cumulative effects of immigration and fertility are greater. Different immigration assumptions, ranging from low to high, will result in population size differences of 10 percent. Different fertility assumptions will account for differences of 12 to 14 percent. These results are consistent with other studies (Long, 1991) concluding that variability in fertility and immigration outpaces the contribution to long-term population size from mortality, in the U.S. context.

TABLE 3.C1 U.S. Population Size Under Alternative Immigration, Fertility, and Mortality Assumptions, 1995-2050

		Immigration		Fertility		Mortality	
Year	Medium	Low	High	Low	High	High	Low
1995	263	263	263	263	263	263	263
2000	277	275	279	271	274	277	277
2010	302	295	310	296	308	299	305
2020	327	313	341	314	340	320	334
2030	351	330	373	330	372	337	362
2040	370	341	400	337	407	352	385
2050	387	349	426	341	441	360	410

TABLE 3.C2 U.S. Population Size Relative to Medium-Level Assumptions Under Alternative Immigration, Fertility, and Mortality Assumptions, 1995-2050

		Immigration		Fertility		Mortality	
Year	Medium	Low	High	Low	High	High	Low
1995	100	100	100	100	100	100	100
2000	100	99	101	99	100	100	100
2010	100	97	103	98	102	99	101
2020	100	96	104	96	104	98	102
2030	100	94	106	94	106	96	103
2040	100	92	108	91	110	95	104
2050	100	90	110	88	114	93	106

4

Immigration's Effects on Jobs and Wages: First Principles

What impact does immigration have on the U.S. economy? Economic theory points to possible effects on the employment and wages of domestic workers, U.S. trade with other countries, the size and growth rate of the economy, and the prices that Americans pay for goods and services. Given the broad scope of these potential effects, this chapter and its companion, Chapter 5, necessarily cover wide ground. The evidence presented in Chapter 4 relies on theoretical insights of the likely effects, whereas Chapter 5 offers a comprehensive empirical documentation of the actual effects.

Our theoretical presentation in this chapter relies on a "first principles" discussion of immigration's likely impact on domestic labor markets. This treatment highlights the main insights from economic analysis about the effects of immigration. While our primer is written principally for noneconomists, economists may also be interested in the panel's collective judgment (with which some may disagree) about what the essential truths are. In particular, the chapter is not offered as a technical contribution to an extremely rich and growing literature in economics, from which we have borrowed extensively. Moreover, the panel decided not to cover all possible theoretical scenarios, from which an array of alternative outcomes becomes possible. Rather, we believe our most important task is to provide its best professional judgment about which models accurately capture the most salient impacts of immigration on labor markets.

To highlight these essential insights, we start with a very simple model to demonstrate that, on balance, immigration benefits the American economy. This model is then extended to provide a richer set of implications about the distributional impacts of immigration on the wages of domestic workers, the adjustments in the location of domestic employment, and the effects on the prices of domestically produced goods and services. This extension also illustrates how trade with other countries modifies the economic impacts of immigration.

Our initial theoretical model is static—that is, it examines immigration's impact at a moment in time. This issue is addressed in the second half of this chapter, which discusses the channels through which immigration may affect economic growth.

Chapter 5 focuses on the empirical evidence concerning the role of immigrants in the labor market. The issues covered range over the changing relative economic status of immigrants, their ability to assimilate economically, the effects of immigration on the wages and employment of native-born workers, and the impact of immigration on the prices of goods and services.

FIRST PRINCIPLES: LABOR MARKET EFFECTS OF IMMIGRATION

Whether native-born Americans gain or lose, immigration most directly affects the welfare of immigrants themselves. Immigrants come with the expectation that they will gain from immigration. If they had not felt that they would gain, they were free not to immigrate. Economic betterment is only one of many reasons why immigrants come here. Some may come expecting economic loss, but this must be offset by higher perceived gains in other things they value, like political freedom or reunion with their families. These gains are all before the fact. It may turn out that some immigrants are disappointed with life in their new country and some who fail to realize a gain return to their country of origin.[1] Beyond the immigrants themselves, their immigration may have implications for the economic well-being of those who remain in the sending countries. Because immigration reduces labor supply in those countries, the income of other workers rises and the income of other factors of production falls there. But such effects are beyond the scope of the panel's work and are not dealt with in this report.

Baseline Analysis

The easiest way to see how immigration affects economic outcomes is to take a very simple and highly aggregate view of the economy as a system that combines two inputs—one for which immigrants are good substitutes, and the other for which immigrants are complements—to produce a single final good, which we can think of as gross domestic product (GDP).[2] In the very simple

[1]Not all of those who leave should be seen as disappointed immigrants. Many who come and leave (the sojourners) may have fully foreseen—even planned—that they would eventually return home.

[2]These inputs are also assumed to have fixed supplies (completely inelastic supply curves). In addition, we assume for the moment that the production technology is constant returns to scale (for example, a doubling of all inputs leads to a doubling of output). These assumptions are relaxed below.

model, there is no trade between nations, so America consumes what it produces. Even this highly stylized model illustrates fundamental points about the effects of immigration on the domestic economy. Later, we relax some of these simple assumptions to obtain an even richer set of theoretical implications about the effect of immigration on the domestic economy.

This baseline analysis focuses first and foremost on immigration's direct effect on the economy through the addition of workers to the labor force. At the most basic level, immigration increases the supply of labor in the economy. More labor means more goods and services being produced, so that national output (GDP) rises.

Immigration also affects the prices of the inputs that are used to produce these goods and services. Those inputs for which immigrant labor substitutes will suffer as the prices of their services fall. Simply put, "substitutes" means two things that are very similar to one another. As a homely example, red apples and green apples are almost perfect substitutes, so that an increase in the number of red apples would not only reduce the price of red apples, but also simultaneously lower the price of green apples by about the same amount. In the context of immigration, where as we shall see many immigrants are unskilled laborers, the strong presumption is that immigrants are substitutes for domestic unskilled labor.[3] Therefore, an increase in the number of immigrants will generally decrease the wages of domestic unskilled workers.

Immigrants are not substitutes for all domestic workers. A disproportionate number of immigrants are low-skilled relative to native workers, and so tend to be poor substitutes for workers other than the low-skilled—that is, they do not do the same things at all. In the jargon of economics, two factors that are not substitutes are called "complements." For a simple example, think of supervisors and production workers. Suppose that, for every 50 production workers, we need one supervisor. If we increase the number of production workers, we will need more supervisors and their wages will rise. An increase in the number of immigrants, then, will raise the wages of those domestic workers who are their complements. The common presumption is that skilled domestic workers are complements for immigrants, so that an increase in the number of immigrants will raise the wages of domestic skilled labor. Capital may also be a complement to immigrant labor, although the evidence on the complementarity of unskilled labor and capital is more ambiguous than that of skilled and unskilled labor. **In summary, an increase in immigration flows will lead to higher incomes for productive factors that are complementary with immigrants, but lower incomes for factors that compete with immigrants.**

This very simple model implies that an increase in immigration will lead to an increase in national output, an increase in the income of complementary fac-

---

[3]We are considering the effects of the entry of new immigrants. Domestic labor includes both native-born workers and foreign-born workers who immigrated to the United States in the past.

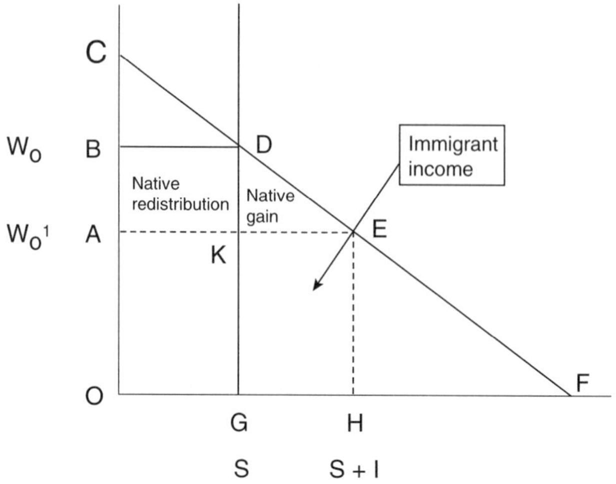

FIGURE 4.1 Effects of an influx of immigrants on a simple model of the labor market.

tors, and a reduction in the income of substitute factors. Since immigrants to the United States are disproportionately low-skilled workers, people usually think of the substitute input as unskilled labor and the complementary input as capital or skilled labor. But large influxes of immigration in some highly skilled workers, such as mathematicians and nurses, imply that some highly skilled natives will also see their wages or job opportunities worsen with immigration while capital or less skilled labor gains.

To sum up, immigration makes national output go up, some domestic workers suffer, and other workers benefit. Although it clearly begets winners and losers, can we make an overall statement that the winners win more than the losers lose, so that in the aggregate native-born Americans are better off? **With plausible assumptions about factor supply and returns to scale, we show that immigration produces net economic gains for the native-born.**

To understand this perhaps surprising result, we use a simple diagram (Figure 4.1). In the simple world portrayed by this diagram, we have two types of domestic workers: those who are perfect substitutes for immigrants (unskilled labor) and those who are complements (skilled labor).[4] Only one good is produced (GDP), and the numbers of unskilled and skilled domestic workers are fixed. Figure 4.1 plots the demand curve (CF) for domestic unskilled workers.

Before immigration, there are *S* domestic unskilled workers, who are all paid

[4]In particular, in this simple world there is no capital, so that workers receive all the income produced by selling the single good.

a wage W_o (the wage that equates demand and supply), so that the total amount that domestic unskilled workers are paid is *S* times W_o, or the area OBDG. Although we deal explicitly only with unskilled workers in this diagram, we can also determine how much skilled domestic workers are paid. To see this, note that the height at each point along the demand curve is the value of the extra national output produced by another unskilled worker.[5] Therefore, total national output (GDP) is the area underneath the demand curve up to *S* unskilled workers (OCDG) so that the remainder (BCD) is the amount paid to domestic skilled workers.

Now let new immigrants come into this country, increasing the supply of all unskilled labor in the work force to $S + I$. The new wage that equates the demand and supply of unskilled labor falls to W_o^1; that is, the wage of substitute domestic unskilled workers falls to W_o^1. Unskilled domestic workers are clearly worse off. Since the total amount that all unskilled domestic workers are paid falls to OAKG, the domestic unskilled workers lose ABDK as a result of immigration. Unskilled immigrants are paid the same wage as domestic unskilled workers so, as a group, immigrants receive the area GKEH.

What about skilled domestic workers? Before immigration, they received the area BCD, but what do they get now? Once again, we can calculate their incomes as a residual. With these new immigrants added to the workforce, total national output (GDP) will rise, so that it now equals the area under the demand curve up to the total number of unskilled workers, $S + I$. Instead of their pre-immigration incomes of BCD, domestic skilled labor now receives the area ACE (everything that isn't paid to either unskilled domestic workers or immigrants). Total GDP is now the area OCEH, so that the value of domestic output has increased by the area GDEH. But new immigrants get only the rectangle GKEH, so that, on net, domestic workers must gain by the size of the triangle KDE. Immigration thus raises national output and national output per domestic worker.

One way of seeing that the native-born must gain from immigration in this simple model is to recognize that new immigrants help produce new goods and services, but they are paid less than the total value of these new goods and services. The rest goes to domestic residents, who collectively are better off than before, by the triangle KDE.[6]

Figure 4.1 also illustrates that, although the net gain is positive domestically, some workers may lose and others may gain. In fact, although domestic unskilled workers lose ABDK, domestic skilled workers gain ABDE. The area in common

---

[5]Technically, the height is the marginal product of unskilled labor.

[6]The fact that immigrants are not paid the total value of the new goods and services does not mean that immigrants are in any sense "exploited." Some of the extra output produced should be credited to native workers, who are now being worked more intensively. For example, if native workers were only supervisors and immigrants were only production workers, each native worker would be supervising more immigrants.

is the rectangle ABDK, which is simultaneously (and equally) a loss to domestic unskilled workers and a gain to skilled domestic workers.

Therefore, although immigration yields a positive net gain to domestic workers, that gain is not spread equally: it harms workers who are substitutes for immigrants while benefiting workers who are complements to immigrants. Most economists believe that unskilled domestic workers are the substitutes, so their wages will fall, and skilled domestic workers are complements, so their wages will rise.

The potential size of this redistribution among the native-born compared with the size of the net national gain is one reason why our national political debate stirs such strong emotions. As Figure 4.1 indicates, at least in this simple economy, the magnitude of the redistribution rectangle is proportional to the number of unskilled domestic workers. In addition to being a triangle (which alone would make it half as large as the redistribution rectangle), the size of the net national gain is proportional to the immigrant flow (generally a much smaller base). Consequently, the redistribution among domestic workers could be large relative to the positive gain to the nation as a whole. There is a good argument that specific policies should be based only on whether a national gain or a national loss exists, and that we should use other policies to achieve our desired income distribution. However, the magnitude of redistribution relative to the aggregate national gain is clearly one important element in the national political debate.[7]

From the diagram, it is also clear that the **magnitude of the net gain to the domestic economy may depend on the magnitude of the loss to substitute domestic labor**. The area of the triangle in Figure 4.1 that represents the net gain to the domestic economy is equal to one-half multiplied by the number of new immigrants times the fall in the wages of domestic unskilled workers. Since the number of immigrants is fixed, the bigger the drop in the wages of domestic unskilled labor, $(W_o - W_o^1)$, the larger is the net rise in the incomes of domestic workers. If the wage of domestic unskilled workers did not fall, no domestic worker (unskilled or skilled) would gain or lose, and there would be no net domestic gain from immigration. In this case, the value of all the new domestic output immigrants produced would go to the immigrants themselves.

There is a direct correspondence between the fact that some domestic workers suffer wage reductions and the fact that we gain as a nation. This wage reduction is, in fact, the reason that the nation as a whole gains from immigration. This simple point is often lost in the voluminous empirical literature, which

---

[7]It is the case that the gain from immigration could compensate the losers since the size of the total gain exceeds the size of the total loss. This is the concept of Pareto optimality. A policy is a Pareto improvement if it results in a net gain. Such a policy is an improvement in the sense that it would be possible to compensate those for whom the policy produces a loss by redistributing income from those who receive a gain, and hence all parties could potentially be made better off.

searches long and hard to find those native-born Americans who experience wage reductions that are then labeled the "cost" of immigration. Although these wage declines are real losses to these affected workers, they are also the source of a national "gain" from immigration.

The gains and losses of immigration are therefore closely intertwined. As long as immigrants substitute for some natives, the larger the loss to those natives, the greater the benefits of immigration to the aggregate domestic economy. Similarly, if immigration has little effect on the aggregate economy, it must have little adverse effect on native workers for whom the immigrants are good substitutes.

This analysis focuses attention on the extent to which natives and immigrants are similar and whether they are substitutes or complements at workplaces. If immigrants have skills that substitute for those of some native workers, those native workers will lose from immigration. If immigrants have skills that complement those of other native workers, those native workers will gain from immigration. In the extreme, if natives and immigrants had utterly different distributions of skills—if, say, all immigrants had less than a grade school education and all natives were high school graduates or better—immigrants might be complements to all native labor. Then immigration would improve the economic position of all natives and harm none. Immigrants might also take jobs that no native would or could take. This would enable the economy to produce goods or services that it would otherwise not produce.

Finally, to close the logical possibilities, assume for a moment that the immigrants who arrive are exactly the same as the domestic workers who are already here. If immigrants have exactly the same skill distribution as domestic workers (the same fractions are unskilled and skilled workers) and if they have brought sufficient capital with them to maintain the U.S. capital/labor ratio, then natives will neither benefit nor lose from immigration. In this case, all inputs and national output will increase by the same amount and the wages of all workers will remain constant.[8] **It is only because immigrants and native workers differ from one another that immigration yields a net national gain. These differences between natives and immigrants, which may well be a legitimate source of concern about the ability of immigrants to assimilate socially and culturally, are the very reasons why the nation gains economically from immigration.**

This analysis directs attention at differences between the skill distributions of natives and immigrants in analyzing the economic effects of immigration. Table 4.1 gives the distributions of natives and immigrants by educational attainment in the 1990 Census of Population. Columns 1 and 2 show the distributions for the two groups for the United States as a whole, and Columns 3 and 4 the

---

[8]This assertion depends on the assumption of constant returns to scale, which is relaxed below.

TABLE 4.1 Percentage Distribution of Immigrants and Natives by Educational Attainment, 1990, United States and California

Years of Educational Attainment	United States		California	
	Native	Immigrant	Native	Immigrant
Less than 9	4.2	23.4	2.2	28.6
9-11	15.0	16.0	11.9	17.4
12	32.0	20.1	24.0	16.7
13-15	29.5	21.1	37.5	20.5
16	13.8	12.0	16.4	11.0
16+	6.6	8.4	7.9	5.8

Source: Calculated from U.S. Bureau of the Census (1993).

distributions for the two groups for California. The educational attainment of immigrants differs substantially from that of natives. Many among the immigrants have very low levels of education, particularly in California, and thus may be complementary with most American workers. Many among the immigrants have college degrees or better, and thus may compete with native college graduates and be complementary with less skilled Americans. Many also have 9 to 11 years of education and may compete with native high school dropouts and be complementary with more skilled Americans. But the salient finding in the table is the large proportion of immigrants with less than nine years of schooling, 23.4 percent in the United States and 28.6 percent in California, who may be complementary with most native American workers.

New immigrants lower the wages of groups for which they are close substitutes. The closest substitutes for newly arriving immigrants may well be prior waves of immigrants, rather than native workers. We show in Chapter 5 that, in terms of the jobs they do, newly arriving immigrants most closely resemble their immediate predecessors. Therefore, the bulk of the wage reduction induced by new immigrants may be concentrated on prior immigrant waves.

In sum, the baseline analysis suggests that immigration raises national output and on net improves the economic well-being of the native-born. Immigration also redistributes income from workers who compete with immigrant labor to factors that complement immigrant labor. The analysis also implies that Americans benefit most from immigrants whose skills are very different from those of natives.

Model Extensions

This very simple model effectively highlights many of the fundamental implications about the economic effects of immigration, but other implications can be illustrated only by taking a broader perspective. These implications include the effect of immigration on the prices of the goods we consume, the displacement of native workers (that is, the potential changes in where they are employed), and the relation between immigration and international trade.

As before, we initially assume that the United States is a closed economy—that is, it does not trade with other countries, and that total supplies of domestic factors (skilled and unskilled labor) are fixed. The United States then still must consume only what it produces. The fundamental extension is that we now let the U.S. economy produce two goods instead of only one. Although this change may sound trivial, it allows immigration to alter the relative prices of goods and services, so that domestic consumers can now gain or lose depending on which prices change the most. It also allows domestic labor to choose the sector of the economy in which they will work, so that sectoral displacement of domestic workers is possible. Because the analytics of the model can quickly become quite complicated, we present only a brief summary of results in the text. Appendix 4.A presents a detailed model on the analytics of the gains from immigration in this two-good, two-factor case.

In this simple economy, we now have two goods (call them X and Y) being produced efficiently with both unskilled and skilled labor.[9] Both goods need both types of labor, but they differ in the relative amounts of each factor they need. For convenience only, assume that good X needs a lot of unskilled labor relative to skilled labor, and good Y definitionally is the opposite. These factor proportions are crucial because they determine which sector immigration will affect more.

Without immigration, and with no international trade, our hypothetical economy efficiently produces and consumes a certain amount of good X and a certain amount of good Y.[10]

What happens to this economy if there is an inflow of immigrants? Once again, assume that these immigrants are unskilled compared with domestic workers. This relative increase in the supply of unskilled labor will, as in the very simple economy, lower the wage of unskilled labor relative to the wage of skilled labor. As before, unskilled domestic labor suffers a loss and skilled domestic labor a gain from immigration. Because good X uses more unskilled labor relative to skilled labor, this increase in immigration will also lower the price of good X relative to the price of good Y.

These changes in relative prices have a number of important consequences. Because the relative price of good X falls, domestic consumers will want to consume more X and less Y. Among native consumers, those who like good X the

[9]As before, each good's production function is characterized by constant returns to scale.

[10]This situation is depicted graphically in Appendix 4.A: Figure 4.A3, which plots the maximum amounts of X and Y that can be produced efficiently domestically. This situation is depicted as point A on this graph.

most—who consumed relatively more of it before immigration—will gain the most from its falling price, and those who like good Y the most will gain the least. The example is not fanciful. Immigrants are highly concentrated in certain sectors of the economy, so that relative price effects are possible. Many observers have argued that one of the primary effects of immigration is that it has reduced the cost of household service (cleaning house, caring for young children), a benefit that may be largely confined to the well-to-do. In Chapter 5, we go beyond mere speculation by providing solid empirical evidence on how widely concentrated or dispersed these price effects are across domestic consumers.

With this expanded model, **immigration has distributional effects: skilled domestic labor and domestic consumers of immigration-intensive products gain, and domestic unskilled labor and domestic consumers of goods not produced by immigrants lose or gain the least.** But can we go beyond simply distributional gainers and losers to whether these cumulative domestic gains or losses are positive or negative in the aggregate? It turns out that we can, and, on net, the native-born will still gain from immigration.[11]

Domestic workers will shift their production to good Y, the good that they are better at, to take advantage of its higher relative price. **One source of the native gain from immigration is that it allows the nation to use domestic labor more productively, specializing in producing goods in which we are relatively more efficient.** In short, if immigrant labor can produce something for $3.00, what do we gain from producing it ourselves for $3.50? We can let immigrants produce it and pocket the 50 cents we save.

Because of the shift in domestic production, some domestic workers, especially the less skilled ones, who had been working in industry X, may now have to move to industry Y. **In addition to wage effects, immigration has "displacement" effects. Some domestic workers will be "displaced" by immigrants, in the sense that they will now have to work in a different industry.**

In the simple model, we are assuming that the process of displacement is costless, in that displaced workers will eventually find employment in the other sector. This is a good characterization of the long run, but in the short run adjustment does have costs. It may take time to find this new job, with all the anxiety associated with that search. Changing jobs may mean moving out of one's neighborhood, city, or even region, with a loss of family, friends, and familiar schools and churches. Many Americans who perceive themselves to be displaced by immigrants resent having to make this adjustment. "Perceive" is an important word in this sentence because an attribution problem emerges when it comes to

---

[11]To see this visually, return to Appendix 4.A: Figure 4.A3. Before immigration, the economy was producing and consuming at point A. Immigration lowers the price of good X relative to good Y. Let this new relative price be depicted by the slope of the line L_0L_0. After compensating immigrants for their contributions, the domestic budget corresponds to all points on the line L_0L_0.

immigration. Some may associate their displacement with immigrants when the real causes lie elsewhere.

Whatever its costs, more efficient domestic production is not the only gain from immigration. **There is also the gain associated with specialization in consumption. Just as the presence of immigrants allows natives to specialize in production, it allows them to consume something different from what they can produce themselves.**[12] As a nation, we may be very good at producing good Y, but we really like good X. Immigration is one way we can have the best of both worlds; making what we are good at and also consuming what we like. The welfare gain to natives from immigration thus can be decomposed into two parts: the gain from shifting production toward more valuable activities that use the relatively more skilled native labor, and the gain in consumption toward commodities whose cost has fallen.[13]

In sum, the net welfare gains from immigration stem from two sources. By having immigrants specialize in the production of goods requiring a lot of low-skilled labor, it allows us to shift our domestic production toward those goods (Y) in which natives are relatively efficient (those that need a lot of skilled labor) and away from those that can be produced more cheaply by immigrants. The second component is the gain in consumption. Before immigration (and with no international trade), we could consume only that which we could produce domestically. **Immigration breaks this rigid link between domestic consumption and domestic production, allowing us to produce goods of which we are relatively efficient producers and to consume those goods that conform to our tastes.**

The models thus far highlight the potential substitution of immigrant labor for some competing native workers and the possible redistribution among native workers. Such models may well exaggerate the harm and understate the economic benefits from immigration. Immigrants may not directly substitute for many domestic workers at all if immigrants produce goods and services that largely would not otherwise have been provided. For example, we might well not have any domestic textile industry (or any domestic workers, most of whom are unskilled, in it) if it were not for immigrants. In this case, the gains from immigration are not reflected in wages at all, but in the lower domestic prices of goods related to textiles. All domestic consumers gain in this case, including unskilled domestic labor.

These purely domestic gains from immigration do not involve only substitutes for imports. As we shall see in the next chapter, immigrants are extremely

---

[12]In Appendix 4.A: Figure 4.A3, domestic factors alone would produce at point C, but domestic consumers will consume at point E.

[13]In Appendix 4.A: Figure 4.A3, the overall welfare gain to domestic workers is represented by the difference between U_2 and U_0. The movement from A to D represents the gain associated with shifting consumption, and the movement from D to E represents the gain associated with shifting production from A to C.

specialized in the activities in which they work. Even though their numbers are small, immigrants numerically dominate some activities, especially in services that cannot be imported. Such activities include household and child care service in private homes and the ownership, cooking, and staffing of ethnic restaurants. Although one could speculate that a native-born cook is displaced by a foreign-born Chinese cook in a Chinese restaurant, many of us may no longer believe that the food we are eating is really Chinese if it is not prepared by a Chinese cook. The more realistic alternative, absent immigration, is not that native-born cooks will staff Chinese restaurants, but that there will be a lot fewer Chinese restaurants around. All domestic consumers, especially those who like Chinese food, would lose. Similarly, many Americans would have to do without household help entirely if not for immigrants, who almost completely dominate that field. In this case, once again, there would be few domestic losers and only domestic gainers from the lower price of household service.

To the extent that immigrants specialize in activities that would otherwise not have existed domestically at that scale, immigration benefits all the native-born. In this case, there is little substitution against domestic workers, and domestic consumers gain from the availability and lower prices of these new services.

Immigration and Trade

As the previous section strongly hinted, immigration is in many ways similar to international trade in products. **Viewed through immigration lenses, trade is a form of immigration in which workers from foreign countries are embodied in traded goods rather than coming to the United States and producing those goods here.** The primary effect of both immigration and international trade is to allow us to specialize in producing those things we are good at and to consume something other than what we can produce ourselves.

Exactly the same reasons that explain the net national gain from trading with other countries explains the net national gain from immigration. First, a gain arises from shifting productive resources toward more valuable activities. Another gain flows from shifting consumption toward commodities whose cost has fallen. Although some people in the trading countries may be harmed by this specialization, the important lesson, as we have seen, is that the gains from trade outweigh the losses. The winners can afford to compensate the losers and have something left over.

Broadly speaking, immigration and international trade are alternative ways to achieve the same goal. Through either mechanism, we can obtain inputs that are relatively more abundant overseas than they are in our own country. Given the high level of human capital (skill) in the United States, we can import low-skilled workers (through immigration), or we can import the goods such workers make.

That immigration and trade are substitute ways to obtain the same output suggests that changes in the number of immigrants will have less effect on native incomes in the presence of relatively free trade than they otherwise would. Trade with other nations will move us closer to our desired consumption of X and Y,[14] so that the remaining gains achievable from immigration are lower.

For example, assume that the United States reduces the number of immigrants working in textiles, so that domestic prices for textiles rise. Domestic consumers might then buy foreign-produced textiles (now relatively cheaper), reducing the demand for native textile workers as much as immigration would have done. Commensurately, an increase in immigration could simply reduce textile imports, with no effect on the demand for native labor. In the limit, if trade and immigration were perfect substitutes, either would by itself produce the same outcome on native labor.[15]

But there are differences between immigration and trade that imply that these two paths for economic adjustment are not perfect substitutes in their effect on the labor market. One difference is that immigration reflects the movement of a stock of workers: an immigrant who comes permanently to the United States competes with natives for every year of his or her working life. Trade is a flow, dependent on exchange rates and trade policies: this year's trade deficit may turn into next year's trade surplus, and this year's import industry may turn into next year's export industry.

A second difference between the effects of immigration and trade is that natives can escape competition with imports by working exclusively in nontraded goods, such as government and retail trade, and various nontraded services. But they cannot escape competition with immigrants, who can substitute for them in both traded and nontraded goods and services.

Trade economists stress how trade affects the distribution of output and employment among industries, and the economic advantages that accrue from each country doing what it does relatively best—the concept of comparative advantage. If the United States has a comparative advantage in, say, goods that use highly skilled labor, we will export those goods and import goods that use less skilled labor, which raises U.S. and world income. As a result, the composition of our national output will shift toward sectors in which the United States is relatively more efficient and away from sectors in which it is relatively less efficient than other countries.

Immigration should also affect the industrial composition of output and employment and the exchange rate and terms of trade as well. When immigrants come into the United States and work in import-intensive activities, resources will shift toward those sectors. Absent immigration, the garment industry in the

---

[14]Point E in Appendix 4.A: Figure 4.A3.

[15]Taking the argument a step further, in a world with highly mobile capital, absent trade and immigration, capital might move across countries, producing similar outcomes.

United States might be much smaller or even not exist. The immigrant-induced increase in import-competing activities should reduce imports of textiles. If all else was the same, this would raise the value of the dollar on world markets, since we would demand less foreign currency to purchase imports. The terms of trade (the price at which we sell our exports compared with the price of imports) would thus shift in our favor. At the same time our comparative advantage would be smaller and we would be gaining less from trade. In the extreme, immigration could equalize the composition of labor skills and capital/labor ratios across countries, eliminating incentives for much of trade. In principle, so too might international flows of capital. That international trade has grown so rapidly implies that the world is very far from such a situation.

When immigrants come and work in nontraded sectors, such as restaurants, the nation's industrial composition and pattern of trade are also affected. An increase in the number of restaurants will shift resources to that sector and to food and beverages and related activities, drawing native complementary labor and capital from other industries, including the export and import-competing sectors. The traded goods sectors will decline, and so will the foreign exchange value of the dollar (for we will be producing fewer exports and importing more foreign goods) until the nation's balance of international trade reaches some sort of equilibrium.

By contrast, immigrants who come and work in export-intensive industries shift the industry mix toward those sectors, increasing the nation's comparative advantage in those goods. If more foreign engineers come to the United States, U.S. engineering firms will have a greater supply of labor and thus a competitive edge over companies in countries whose engineers came to the United States. Exports of U.S. engineering will expand, and, if we are a big producer of those goods, their prices could change as well.

All of these possibilities depend critically on the kind of immigrants the nation attracts and on the sectors in which they find employment. Although there are no firm estimates about the overall magnitude of the relation between immigration and trade (let alone about them and capital flows), the statistics in Table 4.2 suggest that, on average, immigrants are disproportionately employed in import-competing sectors and thus that they largely substitute for imports. Analyses that ignore this pattern may overstate the possible adverse effects of immigrants on low-skilled natives.

Looking at immigration in this way suggests that immigrants are more likely to work in import-intensive industries than in export-intensive industries. In fact, given the weighting calculation provided in the table, 12.8 percent of workers in import activities are immigrants, whereas only 10.1 percent of workers in export activities are immigrants (see Table 4.2). At the industry level too, immigrants are more involved in import activities than in export activities. In the top 10 percent of importing industries, immigrants make up 19.9 percent of the workforce, compared with 9.0 percent of workers in the top 10 percent of export-

TABLE 4.2 Percentage of Immigrants in Import-Intensive, Export-Intensive, and Other Industries, 1990

Industry	Percentage of Immigrants
Import-intensive manufacturing industries	12.8
Top 10% of import-intensive	19.9
Export-intensive manufacturing industries	10.1
Top 10% of export-intensive	9.0
Agriculture	14.7
Service industries (nonmanufacturing; nonagricultural)	8.7
Retail trade	10.4
Personal services (nonhousehold)	15.6
Household services	31.4

Source: Calculated from U.S. Bureau of the Census (1993). Percentage of immigrants in import-intensive and export-intensive industries defined as a weighted average percentage of immigrants in an industry, where the weights are the industry share of imports or exports. See Borjas et al. (1997).

ing industries.[16] Finally, immigrants are more likely to work in manufacturing than in services (which are usually nontraded), but they are overrepresented in several service sector areas.

Returns to Scale, Bottlenecks, and Externalities

There are other channels by which immigration can affect the domestic economy and native workers. In addition to its direct effects through increasing the labor supply, immigration may have indirect effects on national output and the job market. It may create externalities of various forms, for instance, through economies of scale in production; or it may alter the demand for products, or change the composition of industrial output and the terms of trade (the price of exports relative to imports).

[16]However, in agriculture, a major U.S. exporter, immigrants are an important input, making up 14.7 percent of the workforce.

Assume that the U.S. economy is subject to increasing returns to scale, in the sense that having a larger economy raises the productivity of domestic labor and capital. Perhaps some industry needs a critical mass to take advantage of modern technology. If immigration gives the economy that mass, it can increase GDP by more than the triangle in Figure 4.1.

Alternatively, assume that the U.S. economy is subject to decreasing returns to scale, in the sense that having a larger economy reduces the productivity of domestic labor and capital. Perhaps the presence of more people worsens congestion in cities or pushes pollution above some critical value. In this case, immigration will increase GDP by less than the triangle in Figure 4.1 or may even reduce it.

Some economists believe that increasing returns—agglomeration effects—help explain the pattern of economic growth. Some industries claim that they need certain kinds of immigrant workers to survive. In the 1960s, Europe admitted many guest-workers to meet high demand for labor, presumably facilitating rapid economic growth. On the other side, some believe that decreasing returns—crowding effects—threaten economic growth.

No strong evidence suggests that any of these effects dominates the aggregate economy, although one can cite examples of each. Some claim, for instance, that the success of the Silicon Valley high-technology industry depends on the benefits of having lots of firms engaged in the same line of work, and that the availability of foreign engineers and computer experts helped create the critical mass. On the other side, lengthened commuting time reflects possible diseconomies of scale due to a larger population, to which immigrants contribute. Hard evidence on the magnitude of returns to scale could alter the baseline analysis, but at present we simply note the possibilities that immigration may have effects beyond raising the supply of labor.

In our baseline analysis, we assume that the U.S. economy is characterized by constant returns to scale—that is, growth in the size and scale of the economy neither reduces nor increases the productivity of labor and capital. Potentially, factors such as increases in congestion in cities and rising pollution levels could cause productivity to fall as the size of the population increases. Conversely, many theorists of economic growth and economic historians point to the possibility of increasing returns to scale, that is, economic output increasing more than proportionately to an increase in factor inputs like labor. Similarly, agglomeration effects may lead to cost decreases as the scale of economic activity expands. We believe that the assumption of constant returns to scale is the most reasonable starting point for the analysis of effects of immigration. Existing research has not convincingly demonstrated that, in the aggregate, either decreasing returns due to fixed factors or congestion effects, or increasing returns, are more compelling alternatives. We caution, however, that this assumption of constant returns to scale is intended for analysis of marginal changes from the existing situation. The empirical work on economic growth is based, of course, on historically observed magnitudes of immigration and historically observed characteristics of immigrants and their children. We would not extrapolate far beyond current levels and say that immigration flows much larger than those considered in our demographic projections would always produce economic gains. With far larger flows, and over long periods of time, the uncertainty about increasing or decreasing returns to scale would have to be resolved with sound empirical evidence.

Plausible Magnitudes of Effects

In this section, we have argued that immigration has a direct effect on labor supply that should increase GDP, possibly at the cost of reduced wages for workers who compete with immigrants. The largest benefits accrue when immigrants are complementary with most U.S. workers, when trade and immigration are poor substitutes, and when immigrants specialize in products and services that otherwise would not have been produced domestically. The largest costs occur when immigrants substitute for most U.S. workers. When trade and immigration are good substitutes, neither benefits nor costs are large.

How large might the immigration-induced benefits and costs be from the past flows of immigrants into the United States? This is a difficult question, but under plausible assumptions, we can indicate the magnitudes of the effects, barring huge positive or negative externalities.[17] Assume that the native labor force consists of workers with less than a high school education, for whom the majority of immigrants are a good substitute, and workers with high school or more education, who are complements with most immigrants. Suppose that immigration raised the ratio of workers with less than a high school education to other workers by about one-third. According to Table 4.1, nearly 20 percent of the native workforce would fit into the substitute group and 80 percent into the complementary group of workers. Further assume that changes in immigration do not spawn offsetting changes in trade patterns, which would reduce the effects of immigration.

Under these assumptions, the increase in the number of immigrants raises the nation's stock of less-skilled workers relative to that of more-skilled workers, which should reduce the pay of the less skilled and raise the pay of the more skilled. The magnitude of the effect on labor incomes will depend on the responsiveness of wages to changes in relative inputs. The labor demand literature (reviewed in Hamermesh, 1993) suggests that a 10 percent increase in the relative supply would reduce wages by about 3 percent. Given such a relationship, the 33 percent increase in the relative supply of less-skilled workers would have reduced the wages of native high school dropouts by about 10 percent.

---

[17]A more detailed discussion of such calculations appears in Appendix 4.B.

Assume for simplicity that the 20 percent of the workforce who are unskilled earn 10 percent of labor incomes (they earn less than their share of the workforce because they are less skilled). Then, their share of GDP fell by roughly 1 percentage point (= .10 loss of wages × 10 percentage share of labor income). This in turn implies a 1.2 percent gain in share of GDP going to complementary native inputs and, using the model in Figure 4.1, a gain in total GDP of about 0.2 percent.[18] With a GDP of roughly $7 trillion, this percentage gain translates into a gain to the total economy on the order of about $14 billion.

This calculation is, we stress, simply an order-of-magnitude estimate. If the loss of wages to less-skilled natives is larger than 10 percent, the gain to other inputs and the aggregate economy will be larger. If more natives are complements with immigrants, the losses will be concentrated on a smaller group of natives and the gains more widely distributed. If trade is a good substitute for immigration, the effects will be smaller. Most important, our measures do not take into account the domestic benefits received from the lower prices of newly available services that do not directly compete with domestic labor.

Is this $14 billion a large or small effect? If it is measured relative to the total size of the economy (GDP), it looks modest indeed. Even the swelling in immigrant flows in the 1980s was unlikely to move the U.S. economy very much. Indeed, in that massive economy, no single factor can have a huge effect on relative earnings or on GDP. Using GDP as the reference standard certainly cautions us against exaggerating the possible impacts of immigration. The other view is that $14 billion is a lot of money, and that it is a net economic gain domestically. Very few other public policies would meet the test of yielding that much gain. Many factors that have only modest or moderate effects on the economy can cumulate to economic success or failure.

Others have made somewhat more sophisticated calculations of the size of the gains from immigration. Although they have not arrived at exactly the same number, their estimates are of similar magnitude. Assuming no response of the supply of capital to immigrant-induced higher returns, Borjas (1995) estimates that the approximately 10 percent of the American workforce who are immigrants added roughly 0.1 percent (one-tenth of one percent) to the GDP accruing to other Americans—or about $7 billion in a $7 trillion economy. Under the same assumption, Johnson (1997) estimates that a hypothetical increase in unskilled immigrants by 10 million (roughly 8 percent of the U.S. workforce) would raise national output accruing to natives by just $2.5 billion—or about 0.036 percent of GDP. Borjas et al. (1997) estimate a gain to natives of $9.1 billion—

[18]The gain in total GDP is the area labeled "Native Gain" in Figure 4.1, which is 1.65 percent of the part of GDP going to unskilled labor (calculated as the 10 percent decrease in wages times the 33 percent increase in supply times one-half). Multiplying that figure by unskilled labor's share of GDP (10 percent) to express the gain in terms of GDP, one obtains 0.165 percent. The gain to complementary native inputs is just the sum of the loss to unskilled natives and the net gain.

or about 0.13 percent of GDP. These are all small numbers relative to the size of the economy, so that such effects would be hard to detect in any aggregate data, given the many factors that influence GDP.[19]

All of these assessments place the economic gains to the country from immigration in the same rather modest range of magnitude: from $1.1 billion to $9.5 billion in a $7 trillion economy. This consensus reflects what economists view as plausible values of the relevant elasticities of factor prices to changes in labor supplies, or of the economic parameters that govern an aggregate production function. These empirical estimates suggest a net gain from immigration of from $1 to $10 billion dollars a year. While this is a small number relative to GNP, it is not a trivial number in absolute terms. Not many changes in policies would produce benefits as large as that number.

Overall, barring sizable immigration-induced economies or diseconomies of scale, the most plausible magnitudes of the impact of immigration on the economy are modest for those who benefit from immigration, for those who lose from immigration, and for total GDP. The domestic gain may run on the order of $1 to $10 billion a year. This gain may be modest relative to the size of the U.S. economy, but it remains a significant positive gain in absolute terms.

GROWTH AND IMMIGRATION

To this point, our discussion about the effects of immigration on labor markets has been entirely static. That is, we have been asking what would happen to GDP or domestic wage levels at a moment in time. But immigration may also alter the rate at which economies or wages expand over long periods of time. In fact, some have argued that immigration has been a driving force in promoting the long periods of substantial economic growth of the U.S. economy.

The impact of immigration on growth is a more subtle and difficult topic than its effects on labor markets at a moment in time. On this topic, unfortunately, speculation and undocumented assertions often carry the day. Because it is necessary to know so many additional parameters, there is nowhere near the same body of solid scientific empirical evidence available on growth as exists for static labor market effects. Given the lack of such evidence, we again go back to a first-principles approach that first outlines how and through which pathways

---

[19]When capital flows respond to immigration-induced higher returns, the gains accruing to U.S. natives are even lower. In this case, the gain to capital draws in additional capital, so that the return to native capital is ultimately driven back down. Johnson (1997) estimates that the gain to natives in this case is a bare $1.1 billion, all of which accrues to skilled labor given his assumption that immigrants were entirely unskilled. Borjas et al. (1997) estimate that the gain to natives is $3.5 billion when capital is completely elastic in supply. The gains accrue to skilled labor because immigrants are disproportionately unskilled.

immigration may affect economic growth rates. As in the static labor market approach, we then rely on a plausible set of parameters to assess how large or small the empirical effects may be. Our conclusions regarding immigration's effects on economic growth should be regarded as suggestive, until more solid scientific evidence becomes available.

Growth and Immigration in Historical Context

At least as far back as Adam Smith's *Wealth of Nations* (1776), the question of why and how the economies of nations grow, and why these growth rates are different in different nations over extended periods of time, has been a central concern of economists. When the perspective shifts from the static short-run model to long-run growth, the long run to which we refer is not simply a few years or decades. Rather, the perspective moves to generations and centuries, as we evaluate whether immigration can serve as a significant force (either positive or negative) in temporarily or permanently altering trajectories of native per capita incomes.

Our treatment of immigration must first be embedded in a plausible model that isolates the salient factors that influence the growth of economies. One of the earliest and still most widely read essays on the subject was that of Thomas Malthus (1798). Writing at the dawn of the Industrial Revolution, Malthus assumed that populations would grow exponentially with time but that food supply would grow at most linearly. The implications of those assumptions for income and wealth bequeathed both the adjective "Malthusian" to the English language and the moniker the "dismal science" to economics.

Today, the perspective is different. First and foremost, the developed nations have enjoyed a period of unprecedented prosperity and rising incomes far beyond the limits anticipated by Malthus. Consequently, the theory of economic growth has been reconsidered (more than once) in the interim. Second, the experience of nations is far from uniform. The richest, for the most part, have enjoyed increasing levels of per capita income for at least a half-dozen generations. Some have moved in only a generation or two from income levels associated with subsistence agriculture to the levels of the rich nations—notably, several East Asian economies in recent years. Still others appear to be stagnant, showing little or even negative growth rates over several decades. These widely different records are both a puzzle to be explained and a potential laboratory for understanding the factors that prevent growth and the attainment of prosperity as well as the environment that sustains steady growth.

The growth and prosperity of the Industrial Revolution were accompanied by unprecedented levels of voluntary migration. However, no obvious simple empirical relationship appears to link international migration and economic growth. Some countries that grew rapidly over the past six generations, most notably the United States and Canada, had high levels of immigration for some of that period. Among countries with high levels of emigration, some, for example Germany and the Scandinavian countries, experienced similar growth rates and today have comparable levels of per capita income; others, for example Ireland and Mexico, have not had the same growth patterns.[20]

A Simple Framework for Economic Growth

Since the factors that sustain or prevent economic growth and the role of migration in this process (if any) are not obvious from history, a simple conceptual framework is necessary for interpreting the experience of nations. As before, such a framework reduces the economies of nations to a few essentials and then examines what happens to growth rates, per capita income, and wealth in the long run. In particular, this approach abstracts from the rich diversity of goods and services produced in a developed economy to a single good (GDP). A portion of the single good is consumed today, with the other portion devoted to investment, so that we can consume more in the future. In the model, the single good is produced using three inputs: physical capital (plant, equipment, and so on) and two types of labor—unskilled and skilled. Physical capital and skilled labor both depreciate (machines break down, skills become obsolete) and grow through additional investment (for example, new machines, schooling). Unskilled labor in this simple model requires no investment.

An important feature of this framework is the set of assumptions made about technology. Technology is the set of rules that determine the amount of the single good that can be produced with specified levels of inputs (capital, skilled labor, and unskilled labor, in the example). For a given technology, however, a common reference point of almost all analyses of economic growth is the same assumption of constant returns to scale that we made in the static model. If all inputs change in a certain proportion, then output changes in the same proportion.[21] As before, this assumption implies that wages and returns to capital depend only on ratios of factors and not on the scale of the economy.

---

[20]The pattern of migration from rich nations to poor nations is interesting. Large flows have been associated with colonization, for example, from Spain to Latin America and from England to the North American colonies and then Australia. This migration involved the imposition of the immigrants' culture and economy, and within a generation or two the income level of the country of origin was realized. There have been no significant migrations from established richer countries to established poorer ones. Looking more closely at the United States, rates of immigration have varied widely over time, peaking at nearly 1 percent of the population per year in the 1850s, 1880s, and 1900s (see Figure 2.2), and dropping to less than 0.1 percent. This historical experiment is not well suited to drawing conclusions about links between immigration and growth using simple empirical methods.

[21]The scale-free technology also implies that the ratio of output to any factor of production depends only on the relative amounts of the factors and not their absolute levels (Varian, 1984: Chapter 2).

In the simplest variant of this model, population growth is taken as given: it can be either positive or negative, and it can be increased through fertility or immigration or decreased through mortality or emigration. A fixed fraction of output (GDP) is devoted to investment in physical capital used in production and to investment in the resources that produce skilled workers, with the allocation such that the returns to investment are the same in both forms of capital. New investment must be just great enough both to replace the capital and skilled labor lost through depreciation and to provide enough new capital and skilled labor to "scale up" these factors along with the increase in population.[22] When this point is reached, all three factors continue to grow at the same rate, but all ratios—including the wages of skilled and unskilled workers and the rates of return to owners of capital—remain the same.

Immigration in the Simple Framework

This simple framework has several interesting implications for immigration. Suppose a base case in which there is never any immigration or emigration. Contrast this with a case in which there is migration, and migrants, as a group, carry with them the same mix of factors of production as natives. That is, the proportion of skilled workers is the same among migrants as among natives, and migrants bring in (or take out) the same amount of physical capital, on average, as natives.

In this case, immigration has no effect on the ratios of the factors of production in the economy, and consequently—because of the assumption of constant returns to scale—it has no effects on output per person or the distribution of income. Immigration will affect only the size of the economy: more GDP will be produced. The United States will be a bigger economy, but the average income of all of its inhabitants will remain unchanged. If immigration is confined to a limited period of time, it will change only the level, but not the growth rate, of GDP. That is, U.S. output will grow faster during the periods of immigration but will then revert back to its normal growth rate when immigration ceases.

If immigration is sustained permanently in relation to the size of the country, it will alter both the level and the growth rate of GDP but will leave income per capita unchanged. For example, if immigration is +0.5 percent of population

[22] If important factors of production are fixed (say, land), then returns to scale can be decreasing. Conversely, if there are positive returns to proximity of factors (like decreasing transportation costs), then returns can be increasing. Bringing empirical evidence to bear on this problem has proven difficult, and the evidence is mixed (Hall, 1988; Burnside et al., 1995). If investment is too little to keep the capital-labor ratio constant, then the ratios of capital and skilled labor to unskilled labor will fall. As they fall, less is lost to depreciation, until eventually the loss just matches the level of investment. Similarly, if investment is more than enough, these factors grow relative to unskilled labor, until investment is just sufficient to sustain the ratios of the three factors.

each year, then it will permanently affect the growth rate of total output (GDP), also by +0.5 percent. But it will not change the well-being of natives as measured by their per capita incomes because there is no long-run impact on the ratios of factors.

Therefore, given constant returns to scale, immigration will not affect long-run growth in per capita incomes of natives if immigrants are just like native-born workers. As in the static case, immigration can have permanent economic effects on native-born growth paths only if immigrants are different from the native-born.

Once again, for migration to have even temporary effects other than simply the scale of the economy, migrants must differ from natives with respect to the distribution of the factors of production they carry with them. For example, if capital and unskilled workers substitute well for each other in production, then a long-run increase in the number of unskilled workers in the economy can lower the returns to capital, as well as lowering unskilled wages and raising skilled wages.

The extent to which these factors substitute for or complement one another has been extensively studied; Hamermesh (1986) provides an extensive review. These studies find that unskilled workers and capital are weakly complementary. They also indicate that changes in factor supplies induce less than proportional changes in wages and the return to capital. If in the long run the fraction of unskilled workers in the labor force increases by 1 percent, then the ratio of unskilled workers' wages to skilled workers' wages will decline, by at most 0.5 percent. The effect on the return to capital is smaller; it is more likely to increase than decrease, but not by more than 0.2 percent. These studies also find that about half of income is returned to unskilled workers and the remainder is divided roughly evenly between capital and skilled workers. Thus, an increase in the number of unskilled workers equivalent to 1 percent of the labor force will have the effects on relative wages just described, with a 0.5 percent increase in output and little change in the return to capital.

Even if immigrants were disproportionately less skilled and owned proportionately less capital than natives, the permanent effects of immigration would be less than these demand effects alone suggest, however. The higher relative wages of skilled workers will make investment in skill acquisition more attractive to both natives and immigrants. Some natives who were unskilled before the immigration will remain unskilled and have lower wages, but some will move to skilled jobs at higher wages.[23]

---

[23]Some empirical support for this effect lies in the fact that an increase in the ratio of wages of college graduates to wages of high school graduates by over 20 percent since 1977 has been accompanied by a substantial increase in the proportion of high school students going on to college. (The association of the change in relative wages with immigration is more tenuous.)

Persistence of the Effects of Immigration on Growth

A critical feature in determining the impact of immigration on long-run economic growth is the factor mix that accompanies the immigration. A second critical feature is whether the change in the factor mix associated with immigration is temporary or permanent.

How long these effects on growth persist depends on the fertility rates of immigrants and their children and on the rate of generational assimilation of the new immigrants. High fertility of immigrants (and of their descendants) relative to that of the native-born increases the relative weight given to the characteristics of the immigrant population and perpetuates any differences between immigrants and the native-born. The available evidence suggests, however, that the fertility rates of immigrants and their descendants converge toward the national norm within two generations. Consequently, there is little reason to believe that differential rates of population growth will produce any long-term impact of immigration.

Similarly, if the children of immigrants born in the United States distribute themselves among the skilled and unskilled labor force and also save and invest in the same way as natives, the effects of an increase in immigration over one generation will be negligible one generation following that.[24] The only long-run effect of a generation of increased immigration will be an economy that is somewhat larger; the growth rate and distribution of income will be unaffected. To put it simply, **if the children of immigrants are just like the children of the native-born, we are back to the case in which all we are doing is scaling up the population and economy with no impact on per capita incomes. A generation of increased immigration then can alter long-run growth paths only if generational assimilation, both economic and demographic, is never complete.**

If assimilation takes longer, impacts on wages will be more persistent, increasing incentives for natives to invest in better job skills. If descendants of immigrants never assimilate, this investment will maintain a ratio of unskilled to skilled workers higher than that for the descendants of those who were native at the time of the immigration. If the natural rates of increase of the two descendant groups are the same, the impacts on wages and returns will persist, and the proportion of natives in skilled jobs will rise.[25]

The rate of assimilation and the degree to which natives and immigrants invest in skills and capital in response to wage and factor price differentials are

[24]This abstracts from secondary effects, such as the physical capital required to transform immigrant children into skilled workers, which immigrants did not bring with them.

[25]In the extreme case in which immigrant descendants never assimilate and have a higher rate of natural increase, the nation to which they have immigrated eventually takes on the same economic characteristics as the one from which they came.

the keys to predicting the long-run impacts of immigration. A historically based working assumption is that the grandchildren of immigrants have the same economic characteristics as all natives whose grandparents were natives, and that the characteristics of immigrants' children are somewhere in between those of their parents and those of their own children (Borjas, 1995).

We can illustrate these effects with a simple numerical example in a society that consists of three generations: immigrants, their children (the second generation), and their further descendants (third and later generations). Begin with a domestic labor force in which one-fifth of the labor force is skilled and four-fifths is unskilled. Further suppose that the skilled wage is twice the unskilled wage. A bit of arithmetic shows that under this scenario one-third of labor income goes to skilled workers and two-thirds to the unskilled.[26] To capture the extremes, suppose that the characteristics of immigrants are quite different: they are all unskilled. The grandchildren of immigrants will look the same as the original native-born (one-fifth skilled), and the children of immigrants are in between (one-eleventh skilled).[27]

The next set of assumptions refers to the steady-state population weights. Suppose that there is one immigrant for every two children born to natives, so that one-third of the population is immigrant in the steady state. With these assumptions, eventually 19.7 percent of labor returns will go to skilled workers (compared with one-third without immigration), and 10.9 percent of the labor force is skilled (compared with 20 percent without immigration).[28] If a skilled worker owns three times as much capital as an unskilled worker, on average, then the demand elasticity estimates surveyed in Hamermesh (1986) imply a decrease in the unskilled wage of 10 to 15 percent, an increase in the skilled wage of 15 to 20 percent, and an increase in the return to capital of about 5 to 7 percent. (These results are not very sensitive to assumptions about capital ownership.)

---

[26]To see this, let w represent the wage of the unskilled (and so $2w$ gives the wage of the skilled) and L represent the total number of workers. Total labor income going to skilled workers (who represent one-fifth of L, or $.2L$) is $2w(.2L) = .4wL$, and the unskilled receive $w(.8L)$. Total labor income is then $w(.8L) + 2w(.2L) = 1.2wL$, and the share of the skilled is one-third of that amount.

[27]This puts the second generation exactly half-way between the immigrant and third (and beyond) generations in terms of the fraction of income going to skilled workers within that generation. One-third of the income of the third generation goes to skilled workers, compared to one-sixth of the income of the second generation, and none of the income of the immigrant generation.

[28]In the steady state, one-third of the population is immigrant. Of the remaining two-thirds, one in three has immigrant parents, so two-ninths of the population is second generation. The remaining four-ninths of the population is third generation and beyond. Adding together the skilled portion of the population in each of those generations, we have 2/99 from the second generation (two-ninths of the population, of whom 1 in 11 is skilled) and 4/45 from the third and higher generations (two-ninths of the population, of whom 1 in 5 is skilled), so 10.91 percent of the population is skilled, leaving 89.09 percent unskilled. Following the method in the previous footnote, the share of income going to skilled workers would then be 10.91 times two, divided by $(10.91 \times 2 + 89.09 \times 1)$ to get 19.7 percent.

Even a modest response in the supply of factors implies that these figures are well above the equilibrium levels, however. Suppose that in response to the increase of about 35 percent in the relative wage of skilled workers, 10 percent more of the native labor force were to acquire skills, and that immigrants' children continue to be about half as skilled as natives. Then making the same assumptions about capital ownership, nearly 17 percent of the labor force will be skilled and about 28 percent of labor income will go to the skilled.[29] The unskilled wage will drop by 3 to 5 percent, the skilled wage will increase by 4 to 6 percent, and the return on capital will increase by about 2 percent. Thus, even after making strong assumptions about the number and composition of immigration and making conservative assumptions about the supply response, the effects on relative wages and factor prices are relatively small. Since the steady-state number of immigrants is more akin to 1 in 10 than to 1 in 3, as in this example, the effects are smaller still.

For a number of reasons, immigration will have a relatively small effect on growth rates of per capita incomes of natives. First, generational assimilation will tend to mitigate the initial static effects. This mitigation occurs in part because fertility rates of immigrants eventually converge to the native-born norm. In addition, the very success of immigrants in their assimilation across generations implies that they will eventually be like natives in terms of skill ratios, and that their long-run effect on rates of economic growth are nil. Finally, by increasing the returns to acquiring skill, immigration provides incentives for some domestic workers to acquire more skill.

Changes in Technology

Our simple framework indicates that the characteristics of immigration are one key to understanding its impact on the level and distribution of economic output in the long run. The assumption of constant returns to scale is also central. The only way this framework can generate steady growth in per capita income over a long period is through capital that grows at an accelerating rate. By all accounts, capital per worker has grown steadily, but without acceleration, in developed countries. Nor have returns to capital steadily fallen.

A changing technology—one that raises the productivity of the factors of production—can account for the observed sustained improvements in per capita income in developed countries. We can think of changing technology such that each year a worker (skilled or unskilled) is equivalent to slightly more than one

[29]This follows from the same sort of calculations outlined in the previous footnotes. The fraction of skilled workers in the third generation and beyond is changed from 20 percent to 30 percent, while the fraction of skilled workers in the second generation is changed from one-eleventh to 3/23 (which puts the second generation half-way between the immigrant and third generations in terms of labor income going to skilled workers).

worker in the technology of the previous year. For example, take 100 workers in year 1 who become 10 percent more productive by year 2. By year 2, these same 100 workers are equivalent to 110 effective workers (doing the same work that it would take 110 workers in year 1). Even though the number of actual workers might be unchanging, the number of effective workers is growing steadily, just as if there were a positive rate of natural population increase in the simple framework.

Given this way of thinking about improved technology, our earlier results extend easily to the framework with a changing technology. In the long run, capital grows at the same rate as the number of effective workers. But the growth rate of effective workers exceeds the growth rate of actual workers by the rate of technical progress. Thus, capital grows at a steady rate. The ratio of capital to the actual number of workers is forever increasing, but it is constant relative to the effective number of workers. With this type of technical progress, there is no growth in wages relative to the number of effective workers, but wages per actual worker are growing. In this case, the return to capital remains constant rather than falling. These characterizations and conclusions agree, broadly, with what is observed in developed countries (Baumol et al., 1989).[30]

The limitation of this approach is that it doesn't explain why technical progress occurs.[31] At its core, technical change represents the production of new knowledge or the productive application of old ideas. One line of attack in recent models is to investigate how inventions and new ideas find their way into an economy (Grossman and Helpman, 1994).[32]

Nations not at the frontier can achieve change by transferring technology from more developed nations, with appropriate modifications. Explaining why some nations do not grow, or explaining why certain nations have moved from stagnancy to approach the highest levels of per capita income, involves examination of the conditions for transfer.[33]

---

[30]The analysis of the effects of immigration, with this kind of technical change, is essentially the same as in the simple framework if we replace "worker" with "effective worker." It is also necessary to assume that each immigrant, skilled or unskilled, becomes the same number of effective workers as each native worker. A different assumption leads to four rather than two kinds of workers, and thus to a more involved analysis requiring assumptions more difficult to ground in solid empirical findings.

[31]To explore the origins of growth successes and failures more deeply requires some accounting for the conditions under which growth can occur. Recent work has done exactly that, developing endogenous growth models that push back the level at which assumptions are made.

[32]Although there is much public-sector research, there is more research and development in the private sector; and the results of public-sector research usually are brought to actual application in the private sector. Firms will not pursue research and development unless they expect to profit from it. Profit cannot be realized if the results are publicly and costlessly available; some sort of monopoly over the fruits of this activity, even temporary, is needed if it is to take place. Patent systems are a leading example of a public policy that provides such monopolies.

[33]Most prominent among these are property rights, including freedom from threat of expropriation and civil unrest; and transaction costs, including forms of social capital that avoid the need for explicit contracts about commercial minutiae (Fukuyama, 1995).

Immigration and Changes in Technology

Observed patterns of migration underscore the importance of endogenous growth (that is, growth that can be manipulated). In particular, the simple framework with exogenous growth (that is, growth over which people have no control) implies that returns to skilled labor should be high when the level of skilled labor is low, since returns to all factors are decreasing. Yet we do not observe migration of skilled labor from rich nations with high proportions of this factor to poor nations with low proportions. This fact has been cited as one of the most telling conflicts between the exogenous growth framework and observed behavior (Lucas, 1988; Romer, 1994). In the case of the most highly developed nations, endogenous growth models suggest an avenue of influence of immigration on growth beyond the mix of factors in the simple framework. These models highlight the role of research and development in sustaining economic growth.

Immigrants are important in many research and development sectors in the United States: they are disproportionately represented in many research laboratories, in the community of Nobel laureates recognized for work in the United States, in postgraduate programs in the sciences and engineering, and increasingly on the faculties of U.S. universities. The system of postgraduate education in the United States has long been central in this process. Widely recognized as the best in the world, this system brings in large numbers of graduate students from other countries, tries (usually successfully) to keep the best in the United States, and returns the others. Those who stay concentrate in research and development sectors important to sustaining economic growth, and those who return are among the most skilled in their countries of origin.

Another mechanism through which immigration may affect growth involves immigrants who exhibit extraordinary entrepreneurial ability. Entrepreneurs, especially the successful ones, create wealth and jobs well beyond their numbers. They often supply the energy, ingenuity, ideas, and capital that are the sinews of economic growth.

Although no direct systematic evidence exists on differences in entrepreneurship between natives and the foreign-born, some indirect evidence indicates the extent to which immigrants are self-employed. Table 4.3 lists rates of self-employment for the two groups in the 1990 census. It reveals essentially no difference in the probability of self-employment between immigrant and native-born workers. Self-employment varies considerably among source countries, running from a little less than 1 in 5 among European men to about 1 in 20 among Mexican women. With these data, however, it is difficult to argue that self-employment and any entrepreneurship associated with it mark a critical distinction between immigrants and the native-born.

In addition, immigration is a very unlikely vehicle for increasing total national savings. Because immigrants still represent only about 8 percent of the population, savings differences between immigrants and the native-born would

TABLE 4.3 Self-Employment Rates by Region of Birth and Education Level

	Percent Self-Employed	
Group	Men	Women
Natives	13.1	7.2
All foreign-born	13.1	8.3
Foreign born, by region		
Europe	18.4	10.2
Asia	15.9	9.8
Mexico	7.2	5.7
Other America	11.1	6.5
Other	11.2	7.1
Foreign born, by education level		
8th grade or less	9.6	6.8
Grades 9-12, no degree	11.8	8.5
High school degree or certificate	13.4	8.8
Some college	14.1	8.4
Bachelor's degree or greater	15.6	8.9

Source: Calculations based on reported class of worker at the time of the census, in sample of employed people ages 25-64 from the 1990 Census Public-Use Microdata Sample.

have to be extremely large to alter aggregate savings.[34] Although there exists little firm evidence about savings differences between immigrants and the native-born, it is more likely that immigrants actually save less than the native-born. Low-income families tend to save very little and the preponderance of immigrant families in the low-income deciles implies that their savings rate is likely to be low.

The Impact of Immigration on Income, Wealth, and Growth

The theory of economic growth identifies several features of the economy that are keys to determining the impact of immigration on income and wealth in the long run: the skill mix of the immigrant population, the ability to substitute

[34]For example, assume that the native-born save 10 percent of their income and represent 92 percent of the population. If immigrants saved at twice the rate as the native-born (i.e., 20 percent, which is extremely unlikely), then national savings would rise to only 10.8 percent.

different labor skills and capital in production, the rate at which immigrants enter the economy, the rate of economic assimilation of immigrants, the response of investment in labor skills and physical capital to changes in factor returns, and the participation of immigrants in research and development. The evidence points to a substantial capacity of the economy to absorb immigrants. **The rate of immigration can have important consequences for the absolute size of the economy (as documented elsewhere in this report), but it is not likely to have major long-run consequences for the distribution of income or the rate of capital formation. The very success of immigrants in assimilating economically across generations mitigates their potential to alter long run-growth rates.**

CONCLUSIONS

To summarize the main findings of this chapter, as a nation, on net, we gain economically from immigration for several reasons. On the production side, immigration allows domestic labor to specialize in producing goods at which we are relatively more efficient. Specialization in consumption also yields a gain. Immigration thus breaks the rigid link between domestic consumption and domestic production. From this perspective, its effects are comparable to those of international trade. Because the two processes are so similar, when trade is relatively free, changes in the number of immigrants will affect the incomes of the native-born less than they would have without trade.

Even when the economy as a whole gains, though, there can be losers as well as gainers among different groups of U.S. natives. The gainers are the owners of productive factors that are complementary with immigrants—native higher-skilled workers, whose incomes will rise. Those who buy goods and services produced by immigrant labor benefit, too. But there may also be losers: the less-skilled native workers who compete with immigrants and whose wages will fall. To the extent that immigrants specialize in activities that otherwise would not have existed domestically, immigration can be beneficial for all the native-born. In this case, there is little substitution against native workers, and native consumers gain from the lower prices of these services.

Overall, immigration is unlikely to have a huge effect on relative earnings or on gross domestic product per capita. Many other factors are far more critical to the U.S. economy than is immigration, including savings and investment and the human capital of U.S. workers.

In the long run, assuming constant returns to scale, immigrants can affect rates of economic growth only to the extent that they differ from the native-born—if, for example, they arrive with a different mix of skills from those possessed by the native-born. To affect growth rates, this difference between immigrants and natives must persist over each new generation. If the grandchildren of immigrants come to be just like the native-born, all that immigration does is augment the population and the scale of the economy; it scarcely changes per capita income in the long run.

REFERENCES

Baumol, W.J., S.A.B. Blackman, and E.J. Wolff
1989 *Productivity and American Leadership: The Long View.* Cambridge: MIT Press.

Borjas, G.J.
1995 The economic benefits from immigration. *Journal of Economic Perspectives* 9:3-22.

Borjas, G.J., R.B. Freeman, and L.F. Katz
1997 How much have immigration and trade affected the U.S. job market? *Brookings Papers,* forthcoming.

Burnside, C.A., M. Eichenbaum, and F. Rebelo
1995 Capital utilization and returns to scale. *NBER Macroeconomics Annual.*

Fukuyama, F.
1995 *Trust: The Social Virtues and the Creation of Prosperity.* New York: The Free Press.

Grossman, G.M., and E. Helpman
1994 Endogenous innovation in the theory of growth. *Journal of Economic Perspectives* 8:23-44.

Hall, R.E.
1988 The relationship between price and marginal cost in U.S. industry. *Journal of Political Economy* 96(5):921-947.

Hamermesh, D.S.
1986 The demand for labor in the long run. In O. Ashenfelter and R. Layard (editors), *Handbook of Labor Economics.* Amsterdam: Elsevier Science Publishers.
1993 *Labor Demand.* Princeton, NJ: Princeton University Press.

Johnson, G.E.
1997 Estimation of the Impact of Immigration on the Distribution of Income Among Minorities and Others. University of Michigan, mimeo, February.

Lucas, R.E., Jr.
1988 On the mechanics of economic development. *Journal of Monetary Economics* 22:3-42.

Malthus, T.R.
1798 *An Essay on the Principle of Population.* First edition published 1798. New York: Random House (1960).

Romer, P.M.
1994 The origins of endogenous growth. *Journal of Economic Perspectives* 8:3-22.

Smith, A.
1776 *An Inquiry into the Nature and Causes of the Wealth of Nations.* Dublin: Whitestone.

U.S. Bureau of the Census
1993 *1990 Census of Population.* Washington, D.C.: Department of Commerce.

Varian, H.R.
1984 *Microeconomic Analysis.* New York: W.W. Norton and Company.

APPENDIX 4.A
IMMIGRATION IN THE TWO-GOOD, TWO-FACTOR MODEL

Consider a simple closed economy that produces two goods, x and y, using two factors of production, labor and capital. Let x and y be produced by constant-returns-to-scale production functions, F and G, respectively. We can write the following equations:

$$x = F(L_X, K_X) = L_X F(1, K_X / L_X) = L_X f(k_X) \quad (1)$$

$$y = G(L_Y, K_Y) = L_Y G(1, K_Y / L_Y) = L_Y g(k_Y) \quad (2)$$

$$L = L_X + L_Y \quad (3)$$

$$K = K_X + K_Y \quad (4)$$

The Edgeworth box in Figure 4.A1 presents all feasible combinations of x and y that can be produced given this economy's endowments of labor and capital. Assume that good x is relatively intensive in its use of labor and that good y is intensive in its use of capital. The O_XO_Y locus traces all the efficient combinations of production where the marginal rates of substitution between capital and labor are the same in the two sectors.

Suppose that production takes place at point A. The capital-labor ratio in sector x is then given by the slope of R_0. Similarly, one can connect the O_y with

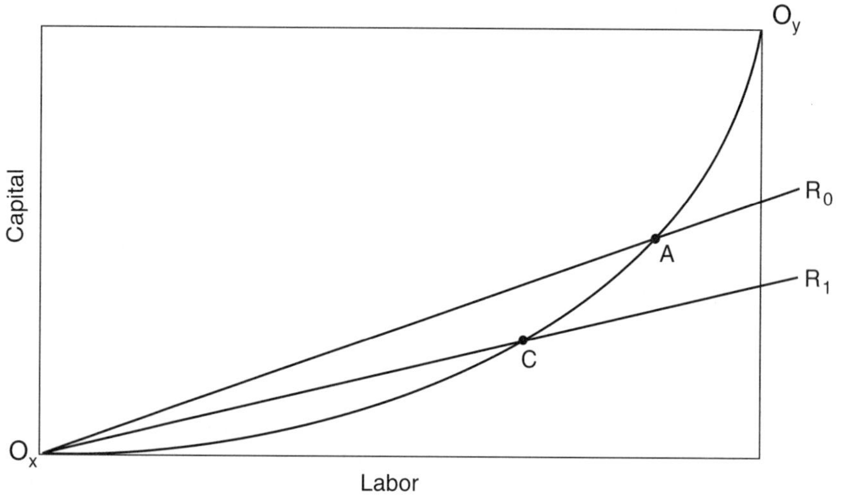

FIGURE 4.A1 Edgeworth box.

point A and take the slope of that radius to arrive at the capital-labor ratio in sector y. It is easy to see that, if we move production from A to, say, point C, the equilibrium capital-labor ratios will fall in both sectors. In fact, each point on the efficiency locus corresponds to different capital-labor ratios within each sector, with the range of possible capital-labor ratios being bounded by the available quantities of labor and capital.

From equations 1 and 2 it follows that the marginal physical products are functions of the capital-labor ratio only:

$$x_L = f(k_X) - k_X f'(k_X) \quad \text{and} \quad x_K = f(k_X) \tag{5}$$

$$y_L = g(k_Y) - k_Y g'(k_Y) \quad \text{and} \quad y_K = g'(k_Y) \tag{6}$$

By dividing the marginal physical product of labor by the marginal physical product of capital in both equations 5 and 6 and by taking the total differential, it follows that capital-labor ratios are strictly increasing in the marginal rate of substitution between capital and labor, independent of the endowments,

$$d(k_X)/d(\omega) = f'(k_X)/(f''(k_X) + \omega) \tag{7}$$

and

$$d(k_Y)/d(\omega) = g'(k_Y)/(g''(k_Y) + \omega) \tag{8}$$

where $\omega = x_L/x_K = y_L/y_K$.

Preferences determine where production will take place. The Y_0X_0 locus in Figure 4.A2 traces efficient production in $y - x$ space. One can imagine a set of social indifference curves such that the highest possible level of welfare, given the budget as represented by the production frontier Y_0X_0, is obtained at point A. Both production and consumption take place at point A.

What happens to this economy if we allow an inflow of immigrants? For simplicity, assume that the new immigrants bring no capital with them, so that they add only to the stock of labor in the economy. With x being relatively more labor intensive, immigration allows relatively more x to be produced, and the production frontier will expand to, say, Y_1X_1. If the price of x in terms of y, given by the tangency to the production frontier Y_0X_0 at point A, does not change, consumers (natives and immigrants) will have an excess demand for y and an excess supply of x. The relative price of x will have to fall to restore equilibrium. Preferences determine the size of that change. Thus, immigration has changed relative prices, lowering the price of the good that uses labor intensively in terms of the good that uses capital intensively.

Suppose the new production point is given by point B. The question that

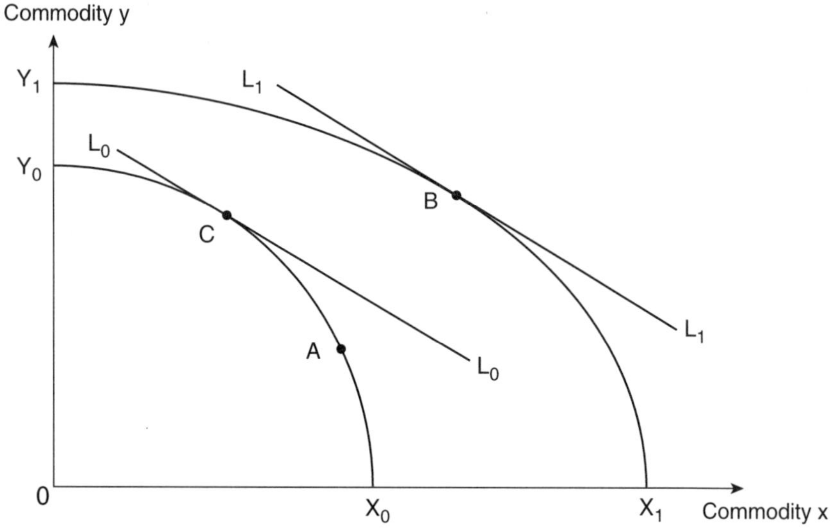

FIGURE 4.A2 Production possibilities with and without immigrants.

arises is whether domestic workers are better off because of the immigration. To see that they are, first realize that the domestic budget is given by the tangency of the new price line at the old production frontier. That is, the difference between the two frontiers is made up of payments to the new immigrants. Given constant returns to scale, national income, Y, in terms of y must add up the payment to the factors of production. That is,

$$Y = y + px = G_L(L_y + I_Y) + G_K K + p\,F_L(L_X + I_X) + p\,F_K K_X \tag{9}$$

which, with $p = G_L/F_L = G_K/F_K$, simplifies to

$$Y = G_L(L + I) + G_K K \tag{10}$$

where I represents new immigrant labor. Similarly, at the old production frontier national income at point C is given by

$$Y^* = G^*_L L + G^*_K K \tag{11}$$

The difference between Y and Y^* is equal to the compensation of new immigrant labor if and only if $G_L = G^*_L$ and $G_K = G^*_K$. Ruling out factor-price-intensity reversals, relative prices at B and C are the same and imply equal marginal rates of substitution between capital and labor. Since the marginal rate of substitution uniquely defines capital labor ratios, which in turn define the marginal physical

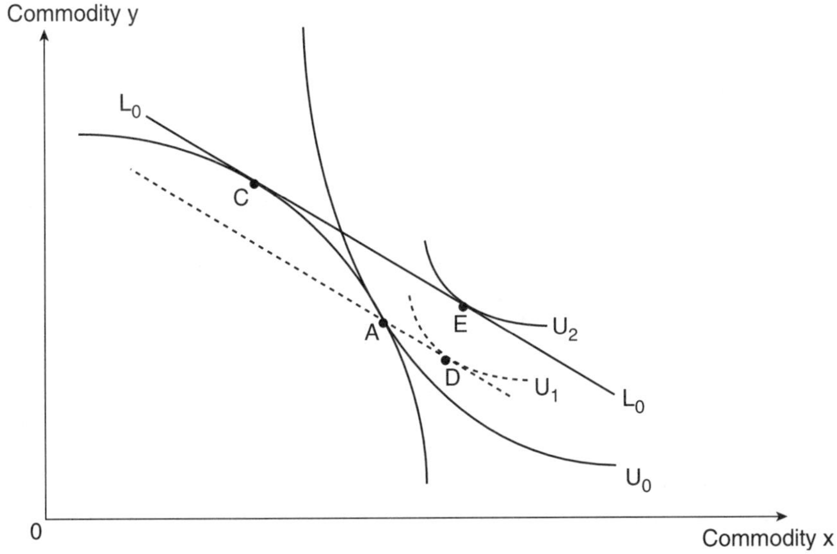

FIGURE 4.A3 The gain from immigration in a model with two factors and two goods.

products given in equations 5 and 6, it follows that the marginal physical products are equal at B and C and thus the difference between L_0L_0 and L_1L_1 gives the compensation to new immigrants.

L_0L_0 thus corresponds to the budget for domestic workers after immigration has taken place. Domestic workers have shifted their production from A to C to take advantage of the higher relative price of good *y*. The presence of new immigrants allows domestic workers to specialize in production and to consume outside the old production frontier. Consumption and production are no longer constrained to be the same. At the new relative price, a higher social indifference curve can be attained and domestic workers thus experience an overall welfare gain. This welfare gain can be decomposed into two parts: the gain from shifting production toward more valuable activities, and the gain from shifting consumption toward commodities whose cost has fallen. In Figure 4.A3 the overall welfare gain is represented by the difference between U_2 and U_0. The movement from A to D represents the gain associated with shifting consumption, while the movement from D to the new consumption equilibrium at E represents the gain associated with shifting production from A to C.

APPENDIX 4.B
ASSESSING THE LABOR MARKET BENEFITS AND COSTS OF IMMIGRATION

In standard models of immigration and trade, the income losses of natives who compete with immigrants are more than matched by the income gains of natives whose skills or capital complement those of immigrants. How large might these gains and costs be?

To answer this question, economists use variants of the model shown in Figure 4.1. By aggregating groups of workers into a small number of complements or substitutes for immigrants; by assessing the extent to which these workers are complementary with or substitutes for capital or (what amounts to the same thing) of the responsiveness of factor prices to a change in immigrant labor supply; and by assessing the potential response of capital and labor supplies to immigration; one can put numbers to the labor market benefits and costs of alternative immigration flows.

The basic framework for estimates is a production function $Q= f(K, S, L)$, where Q is output, K is capital, S is skilled labor, and L is unskilled labor. Under constant returns the income received by residents is

$$Q = F_K K + F_S S + F_L L \tag{1}$$

where F_K, F_S, F_L are the marginal products of capital, skilled labor and labor, respectively. Output is divided between capital, skilled labor, and unskilled labor according to their marginal products and magnitudes.

If immigrants contribute more to the supply of unskilled than of skilled labor, as in the United States in the past three or so decades, then under virtually any plausible assessment of the effect of immigrants on the marginal productivity of skilled labor, unskilled labor, and capital, unskilled labor will lose and skilled labor and capital will gain. However, even the smaller number of immigrants who add to the nation's skilled labor can reduce the earnings of skilled labor as well, with the result that the sole beneficiary of immigration is capital. If increased labor supplies in the United States induce capital to move to the United States, however, U.S. capital will not gain at all: it will simply reallocate from other countries to the United States.

Formally, let I be the increase in immigrant labor to the United States. Assume for simplicity that this increase consists entirely of unskilled labor (what matters is whether the immigrant supply consists disproportionately of skilled or unskilled labor). With a constant returns to scale production function, the change in the national income, Δ, accruing to current U.S. residents depends on the amount of their factor resources and the effect of the immigrant supply on factor prices:

$$\Delta = (\partial f_K/\partial I)K + (\partial f_S/\partial I)S + (\partial f_L/\partial I)L \tag{2}$$

The effect of unskilled immigrants on the factor prices of capital and skilled workers will be positive, but it will be negative on the wages of unskilled labor. The economic analysis in Chapter 4 explained why (barring external diseconomies of scale) Δ will be positive.

To turn this expression into a quantitative estimate of the effects of immigration on the income accruing to natives, we need estimates of the effects of immigrants on the factor prices, and/or on the marginal productivities of the factors.

Economists have some knowledge of the interrelations among factors, but this knowledge is not hard and firm. Different analysts have made somewhat different assumptions about the parameters governing the interrelations, which yield somewhat different estimates of the magnitude of effects. Still, a general consensus has emerged that, overall, the net gains to the United States of immigration are rather modest measured relative to gross domestic product (GDP).

Assuming no response of the supply of capital to immigrant-induced higher returns, Borjas (1995) estimates that the approximate 10 percent of the American workforce who are immigrants added roughly 0.1 percent (one-tenth of one percent) to the GDP accruing to other Americans—or about \$7 billion in a \$7 trillion economy. Under the same assumption, Johnson (1997) estimates that a hypothetical increase in unskilled immigrants by 10 million (roughly 8 percent of the U.S. workforce) would raise national output accruing to natives by just \$2.5 billion--or about 0.036 percent of GDP. Borjas et al. (1997) estimate a gain to natives of \$9.1 billion, or about 0.13 percent of GDP. These are all small numbers, which would be hard to detect in any aggregate data, given the many factors that influence GDP.

When capital responds to immigrant-induced higher returns, the gains accruing to U.S. natives are even lower. In this case, the gain to capital—the major complement to immigrant labor—draws in additional capital, so that the return to native capital is ultimately driven down. In terms of our equation, $\partial f_K/\partial I = 0$, Johnson (1997) estimates that the gain to natives in this case is a bare \$1.1 billion, all of which accrues to skilled labor, given his assumption that immigrants were entirely unskilled. Borjas et al. (1997) estimate that the gain to natives is \$3.5 billion when capital is completely elastic in supply. The gains accrue to skilled labor because immigrants are disproportionately unskilled.

All of these assessments place the economic gains to the country from immigration in the same modest range of magnitude: from \$1.1 billion to \$9.5 billion in a \$7 trillion economy. This consensus reflects what economists view as plausible values of the relevant elasticities of factor prices to changes in labor supplies, or of the economic parameters that govern an aggregate production function.

To see how virtually all such calculations yield relatively modest estimates of the gains to immigration, consider a simpler but extreme model with two factors, capital and skilled labor taken as one input, and unskilled labor (high school dropout workers) taken as a second factor. Assume that unskilled labor makes up 20 percent of the U.S. workforce and that unskilled labor earns 10 percent of U.S. GDP—all reasonable order of magnitudes for high school dropout labor. Now let immigration increase the supply of unskilled labor by 33 percent. The gain to natives in terms of additional GDP from this flow of immigrants would be the triangle in Figure 4.1, which is one-half the change in labor supply times the change in the wage of unskilled labor. The change in the supply of labor that substitutes for immigrants is 0.33. If the elasticity of the wage of unskilled labor to this change was, say, 0.3, the wage loss to these workers would be about 10 percent. The triangle would be 1/2 (.33) (.10) for a group whose earnings represent 10 percent of GDP. Thus, relative to GDP, the gain to all natives would be about 0.2 percent or $14 billion in a $7 trillion economy. Immigration in this case has reduced the pay of a relatively modest number of U.S. workers by 10 percent while increasing the total GDP accruing to natives by 0.2 percent.

5

Immigration's Effects on Jobs and Wages: Empirical Evidence

Building on our first-principles treatment of the economic effects of immigration, this chapter focuses on the empirical evidence concerning immigrants' role in U.S. labor markets. We first address the changing economic status of the immigrants themselves: What is the size of the economic gain to immigrants? What is happening to the labor market skills of recent immigrants compared with those of native-born workers? Are immigrants able to assimilate economically into the U.S. labor market? Most of the literature has examined these issues for male immigrants; to gauge the labor market success of immigrant women, we make comparisons between female immigrants and female natives similar to those we make for men.

The section that follows directly addresses the issue of the impact that immigrants have on native workers' earnings and employment. We start our treatment of this central issue with a theoretical discussion that places some constraints on how large or small these impacts on native workers can be. This theoretical treatment is complemented by a summary of the empirical evidence on the size of the wage and employment effects on native workers.

The bulk of research has looked for the effects of immigration on labor market outcomes. However, immigration may also alter product markets, raising or lowering the prices of alternative goods and services by different amounts. Since Americans do not consume all goods in the same proportions, some may gain more than others as these prices change. The final section of this chapter presents new evidence on the impact of immigration on the prices of goods. By doing so, it attempts to identify the American households that benefit the most and those that gain the least from these changing prices.[1]

THE ECONOMIC GAIN TO IMMIGRANTS

In the previous chapter, we argued that immigrants expect that they themselves will gain from immigration, or they would not come. But how large are these economic benefits to immigrants? Although the question is straightforward, it is amazing how little direct evidence exists on the magnitude of their actual economic benefits. Some thorny conceptual issues beset comparison of standards of living across countries, but the primary reason for the lack of knowledge is that survey data contain little information about immigrants' lives before they came to America. As a not atypical example, the decennial census questionnaire asks no direct questions about how immigrants fared in labor markets at home.

Given this paucity of direct evidence, the best we can do is make some simple contrasts between what immigrants earn here compared with average wages in the major sending counties.[2] There are two salient facts in describing wages in the United States relative to those of potential sending countries. First, wages in the United States are high relative to those in the less economically developed sending countries, such as the Philippines, Mexico, and the other Central and South American countries. Second, dispersion in wages in the United States is high relative to that in most of the developed sending countries, including those in Western Europe and Canada.

The implication is that immigration to the United States should be attractive to most workers from less economically developed countries and that skilled workers from many developed countries may want to emigrate into the United States.[3] These implications appear to be broadly consistent with migration patterns—for example, unskilled labor from Mexico and skilled labor from Western Europe.

As a rough gauge on relative standards of living, Table 5.1 lists gross domestic product per capita for the principal source countries. This table illustrates the

---

[1]There are other interesting issues that the panel did not consider because it was necessary to limit the scope of the report. Among them are the effects of immigration on family income (as opposed to individual earnings) and the contribution of immigration to the rise in individual and family income inequality over the past 20 years.

[2]One difficulty with such comparisons is that immigration may be highly selective relative to home country traits.

[3]These implications are strictly true as long as productivity differences among workers do not fully account for these wage differences between the United States and the sending countries. The extent to which productivity differences can fully account for these differences is a source of considerable debate. Unlimited free trade or immigration would imply that wages would tend to equalize across nations (factor price equalization). Current estimates of productivity adjustments suggest that productivity-related factors can explain only some of these intercountry wage differences, leaving large wage differences and large gains from migration.

TABLE 5.1 Per Capita Gross Domestic Product Measures, for Selected Countries, 1992

Region and Country	GDP Per Capita Relative to U.S.	GDP Per Capita
Europe		
Austria	73.2	16,989
Czechoslovakia	23.2	5,066
France	78.5	18,232
Germany	87.0	20,197
Greece	39.0	8,203
Hungary	24.9	5,780
Italy	72.0	16,724
Poland	21.1	4,907
Portugal	41.3	9,005
U.S.S.R.	41.9	8,780
United Kingdom	70.2	16,302
Yugoslavia	25.0	5,467
Asia		
Cambodia	NA	NA
China	7.9	1,838
India	7.0	1,633
Iran	17.9	4,161
Japan	85.8	19,920
Korea	42.1	9,358
Laos	7.7	1,710
Lebanon	NA	NA
Philippines	9.4	2,172
Taiwan	45.1	9,850
Vietnam	NA	NA
North and South America		
Argentina	25.3	5,532
Canada	90.3	20,970
Colombia	18.3	4,254
Cuba	NA	NA
Dominican Republic	12.6	2,918
Ecuador	14.7	3,420
Guatemala	12.4	2,888
Haiti	4.6	957
Jamaica	13.4	2,978
Mexico	33.9	7,867
Nicaragua	6.6	1,441
Panama	17.7	4,102
Peru	11.3	2,602

continued on next page

TABLE 5.1 Continued

Region and Country	GDP Per Capita Relative to U.S.	GDP Per Capita
Africa		
Egypt	9.8	2,274
Ethiopia	NA	NA
Nigeria	4.9	1,132
South Africa	16.7	3,885
Oceania		
Australia	79.7	18,500
United States	100.0	23,220

Note: GDP = gross domestic product; NA = not available. GDP figures are in constant dollars adjusted for changes in terms of trade. 1991 data was used for Greece, Jamaica, Korea, and Laos. 1990 data was used for Argentina, Czechoslovakia, Nicaragua, Portugal, Taiwan, and Yugoslavia. 1989 data was used for Haiti and U.S.S.R.

Source: National Bureau of Economic Research, Penn World Data Set. WWW site. National Bureau of Economic Research, February 4, 1997.

tremendous variation in incomes among the sending countries as well as the large gap between some of these countries and the United States. For example, gross domestic product (GDP) per capita in the United States is roughly 7 times as large as that in Ecuador and 15 times as large as that in Nicaragua. The disparity is three to one with the largest source country, Mexico.

With the exception of Japan, income disparities are also quite large with many of the Asian sending countries—a ratio of 11 to 1 with the Philippines and 14 to 1 with India and China. The disparities with Western Europe are considerably smaller, and with many of the Eastern European nations they run as much as 5 to 1. Collectively, the data in Table 5.1 suggest that many immigrants experience large economic benefits from migrating to the United States.

Immigrant wages in the United States typically far exceed those in their home countries. How do they compare with the wages of native-born workers? And what factors account for any immigrant wage deficit that may exist? Tables 5.2 and 5.3 answer the first question. For example, the hourly wages of foreign-born men in 1990 were 7 percent lower than those of native-born male workers, and annual earnings were 15 percent lower (Table 5.2). These gaps vary greatly across the sending countries, ranging from wages that are only one-half of native wages among recent Mexican male immigrants to wage premiums among European and Canadian male immigrants.

Recent arrivals earned considerably less than natives throughout the last three decades. The wage gap between recent immigrants and natives widened substantially in more recent years: in 1970 the gap for men was about 10 percent of native wages; in 1990 it was 22 percent. Gaps in men's annual earnings were larger than those in hourly wages but showed a similar trend, widening from about 19 percent in 1970 to about 35 percent in 1990.

TABLE 5.2 Average Hourly Wages and Earnings of Foreign-Born and Native Men in 1970, 1980, and 1990, Civilian Employed, Ages 25-64, 1995 Dollars

Nativity and Time of Arrival	1970 Hourly	1970 Annual	1980 Hourly	1980 Annual	1990 Hourly	1990 Annual
Native-born	$19.00	$37,212	$19.83	$37,591	$19.41	$37,551
All foreign-born	19.29	36,043	18.93	34,164	18.06	31,935
Recent arrivals	17.08	30,156	16.18	27,107	15.17	24,318
Europe and Canada	19.20	35,779	20.04	36,648	21.52	41,957
Asia	18.09	29,863	17.54	29,548	16.97	28,026
Africa and Oceania	19.03	27,439	18.06	29,387	19.95	25,446
Other America[a]	15.00	26,259	14.68	23,035	13.04	19,594
Mexico	11.74	20,165	12.11	18,911	9.71	14,251
Earlier arrivals	20.40	38,981	20.71	38,750	20.06	37,228
Europe and Canada	21.69	41,942	22.45	43,299	24.07	47,270
Asia	20.00	37,980	24.00	46,883	24.67	46,385
Africa and Oceania	17.77	33,477	24.25	46,833	19.05	36,746
Other America[a]	17.87	32,506	18.19	33,011	18.78	33,564
Mexico	13.57	24,498	15.97	26,153	13.17	21,846

Notes: Recent arrivals are defined as foreign-born men who arrived in the 10 years preceding the census year, and earlier arrivals include all other foreign-born men in the sample. Hourly wages are computed by dividing annual earnings from wages and self-employment income by weeks worked and average hours per week. The sample is men aged 25-64 years who worked at some point in the preceding year, were not self-employed, did not reside in group quarters, and were not in the armed forces at the time of the census.

[a] "Other America" includes Central America, the Caribbean, and South America.

The widening gap between recent immigrants and natives is accounted for at least in part by the shift in immigrants' home countries: immigrants in 1990 included large numbers from Latin America and Asia, whereas in 1970 a larger share came from Europe. Recent male immigrants from Europe did well relative to natives throughout this period, moving from a slight deficit in earnings relative to natives in 1970 to substantially higher earnings in 1990. In contrast, recent male immigrants from the countries that are now the dominant sources (in Asia and Latin America) earned much less than natives. For instance, wages and annual earnings of recent male immigrants from Mexico were less than half those of native-born workers, and they were also substantially below those of recent male immigrants from other regions.[4]

[4]Male immigrants who had been in the United States for more than 10 years at the time of the census have much better labor force outcomes than did more recent arrivals. This group had somewhat higher wages than did natives in each of these years, but also had some decline in wages and earnings relative to natives, although the magnitude of that change was much smaller. Earlier arrivals as a group fared well relative to native-born workers, but there were substantial differences across region of origin for this group as well, with earlier immigrants from Mexico, Central America, and the Caribbean having substantially lower wages than those from Europe and Asia.

TABLE 5.3 Average Hourly Wages and Earnings of Foreign-Born and Native Women in 1970, 1980, and 1990, Civilian Employed, Ages 25-64, 1995 Dollars

Nativity and Time of Arrival	1970		1980		1990	
	Hourly	Annual	Hourly	Annual	Hourly	Annual
Native-born	$12.70	$14,899	$12.63	$16,805	$13.42	$20,196
All foreign-born	13.02	15,338	12.63	16,604	13.23	19,154
Recent arrivals	11.82	13,894	11.71	14,606	11.64	15,157
Europe and Canada	12.46	14,254	11.98	14,953	14.76	18,841
Asia	13.71	15,196	12.61	16,743	12.84	17,669
Africa and Oceania	9.99	12,870	13.81	15,807	12.81	16,863
Other America[a]	10.81	14,086	11.10	13,255	10.22	13,178
Mexico	10.11	8,823	9.47	10,067	8.08	8,738
Earlier arrivals	13.62	16,082	13.11	17,663	14.06	21,242
Europe and Canada	13.75	16,378	13.06	17,561	14.40	21,963
Asia	13.70	16,285	15.23	21,975	16.53	26,175
Africa and Oceania	14.72	16,261	13.81	19,570	14.54	21,832
Other America[a]	13.42	16,533	13.07	18,064	13.97	21,195
Mexico	10.97	11,770	11.11	12,448	9.89	12,803

Notes: Recent arrivals are defined as foreign-born women who arrived in the 10 years preceding the census year, and earlier arrivals include all other foreign-born women. Hourly wages are computed by dividing annual earnings from wages and by weeks worked and average hours per week. The sample is women aged 25-64 years who worked at some point in the preceding year, were not self-employed, did not reside in group quarters, and were not in the armed forces at the time of the census.

[a] "Other America" includes Central America, the Caribbean, and South America.

Similar patterns appear in comparing the hourly wages and annual earnings of native and foreign-born women (Table 5.3). Recent arrivals have lower wages and earnings than native women; this gap has widened over time, whereas earlier arrivals fare well relative to natives throughout the period. The same diversity in economic outcomes exists across sending countries. However, the wage gap between recent arrivals and others is generally smaller for women than for men, as is the variation in wages across region of origin.

One gender difference of note involves the changing standard (native-born wages) to which immigrants' wages are being compared over time. For men, the wages of natives were quite flat over the past few decades and, consequently, the growing gap implies an absolute decline in the real wages and earnings of recent immigrants. In contrast, the real wages of native-born women have been rising, so that the widening of the gap among women is consistent with flat or rising wages of immigrants.[5]

[5]The other noticeable gender difference is that, for women, the widening in the gap between recent immigrants and natives was much more dramatic for earnings than for wages. For men, the change in

Mean wage disparities between immigrants and the native-born hide considerable diversity. One way of measuring this diversity across the full distribution of wages is to first rank natives by their wages into 10 equal deciles. If natives and the foreign-born had precisely the same wage distribution, 10 percent of the foreign-born would also be placed in each of those deciles. These distributions are presented in Table 5.4 for the six largest immigration states, for California taken alone, and for Los Angeles.

This table demonstrates that immigrants are disproportionately at the bottom of the wage distribution. This concentration is particularly strong in places where immigrants make up a substantial share of the population. For example, in the six states receiving the largest number of immigrants between 1980 and 1990 (California, Florida, Illinois, New York, New Jersey, and Texas), 17.7 percent of immigrants fall in the bottom decile of the native wage distribution. For the state with the highest concentration of immigrants, California, this proportion is 22.7 percent, and for a high-immigration city, Los Angeles, it rises to 29.5 percent.[6]

The overrepresentation of immigrants in the bottom rung of the wage ladder is even more dramatic for the most recent arrivals. For those immigrants who arrived within five years of the 1990 census year, 27.5 percent have wages in the lowest wage decile in the top six immigrant states, compared with only 13.7 percent of those who came before 1980. The concentration is even more pronounced in California and Los Angeles. For example, 44.5 percent of all recent immigrants living in Los Angeles in 1990 have wages below that of a native-born worker at the lowest decile. In large immigrant cities like this, immigrants earn wages that place them disproportionately in the lowest economic stratum.

What explains these wage disparities between the native-born and immigrants, especially those from sending countries, such as Mexico, whose wage deficits are huge? The disparities could be due to differences in the skills that immigrants and the native-born bring to the labor market, or to overt or covert discrimination against immigrants. Such discrimination would not be difficult to exercise, because the foreign-born may be easy to identify. Skill differences could emerge for a number of reasons, including the schooling gap (in both quantity and quality) between immigrants and natives and the quality of their respective labor market experiences. The latter may be particularly relevant for older immigrants, whose experience in their home countries may not be as highly valued in the U.S. labor market.

For the most part, the available studies attribute much of the wage gap between many immigrant groups (particularly those from poorer countries) and na-

---

the gap was only 4 percent larger for earnings than for wages, whereas for women, the change in the gap was 12 percent larger for earnings. This reflects the rapid increase in employment rates experienced by native women.

[6]This is not just an artifact of the larger share of immigrants in the population; no matter what that share, the sum of the representation of immigrants in each of the deciles has to be 100 percent.

TABLE 5.4 Distribution of 1990 Hourly Wages of the Foreign-Born by Native Wage Decile, for Immigration States, California, and Los Angeles (percentage)

				Foreign-born, by Time of Arrival		
Area	Decile	Natives	Foreign-born	1985-90	1980-84	Before 1980
Immigration States	1	10	17.7	27.5	21.8	13.7
	2	10	14.5	19.4	17.8	12.1
	3	10	12.0	12.4	13.6	11.3
	4	10	10.1	9.1	10.5	10.3
	5	10	9.0	7.0	8.6	9.6
	6	10	8.1	5.8	7.3	9.0
	7	10	7.2	4.7	5.7	8.4
	8	10	7.0	4.4	5.1	8.3
	9	10	6.9	4.3	4.7	8.3
	10	10	7.5	5.5	4.9	9.0
California	1	10	22.7	37.0	27.1	17.0
	2	10	17.8	21.0	21.0	15.6
	3	10	12.1	11.2	12.9	12.1
	4	10	9.3	7.2	9.2	10.0
	5	10	8.0	5.5	7.5	8.9
	6	10	6.6	4.1	5.5	7.7
	7	10	6.1	3.6	4.6	7.4
	8	10	5.8	3.4	4.2	7.2
	9	10	5.5	3.1	4.0	6.8
	10	10	6.0	3.9	4.1	7.2
Los Angeles	1	10	29.5	44.5	35.9	22.4
	2	10	18.0	19.3	19.9	16.9
	3	10	11.7	10.1	11.3	12.4
	4	10	8.4	6.2	8.2	9.2
	5	10	6.9	4.6	6.0	7.9
	6	10	6.0	3.6	4.9	7.1
	7	10	5.1	3.1	3.7	6.3
	8	10	5.1	2.8	3.7	6.3
	9	10	4.6	2.7	3.1	5.7
	10	10	4.7	3.1	3.3	5.9

Notes: The states included are California, Florida, Illinois, New York, New Jersey, and Texas. The foreign-born are assigned to a decile if their wage falls above the cutoff point for the next lower decile and at or below the cutoff point for the next higher decile. Cutoff points are defined to put 10 percent of wages of the native-born in each decile (within the given area), so the percentage in the native column is 10 by definition. However, since many individuals can have the same wage, applying that assignment rule to natives assigns slightly more or less than 10 percent in some cases.

tives to underlying skill differentials. In particular, a great deal of evidence suggests that much of the wage differential between Hispanics and non-Hispanics is due to differences in observed socioeconomic characteristics, particularly education and English language proficiency. For example, Reimers (1983) found that differences in observed socioeconomic characteristics accounted for 27 of a 34 percentage point wage difference between white non-Hispanic men and men of Mexican ancestry. Her results indicated that, for men of Cuban ancestry, adjusting for observable differences more than accounted for the entire wage differential, whereas for "other Hispanic" men, observable characteristics accounted for roughly half of a 23 percent wage differential. McManus et al. (1983) found that there was no statistically significant difference in wages between non-Hispanic white men and Hispanic men who were proficient in English, once adjustments were made for other differences in socioeconomic characteristics. Similarly, Smith (1997) found that, after controlling for differences in education, geographic location, language, and time since immigration, there was little remaining wage difference between Hispanics and native-born whites. The evidence, therefore, is not consistent with the hypothesis that widespread labor market discrimination results in substantially reduced wages for immigrant Hispanic and Asian groups.

Our conclusion about the relatively minor role that discrimination plays in aggregate labor market outcomes of immigrants should not be misunderstood. In particular, it is not meant to deny that immigrants in their daily lives encounter many instances of verbal and nonverbal abuse. Such abuse occurs with far too great frequency, and it stings. The import of our conclusion is that discriminatory actions of this kind do not lead to a significant wage penalty in the labor market.

To sum up, most immigrants who come to the United States enjoy substantial economic benefits, in that wages are considerably higher here than in their home countries. There is a great deal of diversity among immigrants in their incomes in the United States. For both male and female immigrants, the lowest wages are received by recent immigrants and by immigrants from Mexico, Central America, and South America. The size of the wage gap between recent immigrants and natives has widened substantially in recent years. Finally, there appears to be little evidence of substantial wage discrimination against immigrants.

TRENDS IN IMMIGRANT SKILLS

We have argued in this volume that the skill composition of immigrants helps determine the distributional impact of immigration on the employment opportunities of native-born workers. In Chapters 6 and 7, we argue that it also helps determine expenditures in social insurance programs. Trends in the skills of immigrants relative to those of the native-born are important because they help us answer another critical question: How successful are immigrants in assimilating economically into the U.S. labor market? This issue is dealt with in the section on economic assimilation below.

Are there intrinsic differences in relative productivity across immigrant cohorts? If so, why? Such cohort effects can arise from changes in immigration policy; one consequence of the major changes in policy embodied in the Immigration and Nationality Act Amendments of 1965, for example, may have been to deemphasize the role of skills in allocating entry visas. Later immigrants may thus have been less skilled relative to the native-born than those who came earlier.

Cohort effects may also stem from changes in economic or political conditions in the source countries and in the United States. Even if the United States had not adopted the 1965 amendments, the improvements in economic conditions in Western Europe would have reduced the number of immigrants from these historical source countries. If skill levels vary across countries or if skills from different countries are not equally transferable to the United States, then the changing mix in national origins of the immigrant flow generates cohort effects.[7]

To determine whether such cohort effects indeed exist, it is instructive to summarize the key trends in some measures of skills over the past three decades.[8] Table 5.5 reports both the distribution of educational attainment as well as the percentage wage differential between immigrant and native workers over this period; it presents data on men and women separately.

While comparing the skills and wages of immigrants with those of the native-born, it is important not to lose of sight of trends in the absolute skill levels of newly arriving immigrants. Table 5.5 shows, for example, that the education levels of new immigrant cohorts (men or women) have been rising over time. If education is a proxy for skill, the labor market skills that immigrants bring with them thus have been improving over time—but so have the skills of native-born Americans. The question, then, is whether the secular rate of improvement in immigrant skills has kept up with that of the native-born.

Education may be the central credential an immigrant carries when he or she arrives in the United States. Many immigrants come with impressive schooling. In fact, a larger proportion of recent new immigrants have at least a bachelor's

[7]Cohort effects are also observed when there is nonrandom return migration. If low-wage immigrant workers return to their source countries, the survivors from the earlier waves will tend to have relatively higher earnings than more recent waves. This issue is dealt with in the section on emigration below.

[8]The statistics presented in this chapter are typically obtained from calculations that use the Public Use Samples of the U.S. decennial census. For the most part, native and immigrant wages are calculated in the subsample of civilian workers who are between the ages of 25 and 64, and who are not self-employed. It is common to restrict the analysis of wage data to salaried workers because the income of self-employed workers reflects both a return to the workers' human capital as well as a return to the physical capital invested in the firm. The census does not provide any information on these separate components of a worker's income.

TABLE 5.5 Socioeconomic Characteristics of Immigrants and Natives in the United States, 1970-1990

Group/Variable	1970	1980	1990
MEN			
Natives			
Mean educational attainment (in years)	11.4	12.7	13.2
% less than high school diploma	40.2	22.7	14.4
% college graduate	15.0	22.9	26.3
All immigrants			
Mean educational attainment (in years)	10.7	11.6	11.6
% less than high school diploma	48.9	37.7	37.1
% college graduate	18.2	25.0	26.2
Percent wage differential between immigrants and natives	–0.7	–9.5	–16.0
Recent immigrants (less than 5 years in U.S.)			
Mean educational attainment (in years)	11.1	11.7	11.8
% less than high school diploma	46.0	37.5	36.2
% college graduate	27.7	29.6	30.5
Percent wage differential between immigrants and natives	–17.0	–27.4	–32.4
WOMEN			
Natives			
Mean educational attainment (in years)	11.1	12.1	12.8
% less than high school diploma	40.7	26.0	16.7
% college graduate	9.0	14.3	20.4
All immigrants			
Mean educational attainment (in years)	9.9	10.9	11.2
% less than high school diploma	52.1	39.4	37.4
% college graduate	7.9	14.6	19.3
Percent wage differential between immigrants and natives	1.8	–2.5	–5.3
Recent immigrants (less than 5 years in U.S.)			
Mean educational attainment (in years)	9.8	10.6	11.2
% less than high school diploma	52.8	42.2	37.4
% college graduate	13.0	19.3	24.1
Percent wage differential between immigrants and natives	–11.5	–15.0	–22.0

Source: Tabulations from 1970, 1980, and 1990 Public Use Samples of U.S. Census of Population. Educational attainment for men and relative wages for both men and women are calculated in the sample of those aged 25-64 years who did not reside in group quarters, who were not self-employed, and who were employed in the civilian sector. Educational attainment for women is based on the sample of women aged 25-64 years who did not reside in group quarters.

degree than is true of the U.S. population as a whole; 10 percent have advanced degrees, compared with 7 percent of the U.S. population.[9] At the same time, most recent immigrants have much lower levels of schooling than do other residents of the United States. More than 1 in 4 have only an eighth-grade education

[9]This may be due in part to the existence of immigration admissions criteria that make it easier to gain entry if one has a bachelor's or an advanced degree.

or less, compared with only 1 in 10 in the U.S. population. One in eight new immigrants has only four years of schooling or less.

In 1970, almost half (48.9 percent) of male immigrants enumerated by the census were high school dropouts, and only 18.2 percent were college graduates. On average, immigrant men had 10.7 years of schooling. In contrast, a somewhat smaller fraction of native-born men were either high school dropouts (40.2 percent) or college graduates (15.0 percent). The typical native male worker had 11.4 years of schooling in 1970. The 1970 distribution of educational attainment in the male immigrant population compared favorably with that of native male workers: the typical immigrant was slightly more likely to be a high school dropout, but also more likely to be a college graduate. Given their similar skill levels in 1970, it is not surprising that the wage rate of the typical male immigrant was only 0.7 percent *lower* than the wage rate of the typical male native worker.[10]

This situation changed dramatically by 1990. By that year, 37.1 percent of male immigrants were high school dropouts, as compared with only 14.4 percent among native men. Male immigrants were now more than twice as likely as the native-born not to have completed a high school education. Similarly, about 26 percent of *both* male immigrants and male natives were college graduates. On average, the typical male immigrant had 11.6 years of schooling compared with 13.2 years for natives, an education gap of 1.6 years. Partly as a result of the widening education gap between immigrants and natives, the typical male immigrant earned 16.0 percent less than male natives in 1990.

Part of this decline in the relative economic status of immigrants can be attributed to cohort effects. The best way of tracking the changing character of new immigrants over time is to examine only the attributes of recent immigrant arrivals. Table 5.5 accomplishes this by isolating the latest immigrant wave enumerated in each of the censuses—namely, those who have been in the United States less than five years. In the 1970 census, the most recent immigrant wave refers to those who arrived between 1965 and 1969; in the 1980 census, it refers to the 1975-79 arrivals; and in the 1990 census, it refers to the 1985-89 arrivals.

As the table shows, the educational distribution of the most recent male arrivals enumerated in 1970 was more skewed toward the higher skill levels than that of native men. About two-fifths of both male natives and recent male immigrants were high school dropouts, but 27.7 percent of male immigrants were college graduates, almost double the college graduation rate of the native workers.

By 1990, however, the relative educational attainment of the most recent male immigrants had declined substantially. In particular, they were now about twice as likely as the native-born to be high school dropouts, and they had roughly

---

[10]Actually, the census reports the wage in the calendar year prior to the survey, so that the wage differentials are measured as of 1969. To prevent any confusion about the timing of the variables, we always refer to the data in terms of the census year.

the same rate of college graduates. Partly as a result of the widening gap in educational attainment, the relative wage of the most recent male arrivals dropped from –17.0 percent in 1970 to –32.4 percent in 1990.

The patterns of schooling for immigrant and native women are similar in many ways to those for men. Relative to the education of native women, education levels among immigrant women have also fallen over time. Although the fraction of immigrant women who have less than a high school education shrank, the decline was not nearly so large as that for native women. Among immigrant women, that fraction fell from 52.1 percent in 1970 to 37.4 percent in 1990, and for native women it dropped from 40.7 to 16.7 percent over that same period. Immigrant women remain far more likely than native women to have very low levels of education.

At the same time, the proportion of immigrant women who have a college degree has improved, and, on this dimension, immigrant women have essentially kept pace with native women. Twenty-seven years ago, immigrant women were slightly less likely to be college graduates than were native women, a difference that has remained relatively constant since.

As was the case for men, secular trends are more apparent if we examine data only for recent immigrants. The decline in the relative position of immigrant women appears actually to have accelerated during the 1980s. Relative to their respective populations, the fraction of high school dropouts among recent immigrant women was about 16 percentage points higher than that among native-born women in 1980. By 1990, that difference had expanded to 21 percentage points.

In addition to these gaps in years of schooling, many immigrants experience a competitive disadvantage because the quality of their limited schooling was also poor. Because of the poverty of the countries from which they came, their schools were often characterized by limited instructional resources.

In light of this growing gap in immigrant-native differences in schooling, it is not surprising that relative wages follow a similar path. Among recent immigrants, for example, the wages of female immigrants trailed those of native-born women by 11.5 percent in 1970; this wage deficit had grown to 22.0 percent by 1990.

In sum, there is considerable evidence that the skills (as measured by schooling) of new waves of immigrant men and women have improved over the last few decades. At the same time, they have been declining relative to those of native-born Americans. This decline appears across a number of measures, including education levels and wages.

DIFFERENTIALS ACROSS NATIONAL ORIGINS AND THE DECLINE IN IMMIGRANT SKILLS

Why have the labor market skills of immigrants declined relative to the native-born? One possible reason is the changing mix of countries of origin. To explore this possibility, Tables 5.6 and 5.7 illustrate the huge differences in educational attainment and earnings across national origin groups in 1990, for men and women, respectively.

The variation in schooling levels across these sending counties is enormous for both men and women. Mean years of schooling among men range from 8 years for immigrants from Mexico or Portugal, to about 15 years for immigrants from such diverse countries as Austria, India, Japan, and the United Kingdom. Similarly, male immigrants from El Salvador or Mexico earn 36 to 37 percent less than natives, while male immigrants from Australia or South Africa earn 34 to 44 percent more than natives.

The patterns for women are similar: countries with high levels of education and relative wages for immigrant men also have high levels of education and relative wages for immigrant women. However, the dispersion in both measures tends to be somewhat smaller among immigrant women. Male and female immigrants from Taiwan, for example, have the highest average level of education among immigrants—16.4 years for men and 14.9 for women. However, at the other end of the distribution, Mexican immigrants have among the lowest average levels of education among both men and women immigrants, but the levels for women—8.3 years—are not as low as those for men—7.7 years.[11]

In view of these sizable earnings differentials across national origin groups, the changes in the source countries may explain part of the decline in immigrants' relative earnings. To see whether it does, immigrant flows are separated into five regions: Europe or Canada, Mexico, other Latin America, Asia, and other countries. Table 5.8 gives the fraction of the immigrant flow that originates in each of these regions, as well as the relative wage of immigrants from each region in the 1990 census (that is, the percentage differential in wages between each group of immigrants and natives). The average relative wage of immigrants in 1990 can be defined by:

$$\overline{w} = \sum p_i w_i , \qquad (1)$$

where p_i gives the fraction of the immigrant flow that originates in region i as of 1990, and w_i gives the relative wage of immigrants originating in that region.

Consider the following counterfactual exercise: What would be the average wage of immigrants in 1990 if the national origin composition of the immigrant flow had not changed between 1970 and 1990? Table 5.8 also reports the na-

[11]These differences cannot be attributed to the fact that some national origin groups have lived in the United States for longer periods. There is substantial dispersion in both educational attainment and relative wages even among male and female immigrants who have been in the country more than 10 years.

TABLE 5.6 Educational Attainment and Wages of Immigrant Men in 1990, by National Origin Group

	Educational Attainment (years)		Percentage Wage Differential Between Immigrants and Natives	
Country of Birth	All Immigrants	Pre-1980 Arrivals	All Immigrants	Pre-1980 Arrivals
Europe				
Austria	14.5	14.3	37.5	38.2
Czechoslovakia	14.5	14.6	27.1	37.6
France	14.8	14.0	28.1	27.7
Germany	13.9	13.7	22.8	22.1
Greece	11.8	11.6	2.5	5.4
Hungary	13.6	13.4	26.5	29.6
Italy	11.0	10.8	17.8	18.3
Poland	12.7	12.3	3.3	20.5
Portugal	8.3	8.4	–1.8	–0.1
U.S.S.R.	14.2	14.1	29.9	26.6
United Kingdom	14.6	14.3	37.3	37.1
Yugoslavia	11.7	11.4	15.2	21.1
Asia				
Cambodia	10.2	11.5	–28.5	–16.6
China	12.8	13.2	–18.3	0.4
India	15.9	16.6	17.6	51.6
Iran	15.5	15.9	9.9	19.1
Japan	15.1	14.7	54.2	23.2
Korea	14.2	14.8	–7.5	12.0
Laos	10.0	10.5	–29.5	–24.6
Lebanon	14.2	14.0	–1.3	9.7
Philippines	14.1	14.1	–5.1	8.5
Taiwan	16.4	17.2	19.5	48.5
Vietnam	12.3	13.3	–16.4	–2.2
North and South America				
Argentina	13.3	13.1	6.4	16.4
Canada	13.8	13.6	25.7	25.4
Colombia	12.0	12.3	–15.6	–3.5
Cuba	11.7	12.3	–13.7	–5.0
Dominican Republic	10.2	10.5	–20.8	–15.6
Ecuador	11.5	11.9	–17.7	–7.2
El Salvador	8.6	9.6	–35.8	–25.2
Guatemala	9.2	10.3	–34.6	–21.6
Haiti	11.3	12.3	–25.2	–7.8
Jamaica	12.0	12.4	–6.7	0.4
Mexico	7.7	7.6	–37.2	–30.8
Nicaragua	11.6	12.2	–31.3	–10.8
Panama	13.4	13.5	6.0	14.9
Peru	12.9	13.1	–18.4	3.7

continued on next page

TABLE 5.6 Continued

Country of Birth	Educational Attainment (years) All Immigrants	Pre-1980 Arrivals	Percentage Wage Differential Between Immigrants and Natives All Immigrants	Pre-1980 Arrivals
Africa				
Egypt	15.5	15.6	15.3	41.1
Ethiopia	13.7	15.4	–14.0	7.7
Nigeria	15.8	16.5	–17.1	–4.4
South Africa	15.8	15.8	44.4	55.2
Australia	15.2	15.0	34.5	26.1

Source: Tabulations from the 1990 Public Use Sample of the U.S. Census of Population. The statistics are calculated in the subsample of men aged 25-64 years who work in the civilian sector, who are not self-employed, and who do not reside in group quarters. The educational attainment of native men in 1990 is 13.2 years.

tional origin composition of the immigrant flow in 1970, which we denote by q_i for region *i*. The predicted 1990 wage of immigrants had there been no change in national origin between 1970 and 1990 is given by:

$$\overline{w} = \sum q_i w_i , \qquad (2)$$

and these numbers are given in the last rows of Table 5.8.[12]

The average wage of male immigrants in 1990, therefore, would have been 0.2 percent lower than that of natives had there been no change in national origin; the actual wage was 17.2 percent smaller. Since the wage of immigrants in 1970 was 1 percent lower, the relative standing of immigrants would not have changed had the national-origin mix not changed.

The picture is similar for immigrant women. The majority who worked in 1970 were from Europe or Canada, source countries with high levels of education and wages. By 1990, those countries accounted for only about one-quarter of the immigrant women in the labor force, and Asia, Latin America, and the Caribbean had greatly increased their shares. Of the decline of about 7 percent in relative

[12]This sort of calculation is known as direct standardization in demography and biostatistics. Direct standardization is often used, for example, in fertility and mortality analysis to apply weights from a standard age distribution to a set of age-specific vital rates, yielding age-standardized birth or death rates.

TABLE 5.7 Educational Attainment and Wages of Immigrant Women in 1990, by National Origin Group

	Educational Attainment (years)		Percentage Wage Differential Between Immigrants and Natives	
Country of Birth	All Immigrants	Pre-1980 Arrivals	All Immigrants	Pre-1980 Arrivals
Europe				
Austria	13.5	13.5	17.4	17.1
Czechoslovakia	13.6	13.4	12.0	16.0
France	14.0	13.6	13.7	11.9
Germany	13.0	12.9	–0.3	–0.5
Greece	11.3	11.1	–1.1	–0.3
Hungary	13.3	13.2	17.7	20.9
Italy	10.5	10.3	2.6	1.5
Poland	12.3	12.0	–1.4	5.3
Portugal	8.3	8.4	–8.5	–6.1
U.S.S.R.	14.1	14.0	28.6	23.8
United Kingdom	13.3	13.2	7.9	7.5
Yugoslavia	11.1	10.9	6.0	7.3
Asia				
Cambodia	8.8	10.0	–17.0	–12.0
China	11.7	12.1	–10.7	2.1
India	14.9	15.1	20.1	37.5
Iran	14.7	15.0	16.7	27.3
Japan	13.0	12.7	3.7	–0.6
Korea	12.6	12.8	2.2	10.0
Laos	8.2	8.4	–19.6	–16.2
Lebanon	13.2	12.8	17.6	13.3
Philippines	14.2	14.2	17.4	28.8
Taiwan	14.9	14.9	25.2	31.6
Vietnam	11.5	12.1	–1.8	1.0
North and South America				
Argentina	13.2	13.2	11.3	17.7
Canada	13.5	13.4	16.3	14.9
Colombia	11.8	11.9	–7.0	–0.0
Cuba	12.1	12.4	–4.1	1.8
Dominican Republic	10.0	10.4	–11.1	–2.4
Ecuador	11.7	11.8	–7.2	–4.8
El Salvador	8.6	9.4	–24.8	–16.4
Guatemala	9.0	9.9	–28.0	–15.9
Haiti	11.1	12.3	–6.0	11.8
Jamaica	12.5	12.8	14.5	23.8
Mexico	8.3	8.5	–25.3	–22.4
Nicaragua	11.2	11.7	–20.8	–3.7
Panama	13.0	13.1	13.8	18.0
Peru	12.7	12.7	–1.8	8.6

continued on next page

TABLE 5.7 Continued

Country of Birth	Educational Attainment (years)		Percentage Wage Differential Between Immigrants and Natives	
	All Immigrants	Pre-1980 Arrivals	All Immigrants	Pre-1980 Arrivals
Africa				
Egypt	14.9	14.9	29.4	38.1
Ethiopia	13.4	14.3	4.7	12.2
Nigeria	15.0	15.3	11.9	29.1
South Africa	14.5	14.2	13.8	15.1
Australia	14.1	14.1	29.1	27.1

Source: Tabulations from the 1990 Public Use Sample of the U.S. Census of Population. The statistics are calculated in the subsample of women aged 25-64 years who work in the civilian sector, who are not self-employed, and who do not reside in group quarters. The educational attainment of native women in 1990 was 13.2 years.

wages of immigrant women over that period, the shift across regions in country of origin accounted for three-quarters.

This simple exercise points to a striking result: **the relative decline in the economic status of both male and female immigrants can be attributed essentially to a single factor—the changing national-origin mix of the immigrant flow. If that mix had not changed in the past few decades, we would not have seen much change in the relative wage of immigrants.**[13]

WHO ARE THE IMMIGRANTS?

One limitation of using conventional surveys to track changes in the status of immigrants over time is that the foreign-born population included in these surveys is not made up exclusively of legal immigrants. Though they are not permitted to live or work in this country, as many as 50 percent of illegal immigrants participate in surveys such as the census, according to current demographic estimates. Moreover, many nonimmigrants—for example, students and temporary workers—are included because they are residents of the United States at the time of the survey.

[13]This exercise uses a very rough measure of national origin, the continent of arrival. Nevertheless, both Borjas (1992) and LaLonde and Topel (1992) show that the same result was obtained when the analysis considered a more detailed breakdown in terms of actual country of origin. The exercise does not take into account general equilibrium changes in relative wages that might have resulted from the shift in the national origins of immigrants.

TABLE 5.8 Link Between Changes in National Origin Composition and Relative Skills of Immigrants

Region of Birth	Percentage of Immigrant Men Originating in Region		Relative Wage of Immigrant Men in 1990	Percentage of Working Immigrant Women Originating in Region		Relative Wage of Immigrant Women in 1990
	1970	1990		1970	1990	
Asia	10.8	25.3	–.045	9.1	27.9	.045
Europe and Canada	60.8	20.5	.166	63.1	25.4	.053
Mexico	10.0	24.9	–.512	5.9	14.8	–.370
Other America	13.8	22.2	–.254	16.5	25.9	–.103
Other	4.6	7.1	–.179	5.3	6.1	–.021
All regions			–.172			–.055
All regions, adjusted			.002			–.002

Source: Tabulations from the 1970 and 1990 Public Use Samples of the U.S. Census of Population. The statistics are calculated in the subsamples of men and women aged 25-64 years who work in the civilian sector, who are not self-employed, and who do not reside in group quarters. The relative wage of immigrants in 1990 refers to the log point differential between the immigrant group and native men.

Because the census and household surveys do not distinguish among legal immigrants, illegal immigrants, and nonimmigrants, the three groups are commingled in the tables in this chapter. In consequence, the trends the tables reveal obviously do not represent legal immigrants alone, desirable as that would be. Even though legal immigrants account for most of the foreign-born surveyed, we have no way of knowing whether, for example, the decline in the skills of the foreign-born was due entirely to illegal immigrants—because their education was declining over time or because they accounted for an increasing fraction of the foreign-born in the survey.

Nor do the available data shed light on the influence on these trends exerted by the mix of immigrants that is determined by the preference categories under which they were admitted. So we do not know whether changes in immigration policy in favor of, say, the better educated or the more highly skilled would alter these trends.

We can gain some insight on these issues from data the Immigration and Naturalization Service (INS) collects in giving "green cards" to those newly becoming permanent residents. Among other things, the demographic data include age, sex, and marital status, and the economic data include the occupation reported by the immigrant.[14] These data are collected on a monthly basis, so that they are ideal for tracking trends across new immigrant cohorts.

Although income is not reported in the INS data, occupation, a key correlate of income, is a measure of an immigrant's economic status. It would be difficult to gauge the overall trend in economic status by directly examining changes in the fraction of immigrants in each of the 25 INS occupational categories. Instead, we use a summary measure created by taking average earnings of U.S. men in each occupation and then assigning such a value to each immigrant based on the occupation they reported—a value we will term "occupational earnings."[15] Table 5.9 presents these numbers for six broad occupation categories, along with the distribution of new permanent residents across these categories for three entry cohorts—1977, 1982, and 1994.[16]

Average occupational earnings appear below the figures giving the occupa-

[14]Reported occupation may or may not correspond to an immigrant's occupation once employed in the United States. For employment-preference immigrants, who generally enter with arrangements for employment, there is likely to be a close correspondence between reported and actual occupation. Immigrants admitted as refugees or on the basis of family ties may not know what sort of employment they will have once they are settled in the United States, in which case reported occupation may correspond to their occupation in their country of origin or to expected occupation in the United States.

[15]In particular, we use the average annual earnings of full-time, full-year male workers in an occupation, based on census data from 1980 for those aged 21 to 65 years.

[16]The figures for fiscal year 1994 exclude both aliens legalized under provisions of the Immigration Reform and Control Act and legalization dependents who became permanent residents in that year.

TABLE 5.9 Occupation, Immigrants Aged 21-65 Years at Admission to Permanent Residence: Fiscal Year 1977, 1982, and 1994 Cohorts

		FY 1977 Cohort		FY 1982 Cohort		FY 1994 Cohort	
Summary Occupation Group	Average Income	Men	Women	Men	Women	Men	Women
Managerial and professional specialty occupations	$31,199	33.3	30.1	30.3	27.9	32.2	33.2
Technical, sales, and administrative support occupations	$18,882	11.8	22.9	12.4	24.4	12.1	21.0
Service occupations	$13,751	9.1	19.8	10.3	21.8	14.5	21.7
Farming, forestry, and fishing occupations	$13,301	4.9	0.9	6.2	4.1	4.4	3.2
Precision production, craft, and repair occupations	$18,254	16.4	1.9	17.7	9.9	11.1	14.9
Operators, fabricators, and laborers	$15,599	24.5	24.4	23.1	11.8	25.7	14.9
Percentage reporting occupation		86.6	40.7	77.9	44.1	69.9	38.5
Average occupational earnings, 1979 dollars		$21,267	$18,888	$20,010	$18,609	$19,648	$18,767
Number aged 21-65 years		130,011	152,654	173,185	173,201	216,306	266,130

Note: Figures for fiscal year 1994 exclude both aliens legalized by provisions of the Immigration Reform and Control Act and legalization dependents.

Source: Immigration and Naturalization Service Public Use Files.

tional distribution. For each year, these are based on the same set of occupational earnings from the 1980 census, so changes in the average value over time occur only through shifts in the distribution of immigrants across occupations. Thus, a decrease in the fraction of new immigrants in the relatively highly paid managerial and professional specialty occupations will lead to a fall in average occupational earnings.

Among male immigrants, average occupational earnings fell 7.6 percent between 1977 and 1994. Using the same methodology, incomes of native-born men rose 1.5 percent. Therefore, the same general trend of declining relative quality of immigrant cohorts is found using legal immigrants only. Similarly, among immigrant women, occupational income declined 0.6 percent between 1977 and 1994, and that of native women rose 4.1 percent. These trends are broadly consistent with the earlier evidence on trends among recent immigrants in conventional household surveys. The occupational earnings of immigrant men declined 9.1 percent relative to those of natives, and immigrant women experienced about a 5 percent relative decrease.

This analysis can be taken a step further by examining how average occupational earnings vary depending on the visa class of admission to permanent residence (see Table 5.10). New immigrants admitted under employment-preference visas have substantially greater earnings than those in other categories. Male employment principals had the highest occupational earnings, followed by their wives, women admitted as employment principals, and the spouses of those women. At the other end of the spectrum, refugees or asylees and their spouses have the lowest occupational earnings, and the various family-preference immigrants fall between these extremes.

The other columns in the table list changes in average occupational earnings relative to their 1977 level, first for 1982 and then for 1994. For both men and women, the most substantial changes are declines in earnings among employment principals and their spouses. These decreases occurred between 1977 and 1982, with some recovery (particularly among women) by 1994. A closer look at the change in occupational distributions reveals that the change in occupational earnings was driven largely by a dramatic fall in the number of physicians being admitted. This decline was driven by changes in U.S. immigration policy that made it much more difficult for physicians to enter as employment principals. The other substantial decline in occupational earnings was among male refugees and asylees, suggesting that the composition of refugees was shifting toward those whose occupational prospects were not so good.

Occupational earnings also differ substantially across country of origin, a pattern illustrated in Table 5.11. Immigrants from Mexico have the lowest average incomes, and those from Vietnam and the Dominican Republic have only modestly higher averages. In contrast, immigrants from India have the highest average incomes. There were very large declines in the occupational earnings of immigrants from some areas over this period—namely Vietnam, India, and Af-

TABLE 5.10 Occupational Earnings Among Immigrants Aged 21-65 Years at Admission to Permanent Residence, by Visa Class and Fiscal Year of Admission, Fiscal Year 1977, 1982, and 1994 Cohorts

	Men			Women		
Visa Class	Occupational Earnings for 1977 cohort	% Change in Occ. Earnings, 1977 to 1982 cohorts	% Change in Occ. Earnings, 1977 to 1994 cohorts	Occupational Earnings for 1977 cohort	% Change in Occ. Earnings, 1977 to 1982 cohorts	% Change in Occ. Earnings, 1977 to 1994 cohorts
Spouse of U.S. citizen	$19,314	–2.0	–2.9	$18,859	0.1	0.6
Parent of (adult) U.S. citizen	19,783	1.4	–3.4	17,078	7.8	2.9
Employment principal	33,126	–21.7	–19.9	25,278	–25.5	–15.2
Spouse of employment principal	24,570	–6.4	–8.3	26,304	–14.8	–11.3
Sibling principal	20,818	0.5	–4.2	18,794	0.2	0.0
Spouse of sibling principal	20,709	4.6	–1.9	19,543	–0.5	–1.6
Refugee/asylee principal	18,478	–3.5	–8.6	17,091	2.4	–3.1
Spouse of refugee/asylee principal	17,708	–0.6	0.4	16,605	5.1	0.4
All immigrants		–3.7	–5.1		–0.6	–0.5

Note: Percentage changes are based on differences in the logarithm of occupational earnings, which are then converted to percent changes using 100(exp(d)–1), where *d* = difference in logs.

Source: Immigration and Naturalization Service Public Use Files.

TABLE 5.11 Cohort Percent Change in Occupational Earnings Among Immigrants Aged 21-65 Years at Admission, Relative to the Fiscal Year 1977 Cohort, by Region and Selected Countries of Birth

Region/ Country of Birth	Men 1977 Levels	Men FY 1994	Women 1977 Levels	Women FY 1994
North/Central America	$17,970	–5.0	$16,851	0.0
Canada	24,925	–5.4	20,274	4.1
Cuba	18,211	–6.6	16,890	3.5
Dominican Republic	17,465	–1.2	17,976	17.7
Haiti	18,744	–0.6	17,281	11.2
Mexico	16,494	–1.3	15,841	–2.8
South America	19,487	–3.2	17,859	5.8
Africa	22,904	–23.1	20,504	–8.9
Asia	22,061	–11.7	20,264	–6.1
China, mainland	20,901	–5.5	19,490	–2.3
Hong Kong	22,946	3.2	20,529	12.0
India	27,384	–21.5	27,206	–18.2
Japan	21,428	11.7	19,316	1.9
Korea	21,273	–1.9	19,571	–5.8
Philippines	21,962	–8.5	20,212	–2.9
Taiwan	25,619	0.5	22,235	1.9
Vietnam	17,122	–27.6	16,829	–15.5
Europe	20,388	2.0	19,203	0.2
Ireland	20,246	8.6	19,061	0.1
Italy	19,098	10.2	18,746	21.0
Poland	18,848	0.2	18,677	4.8
Oceania	21,700	0.6	18,942	–2.0
All immigrants	21,267	–5.1	18,888	–0.5

rica, the last two being the earlier source of many physicians, whose entry was restricted during this period. The fall in occupational earnings among the Vietnamese reflects the changing composition of Vietnamese refugees.

To sum up, the decline in the relative skills of the foreign-born over the last few decades is not due exclusively to illegal immigrants or nonimmigrants. The data suggest that the relative skills of legal immigrants have also been falling over this period. In part, this decline reflects more severe limitations on entry placed on certain highly skilled immigrants (physicians) and the changing country of origin of refugees and other legal immigrants.

ECONOMIC ASSIMILATION

To what extent do immigrants make up some of their initial wage deficits as they continue their lives and careers in the United States? Some of the economic

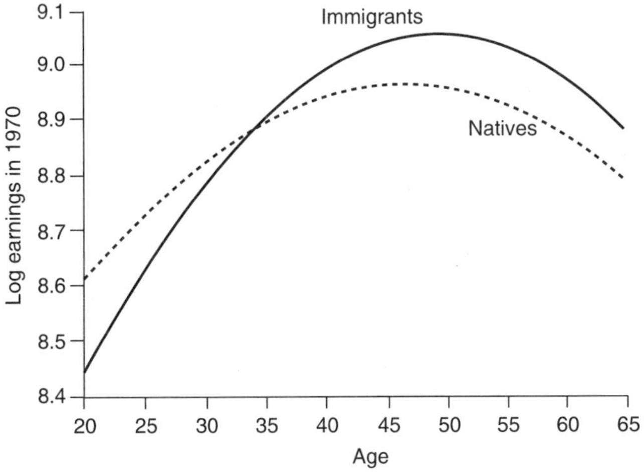

FIGURE 5.1 Cross-sectional age-earnings profiles of immigrants and natives in the United States, 1970.

consequences of the gap between wages of the native-born and of immigrants when they first arrive in this country could be ameliorated if the gap narrowed over time, as immigrants accumulate job experience in the U.S. labor market—in a process of economic assimilation. To learn whether immigrants indeed assimilate economically, we must follow individual immigrants or groups of immigrants over their careers and compare their outcomes with those of comparable native-born workers as their careers progress. Early research (Chiswick, 1978; Carliner, 1980) on this issue instead simply compared the earnings of immigrants and native workers of different ages at a point in time using a single *cross-sectional* data set.

The essential nature of the cross-sectional evidence is summarized in Figure 5.1, which illustrates the predicted age-earnings profiles of immigrants and natives implied by the 1970 census. At the time of arrival, immigrants earn about 17 percent less than natives. Because immigrants experience faster wage growth, their earnings appear to overtake native earnings within 15 years of arrival. After 30 years in the United States, the typical immigrant earns about 11 percent more than a comparable native worker.

These cross-sectional data lend support to a very optimistic view of rapid economic progress (or assimilation) of immigrants within their own generation. In this view, at the time of arrival, immigrants earn less than natives because they lack many of the skills that the U.S. labor market rewards (such as English proficiency). As these skills are acquired, the human capital of immigrants grows relative to that of natives, and immigrants experience faster wage growth than natives.[17]

The basic problem with the optimistic interpretation of the cross-sectional data is that it draws inferences about how earnings of different cohorts of immigrant workers evolve over time from a single snapshot of the immigrant population (Borjas, 1985). But we already know that newly arrived immigrants are inherently different from those who migrated 20 years ago. If so, the situation of an immigrant worker who is 40 years old in 1990 cannot be used to predict the economic situation 20 years hence of an immigrant worker who is 20 years old in 1990. Because the relative labor market quality of newly arriving immigrant cohorts has been declining, a cross-sectional comparison of immigrants by age will tend to paint far too optimistic a rate at which immigrants will be able to assimilate.

Table 5.12 follows wage growth of specific cohorts of male immigrants and male natives across U.S. censuses.[18] To illustrate the way to read these tables, consider those immigrants who arrived when they were between 25 and 34 years old in the late 1960s. These immigrants are first compared with natives in the same age groups in 1970. Then 10 years later, the wages of this same immigrant cohort are compared with those of natives who are now 10 years older (35 to 44 in 1980), and 20 years later to natives aged 45 to 54 years in 1990. A similar comparison for women is presented in Table 5.13. These data are stratified by schooling levels in the appendix to this chapter.

Let us start with male immigrants who arrived between 1965 and 1969 and who were relatively young at the time of arrival (that is, aged 25 to 34 years at the time of the 1970 census). These immigrants earned 11.2 percent less than native men in 1970, but only 3.1 percent less by 1990. Over a 20-year period, therefore, the wage of this immigrant cohort relative to that of native men increased by 8 percentage points. Once schooling levels are controlled, wage convergence is almost total for this immigrant cohort (see Appendix A: Table 5.A1).

A similar pattern of wage growth is experienced by other male immigrant cohorts who arrived at younger ages. For instance, examine the immigrant cohort that entered the United States between 1975 and 1979 and who were around age 30 at the time of arrival. These immigrants earned 21.8 percent less than natives

---

[17]By itself, even this optimistic view would not explain why immigrants appear eventually to earn more than the native-born. After all, why would immigrants accumulate more human capital than natives? That immigrants not only catch up but eventually overtake natives was instead interpreted in terms of how selective immigrants were to begin with. On the selection argument, immigrants were seen as more able, more highly motivated (Chiswick, 1978: 900), and harder workers than natives (Carliner, 1980: 89). This assumption was often justified by arguing that only the most driven and most able persons have the ambition and wherewithal to pack up, move, and start life anew in a foreign country.

[18]The important caveat to this methodology involves possible emigration from an original cohort. This issue is explored below.

TABLE 5.12 Observed Relative Wage Growth of Specific Cohorts of Immigrant Men (Percentage Wage Differential Between Immigrants and Natives, by Age Group and Year of Arrival)

	Year		
Cohort/Age Group	1970	1980	1990
1960-1964 arrivals			
15-24 in 1970	—	1.1	3.9
25-34 in 1970	3.0	−1.1	0.0
35-44 in 1970	−6.1	−6.8	1.9
45-54 in 1970	−13.5	−11.6	—
1965-1969 arrivals			
15-24 in 1970	—	−5.6	−7.5
25-34 in 1970	−11.2	−6.6	−3.1
35-44 in 1970	−17.3	−15.7	−8.2
45-54 in 1970	−23.7	−21.3	—
1970-1974 arrivals			
25-34 in 1980	—	−12.7	−12.4
35-44 in 1980	—	−18.1	−17.0
45-54 in 1980	—	−26.4	−20.0
1975-1979 arrivals			
25-34 in 1980	—	−21.8	−16.3
35-44 in 1980	—	−24.3	−24.1
45-54 in 1980	—	−29.8	−26.1
1980-1984 arrivals			
25-34 in 1990	—	—	−20.0
35-44 in 1990	—	—	−26.0
45-54 in 1990	—	—	−34.2
1985-1989 arrivals			
25-34 in 1990	—	—	−24.5
35-44 in 1990	—	—	−28.9
45-54 in 1990	—	—	−35.8

— = cohort is outside the 25-64 age range.

Source: Tabulations from the 1970, 1980, and 1990 Public Use Samples of the U.S. Census of Population. The statistics are calculated in the subsample of men aged 25-64 years who work in the civilian sector, who are not self-employed, and who do not reside in group quarters.

in 1980 and 16.3 percent less than natives in 1990. Comparably aged male immigrants who arrived between 1965 and 1969 had a similar experience: they earned 11.2 percent less than natives in 1970 and 6.6 percent less in 1980.

Men who enter the country at older ages tend to face more adverse economic opportunities, both initially and throughout their working lives. Men who arrived in the late 1970s and who were roughly aged 25 to 34 years at the time of arrival

TABLE 5.13 Observed Relative Wage Growth of Specific Cohorts of Immigrant Women (Percentage Wage Differential Between Immigrants and Natives, by Age Group and Year of Arrival)

	Year		
Cohort/Age Group	1970	1980	1990
1960-1964 arrivals			
15-24 in 1970	—	3.8	9.3
25-34 in 1970	2.1	1.6	3.6
35-44 in 1970	0.5	–1.9	2.9
45-54 in 1970	–4.9	–4.6	—
1965-1969 arrivals			
15-24 in 1970	—	0.4	-0.0
25-34 in 1970	–7.5	5.3	4.2
35-44 in 1970	–10.9	–5.2	–1.6
45-54 in 1970	–20.4	–10.3	—
1970-1974 arrivals			
25-34 in 1980	—	–4.8	–2.2
35-44 in 1980	—	–4.2	–1.5
45-54 in 1980	—	–12.2	–9.3
1975-1979 arrivals			
25-34 in 1980	—	–13.7	–5.5
35-44 in 1980	—	–13.8	–11.2
45-54 in 1980	—	–21.6	–12.7
1980-1984 arrivals	—		
25-34 in 1990	—	—	–11.0
35-44 in 1990	—	—	–16.1
45-54 in 1990	—	—	–21.3
1985-1989 arrivals			
25-34 in 1990	—	—	–16.9
35-44 in 1990	—	—	–24.8
45-54 in 1990	—	—	–28.9

— = cohort is outside 25-64 age range.

Source: Tabulations from the 1970, 1980, and 1990 Public Use Samples of the U.S. Census of Population. The statistics are calculated in the subsample of women aged 25-64 years who work in the civilian sector, who are not self-employed, and who do not reside in group quarters.

earned 21.8 percent less than natives at the time of entry; men aged 45 to 54 years who entered the country at the same time earned 29.8 percent less than natives at the time of entry. This gap narrows little, if at all, over their lifetime. These much larger wage disparities among older immigrants, even after we control for time since entry into the United States, suggests that their prior work experience is not valued highly in the U.S. labor market.

Although some patterns appear, especially when we stratify by schooling levels and age, no systematic pattern appears between the size of the initial immigrant wage deficit relative to native-born workers and the rate at which the two converge. The historical pattern suggests that the wage gap between young male immigrants and male natives may narrow by about 10 percentage points during the first two decades after immigration. This rate of convergence may have been sufficient to allow earlier male cohorts to catch up economically with natives. Because of the sizable cohort effects, however, more recent male cohorts are starting out at a much greater disadvantage. Although they may close their wage gap at the same pace that earlier cohorts did, the greater distance they have to travel implies that it will be very difficult, if not impossible, for them to fully close it.[19]

Following a given cohort of immigrant women over time, one finds that the gap in wages between immigrants and natives narrows somewhat. The gap for those entering between 1970 and 1974 narrows by about 3 percentage points for each of the age groups (see Table 5.13). The 1975-1979 cohort starts out with larger wage gaps in 1980, but has larger gains—about 8 percentage points for the 25 to 34 and 45 to 54 age groups, but less than 3 percentage points for the 35 to 44 age group. Like immigrant men, immigrant women make small gains relative to natives over time, but because the wage gap for women is narrower to begin with, immigrant women come closer to catching up to natives than do immigrant men.

During the past few decades, the labor market underwent a number of other structural changes that may have affected the economic prospects of newly arriving immigrants. The most important change was the sharp widening in wage inequality in the labor market over the last two decades; these historic changes did not affect all skill groups equally (Murphy and Welch, 1992). In particular, the wage gap between highly educated and less educated workers widened considerably, as did that between workers with many years of experience and new labor market entrants and that among workers within narrowly defined occupation and industry cells. The simplest summary is that, across many dimensions, those with less skill saw their wages fall significantly relative to those with more skill.

These changes in the wage structure are unlikely to have affected the earnings of immigrant and native workers by the same percentage, since immigrants are relatively less skilled. Because the wages of unskilled labor (including the

---

[19]Duleep and Regets (1992) use decennial census data to estimate correlations between wage growth and entry wages across national origin groups. These correlations tend to be negative, leading them to conclude that the low entry wage of the immigrants who arrived in the late 1980s did not represent their true quality because they would eventually experience faster wage growth than earlier immigrants. The raw data presented in this volume, however, do not support this assertion.

native-born) fell over the last two decades, the relative wage of immigrants would have fallen over time *even if immigrant skills had remained constant.*[20]

It is very unlikely, however, that this changing wage structure can fully account for the downward trend in relative wages across successive immigrant cohorts, or for the slow pace of wage convergence between immigrants and natives. The same general trends appear in educational attainment, a measure of skill that is invariant to changes in the wage structure. Such data clearly show that the relative decline in skills cannot be attributed solely to the changing wage structure of the United States.

The average rates of wage convergence reported for all immigrants hide a great deal of variation across national-origin groups. To show this diversity, Table 5.14 presents a similar tracking of the wage experience of male immigrants separately for Mexican and non-Mexican immigrants.[21] Male Mexican immigrants, who also happen to have some of the lowest initial wage levels, experienced essentially no career wage convergence whatsoever—in fact, they may have experienced a *decline* in their relative wage over time (see also Smith, 1997). In contrast, immigrants (from Europe, China, Korea, and Japan) experienced a great deal of wage convergence over the 1970-1990 period. Within their own work careers, Mexican immigrants have a much more difficult time closing their sizable wage gaps with natives.

The decline in wages of initial entry cohorts appears to characterize non-Mexican as well as Mexican immigrants. Controlling for age and time since immigration, the wage gap for new immigrants has widened substantially over time. For example, Mexican male immigrants 25 to 34 who arrived between 1965 and 1969 had an initial wage gap of 39.8 percent; this gap had broadened to 51.1 percent among men of the same ages who came 10 years later.

In sum, the typical immigrant experienced a modest amount of economic assimilation during his or her time in the United States, but this average hides a great deal of dispersion across national-origin groups. In particular, Mexican immigrants, who have very high initial wage gaps with native-born workers, experience no wage convergence with natives during their time in the United States. In contrast, immigrant groups from Europe and Asia experienced significant wage convergence with native workers.

---

[20]Essentially, this argument claims that period effects influence the wage of immigrants and natives by the same relative amount. Period effects refer to those changes in economic conditions that are associated with calendar time. For example, we may be experiencing a boom in some years and an economic recession in others.

[21]The data for women are included in Appendix A: Table 5.A3. The patterns are quite similar to those obtained for men.

TABLE 5.14 Observed Wage Growth of Specific Cohorts of Immigrant Men from Mexico and from Countries Other Than Mexico

	Year		
Cohort/Age Group	1970	1980	1990
Immigrants from Mexico			
1960-64 arrivals			
15-24 in 1970	—	–11.2	–20.0
25-34 in 1970	–24.0	–26.9	–35.9
35-44 in 1970	–37.6	–35.7	–35.9
45-54 in 1970	–41.9	–41.0	—
1965-69 arrivals			
15-24 in 1970	—	–18.9	–29.2
25-34 in 1970	–39.8	–31.9	–39.5
35-44 in 1970	–52.2	–38.2	–44.7
45-54 in 1970	–49.0	–36.7	—
1970-74 arrivals			
25-34 in 1980	—	–27.0	–35.9
35-44 in 1980	—	–38.7	–47.2
45-54 in 1980	—	–45.8	–47.8
1975-79 arrivals			
15-24 in 1980	—	–40.0	–43.2
25-34 in 1980	—	–51.1	–52.7
35-44 in 1980	—	–53.6	–54.5
1980-84 arrivals			
25-34 in 1990	—	—	–37.4
35-44 in 1990	—	—	–51.1
45-54 in 1990	—	—	–57.3
1985-90 arrivals			
25-34 in 1990	—	—	–44.7
35-44 in 1990	—	—	–55.1
45-54 in 1990	—	—	–62.1
Immigrants from Countries Other Than Mexico			
1960-64 arrivals			
15-24 in 1970	—	5.7	12.0
25-34 in 1970	9.1	7.1	10.0
35-44 in 1970	–0.5	–0.1	9.7
45-54 in 1970	–11.8	–5.7	—
1965-69 arrivals			
15-24 in 1970	—	2.1	4.6
25-34 in 1970	–7.5	0.2	6.5
35-44 in 1970	–14.0	–12.9	–4.1
45-54 in 1970	–20.7	–19.6	—
1970-74 arrivals			
25-34 in 1980	—	–3.5	5.6
35-44 in 1980	—	–11.3	–5.2
45-54 in 1980	—	–22.3	–14.0

continued on next page

TABLE 5.14 Continued

Cohort/Age Group	Year 1970	1980	1990
Immigrants from Countries Other Than Mexico (continued)			
1975-79 arrivals			
15-24 in 1980	—	−15.4	−4.2
25-34 in 1980	—	−17.6	−14.4
35-44 in 1980	—	−24.4	−20.1
1980-84 arrivals			
25-34 in 1990	—	—	−10.1
35-44 in 1990	—	—	−20.5
45-54 in 1990	—	—	−29.5
1985-90 arrivals			
25-34 in 1990	—	—	−15.8
35-44 in 1990	—	—	−22.5
45-54 in 1990	—	—	−29.2

— = cohort is outside 25-64 age range.

Source: Tabulations from the 1970, 1980, and 1990 Public Use Sample of the U.S. Census of Population. The statistics are calculated in the subsample of men aged 25-64 years who work in the civilian sector, who are not self-employed, and who do not reside in group quarters.

EMIGRATION

A significant fraction of immigrants residing in the United States eventually return to their country of origin. The Census Bureau makes population projections by assuming that 30 percent of immigrant flows return to their countries of origin (or migrate elsewhere). The changing composition of immigrant cohorts across censuses suggests that the wage convergence derived by tracking this group over time might be biased if the typical return migrant differs from the typical immigrant who chooses to remain in the United States. If return migrants are disproportionately workers who have lower than average wages, intercensus tracking of immigrant cohorts may indicate an improvement in relative wages, even if none has taken place. Alternatively, the rate of wage convergence would be underestimated if return migrants are the more successful members of the original immigrant cohort.

The United States does not collect information on the number or skill composition of return migrants, so the available data do not permit a systematic study of the potential biases introduced by return migration. Nevertheless, there is a simple way of ascertaining the relative importance of this bias. Let $\overline{w}_o$ be the average (log) wage of a cohort of immigrants at the time of entry (period 0) relative to the wage of natives, and let w_I^s be the average relative (log) wage of the sample of survivors in period 1 (that is, the average wage of those immigrants who chose to remain in the United States relative to the wage of natives in period 1). A fraction *r* of the immigrants will leave the United States between periods 0 and 1; assume that there is no sample attrition in the native population. We can then write the *observed* rate of wage convergence over this period for this particular cohort of immigrants as:

$$w_1^s - \overline{w}_o = w_1^s - [(1-r)w_0^s + rw_0^R] \quad (3)$$

where w_0^S is the average relative entry wage of immigrants who remained in the United States; and w_0^R is the average relative entry wage of the immigrants who returned home. We can rewrite equation 3 as:

$$w_1^s - \overline{w}_o = (w_1^s - w_0^s) + r(w_0^s - w_0^R). \quad (4)$$

Equation 4 shows the relationship between the observed rate of wage growth and the true rate of wage growth ($w_1^S - w_0^S$) experienced by the sample of survivors. Note that the observed rate of wage growth is a biased measure of the true rate as long as the sample of survivors differs from the sample of return migrants (that is, as long as $w_0^S \neq w_0^R$).

No direct empirical evidence tells us about how much the entry wage of immigrants who remain in the United States differs from the entry wage of immigrants who do not. Equation 4 suggests, however, that the observed rate of wage convergence estimated by tracking cohorts across censuses cannot be far off the mark for reasonable parameter values. Suppose subsequent emigration rates are about 30 percent and out-migrants are the successes (they have higher wages than those who remain in the United States).[22] If immigrants who leave earn about 30 percent more than those who stay, equation 4 then indicates that the true rate of wage convergence is about 9 percentage points higher than the observed rate of wage convergence. The data in Table 5.12 suggest, however, that even if we add 9 percentage points to the wage growth experienced by the surviving immigrants, the wage of recent immigrants will remain far below that of native workers.

TRENDS IN EMPLOYMENT

Although most research focuses on wages of immigrants and natives, there are other salient labor market outcomes. One of the most important involves the likelihood of working. Trends in employment propensities for males are documented in Table 5.15, which lists employment rates for male immigrants relative to those of native-born men; Table 5.16 presents parallel evidence for women.

---

[22]If the out-migrants are persons with relatively low wages, then the estimated rate of wage convergence reported in Table 5.12 overestimates the actual rate.

TABLE 5.15 Observed Growth in Relative Employment Rates of Specific Cohorts of Immigrant Men (Difference Between Immigrant Men and Native Men in Percentage of the Population That Is Employed, by Age Group and Year of Arrival)

	Year		
Cohort/Age Group	1970	1980	1990
1960-64 arrivals			
15-24 in 1970	—	0.2	0.4
25-34 in 1970	0.4	1.5	2.4
35-44 in 1970	0.9	3.2	12.0
45-54 in 1970	1.1	13.0	—
1965-69 arrivals			
15-24 in 1970	—	–0.4	–1.4
25-34 in 1970	–5.4	1.0	2.4
35-44 in 1970	2.3	3.1	12.0
45-54 in 1970	–1.6	10.8	—
1970-74 arrivals			
25-34 in 1980	—	–1.1	–0.2
35-44 in 1980	—	0.3	1.4
45-54 in 1980	—	1.6	13.1
1975-79 arrivals			
15-24 in 1980	—	–11.4	0.7
25-34 in 1980	—	–7.8	0.4
35-44 in 1980	—	–7.8	11.8
1980-84 arrivals			
25-34 in 1990	—	—	–1.2
35-44 in 1990	—	—	–2.1
45-54 in 1990	—	—	–2.0
1985-90 arrivals			
25-34 in 1990	—	—	–9.6
35-44 in 1990	—	—	–9.3
45-54 in 1990	—	—	–9.0

— = cohort is outside 25-64 age range.

Source: Tabulations from the 1970, 1980, and 1990 Public Use Samples of the U.S. Census of Population. The statistics are calculated in the subsample of men aged 25-64 years who did not reside in group quarters.

Since these tables have exactly the same format as those that tracked cohort-specific trends in wages, they can be used to examine both changes in employment across immigrant cohorts as well as career trajectories in relative employment rates of immigrants.[23]

[23]As was the case in examining relative wage growth by tracking cohorts over time, selective emigration may explain part of this convergence of employment rates.

TABLE 5.16 Observed Growth in Relative Employment Rates of Specific Cohorts of Immigrant Women (Difference Between Immigrant and Native Women in Percentage of the Population That Is Employed, by Age Group and Year of Arrival)

	Year		
Cohort/Age Group	1970	1980	1990
1960-1964 arrivals			
15-24 in 1970	—	–2.1	–4.1
25-34 in 1970	–3.5	–3.3	–3.7
35-44 in 1970	–0.7	0.9	5.1
45-54 in 1970	5.9	9.3	—
1965-1969 arrivals			
15-24 in 1970	—	–4.4	–6.8
25-34 in 1970	–0.0	–1.3	–1.4
35-44 in 1970	3.8	5.1	6.1
45-54 in 1970	3.3	9.8	—
1970-1974 arrivals			
25-34 in 1980	—	–6.3	–8.2
35-44 in 1980	—	–0.7	–3.9
45-54 in 1980	—	4.1	5.3
1975-1979 arrivals			
25-34 in 1980	—	–13.7	–7.1
35-44 in 1980	—	–12.1	–5.4
45-54 in 1980	—	–10.8	1.6
1980-1984 arrivals			
25-34 in 1990	—	—	–11.1
35-44 in 1990	—	—	–10.7
45-54 in 1990	—	—	–9.1
1985-1989 arrivals			
25-34 in 1990	—	—	–22.3
35-44 in 1990	—	—	–21.4
45-54 in 1990	—	—	–20.5

— = cohort is outside 25-64 age range.

Source: Tabulations from the 1970, 1980, and 1990 Public Use Samples of the U.S. Census of Population. The statistics are calculated in the subsample of women aged 25-64 years who did not reside in group quarters.

Each number in these tables expresses the difference between the percentage of immigrants and natives of the same ages who are employed. For example, men who arrived between 1965 and 1969 and were aged 25 to 34 years in 1970 had an employment rate in 1970 that was 5.4 percentage points lower than that of natives aged 25 to 34. Ten years later, they were 1 percentage point more likely to be employed than were natives of the same ages (now 35 to 44). By the time they were ages 45 to 54 in 1990, this group of immigrants had a 2.4 percentage point higher employment rate than did their native counterparts.

For both men and women, there are two salient trends in these employment rates. First, the employment rates of newly entering immigrant cohorts have been declining relative to those of natives. Second, most of that initial employment deficit seems to disappear the longer the immigrants remain in this country.

Finding employment apparently has been much more difficult for new entrants in recent years. For example, in 1970, men aged 25 to 34 years who had been in the country less than five years had an employment rate 5.4 percentage points lower than that of natives. By 1980, the employment deficit had deepened to 11.4 percentage points, and it was 9.6 percentage points for that age group in the newest entry cohort in 1990.

Even more dramatic cohort trends in relative employment appear for women. In their first five years in the United States, women aged 25 to 34 years had exactly the same employment rate as native-born women in 1970; but, by 1980, a deficit of 13.7 percentage points had opened, and by 1990 it had widened to 22.3 percentage points. The reason was not that immigrant women weren't employed at the same rate; in fact, their employment rate remained essentially the same. It was, rather, the striking expansion in the other part of the comparison, the employment among native-born women: in 1970, barely half of these women worked; by 1990, two-thirds of them did.

Although successive cohorts of new immigrants have ever wider employment deficits against their native counterparts, the gaps consistently narrow the longer immigrants remain in the United States.

For men, the end result has generally been employment rates equal to or above those of natives.[24] The situation for immigrant women is more complicated. The data in Table 5.16 do indicate that their initial employment gap is substantially reduced as their stay lengthens. However, there is not yet enough time in the United States to know whether these large employment gaps for recent immigrant women will ultimately close altogether. For immigrants arriving in the 1970s and 1980s who began with a large deficit, the initial rise has not yet generally brought their employment rates up to those of natives.

What factors explain these large differences in employment rates between immigrant and native women? Shifts in the national origins of new female immigrants can account for approximately one-third of the relative decline in employment between the cohorts who entered before 1970 and those entering in the

[24]Each of the cases in which immigrants show very high employment rates relative to natives occurs when a cohort is aged 55 to 64 years. Employment rates for natives drop dramatically at these ages—for example in 1980, 87 percent of men aged 45 to 54 years worked, compared with 64 percent of men aged 55 to 64 years in 1990. Employment rates among immigrants also drop at these ages, but the drop is considerably smaller—for example, among men who arrived in the United States between 1970 and 1974 and were aged 45 to 54 years in 1980, 89 percent worked, compared with 77 percent for that cohort in 1990.

1980s, according to Funkhouser and Trejo (1996). These authors also find that the change in distribution of education and the decline in English proficiency among more recent immigrants play a supporting role.[25]

Moreover, the low rates of employment among newly entering female immigrant cohorts may simply be a consequence of current immigration policies. The entry years to which we refer in these tables do not mark the date these women became legal immigrants but rather the date they entered the United States. Many arrived as spouses with visas that explicitly prohibited or severely limited their working in the United States. Once these restrictions were removed, employment rates of immigrant women converged toward those of native-born women.[26]

For both men and women, the employment rates of new immigrant cohorts have been declining relative to those of native workers. Immigrants catch up relatively quickly, however, so that after some years they exhibit employment rates quite similar to those of natives.

OCCUPATIONS AND JOBS

Our first principles discussion in the previous chapter suggested that immigrants and native-born workers may hold quite different jobs. To see how far this is true, we pay special attention to the concentration of immigrants in certain occupations. We know that immigrants, relative to natives, are overrepresented at both ends of the educational spectrum. And it may be that this concentration is reflected in the jobs they hold: immigrants may be disproportionately included in both some very low-skilled and some very highly skilled occupations.[27]

Tables 5.17 and 5.18 examine two groups of occupations with above-average representation of immigrants: those that require a great deal of formal skill and those that require relatively little skill. For the occupations listed, the first and third columns provide the fraction of all labor that is foreign-born at the

---

[25]Potentially, differences in family structure may also be important in affecting comparisons of immigrant and native women. Chapter 2 presented evidence that immigrant women were more likely to be married and have more children than native women of comparable ages. However, Funkhouser and Trejo document that the difference between natives and immigrants in rates of childbearing and marriage are not large enough to be a primary determinant of the differences in their rates of employment.

[26]One of the important missing pieces of information is what employment rates of immigrant women were in their home countries. Such data are required to know the direct impact of immigration on the likelihood of working for immigrant women.

[27]Twelve percent of all hours worked by natives were accounted for by those who had neither graduated from high school nor received an equivalent degree: the comparable figure for immigrants was 32.0 percent. This share was even larger for recent immigrants—34.5 percent. Immigrants are also overrepresented at the high end of the educational distribution, but not nearly so extremely as at the low end. Among native workers, 3.5 percent of hours in 1990 were worked by those having a professional degree or a PhD, compared with 5.5 percent among immigrants.

national level and for the six largest immigration states, respectively.[28] The second and fourth columns list the proportions of recent immigrants in all foreign-born labor in the occupation. In both tables, separate listings are provided for men and women.

How were the particular occupations listed selected? In Table 5.17, which lists the top 20 high-education occupations, the ranking is in terms of the proportion who are foreign-born. Occupations are designated as "high education" if the percentage of native-born employees with professional degrees or PhDs is above the national average for native-born workers.[29] These occupations mainly involve college teaching, science, and the health field. The predominance of college professors is particularly striking in the list of occupations for men. That immigrants predominate among foreign language teachers is not surprising, but they also account for a very large fraction of many other disciplines. For example, more than one out of every four physics professors is an immigrant, as is about one out of every five doctors.[30]

The relative fraction of all immigrant workers who are new immigrants offers some hint about whether any of these occupations serve as entry-level jobs for new immigrants. Many new male immigrants are dental assistants, and a popular field for new female immigrants is teaching economics. The fraction of new immigrants in a field also may tell us something about the job prospects in that occupation. For example, male immigrants display about the same overall fraction in both the math and sociology teaching, but the proportion of the foreign-born who are new immigrants is four times as large.

Table 5.18 provides a parallel list of the 20 low-education occupations with the greatest immigrant representation. A low-education occupation is defined as one in which the percentage of native-born employees with less than a high school

---

[28]These distributions are characterized using shares of hours worked rather than the relative shares of numbers of workers. Using relative hours shares more precisely measures the concentration of immigrant labor in different occupations. As a reference point, immigrants accounted for 9.3 percent of total hours worked in 1990 among male workers between the ages of 25 and 64. Recent immigrants, those who arrived between 1980 and 1990, accounted for 3.5 percent of total hours, and pre-1980 immigrants accounted for the other 5.8 percent. Among female workers, the average immigrant share was slightly smaller, with an overall share of 8.7 percent and the share of recent immigrants of 2.8 percent.

[29]Among native men in occupations classified as high education in which immigrants are overrepresented, 44 percent of all hours are accounted for by those with a professional degree or PhD, and only 8 percent have less than a high school diploma. Among native women in high-education occupations with an overrepresentation of immigrants, 14 percent have a professional degree or PhD, and only 7 percent have less than a high school diploma.

[30]Overall, 5.7 percent of male immigrant employee hours are spent in high-education occupations, with an overrepresentation of immigrants, compared with 3.3 percent for native men. Among women, these numbers are 7.4 percent for immigrants and 5.7 percent for natives.

TABLE 5.17 Top 20 High-Education Occupations, Ranked by Immigrant Share of Hours Worked

Occupation	National Share of Hours Worked		Share of Hours Worked in 6 Immigration States[a]	
	All Immigrants	Recent/ All	All Immigrants	Recent/ All
Men				
1. Foreign language teachers	38.5	33.2	37.1	42.8
2. Physics teachers	30.8	38.6	39.0	32.1
3. Health record technologists and technicians	29.6	39.2	46.9	40.3
4. Medical scientists	29.0	69.6	40.7	65.8
5. Dental assistants	25.4	71.6	38.3	73.0
6. Political science teachers	24.9	43.7	43.2	55.5
7. Social science teachers, n.e.c.	21.8	32.8	47.5	74.7
8. Medical science teachers	21.2	20.9	24.6	17.1
9. Physicians	19.0	22.3	25.2	23.0
10. Engineering teachers	18.0	42.8	24.4	41.4
11. Computer science teachers	16.8	44.1	20.9	11.9
12. Economics teachers	16.5	31.9	27.1	34.1
13. Physicists and astronomers	16.0	45.1	20.2	50.1
14. Earth, environmental and marine science teachers	16.0	49.6	33.6	62.0
15. Postsecondary teachers, subject not specified	15.9	43.6	19.6	42.5
16. Chemists, except biochemists	15.8	38.6	21.6	37.5
17. Health specialties teachers	14.8	31.2	13.3	26.6
18. Chemistry teachers	14.4	26.6	19.0	16.9
19. Sociology teachers	14.2	14.5	21.7	0.0
20. Mathematical science teachers	13.8	59.2	14.4	55.2
Women				
1. Foreign language teachers	39.8	39.7	50.0	33.7
2. Political science teachers	31.9	43.3	53.0	100.0
3. Physicians	23.4	27.2	31.8	27.2
4. Dentists	23.4	29.1	35.8	30.8
5. Chemists, except biochemists	21.0	37.2	32.2	38.5
6. Artists, performers, and related occupations	20.5	31.0	25.1	31.2
7. History teachers	17.8	20.0	2.0	100.0
8. Social science teachers, n.e.c.	17.0	64.9	38.3	100.0
9. Architects	16.2	37.5	25.4	40.4
10. Medical scientists	16.1	47.3	20.8	47.8
11. Actuaries	15.2	19.6	18.2	18.1
12. Biological and life scientists	15.1	41.0	21.6	42.9
13. Physicists and astronomers	14.7	47.7	18.1	25.4

continued on next page

TABLE 5.17 Continued

Occupation	National Share of Hours Worked: All Immigrants	National Share of Hours Worked: Recent/ All	Share of Hours Worked in 6 Immigration States[a]: All Immigrants	Share of Hours Worked in 6 Immigration States[a]: Recent/ All
14. Science technicians, n.e.c.	14.4	48.3	26.9	46.9
15. Chemical engineers	14.3	24.9	17.3	19.9
16. Economics teachers	13.5	56.1	9.8	100.0
17. Social work teachers	13.4	0.0	22.3	0.0
18. Pharmacists	12.3	21.8	24.5	21.9
19. Computer science teachers	12.2	16.5	23.2	21.3
20. Statisticians	11.5	33.1	16.5	33.1

[a]High immigration states are California, Florida, Illinois, New Jersey, New York, and Texas.
Note: High education occupations are defined as those in which at least 3.46 percent of all hours worked by native workers are accounted for by those with a professional degree or a PhD, and less than 12.19 percent of native hours are accounted for by those with less than a high school diploma or equivalent (3.46 percent and 12.19 percent represent the overall fraction of hours accounted for by workers in the respective education groups). For the country as a whole, immigrants accounted for 9.3 percent of all hours worked by men, and 8.7 percent of all hours worked by women, with recent immigrants accounting for 3.5 percent among men and 2.8 percent among women. In high education occupations in which immigrants are overrepresented, immigrants account for 15.2 percent of male employment, and 11.2 percent of female employment. Of all hours worked by immigrants, 5.7 percent are accounted for by such occupations among men, and 7.4 percent among women. The analogous numbers for natives are 3.3 percent for men and 5.7 percent for women. Occupations for which there were fewer than 10 observations in the Census Public Use Microsample (PUMS) sample are excluded.

Source: Tabulations from the 1970, 1980, and 1990 Public Use Samples of the U.S. Census of Population. The statistics are calculated in the subsample of men and women aged 25-64 years who did not reside in group quarters.

diploma is below the percentage among all native-born workers.[31] These occupations separate into those that appear to be relatively menial and those that are skilled crafts that require little formal schooling. This last category includes, for example, tailors, dressmakers, cooks, and jewelers; the former includes farm laborers, parking lot attendants, and private household cleaners and servants.

The concentration of immigrants is much more dramatic for the low-education occupations than for the high-education occupations, reflecting the greater

[31]Among native men in occupations classified as low education in which immigrants are overrepresented, 27 percent of all hours are accounted for by those without a high school diploma or equivalent, and 5 percent have at least a college degree. Among native women in low-education occupations with an overrepresentation of immigrants, 28 percent do not have a high school diploma or equivalent, and 5 percent have at least a college degree.

TABLE 5.18 Top 20 Low-Education Occupations, Ranked by Immigrant Share of Hours Worked

	National Share of Hours Worked		Share of Hours Worked in 6 Immigration States[a]	
Occupation	All Immigrants	Recent/ All	All Immigrants	Recent/ All
Men				
1. Tailors	58.8	29.5	75.1	31.7
2. Waiters'/waitresses' assistants	55.2	68.3	70.0	68.7
3. Cooks, private household	52.8	58.9	78.0	54.9
4. Dressmakers	49.5	58.9	74.1	54.6
5. Housekeepers and butlers	47.6	66.1	46.8	48.8
6. Graders and sorters, agricultural products	43.6	44.1	66.5	42.0
7. Nursery workers	41.9	56.1	61.0	54.4
8. Waiters and waitresses	40.5	50.7	53.7	49.8
9. Cooks	39.0	51.6	54.9	51.0
10. Miscellaneous food preparation occupations	38.1	65.5	59.9	65.8
11. Textile sewing machine operators	37.5	56.2	77.1	59.0
12. Precious stones and metals workers (jewelers)	35.3	41.3	53.4	43.1
13. Parking lot attendants	35.0	61.4	48.9	61.4
14. Shoe repairers	34.4	41.2	56.9	41.4
15. Taxicab drivers and chauffeurs	32.2	51.1	44.7	50.9
16. Kitchen workers, food preparation	31.9	52.1	46.0	52.3
17. Private household cleaners and servants	31.9	55.4	46.5	53.3
18. Solderers and brazers	31.5	50.1	60.3	49.8
19. Food counter, fountain and related occupations	30.2	49.7	44.7	51.3
20. Bakers	29.5	46.5	46.9	50.0
Women				
1. Production samplers and weighers	47.1	21.1	75.6	22.4
2. Housekeepers and butlers	45.8	63.2	62.4	62.8
3. Tailors	45.7	32.5	70.2	34.8
4. Miscellaneous precision apparel and fabric workers	43.5	31.1	60.2	35.8
5. Graders and sorters, agricultural products	43.4	39.8	62.3	37.9
6. Private household cleaners and servants	37.5	57.3	58.6	58.0
7. Dressmakers	37.2	35.4	60.2	38.8
8. Patternmakers, layout workers, and cutters	34.0	29.4	4.1	100.0

continued on next page

TABLE 5.18 Continued

Occupation	National Share of Hours Worked: All Immigrants	National Share of Hours Worked: Recent/All	Share of Hours Worked in 6 Immigration States[a]: All Immigrants	Share of Hours Worked in 6 Immigration States[a]: Recent/All
9. Cooks, private household	31.6	46.0	51.9	45.0
10. Numerical control machine operators	29.1	33.3	65.4	51.0
11. Textile sewing machine operators	27.3	41.1	72.9	43.2
12. Farmworkers	25.8	42.3	53.3	40.9
13. Child care workers, private household	24.8	68.1	44.3	69.1
14. Electrical and electronic equipment assemblers	23.4	34.1	42.3	36.6
15. Graders and sorters, except agricultural	23.1	35.6	49.4	35.1
16. Inspectors, agricultural products	23.1	53.0	32.6	54.7
17. Maids and housemen	23.0	45.0	42.2	45.3
18. Parking lot attendants	23.0	42.4	43.1	45.8
19. Precious stones and metals workers (jewelers)	22.8	45.6	40.0	43.2
20. Elevator operators	22.7	51.7	35.7	36.0

[a]High immigration states are California, Florida, Illinois, New Jersey, New York, and Texas.
Note: Low education occupations are defined as those in which at least 12.19 percent of all hours worked by native workers are accounted for by those with less than a high school diploma or equivalent (12.19 percent represents the overall fraction of hours accounted for by workers with less than a high school diploma). For the country as a whole, immigrants accounted for 9.3 percent of all hours worked by men, and 8.7 percent of all hours worked by women, with recent immigrants accounting for 3.5 percent among men and 2.8 percent among women. In low education occupations in which immigrants are overrepresented, immigrants account for 16.3 percent of male employment, and 15.1 percent of female employment. Of all hours worked by immigrants, 38.0 percent were accounted for by such occupations among men, and 45.0 among women. The analogous numbers for natives were 20.1 for men and 24.2 for women. Occupations for which there were fewer than 10 observations in the Census Public Use Microsample (PUMS) sample are excluded.

Source: Tabulations from the 1970, 1980, and 1990 Public Use Samples of the U.S. Census of Population. The statistics are calculated in the subsample of men and women aged 25-64 years who did not reside in group quarters.

overrepresentation at the low end of the education distribution. For example, the majority of tailors are immigrants, and so are close to half of all housekeepers and butlers.[32]

[32]Overall, 38.0 percent of male immigrant employee hours are spent in such occupations, compared with 20.1 percent for native-born men. For women, the analogous figures are 45.0 percent for immigrants and 24.2 percent for natives.

The degree to which immigrants dominate some of these fields is remarkable. In the large immigrant states, three out of every four tailors, cooks, and textile workers are immigrants. A majority of taxicab drivers and service workers in homes are immigrants. These jobs are consistent with our first principles expectations. Some industries, such as textiles, that are dominated by immigrants are substitutes for trade in the same products and would not exist domestically without immigrants. Other jobs employing many immigrants are in the nontraded goods sector (restaurant and private household work). These services would not exist on the same scale without immigrants, and the main economic impact may well be in the form of lower prices.

The second and fourth columns in Table 5.18 give the percentage of all immigrant hours that are worked by recent immigrants—an indicator of entry-level jobs for new immigrants. For example, in the country as a whole, immigrants work about 53 percent of all the hours any man works as a cook in a private household. Of all the hours that all immigrant men work as cooks, new immigrants account for about 59 percent. That means that the new immigrants account for 31 percent (0.528 times 0.589) of all the hours any man—native- or foreign-born, new or established immigrant—spends cooking for private families. A common entry point for low-skilled male immigrants is waiting on tables, often in ethnic restaurants owned by older immigrants with the same ethnic background. New low-skilled female immigrants clean houses and often care for the children who live in them. Within these low-education occupations, the share of recent male immigrants as a fraction of all male immigrants exceeds 60 percent for such jobs as waiters' or waitresses' assistants, miscellaneous food preparation, and parking lot attendants. New female immigrants account for over 60 percent of the hours worked as housekeepers and child care workers in private homes by all foreign-born labor.

Each of these tables contains data based on employment in the six states with the largest inflows of immigrants between 1980 and 1990—California, Florida, Illinois, New Jersey, New York, and Texas. Not surprisingly, given the much greater share of immigrants in the labor market in these states (17.6 percent for men and 16.1 percent for women), immigrant shares in these occupations are generally higher there. But not by a uniform degree: the difference between the shares for the nation and for the high-immigration states is much larger for the low-education occupations. Averaging across the occupations in the two lists, the average difference between the national share and the six-state share is about 6 percent for the high-education occupations, and about 18 percent for the low-education occupations.

These figures suggest that, to some extent, immigrants with high skills and high education see the market for their services as national in scope. They are not as geographically concentrated as low-skilled immigrants are, and they are as likely as not to work with and for native-born Americans. In contrast, low-wage immigrants work largely in the big immigrant states. Their labor market bound-

TABLE 5.19 Top 20 Medium-Education Occupations, Ranked by Native Share of Hours Worked

Occupation	National Share of Hours Worked		Share of Hours Worked in 6 Immigration States[a]	
	All Immigrants	Recent/ All	All Immigrants	Recent/ All
Men				
1. Tool and die maker apprentices	0.0	—	0.0	—
2. Supervisors, firefighting and fire prevention occupations	0.9	0.0	1.8	0.0
3. Classified ad clerks	1.0	100.0	2.0	100.0
4. Forestry and conservation scientists	1.3	5.0	1.7	0.0
5. Firefighting occupations	1.3	20.1	2.1	20.0
6. Administrators, protective services	1.5	16.6	3.3	18.7
7. Sheriffs, bailiffs, and other law enforcement officers	1.7	16.1	2.9	16.4
8. Postmasters and mail superintendents	1.9	24.8	3.1	26.3
9. Supervisors, police and detectives	1.9	16.7	2.9	16.0
10. Fire inspection and fire prevention occupations	2.0	15.1	3.1	20.7
11. Telephone line installers and repairers	2.2	18.6	4.5	20.9
12. Power plant operators	2.3	19.8	5.3	20.4
13. Police and detectives, public service	2.3	12.8	3.9	13.0
14. Locomotive operating occupations	2.5	16.3	5.3	13.2
15. Correctional institution officers	2.6	23.6	4.3	26.4
16. Teachers, secondary school	3.2	22.7	4.9	28.4
17. Commissioned officers and warrant officers	3.4	23.0	4.4	22.4
18. Broadcast equipment operators	3.4	27.7	6.1	33.5
19. Teachers, elementary school	3.5	26.9	6.4	28.6
20. Air traffic controllers	3.6	23.9	6.4	23.4
Women				
1. Mining engineers	0.0	—	0.0	—
2. Helpers, extractive occupations	0.0	—	0.0	—
3. Supervisors, firefighting and fire prevention occupations	0.0	—	0.0	—
4. Captains and other officers, fishing vessels	0.0	—	0.0	—
5. Patternmakers and model makers, wood	0.0	—	0.0	—
6. Supervisors, forestry and logging workers	0.0	—	0.0	—

TABLE 5.19 Continued

	National Share of Hours Worked		Share of Hours Worked in 6 Immigration States[a]	
Occupation	All Immigrants	Recent/ All	All Immigrants	Recent/ All
7. Postmasters and mail superintendents	1.3	5.9	4.2	3.8
8. Supervisors, material moving equipment operators	1.6	0.0	3.8	0.0
9. Power plant operators	1.9	0.0	5.6	0.0
10. Correctional institution officers	2.0	11.4	3.3	10.6
11. Sheriffs, bailiffs, and other law enforcement officers	2.1	12.2	2.9	20.6
12. Speech therapists	2.1	27.7	3.5	21.0
13. Supervisors, police and detectives	2.3	9.5	3.8	12.0
14. Meter readers	2.4	9.0	5.3	13.2
15. Air traffic controllers	2.4	25.4	4.1	33.0
16. Dispatchers	2.4	14.0	4.4	15.3
17. Railroad conductors and yardmasters	2.5	0.0	4.9	0.0
18. Commissioned officers and warrant officers	2.5	36.0	4.6	45.9
19. Mail carriers, postal service	2.7	29.0	5.1	27.8
20. Firefighting occupations	2.8	0.0	4.9	0.0

[a]High immigration states are California, Florida, Illinois, New Jersey, New York, and Texas.

Note: Medium-education occupations are defined as those in which less than 12.19 percent of all hours worked by native workers were accounted for by those with less than a high school diploma or equivalent, and less than 3.46 percent of all hours worked by native workers were accounted for by those with a graduate or professional degree (12.19 percent and 3.46 percent represent the overall fraction of hours accounted for by workers in those education groups). For the country as a whole, immigrants accounted for 9.3 percent of all hours worked by men, and 8.7 percent of all hours worked by women, with recent immigrants accounting for 3.5 percent among men and 2.8 percent among women. In medium-education occupations in which immigrants were underrepresented, immigrants accounted for 6.6 percent of male employment and 5.7 percent of female employment. Of all hours worked by immigrants, 25.4 percent were accounted for by such occupations among men, and 32.5 among women. The analogous numbers for natives were 37.2 for men and 51.3 for women. Occupations for which there were fewer than 10 observations in the Census Public Use Microsample (PUMS) sample are excluded.

Source: Tabulations from the 1970, 1980, and 1990 Public Use Samples of the U.S. Census of Population. The statistics are calculated in the subsample of men and women aged 25-64 years who did not reside in group quarters.

aries appear to be much more local in scope, and many of them work with and for other immigrants.

If immigrants are highly concentrated in certain jobs, they are almost invisible in others. Table 5.19 lists the 20 medium-education occupations in which immigrants have the lowest representation. Medium-education occupations are those in which the native-born with either low or high education levels are underrepresented compared with their overall representation among all native-born workers. For men, these are primarily public-sector occupations, such as firefighters and law enforcement officers. The list for women also includes public-sector occupations, but a number of others appear to be occupations that are traditionally male, such as mining engineers, helpers in extractive occupations, and captains of fishing vessels.

All in all, the data suggest that the jobs of immigrant and native workers are different. One can find jobs that are dominated by immigrants at both the high and the low end of the educational distribution: teachers and scientists at the high end, service workers and what are sometimes referred as crafts people at the low end. Immigrants are less prominent in jobs that require intermediate levels of education.

Some of the heterogeneity in the skills of recent immigrants is an artifact of the preference categories in which they were admitted. Employment-preference immigrants are heavily concentrated in two highly skilled kinds of occupation: executive, administrative, and managerial posts and professional specialties. A sizable proportion of refugees and of those admitted to reunite with their families are concentrated in the low-skilled occupations; they are employed as service workers and as operators, fabricators, and laborers.[33]

To sum up: mirroring the situation in education, although foreign-born men are somewhat more likely to be in the high-education, high-paying jobs, they are far more commonly found to be working in the low-education, low-paying jobs. Compared with natives, immigrant men are found in some occupations requiring high levels of education, such as college teachers of foreign-languages and medical scientists, as well as in some occupations requiring little schooling, such as tailors, waiters' and waitresses' assistants, and housekeepers and butlers. The picture for immigrant women is similar to that for immigrant men. They are disproportionately employed in some high-education occupations, such as foreign language teachers and physicians, but they also make up a large share of employment in many more

[33]The occupational distribution of immigrants is based on reports in applications for visas. Because employment-preference immigrants are likely to have a pending job offer in the United States, their occupation in the United States will probably conform fairly closely to the one they reported on their application. The jobs other immigrants will have here may be subject to more uncertainty, and so the occupation they cite on their application may tell little about the job they eventually have in the United States.

occupations that require little schooling: tailors, graders and sorters of agricultural products, and private household service workers.

IMPACT OF IMMIGRANTS ON NATIVE EARNINGS AND EMPLOYMENT

To this point, we have talked mostly about the economic impacts of immigration on immigrants themselves. But do immigrants alter the earnings and employment opportunities of natives? If so, how much? Are all native groups equally affected by the entry of immigrants into the labor market?

In this section, we summarize the empirical evidence about the impacts that immigrants have on the wage structure of natives. Again, this summary is guided by the first principles discussion in the previous chapter. Although immigration yields a positive net economic gain to the native-born, there may be some winners and losers among native-born workers. In general, we should expect that the wages of native-born workers who are complements (the more skilled) should rise, and the wages of those who are substitutes (the less skilled) for immigrants should fall.

What determines the magnitude of these potential effects? Recall the example presented in Chapter 4 in which we drew the demand curve for domestic unskilled labor (Figure 4.1). An increase in the number of immigrants lowered the wage of substitute labor by $W_o - W_o^1$ while the wages of skilled labor rose. One critical parameter that will determine how much wages may change is the steepness of this demand curve for labor. If this curve is very steep, wages of unskilled domestic labor will fall a lot. If it is very flat, wages will hardly change at all. The technical term used to describe this steepness is the elasticity of the demand for labor. Demand curves will be very elastic (flat in Figure 4.1) when there are good substitutes for this type of labor, and relatively inelastic (steep in Figure 4.1) when good substitutes are unavailable.

What does the literature on labor demand suggest that we would expect to find empirically? According to Hamermesh's extensive review (1993), the best point estimate is an elasticity of demand for labor of about 0.3. That is, the empirical evidence suggests that a 10 percent increase in the size of the labor force will reduce the wage of competing workers by about 3 percent of that change. During the 1980s, immigration increased the supply of all workers by about 4 percent. Therefore, immigration may reduce the wage of competing native workers by only about 1.2 percent.[34]

---

[34]The theoretical discussion in Hamermesh (1993: 22-28) allows us to construct an exact expression relating two relevant elasticities. In particular, the output-constant elasticity of labor demand, which we denote by e, and which gives the percentage change in the number of workers hired for a given percentage change in the wage, is equal to $-(1 - s)\sigma$, where s is the share of income that accrues to workers, and σ, is the elasticity of substitution. The elasticity of factor price (defined as the

The weight of the empirical evidence suggests that the impact of immigration on the wages of competing native-born workers is small—possibly reducing them by only 1 or 2 percent. Why does this effect seem so small? One reason is that it is easy to exaggerate the importance of immigration. Although immigration touches some hot button issues, the American economy is extremely large and complex, running at $7.6 trillion a year. This economy is the end result of ten of thousands of factors, many of which are far more critical than the country's immigration policy. Such factors include the rate at which the country saves and invests and the human capital of its own workers. It is simply not plausible that immigration, even across a decade, by increasing the supply of workers by 4 percent could seriously impact such an economy. However, although it is easy to exaggerate the aggregate effects of immigration, they should not be minimized. As measured by changes in wages, the economic benefits of immigration run as much as $10 billion a year. In addition, the economic benefits of immigration that operate only through lower prices, without displacing or disadvantaging competitive domestic labor, add to the positive effects of immigration.

Another reason why the potential effects seem small is that the aggregate increase in the supply of labor caused by immigration is itself small. And although the effect on the aggregate wage may be small, the effects in other dimensions may be larger. The two dimensions that have preoccupied the literature are subgroups of workers and local labor markets. The increase in the supply of workers may be larger for some types of workers—for example, less educated and black workers—because their skill distribution more closely resembles that of immigrants. Similarly, because immigrants are concentrated in relatively few geographic labor markets, native-born workers who live in those local areas may feel heavier impacts.

---

percentage change in the wage for a given percentage change in the number of workers, holding marginal costs constant) is given by $-(1 - s)/\sigma$,. The elasticity of factor price can then be written in terms of the output-constant elasticity of demand, and is thus given by $(1 - s)^2/e$. It is well known that s is approximately 0.7, and Hamermesh concludes that e is approximately –0.3 (pp. 76-105). The elasticity of factor price that holds marginal cost constant, therefore, is about –0.3 (a 10 percent change in labor supply reduces the wage by 3 percent). However, this calculation assumes that the marginal cost of production is fixed. If immigration reduces marginal costs (because it reduces wages), it would lead to a reduction in the price of the output, which would in turn induce an additional reduction in the wages of native workers. No estimates are available about how much larger this impact is likely to be. Estimates of the elasticity of demand for labor vary somewhat depending on the level of skill considered. However, given the range of estimates it is difficult to be precise about how the elasticity for one type of labor differs from that of another. The basic point is that, in the relevant range of these elasticities, the impact of immigration on native wages will be small.

Local Labor Markets and the Empirical Evidence

The basic impetus for an analysis of the economic impact of immigrants in local labor markets flows from the fact that immigrants are highly concentrated in relatively few geographic areas. The increase in supply from additional immigration may be small at the national level, but it may be much larger in some communities with lots of immigrants. Los Angeles is a good example, since one-third of its current population is foreign-born.

The basic framework used by most local labor market studies that attempt to determine the impact of immigrants on native employment opportunities is easy to describe. For the most part, these studies compare the economic performance of natives who live in cities where few immigrants live with the economic performance of natives who live in cities where many immigrants live. If immigration truly has an adverse impact on the earnings of some native workers, we would expect to find that some natives in immigrant cities would have lower earnings or lower employment propensities (or both) than comparable natives who live in labor markets that immigrants have not yet penetrated. Of course, these comparisons require controlling for other factors that could create variation in economic performance across labor markets.[35]

Practically all empirical studies in the literature, beginning with the initial work of Grossman (1982), use this type of spatial comparison to measure the impact of immigration on native employment opportunities. The typical study correlates a measure of the native wage in the locality on the relative numbers of immigrants in that locality (or correlates the change in the wage in the locality over a specified time period on the change in the number of immigrants in the locality).

A number of recent studies have surveyed this extensive literature (Borjas, 1994; Friedberg and Hunt, 1995; Greenwood and McDowell, 1993). Panel A of Table 5.20 reports the Borjas summary of the representative results in this literature. The spatial correlations generally indicate that the average native wage is slightly lower in labor markets where immigrants tend to reside. The point estimates of the elasticity of the native wage with respect to the number of immigrants cluster around zero.[36] Even the most negative effect found in these stud-

---

[35]One of the principal difficulties involves controlling for other factors affecting wages in an area at a point in time. The problem of controlling for demand-side conditions is an obstacle in current research. Borjas et al. (1997) point out that labor markets in immigrant-intensive states, such as California, were relatively robust during the 1970s but ran into difficulty during the 1980s. As a result, changes in wages tend to be positively correlated with immigrant flows during the 1970s and negatively correlated during the 1980s.

[36]This is by no means an exhaustive list of such studies, but the results are fairly typical of this literature. Some examples of other such studies are DeFreitas (1988), Greenwood and Hunt (1995), and Greenwood et al. (1997). Each of these authors finds small effects that cluster around zero.

TABLE 5.20 Elasticity of Native Wages and Native Employment with Respect to the Number of Immigrants in a Locality

Study			
Panel A: Native Wages	Impact of Immigrants on:	Dependent Variable	Elasticity Estimate
Altonji and Card (1991:220)	Less skilled natives	Weekly wages	+.01
Bean, Lowell, and Taylor (1988:44)	Native Mexican men	Annual earnings	–.005 to +.05
	Black men	Annual earnings	–.003 to +.06
Borjas (1990:87)	White native men	Annual earnings	–.01
	Black native men	Annual earnings	+.02
Grossman (1982:600)	All natives	Factor share of native workers	–.02
LaLonde and Topel (1991:186)	Young black natives	Annual earnings	–.06
	Young Hispanic natives	Annual earnings	–.01
Panel B: Native Employment			
Altonji and Card (1991: 220)	Less skilled natives	Employment-population ratio	–.038
		Weeks worked	–.062
Borjas (1990:92)	White native men	Labor force participation rate	–.01
	Black native men	Labor force participation rate	+.04
Muller and Espenshade (1985:100)	Black natives	Unemployment rate	–.01
Simon, Moore, and Sullivan (1993)	Natives	Unemployment rate	+.001
Winegarden and Khor (1991:109)	Young white natives	Unemployment rate	.01
	Young black natives	Unemployment rate	–.003

Source: Borjas (1994).

ies, LaLonde and Topel's (1992) estimate for young black natives, implies that a 10 percent increase in the number of immigrants would decrease the wages of young black natives by only 0.6 percent.

Most of the studies focus on the relationship between native earnings and the immigrant share in the local labor market, but some also estimate the correlation between immigration and native labor force participation rates, hours worked, and unemployment rates. Panel B of Table 5.20, taken from Borjas's survey article, illustrates the findings of such studies. The available cross-city evidence also suggests that immigration has a weak effect on the employment of natives. Altonji and Card's (1991) study, for example, finds an elasticity that would imply that a 10 percent increase in the number of immigrants in a local labor market would reduce weeks worked by less skilled natives by 0.6 percent.

Studies of specific labor markets confirm these findings even when the market receives very large numbers of immigrants. On April 20, 1980, Fidel Castro declared that Cuban nationals wishing to move to the United States could leave freely from the port of Mariel. By September 1980, about 125,000 Cubans, mostly unskilled workers, had chosen to undertake the journey. Almost overnight, Miami's labor force had unexpectedly grown by 7 percent. Card's (1990) analysis of the data indicates that the time-series trend in wages and employment opportunities for Miami's workers, including its black population, was barely nudged by the Mariel flow. The trend between 1980 and 1985 was similar to that in other cities, such as Los Angeles, Houston, and Atlanta, which did not experience the Mariel flow.

The evidence also indicates that the numerically weak relationship between native wages and immigration is observed across all types of native workers, white and black, skilled and unskilled, male and female. The one group that appears to suffer significant negative effects from new immigrants are earlier waves of immigrants, according to many studies. For instance, Grossman (1982) reports that a 10 percent increase in the number of immigrants reduces the immigrant wage by 2 percent, and Altonji and Card (1991) conclude that a 10 percent increase in the number of immigrants reduces the immigrant wage by at least 4 percent.

Many of the studies make a particular effort to measure the impact of immigration on the wages and employment of specific subgroups of the native population, particularly black Americans. Because immigrants are relatively unskilled, some suspect that black workers may be particularly hard-hit by immigration. However, a look at Table 5.20 reveals that the estimated effects on both employment and wages are small even when estimated separately for blacks. **None of the available evidence on spatial correlations suggests that in the aggregate the economic opportunities of black Americans are substantially reduced by immigration.**

One reason for this perhaps surprising result is that black Americans and immigrants live in quite different areas of the country. For each black American

TABLE 5.21 Distribution of Native-born Black Americans Aged 25-64 Years, by the Percentage Immigrant in the Area in Which They Live

Percentiles of the Black Population	Percentage of Immigrants Living in Same Area
10	1.0
30	2.0
50	4.2
70	8.2
80	15.1
90	27.4
95	35.1

Note: The percentiles are defined after ranking black Americans according to the percentage of the population aged 25-64 years that is foreign-born in their area of residence. For example, 10 percent of native-born black Americans live in areas where less than or equal to 1.0 percent of the population is foreign-born.

Population areas are based on the more than 1,000 Public Use Microdata Areas (PUMAs) defined for the 1990 census.

Source: 1990 Census Public Use Microdata files.

between the ages of 25 and 64, we computed the fraction of his or her area's population who were immigrants.[37] The black population was then ranked by that fraction. As Table 5.21 shows, 30 percent of blacks live in areas where immigrants account for 2 percent or less of the population. Although 10 percent of the population are immigrants, they are only 4.2 percent of the population where the median black adult resides. Some black adults live in places with heavy concentrations of immigrants, but as such they are very few.

As these numbers suggest, black Americans and immigrants reside in different states: 63 percent of blacks live in states other than the six top immigration states. In those 44 states, only 4 percent of the population are immigrants.

Some black workers have lost their jobs to immigrants, especially when they live in a place with a large concentration of immigrants. But the vast majority do not live in such places, and their economic opportunities are determined by other things.

The absence of any large wage effect on certain subgroups of workers also

[37]For these calculations, areas were defined as the over 1,000 Public Use Microdata Areas (PUMAs) identified in the census Public Use Microdata Sample.

appears at first blush to be inconsistent with some case studies of a particular industry in a particular city (such as the apparel or restaurant industry in New York or Los Angeles). These studies typically trace the employment patterns in an industry as it is penetrated by immigrants. Often, they find substantial "displacement"—in the sense that native workers leave the industry as the immigrants enter it. For example, Waldinger (1996) studied the garment and hotel industries in New York City over the period 1940-90. He found that immigrants' share of employment in these sectors grew as the share of natives, particularly black natives, fell. Mines and Martin (1984) found that new Mexican immigrants working for farm labor contractors expanded their share of employment in the citrus industry in California's Ventura County during the 1970s. As this happened, the employment of established unionized workers (who were largely earlier Mexican immigrants) decreased.

However, such studies are not inconsistent with our overall conclusion that immigrants have no large negative impact on wages. One reason is that such studies systematically examine situations in which displacement might have been thought to be large. But more fundamentally, these case studies are asking a question different from ours: employment displacement may well be very large without any noticeable wage adjustment if the displaced workers find employment often in other industries or in other areas of the country. Although such case studies generally have little information on what happens to individuals who have left the industry in question, the evidence that the wages and employment of natives are not substantially lower in areas with large numbers of immigrants suggests that, if substantial displacement occurs, displaced workers must either find other jobs with similar pay or move to other areas.

Moreover, the empirical literature may have a systematic bias in that it consistently searches for negative wage effects, typically on less skilled or economically disadvantaged groups, while rarely exploring the possibility that the wages of other workers may improve. In fact, they do, for the more skilled, and although the improvement is small, it may be spread over a larger fraction of the workforce.

Do Spatial Correlations Measure the Labor Market Impact of Immigration?

A number of problems arise in using spatial correlations between the wage (or employment) of natives and the presence of immigrants to measure whether immigration adversely affects native workers. In particular, the comparison of economic conditions in different metropolitan areas, as well as the pre- and postimmigration comparison in a particular metropolitan area, presumes that the labor markets are closed (once immigration takes place) and that the immigration flow into an area is exogenous.

Both of these assumptions can be questioned. Local labor markets in the

United States are certainly not completely closed economies. Labor, capital, and goods flow across localities and in doing so tend to equalize the price of labor (the wage rate). As long as native workers and firms respond to the entry of immigrants by moving to areas offering better opportunities, there may be no reason to expect much of a correlation between the wage of natives and the presence of immigrants.

To give an concrete example, suppose that immigration into San Diego lowers the earnings of natives there substantially. San Diegans are not likely to stand idly by and watch their economic opportunities vanish. Some, especially those who compete with immigrants, will move to other cities, and people who were considering moving to San Diego will now move somewhere else instead. As native workers respond to immigration by voting with their feet, the adverse impact of immigration on this Southern Californian labor market is diffused to other communities.[38]

In terms of Figure 4.1, there is a reduction in the supply of competing domestic workers in the local area that may partially or even fully offset the increase in the supply of immigrants. If this is a full adjustment, *all* competing native workers are worse off from immigration by the same amount, not simply those residing in cities where immigrants cluster. If so, the comparison of native economic opportunities across local labor markets will not capture the macro effect of immigration.[39] However, if we accept this reasoning and then move to the national level, we must also accept that the increases in total supply due to immigration are much lower if they are calculated at the national level.

The second reason why the local labor market effect may be small concerns the elasticity of demand for labor in a local area. If demand elasticities are large, we know that wage effects will be small. Elasticities of demand must be considerably larger in local areas than nationally since workers in other areas should be very good substitutes for labor in any one place.

Concern about these spatial correlations has motivated a second strand of research, which has been called the factor-proportions approach. These studies take a national perspective, focusing on the impact of immigration on native labor market opportunities in the *aggregate* economy, rather than in a particular local-

---

[38]This argument also works if it is capital, rather than labor, that moves across cities. Suppose a group of investors is planning to open up a factory employing less-skilled workers in Detroit. They now find that they can open the same factory in San Diego and make higher profits (because of the relatively abundant supply of less-skilled workers in that area). Firms that employ less-skilled workers, therefore, have an incentive to move to San Diego. This process lowers economic opportunities in other cities and attenuates the adverse impact of immigration in the San Diego area.

[39]In addition, immigrants do not simply land in a randomly chosen metropolitan area; presumably they choose areas that offer the best opportunities. Therefore, the spatial correlations that are typically reported in most studies say little about the effects of immigration on native employment opportunities.

ity. They view immigrants as the source of an increase in the national supply of workers with the relevant skill. Because immigration tends to expand the supply of some skill groups more than others, it changes the factor proportions in the economy—for example, the ratio of unskilled to skilled workers. An extensive literature in economics analyzes how wage ratios change when the proportions of different labor inputs change. The factor-proportions approach then uses the estimated elasticities of substitution to simulate how labor market opportunities for particular skill groups must have changed when immigration shifted the relative number of less-skilled workers.

The factor-proportions approach also has its limitations. First, it does not truly estimate the actual impact of immigration on the labor market. Rather, it simulates the impact. In other words, given the existing estimates of the elasticity of substitution among different types of workers—estimates that were derived *outside* the immigration context—these studies calculate what a change in the relative number of skilled to unskilled workers implies for the wage ratio between the two groups. In addition, by its very nature, the factor-proportions approach must be based on an underlying model of the economy. In a sense, the approach does not let the data speak freely. As a result, if the economic model used in the simulations does not accord with the real-world labor markets, the validity of the conclusions comes into question.

Borjas et al. (1992, 1997) used the factor-proportions approach to provide evidence of the macro impact of immigration using time-series data drawn from the Current Population Surveys and the decennial census. The 1980s and early 1990s witnessed a substantial increase in the wage gap between workers who do not have a high school diploma and workers with more education. As we have seen, the decade also witnessed the entry of large numbers of less-skilled immigrants. In their comprehensive study, Borjas et al. (1997) show that the increase in the supply of workers due to immigration was concentrated among high school dropouts. Post-1979 immigration increased the relative supply of dropouts by roughly 15 percent. Over that same period, the relative wages of high school dropouts fell by roughly 11 percent. If wages went down by 3 percent for every 10 percent increase in supply, then the immigration-induced increase in the relative number of high school dropouts lowered wages by 4.8 percent. Alternatively, 44 percent of the decline in the relative wage of high school dropouts between 1980 and 1994 can be attributed to the large influx of less-skilled immigrants who entered the United States during that period (see Borjas et al., 1996).

The Borjas et al. study shows very modest effects of immigration on relative wages of all other groups. For example, since 1979, wages of college graduates relative to high school graduates increased by 19 percent. Immigration had only a very modest impact on the relative supplies of these college graduates relative to high school graduates over this period. Immigration alone would have predicted less than a 1 percent rise in relative wages of college graduates, thereby explaining very little of the rapid rise in the wages of college graduates.

Over the last two decades, immigration has played some role in explaining the declining wages of high school dropouts but little part in the expanding wage inequality for any other group of domestic workers. The negative wage effects of immigration led to about a 5 percent wage reduction among high school dropouts. This wage reduction is concentrated on a declining group of American workers. By 1995, high school dropouts represented less than 10 percent of the American workforce.

IMMIGRATION AND NATIVE MIGRATION

A central linkage between the impact of immigration on local labor markets and the national economy concerns how the internal migration flows of native workers respond to immigration. The economic impacts of immigration on local labor markets will generally be smaller the larger the net internal outflow of native workers induced by inflows of immigrants into an area.[40]

Our evidence on whether internal migration patterns are affected by immigration is contained in Table 5.22. This table shows the 1950-90 trends for the working-age populations of California, a composite group of five other immigrant-receiving states (Florida, Illinois, New Jersey, New York, and Texas), and the rest of the United States. Before 1970—that is, before the decade when the immigrant population began to increase rapidly—the share of natives who lived in California was rising rapidly—from 6.9 to 9.6 percent between 1950 and 1970. At the same time, the table reveals that the share of natives who live in California has remained roughly stable at that level since then. By 1990, only 10 percent of the native population lived in California, a state that experienced remarkable population growth in the 1970s and 1980s.

Most of this population growth can be attributed to immigration. Even though the share of natives who lived in California rose only slightly between 1970 and 1990, the share of the U.S. population residing in California rose from 10.2 percent to 12.4 percent during that period. In other words, the 1970-90

---

[40]There are a number of existing studies of this question (see Filer, 1992; White and Hunter, 1993; White and Liang, 1993; Frey and Liaw, 1996; Frey et al., 1996; Card, 1996). These studies, however, have not yet reached a consensus on whether and how the internal migration decisions of native workers are affected by immigration. Some of the evidence (Filer and White/Hunter) suggests that metropolitan areas where immigrants cluster experienced lower rates of native in-migration and somewhat higher rates of native out-migration. Frey uses the 1990 census data and reports a strong negative correlation between net migration rates of natives and immigration. In contrast, Card (1996), also using the 1990 census, reports that the cross-city correlation between the 1985-90 rate of growth in the number of native workers and the rate of growth in the number of immigrant workers is slightly positive. As we noted earlier, however, this positive correlation may be simply indicating that both natives and immigrants choose to reside in growing, rather than declining, markets.

TABLE 5.22 Percentage of the U.S. Population Living in Particular States

	Percentage of U.S. Population Living in:			Percentage of Natives Living in:			Percentage of Immigrants Living in:		
Year	CA	Other Immigration States	All Other States	CA	Other Immigration States	All Other States	CA	Other Immigration States	All Other States
1950	7.2	26.9	65.9	6.9	25.4	67.7	10.4	44.4	45.2
1960	8.9	27.3	63.7	8.6	26.2	65.2	14.6	44.9	40.6
1970	10.2	27.1	62.7	9.6	26.2	64.2	20.1	43.8	36.0
1980	10.9	26.7	62.4	9.7	25.6	64.8	27.2	41.9	30.9
1990	12.4	27.0	60.7	10.0	25.5	64.4	33.8	40.0	26.1

Note: the "other immigration states" include Florida, Illinois, New Jersey, New York, and Texas. The calculations use the Public Use Samples of the U.S. Census of Population and are based on the sample of persons aged 18-64 years in each of the censuses.

Source: Borjas et al. (1997).

expansion experienced by California can be attributed almost exclusively to immigration.

This basic empirical fact has an important implication in the present context. If the native population in California had grown in the 1970s and 1980s at the same rate that it grew in the 1950s and 1960s, 12.3 percent of natives would have lived in California in 1990.[41] One interpretation of the evidence suggests that the increasing immigration to California displaced much of the native migration that would have occurred between 1970 and 1990. In other words, the increased immigration to California encouraged natives to stop moving there, and this process effectively dispersed the labor market effects of immigration from California to the national economy.

This migration process may play an important role in the estimation of the immigrant effect on native earnings, according to related evidence. If native workers or native capital responds to immigration by moving to other labor markets, the impact of immigration on labor market opportunities will be relatively small when spatial correlations are calculated at the city level (it is easy to move from one city to another), but it will be larger at the state or regional level (it is more costly to move across states or regions). Although there is a great deal of dispersion in the estimated effects, a recent study by Borjas et al. (1996) suggests that the impact of immigration on the wages of natives depends on the level of geography. In particular, the impact of immigration on the native wage is smallest when the comparison is across metropolitan areas, becomes more negative when the comparison is across states, and is largest when the comparison is across census regions.

The evidence leads us to conclude that immigration has only a small adverse impact on the wage and employment opportunities of competing native-born groups. This effect appears not to be concentrated in the local areas where immigrants live; much of it is probably dispersed across the United States as competing native workers migrate out of the areas to which immigrants move. The migration of native labor and native capital across cities (to take advantage of whatever differential economic opportunities initially arise from immigration), as well as the beneficial effect that immigrant groups have on other native groups, suggests the unlikelihood of detecting any sizable negative effect on native workers.

PRICE EFFECTS OF IMMIGRATION

The earlier examination of the occupational distribution of immigrants indicated that the jobs they hold differ from those natives hold, suggesting that in the

---

[41]The share of native population residing in California grew by 2.7 percentage points between 1950 and 1970. Extrapolating this trend to the 1970-90 period implies that the native share would have grown an additional 2.7 percentage points between 1970 and 1990.

absence of immigration jobs performed by immigrants would either have to be filled by natives or would not be performed at all. Thus the presence of immigrants in U.S. labor markets causes a reallocation of labor across different sectors of the U.S. economy, and in so doing changes the mix of goods the country produces, as well as the prices of those goods. As consumers, natives benefit from immigration by consuming goods and services whose relative prices fall in response to this reallocation.

In this section, the question is: Who benefits most from the labor services provided by immigrants? Since we cannot measure prices without immigration, our focus is on the extent to which consumers rely on commodities that are produced by immigrant labor. If, for example, some groups of consumers rely more heavily than others on goods produced primarily with immigrant labor, then it follows that they would benefit more than others from the changes in relative prices due to immigration. Examining how much different consumers rely on goods produced with immigrant labor can provide only a first-order approximation to the price effects of immigration. Such an exercise cannot, for example, inform us of the effects of changes in the wages of those natives who are either complements or substitutes for immigrant labor.

We focus on the relationship between the amount consumers spend on particular goods and services and the cost share of immigrant labor in their production. This type of analysis involves tracing consumption back to the place of production. It is made more complicated by the fact that behind most goods that consumers buy is a lengthy production process. When a typical consumption good reaches the household, it has traveled through several different industries, starting perhaps with natural resources or agriculture, going on through manufacturing, transportation, wholesale trade, and then ending in retail trade, where it is purchased by the consumer. To correctly infer the amount of immigrant labor involved in producing a dollar's worth of consumer spending requires detailed knowledge about the production process along every step of the way.

That knowledge is embodied in economy-wide input-output tables provided by the Bureau of Economic Analysis. These tables are used to determine how much of a commodity gets produced domestically, which industries produce it, and how much labor these industries use in production. The immigrant portion of labor costs is then inferred from immigrants' share of earnings paid to workers in these industries, derived from the 1990 census. For each commodity listed in the input-output tables, the cost share of immigrant labor is calculated by summing up the immigrant cost share in each of the steps in the production process. Commodities are then aggregated into 48 broad expenditure categories. These categories include food (distinguishing between that consumed inside the home and that consumed outside the home), household services, financial and legal services, household goods (appliances, furniture), utilities, housing (rent, maintenance), apparel, education, transportation, and recreation. Appendix 5.B provides the

TABLE 5.23 Share of Consumption Expenditures Attributable to Immigrant Labor

		Immigrant Labor Share	
Income Decile	Total Quarterly Expenditures (1994 $)	All Immigrants	Recent Immigrants
1	$2,901	0.048	0.020
2	3,346	0.047	0.019
3	3,947	0.048	0.020
4	4,816	0.049	0.020
5	5,425	0.049	0.020
6	5,920	0.049	0.020
7	6,813	0.049	0.020
8	7,932	0.051	0.021
9	9,124	0.051	0.021
10	13,003	0.054	0.023

Note: The Consumer Expenditure Survey has a rotating panel design with households being interviewed up to 4 times. To make the household observations comparable, the weighting was adjusted for the number of interviews. For those interviewed only once, the sample weight is multiplied by a factor of 4; for those interviewed twice, the weight is multiplied by a factor of 2; and for those interviewed three times, the weight is multiplied by 4/3.

details about the calculation of the immigrant labor shares and the aggregation into broad expenditure categories.

The categories that have relatively high immigrant labor-cost shares include household services (18.2 percent), services to dwellings (13.5 percent), and laundry, cleaning, and garment services (10.9 percent). Identification of these categories is not surprising given the evidence presented earlier on the occupations and industries in which immigrants are disproportionately employed. Categories with relatively low immigrant labor-cost shares include electricity (1.3 percent) and all other utilities, tobacco products (1.3 percent), and gasoline (1.5 percent).

Who consumes the commodities in these categories is then determined from expenditures on these categories, as reported in the 1994 Consumer Expenditure Survey (CES). By examining the relationship between consumers' expenditures and their other characteristics, we can explore the question of who is most likely to benefit from the price effects of immigration.

As Table 5.23 illustrates, the share of expenditures that can be attributed to immigrant labor in this way is remarkably constant over most of the household income distribution, though it rises at the high end of the distribution. On average, immigrant labor accounts for about 4.9 percent of household consumption expenditures, very similar to the 4.8 percent share among consumers in the bottom 10 percent of the income distribution. Consumer shares are very close to this level through the ninth income decile. Only for consumers with incomes above that level does the immigrant share of expenditures appear to be markedly higher.

TABLE 5.24 Share of Expenditures Attributable to Immigrant Labor by Education and Household Composition

		Immigrant Labor Share	
	Total Quarterly Expenditures (1994 $)	All Immigrants	Recent Immigrants
By Education			
Less than high school	$3,946	0.046	0.019
High school diploma	5,613	0.048	0.020
Some college	6,062	0.051	0.021
College degree	8,522	0.052	0.022
By Household Composition			
Single males	4,013	0.051	0.021
Single females	3,516	0.050	0.021
Single male parents	7,532	0.049	0.020
Single female parents	4,359	0.050	0.020
Husband and wife, no children, both work	5,951	0.051	0.021
Husband and wife, no children	7,827	0.048	0.019
Husband, wife, and children < 6, both work	6,920	0.051	0.021
Husband, wife, and children < 6	9,113	0.049	0.020
Husband, wife, and children > 5, both work	7,737	0.050	0.020
Husband, wife, and children > 5	7,532	0.048	0.020
Others	6,216	0.048	0.019

The share attributable to the labor of recent immigrants parallels that pattern, with consumers spending close to 2.0 percent on goods and services attributable to immigrant labor in all but the highest 10 percent of the income distribution.

An examination of expenditure shares by the education level of the head of household confirms this finding. About 5.2 percent of spending is attributable to immigrant labor among those with a college education, compared with a slightly lower 4.6 percent among those who did not graduate from high school (see Table 5.24). That is not surprising given that those with more education have on average higher levels of income.

Single (childless) males and couples in which both spouses work have the highest fraction of expenditures attributable to immigrant labor—5.1 percent (see

TABLE 5.25 Effects of Income, Age, Education, Race, and Family Composition on the Share of Household Expenditures Attributable to Immigrant Labor

	All Immigrants	
Variable	Coefficient	Standard Error
Logarithm of household income	0.011	0.0000
Age	–0.001	0.0000
Age ≥ 65	0.017	0.0002
Less than high school	–0.014	0.0001
Some college	0.021	0.0001
College degree	0.035	0.0001
Black	–0.004	0.0002
Other	0.006	0.0003
Husband, wife, no children, both work	0.000	0.0002
Husband, wife, and children < 6	–0.000	0.0004
Husband, wife, and children < 6, both work	–0.001	0.0003
Husband, wife, and children > 5	–0.001	0.0003
Husband, wife, and children > 5, both work	–0.001	0.0002
Single male parent	–0.000	0.0006
Single female parent	0.001	0.0003
Single males	0.002	0.0002
Single female	0.002	0.0002
Other composition	–0.000	0.0002

Note: The dependent variable is the share of expenditures attributable to immigrant labor multiplied by 100.

the lower portion of Table 5.24). This is so because these households spend a greater proportion of their income on services, in particular household services and food consumption away from home, both expenditure categories with relatively high immigrant labor shares.

As a final summary, Table 5.25 presents estimates that simultaneously examine the effects of various consumer characteristics—such as household income, education level and race of the head of household, and household composition—on the share of household expenditures attributable to immigrant labor. The estimates come from a linear regression model and so give differences in expenditure shares associated with particular characteristics, holding constant each of the other characteristics of the household. So, for example, the coefficient for college degree indicates that the share of expenditures attributable to immigrant labor among those with a college degree is on average 0.035 percentage point larger than the reference group (high school graduates) after adjustment for associated differences in average income levels, race, age, and household composition.

Controlling for all these variables together does not substantively alter any of the conclusions that one would derive from the simple averages presented earlier.

All of the coefficients are quite small, indicating that consumption of immigrant-intensive commodities is spread rather evenly across different groups of consumers stratified by these attributes. The positive coefficients for those with relatively high incomes, those with high levels of education, and those who would be expected to have less time to spend inside the household indicate that they consume fractionally higher proportions of commodities produced using relatively high proportions of immigrant labor.

Because the price benefits of immigration appear to be largely independent of the household attributes listed in the models, one should not conclude that all households benefit the same amount from immigration. Even within the attributes on which we stratify, some households gain a great deal from immigrants. For example, some households in West Los Angeles hire immigrant labor to care for their children, to chauffeur them to and from school, to tend their gardens and clean their houses, and to cook their meals. They also indirectly buy immigrant labor when they go out to expensive restaurants, have their cars washed, and have their clothes tailored. These households derive considerable economic benefits from immigration, but that subtlety is not captured in the models.

In sum, the benefits of immigration from lower prices are spread quite uniformly across most types of domestic consumers. Benefits from lower prices are higher for households with very high levels of wealth and education.

CONCLUSIONS

Our examination of empirical evidence on how immigration affects labor markets leads to the following general conclusions.

Immigration most directly affects the welfare of the immigrants themselves. Wages are higher in the United States than in less economically developed countries, and dispersion in wages is high relative to most of the developed sending countries. Because of these differences, immigration to the United States should be attractive to most workers from less economically developed countries and to more-skilled workers from many developed countries.

Once in the United States, immigrants on average earn less than native workers. This gap between foreign-born and native workers has widened recently, and recent arrivals and immigrants from Latin America have the lowest wages. The growth in this gap has come about despite improvement in the education levels of new immigrants over the last several decades. Although immigrant education levels have risen, they have not kept pace with the rising schooling of the native-born, and so the skills of immigrants have declined relative to those of the native-born.

This relative decline in wages and skills can be attributed essentially to a single factor—the change in the national origins of the immigrants. Recent immigrants have come increasingly from poorer countries, where average education levels are far below those in the United States. Part of this growing wage gap may stem from the influx of illegal immigrants, but there is also evidence of a growing gap among legal immigrants. With time spent in the United States, the wage gap narrows for some—significantly for immigrants from Europe and Asia, and at least modestly for some others—but not at all for those from Mexico.

Employment rates of recent immigrants have also fallen relative to those of natives. However, immigrants catch up to natives relatively quickly on this dimension, so that their employment rates are quite similar to those of natives after some years in the United States.

A higher proportion of immigrants than of the native-born work in many jobs that call for high levels of education—they are college teachers, medical scientists, economists. But they are even more disproportionately represented in many of the lowest-paying jobs: waiters and waitresses, agricultural graders and sorters, private household workers. Immigrants also account for a disproportionate number of workers in many occupations that require little education but much skill, such as tailors and jewelers.

Potentially, immigration could have large effects on certain parts of the labor market—workers in geographic areas that receive large numbers of immigrants or those with low levels of education. However, the evidence on local labor markets shows only a weak relationship between native wages and the number of immigrants. This evidence also indicates that the numerically weak relationship between native wages and immigration is observed across all types of native workers, skilled and unskilled, male and female, and black and white. Ironically, the one group that appears to suffer substantially from new waves of immigrants are immigrants from earlier waves.

However, the weak observed relationship between native wages and immigration may be due to problems with this approach. If native workers and firms respond to the entry of immigrants by moving to areas offering better opportunities, the wages of all competing native workers fall, not just the wages of natives working in the cities where immigrants cluster. But in this case, because immigration generates only small changes in aggregate labor supply, wage changes will be relatively small.

Looking in particular at workers with low levels of education, over the 1980s immigration was partly responsible for increasing the supply of high school dropouts by 15 percent relative to the supply of workers with at least a high school diploma. Based on an alternative approach using previous estimates of wage responses to changes in supply, the supply increase due to immigration could account for about 44 percent of the total decline in the relative wage of high school dropouts that was observed between 1980 and 1994.

The evidence points to the conclusion that there is only a small adverse impact of immigration on the wage and employment opportunities of competing native groups. This effect does not appear to be concentrated in the local areas where immigrants live, but instead is dispersed across the United States. This dispersal comes about in part because competing native workers migrate out of the areas to which immigrants move.

REFERENCES

Altonji, J.G., and D. Card

1991 The effects of immigration on the labor market outcomes of less-skilled natives. Pp. 201-234 in J. Abowd and R. Freeman (editors), *Immigration, Trade, and the Labor Market.* Chicago: University of Chicago Press.

Bean, F.D., B.L. Lowell, and L.J. Taylor

1988 Undocumented Mexican immigrants and the earnings of other workers in the United States. *Demography* 25(1):35-52.

Borjas, G.J.

1985 Assimilation, changes in cohort quality, and the earnings of immigrants. *Journal of Labor Economics* 3(4):463-489.

1990 *Friends or Strangers: The Impact of Immigrants on the U.S. Economy.* New York: Basic Books.

1992 National origin and the skills of immigrants in the postwar period. Pp. 17-47 in G. Borjas and R. Freeman (editors), *Immigration and the Work Force.* Chicago: University of Chicago Press.

1994 The economics of immigration. *Journal of Economic Literature* 32(4):1667-1717.

1995 The economic benefits from immigration. *Journal of Economic Perspectives* 9:3-22.

Borjas, G.J., R. Freeman, and L.F. Katz

1992 On the labor market effects of immigration and trade. Pp. 213-244 in G. Borjas and R. Freeman (editors), *Immigration and the Work Force.* Chicago: University of Chicago Press.

1996 Searching for the effect of immigration on the labor market. *American Economic Review* 86(2):246-51.

1997 How much have immigration and trade affected the U.S. job market? *Brookings Papers,* forthcoming.

Card, D.

1990 The impact of the Mariel boatlift on the Miami labor market. *Industrial Labor Relations Review* 43(2):245-257.

1996 Immigrant Inflows, Native Outflows, and the Local Labor Market Impacts of Higher Immigration. Unpublished manuscript, Department of Economics, Princeton University.

Carliner, G.

1980 Wages, earnings and hours of first, second and third generation American males. *Economic Inquiry* 18(1):87-102.

Chiswick, B.R.

1978 The effect of Americanization on the earnings of foreign-born men. *Journal of Political Economy* 86(5):897-921.

DeFreitas, G.

1988 Hispanic immigration and labor market segmentation. *Industrial Relations* 27(2):195-214.

Duleep, H.O., and M.C. Regets

1992 *The Elusive Concept of Immigrant Quality.* Washington, D.C.: The Urban Institute.

Filer, R.K.

1992 The effect of immigrant arrivals on migratory patterns of native workers. Pp. 245-269 in G. Borjas and R. Freeman (editors), *Immigration and the Work Force.* Chicago: University of Chicago Press.

Frey, W.H., and K. Liaw

1996 The Impact of Recent Immigration on Population Redistribution within the United States. Paper prepared for the panel. Research Report 96-376. Population Studies Center, University of Michigan.

Frey, W.H., K.-L. Liaw, Y. Xie, and M.J. Carlson

1996 Interstate migration of the U.S. poverty population: Immigration "pushes" and welfare magnet "pulls." *Population and Environment* 17(6):491-537.

Friedberg, R.M., and J. Hunt

1995 The impact of immigrants on host country wages, employment, and growth. *Journal of Economic Perspectives* 9:23-44.

Funkhouser, E., and S.J. Trejo

1996 Female Immigrants in the United States. Paper prepared for panel. Department of Economics, University of California, Santa Barbara, September.

Greenwood, M.J., G.L. Hunt, and U. Kohli

1997 The factor-market consequences of unskilled immigration to the United States. *Labour Economics* 4:1-28.

Greenwood, M.J., and G.L. Hunt

1995 Economic effects of immigrants on native and foreign-born workers: Complementarity, substitutability, and other channels of influence. *Southern Economic Journal* 61(4):1076-1097.

Greenwood, M.J., and J.M. McDowell

1993 The Labor Market Consequences of U.S. Immigration. U.S. Department of Labor, Bureau of International Labor Affairs, Division of Immigration Policy and Research.

Grossman, J.B.

1982 The substitutability of natives and immigrants in production. *Review of Economics and Statistics* 64(4):596-603.

Hamermesh, D.S.

1993 *Labor Demand*. Princeton, NJ: Princeton University Press.

LaLonde, R.J., and R.H. Topel

1991 Labor market adjustments to increased immigration. Pp. 167-199 in J. Abowd and R. Freeman (editors) *Immigration, Trade, and the Labor Market*. Chicago: University of Chicago Press.

1992 The assimilation of immigrants in the U.S. labor market. Pp. 67-92 in G. Borjas and R. Freeman (editors), *Immigration and the Work Force*. Chicago: University of Chicago Press.

McManus, W., W. Gould, and F. Welch

1983 Earnings of Hispanic men: The role of English language proficiency. *Journal of Labor Economics* 1(2):101-130.

Mines, R., and P.L. Martin

1984 Immigrant workers and the California citrus industry. *Industrial Relations* 23(1):139-149.

Muller, T., and T.J. Espenshade

1985 *The Fourth Wave: California's Newest Immigrants*. Washington, D.C.: The Urban Institute.

Murphy, K.M., and F.R. Welch

1992 The structure of wages. *Quarterly Journal of Economics* 57(1):285-326.

Reimers, C.W.

1983 Labor market discrimination against Hispanic and black men. *Review of Economics and Statistics* 65(4):570-579.

Simon, J.L., S. Moore, and R. Sullivan

1993 The effect of immigration on aggregate native unemployment: An across-city estimation. *Journal of Labor Research* 14(3):299-316.

Smith, J.P.
1997 *Hispanics and the American Dream.* forthcoming.
Waldinger, R.
1996 *Still the Promised City?* Cambridge, MA: Harvard University Press.
White, M.J., and L. Hunter
1993 The Migratory Response of Native-Born Workers to the Presence of Immigrants in the Labor Market. Unpublished manuscript, Brown University.
White, M.J., and Z. Liang
1993 The Effect of Immigration on the Internal Migration of the Native-Born Population, 1981-1990. Unpublished manuscript, Brown University.
Winegarden, C.R., and L.B. Khor
1991 Undocumented immigration and unemployment of U.S. youth and minority workers: Econometric evidence. *Review of Economic Statistics* 73(1):105-112.

APPENDIX 5.A
OBSERVED WAGE GROUTH OF MEN AND WOMEN

The following tables (A1-A3) supplement the material on immigrants' characteristics presented in the text.

TABLE 5.A1 Observed Wage Growth of Specific Cohorts of Immigrant Men, by Education Level (Percentage Wage Differential Between Immigrants and Natives, by Age Group and Year of Arrival)

	Year		
Cohort/Age Group	1970	1980	1990
0-8 years of school			
1960-1964 arrivals			
15-24 in 1970	—	7.7	8.9
25-34 in 1970	12.7	7.2	8.1
35-44 in 1970	–1.0	–0.1	5.2
45-54 in 1970	–4.3	–6.7	—
1965-1969 arrivals			
15-24 in 1970	—	6.6	12.6
25-34 in 1970	–2.4	0.1	5.4
35-44 in 1970	–15.7	–8.5	2.8
45-54 in 1970	–15.5	–9.5	—
1970-1974 arrivals			
25-34 in 1980	—	–3.3	4.3
35-44 in 1980	—	–7.9	–10.8
45-54 in 1980	—	–15.6	–8.9
1975-1979 arrivals			
25-34 in 1980	—	–18.0	–7.3
35-44 in 1980	—	–24.9	–17.4
45-54 in 1980	—	–29.8	–22.3
1980-1984 arrivals			
25-34 in 1990	—	—	–9.3
35-44 in 1990	—	—	–16.8
45-54 in 1990	—	—	–24.5
1985-1989 arrivals			
25-34 in 1990	—	—	–17.7
35-44 in 1990	—	—	–25.4
45-54 in 1990	—	—	–34.4
9-11 years of school			
1960-1964 arrivals			
15-24 in 1970	—	12.1	20.7
25-34 in 1970	15.8	7.5	8.3
35-44 in 1970	–1.3	0.5	7.8
45-54 in 1970	–18.7	–8.9	—

continued on next page

TABLE 5.A1 Continued

	Year		
Cohort/Age Group	1970	1980	1990
1965-1969 arrivals			
15-24 in 1970	—	2.2	12.1
25-34 in 1970	–4.1	2.3	1.2
35-44 in 1970	–16.0	–8.4	–1.9
45-54 in 1970	–17.5	–14.5	—
1970-1974 arrivals			
25-34 in 1980	—	–7.8	4.7
35-44 in 1980	—	–12.4	–5.0
45-54 in 1980	—	–25.3	–6.5
1975-1979 arrivals			
25-34 in 1980	—	–20.4	–7.0
35-44 in 1980	—	–21.4	–19.1
45-54 in 1980	—	–27.0	–18.5
1980-1984 arrivals			
25-34 in 1990	—	—	–9.5
35-44 in 1990	—	—	–17.4
45-54 in 1990	—	—	–23.8
1985-1989 arrivals			
25-34 in 1990	—	—	–20.7
35-44 in 1990	—	—	–24.7
45-54 in 1990	—	—	–29.1
High school graduates			
1960-1964 arrivals			
15-24 in 1970	—	–1.5	6.3
25-34 in 1970	4.0	0.0	–1.1
35-44 in 1970	–0.8	–8.3	4.1
45-54 in 1970	–17.2	–13.7	—
1965-1969 arrivals			
15-24 in 1970	—	–3.1	3.0
25-34 in 1970	–15.5	–10.2	–3.4
35-44 in 1970	–16.8	–17.7	–2.6
45-54 in 1970	–24.3	–23.9	—
1970-1974 arrivals			
25-34 in 1980	—	–10.5	–1.0
35-44 in 1980	—	–21.0	–15.9
45-54 in 1980	—	–25.4	–14.5

TABLE 5.A1 Continued

	Year		
Cohort/Age Group	1970	1980	1990
1975-1979 arrivals			
25-34 in 1980	—	–22.1	–10.0
35-44 in 1980	—	–25.5	–18.5
45-54 in 1980	—	–31.7	–21.0
1980-1984 arrivals			
25-34 in 1990	—	—	–13.3
35-44 in 1990	—	—	–22.2
45-54 in 1990	—	—	–30.5
1985-1989 arrivals			
25-34 in 1990	—	—	–21.5
35-44 in 1990	—	—	–28.3
45-54 in 1990	—	—	–34.7
Some College			
1960-1964 arrivals			
15-24 in 1970	—	3.1	5.8
25-34 in 1970	2.0	0.8	1.8
35-44 in 1970	–2.1	–8.0	0.1
45-54 in 1970	–14.7	–13.1	—
1965-1969 arrivals			
15-24 in 1970	—	0.1	–1.9
25-34 in 1970	–15.7	–9.4	–5.6
35-44 in 1970	–3.4	–11.5	–7.3
45-54 in 1970	–12.7	–20.9	—
1970-1974 arrivals			
25-34 in 1980	—	–6.8	–3.5
35-44 in 1980	—	–18.2	–11.7
45-54 in 1980	—	–18.7	–16.9
1975-1979 arrivals			
25-34 in 1980	—	–18.4	–9.0
35-44 in 1980	—	–22.3	–20.0
45-54 in 1980	—	–30.5	–16.2
1980-1984 arrivals			
25-34 in 1990	—	—	–13.8
35-44 in 1990	—	—	–21.3
45-54 in 1990	—	—	–30.9

continued on next page

TABLE 5.A1 Continued

	Year		
Cohort/Age Group	1970	1980	1990
1985-1989 arrivals			
25-34 in 1990	—	—	–23.1
35-44 in 1990	—	—	–24.8
45-54 in 1990	—	—	–32.5
College graduates (including those with graduate degrees)			
1960-1964 arrivals			
15-24 in 1970	—	5.7	8.0
25-34 in 1970	–0.1	2.1	8.6
35-44 in 1970	–11.8	–3.6	10.9
45-54 in 1970	–27.3	–12.7	—
1965-1969 arrivals			
15-24 in 1970	—	7.5	5.3
25-34 in 1970	–16.8	–1.4	5.5
35-44 in 1970	–22.8	–9.4	–1.9
45-54 in 1970	–28.7	–19.8	—
1970-1974 arrivals			
25-34 in 1980	—	1.9	4.7
35-44 in 1980	—	–14.2	–6.4
45-54 in 1980	—	–24.6	–14.1
1975-1979 arrivals			
25-34 in 1980	—	–10.8	–4.3
35-44 in 1980	—	–20.1	–14.7
45-54 in 1980	—	–20.3	–27.2
1980-1984 arrivals			
25-34 in 1990	—	—	–10.5
35-44 in 1990	—	—	–17.5
45-54 in 1990	—	—	–26.2
1985-1989 arrivals			
25-34 in 1990	—	—	–17.9
35-44 in 1990	—	—	–20.9
45-54 in 1990	—	—	–27.5

— = the cohort is outside the 25-64 age range.

Source: Tabulations from the 1970, 1980, and 1990 Public Use Samples of the U.S. Census of Population. The statistics are calculated in the subsample of men aged 25-64 years who work in the civilian sector, who are not self-employed, and who do not reside in group quarters.

TABLE 5.A2 Observed Wage Growth of Specific Cohorts of Immigrant Women, by Education Level (Percentage Wage Differential Between Immigrants and Natives, by Age Group and Year of Arrival)

	Year		
Cohort/Age Group	1970	1980	1990
0-8 years of school			
1960-1964 arrivals			
15-24 in 1970	—	2.6	16.0
25-34 in 1970	17.2	14.4	14.6
35-44 in 1970	21.4	5.7	14.4
45-54 in 1970	13.7	7.9	—
1965-1969 arrivals			
15-24 in 1970	—	8.5	11.3
25-34 in 1970	2.2	9.5	14.9
35-44 in 1970	2.9	3.6	7.0
45-54 in 1970	2.0	–0.0	—
1970-1974 arrivals			
25-34 in 1980	—	2.5	9.2
35-44 in 1980	—	2.2	7.7
45-54 in 1980	—	0.7	4.4
1975-1979 arrivals			
25-34 in 1980	—	–6.6	0.8
35-44 in 1980	—	–4.8	–2.3
45-54 in 1980	—	–8.6	2.8
1980-1984 arrivals			
25-34 in 1990	—	—	–3.0
35-44 in 1990	—	—	–5.7
45-54 in 1990	—	—	–5.5
1985-1989 arrivals			
25-34 in 1990	—	—	–12.2
35-44 in 1990	—	—	–13.1
45-54 in 1990	—	—	–9.8
9-11 years of school			
1960-1964 arrivals			
15-24 in 1970	—	11.8	11.6
25-34 in 1970	13.2	6.3	18.2
35-44 in 1970	12.0	8.0	9.2
45-54 in 1970	10.0	3.5	—

continued on next page

TABLE 5.A2 Continued

	Year		
Cohort/Age Group	1970	1980	1990
1965-1969 arrivals			
15-24 in 1970	—	8.6	17.1
25-34 in 1970	10.1	12.2	10.8
35-44 in 1970	–5.8	9.3	10.3
45-54 in 1970	–4.8	–1.4	—
1970-1974 arrivals			
25-34 in 1980	—	6.1	10.2
35-44 in 1980	—	2.6	0.6
45-54 in 1980	—	–1.3	–2.1
1975-1979 arrivals			
25-34 in 1980	—	–3.9	4.7
35-44 in 1980	—	–11.0	1.4
45-54 in 1980	—	–8.7	–0.4
1980-1984 arrivals			
25-34 in 1990	—	—	1.5
35-44 in 1990	—	—	–0.8
45-54 in 1990	—	—	–8.2
1985-1989 arrivals			
25-34 in 1990	—	—	–7.0
35-44 in 1990	—	—	–10.9
45-54 in 1990	—	—	–15.0
High school graduates			
1960-1964 arrivals			
15-24 in 1970	—	8.4	14.9
25-34 in 1970	8.1	0.9	3.5
35-44 in 1970	–2.0	–1.4	2.2
45-54 in 1970	–8.5	–7.9	—
1965-1969 arrivals			
15-24 in 1970	—	5.1	11.7
25-34 in 1970	–0.7	3.4	2.3
35-44 in 1970	–5.9	–1.3	1.9
45-54 in 1970	–22.7	–8.3	—
1970-1974 arrivals			
25-34 in 1980	—	–2.4	5.2
35-44 in 1980	—	–2.6	4.2
45-54 in 1980	—	–8.1	–1.0

TABLE 5.A2 Continued

	Year		
Cohort/Age Group	1970	1980	1990
1975-1979 arrivals			
25-34 in 1980	—	–9.3	3.4
35-44 in 1980	—	–3.6	–2.2
45-54 in 1980	—	–13.7	–7.0
1980-1984 arrivals			
25-34 in 1990	—	—	–4.0
35-44 in 1990	—	—	–3.7
45-54 in 1990	—	—	–9.8
1985-1989 arrivals			
25-34 in 1990	—	—	–8.8
35-44 in 1990	—	—	–15.7
45-54 in 1990	—	—	–22.8
Some college			
1960-1964 arrivals			
15-24 in 1970	—	5.7	12.7
25-34 in 1970	11.1	4.9	9.2
35-44 in 1970	–1.1	1.2	4.1
45-54 in 1970	8.0	1.2	—
1965-1969 arrivals			
15-24 in 1970	—	8.5	8.6
25-34 in 1970	–8.2	8.6	8.4
35-44 in 1970	–9.8	1.5	6.9
45-54 in 1970	–15.0	–4.0	—
1970-1974 arrivals			
25-34 in 1980	—	1.3	6.2
35-44 in 1980	—	–2.4	5.0
45-54 in 1980	—	–5.7	3.8
1975-1979 arrivals			
25-34 in 1980	—	–7.0	3.6
35-44 in 1980	—	–8.2	–1.3
45-54 in 1980	—	–18.5	1.7
1980-1984 arrivals			
25-34 in 1990	—	—	–2.3
35-44 in 1990	—	—	–7.5
45-54 in 1990	—	—	–15.5

continued on next page

TABLE 5.A2 Continued

Cohort/Age Group	Year 1970	1980	1990
1985-1989 arrivals			
25-34 in 1990	—	—	–12.7
35-44 in 1990	—	—	–18.8
45-54 in 1990	—	—	–23.5
College graduates (including those with graduate degrees)			
1960-1964 arrivals			
15-24 in 1970	—	7.3	13.6
25-34 in 1970	–14.4	0.6	4.4
35-44 in 1970	–20.5	–8.2	0.1
45-54 in 1970	–36.2	–21.7	—
1965-1969 arrivals			
15-24 in 1970	—	9.5	8.9
25-34 in 1970	–24.9	2.0	3.2
35-44 in 1970	–20.6	–12.2	2.6
45-54 in 1970	–39.5	–13.8	—
1970-1974 arrivals			
25-34 in 1980	—	1.7	7.6
35-44 in 1980	—	–5.6	0.6
45-54 in 1980	—	–20.0	–9.8
1975-1979 arrivals			
25-34 in 1980	—	–17.0	–2.1
35-44 in 1980	—	–24.7	–15.2
45-54 in 1980	—	–36.3	–25.6
1980-1984 arrivals			
25-34 in 1990	—	—	–3.0
35-44 in 1990	—	—	–17.2
45-54 in 1990	—	—	–24.2
1985-1989 arrivals			
25-34 in 1990	—	—	–17.8
35-44 in 1990	—	—	–26.2
45-54 in 1990	—	—	–35.4

— = the cohort is outside the 25-64 age range.

Source: Tabulations from the 1970, 1980, and 1990 Public Use Samples of the U.S. Census of Population. The statistics are calculated in the subsample of women aged 25-64 years who work in the civilian sector, who are not self-employed, and who do not reside in group quarters.

TABLE 5.A3 Observed Wage Growth of Specific Cohorts of Immigrant Women from Mexico and from Countries Other Than Mexico

	Year		
Cohort/Age Group	1970	1980	1990
Immigrants from Mexico			
1960-64 arrivals			
15-24 in 1970	—	–9.0	–16.6
25-34 in 1970	–25.2	–20.0	–26.2
35-44 in 1970	–12.9	–21.6	–25.8
45-54 in 1970	–21.6	–21.2	—
1965-69 arrivals			
15-24 in 1970	—	–17.7	–25.6
25-34 in 1970	–31.0	–21.0	–29.4
35-44 in 1970	–36.1	–23.6	–28.3
45-54 in 1970	–33.5	–28.1	—
1970-74 arrivals			
25-34 in 1980	—	–26.0	–31.7
35-44 in 1980	—	–26.6	–34.3
45-54 in 1980	—	–30.8	–35.5
1975-79 arrivals			
15-24 in 1980	—	–33.3	–37.1
25-34 in 1980	—	–32.4	–40.9
35-44 in 1980	—	–34.9	–37.7
1980-84 arrivals			
25-34 in 1990	—	—	–36.6
35-44 in 1990	—	—	–42.3
45-54 in 1990	—	—	–44.2
1985-90 arrivals			
25-34 in 1990	—	—	–40.9
35-44 in 1990	—	—	–42.8
45-54 in 1990	—	—	–46.9
Immigrants from Countries Other Than Mexico			
1960-64 arrivals			
15-24 in 1970	—	7.3	16.0
25-34 in 1970	5.2	4.5	7.4
35-44 in 1970	0.7	0.2	5.1
45-54 in 1970	–4.0	–3.1	—

continued on next page

TABLE 5.A3 Continued

Cohort/Age Group	Year 1970	1980	1990
1965-69 arrivals			
15-24 in 1970	—	5.2	6.5
25-34 in 1970	–5.1	8.5	8.1
35-44 in 1970	–9.1	–3.4	0.3
45-54 in 1970	–18.0	–8.7	—
1970-74 arrivals			
25-34 in 1980	—	0.8	6.3
35-44 in 1980	—	–0.1	4.1
45-54 in 1980	—	–10.3	–6.9
1975-79 arrivals			
15-24 in 1980	—	–10.5	1.8
25-34 in 1980	—	–11.6	–6.2
35-44 in 1980	—	–20.9	–9.6
1980-84 arrivals			
25-34 in 1990	—	—	–3.9
35-44 in 1990	—	—	–12.3
45-54 in 1990	—	—	–18.5
1985-90 arrivals			
25-34 in 1990	—	—	–11.9
35-44 in 1990	—	—	–22.6
45-54 in 1990	—	—	–26.8

— = the cohort is outside the 25-64 age range.

Source: Tabulations from the 1970, 1980, and 1990 Public Use Samples of the U.S. Census of Population. The statistics are calculated in the subsample of men aged 25-64 years who work in the civilian sector, who are not self-employed, and who do not reside in group quarters.

APPENDIX 5.B
CALCULATION OF SHARES OF EXPENDITURES ATTRIBUTABLE TO IMMIGRANT LABOR

This appendix outlines the procedures implemented to calculate labor and immigrant labor shares for all commodities available in the 1987 benchmark input-output tables of the Bureau of Economic Analysis (BEA), explaining how these shares are transformed into labor shares by broad expenditure categories.

THE CALCULATION OF COMMODITY LABOR SHARES

To be able to relate industries of employment to consumer products, the 1987 benchmark input-output (I-O) accounts are used. The BEA constructs these tables from census data once every five years (the 1992 tables are not available until 1997). The I-O tables accounts use two classification systems, one for industries and another for commodities, both using the same I-O numbers. This distinction between commodities and industries is necessary since industries may produce more than one commodity, and commodities in turn may be produced by more than one industry. For example, the commodity 14.0600, fluid milk, gets produced by industries 14.0600 (80.4 percent), 1.0100 (dairy farm products, 13.2 percent), and several other industries with relatively small shares. In turn, industry 14.0600 produces other commodities as well, such as creamery butter, cheese, and so on. The 6 digit I-O accounts thus summarize information for 519 commodities and industries.

The I-O tables are used to determine how much of a commodity gets produced domestically, by which industries it gets produced, and how much labor these industries use. Although not all commodities are consumed by households, they are still used as intermediate inputs in production of other commodities.

To relate a dollar of consumption expenditure to the share of immigrant labor, several steps are undertaken. Industries produce commodities using inputs such as labor and capital in combination with intermediate inputs, which may have been produced by other industries. The "make" table from the I-O accounts shows the dollar value in producer prices of each commodity produced by each industry. From this table, industry shares in producing commodities are determined as follows,

$$j = S \; i \qquad (1)$$

where j and i are vectors of ones representing commodities and industries, respectively. The S matrix is of dimension j by i, its elements representing industry commodity shares, with its rows adding up to one.

The "use" table shows the dollar value, in producer prices, of each commodity used by each industry. It also contains information on an industry's value added. From the use table, a technology matrix is constructed as follows,

$$i = T\ j + V \tag{2}$$

where the elements of T represent the commodity shares in a dollar of industry production and V being the industry's value added. The compensation of employees part of the value added, l, is used to determine an industry's labor share. Let o represent other value added, and we can rewrite equation 2 as,

$$i = T\ j + l + o \tag{2a}$$

Substituting 2a in equation 1 we get,

$$j = [I - TS]^{-1}\ S(l + o) \tag{3}$$

$$= W(l + o) \tag{3a}$$

The term Wl represents the dollar share of labor in the producer price of a commodity.

To obtain the commodity labor share in terms of purchaser, we need to add the labor that is involved in transportation, wholesale trade, and retail trade. Since part of the domestic supply of commodities is imported, the domestic labor share of a dollar's worth of consumption expenditure is given by the commodity labor share in terms of purchaser prices times the domestic share of commodity production.

Let lj denote the share of labor in a dollar's worth of consumption expenditure. The commodity labor shares are then calculated as,

$$lj = d\ [(1 - m)\ Wl + ml_m] \tag{4}$$

where m is the margin (transportation and trade) part of the purchaser price and l_m the share of labor involved in the trade and transportation margin. Shares attributable to labor are calculated in this way for every commodity.

Industries from the I-O tables are matched up with 1990 census industries to obtain immigrant industry labor shares. Immigrants are simply defined as foreign-born, not to American citizens, between the ages of 18 and 64 years, not living in group quarters. The immigrant labor share is defined as the share of total wages that flows to immigrants within every industry.

EXPENDITURE CATEGORIES

In order to relate the commodity labor shares to consumption expenditure data, commodities are mapped into 48 separate categories. A labor share is then calculated for every expenditure category. Commodities are weighted by the amount of personal consumption expenditures (PCE) to determine labor shares by expenditure category. Expenditures on housing are largely allocated to the construction industry. The definition of expenditure categories depends on how easy it is to map an expenditure category to a commodity in the I-O tables. On one hand, for example, expenditures on laundry, cleaning, and garment services can be directly linked to one I-O commodity. On the other hand, expenditures on food inside the home are linked to 50 commodities, most of which fall under "food and kindred products." Expenditure categories range from food (inside the home, outside the home), household services, financial and legal services, household goods (appliances, furniture), utilities, housing (rent, maintenance), apparel, education, transportation (cars, public), and recreation (equipment, fees).

6

Do Immigrants Impose a Net Fiscal Burden? Annual Estimates

INTRODUCTION

Are immigrants an asset or a liability in the provision and financing of public services in the United States? Judging by the 1996 welfare reform legislation restricting the access of legal and illegal immigrants to a variety of federally funded transfer programs, citizen approval in 1994 of Proposition 187 in California denying funding for public services to illegal immigrants, and recent suits by Arizona, California, Florida, New York, New Jersey, and Texas to recover additional funding from the federal government for immigrant services, many people believe the effect of immigrants is both negative and large. This chapter outlines how the fiscal impacts of immigrants on U.S. citizens in a single fiscal year should be measured and provides estimates of that annual impact for residents of California, New Jersey, and the nation as a whole. Chapter 7 extends this analysis to provide estimates of the long-run or dynamic fiscal effects of new immigrant families.[1]

Estimates of the annual and dynamic fiscal consequences of immigration are important for three reasons. First, from the perspective of those wishing to redesign immigration policy, estimates of the annual and lifetime fiscal impacts of new immigrants can be combined with estimates of their effects on the current

[1]Comprehensive surveys of the many studies estimating the fiscal impact of new immigrants on government spending and revenues are Rothman and Espenshade (1992), Vernez and McCarthy (1995, 1996), and MaCurdy et al. (1996).

and future earnings of domestic workers (discussed in Chapter 5) to determine whether they will be net economic contributors to society.

Second, because our system of public finance is a federal system and new immigrants tend to concentrate in particular regions of the country, they may create taxpayer inequities. Regions that receive a high concentration of new immigrants may bear relatively higher fiscal burdens in the short run if new immigrants contribute less in revenues—inclusive of federal and, for local governments, state aid—than they receive in additional public services. If so, residents in these regions shoulder a disproportionate share of the nation's annual fiscal burden of immigration. Apart from these tax inequities for native residents, a disproportionate allocation of immigration's fiscal burdens may also induce an inefficient allocation of labor. Facing relatively high tax burdens because of concentrated immigration, workers may leave productive employment in the fiscally disadvantaged region for less productive jobs elsewhere.

Third, although estimates of the annual fiscal impacts are important for understanding the economic consequences of immigration for the current year, estimates of how an immigrant family consumes public services and pays taxes over time are also important in order to know the full consequences of admitting additional immigrants into the United States. Almost no family stays just one year. On one hand, new immigrants, even those receiving a net fiscal transfer from residents in the *annual* accounting (those with children in school, for example), may ultimately be net contributors to the public sector over their lifetimes, as they pass into years of productive labor force participation. In the dynamic fiscal accounting, native residents will then be net fiscal beneficiaries. On the other hand, new immigrants who help solve our "annual" funding problem for Social Security and Medicare by increasing the population of payroll taxpayers (young adults, for example), are likely to become recipients of those programs later in life. In that case, an annual fiscal gain for native residents may eventually become a long-run fiscal burden. Furthermore, the long-run burdens or contributions of new immigrants can be reallocated among native residents through the choice of tax and debt policies. Today's burdens can be shifted onto future native residents (and immigrants) through increased government borrowing. Only a dynamic fiscal accounting can reveal these redistributions of fiscal burdens or benefits across generations and the true long-run consequences on native residents of new immigration. Finally, only dynamic fiscal accounting allows us to calculate the effects of new immigrants on the long-run economic sustainability of current fiscal policies.

Both annual and dynamic estimates of the fiscal effects of immigration will require decisions along five dimensions. The first four decisions must be made for both annual and dynamic accounting, the fifth for dynamic accounting only.

First, what is the appropriate demographic unit of analysis? The choice will depend on whether the study seeks to provide static or dynamic estimates of fiscal burdens. Since the household is the primary unit through which public services are consumed and taxes paid, it is the most appropriate unit as a general rule and is recommended for static analysis. Dynamic fiscal accounting using households becomes exceedingly difficult, however, as (often arbitrary) forecasts of family dissolution and formation become necessary. Dynamic studies are best completed by estimating fiscal impacts for individuals. If household estimates are required, hypothetical households can then be constructed directly from the individual fiscal profiles.

Second, what is the legal status of new immigrants? Legal status determines what services immigrants can receive and what taxes they will be required to pay.

Third, given immigrants' household composition and legal access to public services, what will be the effects of additional immigrants on the costs of providing those services? Care must be taken to specify the appropriate technology of public services. Some services are "public" goods—national defense is the easiest example—and do not require additional service spending to accommodate new residents; other services are more like private goods—for example, income transfers—and new residents must receive the same spending as current residents if service levels for all are to be held constant. In addition, new immigrants may utilize public services at different rates than current residents.[2]

Fourth, what will be the contribution of new immigrants to public revenues? For certain taxes—income and payroll—immigrant contributions seem clear. Less clear are the property tax contributions of immigrants who own or rent their residences, the corporate tax contributions of immigrants who buy corporate shares, and sales and excise taxes paid by immigrants who remit an unknown portion of their income to their country of origin.

Fifth—and unique to dynamic fiscal accounting—what are the future paths of income and population growth for new immigrants and for current residents, and what are the future paths of government spending and tax rates? In addition, dynamic fiscal accounting requires specification of a social rate of discount, so that future tax revenues and spending needs can be compared in terms of current dollars. The fact that different scholars give different answers to these five questions goes a long way to explaining the wide range of estimates now available for the fiscal impacts of new immigration (see MaCurdy et al., 1996).

The next section outlines the appropriate methodology for measuring the annual fiscal impact of immigrants on native households.[3] Afterward comes a section that applies this methodology to estimate the annual fiscal impact of immigrants in two states with a heavy concentration of immigrants: New Jersey

---

[2]Immigrants may impose a variety of external costs and benefits on society, some of which are not described here. Immigration may be associated with more diverse restaurants in an area, a benefit to some residents that is not directly measured in the fiscal analysis. Some of these social consequences of immigration are discussed in Chapter 8.

[3]Attention is limited in this chapter to the fiscal effects of immigration. The effects of immigration on labor market aspects of economic welfare of native residents are addressed in Chapters 4 and 5.

and California. In addition, estimates of the annual fiscal impact of immigrants on the federal budget are provided. The chapter's final section summarizes the results.

We emphasize here, and again in the conclusion, that any estimates of the annual fiscal impact of new immigrants, our own included, must be used with care. Annual estimates provide only a one-year snapshot of the how immigrant-headed households contribute revenues and withdraw resources from the public treasury. Such numbers do *not* tell us what the final fiscal impacts of a change in national immigration policy will be. To estimate the full fiscal impact of new immigrants, we need to know how those immigrants and their descendants will use services and pay taxes over their lifetimes while in the United States. Those estimates can come only from a dynamic fiscal analysis, the task of Chapter 7. The static analysis presented here provides the building blocks for the dynamic analysis, however, much as snapshots provide the images necessary for a moving picture.

ESTIMATING THE ANNUAL FISCAL IMPACT OF NEW IMMIGRANTS

The annual fiscal impact of immigrants on the economic well-being of native residents can be estimated in two steps.[4] Step one approximates the effect of the added tax burden imposed on native residents to fund the current level of services received by natives and now extended to immigrants. The reader should note that this analysis is carried out under the assumption that there are no behavioral changes in response to changes in the number of immigrants—it is what is known as a "partial-equilibrium" exercise. Step two shows how this added tax burden can be estimated from published data on government spending, taxes, family incomes, and family program participation.

Fiscal Accounting: Step One

Before the admission of immigrants, native residents enjoy consumption of government-provided public services (denoted by g_N) and after-tax income (denoted as y_N) that together determine their economic well-being. Higher levels of public services and more after-tax income improve the well-being of current residents, and reductions in services and after-tax income reduce it. Immigrants may affect the level of services provided to native residents, the level of their taxes and thus their after-tax incomes, or both. The final fiscal effects of immigrants on a typical native resident's economic welfare can be approximated by

---

[4]The methodology outlined here is a general approach—known as economic-incidence analysis—and can be applied to estimate the fiscal effects of any group on another.

the following monetary measure of the *net annual fiscal impact* of immigration on native residents (denoted as NAFI_N):

$$\text{NAFI}_\text{N} = \mu_N \cdot \Delta g_N - \Delta T_\text{N}, \quad (1)$$

where Δg_N is the change in public services received by the native household because new immigrants now share these services, μ_N is the economic value (measured in dollars) the native resident places on these public services, and ΔT_N is the change in taxes paid by the native resident because of new immigration. If NAFI_N is positive, then the fiscal effects of immigration make the typical native resident better off economically. If NAFI_N is negative, then the fiscal effects of immigration make the native resident worse off economically.[5]

[5]NAFI_N provides a first-order approximation of the change in native residents' economic welfare when new immigrants affect the public services that natives receive and the taxes that natives pay. This specification of the fiscal effects of immigration on native residents' economic well-being is part of a more general analysis, one that combines the labor market effects of immigration with the fiscal effects.

If $U_\text{N} = \text{U}(y_\text{N}, g_\text{N})$ represents the economic welfare of a native resident from public services (g_N) and after-tax income (y_N) then a small change in the number of immigrants (denoted as ΔM) affects native resident welfare through changes in y_N and g_N as:

$$\Delta U_\text{N} \simeq (\partial U_\text{N}/\partial y_\text{N})(\partial y_\text{N}/\partial M)\Delta M + (\partial U_\text{N}/\partial g_\text{N})(\partial g_\text{N}/\partial M)\Delta M. \quad \text{(i)}$$

The monetary equivalent of ΔU_N is obtained by dividing through the change in utility by the marginal utility of an extra dollar of income ($\partial U_\text{N}/\partial y_\text{N}$) to a native resident. That is:

$$[\Delta U_\text{N}/(\partial U_\text{N}/\partial y_\text{N})] \simeq (\partial y_\text{N}/\partial M)\Delta M + \mu_\text{N}(\partial g_\text{N}/\partial M)\Delta M, \quad \text{(ii)}$$

where μ_N is now defined to equal $(\partial U_\text{N}/\partial g_\text{N})/(\partial U_\text{N}/\partial y_\text{N})$ and represents the native resident's willingness to pay ($= \Delta y_\text{N}/\Delta g_\text{N}$) for public services.

Changes in a native resident's after-tax income come from two effects: the effects of new immigrants on resident incomes and the effects of new immigrants on resident taxes. Defining after-tax income (y_N) as pretax income (I_N) minus taxes paid (T_N) implies:

$$(\partial y_\text{N}/\partial M)\Delta M = (\partial I_\text{N}/\partial M)\Delta M - (\partial T_\text{N}/\partial M)\Delta M = \Delta I_\text{N} - \Delta T_\text{N} = \Delta y_\text{N}. \quad \text{(iii)}$$

Changes in a native resident's after-tax income (Δy_N) equal the change due to new immigrants' effects on the native resident's pre-tax earnings (ΔI_N) minus the change due to new immigrants' effects on a native resident's tax payments (ΔT_N).

Substituting (iii) into (ii) and defining $\Delta g_N = (\partial g_N/\partial M)\Delta M$ now specifies the first-order approximation to the final effect of new immigrants on a native resident's economic welfare as:

$$\Delta U_\text{N}/(\partial U_\text{N}/\partial y_\text{N}) \simeq \Delta I_\text{N} + [\mu_\text{N}\Delta g_\text{N} - \Delta T_\text{N}], \quad \text{(iv)}$$

Most studies of the fiscal impact of new immigrants make one important assumption, at least implicitly, before using NAFI_N as a measure of the change in current residents' well-being. The studies typically assume that all governments respond to the flow of new immigrants by holding fixed the level of government services provided to current residents—in other words, they assume government policies are adjusted so that $\Delta g_\text{N} \equiv 0$. If immigrants share government facilities and resources with native residents, then new facilities may be needed to provide services to the immigrants and to protect the level of services now provided to native residents. If so, government spending must increase and government taxes must rise. If native residents help pay for this increase in spending, then their taxes must rise. Using this approach implicitly values all changes in government services at their input costs. All fiscal impacts are now felt through changes in native residents' tax payments. With this additional assumption that all changes are made through taxes, the monetary measure for the overall fiscal effects of new immigration on current residents reduces to:

$$\text{NAFI}_\text{N} = -\Delta T_\text{N}, \tag{2}$$

where it must be understood that government spending and residents' taxes are adjusted to protect the level of services now provided to current residents (i.e., $\Delta g_\text{N} = 0$).[6]

If $\Delta T_\text{N} > 0$ and native taxes rise, then $\text{NAFI}_\text{N} < 0$ and native residents are worse off for fiscal reasons following immigration. Conversely, if $\Delta T_\text{N} < 0$ and native residents receive a net fiscal transfer from the new immigrants, then their taxes fall, $\text{NAFI}_\text{N} > 0$, and native residents are better off for fiscal reasons following immigration.

---

which can be rewritten more simply as:

$$\Delta V = \Delta U_\text{N}/(\partial U_\text{N}/\partial y_\text{N}) \simeq \Delta I_\text{N} + \text{NAFI}_\text{N},$$

where ΔV is the monetary value to a native resident of the change in utility caused by new immigration, ΔI_N is the change in pretax incomes, and NAFI_N is the net annual fiscal impact of new immigrants defined as the effect of new immigrants on public services received by native residents ($\mu_\text{N}\Delta g_\text{N}$) minus the effect of new immigrants on native resident taxes (ΔT_N). Chapters 4 and 5 have provided estimates of ΔI_N. This chapter provides estimates of NAFI_N.

[6]The analysis assumes that changing immigration has no effect on the fiscal policies of state and local governments. On the expenditure side of the equation, the analysis assumes that public goods and services are perfectly elastically supplied (with constant marginal and average costs) by state and local governments. This implies that an additional immigrant (or native) household residing in a state or locality has no effect other than as a scale multiplier on the level of public service provision. The analysis also implicitly assumes that the components of state and local revenue do not change as a result of immigration (or in-migration of native-headed families) to various localities. The assumption of exogenous fiscal policies provides useful short-run estimates for state and local government effects. Future work in this area could examine how much immigration affects fiscal policies at various levels of government and incorporate such endogenous effects into the modeling exercise.

Fiscal Accounting: Step Two

The annual fiscal impact of new immigrants on the tax payments of current native residents—ΔT_N—can be estimated from the government budget constraint that equates government spending to government revenues. Government revenues come from taxes on current *native* residents measured as the average tax per native resident times the number of current native residents ($= T_N \cdot N$); from taxes on current *immigrant* residents measured as the average tax per immigrant times the number of current immigrants ($= T_M \cdot M$); and from nonresident revenues such as government borrowing, intergovernmental transfers, proceeds from previously accumulated government wealth, and business taxes not already allocated to resident households equal to A_N per native resident times the number of residents ($= A_N \cdot N$). Similarly, government spending is allocated to provide services to native residents at a cost of E_N per resident times the number of residents ($= E_N \cdot N$); to previous immigrants at a cost of E_M per immigrant times the number of immigrants ($= E_M \cdot M$); and to businesses and nonresidents, including holders of current government debt raised to finance past deficits at a cost of X_N per native resident times the number of native residents ($= X_N \cdot N$). The government's cash-flow balance requires revenues in any year to equal spending in that year:

$$T_N \cdot N + T_M \cdot M + A_N \cdot N \equiv E_N \cdot N + E_M \cdot M + X_N \cdot N, \tag{3}$$

or alternatively,

$$[T_N - E_N] \cdot N + [T_M - E_M] \cdot M + [A_N - X_N] \cdot N \equiv 0. \tag{4}$$

Any changes in the budget must also show a cash-flow balance. If we assume that the number of native residents does not change following immigration and that government spending allocated to native residents remains fixed at current levels, so that service flows to those residents remain constant too, then changes in the public budget following an inflow of ΔM new immigrants becomes:[7]

[7]The full effect of new immigration on the cash-flow balance is represented by:

$$[T_N - E_N] \cdot \Delta N + [\Delta T_N - \Delta E_N] \cdot N +$$

$$[T_M - E_M] \cdot \Delta M + [\Delta T_M - \Delta E_M] \cdot M + [A_N - X_N] \cdot \Delta N + [\Delta A_N - \Delta X_N] \cdot N \equiv 0,$$

and this becomes the expression in the text when $\Delta N \equiv 0$ and $\Delta E_N \equiv 0$. Note that this decomposition ignores second-order terms (such as $\Delta M \cdot [\Delta T_M - \Delta E_M]$) because they will be small relative to the first-order terms.

$$\Delta T_N \cdot N + [T_M - E_M] \cdot \Delta M + [\Delta T_M - \Delta E_M] \cdot M + [\Delta A_N - \Delta X_N] \cdot N \equiv 0. \quad (5)$$

The effect on native residents' taxes of all budget changes that follow from immigration can therefore be specified as:[8]

$$- \Delta T_N = [T_M - E_M] \cdot (\Delta M/N) + [\Delta T_M - \Delta E_M] \cdot (M/N) + [\Delta A_N - \Delta X_N]. \quad (6)$$

This change in native taxes measures the stock of dollars needed to protect the current flow of public services provided to native households following immigration minus any new revenues generated by the new immigrants themselves. This difference, ΔT_N, is what the average native household must pay to protect government services after immigration and $-\Delta T_N$ is the net annual fiscal impact ($NAFI_N$) of this tax change. If $\Delta T_N > 0$ and $NAFI_N < 0$, then new immigrants impose a net fiscal burden on native residents. If $\Delta T_N < 0$ and $NAFI_N > 0$, then new immigrants offer a net fiscal benefit to native residents. Finally, if $\Delta T_N = 0$, then the new immigrants are "fiscally neutral" for native residents.[9]

This budget accounting clarifies the three possible avenues through which new immigrants can change a native resident's tax burden. First, if new immigrants receive the same level of services and pay the same level of taxes as previous immigrants, and spending exceeds (or is less than) taxes, then there is new tax burden (or relief) equal to the net fiscal balance of each immigrant (= T_M

[8]This impact need not be borne only by current native residents. If native residents share the burden of new immigrants with previous immigrants (M), then the measure of the fiscal effects of new immigration on native residents will be smaller and measured by:

$$- \Delta T_N = [T_M - E_M] \cdot (\Delta M/N + M) + [\Delta T_M - \Delta E_M] \cdot (M/N + M) + [\Delta A_N - \Delta X_N] \cdot (N/N + M).$$

The discussion that follows is valid for this adjusted measure of $-\Delta T_N$ as well.

[9]The measure of $-\Delta T_N$ specified here is for a single government. The analysis can be extended to a federalist public system by measuring $-\Delta T_N$ for each level of government, denoted as $-\Delta T_N{}^L$ for the local fiscal burden to be paid by local native residents in the jurisdiction receiving the new immigrants, by $-\Delta T_N{}^S$ for the state fiscal burden to be paid by native state residents in the state receiving the new immigrants, and by $-\Delta T_N{}^F$ for the federal fiscal burden to be paid by all native residents throughout the country. The total fiscal impact of new immigrants will be:

$$-\Delta T_N = -[\Delta T_N{}^L + \Delta T_N{}^S + \Delta T_N{}^F],$$

where:

$$-\Delta T_N{}^i \equiv \{[T_M{}^i - E_M{}^i] \cdot \Delta M^i/N^i\} + \{[\Delta T_M{}^i - \Delta E_M{}^i] \cdot M^i/N^i\} + [\Delta A_N{}^i - \Delta X_N{}^i],$$

for i = L, S, and F.

$- E_M$) times the number of new immigrants (ΔM). This aggregate fiscal balance is then shared among all native residents (N).

Second, if the new immigrants are poorer or less well educated than previous immigrants, then their utilization of public services—particularly, redistributive services and perhaps public education—may well be greater than utilization by previous immigrants. Furthermore, their tax contributions are likely to be lower. If so, then ΔE_M (the expenditures on immigrants) > 0 and ΔT_M (the taxes immigrants pay) < 0, and there will be a need for an upward fiscal adjustment to the initial fiscal balance estimate of ($T_M - E_M$). Of course, if new immigrants are richer and better educated than previous immigrants, then average spending on immigrants may fall ($\Delta E_M < 0$) and average immigrant taxes may rise ($\Delta T_M > 0$), reducing the average tax burden or increasing the average level of tax relief for native residents.

Current spending per immigrant may also decline with new immigration, even if the same level of immigrant services is provided, if there are significant economies of scale in the provision of public services to immigrants. For example, if a public service is a pure public good, such that the same level of services can continue to be supplied without an increase in spending even in face of new immigration, then *average* spending per immigrant following new immigration should be reduced ($\Delta E_M < 0$) to reflect this savings. This savings is assigned to the current native resident as a reduction in the tax burden imposed on them by new immigration. These adjustments to the average fiscal impact of immigration caused by admitting new immigrants ($\Delta T_M - \Delta E_M$) are then multiplied by all previous immigrants (M), and this total adjustment is then shared by native residents (N).

Finally, new immigrants may mean changes in nonresident revenues (ΔA_N), or nonresident spending obligations per native resident (ΔX_N), or both. The most likely direct source of new nonresident monies ($\Delta A_N > 0$) for state and local governments is additional federal aid to states and additional federal and state aid to localities when new immigrants qualify for federally supported public programs. Welfare programs at the state level and education at the local level are the most important examples. New immigrants may also have a positive effect on business tax revenues ($\Delta A_N > 0$) at all levels of government if workers' wages are lowered and returns to capital or to land increase and those higher business profits are then taxed. Offsetting these potential gains is the fact that new immigrants will share the proceeds from the stock of existing national public wealth.[10] Finally, nonresident spending at the state or local level may change (ΔX_N) if new immigrants affect the ability of government to provide services to the business sector, requiring compensating increases in government spending so as to hold

[10]For estimates of the value of federal government holdings of land and mineral wealth, see Boskin et al. (1985). See note 19 below.

business services fixed ($\Delta X_N > 0$). To the extent that the increase in nonresident revenues is larger than any increase in nonresident spending, the additional tax burden of new immigration on the average native resident will decline.

Fiscal Accounting: Implementation

Steps one and two detail how to measure, in principle,. the annual fiscal impact of new immigrants on current residents. Turning theory into practice requires data that first measure the number of current native residents (N), previous immigrants (M), and new immigrants (ΔM); average spending for (E_M) and revenues from (T_M) previous immigrants; the adjustments to average immigrant expenditures (ΔE_M) and revenues (ΔT_M) needed to reflect attributes of the new immigrant population; and changes in nonresident expenditures (ΔX_N) and revenues (ΔA_N) because of new immigration. There are guiding principles for estimating each of these needed quantities.

Measuring Population and Population Changes

Since most government programs will be decided for households, it is appropriate to measure N, M, and ΔM as the number of households in a given governmental jurisdiction.[11] The decennial census defines a household as family members living in the same home.[12] Furthermore, households should be distinguished by their legal status to receive government services and to pay taxes.[13]

[11]The calculation of spending and revenue includes all persons residing in the state on the date of the study. By definition, the static analysis is based on period estimates. All persons residing in the state, including native-born and foreign-born persons who moved into the state from another state, are included in the analysis. The static fiscal analysis takes into account interstate migrants, and the estimates are influenced by the number and characteristics of these migrants as well as of residents who were born in the state.

[12]The fiscal implications of this census definition should be appreciated when estimating the fiscal impact of previous immigrant households on native residents. For example, a previous immigrant couple with four U.S.-born children may, in the year in which fiscal effects are measured, have only two of those children living at home. The other two older children may now be in the workforce. The two older children will be counted in the census definition as native (not foreign-born) residents. In estimating the fiscal costs of previous immigration policies, it would be an error to count taxes and spending for the two immigrant parents and the two children at home and not count the taxes and spending of the two older children now in the workforce. It is most likely that these older children are contributing more in taxes than they are withdrawing in spending (particularly if their own children are not yet born). These positive contributions should be balanced against the net fiscal impacts of the parents and the two children still at home. Only a dynamic fiscal analysis can correctly account for these life-cycle changes; see Chapter 7.

[13]Available census and survey data do not distinguish the legal status of foreign-born respondents. The participation of illegal immigrants in the census and surveys, however, affects the reported public welfare use because they are ineligible for such programs.

Measuring Spending and Spending Changes

Spending per immigrant on government services (E_M) equals the sum of all spending needed to provide the current level of public services or government assistance to previous immigrant households now provided divided by the previous immigrant population. Spending must include the wages and benefits of public employees, the costs of materials and supplies, the payment of land rents, and the depreciation of public capital.[14] If the provided service is a transfer payment, then the costs of that service should equal the transfer paid plus administrative costs required to verify and service the recipient household.

The average level of spending per immigrant can change with new immigrants for one or more of four reasons: (1) New immigrant households are provided with lower ($\Delta E_M < 0$) or higher ($\Delta E_M > 0$) levels of services than previous immigrant households;[15] (2) new immigrant households permit the use of a more ($\Delta E_M < 0$) or less ($\Delta E_M > 0$) productive technology for producing services;[16] (3) new immigrant households use the public facilities less ($\Delta E_M < 0$) or more ($\Delta E_M > 0$) intensely than previous immigrant households;[17] or (4) new immigrant households may permit economies of scale through the sharing of public facilities with previous immigrants allowing a reduction ($\Delta E_M < 0$) in overall spending per immigrant.

Most studies of the fiscal costs of immigration assume that new immigrants are provided with services similar to those for previous immigrants, benefit from an equally productive service technology, and consume those services at the same rate as previous immigrants. These assumptions are reasonable provided care is taken to estimate the average spending on new immigrants from spending on previous immigrants with comparable incomes and family demographics.

Even with matching demographic cohorts, however, there may remain economies of scale in public service provisions. If so, then ΔE_M must be estimated, allowing for potential savings because services can be shared. Average spending declines by:

---

[14]All of these costs are included in most government balance sheets, except perhaps land rents and the depreciation costs of capital used to provide services. One possible measure of land rents and depreciation costs is current-period principal and interest repayments for infrastructure debt. *Most important, principal and interest payments to cover prior fiscal deficits should not be included as part of the estimate of the expenditures necessary to provide public services today to new immigrants and residents.* These past deficit borrowings did not support capital and land acquisition and therefore have no relationship to the costs of providing current-period public services. New immigrant taxes, however, do contribute to these deficit repayments.

[15]For example, the Personal Responsibility and Work Opportunity Reconciliation Act of 1996 restricts immigrant access to federal redistributive programs.

[16]For evidence of the costs of using different production technologies when providing immigrant services in education and welfare, see Clark (1994).

[17]For evidence that new immigrants may use welfare services more intensely than current immigrants, see Borjas and Trejo (1991) and Borjas and Hilton (1996).

$$\Delta E_M = -(1 - \alpha) \cdot E_M \cdot (\Delta M/M), \qquad (7)$$

where α measures the average degree of "privateness" in the provision of services to the immigrant population. The average degree of privateness (α) equals 1 when all services are fully congestible, private goods. As an example, take a crowded swimming pool or a crowded highway: a 10 percent increase in the number of swimmers or cars will typically require a matching 10 percent increase in the size of the pool or the highway if services per user are to remain constant. In this case, government facilities must be increased in direct proportion to the increase in the number of immigrants consuming the public service. Alternatively, when government services are best described by a privateness parameter (α) equal to 0, then those services are not congested and are called "pure public" goods. Pure public goods—an almost empty swimming pool or highway—can absorb an increase in the number of users without a corresponding reduction in the benefits currently enjoyed by service recipients. If government activities are pure public goods, then additional immigrants will not reduce the service benefits enjoyed by current native or immigrant residents.

If all government services are pure private goods ($\alpha = 1$), then there is no adjustment needed to the original estimate of the fiscal costs of taking a new immigrant into the public economy. Here $\Delta E_M = 0$, and estimating the costs of a new immigrant using average spending on previous immigrant households (E_M) is appropriate. Adding a new immigrant means that the same amount must be spent as is currently spent if service levels for old and new immigrants are to be protected. However, if government services are pure public goods ($\alpha = 0$), then an adjustment is required. Here $\Delta E_M = -E_M \cdot (\Delta M/M)$. The final fiscal costs needed to protect the provision of public services following new immigration is estimated as:

$$(-E_M) \cdot (\Delta M/N) + (-\Delta E_M) \cdot (M/N) = (-E_M) \cdot (\Delta M/N) + E_M \cdot (\Delta M/N) = 0. \quad (8)$$

When public services are pure public goods, adding new immigrant households does not require an increase in government spending; the government can provide the same level of benefits to old and new users without an increase in public facilities.

Of course, government services are neither all pure public goods nor all private goods. Typically, the public budget involves a mixture of public and private services.[18] In this general case, the final effect of new immigrants on native resident taxes felt through an increase in government spending will be:

[18]Recent economic research estimating the value of α for various public services finds estimates that range from almost pure public goods ($\alpha = 0$) to fully congestible private goods ($\alpha = 1$). Hanushek (1986) finds no significant effect of changes in class size on student performance for small changes in student population ($\alpha = 0$); Angrist and Lavy (1997) find large changes do matter ($\alpha = 1$).

$$\Delta T_N = \alpha \cdot E_M \cdot (\Delta M/N), \tag{9}$$

where α is the average degree of privateness in the public budget.[19] In the end, the total expenditure burden of new immigrants on native residents equals the average degree of privateness in the service bundle provided to immigrants *times* the average level of spending needed to provide that bundle *times* the number of new immigrants. This total burden is then shared among all current native residents, requiring each native resident to pay ΔT_N.

Measuring Revenues and Revenue Changes

Current taxes paid per immigrant household equal the sum of all taxes paid by previous immigrant households divided by the previous immigrant population. Not all immigrants pay taxes, however. If ρ is the proportion of immigrants who pay taxes, and if the taxes are levied at an average immigrant household's tax rate τ on the average immigrant household's tax base of β per immigrant taxpayer, then summing over each tax (denoted by t) collected by government defines the total taxes paid per average immigrant household as:

$$T_M = \Sigma_t \tau_t \cdot \rho_t \cdot \beta_t. \tag{10}$$

Most important, since the burden of taxes can be "shifted," it is the economic burden of the tax, not its initial legal burden, that must be measured.

Brueckner (1981) and McMillan (1989) find that fire protection services show significant publicness ($\alpha \simeq 0$); Duncombe and Yinger (1993) find fire protection services to be nearly a private good with respect to changes in population ($\alpha \simeq 1$). Craig (1987) presents evidence that police protection is a public good over most neighborhood sizes but in large neighborhoods services can be congested ($\alpha \simeq 1$). Inman (1978) finds that major access highways are pure public goods, except at peak rush hour when congestion is observed. On balance, the evidence is mixed as to the effect of population on the costs of service provision.

The prudent assumption—one that biases *upward* the estimates of the effects of new immigration on public service costs—is to assume that all public services are private goods ($\alpha = 1$). The one reasonable exception to this rule is national defense, for which it seems plausible to assume that the service will remain a pure public good ($\alpha = 0$) for most anticipated levels of new immigration.

[19]This follows from the specification above for ΔT_N allowing for spending changes only:

$$\Delta T_N \equiv E_M \cdot (\Delta M/N) + \Delta E_M \cdot (M/N).$$

From the specification for ΔE_M:

$$\Delta T_N = E_M \cdot (\Delta M/N) - (1 - \alpha) \cdot E_M \cdot (\Delta M/M) \cdot (M/N),$$

$$\Delta T_N = E_M \cdot (\Delta M/N) - (1 - \alpha) \cdot E_M \cdot (\Delta M/N),$$

$$\Delta T_N = \alpha \cdot E_M \cdot (\Delta M/N).$$

Estimating the economic burden of a tax after tax shifting requires assumptions as to how the legal burden of the tax is allocated economically. Do those who bear the legal burden change their economic behavior and "shift" the tax onto those less able to adjust? For example, it is reasonable to assume that workers bear the full burden of an income tax on their incomes from labor since most workers need their jobs (see Pechman, 1985; MaCurdy, 1992). But who bears the burden of an employer tax on worker incomes, like the employer portion of the Social Security payroll tax? Again, and largely because workers need their jobs, current estimates suggest that workers are likely to bear most of the tax's burden through a reduction in worker wages, even though the tax is legally assessed against the employer (see Pechman, 1985). Similarly, in a competitive economy, sales and excise taxes that are legally paid by retail businesses are likely to be passed on to consumers in higher prices for goods; thus, the consumer of the taxed good bears the burden of sales and excise taxes (see Pechman, 1985). The burden of government fees and licenses paid by consumers for the use of government services will likewise be borne by the consumer.

More difficult to assign are the final economic burdens of property taxation and business income taxes. Property taxes are probably best divided between owners of the taxed property and consumers of the services that the property provides. Thus, local property taxes on rental properties will be borne by renters and by landlords; most estimates suggest local renters bear the largest share of the tax's burden (see Grieson, 1974; Aaron, 1975). Local property taxes on owner-occupied housing will be fully borne by the family living in the house as they both "rent" and "own" the property. Property taxes on businesses will be borne by the investors in the business, by the firm's workers if wages can be reduced, or by the firm's customers if prices can be increased; best estimates suggest that business capital bears the burden of that tax (see Mieszkowski, 1972; Aaron, 1975). Similarly, business income taxes may be borne by business capital, by workers, or by customers; again, best estimates suggest that business capital bears the burden of business income taxes (see Shoven and Whalley, 1972; Pechman, 1985).[20]

In summary, current economic evidence argues that immigrants should be assigned the burden of sales and excise taxes and public-sector user fees when they consume the taxed goods and services, should be assigned the burden of labor and all of payroll taxes as they earn labor income, should be assigned all of

---

[20]At the state and local level, however, mobile businesses may be able to escape the burden of business property taxes and business income taxes by exiting to another locality with lower taxes. Only if those business taxes provide a compensating level of business services will the mobile firm stay within the taxing state or locality (see Mieszkowski, 1972; Courant, 1977). It is not unreasonable to assume that business capital is mobile across states and localities, and thus state and local business taxes must be matched by compensating business services. This incidence assumption is made in the two studies reviewed in the next major section below; see notes 29 and 33.

local property taxes as homeowners and almost all if they are renters, and should be assigned business income and property taxes if they own businesses or invest in business equity.

Even if correctly allocated, however, estimates of the average tax payments of new immigrants may not be accurately measured by the revenue contributions of previous immigrant households if new immigrants have different incomes, consumption behavior, or investments than previous immigrants. Three adjustments seem of potential importance. First, do new immigrants participate in the formal, taxable economy at the same rate (ρ) as previous immigrants do? If not, then estimates of immigrant tax contributions must be adjusted downward from the average level for previous immigrants if new immigrant participation is less than that of previous immigrants and adjusted upward if new immigrant participation is greater than that of previous immigrants. Second, do new immigrants have the same tax base (β) measured by taxable incomes, consumption, and investments as previous immigrants? If not, then again, average revenue estimates from previous immigrant households must be adjusted following new immigration, downward if tax bases are smaller and upward if tax bases are larger.[21] Third, if the tax system is progressive, so that tax rates rise as incomes rise, then if new immigrant households have higher (or lower) incomes than previous immigrants, then the average tax rate must be adjusted upward (or downward).[22]

The needed adjustment to the initial revenue estimates from new immigration provided by T_M can be approximated by:

$$\Delta T_M = \Sigma_t[\tau_t \cdot \Delta\rho_t \cdot \beta_t + \tau_t \cdot \rho_t \cdot \Delta\beta_t + \Delta\tau_t \cdot \rho_t \cdot \beta_t], \qquad (11)$$

where $\Delta\rho_t$ measures the change in the share of all immigrants who pay tax t, $\Delta\beta_t$ measures the change in the average immigrant tax base for tax t, and $\Delta\tau_t$ measures the change in the average tax rate of immigrants paying taxes. If new immigrant households are richer than previous immigrants, then the share of immigrants paying taxes is likely to rise ($\Delta\rho_t > 0$), as is the average tax base ($\Delta\beta_t > 0$) and, for progressive taxation, the average tax rate ($\Delta\tau_t > 0$). Thus, the average level of tax revenues collected from immigrants must be adjusted upward to reflect the lower contributions of new immigrants: $\Delta T_M > 0$. However, if new immigrants are poorer than previous immigrants, then the average rates of tax participation, the average tax base, and the average immigrant tax rate will fall, and the level of

[21]The evidence in Chapter 5 that recent immigrants have lower incomes than those who have been in the country for many years points to a downward adjustment, under the assumption that new immigrants are likely to have characteristics much like those who have recently arrived.

[22]Conversely, if the tax system is regressive and tax rates fall as income rises, then if new immigrants have higher (or lower) incomes than current immigrants the average tax rate must be adjusted downward (or upward).

revenues collected from immigrant households is likely to be lower than that now collected from previous immigrants ($\Delta T_M < 0$).

Measuring Nonresident Revenues and Spending

Governments receive revenues from nonresident sources—borrowing, intergovernmental transfers, accumulated public wealth, and nonresident taxes. These revenues (A_N) help current residents to pay for service expenditures not covered by resident taxes. Offsetting the gains from nonresident taxes, however, is government spending for nonresident and, most important, business services and debt repayments for past deficit financing (X_N). Increases in nontax revenues ($\Delta A_N^i > 0$) because of new immigration will reduce the added tax burden of immigration on native residents, and reductions in these revenues ($\Delta A_N^i < 0$) following immigration will add to native residents' burden. The most obvious and important source of additional nontax revenues for state and local governments is increased intergovernmental aid to cover the cost of services to new immigrant households. Matching aid tied to the level of current spending by the state or local government or grants paid per capita will rise with new immigration ($\Delta A_N > 0$); lump-sum grants and project grants independent of population or spending increases do not contribute to nontax revenues ($\Delta A_N = 0$). There may be a possible additional tax benefit from new immigration if it makes labor cheaper and thereby increases the taxed returns to capital or fixed factors of production such as land ($\Delta A_N > 0$). Offsetting these possible gains in nontax revenues for natives, however, is the dilution of native residents' share of the proceeds from national public wealth ($\Delta A_N < 0$).[23]

Finally, but likely to be less important, are changes in government spending for nonresident business services caused by immigration. The most likely case of new immigrants affecting the provision of business services is one in which residents and businesses share the same public facility, for example, a sewer system. In this case, however, if residents receive a direct benefit from that public facility, then the additional expenditures needed to protect the residential, and now business, service flows are already measured through E_M (spending to

---

[23]If W is the value of the national public wealth and r is the rate of return on that wealth, then native residents' share of these proceeds is diluted by the presence of new immigrants sharing in those proceeds: $A_N = (r \cdot W)/(N + M)$ and $\Delta A_N = -(A_N) \cdot [\Delta M/(N + M)]$. Boskin et al. (1985) estimate W measured as government holdings of land and mineral wealth to equal approximately \$994.4 billion in 1981. Inflating this estimate by the rate of growth in the consumer price index to December 1996 implies an estimate of W equal to \$1,750 billion. If $r = .10$ and $(N + M)$ equals the 1994 estimate of 98.175 million households, then A_N = \$1,782 per U.S. household. Admitting (ΔM =) 400,000 new immigrant households (about 1 million new immigrants) will dilute the typical native household's share of the proceeds from public wealth by about \$7.26 per year (= – (\$1782) · (.4m new households/98.175m current households).

provide government services to immigrants) and ΔE_M. Only in the very unlikely case that residents congest a public facility used by business but get no direct benefits themselves will new immigrants force an increase in X_N spending that is not already included elsewhere in the annual fiscal accounting. The final component of X_N spending is payments for past deficit financing. For this, however, new immigrants have no effect on the costs of repaying these historical obligations. For these reasons it seems reasonable to assume that ΔX_N is zero following new immigration.[24]

ESTIMATES OF THE ANNUAL FISCAL IMPACT OF IMMIGRANT-HEADED HOUSEHOLDS

Two recent studies, one of New Jersey by Garvey and Espenshade (1996) and one of California by Clune (1997) prepared for this panel, offer the most careful analyses to date of the annual fiscal incidence of immigrant-headed households on the budgets of local and state governments. In addition, the Clune study estimates the annual incidence effects on the federal budget of immigrant-headed households in California. The first two parts of this section summarize the local and state government results for New Jersey and California, respectively. The third part reports the estimates of the fiscal effects of California immigrants on the federal budget. Together the two studies allow estimates of the average fiscal balance ($T - E$) for immigrant-headed households ($T_M - E_M$) and native households ($T_N - E_N$), the key first step to estimating the net annual fiscal impact (NAFI_N) of new immigrants on native residents. Using these data from the Garvey and Espenshade and Clune studies, the fourth part estimates NAFI_N for the current population of immigrant-headed households on native residents. The final part extends the analysis to estimate the net annual fiscal impact on native residents of new immigration.

Table 6.1 summarizes the basic demographic and economic facts about immigrant-headed households in New Jersey and California and compares them with each state's native household population. Households are defined as all

[24] In the fiscal accounting here, there is no further adjustment to the fiscal balance because new immigrants share a historically given stock of governmental wealth or make contributions toward paying the interests costs of a historically given stock of governmental debt. Here the stock of existing financial assets and liabilities is "allocated" to the residents. Only if new immigrants alter the value of these historically given stocks of government assets or liabilities should a ΔA_N or a ΔX_N adjustment be added to our accounting. This seems unlikely. What is true and what our accounting does record, however, is the fact that new immigrants may contribute more (less) in revenues than they need in service spending. If there is a net contribution, then this surplus can be used to help cover any shortfalls in the historically given governmental wealth accounts. Alternatively, if immigrants impose a net fiscal burden, then this loss can be covered by any surpluses in the governmental wealth accounts.

family members living in the same home. Both legal and illegal immigrant households are included in both the Garvey-Espenshade (1996) and Clune (1996) studies; separate fiscal accounting for the two groups is not possible.

Net Fiscal Burdens in New Jersey: State and Local Budgets

New Jersey ranks fourth among the states in immigration measured by the number of the state's household population whose heads are foreign-born.

Almost half of New Jersey's immigrant population is from Europe or Canada; families from Latin America account for about a third; and families from Asia about a fifth of the state's immigrant population. Compared with native households, immigrant households have more children, earn slightly lower incomes, and use welfare services a bit more often. But there are large variations within the immigrant population. In particular, Asian and Latin American immigrant families have larger families, the Latin American immigrant families have significantly lower incomes, and they use welfare services nearly twice as often as native and other immigrant households.

Garvey and Espenshade (1996) provide the fiscal analysis required to measure the average fiscal balance for immigrant-headed households ($T_M - E_M$) and native households ($T_N - E_N$) for the state of New Jersey. Estimates of the utilization of local and state government services and taxes and fees paid by native and immigrant-headed households are provided for fiscal year 1989-90. The authors develop their estimates of spending received and revenues paid from individual household data, using the Census Bureau's Public Use Microdata Sample (PUMS) of 145,000 New Jersey households for 1990.[25] Previous studies have typically used state-wide averages for local and state spending and assigned the same spending levels to both native and immigrant households.[26] This standard approach allows for differences in program utilization between natives and immigrants (for example, in number of children and welfare eligibility), but it misses potentially important differences in the level of services received once a family qualifies. The Garvey and Espenshade study measures these important differences too.

Each household in the study is assigned to one of five groups by the nativity status of the head of household: native-born households, foreign-born of European/Canadian origin, foreign-born of Asian origin, foreign-born of Caribbean/

[25]The New Jersey study uses the 1990 PUMS data base because of its large sample size for the state. The alternative is to use the more current Current Population Survey data base (used by Clune in his study of California), but it has only a limited number of observations in the smaller states such as New Jersey.

[26]See Rothman and Espenshade (1992), Vernez and McCarthy (1995, 1996), and MaCurdy et al. (1996) for a comprehensive reviews of this literature.

TABLE 6.1 Profile of New Jersey and California Native and Immigrant-Headed Households

	New Jersey Households					
Characteristic	Native	Foreign-Born	Europe/Canada	Asia	Latin America	Other
Households (share of all households)	2.503m (.865)	.392m (.135)	.182m (.063)	.077m (.027)	.111m (.038)	.022m (.007)
Household size	2.68	3.10	2.62	3.59	3.51	3.16
Age of head	50.03	50.01	57.74	42.06	43.98	44.06
Children < 18	.63	.81	.52	1.14	1.02	.99
Adults > 65	.36	.35	.56	.15	.19	.19
Income/household	$61,966	$58,372	$56,873	$76,220	$48,858	$56,288
% receiving AFDC	2.57	2.63	1.01	3.04	4.93	2.99

Note: Household income data are inflated to be measured in terms of December 1996 dollars. Other = Africa or Oceania.

Latin American origin, and foreign-born of African or Oceanic origin ("other"). For each household in each nativity group, estimates are made of the taxes and fees paid to and of services received from local or state governments. For those services that are jointly provided by local and state governments—education is the most important example—each level of government is assigned its own share of total service provision.

Services provided by local governments and included in the Garvey and Espenshade study are general government administration, courts (excluding corrections), police and fire protection services, public works, welfare and public health, recreation and conservation, libraries, vocational education, community colleges, and—most important—K-12 education. The costs of each service are defined to include labor costs (including employee benefits, taxes, and pension contributions), expenditures for materials and supply, and capital costs estimated by the interest payments on local debts. Local governments include county governments as well as municipalities and school districts. Services provided by state government and included in the study are general government administration, public safety and criminal justice, health, community development, transportation, environmental management, employment training, education administration and state aid for K-12 education, higher education, the state share of

California Households

Native	Foreign-Born	Europe/Canada	Asia	Latin America	Other
8.385m (.746)	2.851m (.254)	.345m (.031)	.699m (.062)	1.592m (.142)	.215m (.019)
2.48	3.72	2.18	3.54	4.18	3.41
49.10	43.70	56.00	45.20	40.00	45.80
.64	1.37	.42	1.15	1.70	1.22
.34	.23	.45	.26	.15	.34
$50,518	$37,878	$45,857	$48,096	$30,012	$51,166
4.80	9.80	3.00	8.80	12.50	4.70

Source: New Jersey data are from Garvey and Espenshade (1996: Tables 1 and 2). California data are from Clune (1996: Tables 3a and 4a).

spending on Medicaid, Aid to Families with Dependent Children (AFDC), and Supplemental Security Income (SSI), general state welfare assistance, pharmaceutical assistance for the elderly and disabled, municipal aid to local governments, and property tax reimbursements.[27] All these local and state government services are treated as private goods by Garvey and Espenshade, each requiring a

[27]The PUMS data base allows Garvey and Espenshade to allocate education spending at both the state and local level to native and immigrant households by their geographic location; higher education spending by enrollment status; all state and local transfers to households (Medicaid, AFDC, SSI, general assistance, pharmaceutical assistance) and training programs by participation status and income; state-to-locality aid by geographical location; property tax relief by income and owner/renter status and geographical location; and general municipal government spending by geographical location. Finally, a few state expenditures could not be allocated to individual households through the PUMS data base. These programs include state spending on general government administration, public safety and criminal justice, health, community development, transportation, and environmental management. These expenditures are allocated to all households on a uniform basis, *after* deducting an estimate of general state services provided to the business sector, estimated by state taxes paid by the business sector.

proportional increase in spending to protect the level of services provided to native residents.[28]

Taxes and fees collected by local governments and assigned to households include property taxes and utility taxes. Consistent with current economic analysis, households who are renters are assumed by Garvey and Espenshade to bear the full burden of property taxes on their rental dwelling. Taxes and fees collected by state government and assigned to households include personal income tax, sales and use taxes, automobile and fuel taxes, alcohol and cigarette taxes, estate taxes, personal property taxes, and the realty transfer tax. State taxes on corporations and on banks and financial institutions and local property taxes on business are assumed to be borne by business capital; they are not assigned to New Jersey's household sector (see note 29).

Using the Garvey and Espenshade analysis, Table 6.2 summarizes local and state government revenues paid (*T*) and expenditures received (*E*) for all households in New Jersey, reported for an average ("all") household and for native and immigrant-headed households separately. The original Garvey and Espenshade estimates are for fiscal year 1989-90; Table 6.2 adjusts their estimates by the national consumer price index-urban (CPI-U) price index to reflect the value of services provided and taxes paid as of December 1996. The average New Jersey household, native and immigrants combined (denoted "all" in Table 6.2), receives $3,141 in locally funded services for which it pays $3,141 in local taxes and fees, and $2,715 in state funded services for which it pays $2,715 in states taxes and fees. The household fiscal budgets at both the state and local levels are in balance (expenditures = revenues). This overall fiscal balance for all households is required because (1) the overall state and local budgets must be in balance and (2) by assumption, all business taxes are assigned to provide business services.[29]

---

[28]That is, $\alpha = 1$ for all state and local services; see note 18 above. In fact, current economic evidence suggests that roadways, police protection, and fire protection may allow some sharing in their provision. If so, the estimates here will overstate the true fiscal burden imposed by immigrants on residents and should be viewed as conservative—that is, the Garvey and Espenshade estimates are more likely to overstate than understate true net fiscal burdens.

[29]From the analysis in the preceding section, on estimating the annual fiscal impact of new immigrants, the budget balance for each level of government requires that

$$[T_N - E_N] \cdot N + [T_M - E_M] \cdot M + [A_N - X_N] \cdot N \equiv 0,$$

where T_N and T_M are revenues collected from native and immigrant households, respectively, E_N and E_M are services allocated to native and immigrant households, and A_N and X_N are all revenues and expenditures received from, or paid to, sectors other than the household sector. Included in the nonhousehold sector is the federal government, businesses, and nonresident tourists. Garvey and Espenshade do not include federal revenues from grants-in-aid as state revenues; those outlays are implicitly counted as providing a federal government service and will appear as part of the allocation of federal dollars to households (see below). There are no significant local or state expenditures on

The fiscal balance for native households ($T_N - E_N$) and immigrant-headed households ($T_M - E_M$) measured separately need not equal zero, however; there can be fiscal redistributions within the household sector from one group to the other. Table 6.2 shows that in New Jersey in fiscal year 1989-90 there was a net fiscal redistribution from native households to immigrant households at both the local and state levels of government. At the local level, the average native household in New Jersey paid an additional \$144 per native household to offset the negative fiscal balance of \$922 per immigrant-headed household imposed by current New Jersey immigrants.[30] Table 6.2 reveals that the negative fiscal balance for immigrant households originates from the differentially high spending for immigrant families, particularly on K-12 education services. New Jersey immigrant families have more children than native families do on average (see Table 6.1), and in addition, Asian families in New Jersey tend to live in high-expenditure school districts. Immigrant households also receive more "other services," including local welfare services; this gap is particularly large for Latin American immigrant families. Interestingly, the fiscal gap between native and immigrant households is closed slightly by the fact that immigrant families in New Jersey—particularly those from Europe/Canada and Asia—pay more in local taxes than do native households.

At the state government level, immigrant-headed households in New Jersey are also in negative fiscal balance, by \$562 per immigrant-headed household. To cover this shortfall, native resident taxpayers contribute a positive fiscal balance of \$88 per native household.[31] The main sources of immigrants' negative balances at the state level are higher spending for K-12 education aid (because

---

behalf of the federal government. Thus the federal government does not appear in A_N and X_N. Businesses and, to a lesser extent, nonresident tourists are included in A_N and X_N, however. Expenditures for business and nonresident tourist services (X_N) cannot be estimated directly. Revenues from business and tourists (A_N) can be estimated, however. Assuming businesses and tourists are mobile and will not locate in any state that exploits them fiscally, the analysis assumes $A_N = X_N$. Given this assumption, then $[T_N - E_N] \cdot N + [T_M - E_M] \cdot M \equiv 0$—that is, the full household sector is in fiscal balance. In Table 6.2, balance is achieved by subtracting directly measured business taxes from the Garvey and Espenshade estimates of uniformly allocated state services. The remaining deficit for the household sector is then an estimate of the unmeasured business or tourist taxes in excess of business services. This final residual is also allocated to the business sector and netted uniformly from all households' state services.

[30]This required surplus of \$144 per native household is just sufficient to offset the negative burden of \$922 per immigrant household, so that the overall local government sector remains in balance: (\$144/native households) · (.865 native households/all households) – (\$922/immigrant household) · (.135 immigrant households/all households) = 0.

[31]Again, the \$88 per household contribution from the native population is sufficient to cover the net fiscal transfer of \$562 per household received by the immigrant population and keep the state budget in overall balance: (\$88/native households) · (.865 native households/all households) – (\$562/immigrant household) · (.135 immigrant households/all households) = 0.

TABLE 6.2 Local and State Expenditures, Revenues, and Average Fiscal Balance by Households: New Jersey (1996 dollars per New Jersey household)

	All	Native	Foreign-Born	Europe/Canada	Asia	Latin America	Other
Expenditures[a]							
Local							
K-12 education	$2,273	$2,162	$2,985	$2,730	$4,002	$2,625	$2,792
All other	868	807	1,251	1,075	1,080	1,606	1,471
Total	3,141	2,969	4,236	3,805	5,082	4,231	4,263
State							
K-12 education	1,625	1,585	1,878	1,583	1,985	2,178	1,912
Transfers to households	502	496	530	338	499	928	563
All other	588	566	738	623	813	833	763
Total	2,715	2,647	3,146	2,544	3,297	3,939	3,238
Revenues[b]							
Local							
Property tax	2,949	2,921	3,126	3,485	3,417	2,544	2,967
All other	192	192	188	196	190	182	180
Total	3,141	3,113	3,314	3,681	3,607	2,726	3,147
State							
Income tax	1,515	1,526	1,446	1,581	1,852	1,062	1,302
Sales tax	582	586	562	591	646	483	528
All other	618	623	576	622	624	503	522
Total	2,715	2,735	2,584	2,794	3,122	2,048	2,352
Average fiscal balance[c]							
Local	≡ 0	144	–922	–124	–1,475	–1,505	–1,116
State	≡ 0	88	–562	250	–175	–1,891	–886
Total	≡ 0	232	–1,484	126	–1,650	–3,396	–2,002

Note: Other = Africa or Oceania.

[a]Local government expenditures by community, school district, and county governments include the local share of outlays for K-12 education and an estimate of the household sector's share of "other" local expenditures for such services as public safety, public works, general health, recreation, and the local share of general assistance; see text. State government expenditures include the state share of outlays for K-12 education (school aid), the state's share of transfers to households (AFDC, general assistance, Medicaid, SSI, and miscellaneous state transfer programs), and an estimate of the household sector's share of "other" state expenditures, the most significant of which are expenditures for higher education and municipal assistance, including property tax relief; see text.

[b]Local government revenues collected by community, school district, and county governments include property taxation and a tax on utilities ("all other"). State government revenues include revenues paid by households under the state income and sales taxes and through various excise taxes ("all other").

[c]Average fiscal balance equals total revenues minus total expenditures. If the average fiscal balance > 0, then the average household in this category makes a net contribution to the state or local treasury. If the average fiscal balance < 0, then the average household in this category receives a net

notes continue on next page

immigrants have more children), for transfers to households (because immigrants are poorer), and for other state expenditures (because immigrant families are larger), and lower taxes collected from immigrant families (because immigrant families are on average poorer). *On average*, these spending and revenue differences between native and immigrant-headed families are relatively small, however. Two immigrant groups—families from Latin America and "other" (Africa and Oceania)—account for almost all of the immigrant group's negative fiscal balance. Asians and families from Europe/Canada (actually net *contributors*) impose no significant fiscal burden on native residents at the state level.

Combining the state and local public sectors, native households in New Jersey bear a total net fiscal burden of $232 per native household from the fact that the average immigrant-headed household receives $1,484 per immigrant household more in state and local services than it contributes in state and local taxes (see Table 6.2). There is wide variation across immigrant households as to the total state and local burdens they impose. Immigrants from Latin America are the biggest group contributor to the burden on native households. In contrast, families originating from Europe/Canada actually help native New Jersey households cover the estimated local and state fiscal shortfalls imposed by the other immigrant families.

Net Fiscal Burdens in California: State and Local Budgets

California has the most immigrant-headed households of any U.S. state, both absolutely and as a share of the state's population. In contrast to New Jersey, where immigrant families come predominately from Europe and Canada, more than half of California's immigrant families come from Latin America, and an additional 25 percent come from Asia. As in New Jersey, California immigrant families are poorer on average than California's native residents, have larger families, and use welfare services more often. But, as in New Jersey, immigrant households vary widely in these important attributes. Families coming from Latin America have the lowest incomes and the most children and are the most likely to be on public welfare; in California, these families are the biggest immigrant group.

---

transfer from the state or local treasury. Since the overall state budget must be in balance and (by assumption) state and local business revenues are fully allocated to pay for state and local business services, the overall household sector (column "all") must have an average fiscal balance = 0; see text.

Source: Calculations based on Garvey and Epenshade (1996: Tables 1, 3, and 5). Garvey and Epenshade's expenditure and revenue estimates for FY 1990 are adjusted upward to reflect December 1996 prices as measured by the CPI-U index.

Clune (1997) provides the fiscal analysis necessary to estimate the average fiscal balance for immigrant-headed households and native households for the state of California. The primary data source for Clune's analysis is the Current Population Survey for March 1995, providing detailed fiscal information for 4,590 California households. This survey is supplemented by data from state and local government budgets for fiscal year 1994-95. Like the Garvey and Espenshade study of New Jersey, the Clune study of California identifies program use by individual households. Households are assigned to native or immigrant groups by the country of origin of the household's head: U.S. native, or European/Canadian, Asian, Latin American, or other immigrant (of African or Oceanic origin). For each household in each nativity group, Clune estimates taxes paid and services received at both the state and local levels of government.

Public services provided at the state level to California households include Medi-Cal health care coverage and AFDC and SSI income transfers, state aid for K-12 education, state support for higher education, state police, corrections, and justice, public works, government administration, transportation, environment and recreation, and state assistance to local governments. Services provided by local governments include local spending on K-12 education, community colleges, police and fire protection, transportation, libraries, public health, public works, general low-income assistance, and general government administration. Like Garvey and Espenshade, Clune assumes each of these services is a private good, requiring a proportional increase in spending to protect services for native residents.[32]

Taxes and fees collected by (or in the case of the sales tax, for) local governments include property tax, sales tax, and miscellaneous fees and charges. As in the New Jersey study, renters are assumed to bear the full burden of local property taxation. Taxes and fees collected for the state government and borne by the household sector include personal income tax, sales tax, a state disability insur-

[32]That is, all state and local public services are assumed to be "private" goods ($\alpha = 1$); see note 18 above. For all redistribution programs, Clune estimates an average benefit per recipient and allocates that average expenditure to qualifying households as identified in the CPS data. K-12 education expenditures are estimated as a state-wide average outlay per child ($5,363 per child) and allocated to households by the number of school-age children in the household. Additional bilingual education costs per eligible child ($101/child) are allocated to the households according to the average number of qualifying children per household. For higher education benefits, a state-wide average is estimated and allocated to those households who list a family member attending a state college or university. Costs of incarceration could not be identified by nativity; thus state prison expenditures are allocated equally to all households in Clune's study. As for the New Jersey study, all other state and local expenditures are allocated on an equal per household basis, *after* deducting an estimate of general state services provided to the business sector, estimated by state and local taxes paid by the business sector.

ance tax, fuel taxes, liquor, tobacco, and excise taxes, motor vehicle fees, and estate taxes. As in the New Jersey study, state taxes on corporations and out-of-state tourists are assumed to be borne by businesses and nonresidents and are therefore not included as part of tax burden on California's households.[33]

Based on Clune's estimates of the fiscal incidence of government spending and taxes, Table 6.3 summarizes revenues paid to, and services received from, local and state governments by California households. As with Table 6.2 for New Jersey, the analysis reports expenditures, revenues, and average fiscal balance of an average ("all") California household ($T_. - E_.$), for an average native household ($T_N - E_N$), and for an average immigrant-headed household ($T_M - E_M$), overall and by country of origin. Clune's expenditure and revenue estimates are for fiscal year 1995; the results in Table 6.3 have been adjusted upward by the national CPI-U index so as to reflect December 1996 dollars.

The estimates for California reported in Table 6.3, like those for New Jersey, reflect the assumption that the household sector as whole is in fiscal balance. Thus, the average fiscal burden computed for "all" households equals zero at the local and state levels. Within the household sector, however, we see that in California—as in New Jersey—there is a fiscal redistribution from native residents to immigrant households at both levels of government. When providing local services, the average native household contributes a fiscal surplus of $283 per household to fund a fiscal deficit of $831 per immigrant-headed household (see Table 6.3).[34] When providing state services, the average native household contributes a fiscal surplus of $895 per household to cover an average negative fiscal balance of $2,632 per immigrant household (see Table 6.3).[35] Comparing services received and revenues paid across native and immigrant households

---

[33]State income taxes and payroll taxes are assigned to households according to each household's eligible tax base. State and local sales taxes are allocated to households according to the household's consumption of the taxed goods; downward adjustments (= $72/immigrant household) for income remitted to country of origin are made. Property taxes are assumed to be fully borne by homeowners and renters and allocated according to property tax payments reported in the 1990 PUMS data base for California residents. Fuel taxes and motor vehicle fees, liquor and excise taxes, and tobacco taxes are allocated to households according to car ownership (fuel taxes and vehicle fees), the number of adults of legal drinking age (liquor taxes), and the number of adults over the age of 18 (tobacco taxes). Inheritance and estate taxes are allocated equally to households according to their status as native or 20-year residence.

[34]The contribution of $283 per native household to California local governments just offsets the local government deficit of $831 per immigrant household, so that the overall local government sector remains in balance: ($283/native households) · (.746 native households/all households) – ($831/immigrant household) · (.254 immigrant households/all households) = 0.

[35]The contribution of $895 per native household to California's state government just offsets the state government deficit of $2,632 per immigrant household, so that the overall state government sector remains in balance: ($895/native households) · (.746 native households/all households) – ($2,632/immigrant household) · (.254 immigrant households/all households) = 0.

reveals that immigrant-headed households are larger consumers of K-12 education (due to relatively larger family size) and receive more state transfers to households (due to relatively lower incomes). Native and immigrant households pay nearly the same in local taxes, but the richer native households pay more in state income and sales taxes. Within immigrant groups, families from Europe/Canada are actually net fiscal contributors, even more so than natives, and households from Asia, Latin America, and "other" (Africa and Oceania) receive net fiscal transfers from California's state and local treasuries.

Combining the state and local public sectors, native households pay an additional $1,178 per household in revenues above services received to support a net fiscal transfer to the average immigrant-headed household of $3,463 household (see Table 6.3). As in New Jersey, the immigrant group making the biggest contribution to this net fiscal burden on native households in California is families from Latin America.

Net Fiscal Burdens in California: The Federal Budget

Clune (1997) also provides estimates of revenues paid, expenditures received, and the fiscal balance for the federal budget for households living in California for fiscal year 1994-95; all dollars have been inflated to reflect December 1996 prices. Table 6.4 summarizes these estimates for an average California household ("all") and then provides separate estimates for native households, all immigrant households, and immigrant households by country of origin.

Clune estimates the average California household paid $14,896 in federal taxes and received $13,549 in federal service spending. The difference—$1,347 per household—is the surplus contributed by the typical California household to the "primary" federal budget.[36] Native households contribute more than immigrant-headed households; virtually all the difference is due to the larger tax payments made by the (on average) richer native residents. Native and immigrant families receive about the same aggregate level of benefits from the federal treasury, with native families (which are, on average, older) receiving relatively more in Social Security and Medicare benefits and immigrant families (which are, on average, poorer) receiving relatively more in income assistance transfers

[36]Excluded from the accounting in Table 6.4 are federal government interest payments. Californians' share of federal interest payments equalled $1,995 per household in fiscal year 1995 (measured in 1996 dollars). Like all Americans, Californians ran a federal deficit on the full—primary plus interest payment—budget. The Californians' share of this deficit averaged –$648 per household (= $1,347 – $1,995). This total is smaller than the national average deficit of –$1,672 per household in fiscal year 1995 because Californians are richer (and thus pay more taxes) and younger (and thus use fewer services) than the typical American household, thereby "benefiting" less from federal borrowing.

TABLE 6.3 Local and State Expenditures, Revenues, and Average Fiscal Balance by Households: California (1996 dollars per California household)

	All	Native	Foreign-Born	Europe/Canada	Asia	Latin America	Other
Expenditures[a]							
Local							
K-12 education	$974	$768	$1,581	$435	$1,453	$1,888	$1,561
All other	4,549	4,522	4,627	4,587	4,732	4,587	4,624
Total	5,523	5,290	6,208	5,022	6,185	6,475	6,203
State							
K-12 education	1,537	1,212	2,496	687	2,294	2,981	2,465
Transfers to households	817	594	1,474	698	1,758	1,581	903
All other	780	704	1,003	686	1,140	882	1,086
Total	3,134	2,510	4,973	2,071	5,192	5,444	4,454
Revenues[b]							
Local							
Property tax	1,059	1,092	965	1,117	1,239	776	1,233
All other	4,464	4,481	4,412	4,453	4,467	4,370	4,484
Total	5,523	5,573	5,377	5,570	5,706	5,146	5,717
State							
Income tax	1,738	1,964	1,070	1,549	1,635	620	1,806
Sales tax	688	727	570	662	696	473	736
All other	708	714	701	620	749	703	657
Total	3,134	3,405	2,341	2,831	3,080	1,796	3,199
Average fiscal balance[c]							
Local	≡ 0	283	–831	548	–479	–1,329	–486
State	≡ 0	895	–2,632	760	–2,112	–3,648	–1,255
Total	≡ 0	1,178	–3,463	1,308	–2,591	–4,977	–1,741

Note: Other = Africa or Oceania.

[a]Local government expenditures by community, school district, and county governments include the local share of outlays for K-12 education and an estimate of the household sector's share of "other" local expenditures for such services as public safety, public works, general health, recreation, and the local share of general assistance; see text. State government expenditures include the state share of outlays for K-12 education (school aid), the state's share of transfers to households (AFDC, general assistance, Medicaid, SSI, and miscellaneous state transfer programs), and an estimate of the household sector's share of "other" state expenditures, the most significant of which are expenditures for higher education and municipal assistance, including property tax relief; see text.

[b]Local government revenues collected by community, school district, special district, and county governments include property taxation and a tax on utilities ("all other"). State government revenues include revenues paid by households under the state income and sales taxes and through various excise taxes ("all other").

[c]Average fiscal balance equals total revenues minus total expenditures. If the average fiscal balance > 0, then the average household in this category makes a net contribution to the state or local

notes continue on next page

to households.[37] National defense and other federal government services (state aid, subsidies to business, flood control, and so on) are distributed equally across native and immigrant families.

Among immigrant-headed households, we again observe significant variation in each cohort's net fiscal contribution. "Other" immigrants contribute to the federal treasury at about the same rate as native households, whereas Asian immigrants also make a significant positive contribution. Immigrant households from Europe/Canada and Latin America both receive a net fiscal transfer from the federal primary budget. Immigrant households from Europe/Canada are older and receive significant Social Security and Medicare benefits; Latin American immigrant households have lower incomes and more children and therefore qualify for more federal income assistance. Comparing the estimates here with the national fiscal year 1994 estimates presented in the dynamic analysis presented in Chapter 7 reveals a downward (toward negative) bias in the estimated federal burden in the California sample. The cause of the bias is the lower incomes of immigrants in California. Thus, the numbers here are not representative of the average immigrant household nationwide—the focus of Table 6.5.

The Total Net Fiscal Burden of Current Immigrants

The estimates of local and state fiscal balances from Tables 6.2 and 6.3 can be combined with the estimates of the federal government fiscal balances adjusted for defense spending in Table 6.4 to yield estimates of the net annual fiscal impact ($\mathrm{NAFI_N}$) of all current immigrant-headed households in New Jersey and California on the native residents of those states (see Table 6.5, panel A). Tables 6.2 and 6.3 provide direct estimates of the average fiscal balance ($T_\mathrm{M} - E_\mathrm{M}$), the most important component of $-\Delta T_\mathrm{N}$ and $\mathrm{NAFI_N}$. For state and local budgets, we

[37]Programs included in "transfers to households" in Table 6.4 include the federal share of AFDC, Medi-Cal, and SSI, and direct federal transfers to residents through federal, military, and railroad retirement and disability payments, unemployment compensation, workers' compensation, veterans' benefits, Pell grants, housing benefits, food stamps, school lunches, energy assistance, and the earned income tax credit.

treasury. If the average fiscal balance < 0, then the average household in this category receives a net transfer from the state or local treasury. Since the overall state budget must be in balance and (by assumption) state and local business revenues are fully allocated to pay for state and local business services, the overall household sector (column "all") must have an average fiscal balance = 0; see text.

Source: Calculations based on Clune (1996: Tables 1, 2, 3a, 5a, 6a, and 7a). Clune's expenditure and revenue estimates for FY 1995 are adjusted upward to reflect December 1996 prices as measured by the CPI-U index.

TABLE 6.4 Federal Expenditures, Revenues, and Average Fiscal Balance by Households: California (1996 dollars per California household)

	All	Native	Foreign-Born	Europe/Canada	Asia	Latin America	Other
Expenditures[a]							
Social Security	$3,064	$3,517	$1,728	$4,852	$1,308	$1,221	$1,834
Medicare	1,707	1,883	1,186	2,341	1,448	747	1,725
Transfers to households	3,461	2,977	4,727	3,059	4,672	5,265	3,593
Defense	2,809	2,809	2,809	2,809	2,809	2,809	2,809
All other	2,508	2,439	2,876	2,344	3,117	2,894	2,833
Total	13,549	13,625	13,326	15,405	13,354	12,936	12,794
Revenues[b]							
Income tax	6,733	7,621	4,123	6,153	6,198	2,357	7,207
Social Security	5,100	5,352	4,358	4,374	5,551	3,686	5,434
All other	3,063	3,374	2,163	2,392	2,468	1,855	2,398
Total	14,896	16,347	10,644	12,919	14,217	7,898	15,039
Average fiscal balance[c]							
Federal	1,347	2,722	–2,682	–2,486	863	–5,038	2,245

Note: Other = Africa or Oceania.

[a]Federal expenditures include Social Security and Medicare, direct federal transfers to households, the federal share of AFDC, Medicaid, and SSI transfers, defense, and other expenditures (e.g., transfers to state and local governments). Excluded are federal interest payments on past federal deficits; see text.

[b]Federal revenues include all revenue collected from the household sector: personal income taxation, revenues from Social Security taxes (including employer share), unemployment insurance tax, corporate taxation allocated to the household sector, and various excise taxes.

[c]Average fiscal balance equals total revenues minus total expenditures. If the average fiscal balance > 0, then the average household in this category makes a net contribution to the federal treasury. If the average fiscal balance < 0, then the average household in this category receives a net contribution from the federal treasury.

Source: Calculations based on Clune (1996: Tables 2, 5a, and 6a). Clune's expenditure and revenue estimates for FY 1995 are adjusted upward to reflect December 1996 prices as measured by the CPI-U index. All federal expenditures and revenues are based on Clune's estimates for households living in California.

TABLE 6.5 Net Annual Fiscal Impact (NAFI) Imposed by Current Immigrant-Headed Households on Native Residents in New Jersey and California

A. NAFI Imposed by Current Immigrant-Headed Households on Native Households in New Jersey and California

	Local NAFI	State NAFI	Federal NAFI	Total NAFI
New Jersey	–$144/native	–$88/native	$3/native	–$229/native
California	–$283/native	–$895/native	$4/native	–$1,174/native

B. NAFI Imposed by Current Immigrant-Headed Households on All U.S. Native Households

	Europe/ Canada		Asia		Latin America		Other		All Immigrant-Headed Households		
State Budget	NAFI	Nat'l Share	NAFI	Nat'l Share	NAFI	Nat'l Share	NAFI	Nat'l Share	NAFI	Immigrant Households	Aggregate NAFI
New Jersey	$449	.26	$2,022	.25	–$5,625	.43	$3,052	.06	–$1,613	9.156 million	–$14.77 billion
California	$1,631	.26	$1,081	.25	–$7,206	.43	$3,313	.06	–$2,206	9.156 million	–$20.16 billion

C. NAFI Imposed by Current Immigrant-Headed Households on Average Native Household

	Aggregate NAFI	Native U.S. Households	Native Household
New Jersey Budget	–$14.77 billion	$89.019 million	–$166/native
California Budget	–$20.16 billion	$89.019 million	–$226/native

Source: Calculations based on Tables 6.2, 6.3, and 6.4.

assume that $\Delta T_M = 0$ (new immigrants and previous immigrants pay identical taxes), that $\Delta E_M = 0$ (all services are private goods), and that immigration does not alter the balance between nonresident taxes and nonresident services ($A_N - X_N = 0$).[38] Thus for state and local budgets:

$$\text{NAFI}_N = -\Delta T_N = (T_M - E_M)(\Delta M/N). \qquad (12)$$

For the federal government budget, $-\Delta T_N$ and NAFI_N require an estimate of the average fiscal balance ($T_M - E_M$) at the federal level (see Table 6.4). The federal budget, however, contains an important pure public good—national defense—that need not be increased with additional immigration. Thus there is the need for a ΔE_M adjustment (see the section on fiscal accounting: implementation). Here $\Delta E_M = -\$2,809$ per household.[39] Again we assume $\Delta T_M = 0$ (new and previous immigrants pay identical taxes) and that $\Delta A_N = 0$ and $\Delta X_N = 0$.[40] For the federal government budget therefore:

$$\text{NAFI}_N = -\Delta T_N = (T_M - E_M)(\Delta M/N) - (\Delta E_M)(M/N), \qquad (13)$$

where $\Delta E_M = -\$2,809$ per household.

From Table 6.2, an average immigrant household in New Jersey is seen to have a negative average fiscal balance ($T_M - E_M$) of –\$922 at the local government level and –\$562 at the state government level. In Table 6.5, all current immigrants are treated as "new" immigrants; thus $\Delta M = M$. The average fiscal balances ($T_M - E_M$) are therefore multiplied by the ratio of the current immigrant to the native households (= M/N = .392m/2.503m = .157; see Table 6.1) to give estimates of NAFI_N for New Jersey native residents; Table 6.5, panel A, reports the results. For local governments in New Jersey, NAFI_N equals –\$144 per native household, and for state governments NAFI_N equals –\$88 per native household.

---

[38]Estimates of E_M and T_M are "own government" expenditures and revenues only. Thus state expenditures and revenues exclude federal aid and local expenditures and revenues exclude federal and state aid. In this specification, there is therefore no need to adjust state and local revenues for changes in federal and state aid following immigration; $\Delta A_N = 0$. We do need to include such aid in estimates of E_M for federal and state governments, however, as Tables 6.2 to 6.4 in fact do.

[39]See the section on fiscal accounting: implementation. In this section the adjustment in spending to allow for less than fully private goods is given as:

$$\Delta E_M = -(1-\alpha) \cdot E_M \cdot (\Delta M/M).$$

Since national defense is a pure public good ($\alpha = 0$), $\Delta M = M$ in this analysis, and E_M for defense = \$2,809 from Table 6.4, we have $\Delta E_M = -\$2,809$.

[40]Since there is no aid to the federal government, all business taxes are allocated to the household sector and are thus part of T_M, and the aggregate stock of government wealth is unaffected by new immigrants (see note 24 above), $\Delta A_N = 0$. New immigrants are assumed to not affect the flow of federal services unique to businesses nor the inherited aggregate stock of government debt (see note 24 above), $\Delta X_N = 0$.

Immigrant households in New Jersey impose a total fiscal burden on native residents of –\$232 per household through the state and local sectors, about four-tenths of 1 percent of a typical native family's income (.0037 = \$232/\$61,966; see Table 6.1).

From Table 6.3, an average immigrant household in California is shown to have a negative average fiscal balance ($T_M - E_M$) of –\$831 per household at the local level and –\$2,632 per household at the state level. Again, treating all current immigrant-headed households as new immigrants ($\Delta M = M$) requires multiplying these estimates of ($T_M - E_M$) by the ratio of current immigrants to native households (= M/N = 2.851m/8.385m = .34) to estimate the NAFI_N of California immigrants on native residents. For California's local sector, NAFI_N equals –\$283 per native household, and for California's state sector NAFI_N equals –\$895 per native household) (see Table 6.5, panel A). The total fiscal burden imposed on California native residents through the state and local public sectors because of immigrant-headed households is –\$1,178 per household, or about 2.3 percent of a typical native household's annual income (.023 = \$1,178/\$50,518; see Table 6.1).

Immigrant households do make a positive contribution to the fiscal position of native households through the federal budget, however. Table 6.4 allows us to estimate the NAFI_N from the federal budget for residents of New Jersey and California because of the presence of current immigrants in their states. First, the average federal fiscal balance of ($T_M - E_M$) –\$2,682 per immigrant household reported in Table 6.4 is adjusted for the fact that national defense is a pure public good; defense spending of \$2,809 per immigrant household should not be included in new expenditures and is therefore added to the negative fiscal balance (\$127 = –\$2,682 + \$2,809). Second, the resulting \$127 per immigrant household is multiplied by the number of immigrant households in California (= M = 2.851m) and then divided by the *national* native household population (= N = 89.018m), since all native households in the country share the *federal* contributions and costs of California immigrants. The resulting estimate of NAFI_N from the federal budget for all California immigrant households on California native households is \$4 per native household (= \$127 × (2.851m/89.018m); see Table 6.5, panel A).

The estimates in Table 6.4 for how California immigrants contribute to the national treasury can be used to approximate the contributions of New Jersey immigrants, assuming that they contribute in the same way as their country-of-origin counterparts in California. If so, then the net fiscal contribution of a New Jersey immigrant family, adjusted for defense spending, equals \$520 per immigrant household.[41] Again, this contribution should be aggregated over all New

[41]This estimate follows from applying the New Jersey distribution of immigrant households by country of origin (Table 6.1) to the estimated average fiscal balance adjusted for defense spending for each immigrant cohort in Table 6.4: \$520 per immigrant household = (.063/.135) × (–\$2,486 + \$2,809) per European-Canadian household) + (.027/.135) × (\$863 + \$2,809) per Asian household) +

Jersey immigrant families and then shared by all U.S. native households. In the end, a New Jersey native household benefits from a positive $NAFI_N$ of about $3 (see Table 6.5, panel A).[42]

Combining the local, state, and federal estimates of the net fiscal burdens imposed by immigrant households on native residents in New Jersey and California shows that the average native household bears an overall fiscal burden of $229 in New Jersey and $1,174 in California. The fiscal burden borne by Californians is larger primarily because of the larger burdens imposed at the local and particularly the state levels. Causing these differences are the larger ratio of immigrant to native households in California,[43] California's large share of immigrants in the economically poorer Latin American cohort,[44] and the relatively more generous welfare programs available to California residents.[45]

The analysis in Tables 6.2, 6.3, and 6.4 also allows estimates of the aggregate net fiscal impact on all U.S. native households of the current national immigrant population (Table 6.5, panel B). Two estimates are presented here, using the local and state budgets of New Jersey and California to estimate the net annual fiscal impact of immigrants through the state and local sectors. Because California has relatively more generous welfare programs, the national estimate using

---

(.038/.135) × (–$5,038 + $2,809) per Latin American household) + (.007/.135) × ($2,245 + $2,809) per "other" immigrant household).

[42]This share of the net fiscal contribution of New Jersey immigrant households is estimated as (net fiscal contribution/New Jersey immigrant household) ¥ (number of immigrant households in New Jersey) ÷ (number of U.S. native households) = ($520) ¥ (.439 m) ÷ (89.018 m) = $2.56/U.S. native household, including California native families. To be consistent with the California estimates, the 1994/95 New Jersey immigrant household population of 438,738 was used.

[43]From Table 6.1, the ratio of immigrant to native households in California is .34 (= 2.851m/ 8.385m). In New Jersey the ratio of immigrant to native households is .16 (= .392m/2.503m).

[44]In both California and New Jersey, immigrants from Latin America impose the largest net fiscal burdens on native households. Among the immigrants in California, more than half (= .56 = 1.592m/ 2.851m; Table 6.1) come from Latin America; in New Jersey the share of all immigrants from Latin America is about one-quarter (= .28 = .111m/.392m; Table 6.1).

[45]Comparing "transfers to households" in Tables 6.2 and 6.3 reveals that California immigrant households in each country-of-origin cohort receive from two to four times the transfers per household in New Jersey. More generally, the aggregate sizes of the per-household local-plus-state-sector transfers in California and New Jersey are $8,657 per household (= $5,523 per household + $3,134 per household; Table 6.3) and $5,856 per household (= $3,141 per household + $2,715 per household; Table 6.2), respectively. The state and local public sector is 48 percent larger in California than in New Jersey ($8,657/$5,856 = 1.48). Comparing the net fiscal contribution/transfer to immigrants by country of origin for California and New Jersey shows the transfer to Latin Americans in California is a 47 percent larger net fiscal benefit than that to their counterparts in New Jersey (–$4,977/ –$3,396 = 1.47) and the transfer to Asians in California is 57 percent larger than to Asians in New Jersey (–$2,591/–$1,650 = 1.57). "Other" immigrant households in the two states receive about equal net fiscal transfers, but they are only a small percentage of all immigrant households. The California fiscal disadvantage from the deficit immigrant groups is offset somewhat by the larger net contribution from the Europe/Canada immigrants, presumably because of more progressive state taxation in California.

the California budget can be viewed as an upper-bound estimate of the national net annual fiscal impact. Table 6.5, panel B, reports the total (local plus state plus federal) net annual fiscal impact ($NAFI_N$) imposed by each immigrant cohort for both the New Jersey and California specifications of the state and local budgets.[46] In fact, except for immigrant households from Latin America, today's current immigrants are net fiscal contributors to the overall fiscal position of native U.S. households, primarily because of their large positive net contributions to the federal treasury to help pay for defense spending. The Latin American immigrant cohort is large, however, and their negative net annual fiscal impact more than offsets the aggregate fiscal contributions paid to natives by Canadians, Europeans, Asians, and other immigrants.

Weighting each cohort's contribution by its share in the national immigrant population provides an estimate of the net annual fiscal impact imposed by a national average immigrant receiving either the New Jersey or the California state and local budgets. The national average immigrant imposes a net annual fiscal impact of –$1,613 per immigrant household when receiving the New Jersey budget and a net fiscal burden of –$2,206 per immigrant household when receiving the California budget. The aggregate $NAFI_N$ on native residents for all U.S. immigrants is estimated by multiplying these per-immigrant burdens by the number of immigrant households in the nation as whole. In 1994-95, there were 9,156,000 immigrant-headed households in the United States.[47] The aggregate net annual fiscal impact imposed on native households by all immigrant-headed households in the United States is therefore estimated to range from –$14.77 billion (New Jersey budgets) to perhaps as high as –$20.16 billion (California budgets) (see Table 6.5, panel B).

Sharing this aggregate burden over all 89,019,000 native households in the United States in 1994-95 would imply a net annual fiscal impact per native household ranging from –$166 (New Jersey budgets) to perhaps as high as –$226 (California budgets). This is an annual fiscal burden imposed on a typical native U.S. household by the current stock of immigrant-headed households now in the United States. The burden ranges from about four-tenths of 1 percent to half of 1 percent of the average household income of $45,000 in 1996.[48]

---

[46]For example, the total average fiscal balance for immigrants from Europe/Canada living in New Jersey is the sum of Table 6.2's estimates of that cohort's local and state net fiscal transfer plus the Table 6.4 estimate of that cohort's federal average fiscal balance adjusted for removing defense spending: –$124 + $250 + [–$2,486 + $2,809] = $449. The total average fiscal balance for immigrants from Europe/Canada living in California is the sum of Table 6.3's estimates of that cohort's local and state net fiscal transfer plus the Table 6.4 estimate of that cohort's federal net fiscal transfers: $548 + $760 + [–$2,486 + $2,809] = $1,631. All other cells in Table 6.5, panel B, are calculated in a similar way.

[47]Estimates calculated from the 1994-95 Current Population Survey.

[48]Average household income is estimated as the average for the most recent year available (= $41,428 in 1993) adjusted for inflation.

It is important to stress what the $NAFI_N$ estimates here represent. They *are* estimates of the annual fiscal burdens imposed on native households by current immigrant-headed households in the early 1990s. They *are not* estimates of the annual costs we could expect in all future years from admitting new immigrant families, and they *are not* estimates of the annual fiscal costs today of past immigration policies. To estimate the future fiscal costs, or benefits, of immigration, one must allow for today's fiscally costly young immigrants to leave school, take jobs, and contribute taxes; this requires a dynamic fiscal accounting. To estimate the annual cost today of past immigration policies also requires a dynamic analysis, one that looks back in time. Children born to immigrants in the United States who are now living on their own and earning incomes must be included in this historical evaluation. These contributing, second-generation children are here because of past immigration policies; they are not, however, included in the average fiscal balance for immigrant-headed households calculated here, because these children no longer live at home. Again, only a dynamic analysis can accurately account for the contributions of these individuals. Chapter 7 outlines one approach to dynamic fiscal accounting for immigration.

The Net Annual Fiscal Impact of New Immigrants

Although it is perhaps interesting to know the annual fiscal burden of current immigrant-headed households on U.S. native households, more relevant for contemporary policy debates over immigration policy are estimates of the net fiscal burdens of *new* immigrants on native U.S. households.

Tables 6.6 and 6.7 offer estimates of the net annual fiscal impact of new immigrants on native families living in New Jersey (Table 6.6) and California (Table 6.7), *under the assumption that new immigrant families are just like the current stock of immigrants now residing in the state*. The estimates reported in Tables 6.6 and 6.7 answer this question: What would be the fiscal burden on native residents if the number of immigrant-headed households now in the state were to exactly double?

The net fiscal impact imposed by a doubling of the number of immigrant-headed households is simply equal to the net annual fiscal impact from current immigrant-headed households, now shared by all households in the state or nation (see note 6). Thus, the net fiscal impact of doubling "all immigrants" will be slightly smaller than the burden of previous immigrants because the tax base over which to share the costs of the new immigrants will be larger. Whereas, as we've said, the current stock of immigrant households imposes a $NAFI_N$ on native households of about –\$229 per household in New Jersey and –\$1,174 per household in California, doubling "all immigrants" will impose a net annual fiscal impact on native New Jersey households of \$199 per household (Table 6.6) or

TABLE 6.6 Net Annual Fiscal Impact (NAFI) Imposed by Additional Immigrant-Headed Households on Native Residents: New Jersey (1996 dollars per current New Jersey household)

Immigrant Group	Local NAFI	State NAFI	Federal NAFI	Total NAFI
All immigrants	–$125	–$76	$2	–$199
Contribution by age of household head				
< 65	–$150	–$74	$12	–$212
65+	$25	–$2	–$10	$13
Contribution by region of origin				
Europe/Canada	–$9	$18	$1	$10
Asia	–$42	–$6	$3	–$45
Latin America	–$65	–$81	–$3	–$149
Other	–$9	–$7	$1	–$15

Note: Estimates of the NAFI imposed by New Jersey immigrants through the federal budget are based on Clune's estimates of the average federal fiscal balance by a typical immigrant household living in California in each age group and from each region of origin; see Table 6.4. The per immigrant household estimates were then weighted by the New Jersey immigrant population shares to obtain the federal NAFI estimates reported above.

Other = Africa and Oceania.

Source: Calculations based on Tables 6.2 and 6.4, adjusted for the share of native households in the New Jersey population (= .865) for local and state NAFIs and in the national population (= .0045) for the federal NAFI.

about three-tenths of 1 percent of the state's average household income (.03 = \$199/\$66,371) and will impose a $NAFI_N$ on native California households of –\$876 per household (Table 6.7), or about 1.8 percent of the state's average household income (.018 = \$876/\$48,347).

Tables 6.6 and 6.7 also decompose the net annual fiscal impacts from doubling "all immigrants" into the contributions made by doubling each of various subgroups of immigrant-headed households. For example, doubling all immigrant households doubles the number whose heads are under age 65 and the number whose heads are over age 65. What contributions do these two age groups make to the "all immigrants" totals? In both New Jersey and California, older immigrant households make a positive fiscal contribution at the local government level, paying more in taxes than they use in services (Tables 6.6 and 6.7). These positive contributions partially offset the negative net annual fiscal impact imposed by immigrant-headed households whose heads are younger than 65. At the state level, both age groups contribute to the negative $NAFI_N$ imposed on

TABLE 6.7 Net Annual Fiscal Impact (NAFI) Imposed by Additional Immigrant-Headed Households on Native Residents: California (1996 dollars per current California household)

Immigrant Group	Local NAFI	State NAFI	Federal NAFI	Total NAFI
All immigrants	–$211	–$669	$4	–$876
Contribution by age of household head				
< 65	–$221	–$635	$77	–$779
65+	$10	–$34	–$73	–$97
Contribution by region of origin				
Europe/Canada	$17	$24	$2	$43
Asia	–$30	–$141	$26	–$145
Latin America	–$189	–$528	–$36	–$753
Other	–$9	–$24	$12	–$21

Note: Other = Africa and Oceania.

Source: Calculations based on Tables 6.3 and 6.4, adjusted for the share of native households in the California population (= .746) for local and state NAFIs and in the national population (= .029) for the federal NAFI.

natives by immigrant households. Younger households, however, are responsible for 98 percent (.98 = –$74/–$76; Table 6.6) of the "all immigrant" total in New Jersey (.98 = –$74/–$76; Table 6.6), and for 95 percent of the total in California (.95 = –$635/–$669; Table 6.7). The reason, of course, is the larger number of younger immigrants. The relative contributions of the two age groups to the federal net annual fiscal impact shows that the younger immigrant groups make a net contribution in both New Jersey and California; older immigrants impose a fiscal burden on the federal budget.

Tables 6.6 and 6.7 also report the results of a decomposition by country of origin of the net annual fiscal impact from doubling immigrant-headed households. New immigrants matching the economic and demographic attributes of current immigrants from Europe/Canada will be overall net fiscal contributors ($NAFI_N > 0$). New immigrants matching the attributes of current immigrants from Asia, Latin America, and "other" regions will impose a net fiscal burden on natives ($NAFI_N < 0$). The single biggest group contribution to new net fiscal burdens—75 percent in New Jersey (.75 = –$149/–$199; Table 6.6) and 86 percent in California (.86 = –$753/–$876; Table 6.7)—will be by new immigrants matching the economic and demographic attributes and numbers of current Latin American immigrants.

Finally, the net annual fiscal impact imposed on an average native household nationally from a doubling of the current immigrant population can be estimated. If all states use the New Jersey state and local budget, then the aggregate $NAFI_N$ from a doubling of today's immigrant-headed households will be –\$14.77 billion (see Table 6.5, panel B). If all states used the California state and local budget, then the aggregate $NAFI_N$ from doubling today's immigrant household population will be –\$20.16 billion. These new fiscal burdens will be shared by all 98.175 million current native and immigrant households, implying an additional net fiscal cost per household ranging from \$150 per household (New Jersey budgets) to \$205 per household (California budgets), or a burden of between three-tenths and four-tenths of 1 percent of current national household income (≃ \$45,000).

These estimates of the net annual fiscal impact of doubling the current immigrant-headed household population can be adjusted to reflect the fiscal burdens on native residents of more modest population changes. For example, what will be the net annual fiscal impact on natives of a 5 percent increase in the current immigrant household population—an increase of about 460,000 new households? Such an increase represents an approximate continuation of current immigration policies. Such an increase will raise next year's net fiscal burden of immigrant-headed households by about \$10 per household in New Jersey (–\$9.95 = .05 · –\$199 per household; see Table 6.6) and by about \$45 per household in California (-\$43.80 = .05 · –\$876 per household; see Table 6.7). Nationally, a 5 percent increase in today's immigrant population will lead to an increase in next year's net fiscal burden for all U.S. native households of from \$7.50 per household (–\$7.50 = .05 · –\$150 per household for New Jersey budgets) to \$10 per household (–\$10.25 = .05 · –\$205 per household for California budgets).

CONCLUSIONS

On the basis of this analysis of the annual net fiscal burden of immigrant households on native families, the panel reaches six conclusions:

1. The state and local net annual fiscal impact of current immigrant-headed households on native residents measured as the difference between the costs of state and local services received and state and local taxes paid for New Jersey residents (for fiscal year 1989-90 adjusted to 1996 dollars) is estimated at \$232 per native household. Similarly constructed estimates for the net annual fiscal impact of current immigrant-headed households on native residents for California residents (for fiscal year 1994-95 adjusted to 1996 dollars) is estimated at \$1,178 per native household.

2. There are three central causes for the negative fiscal impact of immigrants on native residents at the state and local levels: (1) immigrant-headed households have more children than native households on average and therefore consume

more educational services, (2) immigrant-headed households are poorer than native households on average and therefore receive more state and locally funded income transfers, and (3) immigrant-headed households have lower incomes than native households on average and thus pay lower state and local taxes.

3. There are, however, important variations within the immigrant population in the size of the net annual fiscal impact imposed on native residents. Current immigrants over the age of 65 are net fiscal contributors to native residents in New Jersey, but they are a small net fiscal burden on native residents in California. However, almost all of the fiscal burdens imposed on native households by immigrants come from immigrant households whose head is younger than 65. Among the younger immigrant households, the net burden imposed on natives is by far the greatest for those immigrants from Latin American countries. In fact, immigrant households of European or Canadian origin make a net fiscal contribution to the native households of New Jersey and California through the state and local budgets in those states.

4. On average, immigrant-headed households in California made a net fiscal contribution to the federal budget in fiscal year 1994-95, receiving less in services and transfers than they paid in taxes. The positive fiscal impact of immigrant households at the federal level arises because they are assumed to impose no additional burden on the federal budget for national defense, specified here as a "pure" public good. The one exception to this pattern is the immigrant-headed households from Latin America; those households were a fiscal burden even at the federal level.

5. New Jersey and California are both states with high immigration, and as a consequence, the net annual fiscal impact of immigrant-headed households on native residents in those states—particularly from the services provided through state and local governments—are high as well. If these net fiscal burdens from immigrant households were shared not just within the states but nationally, then the burden per native resident would fall significantly. Estimates of the net fiscal burden imposed on all 89,019,000 U.S. native households by all 9,156,000 U.S. immigrant-headed households through all levels of government range from $166 per native household to $226 per native household. The lower estimate gives all U.S. immigrant households the New Jersey state and local budget; the higher estimate gives all U.S. immigrant households the California state and local budget.

6. A decision to admit 460,000 new immigrant-headed households—**assuming those households match the economic and demographic attributes of immigrant-headed households now in the United States**—would add about $10 per household to next year's net fiscal burdens for New Jersey residents and about $45 per household to next year's net fiscal burden for California residents. Nationally, admitting an additional 460,000 immigrant-headed households would lead to an increase in next year's net fiscal burden on all U.S. native households

of about \$7.50 per household (New Jersey budgets) to \$10 per household (California budgets).

The estimates of the net annual fiscal impact provided in Tables 6.2 to 6.7 provide a useful snapshot of the current fiscal consequences of today's immigrant-headed households on native residents in the United States. But also like a snapshot, these annual estimates cannot be used to criticize the past nor to predict the future. A simplistic use of the net annual fiscal impacts estimated here will be misleading for at least two reasons. First, both the native and current immigrant populations and the populations of newly admitted immigrants grow over time. The annual fiscal impact estimates provided here must be adjusted for these changing demographics if we are to accurately judge the fiscal burdens or benefits today of prior policies, or to predict the future burdens or benefits of today's choices. Second, annual estimates take people as they are today, but in the future native residents, current immigrants, and newly admitted immigrants will be people who differ both demographically and economically; their fiscal contributions or fiscal burdens will be different too. Children who consume services and pay no taxes today become contributing taxpayers tomorrow. Today's contributing adults will retire in the future and become net beneficiaries of government programs. Estimates of the current net annual fiscal impact of today's immigrant-headed households are not likely to give us very accurate information about the fiscal impact of today's immigrants 20 or more years from now.

The analysis here of the annual fiscal impact of today's immigrant households provides a starting point for understanding the future fiscal consequences of immigration. Predictions as to the long-term fiscal consequences of current or new immigration policies, however, must be based on a truly dynamic analysis of the fiscal incidence of immigration. Such a study must project the demographic and economic futures of current residents and new immigrants and the future paths of government spending, taxes, and debt policies. Only then will we have an honest representation of the long-run consequences of national immigration policies. Such estimates are provided in Chapter 7.

REFERENCES

Aaron, H.

1975 *Who Pays the Property Tax: A New View*. Washington, D.C.: The Brookings Institution.

Angrist, J., and V. Lavy

1997 Using Maimonides' Rule to Estimate the Effect of Class Size on Scholastic Achievement. National Bureau of Economic Research Working Paper No. 5888.

Borjas, G., and S. Trejo

1991 Immigrant participation in the welfare system. *Industrial and Labor Relations Review* 44(Jan.):195-211.

Borjas, G., and L. Hilton

1996 Immigration and the welfare state: Immigrant participation in means-tested entitlement programs. *The Quarterly Journal of Economics* 111(May):575-604.

Boskin, M.J., M.S. Robinson, T. O'Reilly, and P. Kumar
1985 New estimates of the value of federal mineral rights and land. *American Economic Review* 75(5):923-936.
Brueckner, J.
1981 Congested public goods: The case of fire protection. *Journal of Public Economics* February:45-58.
Clark, R.L.
1994 *The Costs of Providing Public Assistance and Education to Immigrants*. Washington, D.C.: The Urban Institute.
Clune, M.
1997 The Fiscal Impacts of Immigrants: A California Case Study. Paper prepared for panel. Department of Demography, University of California, Berkeley, January.
Courant, P.N.
1977 A general equilibrium model of heterogeneous local property taxes. *Journal of Public Economics* 8(3):313-327.
Craig, S.
1987 The impact of congestion on local public good production. *Journal of Public Economics* 32(Apr.):331-353.
Duncombe, W., and J. Yinger
1993 An analysis of returns to scale in public production, with an application to fire protection. *Journal of Public Economics* 52(Aug.):49-72.
Garvey, D., and T. Espenshade
1996 Fiscal Impacts of New Jersey's Immigrant and Native Households on State and Local Governments: A New Approach and New Estimates. Office of Population Research, Princeton University, September.
Grieson, R.
1974 The economics of property taxes and land values: The elasticity of supply of structures. *Journal of Urban Economics* 1(Oct.):367-381.
Hanushek, E.
1986 The economics of schooling: Production and efficiency in public schools. *Journal of Economic Literature* 24(September): 1986:1141-1177.
Inman, R.
1978 A generalized congestion function for highway travel. *Journal of Urban Economics* 5(Jan):21-34.
MaCurdy, T.
1992 Work disincentive effects of taxes: A reexamination of some evidence. *American Economic Review* 82(May):243-249.
MaCurdy, T., T. Nechyba, and J. Bhattacharya
1996 An economic framework for assessing the fiscal impacts of immigration. Department of Economics, Stanford University, September.
McMillan, M.
1989 On measuring congestion of local public goods. *Journal of Urban Economics* 26(Jan):131-137.
Mieszkowski, P.
1972 The property tax: An excise or profits tax? *Journal of Public Economics* 1(April):73-97.
Pechman, J.
1985 *Who Paid the Taxes, 1966-85*. Washington, D.C.: The Brookings Institution.
Rothman, E., and T. Espenshade
1992 Fiscal impacts of immigration to the United States. *Population Index* 58(Fall):381-415.

Shoven, J., and J. Whalley
1972 A general equilibrium calculation of the effects of differential taxation of income from capital in the U.S. *Journal of Public Economics* 1(Apr):281-321.

Vernez, G., and K. McCarthy
1995 The Fiscal Costs of Immigration: Analytical and Policy Issues. DRU-958-1-IF. Center for Research on Immigration Policy, RAND.
1996 The Costs of Immigration to Taxpayers: Analytic and Policy Issues. Center for Research on Immigration Policy, RAND.

7

The Future Fiscal Impacts of Current Immigrants

INTRODUCTION

Chapter 6 is a snapshot of the effects immigrants have on the U.S. fiscal situation, on an existing group of new immigrants at one point in time. It assigns to native-born residents alive at that time the tax burdens and expenditure benefits occasioned at all levels of government by members of different immigrant cohorts at that time. That picture is instructive, but it cannot be used to predict the long-term consequences of current or new immigration policies. This chapter sets out a forward-looking projection of the long-run implications immigration has for the fiscal balance. It fills in the picture drawn by the static calculations.

For our purposes, those static calculations in Chapter 6 have important limitations. These are particularly relevant when we consider the impact of immigrant flows that change in size and character over time, and when we wish to determine how such changes in the immigrant pool will affect fiscal balance.

The limitations in the static calculations stem from four factors. First, because a static calculation takes one group of existing immigrants, it combines members of different immigrant generations in that group who differ from one another. It therefore gives an inaccurate picture of the impact of any particular generation of immigrants. If, for example, elderly immigrants generally have had a higher level of income than younger, more recent immigrants, then the ratio of their Social Security benefits (which are based on their past incomes) to the payroll taxes of the new immigrants (based on their own, lower incomes) will overstate the ratio based on the benefits and taxes of either group separately.

Second, even if immigrants are all the same, tax and expenditure rules may change in the future. Today's Social Security benefits may be more generous than benefits in the future, so we cannot use current benefits to infer the burden that today's immigrants will ultimately impose on the system when they age.

Third, the outcome of the static calculation depends both on the relation of taxes to expenditures at each age over the life cycle and on the relative numbers of immigrants of each age in the population. Because patterns of expenditures and taxes differ over a lifetime, no single snapshot can accurately depict the impact of any individual cohort of immigrants if the population's age structure changes over time. For example, education spending relates primarily to the school-age population, and income tax payments relate to the working-age population. Consequently, increasing cohort size will overstate the cost of educational expenditures relative to the revenue from income taxes when these children enter the labor market. However, because any single cohort receives its education benefits earlier than it pays income taxes, the failure to discount income taxes overstates revenues relative to education spending. In general, unless the rate of growth of populations plus productivity equals the appropriate government discount rate, these effects will not cancel one another.

Fourth, because the government's budget need not be balanced over any particular time period, a deficit (or surplus) will develop equal to the difference between revenues and expenditures. There is no obvious way to assign the incidence of a deficit in a static calculation; if expenditures exceed revenues, this is not an "error" to be corrected. Yet we know that running a budget deficit today alters the fiscal policy choices tomorrow.

Many static calculations suffer from an additional, serious problem if they are based on the analysis of households with immigrant heads. In this case, they miss the effect of the adult native-born children of immigrants who do not live in households headed by immigrants, as we mentioned in Chapter 6. Because these younger people are likely to be making substantial contributions to the fiscal balance, their omission biases the results toward negative outcomes. This difficulty is not intrinsic to the approach, however.

These problems highlight the inherent limitations of static calculations, but they also point to a solution. Using the static as a starting point, we can project revenues and expenditures into the future, taking account of differences in individuals, policies, cohort sizes, and budget deficits to arrive at a more meaningful calculation that assigns revenues and expenditures to groups of immigrants at each date. This approach will yield the net impact of each group, based on the present value of these annual flows.

DYNAMIC INCIDENCE

The methodology of dynamic calculations of incidence is, to a large extent, simply the methodology of static calculations. Initially, we must go through the same exercise of estimating the marginal tax payments and benefits by age of different groups, determining the extent to which the addition of an individual would change expenditures or revenues, holding fixed the fiscal position of those already in the population. Once this is done for the current period, though, we must take several additional steps and make many more assumptions to complete the calculation. These additional steps include projecting future taxes and expenditures, discounting these future flows, and defining the nature of an immigrant "experiment."

Projecting Future Taxes and Expenditures

Because the dynamic calculation is forward looking, it requires estimating the trajectory of taxes and expenditures far into the future. These estimates affect the calculation in potentially important ways, since we are calculating the present value of the difference between taxes and expenditures at each age that immigrants pass through. If the government runs a large deficit in future years, then expenditures will exceed taxes for everyone on average, including immigrants. If taxes are raised in the future to balance the budget, or if expenditures are reduced, the negative impact of immigrants will decline, or the impact will become more positive.

The rules governing taxes and expenditures change every year, and it is impossible to predict precisely how they will evolve over the relevant future. Over the long run, however, any government faces an overall constraint on its ability to use deficit finance, which narrows the range of possible outcomes. In particular, it cannot let its debt grow without limit relative to the economy, as measured by gross domestic product (GDP), without losing credibility in its ability to repay and may eventually face default. To reflect this, it is necessary to assume that the ratio of debt to GDP stabilizes at some point. From this assumption comes the overall changes in taxes net of expenditures necessary in each year, relative to current policy.

To see why it is necessary to make some assumptions about a future fiscal adjustment, consider for a moment what would happen if we simply let taxes and expenditures follow a pattern that adheres to current rules. We initially projected taxes and expenditures each year, assuming a particular rate of economic growth, a particular pattern of immigration, and maintenance of current fiscal rules (except those already slated to change, like Social Security provisions). The results of that projection for the pattern of national debt is displayed in Figure 7.1. This figure depicts the time path of the national debt that will emerge given the present U.S. fiscal picture. Current tax and expenditure policies will cause the debt to explode over time (Auerbach, 1994; Congressional Budget Office, 1996). We can consider a variety of changes in taxes and expenditures that will bring the path of national debt into line with the particular assumption about how it will be stabilized, and measure the incidence for each scenario. For example, we might assume that the debt/GDP ratio is stabilized immediately at its current value; that

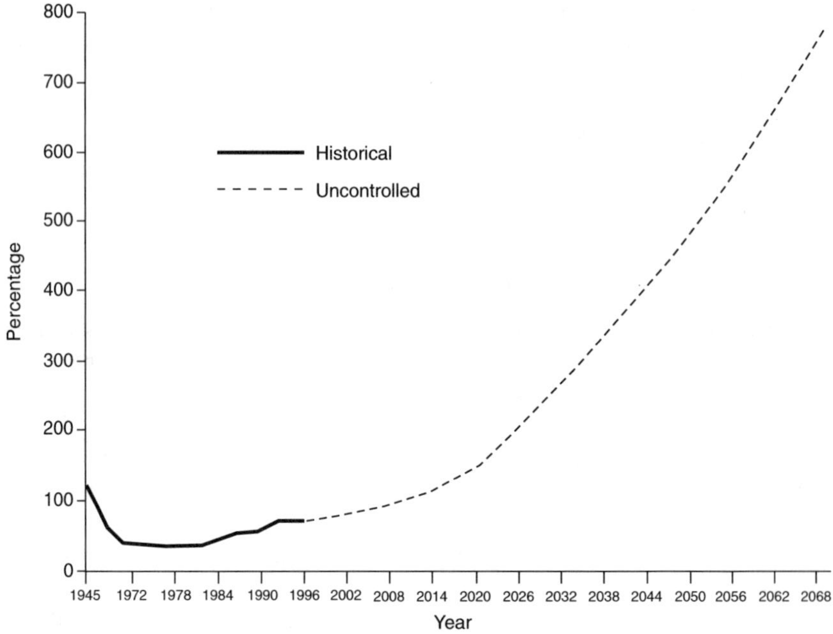

FIGURE 7.1 Gross federal debt as percentage of gross domestic product. (Historical data taken from 1996 Statistical Abstract, Table 512.) Uncontrolled: no fiscal controls on deficit. Adjusted: adjusted to historical data series using 1990 as the base year.

current policy remains in place for 10 years, after which the ratio is stabilized; or that current policy remains in place until the debt/GDP ratio hits 1.0. For each of these scenarios, we can consider the impact of adjustment in income taxes, in transfer payments, in defense spending, or in any combination of these and other components of the budget.

This approach to the government's long-run budget constraint clarifies the appropriate treatment of government debt and deficits under a dynamic incidence calculation. The burden of the debt itself is not assigned directly. Rather, individuals and their descendants are assigned the higher future taxes or lower future benefits that a higher current deficit may necessitate.

In each instance, we perform these calculations as a "partial-equilibrium" exercise. That is, we estimate budget changes needed under the assumption that people do not change their behavior in response to the new conditions. This assumption is unrealistic, but it is necessary given the complexity of the calculation. In any event, this limitation is one carried over from the static-incidence approach, and it is not likely to alter the qualitative nature of the conclusions.

One general equilibrium issue, however, needs to be discussed—how the net increase in the incomes of natives discussed in Chapters 4 and 5 would affect the fiscal calculations. In general, one can think of the total effect of immigration on native after-tax income (in a particular year) as the sum of the net increase in income from labor market effects plus the net fiscal impact in that year. Thinking of the labor and fiscal effects as completely independent seems problematic at first glance, because the increase in income from the labor market effects would presumably lead to additional tax payments, which one would think ought to be considered in doing the fiscal calculation. However, in adding these two pieces together, it is important to realize that it would be double counting to first count a gain in income in the labor market effects and then also count the part of that increase that goes to additional tax payments in calculating fiscal effects.

How should one factor in the increase in incomes of natives in doing the fiscal calculation? The answer depends on what is assumed about the path of future taxes and expenditures. Consider the case in which taxes and benefits adjust to stabilize the debt/GDP ratio at some point. For simplicity, think of benefits as fixed, so debt targets are met through adjustments in taxes. The total amount of tax revenues needed to meet the debt target in a given year is essentially unaffected by the increase in the incomes of natives, although the tax rate needed to generate that level of revenues will fall. Taking into account the income gain to natives may thus lead to a slight shift in the incidence of the tax that would be unfavorable to natives. With a reduced tax rate for everyone and higher income for natives, natives would pay a slightly higher portion of total tax revenues, but this effect would have to be small. Aside from this shift in incidence, it would be correct to simply ignore the additional tax revenues coming from the gain in native income in the fiscal calculations, because it is rebated to natives through lower tax rates.

Discounting Future Dollar Flows

To discount the future flows for each immigrant or immigrant group, we must also settle on an appropriate discount rate. Here, there are a variety of options. The straightforward approach is to use a government borrowing rate, which will provide, in expected value, the present value of future net flows. However, given the uncertainty of the future and the riskiness of future taxes and benefits, it may be more appropriate to discount these flows with a discount rate that reflects their risk characteristics. For example, future income taxes might be discounted with a market discount rate that reflects the riskiness of future income (see Auerbach et al., 1991, for further discussion). Because the "right" discount rate depends on the question being asked, calculations based on a range of discount rates may be appropriate, and that is the approach we follow.

Defining the New Immigration "Experiment"

A dynamic-incidence calculation is intended to enable us to determine the fiscal impact of an additional immigrant of a particular type at a particular date. But we must be more precise regarding this "experiment." An immigrant's arrival has fiscal consequences not only from the immigrant directly, but also from her offspring and their descendants, even though they themselves will be native-born. Thus, we must include in the calculation changes in taxes and expenditures associated not only with the immigrant, but also with her descendants. This process relies on the assumptions made about the characteristics of future immigrants and the speed of assimilation. To calculate the future tax and expenditure flows for immigrants, we must estimate the characteristics of new immigrants, as well as the extent to which the differences between immigrants and natives (in, for example, the birth rate, earnings conditional on education, the fraction of those who are eligible for a benefit that actually apply for it) disappear over time through assimilation. It may also depend on assumptions about the extent to which immigrants marry outside their own ethnic groups, to the extent that this is deemed to influence the rate of assimilation.

Indeed, the dynamic-incidence approach should also allow us to compare the impact of a new immigrant of a particular type at a particular date to that of a comparable native birth. This comparison is useful in separating the fiscal impact of immigration into the impact of population growth generally and the impact of growth through immigration.

KINDS OF IMPACTS

The lifetime fiscal effects of an immigrant and his descendants can be divided into two categories: first, the fiscal benefits or costs of adding one more person to the population regardless of immigrant status and, second, the fiscal benefits and costs associated with the special characteristics of immigrants, such as age at arrival, time since arrival, English language ability, and education. We will briefly discuss these two categories of impacts.

Fiscal Impacts Relatively Independent of Immigrant Characteristics

Any increment to the population, holding all else equal, will have fiscal effects. These arise in part because a larger population helps to bear the cost of so-called public goods—those that provide services to all in the population at a cost that does not rise with the size of the population. National defense, expenditures on veterans, and research on health and science all are public goods.[1] The cost per capita of providing a given level of services declines as population rises because more taxpayers share the unchanging total costs. Also, a larger popula-

[1]For a discussion of empirical estimates of the "publicness" of various kinds of government expenditures, see Chapter 6.

tion helps to bear the burden of the preexisting public debt through tax payments to cover interest or repayment charges.[2]

Much like anyone else in the population, immigrants use services that are costly to provide, or that others can use less freely—so-called congestion costs. Examples include services from roads, sewers, police and fire departments, libraries, airports, and foreign embassies. These services may have a public good aspect, but because they are highly congestible, we treat them as if immigrants raise both the demand for them and the cost of meeting that demand, in proportion to their numbers. Such items have both a capital cost and a current cost, and we account for these separately.

Additional members of the population, whether immigrant or not, crowd the existing social infrastructure, including roads, libraries, airports, sewage and water supply systems, and public buildings. We include in our analysis a cost of investment for each incremental immigrant to replicate the existing social capital stock. We have done this in two ways. First, when we include the present value of a per capita share of government expenditures on congestible goods and services, we implicitly include this capital cost because capital outlays are an item in such expenditures. Second, we use a direct estimate of the per capita value of net public capital (U.S. Department of Commerce, 1994), and use an annual flow of services plus depreciation of this capital, while omitting the capital outlays from expenditures on congestibles.[3] These two methods yield nearly identical results.

Sensitivity of Fiscal Impacts to Immigrant Characteristics

Apart from their simple numbers, the specific characteristics of immigrants influence their fiscal impacts. Immigrants arrive with human resources different from those of the rest of the population. In recent years, for instance, there has been concern that immigrants are disproportionately poor and uneducated. Such immigrants may both pay less in taxes and receive more in benefits than natives do. An immigrant's age at arrival is also important. Natives begin life in the United States when they are born, but an immigrant can arrive at any age; the modal age is around 25. If she arrives after school age, although she may have less education than natives, the public costs of her education have been borne by the sending country. Although she may give birth to children in the United States

[2]Just as a larger population helps dilute the costs of past obligations, it also dilutes the per capita value of publicly owned wealth of various kinds (national parks and forests and publicly owned mineral rights, for example). The calculations below do not include such effects.

[3]The estimate of total net public capital is taken from Survey of Current Business (1994). The annual flow is obtained by multiplying the per capita value, $17,000, by the assumed rate of interest plus a rate of depreciation of 4 percent. The descendants of the immigrant are also taken into account, and a net present value is then calculated.

who will then incur educational costs, these costs will be paid in part by the immigrant parents, who will typically be working and paying taxes.

A child born here or a young immigrant child, however, will not generate incremental tax payments until he or she begins to work, since the parents would have been paying taxes in any case. At the other end of the age spectrum, elderly immigrants, arriving late in their working years or during retirement, will be particularly expensive, since they can qualify for certain kinds of benefits such as Medicaid and Supplemental Security Income, even if they do not qualify for Social Security and Medicare. Consequently, the age distribution of arriving immigrants distinguishes them from native increments to the population, all of whom "arrive" at age 0.

The different fertility, mortality, and emigration rates of immigrants also have effects. On one hand, on average, immigrants have higher fertility and lower mortality rates than natives do, which affect the benefits they receive and the fiscal impact of their descendants. On the other hand, a substantial proportion of immigrants (about 30 percent) return to their country of origin, presumably taking at least their younger children with them, thus substantially mitigating the effect of their higher fertility.[4]

The need for bilingual education for many immigrants makes their public education more costly than that of natives. Cultural factors may influence the extent to which immigrants make use of the benefits for which they qualify. For example, strong family values may reduce the use of nursing homes by elderly immigrants. Finally, immigrants and their descendants are concentrated in certain areas of the country, and these areas may have different taxes and benefits from the rest of the country. For example, the states in which immigrants concentrate on average have higher levels of per pupil expenditures in public schools, and also higher state and local taxes.

To put these various fiscal impacts into perspective, it is useful to consider how important the programs involved are in current federal expenditures. In 1995, for example, expenditures on what we have categorized as public goods accounted for 23.7 percent of total federal outlays. Age-related expenditures made up an additional 55.4 percent of federal outlays, with debt payments accounting for 13.9 percent, and spending on congestible goods or social infrastructure making up the last 7.0 percent. Immigrants affect each of these categories differently in our calculations. New immigrants reduce the burden to natives of public goods and interest on the public debt; on average they are younger than

[4]As noted in Chapter 3, there is little evidence on the characteristics of return migrants. However, there seems good reason to think that they leave few children behind them. Most return migrants leave the United States within the first decade or so of their arrival. Emigration thus cuts short the period during which they could have children in the United States. This also means that children born in the United States are likely to be young when their parents emigrated, making it unlikely that they would leave them behind.

natives when they arrive, so immigrants initially participate less in age-related entitlements.

The annual or cross-sectional estimates of fiscal impacts were done for state and local governments as well as at the federal level. However, it does not make sense to do the longitudinal estimates for individual states or localities, because there is so much mobility from locality to locality and from state to state. Each year, 17 percent of the U.S. population changes residence, 6 percent changes county, and 3 percent changes state. For this reason, it does not make sense to do calculations that are based on the assumption that people remain in the same state over their lifetimes, and that their descendants do the same. When we do these calculations at the national level, we can simply group together all the state and local expenditures. One drawback, however, is that we can easily lose sight of the fact that immigrants and their state and local fiscal impacts are very heavily concentrated in a few states, rather than evenly spread across the nation.

Recall from the introduction that we do not take into account indirect fiscal effects of immigrants arising from any consequences of immigration for the earnings or employment of the existing labor force. This means that we will not consider the possibility that immigrants impose fiscal costs indirectly, by causing native workers to become unemployed or to drop into poverty due to reduced wages. The earlier chapters on the labor market effects of immigration suggested that any such negative effects on native workers are likely to be quite small, and the effects could even be positive. However, the possibility remains that immigration into a particular state may cause some outmigration of workers to other states, resulting in fiscal effects for high-immigration states that we have not taken into account. For the nation as a whole, such effects should average out to zero.

A Word on the Demographic Unit of Account

Many studies of the fiscal impact of immigrants use the immigrant-headed household as the unit of account. Here we use the individual as the unit of account. We do so because it is necessary for longitudinal calculations. If we were to use households, we would have to deal with changing household structure over time through marriage, divorce, widowhood, the departure of growing children, the arrival of additional family members from abroad, death of elderly members, and so on. We would also have to deal with nonimmigrant household members. Using the individual is much simpler in all these respects. Note that our calculations can subsequently be used as the basis of constituting families or households of immigrants when needed for interpreting the results, or for comparing them to results of studies that use the household framework.[5]

[5]The age profiles reflect the average payments of taxes and receipt of benefits for all immigrants at the age in question. Thus attempts to reconstitute specific family configurations by combining the individual profiles at particular ages will also yield families that were implicitly assumed to pay

Some Data Issues

Most of our analysis is based on the Current Population Surveys (CPS) of March 1994 and 1995. The relative merits of several data sets for this purpose—the Current Population Survey, the Survey of Income and Program Participation, the Public Use Micro Sample—are discussed in Appendix 7.C. The number of respondents in the combined CPS sample is roughly 300,000, of which about 29,000 are foreign-born. The 1994 and 1995 March CPS were simply pooled, treating each as a separate sample. Because of the way respondents are rotated from one panel to the next, approximately one-half of the data represent reinterviews of the "same" household a year later.

In principle, these surveys cover illegal immigrants as well as legal immigrants and nonimmigrants (foreign students and foreign business travelers). To the extent that these are included in the CPS, they distort the information about immigrants, particularly those who don't stay very long. The problem may not be trivial, since the number of nonimmigrants in the United States at any time is comparable to the annual inflow of immigrants. At shorter durations in the United States, our calculations could most accurately be said to apply to the foreign-born, rather than to immigrants per se. In practice, we do not know the coverage of illegal immigrants, but we suspect that it is incomplete. In our analysis we cannot distinguish between legal and illegal immigrants. Presumably, illegal immigrants both pay less in taxes and receive less in benefits than other immigrants do.[6]

THE HETEROGENEITY OF IMMIGRANTS AND INTRA- AND INTERGENERATIONAL MOBILITY

The fiscal impacts of immigrants vary greatly depending on a number of their characteristics. The benefits received by immigrants in the United States

---

average taxes and receive average benefits for people of the ages in the family, and these amounts may be out of line with their exact circumstances. However, since both age and education level of self or parent could be taken into account, this does not seem to be a serious problem for constituting families. For example, low-education families would be more likely to receive Aid to Families with Dependent Children, and this would be reflected in the average numbers.

[6]Readers should also note that the calculations in this chapter are based on *estimated* relationships between immigrant status, tax payments, benefit receipts, and the like. That is, we use data to calculate these relationships in the CPS sample, and then make inferences about immigrants and natives in general. Inevitably this introduces some margin of error, as a randomly chosen sample is very unlikely to have exactly the characteristics of the entire U.S. population, and there is some measurement error involved in collecting information through any survey. We have no reason to believe that these are misleading estimates, but estimating these relationships adds additional uncertainty about how close our projections of the effects of an additional immigrant would be to the actual effects.

and the taxes they pay depend strongly on their earnings. Migrants to the United States do not all have the same human resources, which heavily influence earnings. Our analysis captures some of this heterogeneity by distinguishing three categories of educational attainment of immigrants and others: less than high school, exactly high school, and more than high school. For our longitudinal analysis, we need to project educational attainment for the children and grandchildren of immigrants, according to the immigrant's education at arrival. For this purpose we analyzed data from the General Social Survey in a merged sample, calculating intergenerational transition matrices for these three educational categories.

Our analysis distinguishes three lengths of an immigrant's time since arrival: less than 5 years, 5 to 9 years, and 10 years and more. For every age, for every program, and for taxes, we estimate three age schedules from the CPS data, one for each duration. That is, we fully incorporate all the ways in which age and duration of residence here interact for these three duration categories and five-year age groups. The durations were chosen to correspond to potential qualification for entitlement programs, such as Aid to Families with Dependent Children (AFDC) and Old-age, Survivors, Disability, and Health Insurance (OASDHI).[7]

We also analyze the taxes paid by immigrants according to their education, age, and time since arrival. Because immigrants arriving in different periods have had different characteristics, the time of arrival variable may overstate the degree of earnings progress that can be expected of current immigrants. Those who have been in the United States for more than 10 years in 1994-95 may be different from more recent arrivals in ways not fully captured by their education and age.

For this reason we have done the analysis in two ways: first, assuming that the taxes paid by immigrants do follow the progress indicated by the trajectory estimated according to "time since arrival" and, second, assuming that the earnings follow this trajectory only for the first 10 years, and that thereafter the ratio of earnings between immigrants and native-born workers is fixed.[8] There are

[7]For immigrants who arrive after age 55, we constrain benefits after 9 years' duration to conform to those for 5 to 9 years' duration. This procedure avoids confusing qualifiers and nonqualifiers for OASDHI for people at age 70 and above at durations of 10+ years. However, many elderly immigrants whom the data describe as having been in the United States for only a short time, and who therefore would not be expected to qualify for many benefits such as OASDHI, must actually be earlier immigrants who worked in the United States long enough to qualify for OASDHI and other programs, and who have recently returned after a stay abroad. The duration variable will be misleading for such people, and this creates problems for estimates of the costs of elderly first-time immigrants, and for calculating the effects of the 1996 welfare reform legislation on the costs of elderly immigrants. In addition, some elderly first-time immigrants are refugees, who qualify for certain benefits despite their short durations of residence in the United States and lack of U.S. work histories. For these elderly immigrants, the duration variable should have different effects.

[8]Duleep and Regets (1976) compare the 1994 and 1995 CPS data and conclude that the longitudinal changes accurately reflect the cross-sectional duration profiles.

similar concerns about assuming that current immigrants will eventually use government benefits in the same way as immigrants who have been in the United States for more than 10 years in 1994-95, controlling for age and education. However, the case of benefits is quite different from that of taxes.

THE AGE PROFILES OF TAXES AND BENEFITS

We begin by discussing the estimated age profiles of taxes and benefits for 1993-94, which are important building blocks for the later longitudinal calculations. We have used the merged 1994 and 1995 CPS, and occasionally other data sources, to estimate age profiles for 25 different state, local, and federal programs, most of which are disaggregated by educational level, immigrant generation, and, for immigrants, time since arrival.[9] It should be borne in mind that the benefits and taxes estimated from these data will reflect the fact that the U.S. economy ended a recession in the first quarter of 1991. Real gross domestic product growth averaged 2.5 percent in 1992-93; unemployment began to fall in the third quarter of 1992 and averaged 0.6 points lower in 1993 than in 1992. Incarceration costs were estimated using the Public Use Micro Sample (PUMS).[10] The estimated age profiles were adjusted to match national program totals (using the National Income and Product Accounts, NIPA), when weighted by the distribution of the population by age and immigrant status and summed.

---

[9]Specifically, these are Old-age, Survivors, and Disability Insurance (OASDI), Medicare, Medicaid (noninstitutional), Medicaid (institutional), Supplemental Security Income (SSI), AFDC, school lunch, food stamps, Special Supplemental Nutrition Program for Women, Infants, and Children (WIC), energy assistance, rent subsidy, public housing, earned income tax credit, unemployment insurance, elementary and high school, bilingual education, public college, federal student aid, incarceration costs, federal retirement, military retirement, railroad retirement, workers' compensation, state and local retirement, and refugee assistance. Time since arrival is categorized into 0 to 4, 5 to 9, and 10+ years. Immigrant generation is first, second, and third and later, the last representing the majority of the population. Education is categorized into less than high school, high school, and more than high school.

For some items, there is a question of how to allocate benefits to individuals. For example, should AFDC receipts be allocated to the mother or to the children, or proportionately to each? We allocate such costs to the mother. In the longitudinal analysis, we track an immigrant and all the immigrant's descendants, so the AFDC receipts will in any case be attributed to the woman at the age at which the relevant children are in the household. For an immigrant arriving as a young child, and perhaps eventually qualifying for AFDC as a child, it will matter how we handle the attribution, but this is not the most important case. For a measure of the static (cross-sectional) fiscal impact of immigrants, the attribution would matter only if we did not count the costs of U.S.-born children of immigrants as a part of the cost of immigrants; however, it seems clear that such costs should be included. If they are, then attribution does not matter. Most other program items are allocated on an individual basis, with the exception of housing and food stamps. The AFDC discussion applies to these items as well.

[10]Using PUMS, we estimated a logistic regression for probability of institutionalization of the population under 60, by nativity, age, education, and time since arrival. Generally, these incarceration rates were considerably lower for immigrants than for others.

Many of these age profiles for specific programs are interesting in their own right, showing striking differences across generations. We present 5 age schedules representing aggregates of 12 of the 25 individual programs: OASDHI (Social Security benefits including Medicare), Medicaid (including costs for chronic care), SSI, public assistance (AFDC, general assistance, food stamps, and earned income tax credit), and public education (including elementary school, secondary school, and colleges and universities, and bilingual education). Disaggregation by time in the United States (not shown) adds further interesting detail. For example, an immigrant aged 70 years who has been in the United States for 30 years is most likely to be receiving benefits from Social Security and Medicare but is less likely to receive SSI and Medicaid. An immigrant aged 70 years who has been in the United States for only 10 years will probably not qualify for Social Security or Medicare, and so will be more likely draw benefits from SSI and Medicaid.

In addition to these benefits, all of which can be allocated by the age of the recipient, there are other benefits that immigrants receive that are not allocable by age. These are discussed later.

Age Profiles for Illustrative Individual Program Benefits

Figure 7.2 shows the Social Security and Medicare benefits (OASDHI) by age and immigrant generation. Note that here and throughout, third generation refers to the entire population other than immigrants and the children of immigrants. We see that the age schedules are very similar, but that immigrants receive $1,000 to $2,000 less per year in benefits than do second or third generations. This difference presumably reflects lower average earnings throughout their lives, shorter earnings histories in the United States, and, for some immigrants arriving late in life, a failure to qualify at all for benefits.[11]

Figure 7.3 shows that immigrants tend to receive higher Medicaid benefits up to age 80 or so, and lower benefits thereafter. But these differences are surprisingly small, on the order of a couple of hundred dollars. The age profile reflects separate treatment of Medicaid for the noninstitutionalized population, for which information is available from the CPS, and the institutionalized population, for which we made estimates using PUMS.[12] Our analysis indicates that

[11]For both Medicare and Medicaid, the CPS indicates whether an individual is eligible for benefits, but it does not indicate whether benefits were received and, if so, their cost. We have assigned average levels of benefits to all those eligible, conditional on age.

[12]The Public Use Micro Sample from the decennial census contains information on the foreign-born population in institutions, including both nursing homes and prisons. Above age 60, we assume that the institutionalized population is in nursing homes; below age 60, we assume that it is in prison. A logistic regression of the 1990 1 percent PUMS was used to determine proportions in institutions for the population by native-born versus foreign-born status, time since arrival for immigrants, and education. The institutionalization rates for elderly immigrants were about 60 percent as high as those for elderly others. PUMS does not give expenditures per institutionalized person, so we assumed these were the same for immigrants and nonimmigrants.

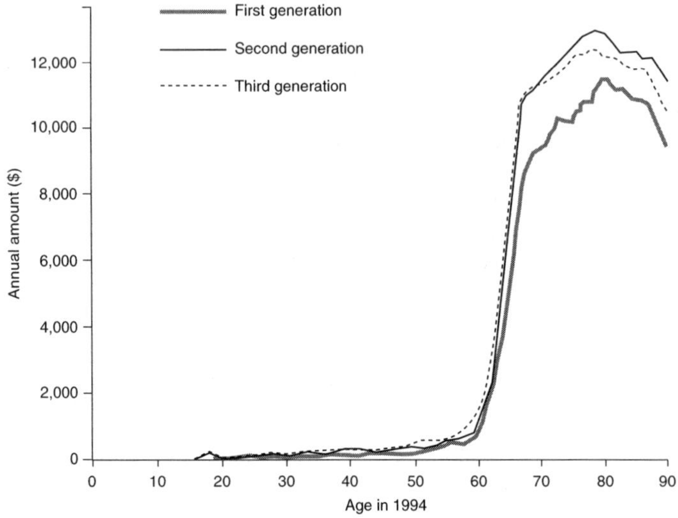

FIGURE 7.2 Estimated age profiles of benefits received from Social Security and Medicare by immigrant generation. Note: Data are from the March Current Population Survey, 1994 and 1995. Data have been smoothed on a moving window of 1,000 observations using a local regression smoother.

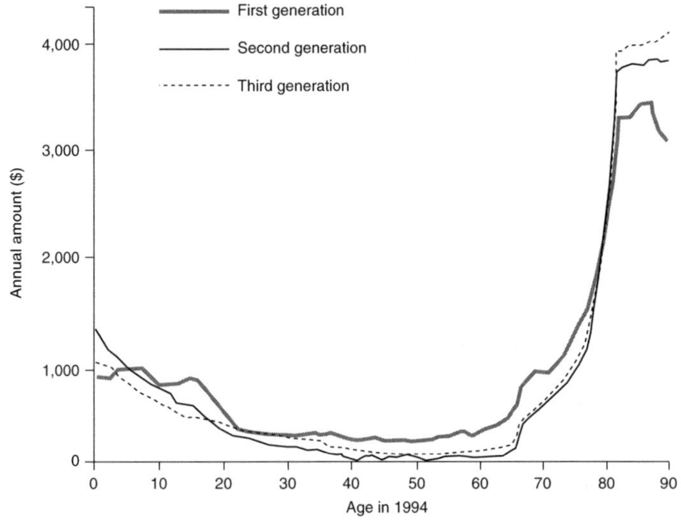

FIGURE 7.3 Estimated age profiles of benefits received from Medicaid by immigrant generation. Note: Data are from the March Current Population Survey, 1994 and 1995. Data have been smoothed on a moving window of 1,000 observations using a local regression smoother.

elderly immigrants are about 40 percent less likely to be in nursing homes than are second- or third-generation elders.

As the age profiles in Figure 7.4 reveal, elderly immigrants rely very heavily on Supplementary Security Income (SSI) compared with the native-born, presumably because many elderly immigrants cannot qualify for Social Security and Medicare.

Figure 7.5 shows expenditures on public education, combining elementary and secondary education with higher education, and reflecting specific educational costs for immigrants, such as bilingual education.[13] For elementary and secondary education, the cost of education is somewhat higher for immigrants and the second generation than for others because states with high proportions of immigrants also have high educational costs per pupil, and state-specific data were used to assign costs by state of residence. For age 15 and above, the CPS furnishes enrollment information, which is also reflected in the profiles; at younger ages, the same enrollment rates are assigned to all children.

Figure 7.6 shows expenditures on public assistance (AFDC and general assistance), food stamps, and the refunded portion of the earned income tax credit. Up to age 30 or so, immigrants receive benefits similar to those for the general population, although higher than those for the second generation. After 30, however, they receive substantially more assistance, on the order of $200 more per person until nearly age 60.

We can now combine all the benefit profiles (see Figure 7.7). It is striking that the benefit levels appear quite similar across all three groups. First- and second-generation immigrants are somewhat more costly during childhood because of the higher educational expenditures in the states in which they live and the costs of bilingual education, but first-generation immigrants who are of college age or who are old are substantially less expensive. The average immigrant does not receive more costly benefits at a given age than natives do; if anything, the opposite is the case. Note, however, that immigrant households are on average larger than native households, so that they may well receive substantially greater benefits than native households, as in the case study of California.

One important lesson to draw from this brief discussion of the age profiles

---

[13]Bilingual students are 44 percent more expensive than average students in the Florida school system, and we assume that this holds in all 50 states (Clark, 1994). About half of first-generation immigrants have limited English proficiency (LEP) (Clark, 1994). We assume that no third or later generation immigrants are LEP and estimate that about a third of second-generation immigrants (36.8 percent) are LEP. Using the proportion of students who are LEP and non-LEP, we estimate the relative costs of each student to the state government. First-generation students are 1.22 times as expensive as the average student ($.51 \times 1.44 + .49 \times 1.00$). Second-generation students are 1.16 times as expensive as the average student ($.368 \times 1.44 + .632 \times 1.00$). If immigrant families tend to live in lower-income areas with lower per pupil expenditures on education, then our procedures will overstate the costs of educating immigrant children.

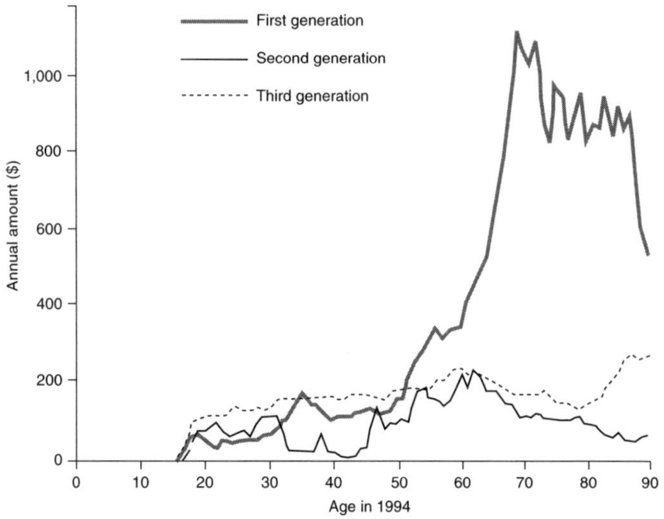

FIGURE 7.4 Estimated age profiles of benefits received from Supplemental Security Income by immigrant generation. Note: Data are from the March Current Population Survey, 1994 and 1995. Data have been smoothed on a moving window of 1,000 observations using a local regression smoother.

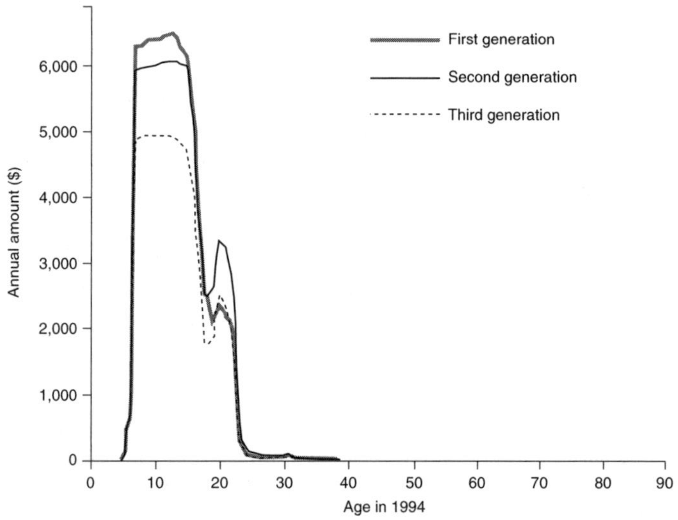

FIGURE 7.5 Estimated age profiles of benefits received from public education by immigrant generation. Note: Data are from the March Current Population Survey, 1994 and 1995. Data have been smoothed on a moving window of 1,000 observations using a local regression smoother.

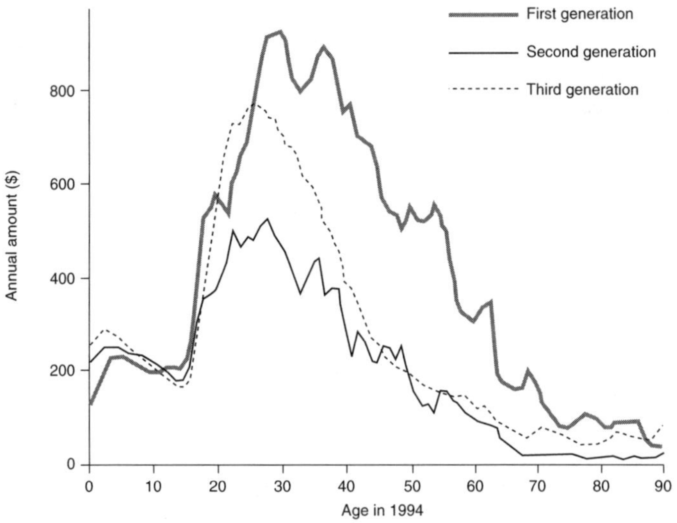

FIGURE 7.6 Estimated age profiles of benefits received from Aid to Families with Dependent Children, general assistance, food stamps, and earned income tax credits by immigrant generation. Note: Data are from the March Current Population Survey, 1994 and 1995. Data have been smoothed on a moving window of 1,000 observations using a local regression smoother.

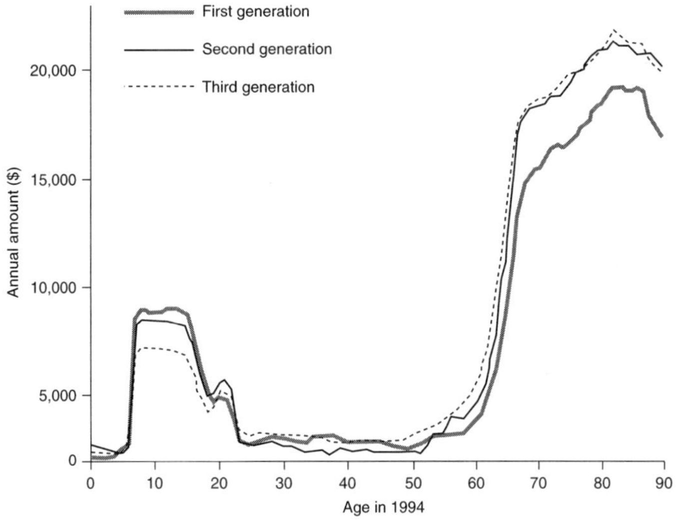

FIGURE 7.7 Combined estimated age profiles of benefits from all programs by immigrant generation. Note: Data are from the March Current Population Survey, 1994 and 1995. Data have been smoothed on a moving window of 1,000 observations using a local regression smoother.

for different programs is that, because the relation of immigrant to native costs varies so much from program to program, it is dangerous to draw general conclusions from the examination of any particular program. General conclusions must instead be based on a full and comprehensive consideration of all government programs and all levels of government.

Tax Profiles

The real difference between immigrants and natives lies in taxes rather than in benefits, as shown in Figure 7.8, which displays total taxes paid by the different immigrant generations in 1994. These plots combine state and federal income taxes, Federal Insurance Contributions Act (FICA) taxes, property taxes, and sales taxes. In addition, federal business taxes and excise taxes are allocated to individuals in proportion to their reported dividend, interest, and net rental income (the CPS does not have data on assets). In contrast to total benefits, there are large differences in taxes paid, with immigrants paying the least at each age, the second generation paying the most, and others paying intermediate amounts. The main reason the second generation pays higher taxes than the third is that it tends to live in states with higher incomes, as does the first generation.

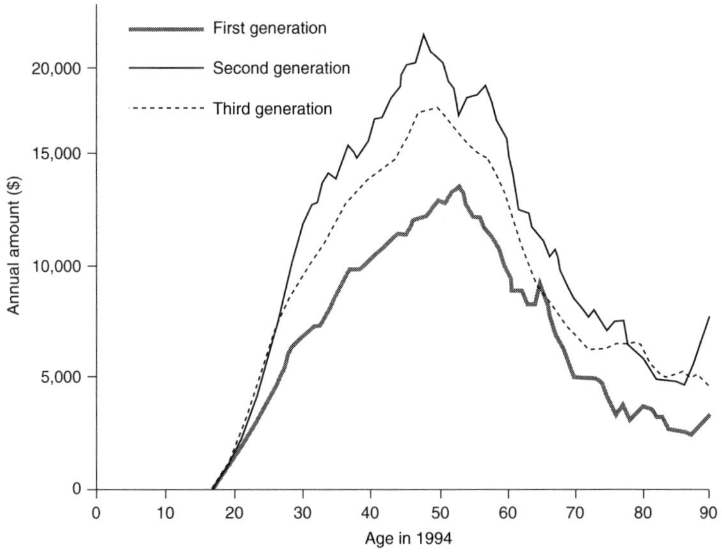

FIGURE 7.8 Estimated age profiles of taxes paid by immigrant generation. Note: Data are from the March Current Population Survey, 1994 and 1995. Data have been smoothed on a moving window of 1,000 observations using a local regression smoother.

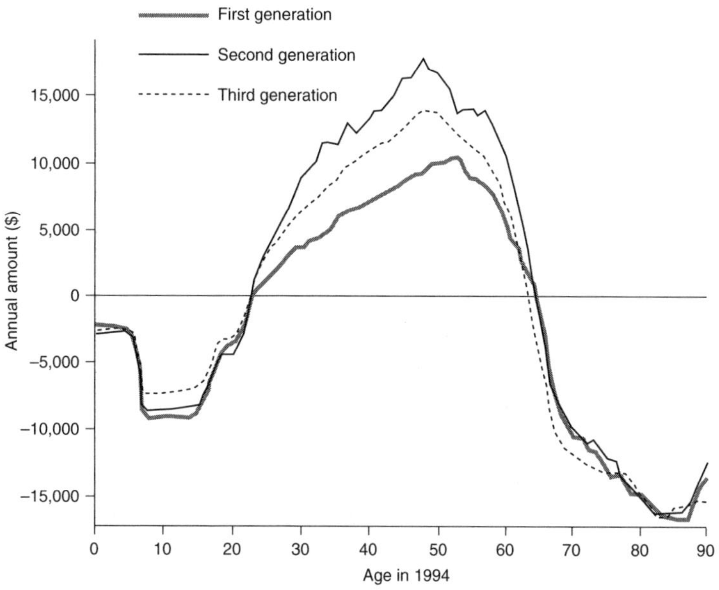

FIGURE 7.9 Estimated age profiles of the annual net fiscal impact of an individual by immigrant generation. Note: Data are from the March Current Population Survey, 1994 and 1995. Data have been smoothed on a moving window of 1,000 observations using a local regression smoother.

These age profiles for taxes are based largely on the CPS, as were those for benefits, and, like the benefit-age profiles, they have been adjusted to match totals given in the National Income and Product Accounts. The CPS imputes tax payments for individuals for federal income tax, FICA, state income taxes, and property taxes. We allocate 70 percent of property tax to renters and 30 percent to the owners of rental properties (for a discussion of the incidence of various kinds of taxes, see Chapter 6). The CPS does not impute state sales taxes. We assume that immigrant households remit $1,250 abroad that is not subject to sales tax (see literature reviewed in the California case study).[14]

In looking at the sum of the benefit profiles just discussed with the costs of government-provided private or congestible goods, a striking pattern emerges: net receipt of benefits in childhood and old age, with a period of net payment of taxes during the working years (see Figure 7.9). Because the variation across age

---

[14]A regression estimated for California (reported in Sheffrin and Dresch, 1995) is used to estimate taxable household expenditures based on adjusted household income, after subtracting the assumed remittance abroad. We then calculate the average sales tax rate that would be needed to generate the NIPA total sales tax revenues for all states combined, and allocate the resulting imputed sales tax payment to the household head.

is so great, the age distribution of immigrants may matter a good deal to the net fiscal impact. It is also clear that the big difference between immigrants and natives is not in the net benefits received in childhood and old age, although differences exist, but rather in the level of the net tax payments during the working years.

For these unstratified results, it must be kept in mind that the second-generation immigrants who are over 30 are the children of immigrants who arrived before 1965, when the composition of the immigration stream was more largely European. There is a danger in treating the second generation as the children of the first-generation immigrants, as the calculations reported below do implicitly. Our actual estimates are based on data disaggregated by the education of the immigrant, and use estimated educational transition rates to project the education of the children and grandchildren of immigrants, depending on their own education.

AGGREGATE CROSS-SECTIONAL FISCAL IMPACTS OF IMMIGRANTS AND THEIR CHILDREN

Although our ultimate goal in this chapter is to estimate the long-term costs of immigrants and their descendants, the benefit and tax profiles just described can also be used to carry out the more common estimate of the net costs or contributions of the foreign-born and their young children in a given calendar year—essentially, the population living in households headed by immigrants. This kind of calculation is often thought to shed light on the current fiscal consequences of past immigration, including the way in which it has affected the age distribution of the population. When governments face constraints on borrowing, it may be particularly relevant compared with present-value calculations.

However, these kinds of calculations have certain conceptual problems, as noted earlier, and they are subject to a practical difficulty as well. When the immigrant population is defined as people living in households headed by immigrants, it is then limited to immigrants themselves and to their most costly descendants—young children. Older descendants of immigrants who have finished their educations and have become taxpayers are included only if they are foreign-born; U.S.-born children who are now adults are excluded, because they no longer live in households headed by immigrants. We illustrate the implications of this exclusion below.

The cross-sectional estimates are obtained by multiplying each age profile by the age distribution of the appropriate population, and summing to find the implied total taxes or benefits. Additional adjustments are made for the costs of providing congestible services at the state, local, and federal levels; at the state and local levels, all government services are treated as congestible. Table 7.1 indicates that the average first-generation immigrant has a substantial annual positive impact on the federal budget (+$1,310), reflecting the young age distri-

TABLE 7.1 Net Fiscal Impact Per Capita by Level of Government and Immigrant Generation (1996 dollars)

	Immigrants (1st)	Children of Immigrants (2nd < 20)	Immigrants + Children < 20	2nd ≥ 20	2nd aged 20-64	Others (3rd +)	Total Population
Federal	+$1,310	–$1,570	+$550	–$1,190	+$4,340	+$1,680	+$1,400
State and local	+490	–4,820	–920	+2,090	+3,000	+360	+290
Total	+1,800	–6,390	–370	+910	+7,350	+2,030	+1,690

Note: Based on the population age distributions derived from the 1994 and 1995 Current Population Surveys (CPS).

bution of the foreign-born, and a smaller positive impact at the state level (+\$490), for an overall large positive impact of \$1,800 in 1994 (these numbers are 1996 dollars).[15] However, the category of immigrants does not include their young children born in the United States. These young children are members of the second generation under the age of 20. They are expensive at the federal level and even more so at the state and local level, for a large net negative impact of \$6,390. Some studies report the net fiscal impact of households headed by immigrants. This group can be closely approximated by combining the immigrants and their young U.S.-born children, as is done in the third column of the table, which shows an overall impact of –\$370. The next column shows that the remainder of the U.S.-born children of immigrants, that is, the older second generation, has an overall positive fiscal impact of +\$910.

Note that, because these calculations are for incremental population members, whether immigrants or natives, no cost is allocated for public goods. This is consistent with the calculations reported in the previous chapter. If we were instead to ask whether immigrants were receiving a good deal, in the sense that the value of services they receive was high relative to the taxes they pay, then we would want to assign to them a pro rata share of expenditures on public goods. If immigrants valued these public goods at more than their net tax payments, then they would be receiving a good deal from government services even though the effect of a marginal immigrant would be a plus to the rest of us. Whether immigrants are better off, however, is not the question we ask here. Instead, we ask how an incremental immigrant would affect the taxes paid or benefits received by the existing population.

Fiscal Effects on the Native-Born Population

So far, we have expressed these impacts in terms of the amount per immigrant and child. But what is the cost to the native-born population? Dividing the total costs attributable to immigrants and their children by the balance of the population yields a cost per native-born of about \$50. Thus, the average native-born paid about \$50 in additional taxes in 1994 because of the 32 million immigrants and their young children in the United States, and the average U.S. household paid about \$125 extra in taxes (= 2.5 times \$50). (However, we shall see that there are problems in measuring fiscal impacts in this way.)

---

[15]Public goods are treated as having zero marginal cost for all members of the population, so their costs are allocated to no one. Also, payments to service the federal debt are not allocated as costs to anyone. Thus, tax payments to pay for public goods and debt servicing will tend to make federal fiscal impacts, as measured in Table 7.1, positive. At the same time, the federal budget was in deficit for the relevant years, which will tend to make the measured federal fiscal impact of all people negative. The balance of these factors leads to the large net positive fiscal impact at the federal level for the total population.

TABLE 7.2 Per Capita Total Benefits and Taxes for Selected Groups (1996 dollars)

	Immigrants + Children < 20	Others (3rd+ generation)	Total Population
All taxes	$5,650	$8,300	$8,170
All benefits	6,010	6,270	6,480
Net impact	–370	2,030	1,690

We can gain some further insight by examining the components of these net impact figures. The per capita benefits of immigrants plus their children are 96 percent as great as the benefits of the third and later generations, and only 93 percent of those for the total population (see Table 7.2). So immigrants and their children do not draw more heavily on benefits than does the general population, as indeed we could already judge from Figure 7.7 above. However, on average they pay only 68 percent of the taxes paid by the third and later generations, and a similar percentage of taxes paid by the total population.

To address one of the pointed questions about the fiscal impact of immigrants, Table 7.3 reports the effects on the Social Security system and on all other benefits, separately. The table shows that immigrants contribute $510 more per capita to Social Security and Medicare than they receive in benefits each year (making a total net contribution of $11.5 billion annually), and the third and later generations contribute $300 more per capita than they receive in benefits. These figures are in stark contrast to the second generation above age 20, which receives $3,700 more per capita each year than it pays into the system. The reason is that second-generation immigrants are on average very old and few work, because of the long period in which rates of immigration were low, and the large numbers of immigrants early in the century.

The difficulties in interpreting the cross-sectional measures of impacts can be illustrated using the numbers in Table 7.1. First, recall that immigrants (first generation) actually have a very positive fiscal impact in the cross section: the average immigrant pays $1,800 more in taxes than he or she imposes on the costs of benefits, and immigrants in total have a positive fiscal impact of $41 billion. Most people would find this figure misleading, however, because it does not include the fiscal impacts of the immigrants' young children born in the United States (second generation). To approximate the members of immigrant households, we can add the members of the second generation under age 20. Each such child has a large negative impact of –$6,390, due to the high costs of public schools. When these are averaged with immigrants, the result is a per capita fiscal impact of –$370. But the immigrants also have U.S.-born children who are

TABLE 7.3 Per Capita Net Taxes Minus Benefits for Old-age, Survivors, Disability, and Health Insurance (OASDHI) and for All Other Benefits (1996 dollars)

Taxes Minus Costs	Immigrants (1st generation)	Immigrants (2nd generation < 20)	Children of 2nd Generation ≥ 20	Others (3rd+ generation)	Total Population
OASDHI	$510	$0	–$3,700	$300	$110
Other	1,300	–6,390	4,610	1,730	1,580
Total	1,800	–6,390	910	2,030	1,690

older and who have grown up, gotten jobs, and begun to pay taxes. These children should also be counted, and, when they are, the per capita figure for net impact rises from –$370 to roughly zero.

What about the older members of the second generation, those over age 65? On reflection, it is clear that they could not possibly be children of the immigrants alive today; their parents would themselves be over age 85, and very few immigrants in the United States today are that old. So let us add just the members of the second generation who are under age 65. Now, the per capita fiscal impact becomes positive again, at more than a thousand dollars a person ($1,340). But not all of those in the second generation are actually children of current immigrants; many are children of former immigrants who have died. And many of these members of the second generation have themselves had children who are imposing costs of schooling. These considerations indicate that the results of cross-sectional calculations must be interpreted with caution.

Consistency with the Case Studies of California and New Jersey

The previous chapter reported on two careful case studies of the fiscal impact of immigrants in two states, California and New Jersey, based on the static, cross-sectional or annual methodology. How consistent are those results with the cross-sectional analysis reported in this chapter? We have reestimated the tax and benefit profiles for New Jersey and California, and adjusted them based on national aggregate underreporting for state and local items rather than adjusting them to match the specific totals for each of these two states (which would be preferable).[16] We group together immigrants with their children under age 20

[16]Nor did we use state-specific data for sales tax rates, congestibles, value of public housing, value of Medicare and Medicaid services, and other taxes and expenditures not reported in the CPS. Instead we use national averages for these items. For example, we use state-specific participation rates in Medicaid, but we use national average costs per participant.

for purposes of comparison to the population living in households headed by immigrants, the basic unit of analysis in the case studies.

Consider the extrapolations to the national level reported in the previous chapter, for net impacts at the state and local level. Based on New Jersey and California, a national range of –\$17.95 to –\$23.34 billion was reported, in contrast with –\$28.5 billion based on the national analysis (with adjustment of age profiles to the aggregate state and local totals reported in the NIPA). Thus the current chapter has additional costs of about \$5 billion, compared with the extrapolation. But the case studies assume that the costs of education are the same for children in immigrant households and native children, whereas in this chapter we impute very substantial costs for bilingual education, amounting in the aggregate to \$5.8 billion. If we were to delete this additional cost, the estimate in this chapter would be \$22.7 billion, falling within the range of the Chapter 6 extrapolations, if closer to California than to New Jersey. Therefore, there is excellent agreement between the national study and these two case studies at the state and local level.

At the federal level, however, the situation is very different. There was no federal component to the New Jersey study, so the extrapolation to a national federal net impact of +\$3.18 billion is based entirely on the California study. The direct national study, however, found a federal net impact of +\$17.1 billion, or more than five times as great. This puts the combined fiscal impact from the national study at –\$11.4 billion, outside the extrapolated range of –\$14.8 to –\$20.2 billion. Although this wide a disagreement in the combined impact is not too troubling, the discrepancy at the federal level merits closer scrutiny.

Concentrating on California, on which the federal extrapolation is based, we find excellent consistency between the numbers we generate and the state calculations:

	Extrapolated from California case study	Implied by national study
Total federal taxes per household	\$10,644	\$10,602
Total federal benefits per household	10,517	10,282
Net fiscal impact per household	127	320

Although the nationally based estimate of the net impact is more than twice the state-based one, the numerical difference is very small, and results from the small difference between the large numbers for taxes and benefits, which separately are in close agreement. The important point is that the results from methods and data used in this chapter agree with the California case study in implying that the positive federal fiscal impact in California is very small, at the same time that a very much larger positive federal impact is found for the nation as a whole. California is simply too different from other states to permit extrapolating from its experience the national federal impact of immigrants. In fact, further exploration reveals that immigrants in California pay far less federal taxes than do those elsewhere, perhaps because they have substantially less schooling. Calculations show that, whereas immigrants in California pay $2,850 per capita in federal taxes, immigrants elsewhere pay $3,824, or nearly $1,000 more. At the same time, immigrants in California receive benefits costing $2,764, whereas immigrants in the rest of the country receive benefits costing $3,022, or about $360 more. This difference in benefits doubtless reflects the older age distribution of immigrants in the balance of the country, whereas the difference in taxes reflects both the age difference and the education difference. Thus, California immigrants have a federal fiscal impact of +$86 per capita, and immigrants in the rest of the country have a federal impact of +$802.

The extrapolation done in the previous chapter controlled for regional heterogeneity by taking ethnic composition into account. However, it turns out that this is not an adequate control, as illustrated by the following figures for federal income taxes paid by ethnic groups in California and in all other states combined:

Immigrant Ethnic Group	California	Other States
White	$1,938	$1,706
Asian	1,533	2,132
Hispanic	435	630

It is also possible to calculate the net fiscal impact by state from the data at hand, and the results are quite striking, as shown in Table 7.4. Whereas the average immigrant, plus her U.S.-born young children, has a negative impact of $369 for the United States as a whole, the total impact is actually substantially positive for New Jersey and is essentially zero for the immigrants in all other states besides California and New Jersey combined. For California, however, it is –$1,313. In California, compared with the United States as a whole (including California), impacts are $400 to $500 more negative at both the state and local and the federal level, adding up to about $950.

The figures for aggregate, rather than per capita, fiscal impacts are also striking. As reported earlier, the aggregate fiscal impact of immigrants and their young U.S.-born children amounts to –$11.4 billion. But the impact for California alone is –$14.3 billion, whereas New Jersey contributes +$2.4 billion and the other states contribute +$0.5 billion. In other words, California alone accounts for the entire national negative fiscal impact of immigrants (at the combined federal and state and local levels)—and then some. Of course, immigrants in some of the states that have been lumped together in "other" may also be costly.

TABLE 7.4 Per Capita Net Fiscal Impacts of Immigrants and Their U.S.-Born Children < 20 (1996 dollars)

Government Level	United States	California	New Jersey	All Other States
Federal	$551	$86	$2,586	$671
State/local	–920	–1,398	–870	–644
Total per capita	–369	–1,313	1,716	27

As for the third and later generations in California and New Jersey, they have more than twice the positive fiscal impact compared with those in the United States as a whole.

This section has these implications:

- The analysis of this chapter is consistent with the case studies reported in the previous chapter.
- It is not possible to extrapolate from the experience of California to the nation; it is too atypical.
- Fiscal impacts, at both the federal and the state and local level, are substantially more negative or less positive in California than in the rest of the country, and, overall, California accounts for the entire negative net impact of immigrants and their young U.S.-born children in the country; in other regions taken together, immigrants and their children have an overall positive impact.

CONSTRUCTING LONGITUDINAL AGE PROFILES

These cross-sectional age profiles and their components from specific programs, with additional disaggregation by education and time since arrival for immigrants, form the building blocks for the longitudinal analysis. They are used to construct longitudinal age profiles on the assumption that each age profile shifts upward at the assumed rate of productivity growth, or 1 percent annually (based on the budget projection assumptions made by the Congressional Budget Office—CBO).[17] The real costs of Medicare and Medicaid per enrollee have been rising particularly rapidly, and are expected to continue to do so in the future. We follow CBO (1996) in using the projections by the trustees of Medi-

[17]Actually, for complicated reasons, we assumed a productivity growth rate of 0.010766 rather than 0.01.

care, as described in their 1996 report (which is more recent than the 1995 report used by CBO), for both Medicare and Medicaid.[18]

Although the federal deficit is currently not very large relative to gross domestic product and is likely to be further reduced by the year 2002, long-term projections reveal that serious imbalances will emerge due to rising health care costs and to the aging of the population, ushered in by the retirement of the baby-boom generations between 2010 and 2030. Current federal taxes and benefits, even if adjusted to meet deficit-reduction targets over the next few years, will not be sustainable in the longer run, and far more substantial adjustments will be required to taxes, benefits, or both. For example, a recent report by the Congressional Budget Office concluded: "CBO projects that, if spending and revenue policies are not changed, deficits and debt will soar to unprecedented levels in the following 20 years. . . . Because the deficits and debt that would result if there are no changes in policy are not sustainable, such changes are inevitable" (p. xxv).

Figure 7.1 illustrated just how unsustainable current fiscal policies are by plotting out the ratio of debt to GDP under our federal budget projections if no changes are made. These projections indicate that if our age-specific profiles of taxes and benefits shift upward at 1 percent per year, the assumed rate of productivity growth (except for Medicare and Medicaid costs as noted), then the debt as a percentage of GDP will rise from its current level of about 60 percent to 100 percent in 2014, 200 percent in 2029, 300 percent in 2039 and 700 percent by 2071. In our baseline scenario, we assume that, starting in 2016, the debt/GDP ratio is frozen by a 50-50 combination of benefit cuts and tax increases.[19] Between now and then, the debt changes according to the CBO budget projections. The implied adjustments shape our results in an important way. At the state and local level, we assume a constant ratio of aggregate state and local debt to GDP, starting in 1994.[20] We assume that the real interest rate paid by all levels of

[18]We have reanalyzed the trustees' projections to produce projections of real costs per enrollee. The trustees also assume that productivity grows at 1 percent annually. Real costs per enrollee are projected to rise at 5.8 percent per year initially, with the rate falling to 2.1 percent by 2005, and to 1.2 percent by 2020; thereafter, it is assumed to rise at the rate of labor productivity, or 1 percent per year, as for all the other age profiles. These projected increases in real costs per enrollee are then used to shift the age profiles for the use of Medicare and Medicaid.

[19]Although our long-term budget projections generally adhere fairly closely to the CBO assumptions, we have used our own estimated benefit profiles and population projections (reported in an earlier chapter) to project governmental costs, as a basis for applying our assumption that, starting in 2016, taxes are adjusted to keep the debt/GDP ratio fixed.

[20]We assume that the state and local budget has a zero primary deficit in 1994, and that the debt/GDP ratio is fixed at the level of 1994. Just as with the federal budget, we use age and immigrant status profiles of publicly provided private goods, together with population projections, to project the demographically driven expenditures for state/local. As with the federal government, we assume each profile rises at the exponential rate of productivity growth, taken to be 1 percent annually. For Medicaid, we follow the projections used at the federal level, which assume somewhat more rapid

government on their debt is 3 percent per year, and this rate is also used to calculate the net present value of an incremental immigrant. Later we will test our results with different budgetary assumptions and with interest rates of 2, 4, 6, and 8 percent.

We assume that these same age profiles, shifted upward as described, also describe the tax payments and benefits received by descendants of immigrants. The descendants are projected based on the fertility of immigrants, which is assumed to converge in two generations to that of the general population, following the assumptions described in Chapter 3. Over their life cycles, 30 percent of immigrants are assumed to return to their countries of origin (Duleep, 1994), taking with them their children under the age of 20 born in the United States. We take into account that these return migrants may or may not be entitled to Social Security benefits, depending on the length of time spent in the United States.[21]

BASELINE RESULTS

Definition of Baseline Scenario and Alternative Scenarios

We will carry out the basic calculations for a baseline scenario, and then examine how results change when we vary certain assumptions, one at a time. Here are the baseline assumptions, and the variants (in parentheses):

- Starting in 2016, and thereafter, fiscal policy will hold the debt/GDP ratio constant at the level of 2016. (Alternatively, the ratio will be constant from now on, or it will never be constant, and taxes and benefits will simply rise with productivity at 1 percent per year.)
- This budgetary adjustment will be achieved by a 50-50 combination of raising taxes and reducing benefits. (Alternatively, all the adjustment will be made to taxes, or to benefits.)
- The real rate of interest is 3 percent. (Alternatively, we use 2 percent and

---

growth for the first few decades. Pension costs require special treatment. We assume that the current number of state/local pensioners was set by state/local employment 30 years ago, and we shift the age profiles of pension receipt upward each year between 1965 and 1994 by the ratio of state/local employees in each year to the number in 1965. (The difference between the mean age of Social Security beneficiaries and FICA taxpayers is 30 years.) The per capita number of state/local employees grows from 4.9 percent in 1970 to 6.1 percent in 1992, for example. After 1994, we allow the age profiles of state/local pensioners to shift upward at 1 percent per year along with all the other age profiles, assuming that growth of state/local government relative to the population size has run its course, and that further growth will just keep pace with population.

[21]Unfortunately, we did not have time to incorporate into our analysis the legislated change in the normal retirement age for Social Security. We believe, however, that doing so would make very little difference.

4 percent. We have also used 6 percent and 8 percent as a rough reflection of the uncertainty of future tax revenues, and the asymmetric valuation placed on the consequences of upward and downward variations.)

- Immigrants continue to receive benefits as they do in 1994-95, for which we have CPS data. (Alternatively, they do not receive SSI, AFDC, Medicaid, food stamps, rent subsidies, energy assistance, public housing, or earned income tax credits during their first five years in the United States, in accord with the welfare reform legislation of 1996 and assuming they become citizens after five years).
- The taxes immigrants pay change as indicated by the cross-sectional data as their stay in the United States lengthens up to 10 years; after that, their taxes relative to the age-specific tax payments by natives are fixed. (Alternatively, their tax payments continue to change to the empirical estimate for durations in the United States of 10+ years.)
- Immigrants arriving after age 55 are allocated the OASDHI benefits estimated from the data. (Alternatively, immigrants arriving after age 55 are assumed to receive no OASDHI benefits, since they would not be able to qualify for them before age 65.)
- Thirty percent of immigrants later emigrate, taking with them all their young children. Consequently, 16 percent of those born in the second generation are assumed to emigrate with their parents. (Alternatively, none of these second-generation children emigrate, and only 20 percent of first-generation immigrants emigrate.)
- Costs of bilingual education raise the cost of educating immigrant and second-generation children by 22 percent and 16 percent, respectively (versus only half of these increases, or an additional 11 percent and 8 percent, respectively).

Net Present Values

Based on these baseline assumptions on the constructed longitudinal profiles and on the demographic assumptions, we can calculate the present value of the taxes paid by the marginal immigrant and his descendants minus the present value of all costs they impose. The effects further in the future have less importance today than do those closer to the present. The government can borrow or lend money, to be repaid in the future, at some real rate of interest, and future fiscal impacts should be discounted at this same rate. In some circumstances, discounting the future is also a way to reflect uncertainty about it, particularly when we care more about negative than about positive departures from our expectations. The net present value, or NPV, of an immigrant's future fiscal impacts is just the sum of all the discounted impacts.

The NPV is conditional on the age of arrival of the immigrant, since this strongly influences the benefits received, the taxes paid, and the number of his or her descendants. It will also vary depending on the education of the immigrant, since this strongly influences earnings and therefore tax payments and the need for public transfers of various kinds. The NPV combines the effect of an immigrant during his own lifetime with the effects of all generations of his descendants born in the United States (children born before coming to the United States are treated as immigrants in their own right, with their own descendants). We consider these two components of the NPV separately for some purposes. We also compare the NPVs of immigrants for various ages at arrival with the NPVs of second and later generations, although in reality the native-born groups can be augmented only at birth, that is, at age zero.

As discussed below, we assign educational categories to children, including infants. There are two ways to do this: (1) according to the ultimate educational attainment of the children, so that the children we show are those who will eventually attain the educational category in which they are plotted or (2) according to the educational attainment of their parents. When the first method is used, the NPV age profiles are smooth with no discontinuities. However, the ultimate educational outcome must be assigned by a complicated procedure, based on the likely family origins of children who eventually attain the educational statuses indicated.[22] We instead plot the results of the second method in our figures, a method that results in sharp discontinuities because the children of parents with low education have a good chance of attaining higher education than their parents, and therefore come to have much higher NPVs than their parents, who are assumed to remain in the low-education category for life. Both methods are valid and will give the same result if used appropriately.

Results

Figure 7.10 presents the NPVs by age and by education for immigrants, which are the core results of this project, indicating the total impact of an immigrant on the combined federal, state, and local budgets, now and in the future. In reading these figures, it should be kept in mind that their meaning is very different from that of the figures depicting cross-sectional age profiles. Here, each single point on the curve summarizes the entire future years for an immigrant arriving at the corresponding age. One cannot trace a given immigrant's impact across the life cycle by moving along the curves. Other points on the curve summarize the entire future years for other immigrants.

Panel A shows the total NPV, and Panels B and C show the NPV for the immigrant's own lifetime and for the immigrant's descendants, respectively.

---

[22]This is done by using intergenerational educational transition matrices to determine the probability distribution of the education of the parents of the children who achieve varying degrees of education.

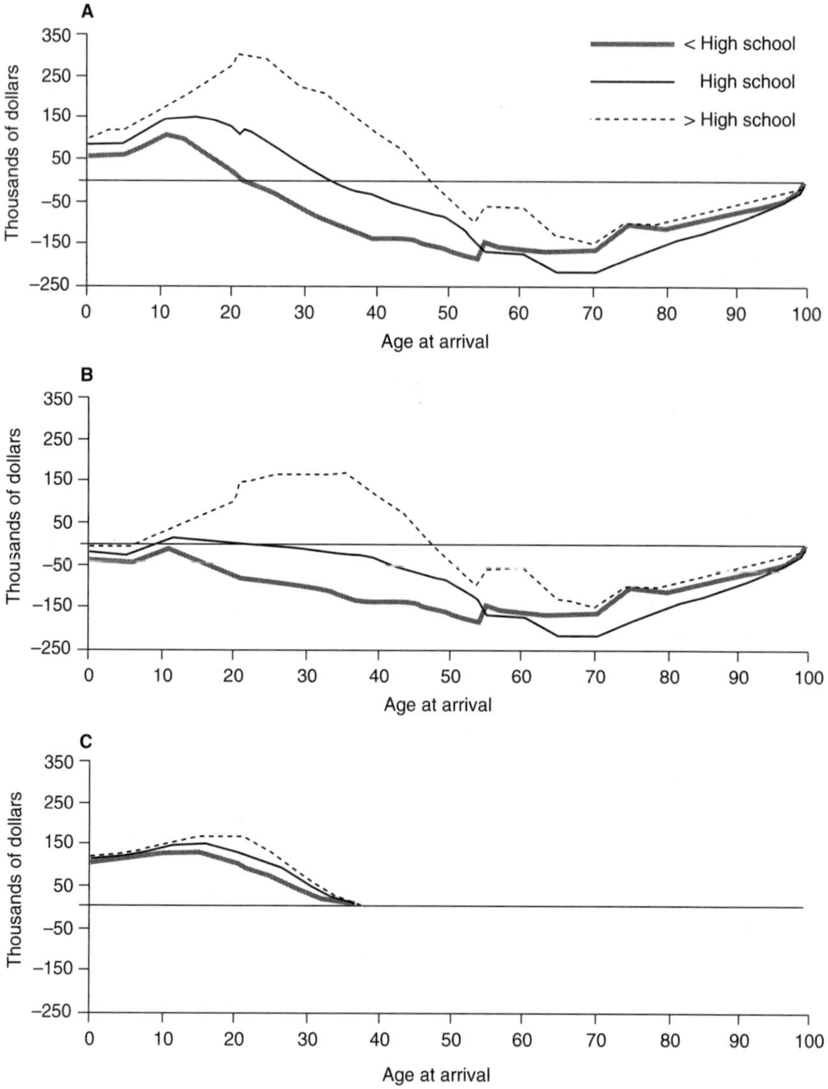

FIGURE 7.10 Net present value of total fiscal impact: **A**, Generation 1 by age at arrival and education status, self and descendants; **B**, Generation 1 by age at arrival and education status, own lifetime; **C**, Generation 1 by age at arrival and education status, descendants.

From Panel A we see that immigrants with more than a high school education (the dotted line) have a positive NPV for all ages of arrival up to the mid-forties, after which the NPV turns negative, reflecting the costs of old-age support programs and the short period of paying taxes before retirement. Note that at age 55 the NPV rises abruptly. This is because an immigrant arriving after that age is assumed not to have time to qualify for OASDHI benefits. For a high-education immigrant arriving at age 21, the NPV is $332,000; he is indeed a substantial contribution. For a high-education immigrant who arrives at age 70, the NPV drops to –$148,000; he is quite costly.

For an immigrant aged 21 years with a high school education, the NPV is $126,000. For arrivals after the mid-thirties, the NPV turns negative, reaching about –$224,000 for an immigrant arriving at age 70. For an immigrant arriving at age 21 with less than a high school education, the low-education category, the NPV is $9,000. Then NPV then turns negative, reaching –$166,000 for an immigrant arriving at age 70. For an infant, the NPV is +$61,000, which reflects the high upward mobility of immigrant children of low-education parents. Panel A makes it very clear that the fiscal impact of an immigrant depends heavily indeed on the immigrant's age and education at time of arrival.

It is also informative to consider Panels B and C together. From Panel C we see that the present value of the descendants of a current immigrant, plotted against the ancestral immigrant's age at arrival, is always positive, regardless of the immigrant's age at arrival and education level. The fiscal effects of descendants shown in Panel C do not reflect any difference in fertility by education. If they did, we would see larger positive impacts for the low-education group and smaller ones for the high-education group. An immigrant who arrives after age 40 or so will not have U.S.-born children, and so for ages above 40, the NPV for descendants drops to zero.[23] From this we can infer that the NPV for the immigrant's own lifetime is going to be less positive or more negative than the total NPV figures of Panel A, an influence that is borne out by Panel B. That panel shows that if we focus on the fiscal effects from the lifetime of the immigrant, the NPVs are substantially negative for those with less than high school education, whatever their age at arrival, and for almost all of those with a high school education. Immigrants with more education who arrive up to their mid-forties still have positive NPV for their own lifetime, with a peak NPV of about $150,000, compared with more than $300,000 for the peak total fiscal impact.

One might be inclined to dismiss the contributions of these descendants to the NPV because they appear conjectural and far in the future. However, the

---

[23]We have used female fertility rates for calculating descendants. Of course, a male immigrant arriving after age 40 could leave descendants. Although immigrants who arrive after age 40 may well bring foreign-born children with them, these children are treated as immigrants in their own right, with their own descendants.

children of an immigrant make important economic contributions throughout much of the immigrant's lifetime. The descendants of an immigrant arriving at age 20, which is close to the modal age of arrival, will begin making contributions when the immigrant reaches the early forties, and will continue to make tax payments that offset the costs of the immigrant's Social Security, SSI, Medicare, and Medicaid benefits when the immigrant is old. We are counting the social costs of investing in the immigrant's children, and we should also count the social return on that investment (see MaCurdy et al., 1996:6-7).

Given the difficulties of forecasting anything very far into the future, some readers may be put off by the very long time horizon in the net present value calculations, and may be concerned that these calculations will be dominated by a variety of assumptions of uncertain validity. Such readers may prefer to skip to Figure 7.15 and the accompanying text, which plots the projected current fiscal consequences of an additional 100,000 immigrants per year without use of the net present value calculation and the long horizons that it entails. Figure 7.15 simply projects the consequences year by year into the future, expressed as a tax cost per U.S. resident, and the reader can consider as many years as he or she thinks relevant.

Figure 7.11 presents NPVs for the federal and state and local governments separately, in Panels A and B, respectively (compare these to the total NPV by the age and education of the immigrant, shown in Figure 7.10A). There is a striking difference between these panels. For the federal government, immigrants with all levels of education arriving early in life—say, before age 30 to 50, depending on education—have a substantial positive fiscal impact as measured by NPV. After these ages, however, they have a substantially negative impact, since the federal government provides entitlements for the elderly, most notably Social Security pensions and Medicare. At the state/local level, the situation is reversed. Young immigrants, regardless of their education, impose substantial net costs up to ages of arrival in the late teens or 30 or so, for the two higher-education categories. For the less educated, the fiscal impact remains negative regardless of age at arrival. At the state and local level, even those who arrive when they are elderly impose only slight fiscal costs, in contrast to the federal level.

Figure 7.12 contrasts the NPVs of immigrants with those of the second and the third and later generations. There are two reasons for expecting that the NPVs of immigrants might be greater than those for natives for a given education level and age at "arrival." First, each immigrant has a 30 percent chance of returning to the country of origin after working for a few years in the United States, but before having become costly at school age; even if she did have children, she would take them along when she returned to her country of origin. In either case, state and local governments would not have to pay for their education. Second, our empirical analysis showed that the children of immigrants with less than high school education tend to get considerably more education than do

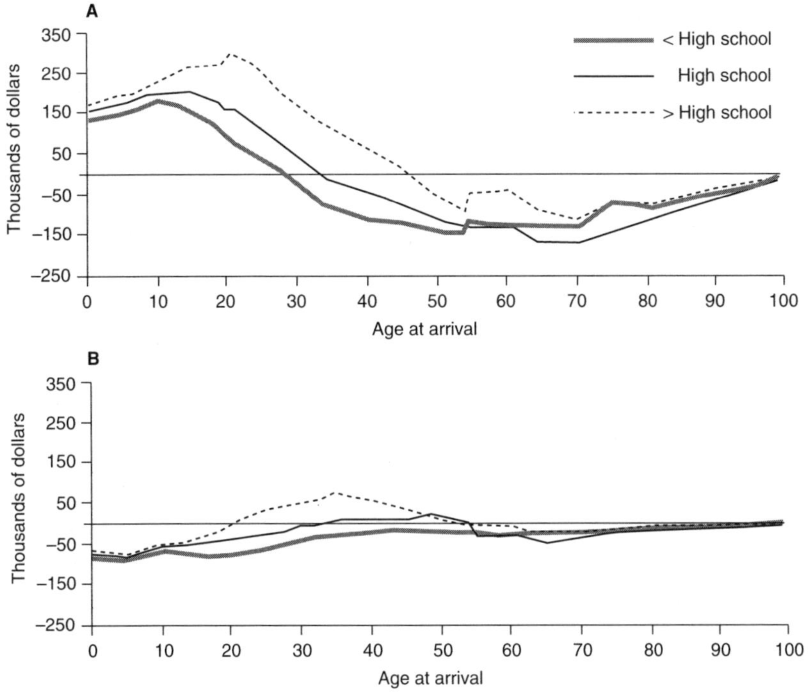

FIGURE 7.11 **A**, Net present value of federal fiscal impact: Generation 1 by age at arrival and education status, self and descendants; **B**, Net present value of state and local fiscal impact: Generation 1 by age at arrival and education status, self and descendants.

the children of low-education natives. This means that the descendants of low-education immigrants contribute more to the total NPV. Figure 7.12 reveals, however, that in general the NPVs of immigrants are somewhat lower than those for natives at each level of education, although this is not true for every age of arrival.

THE AVERAGE IMPACT OF AN INCREMENTAL IMMIGRANT

Because there is a different NPV for every age of arrival and every level of education, and because some of these are large positive numbers and others are large negative numbers, drawing a general conclusion about the fiscal impact of immigration is difficult. To paint the larger picture, we have calculated various kinds of weighted averages of the NPVs across age and education categories, in which the weights are the frequencies of immigrants with these characteristics

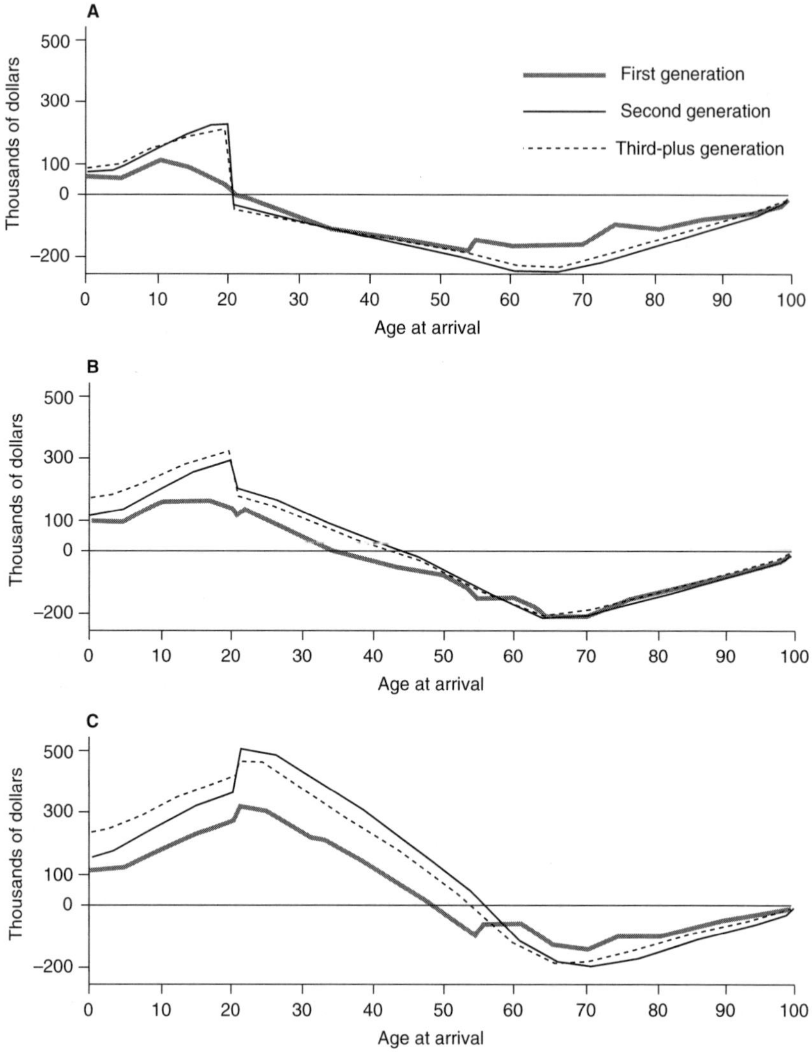

FIGURE 7.12 **A**, Net present value of total fiscal impact: Less than high school education by generation at age at arrival; **B**, High school education by generation at age at arrival; **C**, More than high school education by generation at age at arrival.

arriving in the United States in the past few years.[24] This provides a convenient summary of the implications of the estimates. This idea is appealing, but it suffers from one complication. Children who arrive have not yet completed their education. For those under 20, we have projected the distribution of their completed educations based on the education of their parents, using our estimated probabilities of the upward educational mobility in later generations.

Immigration policy could be varied in terms of the characteristics of the immigrants admitted, or in terms of the numbers admitted, holding characteristics constant. These two different kinds of policy options are informed by different kinds of calculations of the net fiscal impact. We first consider the effects of varying the characteristics of immigrants, and then compare them with the effects of varying their numbers. Before doing so, let us assume for the moment that the only concern of immigration policy is to maximize the net fiscal surplus that immigrants provide to the native-born. To meet that goal we should accept all prospective immigrants who yield a positive fiscal surplus and reject those who impose a fiscal cost. The last immigrant we admit (the marginal immigrant) would cost as much in benefits received as she paid in taxes. In this case, the average fiscal surplus across all immigrants admitted would be a large positive number, since all of them would yield positive fiscal benefits, many of which would be quite large. Our estimates in this chapter show how net fiscal impacts vary with the characteristics of immigrants, but because our simulations contain no feedbacks through the general economy (as explained in the introduction), they do not reflect diminishing returns to immigrants as a result of their hypothetically increasing numbers, and so could not be used to identify the point at which the net fiscal contribution of an incremental immigrant becomes zero. We can, however, identify those immigrants whose characteristics yield a net fiscal impact of zero in the neighborhood of the current volume of immigration.

With this as background, we begin by considering the differences in average NPV by level of education, as shown in the first row of Table 7.5. We see that the average fiscal impact over the life of the immigrants and his descendants is slightly negative for those with less than a high school education; substantial and positive for those with a high school education, and strongly positive, at nearly $200,000 per immigrant, for those with more than a high school education. If the only policy goal were the maximization of the positive fiscal impact of immigrants, the way to accomplish it would be to admit only those with the highest education.[25]

---

[24]That is, we report the weighted average NPV across all age-education combinations, with the relative frequencies of these combinations among recent arrivals supplying the weights.

[25]Given the large amount of net taxes that more highly educated immigrants and their descendants are estimated to pay, one might wonder whether such potential immigrants would continue to select the United States as a destination. Keep in mind, first, that the value of the services that immigrants receive from the government exceeds the costs that we have taken into account because public goods

TABLE 7.5 Average Fiscal Impact of an Immigrant Overall and by Education Level (1996 dollars)

	Education Level of Immigrant			
Group	< High School	High School	> High School	Overall
Immigrants (baseline)[a]	–$13,000	+$51,000	+$198,000	+$80,000
Immigrants themselves	–89,000	–31,000	+105,000	–3,000
Descendants	+76,000	+82,000	+93,000	+83,000

[a]Based on estimated educational transition probabilities.

Row 1 of the table shows the total impact of an immigrant, including the impacts of future descendants born in the United States, and rows 2 and 3 show the components attributable to the immigrant during her own lifetime and to her U.S.-born descendants, respectively. (Note that much of the impact of descendants is actually experienced during the lifetime of the immigrant.) We see that the impacts of the immigrants themselves vary widely by level of education and are substantially negative for all those with less than high school education. By contrast, their descendants have remarkably similar and highly positive effects across the education levels of the immigrant parent, reflecting the considerable upward educational mobility of the children of all immigrants.

Now consider differences in average NPV by age at arrival in the United States. Figure 7.13 shows the average across education levels of the age-specific NPVs, with weights at each age given by the distribution of recent immigrants by educational category. Here we see that, if the only policy goal were making the total fiscal impact as positive as possible, it could be achieved by admitting only

have zero marginal cost but are of value to the immigrant. Second, the fiscal impact of the immigrants themselves is far less positive or far more negative than the total impact, including the impacts of their descendants. Third, all that really matters to the economic incentives to emigrate is the difference between the expected lifetime value of after-tax earnings plus the value of government services received in the United States and those in the country of origin, and this is surely a very large incentive regardless of the fiscal impact. Fourth, potential immigrants may compare the fiscal "deal" they would get in the United States to that they would get in other high-wage developed countries. The United States does not have particularly high taxes in the international context. All governments provide public goods, and this is a big part of the story. The current deficit contributes something to the positive NPVs, but only about half as much as defense spending, and the United States does not have a particularly high ratio of debt to GDP compared with other Western European countries. In other words, these high NPVs are most likely a fact of life for industrial nations. Potential immigrants cannot avoid this situation by shopping around; the United States probably looks better than most in this regard.

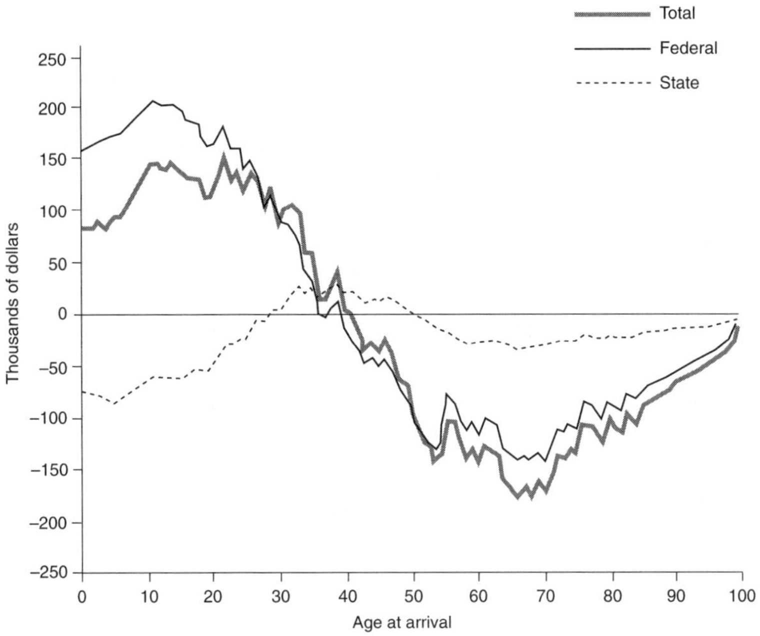

FIGURE 7.13 Net present value of average immigrant by age at arrival.

immigrants of ages 10 to 30. Less restrictively, but still with the narrow goal of avoiding negative NPVs, policy could simply avoid admitting immigrants at ages above 40 or 45. (Figures 7.10 to 7.12 can be consulted for the detail of age-education interactions.) Figure 7.13 also makes clear, however, that, ages at arrival that are good for the federal budget are bad for the state and local budgets, and vice versa.

The curves in Figure 7.13 all refer to individuals of different ages. However, it is a simple matter to constitute families by summing these estimates across the ages of family members at arrival for any desired family configuration. Looking at Figure 7.13 from another perspective, we see that a family with parents of any age at least up to the early forties, with younger children, would have a positive net fiscal impact. Inclusion of elderly family members would substantially reduce it.

These figures indicate the great variation in the fiscal surplus or burdens that immigrants impose. Less-skilled or older immigrants are more likely to be fiscal burdens, and the higher-skilled and young adults are fiscal benefactors of the native-born. In fact, immigration policy has many goals other than purely economic ones, and the composition of current immigrants presumably reflects this diversity of purpose. For example, the less-educated immigrants who impose a fiscal burden are the very same immigrants who provide the economic benefit reported in the labor market chapters.

To see the effect of continuing with this same mix, but increasing the number of immigrants, we consider the expected impact of admitting a randomly chosen immigrant from a pool similar to the pool of actual immigrant arrivals over the past few years. This number is an NPV of +$80,000 (from the last column of Table 7.5).

Of course, all of these numbers are based on a specific set of baseline assumptions, each of which may be questioned, so they should not be taken at face value. In order to investigate the sensitivity of the results to changes in these assumptions, we have redone the entire set of simulations under alternative assumptions, as discussed in the next section. In a subsequent section we present further experiments that will indicate the contributions of different factors to the results.

ALTERNATIVE SCENARIOS

Earlier, we described variations on the baseline scenario. The voluminous results of these alternative calculations are presented in Appendix 7.B in tables 7.B1, 7.B2, and 7.B3, which present results for immigrants in each of the education categories. Each table gives the NPV for selected ages of arrival: 0, 20, 21, 40, and 70. Age 20 is close to the modal age of arrival and often has close to the peak NPV, and 70 is the age of arrival with the greatest negative value.[26] The tables also give the corresponding NPVs of the third and later generations for comparison purposes, along with the difference between immigrant NPV and third-generation NPV. Because variation is so complex, it is difficult to form an impression of the overall effects of the different scenarios on the calculated fiscal impact of an immigrant. Table 7.5 presents NPVs averaged across age at arrival of immigrants, regardless of education, and Figure 7.13 presents NPVs of immigrants of various ages averaged across their education level—Table 7.6 takes both attributes into account. Using the age-education frequencies among recent immigrants, as reported in the 1994 and 1995 CPS, we can average individual immigrants with any combination of age and education.

In this exercise, the baseline results appear to be quite robust, at least regarding the sign of the outcomes. At the state/local level, the average fiscal impact is negative, with present value usually in the range of –$20,000 to –$30,000. At the federal level, however, the average fiscal impact is positive and typically quite large, mostly in the range of $60,000 to $130,000. The average total fiscal impact

[26]The NPV at age 20 is the last that reflects the upward mobility of the children of an immigrant based on the immigrant parent's education; the NPV at age 21 is the first based on the known education of the immigrant him- or herself.

TABLE 7.6 Average Fiscal Impact of an Immigrant (Net Present Value) by Scenario and Level of Government (1996 dollars)

Scenario	State/Local Fiscal Impact	Federal Fiscal Impact	Total Fiscal Impact
Baseline	-$25,000	+$105,000	+$80,000
Alternative scenarios			
Budget assumptions			
No budget adjustment	–25,000	+10,000	–15,000
Immediate budget adjustment	–25,000	+102,000	+77,000
Budget adjustment by taxes	–25,000	+119,000	+95,000
Budget adjustment by benefits	–25,000	+91,000	+66,000
1996 welfare reform act	–22,000	+110,000	+88,000
1996 welfare reform act and no budget adjustment	–22,000	+15,000	–7,000
Interest rates (percent)			
2	–5,000	+223,000	+219,000
4	–27,000	+66,000	+39,000
6	–23,000	+38,000	+15,000
8	–19,000	+27,000	+8,000
Other assumptions			
OASDHI = 0 if arrive > 55	–25,000	+110,000	+85,000
No emigration of 2nd generation	–28,000	+118,000	+90,000
Low emigration of 1st generation	–30,000	+136,000	+106,000
Immigrant taxes increase for 10+ years	–8,000	+132,000	+124,000
Lower bilingual education costs	–23,000	+105,000	+83,000
Benefits fixed with respect to natives	–20,000	+103,000	+83,000

Note: First two columns may not total to third due to rounding.
OASDHI = Old-age, Survivors, Disability, and Health Insurance.

is positive except for two cases, which are viewed as highly unlikely, and its level ranges widely. A few scenarios merit separate discussion.

Starting Year for Fixing the Debt/GDP Ratio

In the baseline scenario, the budget is adjusted starting in the year 2016. Here we consider two alternative scenarios: fixing the debt/GDP ratio starting immediately (which gives very similar results to fixing it starting in 2016), and not adjusting the budget at all, but rather continuing with the status quo, in which tax payments are assumed to grow at the rate of productivity growth, 1 percent per year, as do benefits. It makes little difference whether taxes and benefits are adjusted to fix the debt/GDP ratio immediately or in 2016. Under the first alternative, the average federal NPV declines slightly, from $105,000 to $102,000. Two factors account for this reduction. First, the earlier adjustment may actually lead to lower taxes for a number of years. Second, dealing with the impending budget crisis earlier means that it is sufficiently less severe later on that later taxes will be substantially lower. Also, the relative numbers of immigrants and natives change over time, so altering the timing of tax increases alters the relative burdens between the present value of tax payments by immigrants (including their descendants) and natives.

However, if the debt is allowed to grow with neither tax increases nor benefit cuts, then the positive impact at the federal level is dominated by the state and local negative impact, resulting in a negative total impact. In the status quo scenario, the debt/GDP ratio rises to 3.9 by 2050, and to 11.7 by 2100. This scenario clearly leads to unrealistic debt levels. We believe that the baseline scenario, or perhaps the immediate-adjustment scenario, offers the most realistic basis for assessing the fiscal impacts of immigrants.

It might be thought that, since none of these scenarios involves repaying the debt, nor even preventing its further growth, the calculations must be missing the full contribution of immigrants to the debt burden. In fact this is not so. The present value of all implied interest payments does equal the initial stock of debt under the scenarios with a fixed debt/GDP ratio. Under the no-targets case, debt never has to be controlled, and all interest payments can be made by borrowing rather than by raising taxes, so the effects of debt sharing are inconsequential.

Fiscal Adjustments Entirely Through Taxes or Through Benefits

In the baseline scenario, starting in 2016 the budget is adjusted so that the debt/GDP ratio is held constant thenceforth. The baseline adjustments are shared 50-50 between changes in taxes and in benefits. Here we examine the implications, first, of making all adjustments in taxes while leaving benefit schedules unchanged, and next, of making all adjustments in benefits. It makes a moderate difference (±$13,000) which way government budgets are adjusted, but not enough to affect our conclusions. With higher tax rates, immigrants make a greater contribution to meeting the costs of the retirement of the baby boom generations, and so have a more positive federal and total impact than they would if benefits were reduced.

Effects of the Welfare Reform Legislation of 1996

The Personal Responsibility and Work Opportunity Reconciliation Act of 1996 denies certain means-tested benefits to noncitizens. The legislation did not define these programs and to date they have not yet been defined by regulations.

TABLE 7.7 Increase in Net Present Value (NPV) of Immigrants Under the Welfare Reform Legislation of 1996, by Age of Arrival and Education (1996 dollars)

	Increase in NPV Due to Welfare Reform Legislation of 1996				
	Age at Arrival				
Education	0	20	21	40	70
< High school	$5,000	$5,000	$5,000	$21,000	$15,000
High school	6,000	6,000	6,000	9,000	24,000
> High school	5,000	4,000	2,000	6,000	31,000

We take these means-tested programs to include SSI, AFDC, food stamps, non-emergency Medicaid, energy assistance, rent subsidies, and public housing. Since legal immigrants can become citizens after five years of residence, we have implemented the provisions of this act by assuming that immigrants receive no benefits from the programs just listed during their first five years in the country, and at longer stays receive benefits according to our estimates, as reflected in the baseline scenario. The results of this final scenario are summarized in Table 7.7, which is calculated from data in Tables 7.B1, 7.B2, and 7.B3 in Appendix 7.B. As expected, the NPVs are higher at every age. However, it is striking that, at the most important ages, around 20, the changes are modest.[27] Only near or after retirement age is there a substantial effect. The effect generally declines with education at the younger ages, and it rises with education for arrival at age 70.

The 1996 act, by denying means-tested benefits to immigrants until they become citizens (here assumed to occur five years after arrival), makes the fiscal impact slightly less negative at the state and local level, and makes the impact more positive at the federal level, for an increase of $8,000 per immigrant in the total fiscal impact.

Variations in Interest Rate

The interest rate determines the importance of descendants to NPV relative to the immigrant's own life cycle; the higher the interest rate, the less important are the descendants. We have already seen that, at a 3 percent rate, the NPV

[27]Simple calculations confirm, however, that the magnitude of these effects is consistent with the CBO estimates of savings of $23.7 billion over the next six years, due to reductions in benefits to legal permanent resident immigrants.

contribution of the descendants is always positive, so we expect that lower interest rates will raise the NPV of immigrants overall, and higher ones will reduce it. The interest rate also determines the relative importance of the different stages of the immigrant's own economic life cycle. At low interest rates, childhood, working years, and retirement get similar weights. But as the interest rate rises, the importance of retirement declines relative to the working years, and the importance of the working years declines relative to childhood. For these reasons, we expect our results to be sensitive to variations in the assumed interest rate.

This expectation is borne out by the results shown in the Table 7.6. The interest rate makes a considerable difference to the fiscal impact, particularly when it is low. It is obvious that, as the interest rate is increased, the estimated impacts will sooner or later shrink toward zero for natives as well as immigrants. It is notable, however, that there are no changes of sign within the range of interest rates we have examined.

Assumed Trajectory for Immigrant Workers' Tax Payments

The baseline scenario assumed that the earnings of immigrants follow the empirically estimated trajectory according to "time since arrival" up to 10 years in the United States, and that thereafter the relation of the earnings of immigrants to those of native-born workers is fixed. This assumption was made because some research has found that the observed time-since-arrival trajectories in recent cross-sectional data overstate the amount of convergence toward native earnings that is found in longitudinal data. However, other research using the same CPS data we employ has found that the cross-sectional data on time since arrival accurately describe the longitudinal earnings growth of immigrants measured between successive waves of the CPS (Duleep and Regets, 1997). For this reason, we have also done an estimate in which the CPS time-since-arrival tax profiles are used for stays longer than 10 years, instead of the procedure described above.

This new assumption substantially raises the positive fiscal impact of immigrants because of higher tax payments. This change is seen across all educational levels and is stronger the younger the immigrant (Appendix 7.B).

The remaining scenarios are designed to test the special empirical assumptions on which the estimates were based. The main conclusion here is that these variations make little difference to the outcome.

Many assumptions have gone into these calculations. For some, we have done sensitivity analysis and generally found that none of the assumptions tested individually was decisive. However, there are other assumptions that we have not tested, and we have not tested combinations of departures from baseline.

THE TIMING OF FISCAL IMPACTS

The weighted averages of the total NPV calculations shown in Table 7.6 were mostly positive. For example, in the baseline case, the weighted average of the NPV is +$80,000, composed of –$25,000 at the state and local level, and +$105,000 at the federal level. But how can we interpret such numbers in terms of a current impact on yearly budgets? One approach would be to convert these present values into equivalent equal annual flows. For example, this baseline, average NPV of –$25,000 at the state/local level can be converted into a perpetual negative annual flow of about –$750 per immigrant at 3 percent interest ($750 = .03 \times 25{,}000$). Similarly, the perpetual annualized federal flow would be +$3,150, and the total would be +$2,400 per year. However, this method for converting the long-term present value into an annual impact conceals important features of the annual flows, and it turns out to be far more revealing to calculate these explicitly for each year, using all our information.

The Effects of a Single Immigrant

Consider the actual fiscal impact of an immigrant in each year following his arrival. Figure 7.14 plots the annual impacts discounted at 3 percent for an immigrant arriving in 1994; the NPV is then simply the sum of all the values shown in the figure for each level of government; because they are discounted,

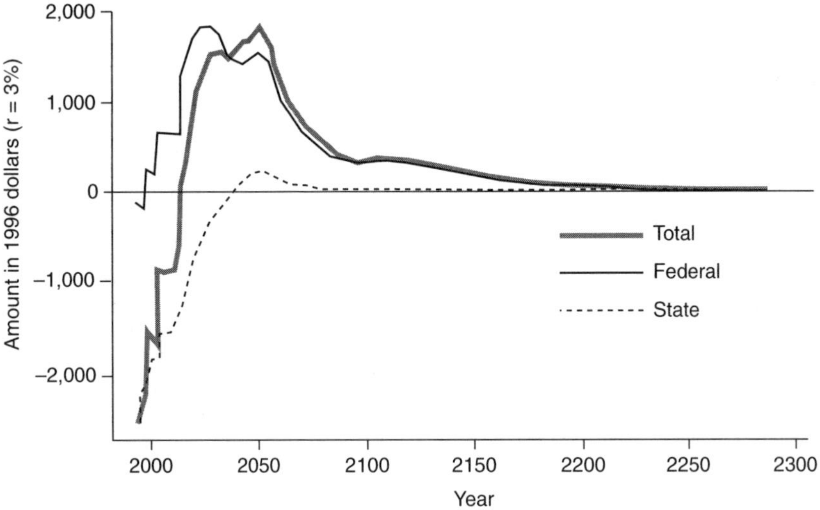

FIGURE 7.14 Present value of annual fiscal impacts: One immigrant arriving in 1994 (discounted at 3%).

they cannot be directly compared with the annualized stream). (The curves actually represent the averages of impacts for immigrants of different ages at arrival and education level, rather than representing any single age at arrival and education level; in all cases, length of time in the United States is taken into account, along with all descendants.) The state and local impact is substantially negative initially, at about –$2,270, and the federal impact is initially close to zero (–$120), for a total impact of about –$2,400. This is very different from the annualized total impact of +$2,430. Indeed, the total impact does not turn positive until 22 years after the arrival of this composite immigrant, and the state/local impact does eventually turns positive, but only after about 40 years. (Note that the impact turns positive just after 2016 when, according to baseline assumptions, taxes are raised and benefits cut in order to control the debt/GDP ratio.) Evidently, even if immigrants have positive NPVs, they nonetheless impose substantial costs in their initial years in the United States.

The immigrants themselves more quickly have a positive fiscal impact at the state and local level; for example, by the 25th year, immigrants have a positive impact of +$910. However, they have also borne children who themselves have had children, and these descendants impose costs of more than $1,660 at the state and local level in the 25th year, so the total impact is still negative, at more than $700. At the federal level, the immigrant has a strong positive effect that is only very slightly offset by the costs of children, at $1,570. After 50 years, both the immigrant and the second generation are making sufficiently positive impacts to offset the substantial costs of the third generation, yielding a positive impact at the state and local level. At the federal level, the composite immigrant is now elderly and has become costly. These costs, however, are more than offset by the second generation, resulting in a strong positive total impact of $1,520.

The NPV calculations are based on projections that reach 300 years into the future, and it would be absurd to claim that the projections into the 23rd century are very reliable. How much do our NPV calculations depend on such long-run outcomes? Since we are discounting at 3 percent, the future is heavily discounted. At 25 years, the discount factor is 0.5; at 50 years, 0.22; at 75 years, 0.1; and at 100 years, 0.05. Calculation of truncated NPVs for varying time horizons shows how much the distant future affects the results. Table 7.8 gives the fraction of the full NPV (based on 300 years) that is achieved with different time horizons.

The approach to the ultimate value is not rapid. Although the total flow turns positive after 23 years, it takes 40 years for the total NPV to turn positive. By 75 years, the planning horizon used for Social Security, more than half the long-run NPV has been reached. It may seem that 50 or 75 years are unacceptably long horizons for measuring the fiscal impacts of immigrants, but reasonable calculations over any shorter period are scarcely possible, since it is very important to include the later-life cycle stage of immigrants in the calculations. But doing that brings in the second generation as schoolchildren, as taxpayers, and as parents

TABLE 7.8 How Quickly the Long-Term Impact of an Immigrant Is Approached

Length of Time Horizon (years)	Percentage of Ultimate Net Present Value Reached by Each Horizon (r = .03%)		
	State and Local[a]	Federal	Total
0	0%	0%	0%
25	172	10	–23
50	184	42	14
75	142	68	53
100	126	79	69
...	...	...	...
300	100	100	100

[a]The percentage for state and local is greater than 100 because early net present values do indeed exceed the terminal value.

and grandparents. Once again, letting the second generation reach its old age in our calculations seems necessary, and indeed a defensible time to stop is impossible to find. For this reason, it seems best to extend the time horizon far into the future, and let the discounting gradually reduce the influence of the future to nothing.

The Effects of a Stream of One Immigrant Per Year

What would happen if we added one immigrant every year henceforth? The fiscal impacts of this one-person immigrant stream can then be multiplied as desired to see the simulated effects of adding, say, 100,000 immigrants each year. Note that this experiment does not permit any feedback from the changed number of immigrants to the trajectory of taxes and benefits (although this could, in principle, be done), so it is most informative about the effects of small changes in the neighborhood of immigrant streams of the current size.

Figure 7.15 plots the fiscal effects of a stream of one composite immigrant per year; the composite is a weighted average of the effects of the various kinds of immigrants. The impact of this stream eventually comes to grow linearly, as does the stock of incremental immigrants. Rather than discounting this stream at 3 percent, as was done above, the figure instead shows the stream discounted at 1.57 percent, which is the long-term growth rate of GDP. Thus, the figure offers a visual sense of the importance of the fiscal impacts relative to the growing GDP. Although the figure gives an idea of the impact of changing immigration policy to admit more or fewer immigrants each year, it is more difficult to use it to get an idea of the current costs of past immigration. The size and composition

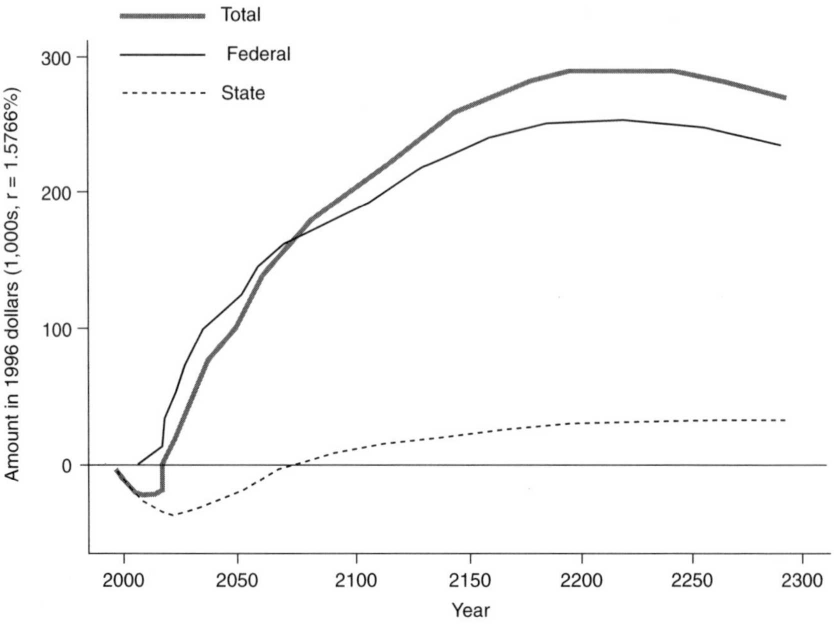

FIGURE 7.15 Undiscounted annual fiscal impacts of incremental stream of one immigrant per year, expressed relative to gross domestic product.

of the immigration stream have changed substantially over the course of this century, but immigrants who arrived early in the century, or before, still exert an influence on current public budgets through their descendants if not through their own old age.

At the state and local level, the fiscal impact remains negative for around 70 years, until late in the 21st century, reaching its most negative level after about 25 years, at around –$35,000. At the federal level, and in total, the effect of the assumed budget adjustment in 2016 is clearly apparent. After 2016, the total (current) fiscal impact turns positive, and very strongly so.

INTERPRETING THE RESULTS

What Accounts for Our Positive Estimates?

What factors drive our estimated results for net present values? To answer this question, we have concentrated on the weighted average NPV, which is +$80,000 for the baseline case (see Table 7.5 or 7.6). We carry out a series of experimental calculations, designed to show the relative contributions of different factors (see Table 7.9). We have not succeeded in coming up with an infor-

TABLE 7.9 What Accounts for the Positive Average Net Present Values: Experimental Calculations (1996 dollars)

Contributing Factor/ Conceptual Experiment	Total Net Present Value	Implied Effect of This Factor
Baseline	+$80,000	—
Applying to any incremental person		
If *public goods* were congestible goods	–$5,000	–$85,000
If *congestible goods* were public goods	+160,000	+80,000
If *interest payments* were a private good	+31,000	–49,000
If *no population aging and health care costs increase* (no budget adjustment scenario)	–15,000	–95,000
Due to special immigrant characteristics		
If immigrants had the same *education* as natives	+121,000	+41,000
If immigrants had the same *age* as natives	+32,000	–48,000
If immigrants paid the same *taxes* by age as natives	+152,000	+72,000
If immigrants received same *benefits* by age as natives	+50,000	–32,000

Note: For the experiments on public goods and interest payments, we simply multiplied the present value of future costs of services from congestible goods by the ratio of the total government expenditures on public goods to the same for congestible goods, and added or subtracted from the average net present value (NPV), as appropriate. This is crude, but it should be approximately correct. For making congestible goods public, we simply added to the NPV the present value of expenditures on congestibles. For education, we assumed that, at each age, the proportional distribution of education for immigrants was the same as for natives. For age, we used the age distribution of the third+ population instead of that of immigrants at arrival to weight the age-specific immigrant NPVs. An alternate way is to use the NPV at age 0 for immigrants, since all natives arrive at age 0. The effects of population aging and rising health care costs are assessed simply by comparing the scenario in which there are no adjustments in taxes or benefits with the one in which these are adjusted immediately, on the grounds that population aging and rising health costs are the only reason that the budget projections show unsustainability in the future. The effects of giving immigrants the tax or benefit profiles of natives are assessed by doing new simulations under these conditions.

mative way of separating and then adding up the roles of mutually exclusive factors; the entries in Table 7.9 count some influences in more than one way. For example, there are entries for tax profiles, benefit profiles, and education, yet education is the main determinant of those profiles. In general, this decomposition is quite rough. Its results depend on just how we formulate alternative scenarios, and often that formulation is somewhat arbitrary.[28]

[28]For example, do we simply eliminate all spending on public goods, or do we imagine that public good spending is really for private goods that grow with the size of the population? In the case of debt, we treat the conventional government debt as one item, and the aging of the baby boom as another. However, we could also think of the aging of the baby boom as mattering because of the implicit debt owed by the Social Security and Medicare systems.

It is interesting that so many different factors appear important in generating the result, and also that none of the experimental changes reported below is sufficient, in isolation, to produce a strongly negative estimate of fiscal impact. For example, if all the expenditures we categorize as provision of public goods (military expenditures are the leading case) were instead treated as private or congestible goods, so that a per capita cost is allocated to immigrants and their descendants, then the average NPV would drop from +$80,000 to –$5,000, just slightly negative, or by $85,000, thus identifying public goods as contributing powerfully to the result. A similar calculation shows that treating congestible goods (roads, police, and the like) as public goods with zero marginal costs would add $80,000 to the NPV, for a total of +$160,000. Readers can draw on their own views about whether various government services are public or private to come up with their own estimate of the overall fiscal impact. The fact that immigrants will pay taxes that go in part to make interest payments on the national debt contributes a sizable $49,000 to their positive average NPV.

We have adhered closely to the assumptions made by the CBO in projecting federal expenditures. One such assumption is that expenditures on the military and on other public goods grow at the rate of population growth plus the growth rate of productivity— that is, they remain a roughly constant share of GDP. This treatment of military expenditures in budget projections may appear inconsistent with our treatment of these as public goods in our fiscal accounting, in which the costs of military services are assumed not to rise with the size of the population. In fact, the two treatments of military are not necessarily inconsistent. As incomes rise, people may choose to spend more on the military, and as population increases, the price to individuals of a given level of military services declines proportionately, which may induce people to demand more.

However, we can show approximately how much difference it would make if we instead projected military expenditures to rise at the rate of productivity growth alone, rather than that plus the rate of population growth, through the following calculation: per capita expenditures on all public goods in the base year (1994) are about $1,400, and these are projected to increase either at 1 percent per year or at 1.5 percent per year, depending on the assumption. Over an infinite horizon, the NPV with growth at 1.5 percent per year would be 1,000/(.030 – .015) = 93,333. With growth at 1 percent per year it would be 1,000/(.03 – .01) = 70,000. The difference is 23,000. Table 7.9 shows that public goods contribute $85,000 to the net present value (NPV), quite close to the figure of 93,000 despite the crudeness of the calculation just described. A better approximation of the consequences of not including population growth in the growth of public goods would be .25 × 85,000 = 21,000 (.25 = 1 – 70,000/93,333). In other words, projecting public good expenditures to grow only at the rate of productivity growth would have an important effect on the estimated baseline NPV, reducing it from $80,000 to $59,000, but this would not change any of our conclusions. By the same line of reasoning we can see that the proportional effect of the change in assumptions declines as the discount rate rises. At a discount rate of 3 percent, the NPV was reduced by 25 percent. At a discount rate of 8 percent, the NPV would be reduced by only 7 percent.

Finally, it appears that the role immigrants play in bearing the cost of the aging of the baby-boom generations and of rising health costs, largely for the elderly, contributes very strongly to their overall positive impact, more so than does any other single factor. In the same way, the fact that natives also will help to meet these projected future cost increases also raises their NPVs. Were it not for the projected future costs arising from aging and health care, the federal budget would now need very little adjustment, and the debt/GDP ratio would remain much the same as it is under current tax and benefit policies. Although immigration does not emerge as an important factor in the Social Security Administration's sensitivity tests of long-run financial soundness (see Board of Trustees of the Federal Old-Age and Survivors Insurance and Disability Insurance Trust Funds, 1996) relative to fertility and mortality, on a per immigrant basis, these contributions are important. All the items just discussed apply to incremental natives as well as to incremental immigrants, although the precise amounts depend on taxpaying propensities.

How do immigrants and natives differ? We see that the relatively lower education of immigrants makes their fiscal impacts less positive, and their age distribution does the opposite. The fact that immigrants pay rather lower taxes than natives at each age substantially reduces their positive impact, although the differences between the benefits received by immigrants at each age and those received by natives actually work to make their impacts more positive, contrary to general belief (the reason can be seen in Figure 7.7).

Why Are NPVs So Negative at the State and Local Level and So Positive at the Federal Level?

When it comes to programs that are age-targeted, state and local governments invest heavily in children, particularly in their education, whereas federal government programs are overwhelmingly directed toward the elderly, for pensions and health care. There are important consequences. First, state and local investments in education pay off in higher tax payments later in life, although only a portion of the payoff is at the state and local level; the remainder is at the federal level, where tax payments are also raised. Second, at the state and local level, an individual or a household typically first receives costly services and transfers, particularly for education, and then in a sense pays for them later in life through taxes. Because of discounting, the future taxes receive a lower present value than the earlier benefits do, creating a negative NPV.[29] At the federal

[29]The effective discount rate here is the difference between the actual discount rate, say 3 percent, and the rate of productivity growth, 1 percent, at which most benefit profiles are rising over time. Taxes are rising at least at the rate of productivity growth, and, under federal budget adjustments, at a higher rate.

level, the opposite occurs: workers pay taxes first, and receive their pension and health care benefits about 30 years later on average. Discounting gives these benefits a lower present value than the present value of tax payments, creating a positive NPV. The state and local NPVs for natives at birth are themselves highly negative for these reasons, at –$45,000 (not shown).

Although the positive fiscal impacts of incremental immigrants are evenly shared by the entire population, the state and local negative impacts are restricted to states that receive immigrants. We cannot say, based on the calculations we have done, whether the total fiscal impact, summing at the federal, state, and local levels, is positive or negative for residents of high-immigration states such as California. We can say only that it is positive for the average U.S. resident under the baseline set of assumptions.

Large NPVs Translate Into Small Annual Effects for the Average Citizen

To understand the costs of immigration at a simple level, suppose that the annual immigrant flow were to increase by 100,000 while its composition remained the same.[30] Further suppose that a payment of $25,000 were made by U.S. residents to cover the net state and local cost of each immigrant at the time they entered the country, for a total of $2.5 billion per year. This cost would be divided among the 260 million U.S. residents (including the foreign-born), each of whom would pay about $10 per year. However, for certain states, in particular California, the costs per individual and per household would be far higher, because of the concentration of immigrants and the special characteristics of these immigrants and of the states themselves.

Now, using the same approach, suppose that each immigrant deposits $105,000—the NPV at the federal level—with the federal government at the time of arrival; each new resident will gain $40 due to an increase of 100,000 in the size of the immigrant flow. Taking these numbers at face value, the federal, state and local taxes of the average resident would decline by about $30. For a household, the extra immigrants would mean a gain of about $80. Despite the large size of the NPVs we have calculated, the size of these annual flows is surprisingly small on a per person basis.

These calculations show how, over time, the large NPVs affect the average taxpayer only a little—but they do not capture the shift over time, whereby immigrants are costly in early years and may be net contributors in later years.

[30]These calculations are informative only if an additional 100,000 immigrants each year constitutes a small change relative to current levels of immigration. In the past few years, immigration has been in the 850,000 to 1 million range, so 100,000 would represent about a 10 to 12 percent change.

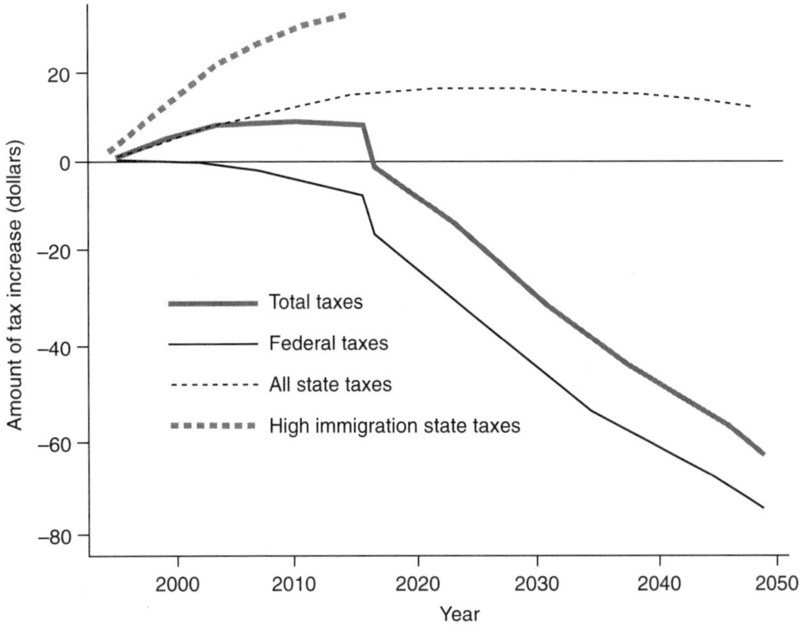

FIGURE 7.16 Per capita tax increases due to 100,000 additional immigrants per year.

Figure 7.16 reveals this pattern, using the same factors as the calculations just reported, aside from timing. It shows state and local costs of about $10 per U.S. resident, consistent with our earlier calculation. However, the federal effects are delayed, so the overall stream of combined favorable effects starts off near zero, lower than the $30 our calculations suggested, but soon grows to be larger than our calculations suggested. Figure 7.16 also shows the average state and local effect for the six states of high immigration, and it is more than twice the national average, for obvious reasons.

SUMMARY

The most striking difference between immigrants and natives is not in benefits received, but rather in taxes paid. Because immigrants on average have less education, at each age they earn less and pay substantially lower taxes, of all kinds and to all levels of government. Nevertheless, the average immigrant pays nearly $1,800 more in taxes than he or she costs in benefits, due to the special age distribution of immigrants, which is heavily concentrated in the working years, with relatively few foreign-born children and relatively few elderly. However, it is more useful also to take account of native-born children—those under age 20—with immigrant parents. In this calculation, the average immigrant or child pays nearly $370 less in taxes than he imposes in costs, in sharp contrast with the average native, who pays $2,030 more in taxes than he imposes in costs. Immigrants and their children form a relatively young population. Because it is federal government programs that assist the elderly, and there are relatively few elderly immigrants, the average immigrant (including native-born children under 20) has a positive federal balance of taxes and benefit costs of nearly $550. Because state and local governments provide for public education, the balance at this level is –$920.

Calculations of this sort are interesting, but they do not enable us to assess the fiscal impact of an incremental immigrant. To do this, we need to make a forward-looking calculation of the present value of taxes and costs over the lifetime of an immigrant, taking account of the taxes and costs associated with his or her descendants.

Such calculations reveal that the fiscal impact of an immigrant varies widely depending on age at arrival in the United States and on educational attainment. The fiscal impact typically rises with age from birth, peaking between ages 10 and 25 at positive values, and then declining gradually to a trough in the late sixties, at which point the impact is highly negative. This curve is higher, the higher the education of the immigrant. There are many immigrants who impose net fiscal burdens on the native-born, and many others who afford them net fiscal benefits. This diversity must be reviewed alongside estimates of average fiscal impact when formulating immigration policy.

Fiscal impacts are quite different by level of government. At the federal level, they are positive for immigrants in all educational categories from birth until the late twenties. After this, as old age draws nearer, they turn negative. At the state and local level, immigrants of all educational categories have negative impacts from birth until after school age, and for low-education immigrants the balance never turns positive.

The descendants of immigrants make a considerable positive contribution to the fiscal impact for all education levels of immigrants, and they should be included in the calculation. The substantial costs of educating the children of immigrants are included, so it is important that the eventual social return in the form of taxes also be included. Taxpaying children overlap the life cycles of their immigrant parents and help to pay the public costs they impose as they age.

In all this detail, it is difficult to discern the larger picture. To show the overall implications of these estimates, we derive summary measures by averaging fiscal impacts (NPVs) across all ages, weighting by the actual age distribution of recent immigrants in each education category. Immigrants with less than a high school education have a fiscal impact of –$13,000, immigrants with a high school education have an impact of +$51,000, and those with more than high school have an impact of +$198,000.

In the same way, we can average the NPVs across education for each age at arrival, and in this way summarize the effect on NPVs of the age at arrival of immigrants. Here, we see that immigrants arriving between their early teens and late twenties have the highest positive fiscal impacts, and immigrants arriving in their mid-sixties have equally large negative impacts.

When we simultaneously average across both age and education to get a single summary measure of net fiscal impact based on the characteristics of recent arrivals, under our baseline assumptions, we find an average value of +$80,000.

These summary measures mask important differences between the federal and the state and local levels. At the state and local level, the average NPV is –$25,000, and at the federal level it is +$105,000. Ages of arrival at which immigrants generate the most positive fiscal impacts at the federal level are the very ages at which they generate the most negative impacts at the state and local level. Although the positive impact at the federal level is shared evenly by the U.S. population, the negative state and local impact is highly concentrated in a few states, with a particularly heavy cost in California.

Because we project so far into the future and by necessity have to make so many assumptions, there is considerable uncertainty about exactly what these NPVs of immigrants will be. We tested the sensitivity of the analysis to variation in the assumed interest rate, the date of adjusting the federal budget, budget adjustments through tax changes or benefit changes, assumed trajectory of immigrants' tax payments with time since arrival in the United States, and a number of other assumptions. Under the reasonable set of baseline assumptions that the panel adopted (chosen before we knew what the answers would be), the average NPV of immigrants was positive. This is an important result because an exclusive reliance on annual budget impacts would have led us to the opposite conclusion. Under many other sets of assumptions, these NPVs remain positive. But there are other sets of plausible assumptions (slightly higher interest rates, less intergenerational assimilation in the future, a smaller share of public goods, marginal costs exceeding average costs, possible displacement effects of native workers) that are by no means implausible and would produce negative fiscal impacts of immigrants. This uncertainty is not surprising given how far we must project into an uncertain future. At a minimum, our results show that a reliance solely on annual budget accounting is an extremely shaky way to draw conclusions about the true fiscal impact of immigrants.

We also examined the effects of the Personal Responsibility and Work Opportunity Reconciliation Act of 1996, by assuming that in their first five years in the United States, immigrants received no benefits from certain means-tested programs including SSI, Medicaid, food stamps, and AFDC. This new policy raises the fiscal impact per immigrant by $8,000, on average, making it more positive, or less negative.

Under the baseline assumption, a number of factors contribute to the positive average NPV: Allocating a pro rata cost to immigrants for public goods would change the average NPV to slightly negative, whereas ignoring the costs of congestible goods would double the positive NPV. Help from immigrants in paying the substantial costs of future population aging and rising health care costs for the elderly is also a major factor. Special characteristics of immigrants also act to raise the NPV: they tend to arrive in the early working years; some of their children are likely to be educationally upwardly mobile, and they receive lower benefits than others. By contrast, that immigrants have lower education than natives, and consequently pay less in taxes, reduces the NPVs.

While the average long-term fiscal impacts of immigration are generally found to be positive, an increase in the annual flow of immigrants would, for a couple decades, have a negative fiscal impact overall. The timing and extent of such a period would depend on federal fiscal policy. At the state and local level, the annual fiscal impact would remain negative for many decades, and the overall NPV would be negative. At the federal level, the annual fiscal impact would be positive from the start.

We have also calculated the annual fiscal impact per U.S. resident of an increase of 100,000 per year in the immigrant flow under the baseline assumptions (change the sign for a decrease). We found it to be roughly +$30 per person, composed of +$40 at the federal level and –$10 per person at the state and local level. This average amount per person strikes us as rather low, despite the large NPVs. However, it should be kept in mind that an earlier period of greater deficits is followed by a later period of greater returns. With due account taken of the many uncertainties in our estimates, it appears unlikely that immigrants and their descendants impose worrisome costs at the combined federal and state and local levels for the average U.S. resident. Indeed, our calculations suggest that immigrants may instead, on average and in the long run, have a positive fiscal impact. Nonetheless, immigrants with certain characteristics, such as the elderly and those with little education, may be quite costly. And residents of certain states with large shares of immigrants without doubt bear higher costs that in some cases may not be offset by the broadly shared gains at the federal level.

KEY CONCLUSIONS

- Households headed by immigrants include the native-born school-age children of immigrants, who incur high costs of public education. However, they do not include the working-age native-born children of immigrants, who typically have a positive fiscal impact. For this reason, cross-sectional or current fiscal impacts estimated for immigrant-headed households are biased toward negative numbers.
- The relative intensity of program use by immigrants and natives at the federal, state and local levels varies significantly from one program to another. For example, immigrants and their young children use bilingual education, SSI, public assistance, and Medicaid more heavily than others in the population, but they also use Social Security and Medicare more lightly than do others.

- The implication of this diversity is that we must be comprehensive in our examination of program use to obtain an accurate assessment of the fiscal impacts of immigration. We find that the pattern of per capita overall program use at each age is very similar for immigrants and others, with immigrants and their children imposing somewhat higher costs at the young ages, and lower costs above age 50. The cost of benefits used by immigrants and their young children is actually 8 percent less per capita than the costs of benefits used by the rest of the population, in part because their age distributions differ.
- On average, immigrants pay considerably lower taxes at each age than do others, and overall they and their native-born children under the age of 20 pay about one-third less than does the rest of the population, again due in part because of their age distribution.
- In assessing the long-term fiscal impact of immigrants, it is important to take into account the likely descendants of the immigrants, and the likely educational attainment of these descendants.
- The long-term (net present value) fiscal impact of an immigrant varies greatly across different types of immigrants. Some groups of immigrants bring net fiscal benefits to natives, and others impose net fiscal costs. Among other things, these fiscal effects depend heavily on the characteristics of immigrants, including age at arrival in the United States, educational attainment, and time spent in the United States. The net present value typically peaks for ages at arrival of 10 to 25, and then declines to a trough for those arriving in their late sixties. This curve is higher, the higher the education. Under our baseline assumptions, the average fiscal impact (net present value) of an immigrant with less than a high school education is –$13,000, and that for an immigrant with more than a high school education is +$198,000. Similarly, older immigrants impose significant fiscal burdens, and younger immigrants produce fiscal surpluses.
- Averaging across these characteristics, immigrants under our baseline scenario have a negative fiscal impact at the state and local level, but a larger, positive impact at the federal level, resulting in an overall positive impact for the United States.
- Under most scenarios, the long-run fiscal impact is strongly positive at the federal level, but substantially negative at the state and local level. The federal impact is shared evenly across the population, but these negative state and local impacts are concentrated in the few states that receive most of the immigrants.
- The average fiscal impact of immigrants under the baseline assumptions is positive in part because they tend to arrive at young working ages, in part because their descendants are expected to have higher skills and incomes, in part because they pay taxes for some items, such as national defense and interest on the federal debt, for which they do not impose costs, and in part because they will help to pay the public costs of the aging baby-boom generations.

• The 1996 Personal Responsibility and Work Opportunity Reconciliation Act, by prohibiting new immigrants from receiving means-tested benefits for a period after arrival, will make the long-term fiscal impact per immigrant more positive by about $8,000.

• If the long-term federal budget imbalance is not addressed—which is not a realistic policy option—the overall fiscal impact of immigrants will be slightly negative; if the debt/GDP ratio is held constant starting immediately, or starting in 2016, the overall fiscal impact will be positive. It will be more negative if discount rates are higher, and if budgetary imbalances are addressed by reducing benefits rather than by raising taxes.

• Although the average long-term fiscal impacts of immigration are generally found to be positive under most scenarios that we tried, the overall annual fiscal impact of an increase in the annual flow of immigrants would be negative for a couple of decades before it turned positive. The timing and extent of such a period would depend on federal fiscal policy.

REFERENCES

Auerbach, A.J.

1994 The U.S. Fiscal Problem: Where We Are, How We Got Here, and Where We're Going. NBER working paper #4709. Cambridge, MA: National Bureau of Economic Research.

Auerbach, A.J., J. Gokhale, and L.J. Kotlikoff

1991 Generational accounts: A meaningful alternative to deficit accounting. Pp. 55-110 in David Bradford (editor), *Tax Policy and the Economy*. Cambridge, MA: MIT Press.

Board of Trustees of the Federal Old-Age and Survivors Insurance and Disability Insurance Trust Funds

1996 *Annual Report of the Board of Trustees of the Federal Old-Age and Survivors Insurance and Disability Insurance Trust Funds.* Washington: U.S. GPO.

Clark, R.L.

1994 The Costs of Providing Public Assistance and Education to Immigrants. PRIP-UI-34, Program for Research on Immigration Policy, The Urban Institute.

Congressional Budget Office of the United States

1996 *The Economic and Budget Outlook: Fiscal Years 1997-2006* Available from U.S. Government Printing Office, Washington, D.C.

Duleep, H.O.

1994 Social security and the emigration of immigrants. Pp. 97-128 in *Migration: A Worldwide Challenge for Social Security*. Geneva: International Social Security Association.

Duleep, H.O., and M.C. Regets

1997 Measuring immigrant wage growth using matched CPS files. *Demography* 34(2):239-249.

MaCurdy, T., T. Nechyba, and J. Bhattacharya

1996 An Economic Framework for Assessing the Fiscal Impacts of Immigration. Paper prepared for the Panel. Department of Economics, Stanford University, September.

Sheffrin, S., and M. Dresch

1995 *Estimating the Tax Burden in California.* Berkeley, CA: California Policy Seminar.

U.S. Department of Commerce

1994 Fixed Reproducible Tangible Wealth in the United States: Revised Estimates for 1991-1993 and Summary Estimates for 1925-1993. Survey of Current Business, Bureau of Economic Analysis.

APPENDIX 7.A
INTERGENERATIONAL EDUCATIONAL MOBILITY

The General Social Survey (GSS) has been carried out every year since 1972 by the National Opinion Research Center (NORC). It collects information on the nativity of the respondent's parents and grandparents, on the respondent's education, and on the education of the respondent's parents. We categorized all educational attainments as less than high school, high school, or more than high school. For a specific generation of respondent (first, second, or third, based on the nativity questions), we created a set of all linked pairs of parent-child educational attainments, using the information on education of respondent and of each parent of the respondent. We then treated the parents as the reference unit, and for each parental level of education, we calculated the proportional distribution of the children by educational attainment. Even within parental education categories, the children of higher-fertility parents have lower educational attainments. However, we did not weight for this, since the overrepresentation of such children in the sample simply reflects the higher fertility of their parents, which we wish to be reflected in the results for the average parent. We ignore differences in fertility by education of parent, which could bias the results in the optimistic direction.

It is well known that the characteristics of immigrants have been changing over the past several decades. Our controls for educational attainment may be insufficient to capture these changes. As a further control, we estimated separate transition matrices by ethnic origin group for Hispanics, Asians and all others, by immigrant generation and education group. We then formed a weighted average of these matrices for each generation and each education group, with weights equal to the ethnic shares in each generation. For first-generation immigrants we used the educational distribution of recent immigrant flows and base changes in the ethnic shares of subsequent generations on fertility differences between ethnic groups. These weighted average matrices were then used to project educational mobility in the analysis.

To estimate the transition matrices for Hispanics and others, we used educational outcomes for all children age at least 21 years, and born after 1960, in every GSS since 1972. For Asians, sample sizes were quite small, so we had to consider all children age at least 21 years and born after 1950. Even so, numbers were small, so we assumed that their dropout rates at each level of education were proportional to the corresponding dropout rates of others, with a different constant of proportionality estimated for each level of parental education. From these fitted dropout rates, we estimated the distribution of educational outcomes. The resulting matrices by immigrant generation, ethnicity, and educational attainment of parents were used as described in the preceding paragraph.

We also used an alternative procedure to estimate these transition matrices in which we weighted the sample in various ways. (1) Early-born cohorts are represented in many different years of the survey, while later-born cohorts are represented fewer times (only once in the extreme case). We therefore weighted by the inverse of the number of times a cohort would be represented in the combined surveys. (2) Blacks were oversampled, and we have weighted to remove this effect. (3) Adults in households with more adults present are less likely to be represented, given our procedures, so we weighted by the number of adults. The various weighting procedures did not change the results in any important way.

The estimated distributions of each generation's education by the education of the original immigrant are shown in Figure 7.A1. It can be seen that there is substantial upward educational mobility for the children of low- and medium-education parents, and by the fourth generation (the great-grandchildren of immigrants), the implied educational distributions are essentially identical, regardless of the educational status of the original immigrant. Although in general it can be said that each generation is better educated than the one preceding it, an important exception is seen in the educational attainment of the grandchildren of immigrants. Grandchildren (third-generation immigrants) whose immigrant forebear had at least a high school education are less well educated than their parents (second generation immigrants). Compared with the general population, we find greater upward educational mobility for the children of first-generation immigrants. However, educational mobility for children of the second-generation immigrants is much lower than that found in the general population.

It would not be right to use the transition matrix estimated for U.S.-born children of immigrants to project the educational attainment of all the foreign-born children of immigrants, since they will have different English language skills and educational backgrounds. For a foreign-born child who arrives in the United States at a young age, this transition matrix is probably appropriate; but for one who arrives as a teenager, it would be much less so. Inspection of transition probabilities estimated from the GSS for foreign-born children shows that these have had somewhat less upward educational mobility than the transition matrices for U.S.-born children of immigrants would suggest. Presumably the ultimate educational attainment of foreign-born children will depend on their age at arrival in the United States. In order to take this into account, we have modified the educational transition probabilities that were estimated for first-generation children. For foreign-born children arriving at ages up to 12 years, we retain the estimated second-generation probabilities. From age 12 on, for children of low- or medium-education parents, we assume the probabilities of upward mobility decline linearly to 0 at age 20. For children of parents with higher education, we leave the probabilities as estimated. In this way we construct different transition matrices for foreign-born children, and for the U.S.-born children of foreign-born parents.

Figure 7.A1 shows that we project that 52 percent of the grandchildren of immigrants will attain more than a high school education (> HS) and a higher

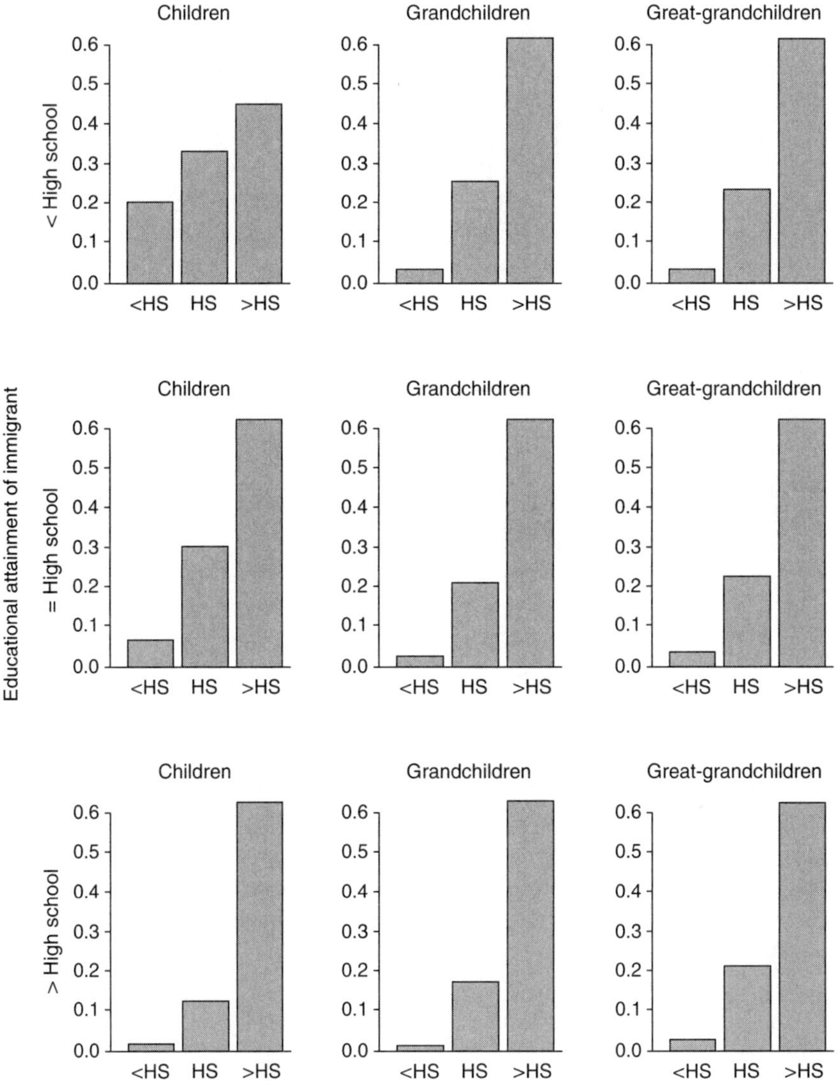

FIGURE 7.A1 Educational attainment of descendants of immigrant by educational attainment of original immigrant.

percentage (67) of the great-grandchildren. Currently, about 52 percent of the total U.S. population aged 25 to 34 years has more than a high school education (U.S. Statistical Abstract, 1995, Table 240:158). By coincidence, this figure is identical to our projection for the grandchildren of immigrants. It is somewhat lower than our projection of 67 percent for the great-grandchildren of immigrants. These figures are not really comparable since our projections refer to educational distributions 30 to 40 years in the future rather than the current levels. Average educational attainment in the U.S. has been rising and it is reasonable to assume that significantly more than 52 percent of the great-grandchildren of nonimmigrants will attain more than a high school education. Indeed, our analysis of the intergenerational educational matrices for the nonimmigrant population indicates a long-run educational distribution in which 72 percent of the population attains more than a high school education.

APPENDIX 7.B
NET PRESENT VALUES FOR IMMIGRANTS AND NATIVES, BY SCENARIO

Tables 7.B1 to 7.B3 present data on the net present values for immigrants, by age of arrival and for native-born residents, in the third and later generations, at current ages, for various alternative assumptions.

TABLE 7.B1 Less Than High School Education

	Immigrant Age at Arrival				
Scenario	0	20	21	40	70
Baseline	60	33	7	−141	−166
2% discount	298	228	181	−192	−181
4% discount	−9	−12	−29	−104	−154
6% discount	−43	−27	−36	−59	−133
8% discount	−44	−24	−29	−35	−117
100% taxes	87	52	23	−160	−167
100% benefits	33	15	−8	−123	−166
Balance budget now	51	25	−0	−140	−161
Never balance budget	−56	−109	−129	−164	−167
Never balance budget + welfare reform	−50	−105	−123	−143	−152
Duration 10+ taxes	99	67	37	−119	−166
Duration 5-9 benefits	62	36	9	−142	−166
Welfare reform act	65	38	12	−120	−151
Elderly immigration with zero OASDHI	60	33	7	−141	−73
No emigration 2nd gen	72	50	23	−141	−166
Lower emigration	103	47	14	−174	−189
Lower bilingual education	65	35	8	−143	−168

Native (3rd + Generation) Current Age					Difference				
0	20	21	40	70	0	20	21	40	70
92	234	–54	–134	–223	–33	–200	61	–8	57
362	487	85	–190	–245	–64	–259	96	–2	65
12	147	–72	–92	–204	–21	–159	43	–12	50
–32	79	–60	–42	–173	–11	–106	24	–16	39
–39	51	–46	–17	–148	–6	–75	17	–18	31
124	266	–47	–155	–224	–37	–213	70	–5	57
61	202	–61	–112	–222	–28	–187	53	–11	56
83	229	–58	–129	–213	–32	–203	58	–10	53
–41	82	–183	–164	–225	–15	–191	55	–0	57
–41	82	–183	–164	–225	–9	–187	60	21	72
92	234	–54	–134	–223	7	–167	91	15	57
92	234	–54	–134	–223	–30	–198	63	–9	57
92	234	–54	–134	–223	–27	–196	66	13	72
92	234	–54	–134	–223	–33	–200	61	–8	150
92	234	–54	–134	–223	–21	–184	77	–8	57
92	234	–54	–134	–223	11	–186	68	–40	34
92	234	–54	–134	–223	–27	–199	62	–9	55

TABLE 7.B2 High School Education

Scenario	Immigrant Age at Arrival 0	20	21	40	70
Baseline	92	146	126	–32	–225
2% discount	353	391	351	–68	–248
4% discount	10	70	58	–6	–205
6% discount	–35	21	16	21	–172
8% discount	–40	8	5	31	–146
100% taxes	123	175	152	–48	–226
100% benefits	61	117	100	–15	–224
Balance budget now	83	138	118	–29	–216
Never balance budget	–26	–2	–16	–56	–227
Never balance budget + welfare reform	–21	4	–9	–47	–203
Duration 10+ taxes	133	184	161	–0	–225
Duration 5-9 Benefits	94	138	117	–44	–225
Welfare reform act	98	152	132	–23	–201
Elderly immigration with zero OASDHI	92	146	126	–32	–142
No emigration 2nd gen	104	164	142	–31	–225
Lower emigration	145	185	159	–44	–261
Lower bilingual education	97	149	128	–31	–227

TABLE 7.B3 More Than High School Education

Scenario	Immigrant Age at Arrival 0	20	21	40	70
Baseline	117	288	333	132	–149
2% discount	395	594	641	116	–163
4% discount	26	174	211	140	–137
6% discount	–28	80	107	140	–116
8% discount	–37	44	64	131	–101
100% taxes	152	332	379	119	–150
100% benefits	82	245	287	144	–148
Balance budget now	108	281	326	138	–142
Never balance budget	–4	127	173	101	–150
Never balance budget + welfare reform	1	130	176	107	–119
Duration 10+ taxes	162	352	407	200	–149
Duration 5-9 Benefits	120	294	343	147	–149
Welfare reform act	122	292	335	138	–118
Elderly immigration with zero OASDHI	117	288	333	132	–54
No emigration 2nd gen	129	307	351	132	–149
Lower emigration	177	364	418	149	–170
Lower bilingual education	123	293	338	134	–150

Native (3rd + Generation) Current Age					Difference				
0	20	21	40	70	0	20	21	40	70
171	342	182	18	–209	–79	–195	–56	–49	–16
495	637	394	–19	–230	–142	–246	–43	–49	–18
61	228	115	43	–190	–51	–158	–57	–49	–15
–10	130	67	68	–160	–24	–108	–51	–47	–12
–28	85	47	75	–136	–13	–77	–42	–44	–10
214	383	205	–1	–210	–91	–208	–54	–47	–16
129	300	158	37	–208	–68	–183	–58	–52	–16
161	336	177	23	–197	–78	–198	–59	–52	–19
31	182	44	–16	–210	–57	–184	–60	–40	–16
31	182	44	–16	–210	–51	–178	–54	–31	7
171	342	182	18	–209	–38	–157	–21	–18	–16
171	342	182	18	–209	–78	–203	–65	–62	–16
171	342	182	18	–209	–74	–190	–50	–41	7
171	342	182	18	–209	–79	–195	–56	–49	67
171	342	182	18	–209	–67	–178	–40	–49	–16
171	342	182	18	–209	–26	–156	–23	–62	–52
171	342	182	18	–209	–74	–194	–54	–50	–18

Native (3rd + Generation) Current Age					Difference				
0	20	21	40	70	0	20	21	40	70
245	442	503	244	–191	–128	–154	–170	–112	42
621	780	846	235	–211	–226	–186	–205	–118	48
106	303	354	246	–173	–80	–129	–143	–107	37
9	174	212	236	–145	–37	–94	–105	–95	28
–18	115	143	217	–122	–19	–70	–79	–86	21
298	494	557	231	–192	–146	–162	–179	–111	42
192	391	448	257	–190	–110	–146	–161	–113	42
234	437	498	255	–176	–126	–157	–172	–117	35
95	273	334	199	–193	–100	–146	–161	–98	43
95	273	334	199	–193	–94	–143	–158	–92	73
245	442	503	244	–191	–82	–90	–96	–44	42
245	442	503	244	–191	–124	–149	–160	–97	42
245	442	503	244	–191	–122	–151	–167	–106	73
245	442	503	244	–191	–128	–154	–170	–112	137
245	442	503	244	–191	–115	–136	–152	–112	42
245	442	503	244	–191	–67	–78	–84	–95	20
245	442	503	244	–191	–123	–149	–165	–110	41

APPENDIX 7.C
DISCUSSION OF DATA SETS FOR THE STUDY OF FISCAL IMPACTS

Most analyses of the use by immigrants of government entitlement programs are based on one of three data sets: the Public Use Microsample (PUMS) of the decennial U.S. Census of Population, the Survey of Income and Program Participation (SIPP), or the Current Population Survey (CPS). Each has advantages and disadvantages. PUMS is the largest sample, containing data on 12.5 million individuals in 1990, of whom about 9 percent, or about 1 million, are foreign-born. Because special efforts were made to include responses from illegal immigrants, it is possible that these are reasonably well represented in the sample. The large size of the PUMS means that estimates have relatively small sampling error and that it is possible to disaggregate by characteristics of immigrants such as education, time since arrival, country of origin, and place of residence in the United States. However, PUMS contains fewer of the necessary programmatic data items compared with SIPP or the March CPS, is updated only every 10 years along with the decennial census, and has limited possibilities for intergenerational analysis.

Compared with the decennial census and CPS, SIPP has a smaller sample size, and only by combining panels is it possible to get enough respondents to include an acceptable number of immigrants. In work for this report, Peter Brandon combined seven SIPP panels, 1986-93, to obtain a total sample size of 290,000 individuals, including 33,000 foreign-born. SIPP distinguishes foreign-born from native-born respondents, and for children up to age 15 reports whether their parents are immigrants. For older children, it does not provide this information. The real strengths of SIPP are that it contains more accurate monthly data on program participation and expenditures and richer information on wealth and income sources, than either PUMS or the March CPS.

CPS, starting in 1994, supports separate study of first and second-generation immigrants and the remainder of the population. The sample size is about 150,000. Combining the 1994 and 1995 surveys yields about 300,000 respondents, with about 30,000 foreign-born. Like SIPP, CPS provides rich detail about program use, but these data are thought to be less reliable than those in SIPP.

For our national-level longitudinal analysis, we have relied largely on CPS, viewing it as a good compromise between the sample size of PUMS and the detail of SIPP. Additional work for the panel pools seven waves of SIPP as a basis for assessing the national work done using CPS. The case study for California derives program participation rates from the March CPS but uses average costs per participant from other sources. The New Jersey case study was based on PUMS.

8

Social Dimensions of Immigration

In addition to the demographic, labor market, and fiscal effects of immigration summarized in the previous chapters, how immigrants and their children will fit into American society now and in the future depends also on other aspects of immigration. In this chapter, we review research bearing on some key questions about the social dimensions of immigration. The first set of issues concerns the integration of immigrants and their children into American society: social and spatial mobility across generations, competence in the English language, naturalization, and intermarriage and ethnic identity. The next set of issues concerns the effects of immigration on American institutions, focusing on two extremes with side-effects for the rest of the population—excellence in science and the arts and participation in crime. The social consequences of immigration are not only the outcomes of immigrants' own values, skills, and motivations, but also reflect the reactions of the resident population. This chapter concludes with a discussion of interethnic relations and public opinion on immigration, especially regarding concerns about the economic effects.

These issues do not exhaust the ways in which immigration has shaped American society and how immigrants have responded to their new environment.[1] But they do serve both to illustrate the potential contribution that social

[1]There are many other issues involving social consequences of U.S. immigration that do not receive detailed discussion in this chapter. Two examples are studies of the effects of immigrants on schools and the role of immigrant entrepreneurs in creating new businesses.

science research can make to policy debates and to identify gaps in current understanding.

Assessments of the social consequences of immigration often arouse strong reactions. Some critics of contemporary immigration policy conclude that the arrival of predominantly nonwhite immigrants displaces native workers, swells the largely minority "underclass," and exacerbates racial and ethnic conflict (Brimelow, 1995; Bouvier, 1991; Lamm and Imhoff, 1985). Others conclude that the new immigrants strengthen and reinforce the best in American traditions, revitalize decaying neighborhoods and stagnant industries, and add new talents and energies to the U.S. civic culture (Binder and Reimers, 1995; Simon, 1989; Portes and Rumbaut, 1996).

Contemporary reactions have historical parallels. Before the enactment of restrictions on immigration in the 1920s, intense debates erupted over whether the new immigrants from Eastern and Southern Europe could ever be assimilated.[2] Contemporary fears about the social consequences of immigration are typically expressed in less graphic language than those in the past, but the sentiments are not dissimilar.

Although it is not possible to resolve all controversies over the impact of immigration, enough is known to allay some of the widely held concerns that immigration has exacerbated the social problems that confront American society in the late twentieth century. Over time, many immigrants, and especially their children, have become integrated into the mainstream of American society (Alba, 1995; Hirschman, 1983; Lieberson, 1980; Portes and Rumbaut, 1996), and immigrants have made significant contributions to many American institutions. It is also true that some immigrants have participated in crime, and interethnic tensions and violence, sometimes directed at other immigrants, have surfaced. But the weight of both the historical and the current evidence is that immigrants are no more likely to participate in socially disapproved activities than are native-born Americans. Although there is no assurance that past trends will always continue, the new Americans who have arrived in recent decades are likely to also be absorbed into the primary institutions of American society. As with many past waves of immigrants, they will also redefine the character and content of American culture in the process.

---

[2]At the beginning of the twentieth century, many scholars believed that Southern and Central European "races" were genetically inferior to the Northern and Western European groups who had emigrated to the United States in earlier times and had defined American culture (Ross, 1914; Grant, 1916; for a masterly review of American nativism, see Higham, 1955). For example, in a full page ad in the Sunday *New York Times* on June 22, 1913, William Ripley, a Harvard economics professor, wrote that "the hordes of new immigrants" were "a menace to our Anglo Saxon civilization." Another economist, Robert Foerster, toured Latin America to investigate the effects of immigration from the rest of the Western Hemisphere for the U.S. Department of Labor. "He concluded, in a report published by the government in 1925, that broad entry by Latin Americans would 'lower the average of the race value of the white population of the United States'" (Muller, 1993:41).

INTEGRATION OF IMMIGRANTS INTO AMERICAN SOCIETY

An often-heard criticism is that immigrants do not adapt to American society and culture, thus balkanizing the American population. The idea of a common society in which all members are fully incorporated and socially equal has been more of an ideal than a reality in American history. America has always been characterized by variations in socioeconomic and cultural status associated with groups defined by national origin and color as well as by great variation even within national-origin groups. A more realistic concept, then, might be integration into the "normal" diversity of American society.

Issues of immigrant assimilation are important for several reasons in this report. Chapter 3 noted that some immigrants, particularly those from Latin America, have higher fertility. Our analysis suggests that the initial higher fertility among Hispanic immigrants will decline for their native-born descendants. These fertility declines possibly reflect the integration of Hispanic immigrants and their children into a society with lower childbearing norms. The assimilation of immigrants in the labor force may have repercussions for the pattern of geographic mobility as well as for their economic success. These, in turn, affect the labor market and the fiscal impacts discussed in previous chapters.

Social and Spatial Mobility

Immigrants tend to cluster in certain geographic areas and occupations. Since they usually depend on the assistance of kin and others in their primary networks, ethnic neighborhoods and enterprises are often essential stepping stones for their social and economic adaptation. Even when government policy tries to disperse new arrivals around the country, as with the case of Cuban refugees in the 1960s and Vietnamese refugees in the 1970s, secondary migration has led to a reconcentration of immigrants. Since ethnic areas often tend to look, sound, and smell different from other areas, some of the native-born population will see immigrant neighborhoods as evidence that new immigrants are not adapting to American society. The historical evidence makes clear, however, that ethnic residential concentrations and ethnic economies are initial efforts by the first generation to get a foothold in American society. Most historical and contemporary research shows that assimilation is a generational process (Lieberson, 1980, 1996). Immigrants who arrive as adults are sometimes slow to learn English, and many older immigrants continue to have close attachments to the countries of origin long after their arrival. In contrast, the second generation, including immigrants who arrive as children or adolescents, typically become "American" in language, behavior, and outlook.

Between the two world wars, the children of immigrants from Southern, Eastern, and Central Europe made significant socioeconomic gains, particularly in educational and occupational attainment (Lieberson, 1980; Perlmann, 1988;

Hirschman and Kraly, 1990). And by the 1960s, there were only modest differences in socioeconomic status and in intergenerational mobility among whites, whatever their national origins (Duncan and Duncan, 1968; Featherman and Hauser, 1978: Chapter 8). The upward movement of Asian immigrants and their descendants was slower but, by the 1960s, Asian Americans were at least at parity with whites in terms of education and occupational status, although an income gap remained (Nee and Sanders, 1985; Hirschman and Wong, 1984). Generationally, the major disadvantaged groups in American society are not immigrants and their children; they are African Americans, American Indians, and Puerto Ricans.

Considerable uncertainty still surrounds the social and economic fortunes of the waves of immigrants who arrived in recent decades. Although it is too early to draw definitive conclusions, most studies show that, with few exceptions, recent immigrants and their children (the second generation) are doing relatively well (Barringer et al., 1993; Jasso and Rosenzweig, 1990; Portes and Rumbaut, 1996). This does not mean that parity has been reached, nor even that all recent groups of immigrants have escaped poverty, but simply that most of the newcomers are not completely isolated from the mainstream of American society: they work, live in neighborhoods, and go to school in proximity to the native-born population.

One of the most important indicators of social adaptation is the level of integration (or segregation) in residential areas. Residential integration is considered the linchpin of interethnic relations, since it opens the door to informal association in schools, playgrounds, and other places where close personal bonds and friendships are formed. In the initial years after arrival, the massive waves of immigrants in the early twentieth century clustered tightly together, but rising income levels and the passage of generations blurred residential segregation within a few decades (Lieberson, 1980: Chapter 9). The rapid pace of immigration in the last three decades has also created many new ethnic areas in major cities around the country. These have been interpreted by some as a sign of balkanization and a harbinger of long-term trends. But empirical research suggests that this may be simply a short-term response.

Some evidence in favor of eventual assimilation is registered in the consistent association between social class (as measured by education, occupation, and income) and residential integration (including suburbanization) among Hispanic and Asian Americans (Frey, 1995). As the ability of immigrants and their children to afford better housing grows, they seem to choose neighborhoods with more amenities over areas with more neighbors with similar ethnicity. This association contrasts with the trend for blacks, who—even if they have higher economic status--have continued to live in segregated neighborhoods (Massey and Denton, 1993). If immigrants, including Hispanics and Asians, have also faced discrimination in the housing market, it has been much less than that experienced by blacks.

Evidence for residential segregation for Hispanics and Asians, taking immigrants and native-born persons together, has come from several recent censuses. Asians, as a group, display low to moderate levels of segregation from whites (Massey and Denton, 1992; Fong, 1994). Asians tend to be highly suburbanized and, because they have low levels of segregation within suburbs, their overall levels are reduced. Asian-white segregation is reduced as the socioeconomic status of Asians increases, with very low segregation levels for higher education and income levels. Taken as a whole, "Asians appear to experience few barriers to residential mobility and display remarkably low levels of segregation" (Massey and Denton, 1992:170).[3]

One difficulty with using the census is that the geographic areas identified are at a very high level of aggregation. Borjas (1995) used data from the National Longitudinal Survey of Youth to look at the probability that other survey respondents living in the same zip code area had the same ethnic background as the respondent.[4] These segregation indices are shown in Table 8.1. Some ethnic groups display high levels of segregation. The average black respondent lived in a neighborhood that was 63 percent black, and the average Mexican respondent lived in a neighborhood that was 50 percent Mexican. The typical respondent lived in a neighborhood with a much lower index: only 30 percent of the respondents had a similar ethnicity. Many other immigrant groups, including Chinese, Filipinos, other Hispanics, Polish, and particularly the older immigrant groups (the Irish and the Italians) had much lower segregation indices. These indices imply that, except for Mexicans, geographic segregation for immigrant groups is not particularly great.

Moreover, segregation weakens as the generations succeed one another. Because the 1970 census included a question about the nativity of the parents of the respondent, it permits researchers to classify people as foreign-born, native-born of foreign-born parents, and native-born of native-born parents—providing information on the first, second, and third and later immigrant generations.[5] In

[3]Although we highlight general segregation patterns for Hispanics and Asians above, there are widespread differences within nationality groups of the population. For example, Cubans are highly segregated from both blacks and whites, and Mexicans are highly segregated from blacks but only moderately segregated from whites. Asians as an overall group are highly segregated from blacks. Within the Asian population, the Japanese have the lowest segregation from whites. The Vietnamese evidence the highest segregation levels. Other Asian groups fall between the two extremes. Because the Japanese have resided in the United States for several generations and the Vietnamese are among the most recent immigrant groups, these results are consistent with a story of declining segregation with generational assimilation.

[4]This survey was not designed to be a survey of immigrants. Rather, we cite these results as evidence that segregation varies among ethnic groups, some of whom are heavily affected by recent immigration.

[5]Questions about parental nativity were omitted from the 1980 and 1990 censuses. Immigration researchers have argued that it would be valuable to include a question on parental nativity in the future (Edmonston, 1996).

TABLE 8.1 Residential Segregation Indices by Ethnicity, 1979

Ethnicity	Percentage of Population in the Neighborhood with Same Ethnic Background
Black	63.4
Chinese	3.5
Cuban	33.3
English	23.9
Filipino	5.0
German	25.7
Irish	14.3
Italian	16.3
Mexican	50.3
Other Hispanic	9.3
Polish	12.8
Puerto Rican	29.8
All[a]	30.4

[a]The total sample includes all reported ethnic groups. There are more groups than are shown in this table.

Source: Analysis of National Longitudinal Survey of Youth data, for persons aged 14 to 22 years, in 1979; reported in Borjas (1995: Table 4).

1970, the typical immigrant lived in a neighborhood that was 33 percent either first- or second-generation (Borjas, 1995). But members of the second generation lived in neighborhoods that were 28 percent first- or second-generation, and those in the third and later generations lived in neighborhoods that were only half as segregated, with 14 percent first- and second-generation.[6]

This generational desegregation did not proceed at the same pace for Hispanics, however.[7] The typical third-generation Hispanic lives in a neighborhood that is 29 percent Hispanic (Borjas, 1995:367). **With the notable exception of Mexican immigrants, the geographic concentration of most immigrant groups is not great, especially compared with geographic segregation among black Americans. The available evidence also indicates that geographic segregation weakens as later generations succeed the immigrant generation.**

[6]Cross-sectional data on immigrant generations do not reveal the inter- and intragenerational dynamics of spatial mobility. Cohort observations would reveal much higher mobility than is indicated by cross-sectional data.

[7]They were the only ethnic group identified separately in the data about nativity.

Once again, the notable exceptions to these trends are Mexican immigrants, who tend to live close to other Mexican Americans across each generation.

Intermarriage and Identity

There has always been variation in the experience of different ethnic groups with social mobility and ethnic or racial identification. East European Jews achieved a great deal of social mobility by the second generation, but Italian Americans took several generations to reach parity with native whites of native parentage (Lieberson, 1980; Alba, 1986). Overall, however, the remarkable progress of once-stigmatized groups like Greeks, Slavs, Irish, and Italians merits Andrew Greeley's description of it as an "ethnic miracle" (Greeley, 1976). Succeeding generations of some non-European groups have also experienced upward mobility. The increase in education and income across the generations of Japanese Americans has been so great that they have the highest income of any ethnic group in the United States (Waters and Eschbach, 1995).

In the nineteenth century, the Irish were seen as a "race" apart from other European groups. They were stereotyped for their criminality, lack of education, and poor family values and were often portrayed as apes in cartoons of the time. In the mid-nineteenth century, Negroes were referred to as "smoked Irish" (Ignatiev, 1995). If those debating immigration restriction in the early part of the twentieth century had done population projections to predict the "race suicide" they believed new immigrants were causing, they would have projected the numbers of Southern and Central Europeans and Irish and shown how these growing groups would have made white Protestants a minority by some date in the far-off future. Yet we now know that such predictions would have been wrong for several reasons.

Most important, they would have failed to predict the decline in the relevance of the boundaries separating European groups from one another. The children and grandchildren of immigrants from Italy, Poland, and Greece—groups that were once seen as "unassimilable" and racially distinct—intermarry with others of different ethnic origins to such an extent that the descendants of most white European groups are virtually indistinguishable. Indeed, the descendants of all immigrant waves from Eastern and Southern Europe have reached equality with white Protestants in education, income, occupational specialization, and residential distributions (Lieberson and Waters, 1988).

At the turn of the century, marital "endogamy was castelike for new ethnics from eastern and southern Europe" (Paginini and Morgan, 1990). Within the space of two generations, social, economic, and cultural changes have led to levels of ethnic intermarriage that would have been unthinkable in the decades immediately following the major waves of immigration. As Alba (1995:13) reports, "in 1990 census data, more than half (56 percent) of whites have spouses whose ethnic backgrounds do not overlap with their own at all . . . . Only one fifth have spouses with identical backgrounds."

Under such conditions of great intermarriage, ethnic identity is increasingly a matter of choice for whites in the United States. An American of Italian, Irish, and Scottish ancestry, for example, can "choose" to identify with one or more of his or her ethnic ancestries and discard or "forget" others (Waters, 1990; Alba, 1990). For example, over 40 million Americans reported Irish ancestry in the 1980 census, a figure far in excess of any reasonable rate of natural increase from the 4.5 million Irish who were immigrants to the United States. Hout and Goldstein (1994) show that the number of Americans who identify as Irish Americans is possible only because of the high rate of intermarriage of persons with Irish ancestry and a very selective identification of Irish identity among offspring with multiple ancestries.

This fluidity of white ethnic categories stands in contrast to the seeming essentiality of race. But this fluidity is partially the result of the primacy of racial issues in American history, which necessitated unambiguous classifications, first to identify discrimination and now to implement affirmative action. But the social and legal forces of racial identity in the United States are also idiosyncratic, the product of complex and contingent processes, and subject to change over the coming decades.

Rates of intermarriage have been growing since 1960 for all groups, even for those defined as "racial" groups (Sandefur and McKinnell, 1986; Kikumura and Kitano, 1973; Kitano et al., 1984; Gurak and Fitzpatrick, 1982; Lieberson and Waters, 1988). Although it is still the case that only a small proportion of marriages by whites are to nonwhites and Hispanics (2 percent), the rate of increase in recent decades has been dramatic: "In 1960 there were about 150,000 interracial couples in the United States. This number grew rapidly to more than 1.0 million in 1990. When marriages with Hispanics are added the intergroup marriages totaled about 1.6 million in 1990" (Harrison and Bennett, 1995:165).

As we noted in Chapter 3, although 97 percent of whites and 94 percent of blacks married within their own groups in 1990, 70 percent of Asians and 73 percent of Hispanics did so. The percentage of intermarriages increased between 1980 and 1990, as younger people married outside their group to a greater extent. Intermarriage rates were much higher for native-born Asians and Hispanics in 1990. Among younger married persons in 1990, aged 25 to 34 years, 65 percent of native-born Hispanics had a Hispanic spouse (see Table 8.2). Among younger Asians, 53 percent of men had an Asian wife and 46 percent of women had an Asian husband.

Intermarriage rates vary regionally, with lower intermarriage rates for Asians and Hispanics in areas where there is a heavier concentration of immigrants. Outside the South and the Southwest, younger native-born Hispanics had a non-Hispanic spouse more than half the time (Farley, 1996). Younger native-born Asians living outside California and the other Pacific states had a non-Asian

TABLE 8.2 Race/Ethnicity of Spouses, Aged 25 to 34 Years, 1990

	Race/Ethnicity of Spouse			
Race/Ethnicity	White	Asian	Black	Hispanic
Husband				
White	96.3%	0.9%	0.2%	2.2%
Asian[a]	36.0	52.6	0.6	8.4
Black	5.6	0.8	91.5	1.7
Hispanic[a]	31.6	1.3	1.2	65.0
Wife				
White	96.7	0.4	0.4	2.1
Asian[a]	45.2	45.6	2.2	6.7
Black	2.2	0.2	96.3	1.1
Hispanic[a]	31.4	1.1	2.0	65.0

Note: The calculation of different race/ethnicity is based on five mutually exclusive groups: white non-Hispanic, American Indian, Asian, black, and Hispanic. American Indian estimates are not shown above but are included in the estimates for the total population. Intermarriage is defined as a married person in one of the five groups whose spouse is reported in another group.

[a]Calculated for native-born individuals.

Source: Farley (1996), based on analysis of 1990 census microdata.

spouse three-fourths of the time. Intermarriage rates are highest for younger married whites in California, where 10 percent of women and 12 percent of men had a nonwhite spouse in 1990. Younger black persons are more likely to have a nonblack spouse in the New England, Mountain, and Pacific states, with noticeably higher intermarriage rates in California: 14 percent of black women had a nonblack husband and 32 percent of black men had a nonblack wife.

Intermarriage figures represent the stock of all past marriages as of the census or survey year; data on the flow of new marriages would be a more sensitive indicator of current trends. As pointed out in Chapter 3, more than one-half of births to native-born Asian and Hispanic persons involve a spouse or partner of a different ethnic group. Because births are generally to younger couples (although not all are married), recent fertility data demonstrate increased intermarriage rates for younger persons.

Those who believe that current immigrants from Asia and Latin America and the Caribbean are less assimilable than those from European countries may be making two important errors. First, they may assume current racial categories to be fixed and essential—yet rising intermarriage means that the boundaries between groups may blur in the future. Our ideas of what constitutes a race or a racial difference are likely to be very different in a few decades, just as they are now very different from what they were at the beginning of the twentieth century. Second, they may assume that the cultures of non-European groups will continue to be very different from what they think of as the core American culture. Yet that core American culture has absorbed a number of groups who were defined as racially different in the past, and it may do so again in the future

Both sides of the assimilation equation are in effect moving targets. Groups that seem racially different now may not always seem so, and the core American culture into which groups are assimilating is itself constantly changing and evolving as it absorbs new influences. Immigrants contribute customs of dress and cuisine, national celebrations, and cultural expressions to the mosaic of American society. Some immigrants even discover their ethnic heritage in America as part of their socialization into the American ethnic community of earlier immigrant waves. As time passes and the descendants of earlier immigrant waves mingle through intermarriage, ethnic cultures have become defined as part of general American culture. The Americanization of St. Patrick's Day as a day of public celebration and the marketing of pizza, bagels, tacos, and sushi as American fast food suggest that immigrant culture is quickly incorporated into the broader America cultural framework.

Assimilation and Education

Although the facts of how fast or how well immigrants and their children are being integrated into American society are subject to debate, the deeper questions revolve around the interpretation of the incomplete, and sometimes confusing, empirical record. Observers may agree that a glass is half-full, but then disagree over whether it will soon be filled or remain permanently half-full. Interpretations about the future are inevitably drawn from empirical generalizations about the past and the broader theories generated in light of this history.

On the basis of a close study of immigrants in Chicago during the early decades of immigration in this century as well as ethnic relations in other societies, Robert Park posited a sequential model of interethnic relations of four stages: contact, conflict, accommodation, and assimilation (Park, 1950; Park and Burgess, 1969). Park suggested that assimilation would come about eventually, not that it would be quick or painless. Indeed, the stages of conflict and accommodation (which included, for example, the institutionalized inequality of Jim Crow laws) could be long-term adjustments in many industrial societies.

More recent researchers have moved away from asserting one global dimension of assimilation to delineating specific spheres of assimilation (acculturation and structural, marital, identity, and other dimensions) that may move at different paces (Gordon, 1964). The logic of industrialism is the shift from local and kinship-based employing institutions to bureaucratic organizations, which recruit labor more on the basis of skills and potential productivity than on family background or national origins (Treiman, 1970). Representative political institutions are assumed to empower all groups as potential members of the electorate, once voting rights are guaranteed. Even if these economic and political processes are imperfect and limited, they will act to erode the boundaries of separate and traditional ethnic groups, although the process may take several generations.

In recent years, considerable doubts have been expressed that the assimilation process will work for the post-1965 wave of immigrants and their children the way it did for the immigrant wave of the early twentieth century. One primary difference often noted is that of race. The earlier wave of immigration was primarily from Europe, and the model of assimilation was that of acculturation and socioeconomic mobility into the majority white Anglo-Saxon American society. Although the children of European immigrants often lost their ethnic roots and mother tongue, that was the price to be paid for the acquisition of American culture (defined as that of middle-class whites), which was considered part of upward social mobility. The "exchange" of culture for social mobility may be quite different for the new immigrants, in this view, because they share a racial (or ethnic) identity with minorities that may preclude easy access into the majority white world. If the loss of ethnic distinctiveness leads to their becoming indistinguishable from native-born blacks or Hispanics, then assimilation may mean joining the culture of the urban ghetto.

Immigrants are thought, in some models of assimilation, to have some advantages over native-born minorities in the labor market. Because immigrants evaluate jobs here relative to conditions in their country of origin rather than to an "American" standard, they may be more willing to accept low-paying, "dead-end" jobs than are many native-born Americans. Immigrants often find employment through social networks that reassure employers about their work habits. For immigrants who are nonwhite, employers may take their immigrant status to be more important than their "racial" status.

Herbert Gans (1992) notes the strong possibility that the post-1965 second generation may face socioeconomic decline relative to their parents, if members of the second generation encounter few chances for upward mobility and refuse to accept the low-level and poorly paid jobs that their immigrants parents held. Negative attitudes toward school, opportunity, hard work, and the "American dream" are prevalent among poor American youth of all groups, but are considered most common in the ethnic ghettos with concentrated poverty. If available jobs do not offer wages that allow for upward mobility of the second generation, and minorities face discrimination in the workplace, then the second generation may face downward mobility into the underclass of American society.

Using material from ethnographic case studies and a survey of second-generation schoolchildren in Miami and San Diego, Portes and Zhou (1993) describe the various outcomes of different groups of second-generation youth as "segmented assimilation." Segmentation refers to the variations in opportunities and the range of cultural and social capital—in the form of ethnic jobs, networks, and values—offered to the second generation. Contemporary immigrants are heterogeneous, ranging from highly rewarded professionals who live in upper-middle-class suburbs far from ethnic residential areas to low-skilled workers who work and live at the margins of inner-city economies. Other immigrants come with strong ethnic networks and access to capital that leads to participation in ethnic businesses and residence in ethnic neighborhoods. These different streams of immigration (and many in between) create different "segments" of opportunities that are linked to the identities and allegiances formed as the children of immigrants reach adolescence.

Second-generation youth whose ties to American minorities are stronger, and whose parents lack the ability to provide jobs for and protect them, may develop an adversarial stance toward the dominant white society, similar to that of some members of native-born minorities. Portes and Zhou (1993) contrast Chinese and Korean immigrants with Haitians. Chinese and Korean immigrants are absorbed into ethnic communities with strong kinship (or religious) ties that link the first generation to rich ethnic networks of job opportunities and that reinforce loyalty and obedience in their children (see also Kim, 1981; Min, 1990; Sung, 1987). Haitians, who are often perceived as black Americans, face much greater discrimination from the dominant institutions. Haitian children must also face pressure from their black American peers to adapt to black culture in school. Portes and Zhou stress that this peer culture takes an adversarial view of upward mobility, school success, and the like. Like Gans, they conclude that members of the second generation who identify with America's minority groups are likely to experience downward social mobility (also see Ogbu, 1990).

Becoming an American includes learning about American race classification systems and about American racial attitudes and prejudices. Although first-generation immigrants from Latin America and the Caribbean may not see themselves in terms of American racial categories, the second generation may do so. For instance, a large proportion of Dominicans in New York are dark in color and would be classified as black by most Americans. These immigrants do not identify themselves as black, because in the Dominican Republic to be partly white means to be nonblack (Grasmuck and Pessar, 1995). Will the children of these immigrants adopt the American view and identify as black? What influence will the way others see them have on the way the children of the immigrants see themselves? Some researchers argue that whether immigrants see themselves as "ethnics" or "minorities" will influence political and social outcomes for the group (Skerry, 1993; Smith, 1994). Those in the second generation who have experienced racial discrimination and who identify racially as a minority may be more likely to adopt an oppositional stance. The social and occupational mobility and economic success of the children of immigrants will depend in large part on their educational attainment.

Empirical studies of the assimilation since 1965 are relatively few, and it would be premature to draw strong conclusions. Several studies conclude that second-generation children who maintain a strong attachment to their immigrant identity do better in school (Suarez-Orozco, 1987; Gibson, 1989; Matute-Bianchi, 1991). Children from tight-knit immigrant families see success in school not primarily as an avenue for individual mobility or independence, but rather as a way to bring honor and success to their families. One of the key questions is the direction of causation. Does a strong sense of immigrant identity heighten motivations for success, or do those who are successful tend to identify more with families and immigrant heritage than with their native-born school peers? If the latter is true, then the segmented assimilation hypothesis may be a better account of variations in socioeconomic mobility within immigrant communities than between them.

In their study of the educational progress of the children of immigrants, Portes and MacLeod (1996) show that the children of Cuban and Vietnamese immigrants do much better than the children of Mexican and Haitian immigrants—independent of social class—because the collective identities of these groups have been shaped by the particular mode of their incorporation into American society.

Consistent with this interpretation are the results of studies by Waters and Eschbach (1995) of the types of identities developed by second-generation West Indian youth in New York City. Students from middle-class backgrounds were more likely to maintain ties to their parents' ethnic identities and to resist categorization as black Americans. Poor and working-class youth in segregated neighborhoods were far more likely to reject their parents' stress on West Indian identity and to develop a strong identity as black Americans. These identities were also closely related to perceptions of discrimination and racism in American society. Those who saw discrimination and blocked opportunity developed more oppositional theories of how to "make it" in American society and were more likely to identify with American black youth. The type of identification was highly correlated with levels of educational success and thus future prospects. Similarly, Foley (1991) finds strong differences among Mexican American youth in South Texas, with upwardly mobile Mexican American youth maintaining some aspects of an oppositional identity, yet succeeding academically and valuing academic success in a way that the values of working-class Mexican American youth did not allow.

Kao and Tienda (1995) examined the educational performance of immigrant youth using the National Educational Longitudinal Study of 1988. They found that "Hispanic, black and white students with immigrant parents performed as well as their native born counterparts whose parents were US born, and that Asian students with foreign born parents outperformed their counterparts whose parents were US born" (p. 13). They also found "little difference between the educational performance of first and second generation youth. Yet both groups tend to outperform their third generation or higher counterparts on various scholastic outcomes" (p. 16).

In a study of the second generation in San Diego, Rumbaut (1996:44) finds that, over time and generations in the United States, reading achievement tests go up, but the number of hours spent on homework goes down, as do average grades. In a multivariate analysis of these data, he finds that time in the United States and second-generation status are connected to declining academic achievement and aspirations, net of other factors. Indeed, having one parent who was born in the United States, and having friends who are not also children of immigrants, were associated with lower grades. "Students whose parents are both immigrants outperform their counterparts whose mother or father is native born" (Rumbaut, 1996:48).

Language

A very sensitive issue surrounding immigration is language. Although the United States does not have an official language, most public discourse is in English. Except for the very young, all immigrants arrive with language skills—in their own language. If that language is not English, or if they do not know English as a second language, the critical question is how quickly immigrants acquire English language facility. Of course, many immigrants have English skills even when they first arrive—some because English is the mother tongue in their home country, and others because, though raised in non-English-speaking countries, they have attended English language schools.

Nearly three-fifths of immigrants who arrived in the 1980s reported in the 1990 census that they spoke English well or very well (see Table 8.3). The groups with the greatest ability were immigrants from Canada, followed by those from South America, Europe, Asia, and the Caribbean. Indeed, almost all of those from countries where English is dominant reported that they speak English

TABLE 8.3 English Language Ability of Recent Immigrants, 1990 (percentage)

	Speaks English		
Continent of Origin	Well or Better	Not Well	Not at All
Europe	73.8	17.7	8.6
Asia	63.1	27.2	9.7
Canada	97.4	1.7	0.3
Mexico, Central America	26.2	31.0	41.8
Caribbean	61.1	18.2	20.6
South America	85.8	10.7	3.2
Weighted Total	57.5	26.3	16.2

Source: U.S. Bureau of the Census (1993).

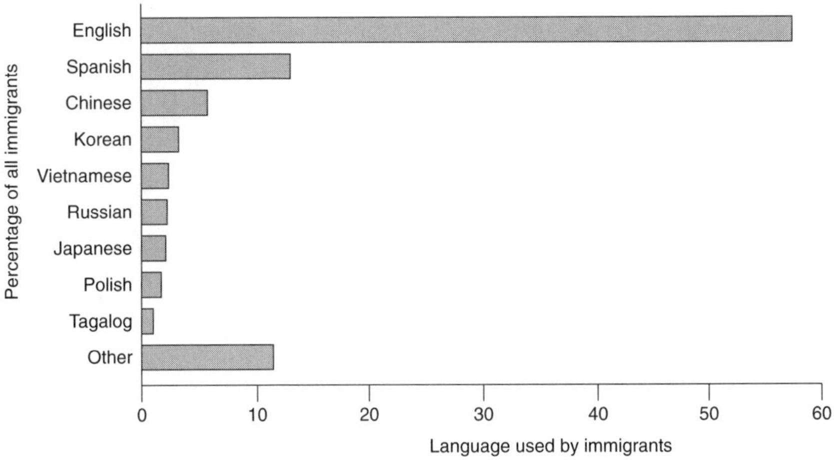

FIGURE 8.1 Language distribution for respondents in a new immigrant survey of the United States.

very well. Where English is an official but not dominant language—Hong Kong, India, and the Philippines—a relatively high proportion of immigrants report high proficiency. The lowest levels of proficiency were reported by those from poor non-English-speaking countries: three-fourths of immigrants from Spanish-speaking countries, and almost half of immigrants from other foreign-language-speaking countries reported that they speak English either not well or not at all. Among those groups, the most common languages spoken were, in rank order, Spanish, Chinese, Korean, and Vietnamese (see Figure 8.1).

Over time and with extended exposure to the new language, immigrants who have arrived without English skills tend to acquire them. As Figure 8.2 suggests, the longer an immigrant from a non-English-speaking country has been in this country, the more likely he or she is to be proficient in English. Among recent immigrants from non-English-speaking countries, 47 percent report that they speak English well or very well within about two years after arrival. The percentage of those with high proficiency increases steadily with length of residence, reaching 88 percent for immigrants who have been here 30 years or more. Among immigrants with long-term residence, only 3 percent report speaking English not well or not at all.

One possibility is that this improvement in English skills over time may be not so much the product of simple everyday exposure or of formal instruction as an artifact of the return to their home countries of a sizable proportion of the immigrants from any entry cohort. Drawing firm conclusions about these notions of the relations between emigration and competence in English is difficult without longitudinal studies. Reviewing the evidence available from decennial

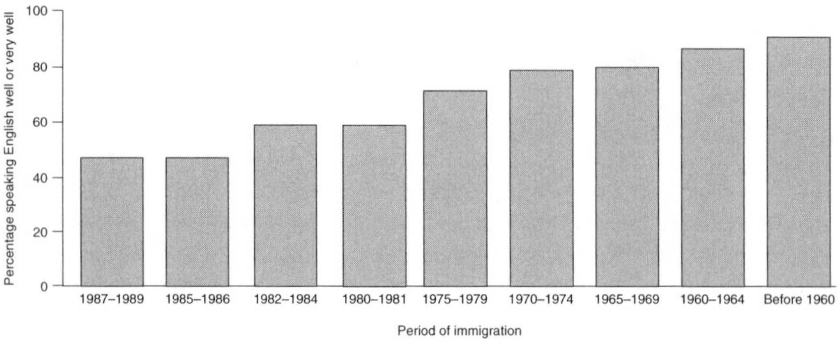

FIGURE 8.2 Percentage of immigrants from non-English-speaking countries who speak English well or very well, by period of immigration, 1990. Source: Stevens (1994).

censuses and from surveys, Stevens (1994) notes that immigrants from English-speaking countries emigrate at a higher rate, and immigrants from Spanish-speaking countries at a lower rate.

The other process affecting English language skills is the language of the children of immigrants. With rare exceptions, native-born persons have competence in English. Many children of immigrants have skills in two languages—English and the language of their parents' country of origin. And although some children of immigrants face special challenges in school because of the bilingual nature of their environment, English language proficiency is almost universal (Portes and Schauffler, 1996).

The data we have assembled suggest that, even though the United States does not explicitly require immigrants to speak English, in the nature of the selection process for immigration many already do when they arrive, and the majority learn it eventually. Virtually all second- and third-generation descendants have good English language skills.

Citizenship and Naturalization

Naturalization is a milepost along the path of many immigrants' adjustment to U.S. society. Although a significant fraction of immigrants remain permanent resident aliens all their lives, many others seek to become U.S. citizens through naturalization. Naturalization brings with it certain advantages. First, naturalized citizens may sponsor immediate family relatives (parents, spouses, and minor children) for immigration without numerical limit. Adult children of naturalized citizens move into a higher preference category, making it easier to bring them into the United States. Second, naturalization confers almost all the rights of citizenship. Naturalized citizens may vote, and they gain broader access to public assistance programs.[8]

Across countries, the rights of citizenship by birth are typically based on two principles: on *descent* from a citizen of the country and on *birthplace*.[9] Most countries base their requirements on a combination of the two, although they often give greater emphasis to one over the other. As Table 8.4 shows, for example, France places greater weight on descent from a French citizen, although a child born in France can claim French citizenship if one of the parents was born in France. The United States, like Australia and Canada, places primary weight on birthplace; however, children born outside the United States to a U.S. citizen can claim U.S. citizenship.[10]

There is more substantial variation in the procedures for acquiring citizenship through naturalization. The United States permits naturalization after five years, about the middle of the 3- to 12-year span across countries. Fees for naturalization range from nothing in France to a high of about $56,000 for the Canton of Geneva, Switzerland (the U.S. fee of $95 is among the lowest); in several countries, including Germany and Switzerland, fees depend on the applicant's income.

The annual number of naturalizations in the United States has been increasing steadily since about 1965, reaching approximately 400,000 in recent years. The year 1996 saw a dramatic increase to 1.2 million—a record.[11] Beyond the simple accumulation of the foreign-born with the requisite length of residence, several factors seem to contribute to this spurt: the large number—3.1 million—of previously illegal aliens who applied for amnesty in 1986, most of whom became eligible for naturalization starting in 1991; the recognition by some per-

---

[8]But they are not eligible to serve as president or vice president, nor, under certain state and federal laws, may they work in certain occupations, such as jobs requiring a security clearance with citizenship as a prerequisite. Naturalized citizens may also be deported under certain conditions.

[9]All countries have naturalization procedures through which citizenship may be acquired. Countries derived from English common law, including Australia, Canada, and the United States, use the term "citizenship," whereas European countries and Japan, for example, refer to the term "nationality." Similarly, European countries and Japan make a distinction between "nationals" and "foreigners," whereas Australia, Canada, and the United States usually refer to the distinction between "native-born" and "foreign-born."

[10]Special rules for U.S. residence of the parents exist, differing for whether or not one or both parents are U.S. citizens.

[11]As of April 1996, according to Immigration and Naturalization Service estimates, 10.5 foreign-born persons with permanent resident visas resided in the United States. Of this population, about 5.8 million persons were eligible to apply for U.S. citizenship. Of course, foreign-born persons do not have to seek citizenship and can continue to reside and work indefinitely with a permanent residence status. About half of the population with permanent visa status population resides in either California (35 percent of the total group) or New York (14 percent): these are two states that could be affected in a major way, through eligibility to vote or to seek public assistance, by large-scale increases in naturalization.

TABLE 8.4.A Citizenship at Birth and Citizenship Acquisition Through Naturalization for Selected Countries

	Citizenship Acquisition/Naturality at Birth[a]			
	Through Parental Descent:			Through Birthplace:
Country	Both Father and Mother Are Citizens	Either Father or Mother Is Citizen	Mother Is Citizen	Born in the Country
Australia		X		X
Canada		X		X
United States		X[b]		X
Belgium	X			X[c]
France		X		X[c]
Germany			X	
Netherlands			X	X[d]
Sweden			X	
Switzerland			X	
United Kingdom		X		

[a]The criteria are for a legitimate birth. Some countries have different requirements for children of unknown parentage. Many countries have special rules for citizenship of adopted children. See Organization for Economic Cooperation and Development (1995:158-161) for more information.

[b]Special U.S. residence requirements apply if only one parent is a U.S. citizen.

[c]One of the parents must have been born in the country.

[d]Both of the parents must reside in the Netherlands.

Source: Interviews with consulate officials at the U.S. Immigration and Naturalization Service and embassies in Washington, D.C.

manent residents that citizenship would broaden their rights to "unlimited" sponsorship of immediate family relatives; and the possible perception by some immigrants that they could safeguard their eligibility for public assistance programs by becoming citizens.

To put naturalization into historical perspective, in 1890 and 1900 over 50 percent of the country's foreign-born residents were citizens. The proportion dropped below that in 1910 and 1920, in association with the large-scale immigration from Southern and Eastern Europe; it then climbed to over 70 percent in

TABLE 8.4.B Citizenship at Birth and Citizenship Acquisition Through Naturalization for Selected Countries

Country	Acquired Naturality/Citizenship[a]						
	Minimum Age	Years of Residence	Good Character	Never Convicted of a Crime	Knowledge of the Language	Renounce Former Citizenship	Application Cost (U.S. Dollars)
Australia	18	3	X	X	X		$67
Canada	18	3		X	X		200[b]
United States	18	5	X	X	X		95
Belgium	18	5		X			192[c]
France	18	5	X	X	X		No fee
Germany	18	10				X	3,000[d]
Netherlands	18	5					300
Sweden	18	5				X	100
Switzerland	20	12					56,000[e]
United Kingdom	18	5					250

[a]In addition to minimum age and period of residence requirements, applicants for naturalization must also satisfy the requirements noted with an X.

[b]There is an application fee of $100 plus a $100 Right of Citizenship fee for adults. Children under 18 years of age need not pay the latter fee.

[c]The registration fee is $192 (Belgian francs 6,000) for applicants aged 22 years and older. For applicants aged 18 to 21 years, the fee is $128 (BF 4,000). There is no fee for children.

[d]The maximum application cost is about $3,000 U.S. (5,000 German marks), or 75 percent of the applicant's monthly income.

[e]The application cost for Swiss citizenship is high and varies by the applicant's income and among Swiss cantons. The highest cost is in the Canton of Geneva, where a high-income adult applicant is charged about $56,000 (75,000 Swiss francs).

1950 and remained relatively high until 1970, after which it declined, reaching about 40 percent in 1990, the lowest level in a century.[12] One reason for this decline is the preponderance among the foreign-born of those who have only recently arrived, and who therefore do not have the requisite years of residence. A second reason seems to lie in the historically low rate of naturalization of Mexican immigrants, who have dominated recent immigration but who have tended to be sojourners. A related factor is that the U.S. foreign-born population now includes a greater number of nonimmigrants who are not eligible to naturalize. As residence of the foreign-born in general lengthens and, as seems likely, more Mexican immigrants seek naturalization, the number of applications will rise and the proportion of the foreign-born who are naturalized citizens will expand.

Several factors may account for the propensity to naturalize. One study of immigrants from all countries who became permanent resident aliens in 1971 reveals that, by 10 years after immigration, 30 percent had naturalized (Jasso and Rosenzweig, 1990:109-115). Among immigrants from Asia, Europe, Africa, and Oceania, the proportion was much higher, at 45 percent, and it was much lower among immigrants from Canada, the Caribbean, and Latin America—only 20 percent of whom became citizens within 10 years. Canadian and Mexican immigrants had particularly low rates.

Gender also plays a role. Adult men, aged 21 to 55 years, are more likely to become citizens than are women, according to census data (Jasso and Rosenzweig, 1990:107-121). Inasmuch as men generally take the lead in sponsoring family members for immigration, this difference may reflect the incentive men have to improve their standing as sponsors of their immediate families. Immigrants from English-speaking countries (other than Canada) are more likely to naturalize than are those from other countries, suggesting that language facilitates integration into U.S. society. **Citizenship is one marker of the eventual assimilation of an immigrant into American society. Although rates of naturalization are at an all-time low, mainly due to Mexican immigrants, the evidence is that propensities to naturalize are now increasing rapidly, in part due to the added benefits attached to citizenship. Citizenship is not an issue for the descendants of immigrants, all of whom are citizens at birth.**

EFFECT OF IMMIGRANTS ON AMERICAN INSTITUTIONS

Questions about immigration often focus on the potential adverse consequences on American society because of their numbers, geographical concentra-

[12]Census data provide information about naturalization, allowing us to calculate the proportion naturalized of current foreign-born residents. These data must be treated with some caution, however, because some foreign-born residents, such as students on nonimmigrant visas, are enumerated in the decennial census but are not eligible for naturalization.

tion, and cultural attributes (Auster, 1992; Brimelow, 1995; Fukuyama, 1993). What is more rarely asked is the alternative question: What have immigrants contributed to American society? Even to pose to the question requires a shift of perspective.

It is not possible to provide a full accounting to this question, in large part because data on the participation and contributions of immigrants and their children in most spheres of American society are simply not available. Immigrants and their descendants may have effects on many institutions that are outside the scope of this report's inquiry. Immigrants affect the quality of American schools, the range and growth of churches in a community, and the interests and views in the local political arena. We limit our attention here, however, and do not examine these important possible repercussions of immigration. Rather, our approach is to present some illustrative information on the roles of immigrants in the development of science, art, and other valued fields in America. Pointing to celebrated cases does show that immigrants have added considerably to the vitality and the richness of our country, but other observers may point to some of the perceived social problems exacerbated by large numbers of immigrants. Therefore, in the next section of the chapter, we examine evidence on the effect of immigration on crime and interethnic tensions in America.

Immigrants in the Sciences and Arts

The United States is acknowledged as a world leader in an extraordinary range of fields of endeavor, from science to sports. The question is what part immigration has played and continues to play in this pursuit of excellence. Of course, since almost all Americans are the descendants of immigrants, the assessment of the contributions due to immigration requires some definition. Our method is to measure the representation of immigrants and the children of immigrants in the top ranks of Americans in diverse fields: American winners of Nobel prizes, recipients of Kennedy Center honors, Olympic medalists, and esteemed scientists and other professionals requiring great talent and dedication.

People with exceptional talent may find it easier to gain admission into the United States. So the overepresentation of immigrants among the extremely talented is, in part, an indication that U.S. immigration admission permits their entry. But the presence of talented immigrants may indicate two other mechanisms. One is that the United States is an attractive place of settlement for world-class scientists, artists, and athletes. The second is the benefit that the United States gains by having this very talented group of individuals settle in this country.

Standard data sources, including most biographical references, rarely report all the information necessary to record the numbers of immigrants among prizewinners or selected professions. Place of birth (and sometimes citizenship) is usually available, but details about the person's naturalization and the nativity of her or his parents are rarely available. This means that estimates of the numbers of the second generation are almost never available. Despite these problems of data, it is fairly clear that Americans with recent foreign roots are overrepresented in any classification of Americans who have brought honor and recognition to the United States.

Nobel prizes are awarded to the most distinguished contributions in the arts and sciences, including the Nobel prize for peace. Winners of prizes in the arts and sciences are named by various Swedish academies; the peace prize is awarded by the Norwegian Nobel Committee. Table 8.5 reports two measures of the proportion of immigrants among Nobel laureates in the five categories of chemistry, physics, physiology or medicine, economics, and literature, for the years through 1995. The base for the proportions is the number of winners (not the number of prizes). The first measure counts as a U.S. winner any person with a U.S. affiliation. The second measure is more stringent, counting as a U.S. winner only persons who both have a U.S. affiliation and are U.S. citizens. Both measures count as an immigrant anyone born outside the United States. Neither measure is fully satisfactory: not everyone with a U.S. affiliation is an immigrant (they could be part-year visitors to the United States); not all U.S. citizens have U.S. affiliations; not all immigrants are U.S. citizens, and not all persons born abroad are immigrants.

As shown in Table 8.5, the proportion of immigrants ranges from 26 to 32 percent by the first measure and from 22 to 27 percent by the second. If immigrants accounted for roughly these same proportions of the U.S. population, these proportions of immigrants among Nobel laureates would be nothing remarkable. But the proportion of foreign-born in the United States reached its peak, 15 percent, in 1910, declined to 5 percent in 1970, and climbed back to 8 percent in 1990. Moreover, the foreign-born population includes persons besides immi-

TABLE 8.5 Proportion Foreign-Born Among U.S. Nobel Laureates, to 1995 (percentage)

Classification	Measure 1	Measure 2
Chemistry	25.6	22.0
Economics	30.8	25.0
Literature	27.3	27.3
Physics	31.8	25.0
Physiology or medicine	30.8	25.0

Note: Measure 1 counts as U.S. winners individuals with a U.S. affiliation; Measure 2 requires both a U.S. affiliation and U.S. citizenship.

Source: Nobel Prize Internet Archive, Web page produced by Almaz Enterprises, data downloaded on January 6, 1997.

grants—foreign correspondents and representatives of foreign corporations, for example. If the comparison were made solely with immigrants in the overall population, the proportions of immigrants among American Nobel laureates would be even more striking.

Immigrants in the United States are represented in all of the fields for which Nobel prizes are awarded. The percentage of U.S. prizewinners who are immigrants includes 26 percent for chemistry, 32 percent for physics, 31 percent for physiology or medicine, 31 percent for economics, and, perhaps surprisingly, 27 percent for literature.[13]

In the United States, two of the highest honors for a scientist or engineer are election to the National Academy of Sciences and the National Academy of Engineering, in recognition of distinguished contributions. The procedures for election involve nomination by an Academy member, with supporting references from several other members, and election at an annual meeting.

The National Academy of Sciences currently has 1,838 members, who represent a wide variety of fields in the physical, biological, and social sciences.[14] As of July 1996, 391, or 21 percent, of the members were foreign-born. The National Academy of Engineering currently has 1,953 members, of whom 245, or 14 percent, are foreign-born.[15] Thus, immigrant scientists and engineers are represented in substantial numbers in both academies of science and engineering.

Kennedy Center honors are given annually to persons who throughout their lifetimes have made significant contributions to American culture through the performing arts. Recipients need not be U.S. citizens; information is available on place of birth but not on immigration status. Of the 90 recipients from 1978, when the award was first given, to 1994, 22—that is, almost one-fourth—are foreign-born. Those recognized have made contributions not only to universal culture, as in music, but also to something largely, often quintessentially, American. Winners include Gregory Peck and Aretha Franklin and, among the immigrants, Claudette Colbert from France, Cary Grant from England, and a true American icon, Bob Hope from England.[16] Again, that immigrants account for 24 percent of the honorees indicates an overrepresentation of immigrants in the ranks of celebrated American achievers.

Immigrant participation in professional sports varies considerably. At one extreme, only 48 of 1,756 players in the 1996 season of the National Football

---

[13]Eleven Nobel prizes for literature have been awarded to residents of the United States. Of these eleven, three were to immigrants, including Isaac Bashevis Singer, from Poland, in 1978; Czeslaw Milosz, from Lithuania, in 1980; and Joseph Brodsky, from Russia, in 1987.

[14]There are also 306 foreign associate members who are excluded from these numbers. The 1,838 members are active or emeritus members in the United States.

[15]There are 146 foreign associate members who are excluded from these numbers.

[16]Examples of recipients who have made contributions to culture beyond anything specifically American include musicians such as Eugene Ormandy and Sir Georg Solti, both from Hungary.

League, or 3 percent, were foreign-born. Of these 48, 11 were born in Canada, 8 in Germany, and 4 or fewer in other countries. At the other extreme, 355 of the 439 players in the 1995-96 season of the National Hockey League (NHL), or 81 percent, were born outside the United States. In one case, the Tampa Bay franchise, not a single player of the 24-player roster was U.S.-born.[17] Over 60 percent of NHL players are from Canada, although there are now a large number of hockey players in the United States from Russia, Sweden, and the Czech Republic.

In between these extremes are immigrants in other professional sports. The National Basketball Association includes 30 foreign-born players of a total of 345 players, or 9 percent. Immigrant basketball players come from around the world, with players from such diverse countries as Lithuania, Yugoslavia, Croatia, Canada, the Netherlands, Italy, Romania, and Nigeria. There are 162 foreign-born baseball players, or 14 percent, of the 1,193 players on the nation's major league baseball teams. Most come from the Dominican Republic, Venezuela, Mexico, Panama, and Cuba.

Immigration and Crime

As Colorado Governor Richard D. Lamm and Gary Imhoff (1985) wrote, "No aspect of immigration is more sensitive, more liable to misinterpretation, and more problematic than the issue of immigration and crime." The fear that immigrants contribute to high levels of crime is a recurrent theme in U.S. history. In 1859, 55 percent of the persons arrested for crimes in New York City were Irish-born and an additional 22 percent were born in other foreign countries (Jones, 1992:114). Yet many of these allegedly criminal acts were for minor actions, including public drunkenness and disorderly conduct; the contribution to more serious crime was much smaller. The gap between popular perceptions about immigration and crime and reality are no narrower today.

Measuring the effect of immigration on crime is mired in a statistical maze. The major limitation from existing crime statistics is that immigrant status is often not known. We often do not know who commits a crime; we especially do not know from victim reports whether the person is an immigrant or a native. Victims are simply not able to tell if a person is an illegal or legal immigrant, or a naturalized or native-born citizen.

Almost all of what is know about immigration and crime is from information on those in prison. But not all crimes are detected, and many perpetrators are never apprehended. For many minor crimes, especially crimes involving juveniles, those who are apprehended are not arrested. Only a fraction of those who are arrested are ever brought to the courts for disposition, and only a minority of

[17] Twenty players on the Tampa Bay team were from Canada. Two players were from the Czech Republic, one player was from Russia, and one from Sweden.

those judged to be guilty are sentenced to jails or prisons. At each stage of the criminal justice process, the data record is incomplete, and there is rarely any information on immigrant status beyond a simple measure of foreign birth or citizenship. The short answer to the underlying question is that it is difficult to draw any strong conclusions on the association between immigration and crime.

Crime measurement is particularly troublesome for illegal immigrants. Immigrants may be apprehended by federal, state, or local authorities for criminal acts, but many illegal immigrants are apprehended by the Border Patrol and other enforcement officers of the Immigration and Naturalization Service (INS). Many illegal immigrants who are apprehended by Border Patrol agents are voluntarily returned to their home countries and are not ordinarily tabulated in national crime statistics. If immigrants, whether illegal or legal, are apprehended entering the United States while committing a crime, they are usually charged under federal statutes and, if convicted, are sent to federal prisons. Throughout this entire process, immigrants may have a chance of deportation, or of sentencing that is different from that for a native-born person.[18]

Nativity and immigrant status can be assessed for prison inmates, however; it is possible to ask inmates about their place of birth as well as to validate their responses by checking with administrative records. Such information is available for federal and state prison inmates in 1991, when prison records were compiled by prison officials for citizens and noncitizens by their current offense and such demographic data as age, sex, and race/ethnicity. We use these inmate data to calculate rates of crime per 1,000 males, aged 18 to 54 years, for citizens and noncitizens (see Table 8.6).

Table 8.6 displays five major categories of crime: violent offenses, property offenses, drug offenses, public order offenses, and other. The first two columns report crime rates for citizens and noncitizens. The third column shows the ratio of the noncitizen crime rate to the citizen rate; values greater than 1.0 indicate that noncitizens have higher crime rates than citizens and values less than 1.0 indicate lower rates.[19]

One finding that is clear from this table is that noncitizens are more likely to be in prison for drug offenses, especially possession of drugs. Almost one-fifth of prisoners serving sentences for drug offenses are noncitizens, even though

---

[18]A related measurement issue concerns information on immigrant status. Except data on noncitizens in the federal criminal justice system, we lack comprehensive information on whether arrested or jailed immigrants are illegal immigrants, nonimmigrants, or legal immigrants. Such information can be difficult to collect because immigrants may have a reason to provide false statements (if they reply that they are an illegal immigrant, they can be deported, for instance). And the verification of these data is troublesome because it requires matching INS records with individuals who often lack documentation or present false documents.

[19]Noncitizens may have had fewer years residing in the United States than citizens, however, and thus less time in which to commit crimes and be apprehended. Hence, incarceration rates do not necessarily reflect differences in current crime rates.

TABLE 8.6 Rate of Sentenced Federal and State Prison Inmates per 1,000 Number of Males, Age 18 to 54 Years, and Ratio of Noncitizen Crime Rate to Citizen Crime Rate, by Current Offense and Citizenship, 1991

Current Offense	Citizen Inmate Rate	Noncitizen Inmate Rate	Ratio of Noncitizens to Citizen Rate
Violent offenses	5.3	2.5	.5
Homicide	1.4	.9	.6
Sexual assault	1.1	.4	.4
Robbery	1.7	.6	.4
Assault	.9	.5	.6
Other	.2	.1	.5
Property offenses	2.9	1.0	.3
Burglary	1.4	.6	.4
Larceny/theft	.6	.2	.3
Fraud	.4	.1	.2
Other	.5	.2	.4
Drug offenses	2.6	5.1	2.0
Possession	.8	2.0	2.5
Trafficking	1.7	3.0	1.8
Other	.1	.1	1.0
Public order offenses	.8	.6	.7
Weapons	.2	.2	1.0
Other	.6	.5	.8
Other	.1	.1	1.0
All offenses	11.6	9.3	.8
Total number of federal and state inmates	712,756	40,634	

Sources: Number of prison inmates is from Harlow (1994:Table 5). Population data for the number of males, age 18 to 54, by citizenship is from tabulations of the microdata from the 1990 census. 1991 population estimates were calculated assuming a population increase of 1.04 percent annual growth rate, the rate of increase for the overall population of males, aged 18 to 54 years between 1990 and 1991.

noncitizens are less than 7 percent of the male population aged 18 to 54 years. For other categories of crime, however, noncitizens have lower rates than citizens. For violent offenses, noncitizens have rates of about one-half those of citizens. For property crimes, noncitizens have rates of about one-third those of citizens. And for public order offenses, noncitizens have rates at about the same rate or slightly lower than those of citizens.

Despite these data, there is, however, often a strong perception that high immigration levels and high crime rates are associated. Indeed, the recent high levels of immigration have coincided with the highest rates of incarceration in modern times. The correctional population—which includes persons in prisons and jails, on probation, and on parole—was less than 1 million in the United States from 1925 until about 1970. It rose gradually from about 1 million to about 2.5 million in 1980, and more rapidly since then, reaching over 5.5 million in 1995.[20]

Several good reasons suggest, however, that the temporal association of high immigration and high crime rates is coincidental and not causal. Some, but not all, of the increase in overall crime rates is due to the increase in the number of young people in the population as the baby-boom cohorts entered their teenage and young adult years. Similarly, crime rates have leveled off, and they have actually begun to decline in the mid-1990s, although immigration remains at very high levels. The rise in the imprisoned population is partly due to changes in sentencing policies, resulting in longer prison sentences; most of the increase results from an increase in arrests, principally connected with drug crimes. Finally, using data from crime reports and Current Population Surveys, Butcher and Piehl (1996) concluded that an influx of recent immigrants into a community has no association with local crime rates.

ATTITUDES TOWARD IMMIGRATION AND INTERETHNIC RELATIONS

Although U.S. history gives evidence of ambivalence toward immigration of long standing, polling data gathered in the decades since World War II provide more detailed evidence on how the American public regards immigrants and immigration. In recent decades, the overall trend has been toward more opposition to immigration, but with frequent oscillations, as illustrated in Figure 8.3. The fraction of Americans who say they think immigration should be decreased from the current level has risen from less than half of the population in polls taken up until the mid-1970s, to roughly two-thirds of the population in more recent polls.

To try to understand this shift, we analyzed a set of polling data from 1995 that included some questions on immigration. Our analysis focused on respondents' answers to the question, "Should immigration be kept at its present level, increased, or decreased?" The multivariate analysis included variables to capture

[20]There is no simple link between crime rates and the size of the correctional population. There are many filters between a crime and imprisonment, including the reporting of the crime, the apprehension of the criminal, the sentencing of the criminal to prison, and the length of incarceration. At each stage, variations can occur.

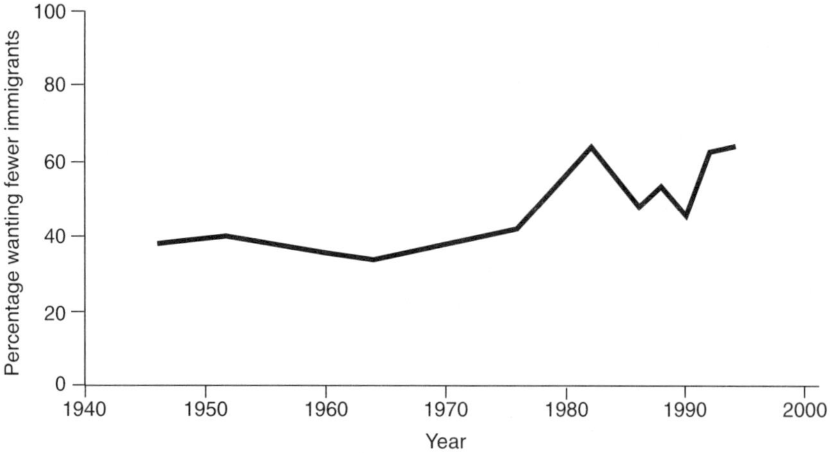

FIGURE 8.3 Trends in American attitudes toward immigration.

differences in attitudes associated with a respondent's age, education, income, race, ethnicity, gender, and region of residence. In addition, we included several variables that described economic conditions in the respondent's state of residence (such as unemployment rates and income levels), along with the fraction of that state's population that was foreign-born. This analysis is described in detail in Appendix 8.A and only the highlights are summarized here.

Why have feelings about immigration hardened? This shift may have arisen from concern about economic conditions: the fraction of Americans wanting less immigration has been positively correlated over time with the unemployment rate. Some evidence also suggests a relationship between economic concerns and attitudes toward immigration from cross-sectional comparisons: in our analysis of polling data, Americans living in states with relatively low rates of economic growth in recent years are more likely to want immigration to decrease.[21] Economic changes are not the only developments whose timing parallels this change in attitudes. The change may be a response to the rise in illegal immigration or to

[21]However, in the same polls no such relationship emerged between unemployment rates and attitudes toward immigration. Others have also found patterns consistent with the idea that economic concerns motivate opposition to immigration. For example, those who say they believe that the U.S. economy is either getting worse or staying the same are more likely to want decreased immigration than are those who think the economy is in very good condition (Espenshade and Hempstead, 1996). When individuals in a New Jersey poll were asked why they wanted a decrease in the current number of immigrants, concerns that there would not be enough jobs to go around, or that immigrants take jobs away from native workers, were the reasons most commonly given (Espenshade, 1997).

the shift in immigrants' countries of origin, although there is little hard evidence on this subject.

Although the majority of Americans now favor decreases in immigration, the strength of this sentiment varies substantially across groups. One might suppose that those who are most likely to face job market competition from immigrants (for example, those with job skills that are common among immigrants) would be most likely to want decreased immigration. This hypothesis, however, does not always fit very well with the observed differences across groups. For instance, residents of states with a high proportion of immigrants in the population do not differ systematically in their attitudes toward immigration from residents of other states (see Table 8.7). Neither did our multivariate analysis find any systematic relationship between attitudes and the fraction of a state's population that was foreign-born. Furthermore, there was no significant relationship between region of the country and attitudes toward immigration, despite the regional concentration of immigrants.

Given the large numbers of recent immigrants with less than a high school education, Americans with low levels of education appear to face the most job market competition from immigrants, and so might be expected to be most opposed to further immigration. Education does, in fact, have an important relationship with attitudes, but not the expected one. At the national level, those with less than a high school education do not stand out as having very different attitudes toward immigration (see Table 8.8). The group that does stand out is Americans

TABLE 8.7 American Attitudes Toward the Current Level of Immigration, 1995 Gallup Polls (percentage of respondents)

	Level of Immigration Preferred		
State	Decrease	Present Level	Increase
States with large numbers of immigrants, combined	64.8	26.3	8.9
California	63.6	24.7	11.8
New York/New Jersey	60.3	32.8	7.0
Texas	80.2	11.9	7.9
Florida	64.5	29.6	5.9
Illinois	57.4	33.6	9.0
All other states combined	66.9	26.3	6.8

Source: Pooled data from Gallup polls taken in June and July 1995. The question asked was "In your view, should immigration be kept at its present level, increased or decreased?"

TABLE 8.8 Attitudes Toward the Current Level of Immigration, by Education Level, 1995 Gallup Polls (percentage)

	Level of Immigration Preferred		
Education Level	Decrease	Present Level	Increase
Less than high school	70.1	22.0	8.0
High school graduate	72.3	19.6	8.0
Some college	64.9	27.6	7.5
College graduate	67.7	27.0	5.3
Graduate school	48.4	43.7	7.9

Source: Pooled data from Gallup polls taken in June and July 1995. The question asked was, "In your view, should immigration be kept at its present level, increased, or decreased?"

with graduate education, a majority of whom do not want to see immigration decreased.[22]

Blacks and Hispanics have more favorable attitudes toward immigration than do non-Hispanic whites: 68 percent of non-Hispanic whites favored decreasing immigration in the polls we analyzed, compared with 57 percent of blacks and 50 percent of Hispanics.[23] These differences in attitudes on the part of Hispanics may be explained by their cultural ties to the large numbers of prospective immigrants from Latin America.[24] However, racial differences in attitudes are harder to explain. The data we presented earlier that indicate that blacks in general do not live near immigrants may be relevant.

Some immigrants appear to be more welcome than others. Americans generally indicate a preference for European immigrants, and immigrants from Asia in turn are generally rated more favorably than are those from Latin America (Espenshade and Belanger, 1996). At the same time, Americans also attributed positive characteristics to both Asian and Latin American immigrants: both groups were seen by a majority of Americans as hard-working and having strong family values (Espenshade and Belanger, 1996).

[22]In the more detailed analysis in the appendix, at the national level only those with graduate education differ significantly from others in their attitudes toward immigration once we control for other characteristics. Within the immigration states, there are larger differences associated with education, and those without a high school degree are indeed most opposed to immigration. However, their attitudes never differ significantly from those of high school graduates.

[23]Our polling data do not identify Asians, but others have found that Asians also generally have more favorable attitudes toward immigration (Espenshade and Hempstead, 1996; Espenshade, 1997).

[24]These data include information on ethnicity but do not identify the foreign-born, so differences associated with the two factors cannot be disentangled from one another.

Americans are particularly concerned about illegal immigration, to the point that they greatly overestimate the proportion of immigrants who are in the United States illegally. In a June 1993 poll, over two-thirds of respondents believed that the majority of recent immigrants were in the country illegally (Espenshade and Belanger, 1996), whereas the U.S. Immigration and Naturalization Service estimates that net illegal immigration in fact accounts for about 20 to 30 percent of annual net immigrant arrivals (*Washington Post*, 1997). This disparity between perceptions and reality complicates the interpretation of Americans' attitudes toward immigration. Part of the recent hardening of attitudes may be due to the widespread media attention paid to the issue of illegal immigration.

To sum up, on the basis of polling data, Americans appear to be more opposed to immigration than they have been in the past. It is not possible to pin down the source of this change in attitudes, although concerns about economic conditions and about illegal immigration seem likely candidates. The majority of Americans now favor decreases in immigration, but there are significant differences across groups in the strength of this sentiment—blacks, Hispanics, and Asians generally have more positive attitudes than do non-Hispanic whites, and Americans with graduate education also have particularly favorable attitudes.

IMMIGRATION AND INTERETHNIC TENSIONS

Is immigration at high levels exacerbating ethnic and racial tensions in American society? Some authors have suggested that increasing competition between new immigrants and black Americans has led to urban unrest in recent years (Miles, 1992; Morrison, 1994). Portes and Stepick (1993) describe the riots in the Liberty City area of Miami as stemming in part from the frustrations of black Americans who see Cuban Americans and Haitian Americans leapfrogging ahead of them into better jobs and housing in the Miami area. Jack Miles (1992) wrote an influential piece in the *Atlantic Monthly* describing the Los Angeles riots of 1992 as reflecting tensions between Latino immigrants and black Americans entitled "Blacks vs. Browns." There have also been noted conflicts between black Americans and Korean immigrants, including a widely publicized boycott of a Korean grocery store in New York City in 1991 and a shooting of a black American teenager by a Korean immigrant shopowner in Los Angeles in the early 1990s. These incidents might lead people to conclude that there is growing ethnic tension in American cities, fueled by the ethnic and racial diversity and the absolute numbers of new immigrants currently being absorbed by gateway cities such as Miami, New York, and Los Angeles.

There is little systematic research into how the presence of new immigrants affects American racial and ethnic attitudes, and into the racial and ethnic attitudes of the new immigrants themselves. Researchers have only just begun to explore interminority racial and ethnic attitudes.

Bobo and Hutchings (1996:958) examined data from the Los Angeles portion of the Multi-City Study of Urban Inequality. They found a complex web of interethnic attitudes with regard to threat and competition from other ethnic groups. More black respondents in Los Angeles perceived that competition with Asians was a zero-sum game than had that perception with respect to Hispanics. And more Hispanic respondents perceived that competition with Asians was a zero-sum game than had that perception with respect to blacks in the areas of housing and job competition. "A similar pattern emerges among Whites, who feel the least threat from blacks and the most from Asians, with reaction to Latinos typically falling in between the two." Asian Americans were found to perceive a greater threat from blacks than from Hispanics (these findings were not statistically significant). Bobo and Hutchings (1996:960) concluded that "Asian American and Latino respondents who are foreign born tend to perceive greater competition with blacks than do their native born co-ethnics." Foreign-born Asian Americans were also more likely to perceive greater competition with Hispanics than were native-born Asian Americans.

Does nativity make a difference in perceptions of discrimination? Using the same data source, Bobo (1995) found that, among Asian Americans, the same proportion of foreign-born and native-born reported discrimination (22 percent). But among the other minority groups there were strong nativity differences, which went in opposite directions. Among Hispanics, the foreign-born were more likely to report discrimination (33 percent compared with 25 percent for the native-born). Among blacks, natives were more likely to report discrimination (62 percent for natives compared with 29 percent for the foreign-born). Waters (1994) also finds that foreign-born blacks are much less likely than American-born blacks to see themselves as victims of discrimination.

Using survey data collected by the *Los Angeles Times*, Oliver and Johnson (1984) found that Hispanics in that city are generally more antagonistic toward blacks than blacks are toward Hispanics. They concluded that the black antagonism arises almost exclusively from economic concerns. Hispanics were almost twice as likely as blacks to agree that the other group is more violent than the average group (39 versus 20 percent). The level of antagonism toward Hispanics was much higher among whites than among blacks. Several recent studies have attempted to measure discrimination against immigrants and minorities. In a survey of hiring practices among Chicago-area employers, Kirschenman and Neckerman (1991) found that employers strongly preferred to hire immigrants over inner-city blacks (see also Neckerman and Kirschenman, 1991; Wilson, 1987). Kasinitz and Rosenberg (1994) found the same preference among employers in the Red Hook section of New York City.

Our reading of these preliminary studies is that interethnic frictions and occasional violent outbreaks between minorities and immigrants are reflections of the conditions of inner-city life where rates of joblessness and poverty are high, and not signs of the inevitability of antagonism between immigrants and minorities. Despite employer preferences for immigrant workers over black youth, national survey data show that black Americans are less hostile to immigrants than are white Americans (see the earlier section on attitudes toward immigration).

CONCLUSIONS

During the interval between the two world wars, the children of immigrants from Southern, Eastern and Central Europe made significant socioeconomic gains, in terms of both educational and occupational attainment. Few socioeconomic or cultural differences now separate the descendants of immigrants from Europe.

There are competing hypotheses about whether present-day immigrants and their children will make the same generational socioeconomic progress. Some scholars predict the possibility of second-generation decline for some national-origin groups in the post-1965 wave of immigrants, and others predict continuity of historical patterns of assimilation.

The future social and economic success of recent immigrants is subject to uncertainty, in part because it is still too early to draw conclusions about the mobility of their children. The early readings are that most immigrants and their children are doing comparatively well. Some descendants of immigrants, current Asian Americans, for example, clearly are at or above parity with whites in terms of education and occupation, although they have less income.

One of the more important indicators of social adaptation is residential integration. On initial arrival and in the early period of residence, past and recent immigrants have tended to settle in certain states and cities, and within particular neighborhoods, creating clusters of people of similar ethnicity. At the turn of the century, most major American cities had large neighborhoods of Italians, Germans, and Irish. Most of those neighborhoods have now changed, and the descendants of the original immigrants are widely dispersed. In recent years, Cuban and Vietnamese refugees have created similar ethnic neighborhoods. With the possible exception of Mexican immigrants, the available evidence suggests that current ethnic neighborhoods will change with time, as children and grandchildren of the immigrants disperse.

Except for young children, all immigrants arrive with language skills. Because public discourse is in English in the United States, the crucial question is how successful immigrants are in adapting to an English-speaking environment. Many immigrants come from countries where English was the dominant language or where they attended English-speaking schools. Almost three-fifths of immigrants who arrived in the 1980s reported in the 1990 census that they spoke English well or very well. Among those immigrants who spoke English with difficulty or not well, most came from non-English-speaking countries, usually Latin America. Although we lack cohort data on immigrants, the available evidence suggests that most immigrants tend to acquire English language skills over time.

Today, after three or more generations of descendants of the original immigrants, offspring of European groups are virtually indistinguishable in terms of education, income, occupation, and residence. Because of extensive intermarriage and the changing patterns of ethnic identification among descendants of European immigrants, the boundaries between different national-origin and ethnic groups—Italians, Irish, Polish, and Jewish, for example—are increasingly blurred. If population projections had been done for groups of European origin at the beginning of the twentieth century, they would have failed to predict the voluntary choices of ethnic ancestries of the present U.S. population.

Under high rates of ethnic intermarriage, ethnic identity becomes quite varied and increasingly a matter of choice. In recent years, ethnic and racial intermarriage has been increasing in this country and is increasingly common among children and grandchildren of Asian and Hispanic immigrants. Current population projections of the future ethnic composition of the U.S. population are especially hazardous because future patterns of intermarriage and the meanings of race and ethnicity are uncertain.

American public attitudes about immigration have long been equivocal. The United States has had periods of large-scale immigration, with considerable public support and welcome, and periods of great distrust and antagonism toward immigrants. In the past 50 years, public opinion polls have allowed us to chart more clearly how the American public views immigration and regards immigrants. Americans have increased their opposition to immigration in recent decades, in part, it appears, because of economic concerns. These attitudes vary greatly, however. College graduates have more positive attitudes toward immigration. Black, Hispanic, and Asian Americans tend to have more favorable attitudes toward immigrants than do non-Hispanic whites.

Public concerns with immigration are centered on illegal immigration, although the average resident greatly overestimates the proportion of immigrants who are illegal. Over two-thirds of respondents believe that most recent immigrants are illegal, whereas the proportion of illegals among total immigrants is closer to 20 to 30 percent.

The scant available data on crime do not allow us to say much about its relationship to immigration. It is hard to draw firm conclusions from the currently scarce information. The crime rate increased from the 1960s until about 1990, then has declined noticeably for the past six years. There is no apparent association in these temporal trends with immigration. From available studies, it appears that overall crime rates have been associated more with other factors, including the changing demographics of the country (with shifts in the number of young men), fluctuations in drug use, and changes in the effectiveness of the police and criminal justice system in reducing local crime. The problems of data of the criminal justice system make it very difficult to reach empirical conclusions on immigration and crime. It appears, however, that the major trends in crime are not being driven by immigration.

REFERENCES

Alba, R.D.

1986 The twilight of ethnicity among americans of European ancestry: The case of Italians. *Ethnic and Racial Studies* 8(1):134-158.

1990 *Ethnic Identity: The Transformation of White America.* New Haven: Yale University Press.

1995 Assimilation's quiet tide. *The Public Interest* 119(Spring): 3-18.

Auster, L.

1992 The forbidden topic: Some conservatives don't want to know about the link between multiculturalism and immigration. *National Review* 44(8):42-45.

Barringer, H., R.W. Gardner, and M. Levin

1993 *Asians and Pacific Islanders in the United States.* New York: Russell Sage.

Binder, F., and D. Reimers

1995 *All the Nations Under Heaven.* New York: Columbia University Press.

Bobo, L.

1995 Surveying Racial Discrimination: Analyses from a Multiethnic Labor Market. Russell Sage Foundation Working Paper #75. September.

Bobo, L., and V. Hutchings

1996 Perceptions of racial group competition: Extending Blumer's theory of group position to a multiracial social context. *American Sociological Review* 61(6):951-973.

Borjas, G.J.

1995 Ethnicity, neighborhoods, and human-capital externalities. *American Economic Review* 85(3):365-390.

Bouvier, L.

1991 *Peaceful Invasions: Immigration and Changing America.* Lanham, MD: University Press of America.

Brimelow, P.

1995 *Alien Nation: Common Sense about America's Immigration Disaster.* New York: Random House.

Butcher, K.F., and A.M. Piehl

1996 Cross-City Evidence on the Relationship Between Immigration and Crime. Unpublished paper. Boston College and Harvard University, September.

Duncan, B., and O.D. Duncan

1968 Minorities and the process of stratification. *American Sociological Review* 33(3):356-364.

Edmonston, B., editor

1996 *Statistics on U.S. Immigration: An Assessment of Data Needs for Future Research.* Committee on National Statistics, National Research Council. Washington, D.C.: National Academy Press.

Espenshade, T.J.

1997 Taking the pulse of public opinion toward immigrants. Chapter 4 in T.J. Espenshade (editor), *Keys to Successful Immigration: Implications of the New Jersey Experience.* Washington, D.C.: The Urban Institute Press.

Espenshade, T.J., and M. Belanger

1996 U.S. public perceptions and reactions to Mexican migration. In Frank D. Bean et al. (editors), *At the Crossroads: Mexican Migration and U.S. Policy.* New York: Rowman and Littlefield Publishers, Inc.

Espenshade, T.J., and K. Hempstead
1996 Contemporary American attitudes toward U.S. immigration. *International Migration Review* 30(2):535-570.
Farley, R.
1996 Increasing Interracial Marriage: Trends Revealed by the Census and Census Bureau Surveys. Unpublished manuscript. Population Studies Center, The University of Michigan, October.
Featherman, D., and R. Hauser
1978 *Opportunity and Change*. New York: Academic Press.
Foley, D.E.
1991 Reconsidering anthropological explanations of ethnic school failure. *Anthropology and Education Quarterly* 22(1):60-86.
Fong, E.
1994 Residential proximity among racial groups in U.S. and Canadian neighborhoods. *Urban Affairs Quarterly* 30(2):285-297.
Frey, W.H.
1995 The new geography of population shifts: Trends toward balkanization. Pp. 271-336 in R. Farley (editor), *State of the Union: America in the 1990s. Volume Two: Social Trends*. New York: Russell Sage Foundation.
Fukuyama, F.
1993 Immigrants and family values. *Commentary* May.
Gans, H.
1992 Second generation decline: Scenarios for the economic and ethnic futures of the post-1965 American immigrants. *Ethnic and Racial Studies* 15(2):173-193.
Gibson, M.A.
1989 *Accommodation Without Assimilation*. Ithaca, NY: Cornell University Press.
Gordon, M.
1964 *Assimilation in American Life: The Role of Race, Religions, and National Origins*. New York: Oxford University Press.
Grant, M.
1916 *The Passing of the Great Race in America*. New York: C. Scribner and Sons.
Grasmuck, S., and P. Pessar
1995 First and second generation settlement of Dominicans in the United States: 1960-1990. In S. Pedraza and R. Rumbaut (editors), *Origins and Destinies: Immigration, Race, and Ethnicity in America*. Belmont: Wadsworth Press.
Greeley, A.
1974 *Ethnicity in the United States: A Preliminary Reconnaissance*. New York: Wiley.
1976 *Ethnicity, Denomination, and Inequality*. Beverly Hills, CA: Sage.
Gurak, D.T., and J. Fitzpatrick
1982 Intermarriage among Hispanic ethnic groups in New York City. *American Journal of Sociology* 87(4):921-934.
Harlow, C.W.
1994 *Comparing Federal and State Prison Inmates, 1991*. Report NCJ-145864. Washington, D.C.: Bureau of Justice Statistics.
Harrison, R., and C. Bennett
1995 Racial and ethnic diversity. Pp. 141-210 in R. Farley (editor), *State of the Union: America in the 1990s. Volume Two: Social Trends*. New York: Russell Sage Foundation.
Higham, J.
1955 *Strangers in the Land: Patterns of American Nativism, 1860-1925*. New York: Atheneum.

Hirschman, C.
1983 The melting pot reconsidered. *Annual Review of Sociology* 9:397-423.
Hirschman, C., and E. Kraly
1990 Racial and ethnic inequality in the United States, 1940 and 1950: The impact of geographic location and human capital. *International Migration Review* 24:4-43.
Hirschman, C., and M.G. Wong
1984 Socioeconomic gains of Asian Americans, blacks and Hispanics: 1960-1976. *American Journal of Sociology* 90(3):584-607.
Hout, M., and J. Goldstein
1994 How 4.5 million Irish immigrants became 40 million Irish Americans: Demographic and subjective aspects of the ethnic composition of white Americans. *American Sociological Review* 59:64-82.
Ignatiev, N.
1995 *How the Irish Became White*. New York: Routledge.
Jasso, G., and M.R. Rosenzweig
1990 *The New Chosen People: Immigrants in the United States*. New York: Russell Sage Foundation.
Jones, M.A.
1992 *American Immigration*, Second edition. Chicago: University of Chicago Press.
Kao, G., and M. Tienda
1995 Optimism and achievement: The educational performance of immigrant youth. *Social Science Quarterly* 76(1):March.
Kasinitz, P., and J. Rosenberg
1994 Missing the Connection? Social Isolation and Employment on the Brooklyn Waterfront. Working Paper of the Michael Harrington Institute, Queens College, New York.
Kikumura, A., and H.L. Kitano
1973 Interracial marriage: A picture of the Japanese Americans. *Journal of Social Issues* 29(2).
Kitano, H., L.K. Chai, and H. Hatanaka
1984 Asian American interracial marriage. *Journal of Marriage and the Family* 46:179-190.
Kim, I.
1981 *The New Urban Immigrants: The Korean Community in New York City*. Princeton, NJ: Princeton University Press.
Kirschenman, J., and K. Neckerman
1991 We'd love to hire them, but—The meaning of race for employers. Pp. 203-234 in C. Jencks and P. Petersen (editors), *The Urban Underclass*. Washington, D.C.: The Brookings Institution.
Lamm, R.D., and G. Imhoff
1985 *The Immigration Time Bomb*. New York: Truman Talley.
Lieberson, S.
1980 *A Piece of the Pie: Black and White Immigrants since 1880*. Berkeley: University of California Press.
1996 Contemporary immigration policy: Lessons from the past. Pp. 335-351 in H.O. Duleep and P.V. Wunnava (editors), *Immigrants and Immigration Policy: Individual Skills, Family Ties, and Group Identities*. Greenwich, CT: JAI Press.
Lieberson, S., and M. Waters
1988 *From Many Strands: Ethnic and Racial Groups in Contemporary America*. New York: Russell Sage Foundation.
Massey, D.S., and N.A. Denton
1992 Residential segregation of Asian-origin groups in U.S. Metropolitan areas. *Social Science Research* 76(4):170-177.

1993 *American Apartheid: Segregation and the Making of the Underclass*. Cambridge, MA: Harvard University Press.

Matute-Bianchi, E.
1991 Situational ethnicity and patterns of school performance among immigrants and nonimmigrant Mexican descent students. In M. Gibson and J. Ogbu (editors), *Minority Status and Schooling: A Comparative Study of Immigrant and Involuntary Minorities*. New York: Garland Publishing.

Miles, J.
1992 Blacks vs. browns. *The Atlantic Monthly* 270(4):41-60.

Min, P.G.
1990 Problems of Korean immigrant entrepeneurs. *International Migration Review* 24(3):436-55.

Morrison, T.
1994 On the backs of blacks. Pp. 97-100 in Nicolaus Mills (editor), *Arguing Immigration*. New York: Touchstone Books.

Muller, T.
1993 *Immigrants and the American City*. New York: New York University Press.

Neckerman, K., and J. Kirschenman
1991 Hiring strategies, racial bias, and inner city workers. *Social Problems* 38(4):433-447.

Nee, V. and J. Sanders
1985 The road to parity: Determinants of the socioeconomic achievements of Asian Americans. *Ethnic and Racial Studies* 8(1):75-93.

Ogbu, J.
1990 Minority status and literacy in comparative perspective. *Daedalus* 119(2):141-168.

Oliver, M., and J. Johnson, Jr.
1984 Interethnic conflict in an urban ghetto: The case of blacks and Latinos in Los Angeles. *Research in Social Movements* 6:57-84.

Organization for Economic Cooperation and Development
1995 *Trends in International Migration: Annual Report, 1994*. Paris: Organization for Econoimic Cooperation and Development.

Pagnini, D.L., and S.P. Morgan
1990 Intermarriage and social distance among U.S. immigrants at the turn of the century. *American Journal of Sociology* 96(2):405-432.

Park, R.
1950 *Race and Culture*. Glencoe, IL: The Free Press.

Park, R.E., and E.W. Burgess
1969 *Introduction to the Science of Sociology*. New York: Greenwood Press.

Perlmann, J.
1988 *Ethnic Differences: Schooling and Social Structure among the Irish, Italians, Jews, and Blacks in an American City, 1880-1935*. New York: Cambridge University Press.

Portes, A., and A. Stepick
1993 *City on the Edge: The Transformation of Miami*. Berkeley: University of California Press.

Portes, A., and M. Zhou
1993 The new second generation: Segmented assimilation and its variants. *Annals of the American Academy of Political and Social Science* 530:74-97.

Portes, A., and D. MacLeod
1996 Educational progress of children of immigrants: The role of class, ethnicity, and school context. *Sociology of Education* 69:255-275.

Portes, A., and R.G. Rumbaut
1996 *Immigrant America: A Portrait*, second edition. Berkeley: University of California Press.

Portes, A., and R. Schauffler
1996 Language and the second generation: Bilingualism yesterday and today. Pp. 8-29 in Alejandro Portes (editor), *The New Second Generation*. New York: Russell Sage Foundation.

Ross, E.A.
1914 *The Old World in the New*. New York: Century Company.

Rumbaut, R.
1996 Paradoxes and Orthodoxies of Assimilation. Paper presented at the Social Science Research Council Conference on Becoming American/America Becoming: International Migration to the United States—Sanibel Island, Florida, January 18-21.

Sandefur, G., and T. McKinnell
1986 American Indian intermarriage. *Social Science Research* 15:347-371.

Simon, J.
1989 *The Economic Consequences of Immigration*. Oxford: Basil Blackwell.

Skerry, P.
1993 *Mexican Americans: The Ambivalent Minority*. New York: Free Press.

Smith, R.C.
1994 "Doubly Bonded" Solidarity: Race and Social Location in the Incorporation of Mexicans into New York City. Paper presented at Social Science Research Council, Conference of Fellows: Program of Research on the Urban Underclass, June.

Stevens, G.
1994 Immigration, emigration, language acquisition, and the English language proficiency of immigrants in the United States. Chapter 6 in B. Edmonston and J.S. Passel (editors), *Immigration and Ethnicity: The Integration of America's Newest Arrivals*. Washington, D.C.: Urban Institute Press.

Suarez-Orozco, M.M.
1987 "Becoming somebody": Central American immigrants in U.S. inner-city schools. *Anthropology and Education Quarterly* 18(4):287-299.

Sung, B.L.
1987 *Chinese Immigrant Children in New York City*. New York: Center for Migration Studies.

Treiman, D.J.
1970 Industrialization and social stratification. Pp. 207-234 in E.O. Laumann (editor), *Social Stratification: Research and Theory for the 1970s*. Indianapolis: Bobbs-Merrill.

U.S. Bureau of the Census
1993 *1990 Census of Population*. The Foreign-Born Population of the United States. 1990 CP-3-1. Washington, D.C.: U.S. Department of Commerce.

Washington Post
1997 New estimates of illegal immigration. February 8, p. A3.

Waters, M.C.
1990 *Ethnic Options: Choosing Identities in America*. Berkeley: University of California Press.
1994 Ethnic and racial identities of second-generation black immigrants in New York City. *International Migration Review* 28(4):795-820.

Waters, M.C., and K. Eschbach
1995 Immigration and ethnic and racial inequality in the United States. *Annual Review of Sociology* 21:419-446.

Wilson, W.J.
1987 *The Truly Disadvantaged: The Inner City, the Underclass, and Public Policy*. Chicago: University of Chicago Press.

APPENDIX 8.A
ANALYSIS OF POLLING DATA

The analysis of polling data is based on two Gallup polls taken in June and July 1995. Both polls included the question, "Should immigration be kept at its present level, increased, or decreased?" The pooled data from the two polls give a sample of 1,754 respondents with complete data. The sample, when weighted, represents U.S. adults in households with telephones. All analysis uses the sampling weights. Several additional variables were matched to these data on the basis of the respondent's state of residence. These variables included 1995 state per capita income and its change since 1992, unemployment rates for the month of the survey and its change since that month in 1993, and the percentage of the state's population that was foreign-born at the time of the 1990 census.

The data were analyzed using probits, with the dependent variable set equal to one if the respondent chose "decreased" as the response, and set equal to zero if the respondent chose "kept at its present level" or "increased." In this context, positive entries in Table 8.A.1 indicate that the characteristic is associated with greater opposition to immigration. The possible responses to the immigration question also allow for use of an ordered probit model in which "kept at its present level" and "increased" were separated into two categories. However, given the small fraction of "increased" responses, using the more complicated model has only negligible effects on the results.

The control variables for age, education, region, income, race/ethnicity, and gender are all dummy variables, which equal one if the respondent reported the value given in that row of Table 8.A.1. The omitted categories in specifying the various dummy variables were non-Hispanic, white, female, high school dropout, living in the West, with household income less than $10,000. The figures reported give the estimated change in probability with a change in the continuous explanatory variables, evaluated at the sample mean of the explanatory variables. For dummy variables, they give the difference in probability from the omitted category, also evaluated at the sample mean.

The results are presented for the nation as a whole, for the six states with high levels of immigration between 1980 and 1990, and for California alone. State-level variables (state per capita income and unemployment rates and their changes over time, along with the fraction foreign-born) were dropped for the analysis of California data, as all observations within the state have the same value for those variables.

No systematic relationship was found between age and attitudes toward immigration, nor between income or region of residence and those attitudes. More education was generally associated with less opposition to immigration, with larger differences associated with education in the high-immigration states and California than for the nation as a whole. Men were generally less likely to want decreased immigration than were women, although the difference between

TABLE 8.A1 Probit Estimates of the Likelihood that Respondents Want Immigration Decreased from Its Current Level, 1995 Gallup Poll

Explanatory Variables	National	High Immigration States[a]	California
Age			
30-39	−.059	−.091	−.271*
	(.033)	(.059)	(.116)
40-49	−.072*	.001	−.219
	(.035)	(.059)	(.119)
50-59	−.022	−.019	−.086
	(.040)	(.068)	(.131)
60 and older	−.007	.037	−.113
	(.040)	(.073)	(.148)
Education			
High school graduate	.037	−.124	−.224
	(.040)	(.078)	(.162)
Some college	−.046	−.216**	−.389*
	(.041)	(.078)	(.164)
College graduate	−.043	−.292**	−.472*
	(.051)	(.098)	(.186)
Graduate school	−.229**	−.399**	−.503**
	(.054)	(.095)	(.189)
Regions			
East	−.012		
	(.047)		
South	.073		
	(.041)		
Midwest	.011		
	(.049)		
Income			
$10,000-20,000	−.012	−.089	−.273
	(.045)	(.089)	(.181)
$20,000-30,000	−.001	−.059	−.220
	(.045)	(.082)	(.167)

TABLE 8.A1 Continued

Explanatory Variables	National	High Immigration States[a]	California
$30,000-50,000	.011	–.007	–.041
	(.044)	(.081)	(.165)
$50,000-75,000	.052	.053	–.025
	(.049)	(.086)	(.168)
$75,000 or more	.021	.055	.136
	(.052)	(.090)	(.167)
Male	–.022	–.065	–.214**
	(.023)	(.041)	(.080)
Black	–.128**	–.110	–.422*
	(.041)	(.072)	(.177)
Hispanic	–.246**	–.271**	–.282*
	(.053)	(.070)	(.113)
Log (state per capita income)	.010	–.232	
	(.172)	(.315)	
Change in state per capita income (3 year change in log [PCI])	–2.384**	.256	
	(.684)	(4.379)	
Percentage of the state's population that was foreign-born in the 1990 census	–.0045	–.0221*	
	(.0039)	(.0091)	
Unemployment rate for state in month of survey	.003	.105	
	(.014)	(.100)	
Change in unemployment rate (over 2 years)	.020	.053	
	(.020)	(.067)	
Sample size	1734	594	185

Notes: * denotes significance at the 5% level, ** at the 1% level. Numbers reported give the change in probability with a change in the continuous explanatory variables, evaluated at the mean. For dummy variables, they give the difference in probability from the omitted category, evaluated at the mean.

[a]California, Florida, Illinois, New Jersey, New York, and Texas.

the sexes was significant only in the estimates for California. Blacks and Hispanics generally had more favorable attitudes toward immigration than did non-Hispanic whites, with (again) larger differences were associated with race and ethnicity in the high-immigration states and California than for the nation as a whole. Among the state-level variables, only the change in state per capita income had a significant relationship to attitudes toward immigration at the national level: residents of states with higher growth rates were less likely to want to see reduced levels of immigration. In the estimates for the six high-immigration states, residents of states with higher fractions of immigrants were less likely to want reduced immigration. Given that the state-level variables take on only six different values for these six states, this is mostly picking up the large difference between attitudes in Texas and those in the other states that is displayed in Table 8.7.

Biographical Sketches

JAMES P. SMITH (Chair) holds the RAND chair in labor markets and demographic studies and was the director of RAND's Labor and Population Studies Program from 1977 to 1994. He has led numerous projects, including studies of immigration, the economics of aging, black-white wages and employment, the effects of economic development on labor markets, wealth accumulation and savings behavior, and the interrelation of health and economic status among the elderly. He is currently co-principal investigator for a pilot project for a new, cost-effective survey that yields adequate sample size of the foreign-born, has known sampling properties, permits longitudinal analyses, and can answer policy questions of particular relevance to immigration. He is a member of the National Science Foundation Advisory Committee for the Panel Study of Income Dynamics and is the public representative appointed by the governor on the California OSHA Board. He has received the National Institutes of Health MERIT award, its most distinguished honor granted to a researcher. He has a Ph.D. in economics from the University of Chicago.

ALAN J. AUERBACH is Robert D. Burch professor of economics and law and director of the Burch Center for Tax Policy and Public Finance at the University of California, Berkeley. He previously taught at the University of Pennsylvania, where he was chair of the Economics Department. In 1992 he served as deputy chief of staff of the U.S. Joint Committee on Taxation. His research has addressed fiscal theory and policy, business finance and investment, the effects of tax provisions on firm behavior, and the impact of changing demographics on fiscal balance. A fellow of the Econometric Society, he testifies frequently before Congress and has consulted for the U.S. Treasury, the Office of Management and Budget, the Finance Ministries of Sweden and New Zealand, the Organization for Economic Cooperation and Development, the International Monetary Fund, and the World Bank. He has a B.A. from Yale University and a Ph.D. in economics from Harvard University.

GEORGE J. BORJAS is a professor of public policy at the John F. Kennedy School of Government, Harvard University; he is also a research associate at the National Bureau of Economic Research. Prior to joining the Harvard faculty, he was a professor of economics at the University of California, San Diego. He has conducted extensive research on many facets of the economic impact of immigration and has written widely on immigration-related issues both for scholarly journals and the popular press. His current research interests include immigration, the role of ethnicity in the U.S. economy, and the impact of international trade on the labor market. He has a bachelor's degree in economics and mathematics from St. Peter's College and M.A. and Ph.D. degrees in economics from Columbia University.

BARRY EDMONSTON is a study director with the Committee on Population. He has been involved in demographic research and teaching at Stanford University and Cornell University, and he was senior research associate with the program for research on immigration policy at the Urban Institute. For the Committee on National Statistics of the National Research Council, he was study director for a panel study on the U.S. census, and also for workshops on immigration statistics and on federal standards for race and ethnicity classification. He has done research on demographic methods, especially on the methodology of population projections, and on questions of immigration and immigration policy. He has a Ph.D. in demography from the University of Michigan.

J. THOMAS ESPENSHADE is professor of sociology and a faculty associate of the Office of Population Research at Princeton University. He was formerly senior research associate and director of the program in demographic studies at the Urban Institute. He is the coauthor *of The Fourth Wave: California's Newest Immigrants* and editor of *Keys to Successful Immigration: Implications of the New Jersey Experience*. He is a member of the academic advisory board for the new immigrant survey at RAND and of the Social Science Research Council's postdoctoral awards committee for the program on international migration; he served on the National Research Council's Panel to Evaluate Microsimulation Models for Social Welfare Programs. His research interests include patterns of undocumented migration to the United States, the fiscal impacts of new immigrants, and attitudes toward U.S. immigration. He is currently directing a study on the contributions of immigrants to the science and engineering workforce in the United States. He has a B.A. in economics from the College of Wooster, an

M.A.T. in mathematics from Yale University, and a Ph.D. in economics from Princeton University.

RICHARD B. FREEMAN holds the Ascherman chair of economics at Harvard University. He is currently serving as faculty co-chair of the Harvard University trade union program. He is program director of the National Bureau of Economic Research's program in labor studies and executive director of the programme in discontinuous economics at the London School of Economics, a major program in economic analysis using neural nets and new data mining tools. His research interests are youth labor market problems, crime and the labor market, higher education, trade unionism, transitional economies, high-skilled labor markets, economic discrimination, social mobility, and income distribution and equity in the marketplace. He is a member of the American Academy of Arts and Sciences, president of the Society of Labour Economists, and vice-president of the American Economic Association. He has served on three other panels of the National Research Council, on high-risk youth, postsecondary education and training in the workplace, and employment and technical change. He has a Ph.D. in economics from Harvard University.

JOHN F. GEWEKE is professor in the Department of Economics at the University of Minnesota and adviser to the Federal Reserve Bank of Minneapolis. He was previously director of the Institute of Statistics and Decision Sciences at Duke University and professor in the Department of Economics at the University of Wisconsin. He is a member of the Committee on National Statistics of the National Research Council and is currently chair of its panel to evaluate the research program of the Economic Research Service of the U.S. Department of Agriculture. He is a fellow of the Econometric Society and the American Statistical Association. His research has included time series and Bayesian econometric methods and applications in macroeconomics and labor economics. He has a B.S. from Michigan State University and a Ph.D. in economics from the University of Minnesota.

CHARLES HIRSCHMAN is professor and chair of the Department of Sociology at the University of Washington, Seattle. He was previously on the faculty at Cornell University and Duke University. His primary research interests include comparative race and ethnic relations, with a particular interest on immigration and ethnic stratification in the United States, and demographic change in Southeast Asia. He is currently the chair of the Committee of International Migration of the Social Science Research Council and vice president of the Population Association of America. He received has a B.A. from Miami University (Oxford, Ohio) and M.S. and Ph.D. degrees in sociology from the University of Wisconsin-Madison.

ROBERT P. INMAN is a professor of finance and economics, University of Pennsylvania, and a research associate at the National Bureau of Economic Research. His published research includes articles on urban fiscal policy, health care finance, tax policy, and political economy. He is the editor of the *Economics of Public Services* (with Martin Feldstein) and *Managing the Service Economy*. He has been a visiting professor of economics at the University of California, Berkeley, and Stanford University and a research fellow at Harvard University, the Australian National University, and the Center for Advanced Study in the Behavioral Sciences at Stanford University. He has an A.B. from Harvard College, an M.Ed. from the Harvard Graduate School of Education, and a Ph.D. in economics from Harvard University.

GUILLERMINA JASSO is professor of sociology at New York University. She was founding director of the theory workshop at the University of Iowa and directs the methods workshop at New York University. Earlier she served as special assistant to the commissioner of the U.S. Immigration and Naturalization Service (1977-1979) and as director of research for the U.S. Select Commission on Immigration and Refugee Policy (1979-1980). Her work is in the areas of international migration, distributive justice, the general scientific theory of behavior, and methods of both theoretical and empirical analysis. She is a member of the Johns Hopkins Society of Scholars and of the Sociological Research Association. She has served on many advisory boards, including panels advising the National Science Foundation, the National Institutes of Health, and the International Institute for Applied Systems Analysis. Currently she is chair-elect of the theory section and of the international migration section of the American Sociological Association. She has a B.A. from Our Lady of the Lake College, an M.A. in sociology and anthropology from the University of Notre Dame, and a Ph.D. in social relations from Johns Hopkins University.

RONALD D. LEE is professor of demography and economics at the University of California, Berkeley, and director of the Center for Economics and Demography of Aging there. He is a member of the National Academy of Sciences and chair of the National Research Council's Committee on Population. His recent research examines intergenerational transfers of resources, and he also works on methods for forecasting population, merging these interests in work on stochastic forecasts of the finances of the social security system. He has also worked on various topics in historical demography. He has a B.A. from Reed College, an M.A. from the University of California, Berkeley, and a Ph.D. in economics from Harvard University.

KRISTIN McCUE served as research associate for the panel's study. A labor economist, she was an assistant professor in the Economics Department at Texas

A&M University from 1989 to 1995. She is now employed at the Congressional Budget Office. She has a Ph.D. in economics from the University of Chicago.

MARY C. WATERS is professor of sociology at Harvard University. She is the author of two books and numerous articles on racial and ethnic identity and immigrant assimilation. Her current research focuses on the racial and ethnic identities of Caribbean immigrants in the United States, patterns of assimilation among young adult children of immigrants from a wide variety of countries in New York City, and patterns of racial intermarriage and identity formation in the United States. She has been a consultant to the Census Bureau on issues of measurement of race and ethnicity and is a member of the review panel of the social sciences and population section of the National Institute of Child Health and Human Development. She has been a Guggenheim fellow, a visiting scholar at the Russell Sage Foundation and is a member of the international immigration committee of the Social Science Research Council. She has a B.A. in philosophy from Johns Hopkins University, an M.A. in demography, and M.A. and Ph.D. degrees in sociology from the University of California, Berkeley.

FINIS R. WELCH is distinguished professor of economics and Abell professor of liberal arts at Texas A&M University. Earlier he was on the research staff of the National Bureau of Economic Research (as director of the program in income distributions) and RAND (as founding director of the labor and population studies program). He is currently chair of Unicon Research, chair of STATA Corp., and president of Welch Consulting. He has specialized in teaching and research on determinants of wage earnings and employment. This work has variously addressed group differences: black/white differences in earnings, female/male differential, Hispanic/Anglo differences, etc. More recently the work has focused on determinants of employment and ages of retirement and of the growth in wage inequality. He has been on the faculty of the University of Chicago, Southern Methodist University, the City University of New York (as executive officer of the Ph.D. program in economics), and the University of California, Los Angeles. He has a Ph.D. is economics from the University of Chicago.

Index

A

Abuse of immigrants, 181
Adaptation of immigrants, 15-16, 18. *See also* Assimilation of immigrants
Admission preferences. *See* Preference system
Admissions
  age structure of, 54-55
  asylees, 38, 42, 44, 64
  attitudes about level of, 391-392
  average annual, 51
  employment-based, 41, 64
  family-sponsored, 28 n.7, 41, 43, 64
  Immigration Reform and Control Act of 1986 (IRCA), 52
  nonimmigrants, 49
  occupational earnings by, 193
  race/ethnicity, 64
  refugees, 38, 41, 42, 44, 64
Africa
  gross national product, 176
  population shifts, 20, 79
African Americans. *See also* Black immigrants; Blacks; *specific country*
  attitudes toward immigration, 13, 392, 394
  employment impacts on, 6, 220, 222-224
  social and spatial mobility, 366
African immigrants. *See also specific country*
  citizenship, 382
  educational attainment, 188, 190
  fiscal impact, 277, 280-282, 290-291
  gender profiles, 190
  household characteristics, 272-273, 290-291
  lotteries, 46
  volume, 177
  wages, 176-178, 188, 190
Age profiles. *See also* Elderly population; Generational perspectives; Time of arrival
  at arrival in U.S., 302, 303-304, 326-332, 334-336, 358-361
  and attitudes toward immigration, 390, 403
  childbearing, 58, 85
  construction of, 323-325
  and crime, 386-387, 388
  and dependency ratios, 107-110
  and economic impacts, 77

educational attainment, 241-248, 312, 355-358
employment, 206-208
and expenditures attributable to immigrant labor, 234-235
and federal benefits, 311-312, 315
and fertility rates, 58, 85, 96, 102, 103, 110
and fiscal impacts, 10, 11, 54, 55, 106, 108, 110, 290-291, 293, 303-304, 323-325, 353
gender composition, 100, 198-204, 205-208, 241-250
heads of households, 272-273
households, 272-273
labor impacts, 54, 77
longitudinal, 323-325
and marital status, 57
median, 101-103
mortality rates, 96
net present value and, 327-336, 342-343
patterns, 54-55
projected, 3-4, 101-110, 122-123
and public assistance, 305 n.5, 309-314, 315
race/ethnicity and, 113-114
school age, 77, 94, 103-104
social impacts, 77, 306 n.5
and taxes, 305 n.5, 308, 314-316, 349-352
time since arrival, 302
and wages, 198-204, 241-250
working age, 77, 105, 110
young adults, 94, 104-105, 291
Agriculture, work force, 27, 29, 52, 149
Ahmed, Bashir, 40
Aid to Families with Dependent Children (AFDC), 10, 30, 272-273, 278, 306 n.5, 307, 308 n.9, 309, 311, 313, 339, 352
Aleuts, 80 n. 3
Alien and Sedition Act of 1798, 14
Aliens of exceptional ability, 42-43
Amerasians, 41, 42, 44, 46
American Indians, 80 n. 3, 114, 366
Amnesty. *See* Illegal immigrants/ immigration
Anaheim, 61
Ancestry, 85, 90-92, 118-122, 123
Anti-Terrorism Act of 1996, 29-30
Arizona, 254
Arts, contributions of immigrants to, 385
Asia, 79. *See also specific country*
Asian immigrants. *See also specific country*
attitudes about, 392
citizenship, 26 n.6, 30, 382
educational attainment, 12, 186, 187, 189, 366
emigration from U.S., 40
English proficiency, 376
exclusion, 23-25, 26
fiscal burden of, 275, 280, 282, 288, 322
gender profiles, 186-187, 189, 191
household characteristics, 271-273, 275, 277, 278, 283, 290-291, 293
integration, 367-368
intermarriage, 370-371
occupational attainment, 366
quotas, 27
segregation indices, 367
skills, 28
volume, 28, 32, 36, 37, 38
wages, 186, 187, 189, 191, 202, 236
waiting lists, 46
Asian population, U.S.
ancestry, 85, 90-92, 119, 120-122
attitudes toward immigration, 392 n.23, 396
defined, 80
exogamy, 90-92, 115-116, 117, 122, 132
fertility, 85-87, 115
intermarriage rates, 91, 113, 132
mortality, 88, 131
population growth and size, 4, 114-115, 117, 121, 122
racial/ethnic attribution, 93, 115-116, 117, 118, 123, 133
size, 114-115
Assimilation of immigrants. *See also* Exogamy; Generational perspectives; Intermarriage
citizenship and, 382
economic, 164, 181-182, 196-205

and education, 372-376
fiscal impacts and, 302
generational perspectives, 12-13, 365-366, 396
historical context, 364
into labor market, 18, 39, 158-160
and policy on immigration, 15-16
racial/ethnic, 374-375, 395-396
residential integration, 366-367
social and spatial mobility, 365-369
Asylum and asylees. *See also* Refugees
admission trends, 38, 42, 44, 64
defined, 22
earnings, 194, 195
excluded groups, 30
international comparisons, 64-65
policy on admissions, 28-29, 38, 40, 41, 42
Atlanta, 223
Atlantic Monthly, 393
Attitudes about immigrants
admissions level, 391-392
crime and violence, 364, 386, 389
economic conditions and, 13, 24-25, 26, 396
illegal immigration, 390-391, 393
intermarriage, 369-372
labor-related, 23, 24-25, 26, 27, 144-145, 364, 390-392
population composition, 119, 383
racial/ethnic, 13, 364, 369-371, 374, 375, 382-383, 392
survey results, 402-405
trends, 46-47, 390
unemployment and, 390, 404
welfare-related, 26
Attribution
Asians, 85, 93, 115-116, 117-118, 120-121, 123, 133, 375
blacks, 84-85, 93, 114, 118-119, 120, 133, 375
defined, 77
and educational success, 374-376
Hispanics, 85, 92 n.17, 93, 115, 116-118, 120-122, 123, 133, 375
and intermarriage rates, 91
Irish, 119, 370, 372
and population analysis, 4, 84-85, 89-90, 92-93, 114, 116-123, 133
racial issues, 370, 374
rates, 114, 115, 116-118, 120-122, 123, 133
social dimensions, 363, 369-370, 374-375
whites, 84, 93, 118, 120, 121-122, 133, 370-371, 396
Aussiedler, 63, 64
Australia, 20, 52, 62, 63, 64, 65, 66, 379
Australian immigrants, 186, 188, 190
Austria, 63, 64, 66, 186, 187, 189
Austria-Hungary immigrants, 24

B

Baby-boom generation, 76, 94, 102, 106, 107-108, 110, 324, 347, 353, 389
Baby-bust generation, 76
Benefits. *See* Public assistance, benefits, and services; *individual programs*
Births
fiscal impacts, 302
to later generations, 83, 130
multiple-ancestry, 84, 90, 92
rates, 34, 85-87, 96-97
underreporting, 85
Black immigrants. *See also* Africa; African Americans; *specific country*
ancestry, 84-85, 90-92, 119, 120
attitudes about, 392, 394, 396, 404, 405
attitudes toward immigration, 13, 392, 395
distribution, 224
education, 375
employment impacts, 6, 220, 222-224
exogamy, 90-92, 118-119 n.46, 132
fertility rates, 85-87, 114
integration, 366, 367, 369
intermarriage, 113, 132
male, 222
mortality, 88, 131
population size and growth, 114, 115, 116, 121, 123
racial/ethnic attribution, 93, 114, 118, 133, 375

segregation indices, 366, 367
unemployment, 222
wages, 222-224
Blacks. *See* African Americans; Black immigrants
Border enforcement, 25, 51
Border Patrol, 26, 29, 51-52, 387
Bracero Program, 27, 30
British immigrants, 23, 28, 36, 46, 186, 187, 189
Bureau of Economic Analysis, 231
Bureau of the Census
emigration estimates, 40
fertility estimates, 85, 86, 87
immigration data, 22, 31, 84, 89, 227, 362, 382 n.12
mortality estimates, 87-88
population estimates, 86, 94 n.20
Public Use Samples, 182 n.8, 224 n.37, 271, 273 n.27, 306, 308, 309 n.12, 362
wage data, 182 n.8

C

California
attitudes of residents toward immigration, 391, 402-405
budget, 277-280, 286
labor market, 226
legislation, 254
net annual fiscal impact, 282-294, 321
population, 228-230
Proposition 187, 254
public services, 278, 283
revenues, 278-282, 283, 315 n.14
spending, 280-282, 283
California immigrants
educational attainment, 141-142
employment, 211-217, 221 n.35, 225
federal budget for, 280-282
fiscal impact of, 8, 9-10, 254, 257, 277-289, 290-291, 321-323
household characteristics, 9, 273, 277, 278, 280, 282
illegal, 51, 254
intermarriage, 371
population composition, 228-230, 277, 287
studies, 8, 321-322
taxes, 278-279, 280, 281, 286-287
trends, 59, 61
wages, 179-180
Canadian immigrants in U.S.; *See also* European/Canadian immigrants
athletes, 386
citizenship, 382
educational attainment, 186, 187, 189
English proficiency, 376
fiscal burden, 9-10, 275, 277, 280, 282, 288
gender profiles, 176-178, 186-187, 189, 191
household characteristics, 271-273, 275, 277
illegal, 26
numerical limits, 46
volume of , 28, 31 n.11, 36, 37
wages, 176-178, 186, 187, 189, 191
Canadian immigration system
admissions, 62, 63, 67
asylees and refugees, 20, 67, 72
citizenship, 379
classes, 67, 71-72
composition of immigrants by type of admission, 64
and economic growth, 154-155
illegal immigrants, 50
national origin of immigrants, 65, 66
percentage of foreign-born, 62-63
planning, 65, 67
point-based preference system, 65, 67, 72-75
Capital
complementarity to immigrant labor, 137
flows, 18, 148, 153 n.19
Capital/labor ratios, 148, 161
Caribbean. *See* Latin America and the Caribbean
Castro, Fidel, 223
Census, 141. *See also* Bureau of the Census
Central America, 174

Central Europe, 365-366, 395
Characteristics of immigrants
age, 54-55
family structure, 55-58
and fiscal impacts, 303-305, 306-308
gender, 52-54
Chicago, 61, 372, 394
Child care. *See* Household services
Childbearing rates, 4, 57, 58, 77. *See also* Fertility rates
Children of immigrants, 9, 41, 42, 43-44, 45, 54, 55, 57, 58, 298, 309, 316-323, 327, 377, 395
China, 62, 175, 176
Chinese Exclusion Act of 1882, 14, 23, 24, 50 n.23
Chinese immigrants, 16, 23, 24, 26 n.6, 28, 42, 46, 50 n.23, 374
Chinese Student Protection Act, 42, 46
Citizens, relatives of, 41-42
Citizenship and naturalization
advantages, 378-379
annual growth of, 379-382
Asian immigrants, 24, 26, 30, 382
eligibility, 22 n.3, 379
historical perspective, 379 n.8, 380, 382
incentives/propensity, 30, 378-379, 382
international comparisons, 379-380, 381
temporal trends, 382
Civil War, U.S., 47-48
Coale-Demeny model life tables, 125
Colbert, Claudette, 385
College enrollments, 104-105, 122
Colorado, 386
Commodity labor shares, 232-235, 251-253
Comparative advantage, 147-148
Congressional Budget Office (CBO), 323-324, 339 n.27, 346
Consumer Expenditure Survey, 232
Consumer price impacts
of immigrant labor, 231-233, 251-253
household composition and, 232-235
occupational distribution of immigrants and, 144, 230-231
Consumer price index, 274
Consumer spending by immigrants
changes, 264-266
measurement of, 264
Consumption of goods
expenditures attributable to immigrant labor, 232-235
specialization in, 145
Crime and violence, 364, 386-389
Criminals, exclusion of, 23
Croatia, 386
Cuba, 386
Cuban Americans, 393
Cuban immigrants, 44, 181, 223, 365, 367 n.3, 375
Cultural impacts
on arts and sciences, 383-386
concerns, 14, 383
family structure and, 55
generational, 82, 383
Current Population Surveys (CPS), 40, 85, 86, 130, 227, 271 n.25, 278, 306, 312, 315, 340, 362, 389
Czech Republic, 386

D

Deaths, 83, 96-98. *See also* Mortality rates
Demographics. *See also* Age profiles; Gender profiles; Race/ethnicity
emigration and, 39-40
foreign residents, 52-55, 80
models, *See* Fiscal accounting model; Population projection model
population effects, 94
unit of account, 255-256, 305; *See also* Households, immigrant
Denmark, 62, 63, 64, 66
Department of the Treasury, Bureau of Immigration, 24, 26
Dependency ratios, 107-110
Deportation, 24, 30
Dillingham Commission, 24-25
Distribution. *See* Geographic distribution of immigrants
Diversity admissions, 25, 29, 42, 44, 46
Dollar flow discount, 301
Dominican Republic, 386

Dominican Republic immigrants, 28, 194, 196
Dynamic fiscal accounting, 255-256
Dynamic incidence calculation
  approach, 298-299
  discounting dollar flows, 301
  revenue and spending projections, 299-301
  time of arrival, 301-302

E

Earnings. *See also* Income; Wages
  annual, 176-178
  disparities, by nativity, 176-178
  domestic, 16, 17, 221-225, 219-228
  and educational attainment, 302, 307
  and fiscal impacts, 302, 307
  gender profiles, 193-196
  national origin and, 194, 196
  occupational, 192-196
  and public assistance, 306-307
  temporal trends, 192-196, 307
  by visa class, 195
Eastern Europe, 20, 175, 176
Eastern European immigrants, 25-26, 27, 31, 36, 68, 364, 395. *See also specific country*
Eastern Hemisphere immigrants, 24, 26, 27
Economic growth
  agglomeration effects and, 150
  assimilation of immigrants and, 9, 181-182, 196-204
  conceptual framework, 155-156
  crowding effects and, 150, 303
  emigration and, 155
  endogenous, 162
  entrepreneurs and, 162-163
  exogenous, 162
  fertility rates and, 158, 160
  fiscal impact of immigration, 8-12, 98, 271, 274, 275-276, 278-279, 284, 291-294
  gains to immigrants, 174-181
  generational assimilation and, 5, 10, 158-160, 164-165
  historical context, 154-155
  labor markets and, 4, 6, 16-17, 151-164, 220
  migration and, 154-155, 157, 162
  persistence of effects, 158-160
  single-good model, 155-158
  technological changes and, 155, 160-163
  two-good model, 166-169
Economic impacts. *See also specific aspects of the economy*
  dollar-exchange rate, 148
  gains to immigrants, 174-181
  labor-market changes, 137-142
  of nonimmigrants, 49-50
  of population change, 77, 98
  prices of goods and services, 135-136, 137, 230-235
  recession, 308
  unemployment, 104
Ecuador, 175, 176
Education, public
  assimilation and, 372-376
  bilingual, 311, 321, 326, 356
  generational perspective, 311, 312, 355-358, 374-376
  policies, 103-104
  public spending on, 273 n.27, 276, 281
Educational attainment
  age profiles, 241-248
  and attitudes toward immigration, 13, 390-392, 396, 403
  and earnings, 302, 307
  and emigration, 39
  and expenditures attributable to immigrant labor, 233-235
  and fiscal impact, 10-11, 307, 327-332, 353, 358-361
  gender profiles, 183-190, 241-248
  generational perspective, 355-358
  labor-market impacts, 77, 141-142, 151, 220
  national origin and, 7, 186-190
  by nativity, 141-142, 182-185
  and net present value, 327-336
  requirements, 46

and self-employment, 163
and social impact, 306 n.5
and taxes, 349-352
temporal trends, 183-185
and wages, 7, 17, 151, 179, 181, 182-191, 227-228, 235, 241-248
Eisenhower, Dwight D., 27
El Salvador, 186, 187, 189
Elasticity of demand, 219-220, 222
Elderly population
benefits, 297, 309-311, 320
changes in, 54, 55, 297
dependency ratio, 107, 108-110
fiscal impacts, 10, 76, 77, 106, 290, 293, 307 n.7, 320
growth, 3-4, 106, 122
health benefits, 76, 77, 106, 110, 304, 309-310, 347
OASDHI, 307 n.7, 309, 320, 326; *see also* Social Security
oldest-old, 85, 106-107, 110, 320
pensions, 76, 77, 106, 110
taxes, 320
Emigration
defined, 21
demographic information, 39-40
and earnings, 182 n.17
estimates, 40
fiscal effects, 40 n.17, 304, 326
illegal immigrants, 38, 39
generational perspective, 83, 89 n.14
modeling, 82, 84, 88, 89, 326
national origin and, 40, 65, 66
policy making, 38-40
and population changes, 34, 35, 38-39, 78
and wages and earnings, 182 n.7, 204-205
Employer sanctions, 2, 25, 29, 52
Employment. *See also* Labor entries; Occupations, immigrant; Workforce, immigrant
age profiles, 206-209
educational attainment and, 209, 236
gender profiles, 162-163, 205-209
by nativity, 206-209, 236
skills and, 236
telephone verification system, 2, 25, 29, 51
temporal trends, 8, 206-209
Employment-based admission preferences
admission trends, 41, 64
Canadian system, 65, 67, 71-75
and earnings, 194-195
international comparisons, 64, 65
legislation, 24, 25, 28, 29, 182
national-origin trends, 46
numerical limits on, 41, 42
and occupational skills of immigrants, 218
waiting lists, 45-46
English language
education, 11, 55, 278 n.32, 304, 311, 311 n.13
generational distribution of immigrants and, 82
primacy, 14, 376-378
proficiency, 13, 181, 197, 302, 311 n.13, 376-378, 395-396
requirements for entry, 25
Entrepreneurs, 162-163, 363 n.1. *See also* Investors, admissions
Enumeration of immigrants
emigration and, 38-40
illegal entry and, 52
racial/ethnic considerations, 80
Environmental impacts, 77 n.2, 98-99
Eskimos, 80 n. 3
Ethnic affiliation. *See* Race/ethnicity
Europe, 78, 150, 162, 175
European/Canadian immigrants, 271-273, 277, 278, 280, 281, 282, 287 n.45, 288, 290-291, 293
European immigrants. *See also specific country*
attitudes about, 119, 392
citizenship, 382
educational attainment, 186, 187, 189
emigration from U.S. 40
entry routes, 31 n.11
fiscal burden, 9-10, 275, 277, 280, 282, 288
gender profiles, 176-178, 186-187, 189, 191

geographic distribution, 59 n.28
household characteristics, 271-273, 275, 277
lotteries, 46
volume, 36, 37, 119
wages, 176-178, 186-189, 191, 202, 236

Exchange visitors, 49
Exclusion, 15. *See also* Preference system
of criminals, 23
of feeble-minded, 50 n.23
of paupers, 23, 50 n.23
race-based, 23-25, 50 n.23
of terrorists, 29-30

Exogamy. *See also* Intermarriage
births, 92
data sources, 91
defined, 77, 89
generational perspective, 91-92, 132
modeling, 89-92, 132
and racial/ethnic composition, 114, 115, 117-119, 132

Expenditures. *See* Public spending; State and local government
Export-intensive industries, 148-149

F

Families. *See also* Households, all
defined, 56 n.23
modeling, 305 n.5, 335
public services utilization, 255
reunification policy, 29, 38, 53, 54, 56, 64, 68, 218
structure, 55-59
tax contribution, 255

Family-sponsored admission preferences
admissions, 28 n.7, 41, 43, 64
and earnings, 194, 195
international comparisons, 64
legislation, 27-28
numerical limits, 41, 42
waiting lists, 44-45

Farmworkers, 27, 29, 52
Federal budget
adjustments, 325, 338
benefits, 325, 338
calculating, 303
for California immigrants, 280, 282, 321-323
capital costs, 303
congestion costs, 303, 315, 316
current costs, 303
deficit, 299-300, 318 n.15, 324, 325
net annual fiscal impact of immigration, 257, 270-294
rate of interest, 325-326, 339-340
taxes, 325

Federal expenditures. *See* Public spending
Federal policy on immigration. *See also* Exclusion; Immigration Reform and Control Act of 1986; Preference system; Quotas
admissions, 12, 333, 364
competing goals, 15-16, 28, 38
current, 37-52, 103
debate, 1, 16-17, 22, 38, 96, 140, 364
determinants, 15-17, 37-38, 354
diversity, 38
emigration and, 38-40
family reunification, 2, 29, 38, 53, 54, 56, 68
humanitarian, 28, 29, 37
illegal immigrants, 50-52
legal immigrants, 40-46
and net fiscal impact, 333, 354
nonimmigrants, 48-50
population impacts of, 95-96
size of government and, 8, 46-48
and skills of immigrants, 194, 196, 218
state/local impacts, 17
target population, 30-31

Federal revenues. *See* Public revenues; Taxes
Females. *See also* Gender profiles
labor force participation, 105

Fertility rates
age and, 58, 85, 96, 102, 103, 105, 110
and economic growth, 158, 160
fiscal impacts, 304
generational perspective, 83, 85, 86, 94 n.20, 158-160, 303
immigrants, 2, 77, 83, 95, 97, 304, 365
and labor force, 105

modeling, 82, 83, 85-87, 94 n.20, 329 n.23
and population change, 2, 34, 94, 95, 97, 111, 134
racial/ethnic distribution, 85-87, 114, 115, 119, 121, 365
Finland, 62, 63, 64, 66
Fiscal accounting model
implementation, 263-270, 285 n.39
net annual fiscal impact, 257-260, 261, 270
nonresident revenues and spending, 260, 262-263, 269-270
population and population change, 263
privateness parameter, 265-266
public service utilization, 258-259, 262
revenue and revenue changes, 259, 260-263, 266-269
social rate of discount, 256
spending and spending changes, 264-266
unit of analysis, 255-256
Fiscal impacts. *See also* Net annual fiscal impact; Net present values; Public assistance, benefits, and services; Public revenues; Public spending; Social Security; Taxes
age-related, 11, 54, 55, 106, 108, 110, 272, 290-291, 293, 307 n.5, 308-314, 318-319, 323-332, 334-336, 358-361
aggregate cross-sectional, 316-323
average, 331, 333-337
baseline scenario, 324, 325-331, 337
benefit expenditures, 8, 299-301, 307, 308-314, 338
budget assumptions and, 324, 325, 337-338
calculations, 303; *See also* Dynamic incidence calculation
case studies, 18-19, 320-323; *See also* California; New Jersey
characteristics of immigrants and, 303-305, 306-308
competing, 16
data sources, 306, 362
debt/GDP ratio and, 299-300, 325, 337-338
deficit and, 299-300, 302-303
discount rates, 298, 301
on earnings, 307
education costs, 326
educational attainment and, 11-12, 307, 353
of emigration, 40 n.17, 326
estimation, *See* Fiscal accounting model
exclusion of nonresident children and, 316-318
federal policy and, 254-255
of fertility rates, 304
generational perspectives, 215, 289, 294, 316-323
geographic distribution of immigrants and, 59, 255, 305
household characteristics and, 271-273, 275, 277, 292-293
illegal immigrants, 254, 306
importance, 254-255
incremental immigrants, 331-336
independent of characteristics of immigrants, 302-305
interest rates and, 337, 339-340
internal migration and, 305
labor impacts and, 255, 258 n.5, 305
on native-born population, 8, 318-320
new immigrants, 10, 257-270, 289-292, 293-294, 301-302, 304-305
of population changes, 98, 289-292
by regional origin of immigrant, 271-273, 275-277, 280-283, 287-288, 290-291, 293
revenue/spending adjustments scenario, 338
scope of study, 18
size of government and, 46-48
state and local, 12, 305, 336-337, 341-343; *See also specific states*
studies of, 8, 362
taxes, 8, 299-301, 314-316, 326, 338, 340
time of arrival and, 301-302, 303-304, 307-308, 340

timing of, 341-344
welfare reform and, 326, 337, 338-339
Florida immigrants, 59, 61, 179-180, 211-217, 228-230, 254, 311 n.13, 391
Food stamps, 30
Foreign-born residents, permanent population changes, 34-36
Foreign government officials, 49
France, 63, 64, 66, 379
Franklin, Aretha, 385
Fraudulent documents, 52
French immigrants, 36

G

Gallup polls, 402
Garment industry, 147-148, 225
Gender profiles. *See also* Females; Males
age and, 100, 198-204, 206-209, 241-250
citizenship and, 382
educational attainment, 183-190, 241-250
emigration, 39
employment, 162-163, 205-209
fertility rates, 96
immigration and, 99-101, 402-404
marital status, 57
mortality rates, 96, 131
national origin, 186-191, 196, 249-250
occupations, 210-218
population distribution, 52-54
wages and earnings, 17, 176-178, 181, 183-191, 193-196, 198-204, 223, 241-250
General Social Survey, 307, 355
Generational perspectives
assimilation, 12-13, 365-366, 396
desegregation, 367-369
economic growth, 5, 10, 158-160, 164-165
education, 311, 312, 355-358, 374-376
emigration, 89 n.14
and English proficiency, 377
exogamy, 91-92, 114
female dominance concept, 128-130
fertility rates, 83, 85-87
fiscal impact, 215, 289, 294, 316-323, 353
immigration, 89, 365
intermarriage, 12-13, 369-370
modeling approach, 81, 82-83, 89, 127-130
and net present value, 327-336, 342-343
population growth, 3, 111-113
public assistance and benefits, 297, 309-314
race/ethnicity, 114, 117, 367-369
taxes, 314-316, 319, 349-352
Geneva, Switzerland, 379
Gentleman's Agreement with Japan (1907), 24
Geographic distribution of immigrants
and fiscal impacts, 59, 304, 305
and labor-market impacts, 6, 59, 61, 220-228
metropolitan concentration, 58-62, 104, 228-230, 304
residential concentrations, 365-367
and wages, 179-180
German immigrants, 23, 28, 36, 395
Germany, 50 n.22, 63, 64-65, 66, 155, 379
Goods and services. *See* Consumer price impacts; Household services; Price of goods and services
Grant, Cary, 385
Great Depression, 26, 31, 32, 35, 68
Great Lakes immigrants, 61
Greek immigrants, 24
Greeley, Andrew, 369
Green cards. *See* Visas, permanent resident
Gross domestic product (GDP), foreign
by country and region, per capita, 174-176
debt ratio, 324 n.19, 337-338, 354
Gross domestic product, U.S.
debt ratio, 299-300, 324, 325, 337-338
growth, 308, 334 n.25
labor contribution, 138, 151-153
labor-market impacts of immigration, 6, 136-137, 152-153, 155, 156, 164, 171-172

per capita, 176
projecting, 299-301, 325, 344-345
state/local allocations, 47
Gross national product, U.S., 47

H

Haitian Americans, 393
Haitian immigrants, 16, 374, 375
Health care, 76, 105, 110, 324
Hispanic immigrants. *See* Hispanics, U.S.; Latin American and Caribbean immigrants
Hispanics, U.S. *See also* Latin American and Caribbean immigrants
ancestry, 4, 85, 90-92, 119-122, 181
attitudes toward immigration, 13, 392, 394, 396, 404, 405
defined, 80
educational attainment, 375
English proficiency, 181
exogamy, 90-92, 115-116, 117-118, 132
fertility rates, 85-87, 115, 121, 365
fiscal burden of, 323
geographic distribution, 26
immigration trends, 38, 322
integration, 366, 367 n.3
intermarriage rates, 91, 113, 121, 132, 370-371
male, 222
mortality, 88, 131
native, 222
population size and growth, 4, 38, 80, 114-115, 117-118, 121, 123
racial/ethnic attribution, 92 n.17, 93, 115, 116-118, 122, 123, 133
segregation indices, 367
wages, 181, 222
Hong Kong, 377
Hope, Bob, 385
Hotel industry, 225
Household services, 144, 146, 149, 232, 234, 235
Households, all
consumer price impacts by composition of, 232-235
defined, 56 n.24, 263, 270-271
education expenditures on, 276, 281
fiscal impacts on, 10, 270, 274, 276, 279, 281
income, 290
modeling, 263; *see also* Fiscal accounting model
renters, 274
spending on public services to, 274, 276, 278 n.32, 280, 281, 283
taxes, 274, 276, 280, 281, 283, 318
Households, immigrant. *See also* Families; Fiscal accounting model
African, 272-273, 277, 280, 290-291
age profiles, 272-273, 290-291, 293, 317
Asian, 271-273, 275, 277, 280, 281, 282, 283, 288, 290-291, 293
California, 9, 10, 273, 277-284, 286, 287-288, 289-292, 293, 320-323
children, 9, 271, 275, 277, 282, 289, 292, 294, 316-318, 319-320
composition, 9, 56, 233-234, 256, 263, 271, 272-273, 275, 277, 280, 282
current immigrants, 282-289
economic status, 9, 272-273, 277, 280, 282, 287, 293
education services to, 9, 273 n.27, 275-277, 278 n.32, 280, 281, 292-293, 321
European/Canadian, 9-10, 271-273, 275, 277, 278, 280, 281, 282, 287 n.45, 288, 290, 291, 293
fiscal impacts of, 9-10, 270-294, 316-323
fiscal redistribution from native households to, 275, 279-280
Latin American and Caribbean, 9-10, 271-273, 275, 277, 280, 281, 282, 287, 288, 290, 291, 293
male-headed family, 56
modeling, 319
new immigrants, 264, 265, 268, 289-292, 294
New Jersey, 9, 10, 271-277, 282, 284, 290, 291, 293, 320-323

size, 56 n.27, 271, 272-273, 277, 293
spending on public services to, 264-266, 271, 274, 276, 279 nn.34,35, 280, 282, 283, 290, 293
taxes, 266-268, 269-270, 271, 274, 275, 280, 283, 286-287, 290, 322
welfare utilization, 55, 265, 271, 272-273, 275, 277, 282, 283
Households, nonimmigrant
age profiles, 272-273, 280
characteristics, 272, 273
education services to, 273 n.27, 276, 281
fiscal burden of immigrants on, 9-10, 265-266, 270-294
fiscal redistribution to immigrant households, 275, 279-280
income, 271, 272-273, 288
number in U.S., 288
size, 56 n.27, 271, 272, 273
spending on public services to, 271, 274, 280, 281, 283
taxes, 265-266, 271, 274, 275, 279 nn.34,35, 280, 281, 283
Houston, 61, 223
Humanitarian assistance, 28-29, 38

I

Illegal immigrants/immigration, 190
amnesty for, 25, 29, 32 n.12, 41, 42, 44, 46, 51-52, 379
attitudes about, 390-391, 393
border enforcement against, 51-52, 386
and crime, 30, 387
defined, 21
developed countries, 20, 50
emigration, 39
employer sanctions, 2, 25, 29, 52
entry routes, 26, 52
estimates, 51-52, 88
fiscal impact, 14, 254, 306
geographic distribution, 60-62
legislation and, 2, 25, 26, 29, 30, 50 n.23
modeling and research, 88, 89, 306
national origin, 26, 51
net, 60
nonimmigrants as, 50, 51
and policy formation, 16
population changes due to, 2, 32, 37, 50-51
public assistance and, 25, 263 n.13
skills, 190, 192, 196, 236
survey participation, 190, 192
telephone verification system, 2, 25
trends, 27, 32, 37
and wages, 7, 236
Illegal Immigration Act of 1996, 25, 29
Illinois, 59, 61, 179-180, 211-217, 228-230, 391
Imhoff, Gary, 386
Immigration
defined, 21
modeling, 82, 88-89, 95, 97
Immigration Act of 1891, 23, 24
Immigration Act of 1924, 24, 68
Immigration Act of 1990, 15, 25, 28, 29, 38
Immigration and Naturalization Service (INS)
admissions data, 22, 31, 32 n.12, 379 n.11, 387 n.18
definition of immigrant, 21 n.1
demographic data, 192
economic data, 192
enforcement by, 387
history, 23
illegal immigration data, 89, 393
Immigration Marriage Fraud Amendments of 1986, 44
Immigration and Nationality Act of 1952, 24
1965 amendments, 2, 24, 27-28, 36, 68, 182
1976 amendments, 25
Immigration Reform and Control Act of 1986 (IRCA), 2, 25, 29, 32, 41, 42, 44, 46
Import-intensive industries, 148-149
Income. *See also* Earnings; Wages
after-tax, 258 n.5
aggregate, 314

and attitudes toward immigration, 390, 403-404
averages, 193
and expenditures attributable to immigrant labor, 234-235
family, 174 n.1
and fiscal impacts, 256, 300-301
free trade and, 147
generational assimilation and, 158-160, 164-165
household, 272-273
labor-market structure and, 137, 142, 147, 151, 156-157, 160, 164-165
measures of, 192
by nativity, 194
rate of immigration and, 137-138, 164
technology transfer and, 161
temporal trends, 268 n.21
India, 62-63, 175, 176, 186, 187, 189, 377
Indian immigrants, 26 n.6, 45, 194, 196
Industrial Revolution, 154-155
Institutional effects of immigration, 382-386
Interethnic relations, 389-390, 394-395
Intermarriage. *See also* Exogamy
ancestry and, 91, 132
attitudes about, 369-371
data sources, 91
and identity, 369-372
by nativity, 132
race/ethnicity and, 4, 12-13, 91-92, 113, 115-116, 119, 121, 123, 132, 369-372, 396
rates, 370-371
International comparisons
of citizenship requirements, 379-380, 381
of immigration, 62-65
of wages, 174-177
International trade, 5, 143, 146-149
Intracompany transferees, 49, 66
Investors, admissions, 29, 42, 43, 45, 49, 72 n.33
Ireland, 155
Irish immigrants 23, 28, 29, 36, 46, 119, 369, 395
Israel, 62, 63, 65, 66
Italian immigrants, 24, 28, 395
Italy, 63, 66, 386

J

Japan, 62, 63, 65, 66, 175, 176
Japanese Exclusion Act of 1924, 24
Japanese immigrants, 23-24, 186, 187, 189, 367 n.3, 369
Job opportunities, 7, 138, 210, 221

K

Kennedy Center for the Performing Arts, 383, 385
Kennedy, John F., 27
Korean immigrants, 374, 393
Kuwait, 62, 63, 66

L

Labor, highly skilled, 138, 150, 162, 164, 194, 196, 209-210, 211-212
Labor, skilled
admissions, 42, 43
complementarity of immigrants and natives, 137-141, 151, 152, 157, 163-164
gender profiles, 186, 209-210, 212-215, 222
migration profiles, 174
wages, 137-141, 143, 159-160, 201, 223
waiting lists, 45
Labor, unskilled
admissions, 42, 43
gender profiles, 209-210, 212-215, 222
migration profiles, 174
needed, 42, 43
numerical limits, 42
occupations, 209-210, 212-215
substitution of immigrants for natives, 137-141, 142, 145-146, 151, 157, 163-164, 219, 227
wages, 137, 141, 143, 159-160, 201-202, 223
waiting lists, 45

Labor market impacts
age of immigrants and, 54, 77, 104
baseline analysis, 5, 136-142, 150
benefit/cost assessment, 170-172
of complementarity of capital, 137
of complementarity of skilled labor, 5, 137-141, 151, 152, 157, 164, 219
on consumption, 145-146, 164, 232-233, 251-252
displacement of native workers, 6, 135, 143, 144-145, 220, 221-224, 236-237, 364
distributional, 144, 373
economic growth, 4, 6, 153-164, 220, 234
educational attainment and, 77, 141-142, 151, 220, 227-228, 235-236
elasticity of demand, 219-220, 222, 226
factor proportions analysis, 226-228
fiscal burdens and, 255, 258 n.5, 305
on GDP, 6, 136-137, 152-153, 155, 156, 164, 171-172
geographic distribution of immigrants and, 6, 59, 61, 220, 221-230, 236-237
of highly skilled workers, 15, 138, 150, 164
on income, 137, 142, 147, 156-157, 160, 164-165
on industrial composition, 147-149
internal migration and, 6, 228-230, 236-237
international-trade analogy, 5, 143, 146-149, 164
local, 221-225, 236
magnitude of effects, 151-153
measure of, 225-228
prices of goods and services, 4, 135-136, 137, 142-143, 164, 215, 230-235
prices of inputs, 137
on productivity, 5, 144, 150
returns to scale, 5, 149-151, 155, 156-157, 160
scope of study, 17-18
skilled workers, 5, 137-141, 143, 155-160, 162, 170
specialization in production, 5, 145-146, 164
substitution for domestic labor, 5, 137-141, 142, 145-146, 151, 157, 163-164, 219, 227
two-good, two-factor model, 143-146, 166-169
unemployment, 18, 104
unskilled workers, 5, 137-141, 143, 155-160, 162, 170, 223
wages, 4, 6, 135, 137-141, 142, 143, 151, 157, 161, 164, 219-220, 230, 235-236
Labor markets
aggregate, 6-7
assimilation into, 18, 39, 158, 164, 181-182
discrimination, 181
elasticity of demand in, 219, 222
supply of workers, 4, 6, 219, 220
wage inequities, 201-202
Lamm, Richard, 386
Land rents, 264
Language. *See* English language
Latin America and the Caribbean, 79
Latin American and Caribbean immigrants. *See also* Hispanics, U.S.
educational attainment, 186-187, 189
English proficiency, 376
fertility, 277, 282, 365
fiscal burden, 9-10, 275, 277, 282, 287, 288, 291, 293
gender profiles, 186, 187, 189, 191
household composition, 271-273, 275, 277
migrant workers, 27
public assistance to, 275, 277, 282
volume of immigrants, 32, 36, 37, 177
wages, 186, 187, 189, 191
Legislation. *See also individual statutes*
anti-terrorism, 29-30
evolution of, 23-30
exclusion, 14, 23-25
humanitarian admissions, 38
and illegal immigration, 2, 26
migrant workers, 27, 29

preference system, 2, 20, 24, 25, 27-29
quotas, 24, 25-26, 27-28
refugees, 25, 28-29
and volume of immigration, 32
welfare reform, 2, 30, 254, 326, 338-339
Life expectancy, 87-88, 94, 131
Literacy requirements, 24-25
Lithuania, 386
Los Angeles, 61, 179-180, 221, 223, 225, 235, 393, 394. *See also* California
Los Angeles Times, 394
Lotteries, 46

M

Males. *See also* Gender profiles
heads of households, 56
Malthus, Thomas, 154
Marital status, 56, 57
Marriage fraud, 44
Maryland, 61
Medicaid, 55, 273, 280, 308 n.9, 309-310, 320, 323-324, 330, 339, 352
Medi-Cal health insurance, 278, 282 n.37
Medicare, 10, 11, 255, 280, 283, 304, 308 n.9, 309-310, 319, 320, 323-324, 330
Men. *See* Gender profiles; Males
Mexican immigrants
agricultural workers, 27, 225
deportation, 26
educational attainment, 186, 187, 189, 375
emigration from U.S., 39
gender profiles, 162, 176-179, 186, 187, 189, 191
geographic segregation, 368-369
illegal, 16, 26, 37, 39, 50, 51
integration, 367
naturalization, 382
number of, 28, 31 n.11, 36, 37
occupational earnings, 194, 196
wages, 137-141, 143, 157, 174, 176, 179, 181, 186, 187, 189, 191, 193, 197-198, 201-203, 224-225, 227, 235-236, 249
waiting lists, 45
Mexico, 65, 155, 162, 174, 175, 176, 386
Miami, 61, 223, 373, 393
Migrant workers, 27, 29, 52
Migration
and economic growth, 154-155
internal, 6, 61-62, 228-230, 305, 365
international, 84
native, 228-230
net, 21, 78, 83
rich nations to poor nations, 155 n.20, 162
secondary, 365
Miles, Jack, 393
Ministers and religious workers, 43
Models/modeling. *See* Population projection model
Mortality rates
age and, 76, 96
fiscal impacts, 304
gender and, 96, 131
immigrant rates, 77, 95
modeling, 82, 83, 87-88, 131
and population change, 34, 35, 77, 95, 96, 134
race/ethnicity and, 88
Multi-City Study of Urban Inequality, 394
Multinational companies, 20, 45-46, 49

N

National Academy of Engineering, 385
National Academy of Sciences, 385
National Center for Health Statistics (NCHS), 85, 92
National defense, 256, 283, 285, 293, 302
National Educational Longitudinal Study of 1988, 375
National Football League (NFL), 385-386
National Hockey League (NHL), 386
National Income and Product Accounts (NIPA), 308, 315
National Longitudinal Survey of Youth, 367
National Opinion Research Center, 355
National/regional origin of immigrants
and educational attainment, 186-190
and emigration, 40, 66
employment-preference, 46

family-preference, 45
fiscal impacts, 271-273, 275-277, 280-283, 287-288, 290-291, 293
gender profiles, 186-191, 249-250
and geographic distribution in U.S., 59 n.28
illegal immigrants, 26, 51
international comparisons, 65, 66
and occupational earnings, 194, 196
and population changes in U.S. 32, 36-37
quotas, 24, 25-26, 27, 36
racial/ethnic classifications, 80 n.4
and wages, 7, 174, 176-178, 186-191, 202-204, 235-236, 249-250

Native American, 80 n.3

Naturalization. *See* Citizenship and naturalization

Nebraska, 61

Net annual fiscal impact (NAFI)
California, 277-282, 320-323
comparability of cross-sectional results with, 320-323
current immigrants, 282-289
defined, 289
federal budgets, 280, 282, 317
modeling, 257-260, 261, 262
on native households, 284, 292
new immigrants, 270, 289-292, 293-294
New Jersey, 271-277, 320-323
per capita, 317
state and local budgets, 271-280, 281, 317

Net immigration
and age structure, 102-110
defined, 77 n.1
emigration and, 39
and geographic distribution, 59 n.28
illegal, 60
international comparisons, 65, 66
modeling, 83, 88-89
population impacts, 3, 4, 33 n.14, 34, 39, 40, 77 n.1, 95, 96, 97-98, 102-106, 108-122
and racial/ethnic composition, 4, 114-122

Net migration, 21, 78, 83, 127, 228 n.40

Net present value (NPV)
age at arrival and, 326-332, 334-336, 358-361
for average citizen, 348-349
educational attainment and, 327-332, 358-361
federal level, 330-331
for immigrants, 358-361
incremental immigrant, 331, 333-336
for natives, 358-361
negative estimates, 347-348
positive estimates, 344-347
single immigrant scenario, 341-343
state and local level, 326-327, 347-348
stream of one immigrant per year, 343-344
time since arrival, 340, 358-361
weighted average, 341, 343-345
welfare reform and, 339

Netherlands, 63, 64, 66, 386

New Deal, 47

New England immigrants, 61

New Jersey
attitudes toward immigration, 391
budget, 271-277, 285-286
education benefits, 321
net annual fiscal impact, 282, 284-292, 321
public services, 271, 272-273, 275-276
revenues, 271, 274, 321
spending, 272-273, 275-277

New Jersey immigrants
employment, 211-217
fiscal impact of, 8, 9-10, 254, 257, 271-277, 282, 284, 287-288, 290, 321-322
household characteristics, 271-272, 275, 277, 284, 290
population composition, 228-230, 271, 275
revenues from, 271
studies, 8, 321-322
trends, 59, 61
wages, 179-180

New York City, 61, 225, 228-230

New York State, 59, 61, 179-180, 211-217, 254, 391, 393
New Zealand, 65
Nicaragua, 175, 176
Nigeria, 386
Nobel prizes and laureates, 383, 384-385
Nonimmigrants, 2, 21, 48-50, 51, 66, 190, 192, 196, 306, 382
Nonresident revenues and spending, 262-263, 269-270
North America, 79, 175
North American immigrants. 187, 189. *See also specific country*
North Carolina, 61
Northern European immigrants, 26
Norway, 63, 64, 66
Norwegian Nobel Committee, 384
Numerical limits on immigration
  annual, 40-41
  country-based, 41, 68
  employment-based preferences, 41
  exempted populations, 41, 46
  family-related preferences, 41
  legislation, 24, 25-27

O

Occupations, immigrant
  earnings by, 193-195
  gender profile, 209-218
  high-education, 8, 209-210, 211-212, 236
  low-education, 8, 209-210, 212-215, 236
  medium-education, 216-218
  public-sector, 218
  temporal trends, 210, 213-217
Oceania, 79, 176, 272-273, 280, 281, 282, 290-291, 382
Office of Immigration, U.S., 23
Oklahoma, 61
Old-Age, Survivors, Disability, and Health Insurance (OASDHI), 307, 308 n.9, 309, 320, 326, 337, 347; *see also* Social Security

P

Panama, 64, 386
Panama Canal Company, 64
Panama Canal Treaty, 64
Parents, 41, 44, 195
Park, Robert, 372
Parolees, 42
Patent system, 161 n.33
Peck, Gregory, 385
Pennsylvania immigrants, 59
Pensions, 76, 105, 110, 326 n.20
Permanent residents
  children of, 41
  visas, *See* Visas, permanent resident
Personal Responsibility and Work Opportunity Reconciliation Act (1996), 2, 10, 30, 254, 264 n.15, 326, 337, 338-339, 351, 354
Personal services (nonhousehold), 149
Philippines, 7, 174, 175, 176, 377
Physicians, 7, 194, 196, 210, 211
Policy. *See* Federal policy on immigration; State and local government
Polish immigrants, 24, 28, 46
Political asylum. *See* Asylum and asylees
Population
  dependency analysis, 107, 108-109
  world, 20, 78-79
Population projection model
  age distribution, 84
  base population, 84-85
  data requirements, 125
  definition of population, 125
  emigration and, 82, 84, 88, 89
  exogamy assumptions, 89-92, 132
  fertility assumption, 3, 82, 83, 85-87, 94 n.20, 130
  generational perspective, 3, 81, 83-84, 89, 91-92, 122, 124
  immigrant-generation approach, 82-83
  immigration assumptions, 82, 88-89, 95
  with international migration, 3, 126-127
  mortality assumptions, 3, 82, 83, 87-88, 131
  net migration, 83, 88-89

with no international migration 125-126
and policy changes, 89 n.13
with population by generations, 127-130
racial/ethnic attribution in, 81-82, 84, 92-93, 133
sensitivity of results, 133
standard cohort-component, 81, 82
Portugal, 186, 187, 189
Poverty, as a basis for exclusion, 23, 50 n.23
Preference system, 28. *See also* Employment-based admission preferences; Family-sponsored admission preferences
diversity admissions, 25, 29, 46
executives, 45
legislation, 2, 24, 25, 27-29, 68
refugees, 25
and skills of immigrants, 2, 194, 196, 218
Price of goods and services. *See also* Consumer price impacts
labor-market structure and, 4, 135-136, 143, 144, 164, 215, 230-235
Priority workers, 42, 45
Professionals, 42, 43, 45-46
Property rights, 161 n.33
Public assistance, benefits, and services. *See also specific program*; Personal Responsibility and Work Opportunity Reconciliation Act
age profiles of recipients, 308-316
fiscal impacts, 255, 256, 257-259, 262, 309-316
generational perspectives on, 297, 309-314, 319-320
household utilization, 55, 265, 272-273, 275, 276-277, 278, 282, 283
legislation, 2, 30, 326, 338-339
new immigrants, 10, 255, 264
payment for, 264
public opinion, 26
spending on benefits, 272-273, 319
utilization modeling, 258-259, 262, 264 n.17
Public goods and pure public goods, 256-257, 265, 285, 302, 334-335 n.25
Public revenues. *See also* Taxes
federal aid to states, 262
fees and licenses, 267, 278
modeling, 259, 260-263, 266-269
nonresident sources, 260, 262-263, 269-270
Public spending
age of immigrants and, 304
on debt, 304, 318 n.15
on education, 275-276, 281
historical trends, 47-48
modeling, 264-266, 269-270
for nonresident business services, 269-270
per capita share, 303
projections, 10-11, 299-301
on public assistance and benefits, 10, 272-273, 304-305
on public goods, 293, 302, 303, 304, 318
Public Use Micro Sample (PUMS), 271, 273 n.27, 306, 308, 309 n.12, 362

Q

Quota Act (1921), 25-26
Quotas
Eastern Hemisphere, 24, 26, 27
legislation, 24, 68
national-origin-based, 24, 25-26, 27, 36, 68
numerical, 24, 25-26, 27-28, 68
skills-based, 24, 27
Western Hemisphere, 24, 25, 68

R

Race/ethnicity
admissions based on, 64
attitudes toward immigrants, 364, 374, 375, 392, 393-394
classifications, 80
and education, 355-358
exclusions based on, 23-24
and expenditures attributable to immigrant labor, 234-235

and fiscal impacts, 322
geographic segregation by, 367-368
interethnic tensions, 393-394
Racial/ethnic distribution
age structure, 113-114
attribution issue, 4, 77, 84-85, 89-90, 92-93, 114, 115-119, 121-122, 123, 370
exogamy and, 114, 115, 117-119
fertility rates, 85-87, 114
generational perspectives, 114, 117, 355-358, 367-368
intermarriage and, 4, 113, 123, 369-372, 396
international comparisons, 64
labor-force participation, 105
modeling, 81-82, 84-85, 87-88, 92-93, 133
mortality, 88, 131
population composition, 4, 34, 37, 77, 80, 113-122, 123
projected, 114-122, 123
Refugee Act of 1980, 25, 28-29, 38
Refugees
admission trends, 38, 41, 42, 44, 64
Canadian system for, 20, 67, 72
defined, 22
earnings, 194, 195, 196
European, 27
international comparisons, 64
legislation, 25, 28-29, 38
policy on admissions, 41, 42, 196, 365
resettlement, 25, 28-29, 38
Relatives of U.S. citizens, 41, 44
Representatives of international organizations, 49
Research and development, 162, 164
Resettlement of refugees, 25, 28-29, 38
Restaurants, ethnic, 146, 213-215
Retail trade, 149
Revenues. *See* Public revenues; Taxes
Robinson, Gregg, 40
Romania, 386
Roosevelt, Theodore, 119
Russia, 62
Russian immigrants, 24, 386

S

San Diego, 226, 373, 375-376
San Francisco, 61
Savings rate, 162-163
Scandinavian countries, 155. *See also specific country*
Scandinavian immigrants, 23, 36
School-age population, 77, 94, 103-104
School enrollments, 3, 77, 103-104, 122
Science and arts, contributions to 383-386
Sciences, contributions of immigrants to, 383-385
Scope of study, 1, 17-19
Seasonal agricultural workers, 27, 29, 52
Self-employment, 162-163, 182 n.8
Service industries
immigrant labor-cost shares, 232
occupations of immigrants, 212-215
workforce, 149
Siblings of immigrants, 42, 43, 45
Silicon Valley, 150
Skills of immigrants. *See also* Educational attainment; Labor, highly skilled; Labor, skilled; Labor, unskilled
and economic assimilation, 181-182
and fiscal burden, 335-336
national origin and, 7, 185-190, 235-236
policy on immigration and, 2, 194, 196, 218
trends, 181-185
and wage disparities, 7, 137-141, 143, 157, 179, 181, 193, 197-198, 201-202, 224-225, 227, 235-236
Smith, Adam, 154
Social dimensions of immigration. *See* Assimilation of immigrants; Attitudes about immigration; Education, public; Exogamy; Geographic distribution of immigrants; Intermarriage
age distributions and, 55, 77
citizenship and naturalization, 363, 378-382
concerns, 14
crime and criminals, 53, 386-389

education, 103-104, 122, 372-376
gender balance and, 53
generational perspectives, 374-377, 395-396
interethnic relations, 389-390, 393-395
literacy, 363, 376-378
of population change, 77
public assistance programs, 30, 55
racial/ethnic identity, 363, 369-372
residential integration, 366-368
segregation indices, 366-369
social and spatial mobility, 363, 365-368
Social Security, 10, 11, 40 n.17, 44, 54, 110, 255, 280, 282, 283, 297-298, 304, 309-311, 325 n.20, 330, 342; *see also* Old-Age Survivors, Disability, and Health Insurance
Social Security Administration, 347
South African immigrants, 186, 188, 190
South America, 174, 175, 376
South American immigrants, 23, 287, 289. *See also specific country*
Southern European immigrants, 25-26, 31, 36, 68, 110, 364, 376, 395. *See also specific country*
Soviet Union, 20, 28 n.8, 64. *See also specific country*
Special immigrants, 42, 45
Special Supplemental Nutrition Program for Women, Infants, and Children (WIC), 308 n.9
Sponsors, 30
Sports, contributions of immigrants to, 385-386
Spouses, 41, 42, 43-44, 45, 195, 209
Standards of living. *See* Gross domestic product
State and local government. *See also* California; New Jersey
budget, 271-277, 285-289, 324 n.20
congestive costs, 303, 316
deficit, 324 n.20
education, 262, 273 n.27, 278 n.32, 311
revenues. *See* Public revenues; Taxes
spending. *See* Public spending
Students, foreign-born, 49-50, 51, 103 n.30
Supplementary Security Income (SSI), 10-11, 30, 44, 55, 273, 278, 282 n.37, 304, 308 n.9, 309, 311, 312, 330, 339, 351
Survey of Income and Program Participation, 306, 362
Sweden, 63, 64, 66, 386
Switzerland, 62, 63, 64, 66, 379

T

Taiwan, 186, 187, 189
Tampa Bay, 386
Taxes, federal, state, and local
and age profiles of immigrants, 305 n.5, 314-316, 320, 349-352
aggregate, 314-316
business/corporate, 9, 256, 262, 267-268, 274, 279, 285 n. 40, 314
disability insurance, 278-279, 283
and earnings, 306
and educational attainment, 349-352
exclusions, 285 n.38
generational perspective, 314-316, 319-320, 349-352
immigrant contributions, 256, 276, 280, 281, 283, 314-316, 326, 339, 340
income and payroll, 256, 267, 274, 276, 278, 283, 314
licenses and fees, 267, 278
modeling, 259, 260-263
native burden, 255, 260-263, 265-266, 279 n.35, 281, 283
net annual fiscal impact, 261
net present value, 326-332, 347-348
new immigrant impact, 256, 260, 261, 262, 265, 268, 340, 349
per capita net, 320
projections, 10-11, 256, 297-301
property and utility, 9, 256, 267-268, 274, 276, 278, 279, 281, 314
sales and excise, 256, 267, 276, 278, 281, 314
shifting burden of, 266-267
state and local, 314
time since arrival and, 307
tourists and tourism, 279

Technology, 155, 160-163, 264 n.16
Temporary workers and trainees, foreign, 49-50
Terminology, 21-22, 56 n.24
Texas, 59, 61, 179-180, 211-217, 228-230, 254, 391, 405
Textile industry, 145-146, 147-148, 215
Time of arrival
and citizenship and naturalization, 382
and earnings, 192-196, 307
and educational attainment, 183-185
and employment, 206-209
and fiscal impacts, 301-302, 303-304, 307-308
and income, 268 n.21
and occupational attainment, 210, 213-217
and wages, 7, 177-178, 183-185, 198-204, 241-250
Tourists and tourism, 49, 50, 51, 274 n.29, 275 n.29
Trade. *See* International trade
Transit aliens, 49
Treaty traders, 49
Truman, Harry S, 27
Turkey, 64

U

Undocumented immigrants. *See* Illegal immigrants/immigration
Unemployment, 18, 104, 105
United Kingdom, 62, 63, 64, 65, 66. *See also* British immigrants
United Nations, 79
U.S. Commission on Immigration Reform, 1, 15, 17-19
Unskilled labor. *See* Labor, unskilled

V

Venezuela, 386
Vietnamese immigrants, 28, 194, 196, 365, 367 n.3, 375, 395
Visa systems
Canadian, 65, 67, 72-75
legislation, 24, 29
Visas, permanent resident. *See also* Employment-based admission preferences; Family-sponsored admission preferences
admissions, 42, 43, 209
allocations, 41-43
conditional, 44
and data collection, 192
lotteries, 46
unused, 41
waiting list, 45
Voting, 30, 78, 226, 273, 372-373

W

Wages. *See also* Earnings; Income
age profiles, 197-204, 241-250
by country, 187-190, 196, 249-250
cross-sectional data, 197-198
discrimination, 179, 181
disparities, by nativity, 176-179, 182-185, 197-202, 241-248
dispersion, 174
early arrivals, 177-178
educational attainment and, 7, 17, 151, 179, 181, 182-190, 227-228, 235, 241-248
elasticity of, 221-222
emigration and, 204-205
factor price equalization, 174 n.3
flows of immigrants and, 227-230
gender differences, 17, 176-178, 181, 183-191, 198-204, 241-250
generational assimilation and, 158-160
geographic distribution of immigrants and, 179-180, 221-222, 225-228
growth/convergence rate, 197-205, 241-250
hourly, 176-178, 179, 180
illegal immigrants and, 7, 236
international comparisons, 174-177
local markets, 221-225
migrant workers, 27
national origin and, 7, 174, 176-178, 186-191, 202-204, 235-236, 249-250

productivity differences and, 174 n.3
race/ethnicity and, 181
redistribution of workers and, 7, 137-142, 151-152, 157, 164
skill levels and, 137-141, 143, 157, 179, 181, 193, 197-198, 201-202, 224-225, 227, 235-236
temporal trends, 177-178, 183-185, 198-204, 241-250
Waiting lists, 44-45
Washington, D.C., 61
Washington immigrants, 61
Washington Post, 393
Wealth of Nations, 154
Welfare. *See* Public assistance, benefits, and services
West Indian immigrants, 375
Western Europe, 174, 175, 176, 182
Western Hemisphere immigration
emigration from U.S., 40
quotas, 24, 25, 68
White immigrants; *see specific area and country*
ancestry, 84, 119, 120
attitudes toward immigration, 13, 394, 396
defined, 80
education, 375
exogamy, 90-92, 118 n.46, 132
fertility rates, 85-87
fiscal impact of 322
intermarriage rates, 90, 91, 113, 132, 370
mortality, 88, 131
racial/ethnic attribution, 93, 118, 121-122, 133, 370-371
population size and growth, 114, 115, 116, 121, 123
unemployment, 222
wages, 222, 223
Whites. *See* White immigrants
Women. *See* Females
Work experience, requirements, 46
Workers. *See* Labor
Workforce, immigrant
in agriculture, 149
in service industries, 149
size of, 77, 105, 110, 122
in traded-goods sector, 148-149
Working-age population, 77, 105, 110
World War I, 25, 31, 35
World War II, 26, 27, 29 n.9, 31-32, 35, 68, 76
Wyoming, 61

Y

Young adults, 54, 55, 104-105
Youth dependency ratio, 107-108
Yugoslavia, 386